BRIDE TO AN ALIEN PRINCE OMNIBUS

KATE STEVENS

3AM PRESS

Title: Bride to an Alien Prince: The Omnibus Edition | Kate Stevens

Description: First edition | 3AM Press

Identifiers: ISBN 9781990551055 (e-book) | ISBN 9781990551062 (paperback)

Subjects: BISAC FICTION / Romance / Science Fiction

Cover art by Getcovers

Star Icon by freepik on flaticon.com

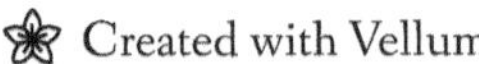 Created with Vellum

KYRIX

BRIDE TO AN ALIEN PRINCE PREQUEL

ONE

MEREDITH

Meredith yawned as the generic pop music playing in Cocoa Love looped to the beginning of the playlist. For the *fifth* time. The damn lyrics literally haunted her dreams at this point. She couldn't even listen to the radio at home without suffering a flashback. Meredith yawned again. If the music didn't kill her, maybe boredom would. Either fate was definitely preferable at this point.

Meredith straightened from where she slouched by the cash register. She shook her head, quickly stretched her arms, and started her thousandth lap of the store. It was an hour after lunch on a Wednesday, leaving the tiny shop empty. She plucked a chocolate from one of the product display bins, unwrapped it, and popped it in her mouth. The only perk of Cocoa Love was the free chocolate.

She dragged her feet, but her lap still only took two minutes. Meredith settled back behind the counter and sighed. Two degrees from expensive colleges and she wasn't even qualified to be the manager of a Cocoa Love. Life was going really well.

If only there were a customer to distract her. Meredith snorted at herself. On one hand, customers made the shift go by faster. On the other, some customers enjoyed being difficult. Meredith was considering her pros and cons when a man in his early thirties strolled into the store, rendering her thoughts useless.

"Welcome to Cocoa Love, would you like a sample?" Meredith pasted on her fakest smile and nearly cringed at the pitch of what she called her customer service voice. The corporate mandate said she had to welcome every customer and offer them a free chocolate. And damn, it got tiring when most people strolled into the store simply for samples and nothing else.

"Hello," the man said, his voice a deep contrast to his rather bland appearance. Something about his face was incredibly unremarkable. His hair was a light brown, the same shade as Meredith's, and his eyes a blank gray. He wore a beige trench coat over a basic suit, almost straight out of *Mad Men*. "I wish you a good afternoon, female."

Meredith blinked at him. Female? What the heck? That was weird, but maybe English was his second language. Not that Meredith faulted him. Spanish was technically her second language, but even after years of schooling, she couldn't string more than a sentence together. 'Dónde está el baño?' and 'Quiero una pizza?' were the extent of her skills.

She kept her smile bright. "Can I help you find anything in particular today?"

He didn't glance around the store, but held direct eye contact with her. "I'm from the Government of Earth. You will answer some questions for me."

Government of Earth? Okay. Double weird. Meredith didn't know what this guy's joke was, but she had nothing better to do. Her bitch manager, Kris, had taken the afternoon off to get a manicure. Meredith would be alone in the store for the next four hours. "Sure, go for it."

The man pulled out a notepad. "Go for it? That is an expression for saying yes?"

"Ummm, yeah? Or, uh, yes?"

He shook his head. "Your people have the oddest language."

Her people? Did he mean Americans? He continued on as if he

hadn't just insulted her entire country. "Then I shall commence with questions. What would you say is Earth's greatest invention?"

Meredith leaned back against the counter and chuckled. "Sliced bread?"

The man didn't laugh at her joke. Meredith didn't mind. She was one of those weird people who enjoyed making jokes purely for her own entertainment. "And you like bread?"

"Hell, yeah, I do. I'd say it makes up half my diet. I'm literally addicted to garlic bread."

His eyebrows raised. "Addiction is not good."

She frowned. "Well, yeah. I'm not *literally* addicted."

He stared at her blankly.

"I meant figuratively?"

He nodded but still didn't seem content in her answer. "Is addiction a common problem for your species?"

Her species? This had to be a prank. Meredith was about to ask where he had hidden the cameras when a high-pitched beeping blared within the man's suit.

In a blink, the ordinary man in front of her turned into a purple-haired, black-horned alien. Meredith gaped. The alien towered over her, at least seven-feet-tall and shirtless, his tight black pants crisscrossed with straps. His chest was almost human-like, if she ignored the azure, dragon-like scales. Meredith couldn't look away from his abs. He was so ripped that his muscles would put bodybuilders to shame.

How much coffee had she drank at lunch? Meredith gripped the counter. "I'm sorry, sir. You need to call an ambulance. I think I'm having a stroke. Unless you normally have blue scales."

He stiffened at her words. His eyes focused on her, something like disbelief in his gaze. She jerked. His eyes were bright purple, his irises slitted like a cat. Meredith needed a paper bag to breathe into. This couldn't be happening—

The man-alien reached for her, his movements a quick blur. Meredith screamed and grabbed for the nearest object. Her hands settled on a spray cleaning bottle. Squirting a freaking alien in the face couldn't end well, but she did it anyway, screaming bloody murder. The alien blocked his eyes and hissed.

"Take that, you bastard."

His eyes narrowed at that. Before Meredith whacked him with the bottle, he pulled something from his belt and flicked his thumb. A slight prick stung her neck. Her knees went weak. He gripped her arm with black-clawed hands to stop her from toppling. A warm flutter spread through her skin at his touch and sparked heat low in her stomach. Was she horny for a horned alien?

Meredith laughed hysterically at her thought as the world went black.

TWO

KYRIX

"Hyra's Graces," Kyrix cursed as the human female slumped into his arms. He had shown his true face to her. He and Bemus had done endless preparation and testing on their cloaking devices. They planned to visit highly populated areas to ask humans a random series of questions. Their devices couldn't fail. Kyrix slammed his fist into the odd table with the mechanical box. It dinged and popped open.

It should have been an easy directive, but Kyrix's life excelled at throwing him complication after complication. His mother was Duchess of Agafyi and Kyrix her heir, but Kyrix was a bastard, his status forever marred. He had been at the top of his class at The Royal Academy, but there were whispers his secret father had pulled strings to get him there. All were obstacles he needed to work to get around. This predicament would be no different.

He whacked the device on his left leg and the light flicked from red to blue. His cloak was back up and running. Kyrix glanced around. The tiny store and mall hallway were thankfully empty. Only one human had seen him then.

He nudged the female, but she remained unconscious. He had

studied humans before venturing into their population, but he hadn't yet gotten used to their appearance. Their shape was like the other advanced species who belonged to the Intergalactic Alliance, but they were rather small and covered in smooth skin instead of scales. The female's skin was a soft cream and hair the color of dalo nuts sprouted from her head. Herkleians had hair, but theirs ranged in color from bright red to orange to turquoise. Kyrix's own was a deep purple beneath his towering horns.

He reached for the dark strands, wondering how they'd feel against his claws. Kyrix pulled back his hand. Now wasn't the time to lust after this strange being. He had spent too long on his ship with only other males for company.

The government of Herkleios had sent five observers to Earth to see if humans had reached a technology level sufficient for contact. The Earthlings had failed the test fifty years ago, but passed the initial tests this time. It had unfortunately extended their expedition by six months. With six months to go, Kyrix couldn't let the human female keep her memories. Once the crew filed their report, the Intergalactic Alliance would decide when to make contact. If word somehow got out before then and Kyrix was responsible, his life would become Hadus regardless of his connections.

Kyrix adjusted the female against his side. If he let her crumple to the floor, she might hurt her head. He tapped the comms device at his hear. Not only did it translate Earth's various languages, it also connected him to his ship. He needed to get her to the medical station on his spacecraft.

"Commander Ezio speaking." The male's voice echoed in his ear, spoken in crisp Herkleian.

Out of all his crewmates, it had to be Ezio on comms duty. "I require transport."

"Why? You haven't completed your shift, *my lord*."

Ezio sneered at the title. He was technically in charge of the crew, but Kyrix was a Lord of Herkleios and didn't answer to the male. They had clashed horns since Command had assigned Kyrix to the expedition. It didn't help that every time Ezio spoke, Kyrix wanted to punch him in the face. "I said I require transport to the *Acacia.*"

A muffled crash reverberated through the comms like Ezio had thrown his earpiece at a wall. Kyrix's hands clenched automatically, his instincts kicking in. He forced himself to loosen his grip. He couldn't bruise the female. The heat of her body radiated at his side and a flare of unexpected arousal coursed through him. He couldn't remember the last time he'd reacted in this manner to a female.

Ezio came back to the comms. "Turn off your jammers. Transporting you in ten seconds."

Kyrix tapped at his gold wristband, which projected a tiny holoscreen, and adjusted his settings to allow for transport. The *Acacia* locked onto his signal. Kyrix secured the female tightly to his scaled chest. She shifted and let out a soft sigh. He almost stopped dead, the sound pulling at his heart. He looked down at her sleeping face. She was beautiful, absolutely beautiful. Kyrix had to get her on the ship before she regained consciousness. He didn't know what he'd do if she woke up.

A tingling sensation brushed across his scale for a second before Kyrix appeared in the transport room. Gold floors and walls decorated the *Acacia*, their surveillance ship, blue symbols marking information points along the wall. It didn't compare at all with the purple-orange meadows and green lakes of his home, Agafyi, but the government didn't care about appearances and neither did any of the crew. Kyrix stomped from the transport platform and through the door, which slid shut after he passed.

He headed straight for the ship's small infirmary. The males on the ship had to administer memory serum if any humans saw their true selves or became suspicious. To date, no one had ever needed to initiate that plan. His crewmates had completed multiple missions on Earth, but that had been Kyrix's first journey to the surface. Naturally, his cloaking device would go to Hadus. Kyrix couldn't fuck up this mission. The deal he made with his father depended on it.

Kyrix's rage spiked at the thought of his sire. He had met his father once, a week before being sent on this expedition. Kyrix had always known the male's identity. His mother had told him at a young age and sworn him to secrecy. But to the people of Herkleios, he was a Lord of Agafyi and that was how it had to remain. It hadn't been a problem until a year ago. His father had made it clear Kyrix's continued existence was tolerated as long as he did exactly as he was told. Namely, stay off the planet until further notice.

Kyrix stormed through the infirmary door. A levitating table of gold occupied a third of the tiny room, the rest cluttered with shelves packed with hundreds of instruments and vials. Detrux glanced up from where he'd somehow fit a small desk in the far corner. The doctor was two decades older than Kyrix, his dark red hair streaked with a few strands of aging gold and his horns already shortening, but the male remained the peak of Herkleian strength and intelligence.

The doctor jolted at the sight of the being in his arms. "Is that a human female?"

Kyrix laid her on the table. It bobbed under her weight, but they built their medical tables to carry a grown Herkleian male. The female was impossibly small in comparison. He reluctantly pulled away from her, the scales on his hands tingling where they had touched her skin. "We need the memory serum."

"Hyra's Graces, Kyrix." Detrux might have grumbled, but he moved quickly, heading straight for his wall of vials. "How did this happen?"

"The cloak started beeping and suddenly, the female asked why I had blue scales."

Detrux shuffled through his vials. "Beamus must be playing with the settings again. Does Ezio know?"

"He transported us aboard." Kyrix kept his answer vague. He hadn't told Ezio and didn't intend to. Kyrix was Ezio's superior, but he didn't have a rank and the rest of the crew was military. He had wanted to attend a military college, but his father's staff had denied the request. Without a clear chain of command, Detrux reported everything to *both* Kyrix and Ezio. If the male knew Kyrix hadn't told Ezio, he'd report to his commander immediately.

Detrux settled on a bottle and approached the female. Kyrix had to stomp on the urge to snarl at his friend. His reaction to this female made little sense. The urge to protect her thrummed through his veins. If he were a superstitious male, he'd almost think she was his fated mate, something out of old Herkleian myth. There hadn't been a matebond reported in over a century.

"Injecting now." Detrux pressed a button on the table's smooth surface. A tube lowered from the ceiling and the doctor inserted the bottle. Micro-injectors in the table's surface would administer the serum intravenously. "She'll wake up and be groggy for the next few minutes. After five, I'll give her a memory test. If everything looks good, we need to return her to the planet. Once she's there, she'll have no memory of our presence."

Kyrix twinged in pain. There was no reason he'd want the human female to remember him, but the thought of never seeing her again wrenched at his chest. He reached out to brush a strand of hair from her face—

The female opened blue eyes the color of the Azov Sea, took one look at Kyrix, and screamed.

THREE

MEREDITH

"What the hell?" Meredith yelled, staring at the same blue-scaled alien she'd seen in her dream. This had to be a dream. She had binged almost every sci-fi show on Netflix. It made sense her imagination conjured up hot, horned aliens who fit her fantasies to a tee. How could this be real life? Why would an alien visit her work?

Meredith shook her head firmly. This was *not* real.

Then she glanced to the right at another freaking shirtless alien. He looked a few years older with bright red hair under his shorter horns. "What in the *absolute* shit?"

"Human," the new alien started.

Meredith scrambled off the table. A freaking floating table. The surrounding room looked straight out of a sci-fi show, if a low budget one at that. It was barely bigger than Cocoa Love. She stumbled into mad-scientist shelves filled with weird devices and vials of colorful liquid. She grabbed one of each in her hands. "What is this? Am I going to be probed? I am *so* not getting probed!"

When Meredith raised the vial over her head, the purple-haired man—male?—stepped forward. "Female, please—"

She glared at him. "Don't call me that. What gives you the right to show up and turn my life upside down? Did you just decide, oh, this human seems irrelevant in her shitty minimum-wage job, let me go ahead and kidnap her?!"

"I apologize." The male bowed. Legitimately bowed. "I never intended to take you, but when my cloaking device failed, I had to bring you to the ship."

Meredith switched between the vial and the thingamabob in her other hand. The device looked more threatening and she gripped it harder. "What are you going to do? Hold me hostage and do weird alien experiments?"

The alien's forehead crinkled. Confused, maybe? Did aliens have the same facial expressions? Meredith didn't know. She hadn't even believed in aliens a few hours ago.

"No one will lay a finger on you," he answered, his deep voice oddly calming. "Once your memory of the incident has faded, we'll return you to your home immediately. I guarantee you'll remain safe."

"So, no probing?"

His forehead creases deepened. Definitely confusion, but he answered, "No probing."

"How long are you going to hold me?" Meredith had left the store unattended, but she didn't care if it got looted. Served her boss right.

"We should have you back within an hour. We have no desire to hurt you. Our mission here is strictly to observe your planet."

"Alright." Meredith dropped the thingamabob. The red-haired alien cringed. Was he the ship's doctor? "Sorry. Hope that wasn't expensive."

"There are three of its kind in existence at the moment."

"Oh shit, I'm sorry." Meredith grabbed the thingamabob and thrust it into the doctor's hands. "Did I break the most valuable device in the universe or something?"

"Valuable in the medical community, yes. It's the smallest body scanner used to assess internal damage."

Meredith wasn't sure if she should feel bad or not. They had kidnapped her after all. Maybe it served them right to have their things broken. She shrugged. "Let's get this show on the road. Give me your magic memory potion."

"Potion?" The purple-haired alien glanced at the doctor.

"Yes. Potion," the doctor said. He plucked one from his shelf. "This one. She must take it with food."

"Sounds good to me." Meredith gestured to the smooth, empty wall she assumed was a door. "After you."

The purple-haired alien stared at the doctor, but whatever his stare meant, Meredith didn't understand. She didn't care, either. She wanted to go home, back to her tiny apartment, and crawl straight into bed. After a long second, the purple-haired male started toward the wall, which split down the middle into a pair of sliding doors. His back rippled with muscle. She'd seen guys with jacked pecs and arms, but to have corded muscles on every inch required extreme dedication. He could probably bench press her easily.

Nervous excitement filled her stomach. Meredith scampered out after him into a wide hallway, all done in shining gold. She didn't see any windows. Was she in space? Kidnapping aside, it was kinda awesome to be on a spaceship with a sexy alien. It was almost like a scene out of one of her fave sci-fi romance novels.

"So... what kind of food do you guys eat? Freeze-dried jerky? Slime?" Meredith asked, trying to fill the deafening silence of the ship as he led her down the long corridor. The alien slowed his steps to keep pace with her. His legs were ridiculously long. He hadn't changed out of his tight leather-like pants, which apparently served as the uniform around here. Meredith hesitated a step to take a quick peek at his toned butt. Heat rushed to her cheeks. Never in a million years would she have imagined checking out an alien's ass.

"Most of our food comes from our home planet," he said, completely unaware of where her eyes roamed, "and is preserved in a suspension fluid to stop aging or rotting."

"Cool, cool." Meredith cleared her throat. She hadn't dated in years. Of course she was checking him out. His blue scales and dragon-like horns didn't matter when he had the kind of body she only dreamed about. She barely suppressed her urge to drool over him. That would definitely be a turn-off. What was she thinking? She was a completely average human. It was unlikely he felt even half the desire she did.

Meredith stuck out her hand. "I'm Meredith, by the way."

The alien stared down at her hand. When he didn't grasp her palm, she reached out and grabbed his hand. His scales were warm to the touch and his fingernails sharp, black claws. Meredith's eyes widened, but she didn't pull away. Her skin tingled where it rubbed against him.

"I am Kyrix Yio'naeus of Agafyi." He glanced at their joined hands, but Meredith didn't want to let go. The tingles spread down her arm and into her chest.

"It's a handshake," she said, answering the question in his eyes.

Kyrix continued to shake her hand, almost as reluctant as Meredith to pull away. "On Herkleios, we tap horns in greeting."

"That's cool." Meredith reached up to tap his horn, but he stiffened and she quickly dropped her hands. She wasn't here to fawn over Kyrix. She needed that memory serum. Hot alien or not, she had a life waiting for her. If she never went home, who would feed her cat?

She stopped dead.

Not because of Kyrix or cats. They had turned a corner to a new section of hallway, one with large windows.

Windows overlooking Earth.

Meredith stumbled toward them and reached out a hand. Outer. Fucking. Space. She looked down on her planet, all green and blue and dotted with bright lights. They hovered over North America. She traced the lights from New York north to Maine. The only place she had ever been. And now she was in space, the stars surrounding her. Her family, her friends, everyone she had ever known was beneath her, getting ready for bed while Meredith was in literal space.

She clutched the window's edge to stop herself from falling. Kyrix stopped at her side. "It's a magnificent view, isn't it?"

"It is." She glanced at him. He wasn't looking out the window, but directly at her. Heat rushed to her face. Meredith stumbled back. Memory potion. That was why she was here. "We should get this over with."

Kyrix backed away and bowed. "After you, Lady Meredith."

Lady Meredith? If only Earth guys had the same manners. Meredith tucked a strand of loose hair behind her ear and continued down the hall. Within a minute, they came to a single door. It slid open when Kyrix approached, revealing a luxury suite. Whoever had decorated this entire ship really liked gold. Maybe these aliens *were* dragons. A small sitting area of levitating chairs circled a floating fire within a gold fireplace. Behind the sofas, gold-embroidered fabrics covered a massive king-sized bed. A bed. Meredith's cheeks burned. She hadn't expected him to bring her into his private rooms.

Kyrix cleared his throat. He had approached an alcove with a levitating table and two gilded chairs, but Meredith had frozen in place, staring intently at the bed. Shaking her head, Meredith crossed the room to settle at his side. "You don't eat with your crewmates?"

"I like to keep to myself. Having my own dining area is a privilege. It would be a shame not to use it."

"You have special privileges?"

"My mother is a duchess. As I don't have any sisters, I'll inherit the title when she passes."

"You're a future duke?" Meredith gaped. She'd been kidnapped by alien royalty. "Do your people normally send dukes on observation missions?"

He stiffened, but said, "It's my duty."

Before Meredith asked another thousand questions, he turned his attention to the large screen on the wall to her left. He tapped a claw against it. Strange, block-shaped letters flicked across the surface. Meredith didn't understand a word. Now that she thought of it, how did she understand Kyrix? What alien spoke English?

"Why can I understand you and not that?"

He tapped his little earbud-like device. "I have a universal translator, both this external version and an implant. When you speak, I can respond in your language. Any language."

"Oh, wow. That'd be really useful." Sometimes customers came into Cocoa Love who didn't speak English well. If Meredith could reply in their own language, her life would be a thousand times easier.

"Here." Kyrix clicked a few buttons and the words turned to pictures. "Now you can understand."

"Can I?" she muttered. Nothing appeared the least bit familiar. All the food was brightly colored, green and red and orange and purple. Like Kyrix himself. Was his planet just as bright? It'd be beautiful. Too bad she'd never get to see it.

Meredith ignored the pang in her chest. She always wanted to travel the world. Portland was terribly boring, all gray buildings and dull parks. She wanted to walk the colorful streets of Morocco, see giraffes in South Africa, and swim in the blue waters of Barbados. Now another location added to her list, a whole different planet. But she could barely save for a flight to New York, much less her own spaceship.

Meredith pressed a button at random. The sooner she drank the serum, the sooner she'd forget about Kyrix and the lure of his planet.

The screen flashed and the button she pressed slid open like a slot. A little tray popped forward, holding a plate with blue meat and a salad of orange leaves, square nuts, and squiggly yellow fruit. The scent that hit her reminded her of fried chicken. Her mouth watered. Kyrix hit his own selection before taking both plates in his massive hands. "You will sit."

"Um, sure." Meredith pulled her chair from the table and plopped into the seat. The stiffness of her pants pulled at her hips. She was still in her Cocoa Love uniform. She resisted the urge to tug at her apron. Kyrix probably already thought she was weird.

He settled in the seat across from her. "Simos meat is my favorite. You have made an excellent selection, Lady Meredith."

"Why, thank you, Lord Kyrix." The words slithered out of her mouth before she thought to stop them. Now she was flirting with the hot alien, too. She cleared her throat. "Don't get me wrong, I love eating. This even smells good, but shouldn't we be focusing on my memory? Do I really need all of this?"

He bared fangs at her. She nearly flinched at the sight of them, but the action wasn't threatening. The alien version of a smile, maybe? "You need to eat."

"I mean, I guess." Meredith pressed a prong-like fork into the blue meat. "Not that I'll remember eating any of it."

"Nonetheless, it's my duty to keep you safe and comfortable here. I'm the reason you're here."

"It wasn't your fault, but thanks anyway." He surprised Meredith. She really felt safe with him at her side. She shook that idea from her head. Soon she'd forget this whole thing and the smoking hot alien would find someone in his own league.

Meredith held out her hand. "Pass the serum over, buddy."

Kyrix stared at her palm for the longest moment, but eventually reached for his belt. He placed the bottle of red liquid on the table. Meredith grabbed the bottle, popped off the lid, and gulped it down. Before she had time to consider her regrets. She couldn't stay here on this ship forever. The slimy liquid trailed down her throat, but she forced herself to swallow.

"Egh." Meredith almost gagged. She quickly cut a piece of the blue meat and took a bite. It tasted exactly like fried chicken. She quickly cut another slice. "How long will it take to work?"

Kyrix pushed at the food on his plate. "Five minutes—"

The sliding doors opened and a large, black-haired alien stormed into the mess hall, a real-life laser gun in his hand. He pointed it at Meredith. "What is this?"

FOUR

KYRIX

Kyrix jumped to his feet and blocked Meredith from Ezio's view. His vision flashed red at the sight of the other male's laser. Pointed at Meredith. *His* Meredith. He wanted to charge forward and impale Ezio with his horns, as warriors did when challenged to a traditional duel. How dare someone threaten his female?

A soft hand settled on his arm. Kyrix turned to find Meredith at his side, no longer protected by his body. He moved to grab her, but she stepped in front of him, facing Ezio and his laser. "I'm Meredith Sinclair. And you are?"

Ezio narrowed his yellow eyes at Meredith. "I am Ezio Yio'aleta of Eritea, Commander of the *Acacia*."

"Oh." Meredith almost faltered, but she didn't back away in fear, even when Ezio approached. His female was brave. She didn't need to be. Ezio was his problem.

Kyrix tried to shove her behind him. "I brought her aboard when I requested transport."

"Why? This goes against every directive we have. You might be highborn, Kyrix, but that doesn't give you the right to bring a toy on board."

"She's not a toy," Kyrix nearly growled. "My cloaking device failed in her presence. She's here for memory serum."

Ezio spotted the empty vial on the table. "And?"

Kyrix looked to Meredith. The lines of hair above her eyes—eyebrows—arched. He didn't know the expression, but Herkleians crunched their foreheads in confusion. Perhaps it was a similar gesture. Ezio was right. The memory serum should have worked minutes ago, erasing all her knowledge of him and this ship. The liquid Detrux had handed him was a booster, nothing more. She shouldn't have been standing, blue eyes clear and aware.

He touched her gently on the shoulder. "I must speak with Ezio, but I promise no one will so much as touch you. I guarantee it."

Meredith searched his gaze, but eventually nodded. Kyrix returned his attention to the commander. Ezio glared at Meredith's shoulder, where Kyrix's hand had touched. Kyrix pushed past the other male to draw his attention. Ezio hated going to Earth's surface and interacting with humans. Kyrix didn't want to leave Meredith alone for a minute in his company.

Once in the hall, Ezio shuffled to the far side of the corridor, away from the open door and Meredith. "Detrux told me there was a human on board, but I didn't believe it. Why are you dining with her?"

Kyrix narrowed his eyes. "As I said, Ezio, my cloaking device malfunctioned. The human saw my true form. I followed the set protocol and brought her aboard for a memory wipe."

"I beamed you aboard half an hour ago," Ezio grumbled. "Memory serum takes minutes to administer. Is there a reason to extend her stay?"

What would Ezio do when Kyrix told him the truth? Nothing good. She threatened the success of their expedition. Their orders didn't allow for the killing of humans, but the crew had to deal with all threats appropriately. If Ezio reported Meredith to Command, what would they order the crew of the *Acacia* to do? But Kyrix couldn't hide the information forever. "Detrux administered the memory serum, but it didn't work. She needed a liquid booster which required food."

"And has she taken the booster?"

"She has."

"When?"

"A few minutes before you came in."

Ezio glared at the door, like he could see Meredith through the metal. "She should have experienced the effects, yes?"

"She should."

"Hadus," Ezio snarled. "Command will not be pleased."

"Since we cannot return her to the surface, I will bring her to the guest quarters." The *Acacia* didn't have many spare rooms, but they had a single guest suite for off-ship visitors. Command intended it for supervisors, scientists or interested dignitaries, not humans immune to their serum. But he didn't want Ezio to lock Meredith in the brig. The one-room cell was cold and barren. It wasn't place for a gentle and kind female.

Just the thought of his Meredith shivering in the brig made him clench his fists, his claws digging into his scales. Kyrix would not let it come to that.

Ezio was oblivious to the movement. "Guest quarters? For a human? I don't think so."

"She poses no threat to Herkleios. There's no reason to jail her."

Ezio narrowed his eyes, but Kyrix stared him down. The male had never challenged him outright. "Fine. Lock her in there and then return to me. Command will want your full report, along with Detrux's."

Ezio sent one last glare toward Kyrix's door before he marched down the hall. As Kyrix turned back to his room, the door slid open. Meredith ventured out, but didn't go far beyond the threshold. "What was that about?"

"Nothing," he replied quickly. Perhaps too quickly, but he didn't want to worry her. He'd bring her to the guest quarters and she'd be none the wiser. After that... he didn't know what he'd do after that.

But no matter what, no one would hurt this female. Not as long as he lived. "You must be tired."

She shrugged. "I guess. I worked a long shift."

He gestured down the hall. Her eyes lingered on the tips of his claws. Humans didn't possess claws, did they? He looked down at her fingers. Her nails were pale and rounded, entirely useless. What purpose could they hope to serve? He wished he could consult his holo-screen on humans, but Meredith had returned her piercing gaze to his face.

"After you, Lady Meredith."

She glanced back at his suite, his plate untouched, but shrugged and walked in the direction he pointed.

"So... what do you do for fun around here?" she said, settling at his side.

"Fun?" He had to walk at half-speed to match her tiny steps. She smelled like zangari flowers, which only bloomed in the light of Herkleios' third moon, Salane. Kyrix had to stop himself from reaching out to her. His entire body tensed. He hadn't laid with a female in almost a year. That was all this was. Nothing more. He tried to focus on what she had asked, but the memory escaped him.

"Yeah, fun. You can't just work all day."

His forehead creased. "That is exactly what I do."

"You need to get yourself a union." His hand twitched. What was a union? She seemed to get that he didn't understand and continued, "It doesn't matter. Don't you get tired?"

He straightened. He was a male in his prime. Did she think him weak? "Herkleian males do not get tired."

"Not even to sleep?"

"To sleep, yes." He puffed out his chest. Her gaze dropped, trailing down his scales to the line of his pants. His cock twitched. Was she as interested in him as he was her? "But we can wake at a moment's notice. Our planet was dangerous for our ancestors. The mountains in Agafyi used to crawl with Therios."

"Therios?"

"Ancient beasts with eight legs and sharp fangs."

Her jaw dropped. Was she hungry again? But she didn't ask to eat, only gasped out, "Pardon me?"

Ah. He had scared her. The Therios had frightened him as a child, too. He had never seen one—thank Hyra—but his mother had told the most terrifying tales. "Our hunters have mostly eliminated them."

She swallowed, a loud gulp. "Mostly eliminated does *not* mean extinct."

"You have nothing to worry about from them, Meredith." He stopped before a door and Meredith stumbled to a halt. He waved his hand before the sensor, which read his DNA. The doors slid open, revealing a hovering bed and a cleaning unit almost side by side in the small room.

She peeked in. "I guess this is me."

"It is." He didn't move. He didn't want to leave this female alone. She was so trusting. Brave, too, for how she had stood up to Ezio, despite the male's laser pointed at her. Their government did not want them hurting Earthlings, but that didn't mean Ezio would interpret their orders that way.

He needed to leave her. Find out what Command ordered. Find out what Ezio had planned. Only then could he keep Meredith safe.

He *would* keep her safe.

He bowed. "I will be back shortly, Lady Meredith."

Her lips twisted. A smile. He had studied those. She didn't hate him, then. "Until later, Lord Kyrix."

FIVE
MEREDITH

Meredith stared at her jail cell of a room. Kyrix hadn't called it a jail, but Meredith knew something was wrong. While he hadn't admitted the memory serum wasn't working, she knew from the tense looks passing between him and Ezio. Meredith was sure Kyrix brought her here so the crew could debate without her overhearing.

She threw herself on the hovering bed. Meredith sat up on the mattress and gave it a bounce. Not bad. It was the only furniture in the room that resembled anything on Earth. A shower-like pod stood in one corner with a bunch of buttons on the inside. There wasn't any lamp or light fixture, but a giant crystal-rock at her bedside emitted a dim glow. Meredith didn't spot a bathroom. Meredith hoped Kyrix returned soon. The aliens already didn't like her and peeing on their floor would make it worse.

Leave it to her to be immune to alien memory serum. Meredith's mother had always jokingly called her a medical marvel. Not because she had any special immunity, but because she always caught the most bizarre ailments. Meredith had never caught the flu, but she'd gotten sick with a throat abscess not once, not twice, but three times.

Meredith was the only person she knew that had gone into septic shock in her twenties.

Medical phenomena aside, her life had been completely average until this point. Meredith went to school, graduated college, got a job she hated like everyone else. Who really enjoyed their job? She saw her family on the holidays, her aunts and uncles pestering her with questions about why she was still single. To which she responded she was perfectly content with her cat, Sir Pounce. She hoped he was okay. He had an automatic feeder since her shifts were all over the place, but he wouldn't be pleased with the state of his litter box.

But now she was on a freaking spaceship. If the memory serum didn't work on her, what would the aliens do? She needed a plan to get off this ship. Kyrix was kind and protective, not to mention the sexiest being she'd ever laid eyes on, but she couldn't be sure the others wouldn't dump her on some barren planet. Or worse. Ezio had already pointed a laser at her. Meredith wasn't just going to sit around and let someone else decide her fate.

She sat up and began taking inventory of the room. The door had locked from the outside. When Kyrix had approached it to get in, it had opened automatically. Whatever scanned him was a technology she didn't understand. There were no communication devices. The best weapon she could scrounge up was the light rock, but she didn't have the strength to make it deadly.

Well, if she was going to die anyway, might as well get clean first. Meredith pulled on the shower-thing-pod's handle and stepped in. One button started flashing. She pressed it. A light flashed at the top and scanned down her body. It tickled her skin, almost like one of those fancy spa lasers. Meredith had gone to a spa once for her eighteenth birthday, as a present from her mom. She hadn't returned. Not only because of the price, but because the technician hadn't stopped talking about her acne and how Meredith needed to wash her face. Little had she known, Meredith had used a six-step beauty routine and tested more products than most people could name.

Once the pod finished its scan, two other buttons flashed. One had a shape on it like a clover. Meredith tapped it. The whole pod flashed white. She yelped. When the light settled, she touched her hair. She had covered it in dry shampoo this morning since she hated showering at night and having to blow-dry her hair. The strands were now smooth and silky, entirely clean. She touched her arm. Her skin was clean, too. In a flash. Meredith laughed. She needed one of these at home.

What would the other button do? Meredith pressed it and the light flashed again. When she glanced down, her Cocoa Love uniform had disappeared. In its place were tight black pants and a similar tank-top. Thank God she wasn't shirtless like all the aliens. She looked like the badass chick on the cover of every urban fantasy novel, but instead of leather, the fabric was soft and flexible. Maybe even more comfortable than the sweatpants she always wore at home.

Meredith pushed out of the shower pod. She normally hated the size of her butt, but it looked great in the reflection of the gold walls. Lululemon had nothing on this sculpting fabric. She was spinning around, trying to get a good look, when the door beeped and opened.

"I hope you're finding everything to your liking—" Kyrix cut off and almost dropped the pitcher of water from his hands.

Meredith couldn't help but grin. No human man had ever stared at her the way Kyrix did now. Maybe he *was* interested in her. Meredith batted her eyelashes. She had no idea how to escape from this ship, but she'd find a way. Whatever happened, she'd probably never see Kyrix again. A pang echoed through her heart. She shrugged it off. After she escaped, she *would* never see him again.

Couldn't hurt to have a little fun with him, then.

"Just missing a little company," she said, patting the bed next to her. Wait, was that too forward?

Kyrix straightened, proudly puffing out his chest. "I'd be happy to keep you company."

Meredith sat on the bed and crossed her legs. She couldn't read his expression, but she hoped he felt the same intoxicating desire she did. He marched to the bed, placed the pitcher on the table, and stood across from her. Meredith wanted to trace her fingers down his hard muscles. What would his scales feel like against her lips? She resisted a blush this time. Badass girls in leather didn't blush.

The tension in the room heated. "So," Meredith asked, tracing circles on the bedsheets. She couldn't just jump him. Meredith's morals didn't allow that. "You like your job?"

Kyrix jerked and his shoulders slackened an inch. "Why would you ask me that?"

"I'm sorry." Damn, this wasn't going well. Meredith had never intentionally seduced anyone. She'd only witnessed it in movies. On her first try, she had struck a nerve. "It's just a common thing people ask on my planet."

Some tension left his shoulders, but his face was still tight. "Do you like your job?"

Meredith snorted. "I don't really care for it. It's just something to pay bills. I'd rather be working on my own than around people all the time."

"My job includes a great deal of back and forth for the sake of diplomacy." He paused, almost like in shock that he was revealing this. "Sometimes I want a moment to be alone and breathe."

"Exactly." His eyes trailed down to her lips. Her chest heaved. She had connected with this alien, more than she had anyone on Earth. She wanted to kiss him. Wanted to trail her hands through his purple hair. Wanted to grip his horns. Wanted to climb into his lap and grind against his hardness.

Meredith stood and bit her lip. How would she even initiate something like that? Did she ask his permission? Before Meredith pondered it further, Kyrix whisked her literally off her feet. He was a good two feet taller than her and in order to reach his lips, she needed a boost. He was happy to provide one. He pressed her back against the wall, his hands cradling her ass while she hooked her legs around his torso.

He teased the opening of her lips until she gave in. He plundered her mouth. His tongue was coarser than a human tongue, but

Meredith didn't mind. She answered his passion back with her own tongue, a deep yearning coming from inside her. Her entire body tingled at his touch, from the back of her neck to her toes. She loved the way he kissed her, loved the way she felt pressed against his firm chest. His scales were hot, nearly burning, but it matched the deep heat pooling in her core.

Kyrix began running kisses across her jaw and down her throat. His fangs grazed at her skin. "Meredith..."

God, she loved the way he murmured her name. But instead of continuing to kiss her, he pulled back. Something like guilt overtook his expression.

"What is it?"

"I can't kiss you like this without you knowing the truth, Meredith." He heaved, but instead of a soft sigh, a low growl escaped his throat. "The serum didn't work on you. We're awaiting instructions from Command on how to proceed, but I can't risk them dragging you back to my planet."

Meredith stiffened. "Fuck. I knew something wasn't right."

"Don't worry. I have a plan."

SIX

MEREDITH

Kyrix waved his hand before the sensor and opened the door. "We have to be quick. The transport room isn't far, but the crew's on alert."

"Are you sure about this?" Meredith poked at the G.I. Joe style belt now swinging from her shoulders. Kyrix had handed her his laser gun, his external translator, and the glowing device that had beeped in the shop, which he'd said had cloaked his appearance. "You really think they'll believe I overpowered you?"

"Ezio doesn't think much of humans. Paxos and Beamus agree with him." He stormed into the hall, but she hesitated to follow. He bared his fangs at her, the only encouragement she needed. "It will throw them off and give me time to knock them out."

Meredith huffed out a breath. "Okay. I can do this."

She marched into the hall, embracing the leather-like pants and a tough girl attitude. She pointed the laser loosely at Kyrix. He had set the mode to stun, so if she did accidentally shoot, no one would die. Thank God. Meredith wasn't prepared to kill anyone, ever.

"This way." Despite his size, Kyrix moved like a panther, sleek and silent. Like the king of the jungle, strolling through his terrain.

Meredith bit her lips, her gaze trailing to his ass. Those tight pants did her in every time.

"Meredith?"

She ripped her gaze to his face. They had made it to the end of another hallway, the same as the last. Kyrix paused by a corner. Unlike the last time she had checked him out, this time he noticed. His slitted eyes roamed down her body and she swore the bulge of his pants got bigger. Way bigger. Almost too big. Her mouth went dry.

He snapped his claws together, a clacking sound. "As much as I want to touch you, we have to get off the ship first."

"We?"

Kyrix paused, like he hadn't even realized he said it. Meredith's heart fluttered at the thought. She had planned on abandoning Kyrix thirty minutes ago. What would it be like if he came with her? She couldn't imagine the big blue alien fitting in her normal human life. But if he wore his cloak and they went somewhere new, somewhere no one knew them... Meredith wanted that. Wanted to get to know him better. Wanted to touch him. Wanted to feel like this forever, her body buoyant at the thought of him.

Meredith always thought people who got married after less than a month of dating were insane, but here she was, ready to change her entire life for a hot alien she'd met hours ago. "Kyrix, I—"

A green-haired alien with brownish-black horns turned the corner. "You finished with the human, Kyrix? I thought I'd pay her a visit before we ship her off..."

The alien trailed off when Meredith came into sight. He didn't jolt into alertness. Confusion entered his red slitted eyes. Exactly like Kyrix had said. His gaze dropped to where she held the laser and his own hand inched closer to the weapon at his belt, but he didn't pull it.

Idiot.

Meredith tightened her grip on the laser. "What are you looking at, asshole?"

Green Hair pulled at his weapon, but Kyrix was quicker. He

lunged forward and slammed into the other male. The two of them plunged toward the ground. They slammed to the floor with a crash. Meredith's hand started trembling, but she held the laser firm. Kyrix got the upper hand, pulling back a powerful fist—

Green Hair pulled a knife.

"No!" Meredith jolted forward. Both Kyrix and Green Hair flinched, but not at her scream.

Meredith had accidentally pulled the trigger.

A wave of blue electricity slammed out of the laser's end and writhed up their bodies. Green Hair took the brunt of it and immediately went slack. Kyrix tumbled to the side. Meredith ran to him. She had shot him. She had freaking shot him. No one should have ever handed her a gun. She worked at a goddamn chocolate shop, for heaven's sake.

"Kyrix." She touched his shoulder, his warm scales radiating into her palm. "Kyrix, are you okay?"

He stared at her for a second, his eyes a mixture of heat and pain. "You have to go."

"No." Meredith tugged at him. "You're coming with me. We're going together, right?"

He sluggishly shook his head. He gestured at his wristband. A red gem flashed on the gold's surface. "Automatic distress call," he all but slurred. "The others... the others will be here soon."

"Kyrix—"

He grazed a knuckle across her cheek. "I told you everything you need to know. Escape, Meredith. You have to... escape..."

He fell to the floor with a thud.

"Kyrix?" She nudged his shoulder, but he didn't stir. She patted his chest until she found his neck, seeking a pulse. Did aliens have pulses? His scales remained warm. Warm meant alive, right? "Kyrix!"

He didn't wake.

Meredith glanced down the hall. Kyrix had given her the code and coordinates to beam back to Portland. He had known this was a possibility. He'd want her to leave. She had to leave. If she went, maybe they had a chance. It'd be easier for him to escape alone. Kyrix hadn't told her how many others were on the ship, but she sensed it wasn't a lot. Their purpose was to observe Earth. That didn't require an entire force, did it? If the crew was small, he could escape.

Meredith swallowed. She stared at his face, memorizing the lines of his jaw, his cheekbones. Almost human, but not. He was too handsome, his scales and horns adding to his beauty. Meredith leaned down and kissed his cheek. "Come find me, will you?"

Meredith grabbed the laser and ran down the hall. She had a horrible sense of direction, but Kyrix had told her when to turn. It was left, left, right. Or left, right, left? Maybe. She didn't have time to think. Meredith turned right and stayed close to the wall.

A single pair of footsteps echoed down the golden hallway. Meredith pressed the top button of the cloaking device like Kyrix had shown her. The light flickered from red to blue. She touched her face. She didn't feel any different. She needed a mirror.

"Kyrix?"

Meredith stifled a yelp. The red-haired doctor had rounded the corner and frowned at Meredith. He didn't pull the laser at his belt. And he had called her Kyrix? The cloak worked, then. She stood straighter and puffed out her chest, like she had watched Kyrix do a few times.

"Your distress signal went off," the male said, moving closer.

"Uh..." Meredith thought fast on her feet. "Must have been an error."

Meredith tried to walk past him, but he didn't get out of her way. "Are you feeling well?"

"Of course." What would Kyrix have said? "I'm always feeling well. I'm in perfect shape."

The male's frown deepened. His scales puckered and flared. "That you are." He started to move past her. "I'll let the others know you're well. Do you know where Paxos is? His distress went off, too."

"No." Meredith lunged forward and grabbed the doctor's hand. If he got to the end of the hall, he'd see the real Kyrix. "I just came from that direction. He's not here."

The doctor frowned down at her hand on his. Shit. The cloaking device only hid her appearance. It wouldn't hide the texture or lower temperature of her human skin. She pulled back, but it was too late. He pulled the laser. Meredith raised her weapon, too. She'd never aimed a gun in her life, but this was a freaking alien laser. How hard could it be?

"What did you do with Kyrix, human?"

She forced her hand to stop quivering. "Get out of my way."

Someone snarled behind her, a growl like a wolf. Meredith shrieked and spun, pressing her back to the wall. Ezio stood behind her, his head thrown back in laughter, the snarling noise coming from him. Meredith hadn't heard Kyrix laugh. Apparently, the Herkleians literally howled. Before she could fully process that, Ezio pointed his own laser at her. Meredith aimed at him, but the doctor hadn't lowered his weapon, either.

Ezio stomped forward, unafraid of Meredith's weapon. "Drop the laser, Earthling."

"No, thank—"

Ezio snatched the laser from her hand and tossed it across the hall. It slammed into the wall with a loud clank. Not only were the Herkleians super strong, but Meredith added super-fast reflexes to their list of advantages.

"Throw her in the brig, Detrux," Ezio snapped at the doctor. The red-haired male put a gentle hand on her arm, but his eyes were unapologetic. "We were kind to you, human, and yet you try this. This time around, we won't be so accommodating."

With a push, Detrux nudged her down the hall. Meredith bit her lip and scampered to stay ahead of him and Ezio. She wasn't giving up. She'd escape this ship and get home. But she couldn't fight two aliens. She needed a better plan.

SEVEN

Kyrix struggled back to consciousness. What had happened? Where was he? He blinked. The hallway. With Meredith. Paxos had rounded the corner. Like Kyrix suspected, the male hadn't considered the delectable female a threat. His mistake. Kyrix had launched himself at his crewmate, but their fight must have spooked Meredith. A crackle of electricity had launched through the air and then... nothingness. Kyrix touched his temple. He had been out for a few minutes. By now, she was probably far from the ship.

A hand touched his shoulder.

Kyrix grabbed for his laser. His claws grazed an empty holster. He'd given his weapon to Meredith. Hyra's Graces. Kyrix spun himself, knocking whoever touched him onto their ass.

"What in Hadus, Kyrix?" a cranky voice shouted in Herkleian.

"Beamus?" Kyrix blinked down at their crew's technician. The male had hair the deepest blue under his two-inch horns. Kyrix pulled away. Beamus wasn't trained in combat. If Kyrix had continued his attack, the male wouldn't have been able to stop him.

He rubbed his back. "What did you do that for? I think he broke something, doc."

"Doubtful," Detrux muttered.

Kyrix scooted back. He slammed into the wall. Paxos lay still on the other side of the hallway, Detrux at the green-haired male's side. A projection from his gold wristband displayed flickering vitals. Kyrix couldn't read them. Would the other male wake soon? Once he did, his crew would know the truth. He might be a Lord of Herkleios, but even he couldn't get away with treason.

At least there was no sight of Meredith. That was a good sign. He jumped to his feet and tried to ram down the hallway, but Detrux blocked his path.

Kyrix's vision flashed red. He needed to know immediately if Meredith had escaped. "What happened?"

"The human tried to escape," Detrux said.

Kyrix's heart sunk. "Tried?"

"She's in the brig."

Hadus. His plan hadn't worked. It had been a desperate attempt, but he had hoped it'd be enough. Kyrix kept his face neutral and blank. They couldn't know he had helped her escape. Kyrix was Meredith's only chance now. He needed to think quickly before Paxos awoke.

"She certainly got the better of you," Beamus muttered, picking at his claws. He threw back his head and howled. "Maybe you'll finally get past your policy of not hitting a female. And of a lesser species, too."

Kyrix's temper flared. "You will *not* speak of her that way."

Detrux's forehead creased. "The human bashed your head in, Kyrix."

"This was supposed to be an easy reconnaissance mission," Beamus muttered behind him. "Why is the human still on board?"

"The memory serum had no effect," Detrux said. "The booster didn't help. We may have found someone entirely immune to the serum's effects."

"Wiping her memory is completely off the table?" Beamus crossed his arm. "So, should we just launch her out of the airlock?"

Kyrix lunged at Beamus with a growl. The male cowered, but that didn't stop Kyrix from punching him in the face. The smaller Herkleian flew into the wall and slumped into an unconscious pile. Hands wrapped around his arms, Detrux pulling him back. He tried to shake the doctor off, but he wouldn't let go. "I can adamantly say that killing an innocent human is not in line with the king's agenda."

"Like you would know." Footsteps sounded in the hallway. Ezio. The male turned the corner, strolling into sight. "You're nothing more than his bastard."

Kyrix stiffened. Ezio knew. The secret he had hidden for all his life, revealed to his crew in an off-hand comment. Kyrix wasn't just the bastard son of the Duchess of Agafyi. He was the bastard son of the Herkleian king, Xenobaccus Yio'hyra.

Detrux's hold on Kyrix's arm loosened. "Kyrix is the king's son?"

"Kyrix is a traitor. Isn't that right, Your Highness?"

Detrux let go entirely. "What are you talking about?"

"I thought to review the security cameras during your little nap." Kyrix stiffened. If Ezio saw the feeds, he knew what Kyrix had done. Before he could argue his case, Ezio pressed the cold tip of a laser against his chest. "You're lucky we can't launch you out the airlock ourselves, Your Highness."

Kyrix didn't flinch this time. Ezio was trying to bait him.

"Why help the human escape? Is this all part of your seduction?"

Kyrix didn't answer. He didn't care what they did to him. All that mattered was Meredith. If he admitted why he freed her, what would Ezio do? He already hated humans. He might hurt her to get to him. Kyrix couldn't allow that.

"You thought we'd believe a pathetic human took a Herkleian warrior hostage? Do you think me a fool?" Ezio dug the laser in deeper. "Throw him in the brig with the human. Maybe some time in there will return him to his senses."

No one responded to Ezio's command. Both Paxos and Beamus remained unconscious on the floor. Ezio and Kyrix looked to Detrux, but he didn't move. Kyrix glared at Ezio. If the commander wanted

Kyrix in a cage, he'd need to do it himself. "Last time I checked, Ezio, I had control of this expedition. You can't throw me in the brig."

Ezio shoved his laser into Kyrix's face. An instant kill shot. "You betrayed your own people, Kyrix. You're not in control of anything anymore."

EIGHT

KYRIX

"Don't have too much fun with the human, Your Highness." Ezio shoved Kyrix into the brig with a hard push. He hit a button on the wall before marching out with a howl. A forcefield buzzed into existence. It not only hindered prisoners from tampering with the door but also stopped heat from radiating through. Chilling air caressed his bare scales.

"Kyrix?"

Meredith squatted in the corner, her arms wrapped around herself. They had taken his laser and cloaking device from her, but left the comms device in her ear. They could speak to each other, then. Kyrix had an implanted device, too, but the external version had quicker translation capabilities. He approached slowly. Her teeth chattered loudly, her body heat dissipating in the cold. Herkleians were always warm, a gift from the dragon goddess Hyra, but Meredith was only human. Throwing her in the brig was a disgrace.

"I'm sorry about shooting you." Her eyes traced his face before settling on the floor, almost in shame.

Kyrix moved to her side and sat beside her. "There's nothing to be sorry about."

"You're not mad at me? I screwed up the plan. You're in here because of me."

"It's not your fault at all." His arm rubbed against hers. His blood heated, arousal flaring through him. "I told them I didn't know how you escaped, but Ezio watched the security footage. It didn't help that I punched Bemus straight in the face when he offended you."

Her eyes widened. She shuffled closer to him. "You fought your crew for me?"

He nodded.

"Seriously?"

"They threatened you." His vision went red at the thought. "Through Hyra's might, I'll never let another male lay a hand on you."

She stiffened. Hyra's Graces. Kyrix shouldn't have said that. It was too much, too soon. Couples mated quickly on Herkleios, but not this quickly. A hundred years ago, matebonded pairs got together in less than a day. But Meredith couldn't be his mate. She was a human. Goddess Hyra wouldn't bless a human with the bond, would she?

"Oh, wow." She started fiddling with her hair. Did it pain her? "Umm, well, thanks for caring so much. I like you, too."

She glanced down, clearly embarrassed by the confession. She had no reason to be. Kyrix had told her he was a lord, the heir to his mother's titles and land, but he wasn't on the ship out of duty. He had lied to her. Meredith deserved the truth about him. "There's something I must tell you, Meredith. I'm the bastard son of the Herkleian king."

Her eyes widened. "Really?"

He nodded.

"Oh." She paused, chewing on her lips. The motion entranced his eyes. "Is that why you're on this mission?"

"Herkleians rarely hide their bastards, as we have the same rights as any other child. When my elder half-brother, the Crown Prince Eryx, abdicated a year ago, his younger brother, Anax, became heir." He paused. Kyrix had never said his reason for leaving Herkleios aloud. When Prince Eryx had announced his abdication, Kyrix's mother had immediately worried. Kyrix hadn't feared until his father showed up. "I'm two months older than Prince Anax. By law, the throne is mine. My father all but banished me. He doesn't want me in the way."

"I'm sorry." She touched his arm and tried for a smile. "But being next in line for a real-life throne is kinda cool, right?"

He bared his fangs at her, a small smile to match hers. "I have no intention of claiming the throne. I don't want to be king. Not only that, but revealing my father cheated on Queen Avra would destroy the Intergalactic Alliance. Their marriage sealed the agreement thirty years ago."

"It's not your fault your dad's a cheating asshole. You shouldn't be punished for being his son."

"I tried telling him I wouldn't challenge Prince Anax, but he couldn't take the risk. He forced me on this expedition less than a week after Anax became Crown Prince. If I return to Herkleios without permission, he'll seize Agafyi from my mother and elect a new Duchess."

Her fingers on his arm starting stroking up and down, a distracting pattern. "I'm so sorry, Kyrix."

He knew he should pull away from her, but he leaned into her touch. "You needed to know. I can't provide for you, Meredith. I can never even return to my homeworld."

She stared at him. "So?"

She said it casually, like it didn't matter. He scanned her face. He had to be missing something. Earthlings and Herkleians had some similar expressions, but not all. What was she thinking? "You do not care?"

"Why would I care?" When she turned, her hand brushed his leg. They had slid closer and closer, seeking warmth and comfort. "Do you care that I work at a chocolate shop?"

His brow creased. Why would he care about her employment?

Selling goods was an honorable career path, necessary to society. "No?"

She smiled. "Then I don't care who your father is or that he's banished you. It doesn't matter to me. What matters is you. I know it's only been a day, but I feel like I've known you forever, Kyrix."

"I feel the same." He had never connected with anyone like he had this tiny female. She was funny and brave and sexy. His gaze trailed to her lips. He wanted to touch her again. Taste her. Feel her moan against his mouth.

Her own gaze dropped to his lips. This close, he felt her breath hitch against his scales. She half-turned away before changing her mind and crawling into his lap. He wrapped her in his arms. Kyrix looked down at her. By Hyra, she was gorgeous. His cock twitched. He couldn't wait any longer.

Kyrix leaned in to kiss her. Their lips touched. It felt insanely good, just like their last encounter. But this time, he wanted more. This time, he was going to take it. Kyrix lashed his tongue harder against hers and dragged his sharp teeth slowly over the bottom of her lip.

She moaned and gripped the sensitive area of his horns. The sensation shivered down his spine. He let out a groan of pleasure. He tore his lips from hers and moved down her throat to the top of her shirt. Kyrix paused, looking into her dazzling eyes. Giving her the option to back out.

"Yes," she huffed out, her lips pink and swollen. "Yes."

That was the only invitation he needed. He drew his claw down the front of her shirt, splitting the black fabric in half. Her breath fluttered. Her skin was pale pink and soft, the mounds of her breasts and valleys of her stomach screaming out for him to touch. She was beautiful. Absolutely beautiful. She was his. His female. He was going to claim every single inch of her.

He lapped his tongue between the peaks of her breasts. She gripped his horns tighter. She tasted like ovtro, his favorite fruit, sweet and succulent and soft. He wanted more of her. Needed more of her. He took one pink nipple into his mouth.

She gasped. He released her. Had he hurt her? His teeth were far sharper than hers.

Meredith clenched his horns. "Don't you dare stop now."

He bared his fangs against her skin. "As you command."

He pulled that hard nipple into his mouth and sucked. She whimpered, soft cries that turned his cock to a steel rod. He needed her, but her pleasure came first. He lapped at one nipple before turning to its lonesome twin, suckling them before lapping at them with his tongue. She arched her back, giving him even better access. He raked his teeth against her, gently. She squirmed under his touch.

"Stop teasing," she murmured into his hair.

"For you, anything."

His cock was rock hard and he longed to be inside her. To fill her until she couldn't take any more of him. But he hesitated. While nothing but lust filled him for his beautiful human, she was much smaller than him. He didn't want to hurt her.

Kyrix would take his time. He would draw out her pleasure until she couldn't even stand.

Meredith was already naked from the waist up, but she quickly rectified that. She pulled off the smooth pants and stepped into the cold air, entirely naked. He drank her in. She was gorgeous, a goddess come to life. It was only fitting that he dropped to his knees before her.

He kissed down her stomach until he came to the heat of her. He retracted his claws and traced a finger against her, a testing glance. She shuddered. His scales came away wet, dampened by her juices. He put that finger into his mouth and sucked, holding her eyes as he swallowed her. Her rich scent burst into the air.

"You are mine, Meredith." He slipped a hand onto her thigh and lifted her leg, hooking it over his shoulder. She gripped his horns with both hands. Good. She would need to hold on.

He didn't hold back this time. He plunged his finger into her depths, then two, stretching her wide. With the ball of his thumb, he thrummed against her clit.

She moaned and widened her leg, opening for him. Wanting him. Craving him. Kyrix, the bastard. Kyrix, who had no land, no title, no future to provide for her. But Meredith hadn't cared. She had embraced him for who he was. He thrust his fingers into her, again and again, her wetness dripping down his scales.

"You're..." The word came out in a breathless rasp. "You're really good at this."

He bared his fangs. "And we're just getting started."

Her scent filled his nostrils, hot and wanting. Kyrix couldn't hold himself back anymore. He had to taste her. He pressed a kiss to her heat.

She gasped, her hands clenching tighter on his horns. "Take me, Kyrix."

"Yes, my lady." He raked his teeth against her clit before taking it into his mouth, teasing, licking, sucking. She started thrashing at his touch, moan after moan escaping her lips. He loved the sounds she made. He craved them. If he died today, killed by Ezio, he'd die a happy male, sated by the sounds of her cries. Sated by bringing his female pleasure. For that was what she was. His human. His female.

His mate.

He couldn't believe it, but he knew deep in his core. She was his mate, like in legends of old. The Herkleian priests had prayed and prayed to Hyra, but she hadn't ever answered why their bonds had faded. But the matebonds hadn't faded, only slumbered. Awakened in his touch of Meredith, her sweet taste on his tongue.

His mate.

He nipped against her clit again before swiping his tongue across her depths. Her body tensed, from the leg over his shoulder to her hands in his horns. With a shriek heard all the way in the heavens, Meredith crashed into climax. Her core gripped at his fingers and her desire melted on his lips. He wanted more, wanted all of her. Kyrix devoured every drop of her wetness.

When her body went slack, her desire spent, he cradled her down into his lap. She curled into him, her cheeks flushed a beautiful red. She grinned lazily at him. His mate. He brushed her hair from her face, her neck. A small star-shaped mark a shade darker than her skin had appeared at her nape. The matebond mark. Each mark was unique and individual, like the couple paired together in the bond. She was his, forever. He wanted to roar his claim to the universe.

She brushed her thumb across the edge of his neck, in the same place. "What's this?"

He tucked her hair behind her ear. She had already experienced too much today. He didn't want to overwhelm her. Earthlings had a concept like mates, but it was purely fictional. How would she react to being bonded to a Herkleian male? "Sleep, naika. You need to rest."

"Naika? That's a pretty word." She yawned, but tried to shake the tiredness from her bones. "I can't sleep yet."

He frowned. "I will keep you safe. I will keep you warm."

"Not that." Her hand slid down to his lap, to the edge of his pants. His cock twitched. "I need to return the favor."

He gently pulled her hand away. He wanted her more than anything. Wanted to feel the heavy weight of him in her hand, wanted to thrust himself into her mouth, into her heat. But he wouldn't, not yet. "There is no need for that. It wasn't a favor but a gift. From me to you, naika."

"But—"

He pressed a kiss to her forehead, to the edge of the mark tying them together. "Sleep, my beautiful Meredith."

NINE

Meredith drifted into consciousness, her body warm and light and floating. She pressed her face against warm azure-blue scales. She inhaled deeply. Kyrix. She had never slept as peacefully as she had in his arms—especially after *that* orgasm. None of her exes had wanted to go down on her. They had expected her to get on her knees for them, but no one had ever done it for her. Not until Kyrix, his fingers and mouth instantly finding the right spots to make her shudder and scream. The coarseness of his tongue had provided an extra layer of delicious sensation.

At her movement, he glanced down at her, his slitted purple eyes caressing her face. Did she wish him a good morning? What if last night was a mistake? She barely knew this male. They hadn't known each other longer than twenty-four hours. What if he only wanted sex from her? Meredith never slept with someone on the first date for that very reason.

But with one look at his face, she knew she was more than a one-night stand for him, too.

He bared sharp fangs in a smile. "Good morning, naika."

Naika. She shivered at the word. She didn't know what it meant, but she loved when he said it. She wanted him to say it over and over for years and years. To think, a day ago she didn't believe aliens existed and now... Meredith was half in love with one. No man had treated her the way Kyrix did, like she was precious, treasured.

The chill of the brig rippled across her skin. Meredith shivered. Would she get the chance to fall completely in love with Kyrix? She was imprisoned on an alien ship. The Herkleian government couldn't allow Earth to discover their existence. They couldn't allow Meredith to keep her memories, but if she did, what would they do with her? What would they do with Kyrix if he tried to stop them? He was a lord, but also the king's banished bastard son.

"So, how long until we're murdered?" she asked cheerfully, trying to keep the mood light.

Kyrix flinched. She immediately regretted the question. This almost didn't feel real to Meredith, but this was Kyrix's normal life—minus the imprisonment. "I'm sorry I didn't protect you," he said, head bowed. "I've failed you, Meredith."

"What are you talking about?" She cupped his cheek, tilting his head to meet her eyes, and smiled. "We're a bag of chips away from a great party here."

"What is a bag of chips?"

She snorted. "That's not important."

Kyrix caressed her cheek. Some emotion entered his eyes, like he wanted to commit the moment to his memory forever. The intensity of it warmed her chest, her cheeks, her core. She squirmed on his lap. A sudden hardness expanded in his pants—and expanded and expanded. She tried not to widen her eyes. He was almost seven feet tall, but she hadn't considered what other, um, parts might be larger, too.

He didn't act on his erection or demand she immediately sate him. He continued stroking across her cheek, his scales like a smooth velvet against her skin.

"What? Why are you looking at me like that?"

He bared his fangs, a sly grin. "Do you not like it?"

"No, I do." She tucked her hair behind her ear. Every time he looked at her, her stomach fluttered. "No one has ever looked at me like that before."

"That's because no one has ever loved you like I do."

Her breath hitched. "Love?"

"Yes, I love you, Meredith." He threaded his claws through her hair before tilting his own head. His purple hair fell to the side, revealing a mark on the back of his neck, almost imprinted onto the scales. Interlocking circles formed a star-shaped mark, no bigger than a coin. She had noticed it last night. Her own neck tickled. "Do you know what this mark means?"

"No?"

"On Herkleios, when two people are fated to be together, this mark appears. Bonding their souls, their essences together forever. A Herkleian will never see their own mark since it's always on the neck, but they'll know it's there. In here." He tapped his claws to his chest, over his heart. "There hasn't been a recorded matebond in the last century. I don't know why they stopped, nor do I know why the goddess had blessed us with one now."

"Us?" The moment she said it, she knew it was true. While Meredith couldn't see the back of her neck, she sensed the symbol there, claiming her as Kyrix's. But Meredith wasn't Herkleian. Soulmates were only myth on Earth. "Go back a second. We're fated to be together?"

"Yes, naika."

"Naika? What does that mean?"

"It's the term bonded mates use to address each other. Naika for a female, naikos for a male." His claws caressed her face, sliding from the top of her neck to her temple and back. She shuddered. "There is no English translation, so my translator uses the Herkleian word."

She reached to the back of her neck and slid her fingers against her skin. The tingling sensation grew. It was there. The truth of his statement echoed within her, but a part of Meredith remained skeptical. She was a simple cashier with two degrees and no prospects.

What had she ever done to deserve a soulmate? "I don't feel anything there."

"It's flat against your skin. I wish I had some kind of mirror to show you."

Meredith swallowed. Even without a mark, she wanted Kyrix. Wanted to be with him. Wanted to get to know him. Wanted to love him. Meredith had wanted and wanted for so long. She couldn't be denied anymore. She shuffled in his lap and made a choice. "I don't need a mirror to see it. The moment you said it, I knew it was true in my gut. You're my mate. We were always meant to be."

Meredith wrapped her hands around his neck and tilted his face towards her. Kyrix didn't hesitate. He claimed her mouth in a possessive swoop. She wrapped her hands in his hair, around his horns. She'd never get enough of this. She opened herself to him. His rough tongue battled with hers, sending shots of electricity through her body. She wanted him, needed him. She pushed onto her knees and straddled his waist, not breaking the kiss—

The door clanked. Meredith pulled away from Kyrix with a gasp. She'd forgotten where she was. Or that she wore absolutely no clothes. She'd found her soulmate in this cell, but that didn't make it any less a prison. What would the Herkleians do with her? She couldn't be parted with Kyrix. Not after they had found each other.

Kyrix stood in a single movement, Meredith still wrapped in his arms. He placed her gently on the floor behind him. "Whatever happens, know I will protect you. Know it in your heart, naika."

Meredith nodded. She knew it. When Kyrix turned to face his crew, she pulled on the smooth, black pants. She wouldn't let her mate stand alone against four other Herkleians. Her shirt was slit down the middle, so she threw her arms through the holes and knotted the front. Meredith hated crop tops—it made little sense to buy half a shirt—but she'd rather wear that than flash the other males.

The forcefield dropped and the door flew open. Ezio pushed into the small space, the green-haired alien behind him. Both glared at

Kyrix, completely ignoring her. "Has your little prison stay cleared your mind?"

Kyrix clenched his fists. Meredith put a hand on his shoulder. He was unarmed and outnumbered. Ezio seemed like the sort of prick to rile others when they were down. He wanted Kyrix to do something stupid.

"Yes." Kyrix rolled his shoulder, shoving Meredith's hand off him. It lashed through her, but she focused on the tingling at their neck, the mark tying them together. Kyrix loved her. He did this for her. "I've had my fill of the Earthling."

Ezio bared his fangs. "I'm glad to hear you say that. I'd have hated to drag you back to Herkleios all tied up."

The green-haired alien stiffened. "Commander?"

Ezio rounded on him with a snarl. "You heard my orders. Lord Kyrix is to go free."

"He tried to kill me."

"You would have deserved it." Ezio turned from Green Hair, his glare re-directed at Kyrix. "Try anything again and I'll be well in my rights to kill you, bastard of the king or not."

Kyrix crossed the small cell to stand at Ezio's side. The chill of the brig bit at Meredith's skin. She tried not to shiver, but she couldn't help herself.

"What has Command ordered us to do with her?" Kyrix asked.

"The scientists at home want to know more about her immunity to memory serum. If others like her are immune, it will cause problems for us in the future." Ezio gestured at Meredith and the green-haired crewmate came forward. She stumbled back into the wall, but there was nowhere to run. "We are putting her on a trans-pod to Herkleios."

TEN

KYRIX

Paxos put a hand on Meredith's shoulder. Kyrix's vision flashed red. His mate. He stamped on the urge to rush forward and impale the other male with his horns. If Ezio even suspected their relationship, their bond, he'd imprison Kyrix permanently. They would shove Meredith into the trans-pod and ship her off to Herkleios, where they'd experiment and prod her. Even after their government contacted Earth, she wouldn't be released. She'd spend the rest of her life in a cage.

He couldn't allow that to happen. Not to his mate. He let Paxos pull her past him, into the hall. Meredith brushed her hand against his. She knew he was doing this for her. For them. When he got them out of this mess, he would beg for her forgiveness. Even if it took him decades on his knees.

Fire stirred in his veins at the thought. He buried his desire for her, too. She had to appear nothing more than a passing entertainment. Ezio couldn't know.

The commander slapped him on the shoulder. "If only Command let us have her for another day. It's been too long since I've had a female."

Kyrix clenched his fists. The other male howled and followed behind Paxos, heading for the trans-pod bay. Ezio would pay for his words. No female deserved to be talked about in that way, especially his gentle mate.

Kyrix needed a plan. The trans-pod bay had three separate shuttles, used for long distance transportation. At full speed, they'd take four days to reach Herkleios. Each pod was equipped with levitating beds that slotted into the wall, a food system, and a forcefield generator for the transportation of prisoners. With one, Kyrix and Meredith could escape, but they wouldn't get far. Someone needed to pre-program the navigation from the *Acacia*. Even if Kyrix forced his way onto one, they wouldn't get far before Ezio re-programmed the pod to return.

To survive, he and Meredith needed the *Acacia*.

When they arrived in the bay, Beamus glanced from where he was programming the pod. Detrux stood off to the corner, medical bag in hand. Would they try to sedate Meredith? They didn't have a male to spare to accompany her. If she remained unconscious for the journey, she wouldn't tamper with their tech.

If so, Detrux would need a moment with her. Out of all his crew, the doctor was the one male who might side with Kyrix. Matebonds were sacred to the Herkleians. To stand against a couple tied together by the mark was to stand in the way of Hyra. Kyrix had to hope the goddess mattered enough to Detrux.

Ezio jerked a thumb toward the doctor. "Paxos—"

Kyrix grabbed Meredith's shoulder. "I'll do it."

"Hey!" Meredith whacked him lightly on the shoulder. "I'm not a sack of potatoes."

"Be quiet, Earthling." He maneuvered her toward Detrux with a snarl. With his body blocking the rest of his crew's view, he rubbed a thumb across her shoulder. He wished he could take her in his arms, proclaim his love, but he couldn't, not yet. Ezio's eyes raked across Kyrix's back, his hand never far from his laser.

Detrux settled his medical bag down on a table and gestured for

Meredith to sit. A stool top levitated out from the floor. "I am sorry for this, Meredith."

She swallowed, eyes locked on the doctor's injector. "What is that?"

"It will make you sleep, nothing more." Detrux pulled a yellow serum from his bag. "The trip to Herkleios is long. We want you to be comfortable."

Meredith glared. "So you can experiment on me once I get there?"

The doctor resisted a flinch, but Kyrix saw the hesitation in his friend's eyes. Detrux was here to see if Earthlings were worthy of joining the Intergalactic Alliance. Imprisoning them for experimentation wasn't something one did to their equals.

"You must look at something first, Detrux." Kyrix gestured to Meredith's neck. Her eyes widened. She brushed away her hair and faced Kyrix, giving her back to the doctor. Kyrix held her gaze. He could spend forever locked in the beauty of her blue eyes.

Detrux frowned, but Kyrix knew the moment he saw the mark. The doctor's entire body stiffened. He stared in shock for nearly a minute before gazing up at Kyrix. "It this...? How?"

"I do not know how, my friend." Kyrix took care to keep his voice light. "Only that it has happened."

Detrux stared harder at the mark. "Do you know what this means?"

Kyrix hadn't considered the implications. All he cared for was his mate. But if Herkleians and Earthlings could form this sacred bond, the fate of both their planets was about to change. "If Meredith can be my mate, her people are worthy of joining the Intergalactic Alliance. If they can join, we have no right to imprison her."

Detrux's eyes flickered over Kyrix's shoulder. "We're outnumbered, Kyrix."

"No, we aren't," Meredith said. "There are three of us, three of them."

The doctor looked skeptical.

"Please." Meredith reached out and touched Detrux's hand, just for a second. "Help us."

Detrux looked down at his Meredith and sighed. Kyrix almost burst with joy. His friend would help. "We need a distraction."

"I can put up a fight?" Meredith suggested.

Kyrix glanced at the doctor. It was their only option. The males nodded. The doctor pulled something from his bag—a small scalpel. He dipped the hilt of the blade in a purple-blue serum that would pass for Herkleian blood and handed it to Meredith. Meredith paled when she glanced at the scalpel's blade.

"When you are ready, naika." He gestured to his bare chest. "Kick me here. I will fall. Ezio and Paxos will come to restrain you. We will take care of them, but you must get our technician, Beamus. He wasn't trained in combat."

She nodded and swallowed. His brave mate. He didn't need to encourage her any more. Meredith raised her bare foot and slammed it into his chest. He actually stumbled back, but threw himself further back, slamming to the floor.

Ezio didn't waste his chance. He rushed forward with a snarl. "Stupid human."

She raised her scalpel, her back to the wall. Detrux slumped behind her, hand pressed against his midsection like Meredith had slashed him. "Asshole alien!"

Paxos rushed to Ezio's side, the two of them facing off against his mate. Paxos howled, a crass sound. "Command won't notice if we have a little fun with her, sir."

Ezio bared his fangs, a cruel grimace. "They certainly won't."

Kyrix had to stop his own howl. Ezio deserved everything coming for him. With a glance at Detrux, the two males moved. Kyrix kicked Ezio's leg as Detrux launched himself at Paxos. Behind them, Beamus shrieked. Meredith didn't give him a moment to pull his laser. She rushed across the room with a battle cry worthy of any Herkleian, scalpel raised. The technician didn't stand a chance.

Ezio thrust out a palm, slamming it into Kyrix's nose. He ripped his attention from his mate. He had his own battle to fight. He rolled to a stand, the other male doing the same.

"You traitor," Ezio snarled.

"I, Lord Kyrix Yio'naeus, heir to the Duchy of Agafyi, challenge you, Ezio Yio'aleta, Commander of the Acadia, to a duel."

Ezio had reached for his laser, but paused at the words. A duel allowed only two weapons: a male's fists and horns. Kyrix had wanted to challenge Ezio since the moment he met. The male probably felt the same. "I accept."

Kyrix rammed forward with a snarl.

The two males crashed, horns locking together. Kyrix punched out, slamming a hand into Ezio's chest. The commander's horns didn't dislodge. Ezio charged forward, forcing Kyrix to stumble back. He held his balance and steadied his legs. He couldn't allow Ezio to throw him.

He put all his strength into his legs, his shoulders. All his love for Meredith, his hopes and dreams for their future. They had a future. Together, no matter what. A day ago, he was lost, banished from his planet because of a genetic connection to a father he'd met once. Now he had a family. Now he had something to fight for.

With a burst of strength, Kyrix launched himself forward.

Ezio lost his balance, dropping to his hands and knees.

The commander's hand went to his belt, to his laser. Using a weapon was against the laws of a challenge, but Ezio had never cared for laws. Kyrix unlocked their horns—

A thin scalpel stabbed straight through Ezio's palm.

Meredith bared her teeth, a savage look. "Remember me, asshole?"

Ezio stumbled. It was all Kyrix needed. He gave the male one last shove and kicked out. His boot connected with Ezio's smug face. The commander slumped to the floor.

Meredith grabbed the male's laser. "You lose, buddy."

Kyrix glanced around. Paxos lay unconscious as Detrux wiped the end of an injector. His friend had a purple-bruised eye, but otherwise appeared unharmed. Meredith had chased Beamus into the trans-pod. The terrified technician had locked himself behind a force-field rather than face his formidable mate. She was right. They had won.

He plucked her off the floor and into his arms. Meredith laughed, that beautiful, tinkling sound, and wrapped a hand around his neck. They had won their future. He kissed his mate. He would never take for granted the softness of her lips.

Ezio grunted from the floor.

Kyrix immediately lowered his mate. Instead of standing in front of her, he stood beside her. Like they always would. She aimed the laser right at the other male's balls. "If you want to keep your parts, Ezio, stay down."

The male spat bright blue-purple blood to the floor. "King Xenobaccus won't let you get away with this, bastard. He'll send ships for you. To kill you and your dirty Earthling like the traitors you are."

Kyrix regretted not letting Meredith stab the male a second time. "Tell my father this, Ezio. If he comes for me, I'll reveal my identity to all of Herkleios. It's a great crime for a father to kill a son. More so for a king to kill his heir. If I come back to Herkleios, that's exactly what I will be. Anax's throne will be mine, as it is by blood right."

Ezio tried to push from the floor with a growl. "You bastard—"

Detrux jammed his injector into the back of Ezio's neck. The male slumped to the floor.

"Hyra's Graces," Detrux muttered. "I thought he would never shut up."

Meredith kicked Ezio's side. The male didn't move. "What are we going to do with them? We can't kill them."

Though Kyrix wished Ezio dead, he agreed with his mate. He glanced back at the trans-pod. "Did Beamus finish the programming?"

Detrux tapped a tablet by the open door. "He did."

"Then put them on the shuttle. Send them back to Herkleios." He grabbed Meredith's hand. "This is our ship now."

ELEVEN

Meredith threw herself onto the middle of Kyrix's levitating bed and leaned back her head. She hadn't sat once in the hours since booting Ezio off the *Acacia*. The designers of this ship had intended it for a crew of five. Two barely managed it, especially when Meredith understood nada about spaceships. Detrux had left them, volunteering to escort Ezio and the others to Herkleios. Kyrix couldn't lock them in the trans-pod's cell if they went unattended, but if he allowed them to roam free, Ezio would signal Command. The doctor needed to go, but it made running the ship all the harder.

"Meredith?"

Meredith jolted awake. Kyrix knelt at the end of the bed. She must have passed out. She wiped the sleep from her eyes. Her mate hadn't changed out of the black, skin-tight pants. It didn't look like he had relaxed at all while she slept. Thanks to Detrux, Meredith and Kyrix had four days to get away, but they had lots to do in the remaining time.

She pressed up onto her arms. "You should have woken me up."

"You were exhausted, naika. You needed sleep."

She reached for his hand. "You need to sleep, too."

"I will." He kissed her palm. "You've been in that ripped outfit all day. I have a bathing room you can use."

He gestured to the door behind him and tried to pull his hand from hers, but Meredith clutched him tighter. She gazed into his purple slitted eyes. Kyrix. Her mate. Heat flushed through her chest. She slipped off the mattress and placed a hand over his heart. With him, she had nothing to fear. "I'll only bathe if you come with me."

Kyrix stiffened under her touch. She wanted him. Needed him. Like he did her. He bared his fangs, a cheshire grin. "As you command, my lady."

She couldn't help but laugh as he scooped her into his arms. She wrapped her hands around his neck, thumbs tracing the interlocking circles of his star-shaped mark. The bond that tied them together for all to see. He kicked through the door into his now *their*—bathroom. Kyrix hit a button by the door. A waist-deep bath tube of jade-like stone materialized in the center of the room. A section in the ceiling opened, pouring streams of hot water and filling the tub in seconds.

Kyrix placed her on the floor near the tub. Meredith didn't plan to waste any time. She wanted her mate. Wanted to feel him inside her, stretching her, filling her. She quickly slid her clothes to the ground. Her skin tingled when it met the ship's open air. Without looking back, she stepped into the tub and leaned back onto the rim.

Kyrix remained still and clothed, his eyes fixated on her. Meredith flashed him a smile and gestured with a single finger, summoning him forward. "Come here, naikos."

And with that, her alien suddenly wasn't wearing any pants. His legs were as blue as his upper body, darkening to a deep sapphire at his cock. Meredith stilled. Not only was he massive, but his shaft was ridged and slightly curved at the end. The sight sent a shock through her system. When he noticed she was staring at him, his mass surged, somehow getting even harder and larger.

Kyrix strutted forward, an intimidating prowl. Goosebumps plucked on her skin. Her nipples hardened to two insistent beads. Meredith slipped deeper into the water as he got closer, inch by tortuous inch. When he climbed into the tub, everything within her tightened, her breaths coming out in puffs. He hadn't even touched her yet, but she was moments away from exploding. His eyes devoured her, claimed her.

Her mate. Her alien.

By the time Kyrix reached her, Meredith couldn't wait. Her hands trailed the scales of his muscular chest to the cords of his neck to the sharpness of his chin. She pulled him down toward her as she surged upwards. Their lips touched. Meredith moaned. She opened herself and he plunged his tongue into her, seeking, claiming.

She sighed into his mouth. He was hers. She was his. Nothing would keep them apart. Never again. She gripped his horns and wrapped one leg around his thigh, pressing her heat against his hardness. He growled into her lips. Her desire only burned hotter, wetter. She couldn't wait. Not anymore.

She gripped his other horn and tugged, stoking the hard blackness. Kyrix shuddered at the touch. He broke their kiss with a final nip to her lips. She stared into those purple eyes and whispered, "I need you now."

Kyrix nearly growled. Meredith started to grin, but he grabbed her other leg, hoisting her up his body. Her back bumped against the bath's far wall. The tip of his cock nudged against her entry. She gasped, the heat in her swelling into a wet inferno.

"You are mine, mate."

Yes. Meredith didn't have the chance to respond. The water brushed against her skin, each wave a caress. She needed him. Needed him inside her. Now. Now. "Now."

Kyrix did as ordered. He slammed into her, filling her to the core.

She gasped, her body pushed to the brink. The curved part of him rubbed right against her g-spot and she shuddered. Every one of his ridges rippled against her sensitive flesh. He was glorious. He was all hers. Her mate. Her naikos.

He braced his hand behind her and thrust. Meredith rocked her hips with his movements. Her back arched. Every touch burst into sparks within her core. Almost too much to bear.

She claimed Kyrix's mouth with her own, wanting every bit of him. Needing every bit of him. She had never wanted a human man like this. Never thought it possible. This kind of passion, the heat inside her, wasn't something she ever thought she deserved.

His fingers dug into her hips with each thrust. Meredith tightened her grip on his horns. She writhed and gasped. He was too much. Too big, too powerful, too alien. A moan escaped from her each time he plunged into her depths. He caught her lips and swallowed her next groan.

She broke the kiss. "I'm not—I can't..."

He didn't stop, wouldn't stop. "Come for me, mate."

Her body clenched around him as the orgasm ripped through her. She had never climaxed like this. Her body rippled and burned, sensation wringing through her every nerve and cell. Kyrix groaned and shuddered, but didn't stop the pound of his hips. Another wave of ecstasy tore through Meredith's core. She screamed his name in the endless rush of heat. Her vision turned into exploding stars.

When she floated back down to Earth—to the *Acacia*—Kyrix pressed a kiss to her forehead and inhaled her scent. She had never been fucked like that before. Meredith wrapped her arms around his shoulders and let her strained body float. Her muscles slackened under the water. Whatever soreness she suffered tomorrow would be worth every second.

She rested her chin on the bend of his shoulder. "So," she started with a satisfied yawn, "where do we go now?"

"Anywhere you want, naika."

She inhaled, breathing in the scent of him. "Literally anywhere?"

"I can't ask you to leave your home. My cloaking device is still glitching but we could find a place on Earth."

Earth was the only place she knew. Her home with her family, her friends. But they couldn't stay here. The Herkleians would find them. Or worse, the American government. What would they do with an alien? She shuddered at the thought. "That's absolutely off the table. I spent my entire life waiting for you. I won't risk anyone finding us. There's no way I'll let anything separate us again."

"I like the sound of that." He pressed a soft kiss to her chin, then lower to her neck.

She clung closer to him. "And we can't go to Herkleios. I won't risk your mother losing Agafyi."

He trailed kisses along her collarbone. "There are hundreds of planets for us to explore, naika."

"Really?" Her voice came out as a gasp. "Hundreds?"

"Not all are inhabited, but there are dozens of planets where species mingle peacefully. There are thousands of cities, as packed and as busy as your Portland."

She shook her head. "I've lived in a city my entire life. It's time to try something new."

He glanced up at her, his lips hovering above her breasts. His claws traced her stomach. "Do you trust me?"

She raised an eyebrow at him. "Of course I trust you."

He retracted his claws and traced a finger along her slit, baring his fangs when she moaned. "Then I know just the place for us."

EPILOGUE

MEREDITH

2 Years Later

Meredith lifted Annabelle's car seat from its cradle and tried her best not to jostle her daughter. Her baby girl would turn six months old in a few days. Meredith scarcely believed it. Annabelle didn't have horns or scales like her father, but her smooth skin was the lightest blue, a perfect match to the pink of her pacifier. Her hair hadn't grown in yet, leaving her head bald and smooth. Meredith had hoped she'd be a brunette like her until Kyrix had told her how his mother had hair a beautiful emerald. Meredith had quickly changed her mind.

Meredith rubbed a gentle thumb across her sleeping daughter's face before facing Kyrix. "I don't know if I can do this."

He wrapped an arm around her shoulder. Almost two full years had passed since Meredith had last stepped foot on Earth. While she loved the life she and Kyrix had carved out for themselves, some days she missed her home, her mother, her friends. They had gone back to her apartment for Sir Pounce, but Meredith had left no letters or notes behind. It had been too dangerous. But now that the Herkleios had officially contacted Earth, Meredith could finally return.

Across a lawn of manicured grass, the red-bricked house Meredith had called home for over a decade looked just as it had the last time she'd seen it. Lights from inside cut squares into the darkness of the night. The *Acacia* had arrived earlier today, but Meredith had waited to go to her mother's. The news was obsessed with the Herkleians. If one of the big blue aliens showed up in a regular suburban neighborhood, every TV station would flock to the area—except for tonight. As part of their treaty with Earth, the Herkleians required a human bride for one of their princes. The poor girl was being introduced to Kyrix's viper of a sire right about now in an inter-galactically-televised event.

But that wasn't the only reason to delay. Meredith hadn't talked to her mom for so long. She almost wasn't sure where to begin. It was easier to stay away.

Kyrix grazed his knuckles across her arm. "You have told me much of your mother, naika. She'll be overjoyed to see you."

"Will she?"

"She will."

Meredith squared her shoulder. Annabelle was half-human. She deserved to have a connection to her human family. Kyrix reached out for their daughter's carrier, and Meredith reluctantly handed her over. She rushed up the steps and rang the doorbell. There was no turning back now. Her heart thudded in her ears as footsteps sounded inside and a familiar voice called out, "One second."

The door opened. Her mom poked out her head, only to stop dead at the sight.

"Hi, Mom."

Her mom gripped the doorframe, but didn't fall over from shock. After a moment, she stepped back and shakily welcomed them inside.

Meredith looked around the foyer. The pictures on the wall hadn't changed, nor had the stool in the corner, where Meredith had first learned to tie her shoes. Her eyes watered. "I missed you, Mom. I really hope you didn't spend this whole time worrying about me."

Her mom wrapped her in a tight hug. Tears trailed down Meredith's face. "I don't know why, but something in me told me you were okay. Regardless of what the police said. I'm happy I was right."

Meredith squeezed her mom back. She had missed this. She pulled back and wiped at her eyes before gesturing at her husband. "This is Kyrix, my husband, and our daughter, Annabelle."

Kyrix dropped into a bow. "It is a pleasure to meet you, Lady Sinclair."

Meredith beamed proudly. What human man would bow to her mom and call her a lady?

"Please, call me Shelley." Her tiny mother opened her arms and gave Kyrix a hug like he wasn't a big, blue alien. "I've seen your people on the news, Mr. Kyrix. I must say, you're all very polite and well-spoken."

"Thank you, my lady."

Meredith reached for the carrier. "Would you like to hold the baby, Mom?"

Her mom peered into the carrier, tracing the lines of her granddaughter's face. "I'd love to."

Kyrix held the carrier in front of him and Meredith undid Annabelle's straps, pulling the baby into her arms. When she handed her daughter to her mom, her baby girl cooed, an adorable sound. Her mom started crying. Meredith's eyes pricked, too.

In that moment, Meredith was incredibly thankful to that shitty chocolate shop for giving her this amazing life.

Thank you for reading! Want more? You can read all about Kyrix's half-brother, Crown Prince Anax, in the first full-length novel in the *Bride to an Alien Prince* series.

ANAX

BRIDE TO AN ALIEN PRINCE, BOOK 1

"How do I get myself into these situations?" Lexi muttered. She pulled at the high neckline of the dress her uncle's assistant stuffed her into. The ornate gown pinched at her shoulders, drowned her in embroidered crystals, and itched thanks to a white shimmering overlay. The damn thing even had a cape. Every step ended with the possibility of her tripping and falling flat on her face.

Her uncle's hand dug into her arm. "You will *not* ruin this for me."

Lexi clenched her fists at her side. When Earth first started receiving messages from deep space, Lexi hadn't believed it. She naively bet her best friend, Olivia, if aliens turned out to be real, she'd marry one. Now, three months later, that was exactly what she was doing. Not that Olivia was making good on the bet, but Lexi still felt like an idiot.

"Smile and don't speak unless spoken to," Uncle Grayson said as they reached a massive set of carved doors. She forced her smile to stay bright when she looked into her uncle's cold eyes.

Grayson Seymour, CEO of Gravitas Technologies, billionaire,

and all-around asshole, had made first contact with Earth's new visitors. When their ships landed, he had personally greeted them, cameras at the ready to document every moment. Her uncle wanted a place in the history books and he'd gotten it. Not only for that first meeting, but for what came next, too.

Like the rest of the world, Lexi sat glued to her TV as her uncle boarded the ship. The existence of aliens had been too surreal, let alone her relationship to the man holding Earth's future in his hands. When his name had lit up her cell phone, Lexi couldn't imagine why calling her would be anywhere on his to-do list. She could count on one hand how many times she'd seen him. He was one of the richest people in America, but Lexi had gone to public school and lived in a picket-fenced bungalow. Lexi never interested Uncle Grayson, especially after her dad had died of cancer when she was sixteen.

But while the Herkleians were eons ahead of Earth technologically, they still held on to more traditional values. It was customary for marriages to seal agreements, joining the two groups into one family. Uncle Grayson had never married and had no children. To have his historical alliance, he needed Lexi. But she hadn't said yes for him. After her dad's death, the hospital had sent her family a bill it'd take a lifetime to pay off. Olivia thought she was crazy to marry an alien for money. Her mom had told her nearly the same thing, but Lexi couldn't watch her family struggle when she had the power to change it.

"Open the doors." At her uncle's command, the staff snapped to attention. Lexi repressed a flinch. Asshole. The betrothal ceremony tonight was at Gravitas Technologies' sleek headquarters in San Francisco. Lexi had scoffed when she'd seen the tacky, gilded envelopes he'd chosen for the event, but the location hadn't surprised her. It was exactly the excuse her uncle needed to boost his company's stock prices.

The doors creaked open and Lexi sucked in a deep breath. She imagined her mom, the relief on her face when the banks stopped calling, their debts paid. Uncle Grayson's grip on her arm tightened, cutting off the circulation at her elbow, but Lexi held onto her grin. Light flared into her eyes from the garish chandeliers and the flash of cameras. The people who swarmed the stairs weren't aliens—at least, Lexi didn't think so—but press from top media companies. Her uncle wanted the event televised across the galaxy. The crystals on her gown caught the light and turned it into a blinding sparkle. She probably looked like a lamp. Lexi tried not to break down into hysterical laughter.

"Mr. Seymour, over here!"

"Miss Alexandra, you look beautiful!"

"Mr. Seymour, what will this alliance mean for your company?"

Her uncle raised a hand. "Thank you, thank you. No questions at this time."

Bodyguards in black gently shoved their way through the press pool, Lexi and her uncle followed in their wake. Her face hurt from all the smiling and she'd only entered the atrium moments ago. Lexi tried to peer over a bodyguard's shoulder. Maybe she could flag down a server for some wine.

Then she saw them.

Her jaw dropped. If her uncle hadn't had his hand on her arm, she'd have tripped over her own skirts. She had seen the Herkleians on TV, but the screen didn't do them any justice. They were humanoid in shape, but the similarities ended there. Instead of skin, they had azure blue scales, iridescent and curved like the hide of a fairytale dragon. Sharp black horns protruded from their heads, some under an inch but others towering antlers. Their horns made their already-tall figures even taller. Even the females stood at over six feet. The males loomed over her uncle's human guests.

The females all wore elaborate ball gowns, fabric weaved into the shapes of bright flower petals and vines, but the males had simpler outfits—tight, sculpted pants and nothing else. In the place of shirts, the males wore a swatch of fabric over their shoulder, the muscles of their chests exposed. They looked like the bodybuilders Lexi tried to avoid the few times she convinced herself to go to the gym. Her mouth watered. Maybe marrying an alien wouldn't be horrible if they looked like that.

Within a crowd of standing Herkleians, an older-looking male and female sat on gilded thrones. The male's hair was a purple so dark it almost looked black, swaying down to his waist like a swath of silk, whereas the female had vibrant red curls piled upon her head and weaved around her horns. The King and Queen of Herkleios, surrounded by their family. All the royals wore white and gold, but the king and queen shined like beacons, glimmering scales and feathers adorning the paler fabric of their robes. Crowns that speared upward into bursting halos sat upon their foreheads.

Uncle Grayson stopped before the thrones and bowed as if he were a true gentleman. "King Xenobaccus, Queen Chryseis, may I present my niece, Alexandra Seymour."

Lexi attempted her best curtsy and managed not to fall on her face. From this close, she noticed the Herkleians had slitted irises. The king's were a bright purple, the queen's a dark orange. Her uncle nudged her in the side, a sharp elbow. Lexi snapped her jaw shut. "It's a pleasure to meet you, Your Majesties."

The queen only glared, but the king bared sharp fangs in what Lexi hoped was their version of a smile. "Well met, Lady Alexandra."

When he spoke, the translator at her ears buzzed. The Herkleians had provided external devices for all the guests, but Lexi would receive an injection once she left Earth for Herkleios. She swallowed. Once she left Earth. Her uncle had said she could return in a year when the courtship ended, but once she married, Lexi would be expected to stay with her husband. This was her last night on Earth.

"Your uncle has told us much about you," the king continued.

Like what? Uncle Grayson didn't know this first thing about Lexi. "Hopefully good things, Your Majesty."

"Of course, of course." The king pushed to a stand, his hand settling on the pommel of a cane decorated with a ruby-looking gem the size of her fist. In the place of fingernails, he had sharp, black claws tipped with jeweled rings. She barely stopped her jaw from dropping again. "Let me introduce my family. Or should I say, *our* family. A few are already enjoying the party, but you'll meet them all soon enough."

Lexi replied with a fake chuckle.

The king started gesturing at the Herkleians around him. Except, Lexi realized, not all were Herkleians. Most had the azure scales, black horns, and colorful hair like King Xenobaccus, but it was easy to spot who else married into the family. There was a female with pink feathers instead of hair and sand-colored skin, while another male was entirely grey, almost like a living statue. Earth's new visitors were part of an alliance of twelve planets, with the Herkleians being the undisputed leaders. Soon, Earth would be the thirteenth planet to join them.

The king introduced her to each member of his entourage. Hatria. Myrtos. Vasilax. A dozen other names she quickly forgot. She smiled and muttered a polite 'hello' to each of them.

"If you wouldn't mind, Lady Alexandra, your uncle and I need to talk in private." King Xenobaccus put a gentle hand on her shoulder. Lexi flinched. His scales were a few degrees warmer than human skin. "Please, enjoy the party."

If only Uncle Grayson was as nice as the Herkleian king. Lexi looked over at her uncle, the only person she knew in the room, but he'd already turned from her, his focus entirely on King Xenobaccus. They strolled towards a group of humans in black suits—dignitaries and ambassadors from around the world. Her betrothal was nothing compared to the treaties and trade agreements being signed tonight.

Gentle music started, an airy sound almost like harps and lyres. Lexi wandered in the music's direction. Both human and alien guests looked on from a distance, no one daring to approach her. Maybe she'd have stared, too, if their situations were reversed, but she couldn't bring herself to meet anyone's eyes.

Smells like she'd never encountered before drifted past her nose. Her uncle hosted the party, but the Herkleians insisted on supplying the catering. She had no idea what to expect, but Lexi hadn't been able to stomach food since breakfast this morning. She approached the buffet. Bright but unfamiliar fruits and tiny pastry-lookalikes laid artfully on cylindrical trays, but the focus of the table was a giant, blue, hairless rabbit, spitted like a roast pig. Nothing looked familiar. Lexi had no idea what anything was, let alone how it tasted.

"You're unfamiliar with the cuisine," a deep voice said from behind her. "I can help you fill your plate."

Lexi spun and met piercing ice-blue eyes. They belonged to a Herkleian male in the white and gold of royalty, his shoulder sash dotted with military medals. The intensity of his gaze caught her entirely off-guard. When her eyes met his, a warm flutter of desire sparked low in her stomach. Lexi took a deep breath to steady herself. Was it normal to feel attraction towards an alien at first sight? While not the largest in the room, he was nearly seven feet of lean muscles she couldn't help but notice. Her eyes traced his broad shoulders, his menacing horns, his washboard abs. A high-tech sword-like weapon hung from his gold belt, drawing her eyes lower to the bulge of his pants. A *massive* bulge. She flushed and quickly re-focused on his slitted blue eyes.

Lexi didn't have a chance to reply before he grabbed a solid gold plate from the table and began filling it with questionable-looking food. "Um, thanks?"

"You're quite small. Do they feed you enough here?"

Lexi went red. No one ever called her small. She could stress-eat an entire pizza on her own and did so occasionally. Lexi glanced at the rest of his family. The females were all quite curvy. Something she had initially missed with her intense focus on the males' hard abs. "Not to be rude, but who are you?"

"Anax." He lifted her hand and pressed his warm lips to her knuckles. "Crown Prince of Herkleios."

"Oh." Her skin tingled where Anax touched. She sucked in a

breath and tried not to faint. Her brain went to mush just standing this close to him. She tugged her hand from his. "Well, I appreciate the offer, but I'm sure I can figure it out myself."

"I'm happy to assist."

Lexi crossed her arms. "I'm fully capable of feeding myself."

He growled, a rumbling sound that sounded almost like laughter. "You certainly are a strong-willed female."

Lexi narrowed her eyes. Hot alien or not, no one talked to her like that. "I'm not some baby. I don't need my daddy to tell me what to eat."

He bared his fangs, a wolfish look. "So I'm your daddy now?"

Lexi's cheeks flared with heat. She had not meant to say that. Lexi prayed daddy didn't have the same alternative meaning on Herkleios that it did on Earth, but given the glint in Anax's eyes, he understood exactly what he'd said. The heat in her cheeks traveled down to her chest.

Lexi ripped her gaze away from his and focused on the buffet. This was her own betrothal. She couldn't be flirting with random Herkleian royals. She circled the buffet to put distance between them and poked at a purple pear-like fruit. The surface was fuzzy like a kiwi. She recoiled. Lexi folded her hands in front of her, trying to appear ladylike.

Across the table, Anax glided from one end of the buffet to another. He reached across the table to spear a chunk of the meat, his abs rippling with the movement. She snapped her jaw shut and returned her attention to anything besides him.

"Here." He settled beside her, an arm's length away, and held the plate for her inspection. "The best of Herkleian cuisine."

When she didn't reach forward, he handed her a two-pronged fork. Lexi speared the pear-like thing. It oozed green juice onto the plate. Lexi's stomach swirled, but a citrus-sweet scent reached her nose. She hesitantly raised the fork to her mouth and took a bite. Her mouth burst with flavor, like a candied orange but better. "Wow, that's amazing."

"It's a tini. Found only in the southern regions near Agafyi. My father loves to hunt in the area and has brought home much of the cuisine."

She stabbed another kiwi-tini. "I love it."

"I'm glad." His eyes traced her lips, watching her chew, but she didn't care, not at the flavor exploding across her tongue. "What's your name?"

She blinked at him. He had introduced himself, but she had never told him her name. "Lexi."

A commotion in the press pool grabbed Lexi's attention. A younger Herkleian male stood in the open doorway. Unlike the other alien royals, his robes were the purest of white and instead of a bare chest, a matching tunic was in place under his shoulder swatch. He couldn't be older than eighteen. Like human boys, he hadn't yet hit his growth spurt, but the Herkleian version of short made him nearly six feet. His shoulders slouched under the pressure of the yelling press, but across the room, Queen Chryseis's gaze pierced into the male. He straightened like a fire was lit under ass.

"One of your brothers?" Lexi asked Anax.

The Crown Prince didn't answer. Lexi turned. Anax stared at the other Herkleian, something on his face. She couldn't read the expression. She glanced back at the younger prince, a nauseous swirling in her gut. He pushed his way through the press pool with the help of her uncle's bodyguards and stopped beside the queen, who took his hand. Together, as one, they turned to Lexi. The queen nudged the boy closer.

"Lady Alexandra." King Xenobaccus broke from his conversation with her uncle and crossed the room to stand at the Crown Prince's side. At her full name from the king's lips, Anax stiffened. "Allow me to present my youngest son, Prince Phintias."

Dread coiled in her stomach. "It's nice to meet you?"

"Ah. Your uncle did not tell you." King Xenobaccus bared those sharp fangs. "Worry not, Lady Alexandra. Today, you're simply betrothed. You'll be married once my son finishes his education. Not for many cycles of this sun. I hope this..."

The world started spinning. This was a mistake. The alien that stood in front of Lexi was just a boy. A freaking teenage boy. But the king didn't stop talking. This was her betrothed.

Uncle Grayson had married her off to an alien child.

TWO

ANAX

Anax strode down a gilded corridor toward the dining room, his boots a stomp against the blue stone floors. *The Queen Niobe* had a mostly modern design for a spaceship, but its royal apartments mimicked the three-hundred-year-old architecture of the Royal Palace. His family always gathered on the sixth day of the week to have their morning meal together. Normally, he didn't mind the opportunity to spend time with his siblings and their spouses, but their spaceship hadn't left Earth until late last night. Not only had Anax not slept, but despite serving a year with the space fleet in his youth, he'd never quite adjusted to long-distance space flight. His head pounded like someone had set a galaf bear loose in his skull.

Anax had hoped his father would cancel the breakfast until they arrived in Eritea, the capital, in four days. But King Xenobaccus hated to break tradition and never cancelled, no matter how considerable the disruption. Even the week Anax's mother, Queen Avra, had died nineteen years ago. His youngest siblings didn't remember that day, but Anax had been twelve and remembered every torturous moment. He wouldn't wish scale rot on his worst enemy. Herkleian medicine had cured thousands of ailments, but not the one that claimed his mother's life.

The doors slid open as Anax approached. Attendants carried platters of fruits and meats from the kitchen but slid out of his way with ease. Anax nodded at each one of them. Anax might be Crown Prince, but that didn't give him the right to disrespect his citizens. In truth, he served them.

The doors slid open as Anax marched into the dining room. A table of solid gold levitated above the floor and reflected the vast domed ceiling, decorated with geometric tiles of various shades of blue. On the wall behind his father's chair, a mural of the goddess Hyra exploded into color. The dragon goddess's scales were the brightest of zafers jewels, her horns towering at nearly five feet long, and the spears of her spine a deep green. His mother had commissioned the mural, and it reminded him of her every time.

The conversation stopped at his late entrance. King Xenobaccus sat at the head, his wife and Anax's stepmother, Queen Chryseis, at his side. She sneered at him, the slightest twitch of her lip. Four of his siblings and their spouses sat in the seats closest to his father. With the exception of Anax and Phintias—and Eryx, who Anax refused to consider—the rest of siblings had married royalty from the other Intergalactic Alliance planets. It had been years since all thirteen of them had been together.

"How kind of you to join us," Chyrseis said politely, though the tone didn't reach her slitted eyes.

He grunted in reply and rested his hand casually on the pommel of his sabre, but his fist clenched the metal tight. Eryx had loved to spar with Chyrseis, but Anax didn't deign to give her the pleasure.

His father raised a hand at the empty spot beside him, across from the queen and Phintias. Anax had expected to see Lady Alexandra sitting beside his teenage brother, but his sister, Bryony, occupied the seat. Fire flared through his blood. A part of him was glad the intoxicating human wasn't in the room. The moment his father had addressed her as Lady Alexandra at the ball, he had known she was his brother's betrothed. That hadn't stopped him from trying to talk to her all night, but she had deftly avoided him. Hours later, Anax still couldn't get her out of his head. He wanted to see her. *Needed* to see her, the ache almost physical.

"Have a seat, Anax," his father said. "The main course is about to be served. We're having zevra today."

"Where is Lady Alexandra?" he asked.

Chryseis's eyes narrowed, but his father thought nothing wrong with the question. "I thought not to trouble her. This is her first experience travelling between planets. She's only human."

Anax stiffened. Her planet was the least advanced of the Intergalactic Alliance, but she didn't deserve the slight. The desire roaring in his veins subsided, overpowered by the strange urge to protect her. "*Only* human?"

The king absent-mindedly waved his hand. "You know what I mean."

"I thought this was a family breakfast."

Annoyance flickered within his father's eyes, but he pushed it down with a sigh. The headstrong males clashed from time to time. "She'll be invited next week once she settles on Herkleios. I promise, son."

Anax held his father's gaze. He could insist his father send a message to Alexandra's room, but he couldn't imagine her in a positive mood if her attendant dragged her from her bed. Anax wanted to make a good impression on her the next time they spoke. This family breakfast wouldn't be it.

After a moment, Anax settled into the heir's seat. Still as uncomfortable as the first time he'd sat in it three years ago. For months after Eryx had left, Anax had refused to touch the chair.

His father tapped his cane against the edge of his seat. Attendants rushed into the room with decadent platters stacked with braised and sauteed foods. Despite all of Herkleios's technological advancement, King Xenobaccus liked to be served the traditional way. After the attendants weighted the table with platters, they scurried from the room, leaving the royals to themselves.

"Are you excited to return to Yazd, Hatria?" Bryony asked.

Hatria's scales deepened to a darker blue with excitement. "I am. The capital has the best music this time of year. Not that I haven't enjoyed spending time with you, father."

"I understand, my dear," the king said.

Bryony clutched Hatria's hand across the table. "You'll return for my wedding, won't you?"

"I wouldn't miss it." Hatria bared sharp fangs at Phintias. "I won't miss yours, either, baby brother."

His brother jerked, gaze flying up to settle on their father's face. He'd been looking at his lap, probably playing Roloi on his holoscreen. "What?"

"When will Phintias get married?" Bryony asked.

Anax stiffened. His pulse raced at the thought of Phintias with Alexandra. He never reacted this way to a female. He seduced them, fucked them, and then forgot them. Maybe if he had her, his obsession would end? She was his brother's betrothed, but he didn't care —*almost* didn't care. It wasn't like Phintias would mind. He'd been dating the same female for three years. Their father didn't consider her an acceptable match, but Anax doubted they had separated as ordered. Either way, it wasn't like Anax could be with Alexandra permanently. He was his father's heir. He needed Herkleian children.

"Not for a year, at least." His father stabbed at his plate, his zevra meat spurting blue across his plate. "But not much longer. Lady Alexandra is eight years Phintias's senior. Her uncle assured me she could breed children past her third decade, but he said the chances of success would lower."

Anax nearly bent the fork in his hand. Breeding. Alexandra with Phintias, his brother. Centuries ago, Herkleians could breathe fire, but ability had faded by the will of goddess Hyra. Something Anax was suddenly thankful for. If he could breathe fire, he'd burn the room to the ground. He put down his fork before he snapped it in two.

Anax needed to stop thinking about Alexandra. It was more than her appearance that drew him in. It was her stubbornness, the sparkle that came to her eyes when she smiled and really meant it. They'd only talked for minutes, but he wanted to know more about her. Learn her likes and dislikes so he could spoil her. If she were a Herkleian female, he'd almost think she was his mate. He repressed a scoff. No Herkleian had experienced a matebond in a century. The goddess Hyra had taken the sacred union as she had the Herkleians' fire.

Across the table, Chryseis narrowed her gaze at Anax's warped fork. He quickly snatched it back into his hand. Eryx had said their stepmother had the guile to rival Hadus, the god of the underworld, banished by Hyra for his betrayal. Anax had thought his brother dramatic, but at the look in Chryseis's eyes, he didn't wish to find out.

Chryseis put her hand on her son's. "Phintias, it would be good of you to give Alexandra a tour of the palace when we arrive."

Phintias pulled away from his mother. "Grex and I were going to take his mother's glider out."

Chryseis bared her fangs, a cautionary smile. "I'm sure you can do that another day, my darling."

"He's been looking forward to this for quite a while," his father said. "I'm sure an attendant can give her a satisfactory tour, Chryseis."

"I'll do it." Anax kept his attention on his father, but he didn't miss the narrowing of Chryseis's eyes. "As your heir, I need to learn all about the newest Alliance planet. What better way than from an Earthing?"

"What a genius idea, my boy." His father tapped his cane twice on the floor. Attendants returned to the room to clear the plates. "You're thinking like a king now."

On any other day, hearing those words from his father would've filled Anax with pride. He had always been the second son, always living in Eryx's shadow. It had pushed him to study harder, serve in the military longer, master the sabre faster. But Anax barely cared, not when he'd soon see the delicious Alexandra again.

THREE

Lexi woke to a pounding in her head. She groaned. Her breath reeked like wine. How much had she drunk last night? Last night... Lexi searched her memory, but everything was foggy.

"My lady?"

Lexi flinched, nearly jumping from the sheets. Someone was in her room. She hadn't had a roommate since Olivia in college, but Liv had a key to her apartment. Not that she ever came in unannounced. She squinted through the drapes of her four-poster bed—

When did she get drapes as soft as silk? Or a four-poster bed, not made of wood but a sleek, twisted gold? And her room wasn't a small LA apartment, but a wide expanse twice the size of her bedroom, with chairs overlooking a hovering fire inside gold metal—both art and fireplace in one. Instead of electronic lights, glowing rocks in the ceiling brightened the room. The entire wall to her right was floor-to-ceiling windows showing hills of magenta spotted with blue-topped trees. A beautiful sight of color, but not one found on Earth.

Because Lexi wasn't on Earth anymore. She was on a freaking spaceship.

The events of the party returned in fractures. After King

Xenobaccus had introduced her to her future husband, Prince Phintias, Lexi had drunk half her body weight to drown her sorrows. Her uncle was marrying her off to a freaking child. She didn't want to believe he'd stoop that low, but Lexi's happiness was never any of Uncle Grayson's concern.

Anax had tried to get close to her again, but she had done her best to avoid him. If Phintias was to be her husband, Anax would be her brother-in-law. Her super-hot, fuckable brother-in-law. Lexi almost whacked herself. She couldn't think of him like that. If she married Phintias—*when* she married Phintias—she'd be a faithful wife. Her ex-boyfriend had cheated on her with his ex, a betrayal that had nearly destroyed Lexi. She'd never do the same thing, even if her marriage were arranged.

"My lady?" the Herkleian female asked again.

Lexi squinted at her. Her hair was the same blue-black as the midnight sky, paired with three-inch horns and slitted yellow eyes. The alien looked at her expectantly. Had they already been introduced? Lexi had met nearly a hundred people last night. "Who are you?"

The female bobbed her head. "I am Kynna, your attendant."

"My what?" Lexi rubbed her eyes. Now that Kynna said that, she noticed the plain design of her gray gown, like what the assistants of the royal family had worn.

"Your attendant, my lady. You won't be marrying the prince yet, but King Xenobaccus wants us to treat you as his family until then."

A sharp pain throbbed between her temples. She was marrying a prince. She had a crush on her fiancé's brother. She had a freaking attendant. "What time is it?"

"It's been twelve hours since we left Earth, my lady. We'll arrive at Herkleios in eighty."

Lexi rubbed at her eyes. Twelve hours of sleep was a lot, even for her. She pushed off her blankets and climbed from the bed, but her vision swirled. Lexi tumbled back to the sheets with a groan.

Kynna appeared at her side instantly. "Are you feeling well, my lady? Space travel can cause disorientation, especially if it's your first time."

"I don't think it's the space travel." Lexi couldn't believe the words out of her mouth. Space travel. A year ago, Lexi didn't even believe in aliens. "It's the wine."

Kynna's forehead scrunched. "The wine?"

"The alcohol I had last night." Kynna nodded, no confusion on her face at the term. Aliens knew what alcohol was, but they didn't understand hangovers? "The next day, it can cause headaches and grogginess."

Kynna's slitted yellow eyes widened. "I did not know that, my lady. Our alcohol doesn't have that effect on us."

"Lucky."

Kynna gestured to the door. "I can get you something to relieve the pain?"

Lexi rubbed at her forehead. She had packed Advil in her suitcases, but the Herkleians probably had a cooler way to get rid of pain. "Thank you."

Kynna bobbed into a curtsy. "There is no need to thank me, my lady."

"Please, call me Lexi."

"I could never do that, my lady."

Before Lexi could argue, Kynna spun on her heels and disappeared from the room. She returned in under a minute, holding two flat, gold circles. Everything Herkleian was gold. They were obsessed with the metal—exactly like dragons. Maybe they *were* dragons? Lexi wanted to ask, but that would probably offend someone.

Kynna held out the tinier gold circle. "I need to attach this to your temple, my lady. It might sting. But I can cure your head pain and also inject your permanent translator."

Lexi stared at the circle, no bigger than a coin. "You can do all that with one device?"

"Our medicine uses nanotechnology, my lady." She pressed the circle to Lexi's temple. It pulsed into her skin with a light prick. "We can cure many ailments with a single tablet like this."

And now, because of Lexi, Earth had access to this technology. Technology that could've saved her father from cancer if he had lived another decade. Tears tingled at Lexi's eyes. She was going to a new world, thousands of light-years from home, but knowing she helped more than her mom made every second worth it.

Kynna tapped gently at the other circle. A white projection flashed out from the gold, almost like a holographic screen. She tapped a few buttons with her black claws. The device warmed on Lexi's skin, but it didn't sting. After a minute, Kynna removed the circle. She placed both within a pocket of her dress, along with the temporary translator at Lexi's ear. "All finished, my lady."

"Really?" Lexi straightened. Kynna was right. The aching in her head had faded and when she moved, her vision didn't swirl. Lexi pushed to her feet. She expected to fall on her ass, but she felt good as new. "Wow."

Kynna's lips twisted, flashing Lexi a hint of fang. "Would you like to get dressed, my lady?"

She glanced down at herself. The dress her uncle had given her was gone, replaced by a sheath of silky fabric. Lexi ran her fingers through it. "What is this?"

"Therios silk, my lady." When Lexi frowned, Kynna continued, "The Therios are almost extinct, but the royal family has access to much of their silks. It was a present from King Xenobaccus, as was the rest of your wardrobe."

Lexi's eyes widened. "The rest?"

"Yes, my lady." Kynna gestured to a circular platform near the fake windows. "If you will."

Lexi approached and tapped the platform with her toes. The designers had embedded a circle of gold into the blue rock. Another piece of Herkleian tech?

Kynna followed behind her. "Step into the circle."

Lexi settled into place, but nothing happened. "What next?"

Kynna tapped at a button on her gold wristband. Suddenly, the circle beneath her erupted with light. It swirled around Lexi. The room disappeared in the brightness. Lexi wanted to grab for Kynna, but the attendant's face remained tranquil. Whatever was happening was absolutely ordinary. On Herkleios, that is.

The light dimmed as quickly as it had erupted. Lexi's jaw dropped. A gown of wispy pink fabric dotted with maroon peony-like flowers had replaced the plain sheath. A belt of gold cinched the dress at her waist before it fell to the floor in a wave of tulle-like fabric. Lexi raised a foot, bringing it to the light. The stems of her heels were sharp pink rock arranged into a mosaic pattern.

Lexi spun. Her dress from last night was worth more than she made in a year at her florist shop, but it had been prim and proper and stiff. This was the gown of an alien princess. Lexi spun again, a happy giggle escaping her lips. She had left behind everything, but maybe her new life wouldn't all be awful.

"Do you like it, my lady?" Kynna wrung her hands together nervously. "We can try another one if you don't. The king provided you with ample options."

Lexi popped off the platform. Her feet didn't ache in the heels as she strutted across the room. Another worthwhile invention for Earth. "I love it."

"I'm glad." Kynna pulled something else from within the pockets of her gown. She opened a small box to reveal a gold bracelet similar to the one Kynna wore. "These are like your smartwatches, but far more advanced. You can accept calls, send messages, or interact with the ship." She pointed at the two little gemstones on the bracelet's face. "The gem on the right will flash blue if you have a notification. Tap it to bring up the screen. The one on the left will remain green when your personal shield is up. It will stop anyone from hacking your device or transporting you without your permission."

Lexi plucked the device from the box, the bracelet no heavier than a feather. "That's amazing."

"It has many other features, but I don't wish to overwhelm you."

"Thank you, Kynna."

"It's my pleasure, my lady." Kynna folded her hands across her front and bobbed into a bow. Once they had known each other longer, maybe Lexi could convince her attendant to treat her like a regular person instead of a princess. "You don't have any events planned until we arrive on Herkleios. Until then, you can adjust and relax."

"Can you show me around? Also, I'd kill for a cup of coffee."

Her slitted eyes widened, nearly horrified. "There's no need to kill, my lady. I can get you anything you need."

"I don't mean that literally." Lexi laughed. It'd take time to get used to Herkleian speech even with a translator. Kynna continued to look alarmed, so Lexi linked her arms with her attendant and gestured at the door. "I want to see everything."

Anax sipped at his krojs, his eyes tracing the ceiling of the domed atrium. Metal arches converged at the peak of the ceiling, twisted with glowing vines and flowers. To an outsider, he appeared enraptured with the architecture, but Anax's entire focus remained on the door. After breakfast, Anax had all but rushed from the royal apartments. When Alexandra woke, her attendant would bring her here, to the dining hall for all the nobles staying on *The Queen Niobe*. He wanted to be near her again. Though she tried to fight it, he knew she felt pulled to him as well.

"Your Highness?" A stodgy voice broke through his concentration. Anax didn't straighten in his seat, but his attention slid over the Lord Petre. The Herkleian's hair had gone completely gold in his old age. "I have petitioned your father, but he hasn't made the time to see me. Do you think perhaps you can speak to him? It's about the mines near Kathis—"

Out of the corner of his eyes, a yellow-haired figure in pink entered the dining hall. Alexandra. She ran her fingers across bright purple flowers near the entrance, the petals nearly the size of her hand. Her lips twisted, a light coming over her face. Herkleians bared their fangs in joy, but humans didn't have fangs. Her smile wasn't any less beautiful for it. He rose from his seat in the corner and walked towards her, nearly entranced. Someone said his name behind him, but he barely noticed.

Alexandra turned to her attendant, who then gestured to the center of the room, where various pitchers and kettles weighted down a levitating bar. She weaved through a small crowd of chatting Herkleians. A few of the aliens glanced in her direction, but they quickly turned their attention back to their own drinks. His perfect opportunity. Anax stalked across the room, like a beast with his prey. He scanned his eyes down her subtle curves. Last night hadn't been an exception. His blood rushed at the sight of her, his cock twitching. For whatever reason, Anax craved this female.

Alexandra scanned the bartop, seemingly lost. After a long moment, she grabbed a mug and filled it with krojs. Anax quickened his step. Nobody had explained krojs to her, it seemed. He settled behind her and cleared his throat right as she brought the cup to her lips.

She spun with a little yelp, her free hand rushing to her chest. When her eyes settled on him, her white skin flushed pink. A beautiful color, in harmony with her dress. He wondered what it meant. Was she impressed with him? Her gaze almost immediately dropped from his face. He had switched out of his tight gold pants, white sash, and military awards for the Herkleian version of casual. His chest was bare, her eyes enchanted by the rippling of his scales, and he wore black shoulder pauldrons, two straps across above his pecs. His pants were black, too, smooth over powerful legs. The jeweled hilt of a sabre rested against his belt.

He glided closer, the movement dragging her from her examination. Her green eyes flickered back to his face. His gaze stabbed through her, reading every hint of her desire. His lips twisted, flashing a bit of fang.

His grin made her stiffen. "Is there something I can help you with?"

He reached out and traced his claws across the edge of her cup. "Krojs is extremely strong. You add a small amount to water to dilute the syrup. If you were to drink this whole cup, you'd be plagued by hallucinations for days."

Alexandra nearly dropped the cup. "Hallucinations?"

Anax took the cup from her hand and placed it on the bar. "Probably. No human has ever tried it."

She threw up her hands. "I just want something with caffeine."

He cocked his head to one side. "What is caffeine?"

"It's liquid energy. I need it to get through my day."

"The quinta fruit has properties that help people stay awake." He grabbed a pitcher at the end of the bar and poured red liquid into a glass. As a Herkleian male, it was his duty to find food for the females around him. A primal instinct, as much as the throbbing in his pants urging him to claim her.

She took the glass from him with an odd purse to her lips. Human faces were almost like Herkleians, but also different in tiny ways. He made it his goal to become an expert in reading her emotions. "You really have a thing for feeding people."

Was it not custom for human males to feed their females? How barbaric. "It's normal among Herkleians. I don't mind in the least."

Anax returned the pitcher to the bartop, his back to her for a moment. He couldn't see her face, but her eyes caressed across his scales, near a touch. No matter her tone, she desired him, too. When he returned his focus to her, she had downed the glass in her hand.

"I think I can take it from here."

He quirked his lip. "As you wish, princess."

She shuddered. "Don't call me that."

"Then what should I call you?"

"You shouldn't call me anything. Better yet, how about you stop speaking to me all together?"

Anax's smile widened, flashing the sharpness of his fangs into the light. Her gaze immediately focused on them. How would it feel to graze his teeth against her skin? His blood pulsed with the thought.

Anax needed to have her. Soon. He almost couldn't control himself when she was near. "And I thought we were having such fun together."

"Look." Alexandra crossed her arms and banished the lust from her eyes. "I'm not interested in this back-and-forth banter thing we seem to have going. As a matter of fact, I'm not interested in speaking to you at all. I am marrying your brother and I will join your family. There will be no funny business between us."

He flinched at the mention of his brother. Alexandra and Phintias, fucking. The thought shouldn't bother him. He had brought a hundred females to his bed, some who had since married and birthed younglings of their own. But none of them had affected him like she did.

Still, he didn't wish to make her uncomfortable. He dropped into a smooth bow. "I will treat you as I would any female family member of mine, Alexandra."

"Lexi."

His forehead furrowed. "Pardon?"

"My name is Lexi." At his confusion, she continued, "Alexandra is my full name. I don't use it. People call me Lexi."

"Ah. I see." He didn't. She had introduced himself as Lexi when they first met, but her name was Alexandra. He had dismissed the first name as irrelevant until now. "Is this a common Earth custom?"

"I guess." She frowned. "You don't have nicknames on Herkleios?"

"What is a nickname?"

"I guess that answers my question," she muttered to herself. Alexandra—Lexi shuffled to the end of the bar and stopped in front of a basket of pastries. Anax couldn't help but follow behind. She enchanted him with every movement. She pursed her lips, considering, and he devoured the expression. Soon, her soft, pink lips would be on his scales. He didn't close the space between them, but he didn't need to. Her eyes stayed on the food, but her mind was on him.

Could she feel the heat radiating from him? Earthling were so cold in comparison.

After a few moments, she raised an eyebrow at him. "Can I help you with something?"

"I would do my family a disservice if I didn't ensure you had settled in well." He gestured at a ganja berry ganit, the pastry one of many in the basket. "Try one."

"What's in it?"

"Ganja berries. They're quite sweet." He paused, a playful look entering his eyes. "I love to suck on them."

Lexi's entire body jolted, like he had hit her with a jolt of electricity. Through the thin fabric of her dress, her nipples hardened into nubs. Eagerly volunteering to be sucked by him. Anax wanted to throw her over his shoulder and carry her from the room. He would strip her naked and make her beg for his tongue, for his cock. But he couldn't. She was right about one thing. She was his brother's future wife, not his.

Lexi panicked, almost like she could read the thoughts in his mind. She grabbed one of the ganits before turning on her heels and marching for the door. But in their conversation, they had circled the bar. Lexi was storming in the wrong direction. Anax brushed a hand against her arm before she could turn again.

Lexi eyed him. "Can I explore the atrium on my own?"

He folded his hands behind his back, the pose of a gentlemale. "You could, but Herkleians are a social bunch and someone will surely approach you. You may think I'm bad, but you might feel differently if left alone to face the courtiers."

Lexi stiffened and eyed the surrounding nobility. "Why? Are they not fond of humans?"

"They're used to all kinds of species at court, but there are some who believe Herkleians are superior." Her skin paled from pink to white. Perhaps in fear? He quickly added, "Fear not, my father has worked hard to make our planet a space where all our allies are welcome."

"Then how could they be worse than you?"

"Because—" Anax leaned in close like he was going to tell her a secret "—they're insufferable gossips."

A noise slipped out of Lexi, a beautiful sound that sent a shiver down his spine. A laugh. He had read about those. Anax howled in response.

His roar halted her laugh immediately, a shudder wracking her body.

"Forgive me, Lexi. That is simply how we show amusement, much like your laughter."

"No, that's alright. I liked it." She flushed that pretty pink color again. Human skin was fascinating. He wanted to touch her again. And again and again.

"I like how yours sounds, too. Like the whistling bird in our gardens."

The pink of her cheeks turned into a bright red. This time she dropped her gaze. Hyra's Graces, had he said something wrong? Her attention focused on the flower display around them, but she had to know he was staring. Had to feel his eyes tracing her skin as hers had traced his scales.

A glance from a lover, not a brother-in-law.

Something he didn't mind, but which obviously bothered her. Before he could say another word, she spun on her heels. "If you'll excuse me, I must get back to my room."

Hadus. He had pushed her too far. He started after her, ready to apologize, to hide his wicked grin and burning desire under the kindly guise of the Crown Prince. He wanted to know her, to claim her, but Anax needed to move slowly. With precision. His temper urged him to rush into things, but patience had always served him well. With his sabre lessons. During his military stint. After Eryx left.

His gaze stayed on her as she rushed from the room, her attendant following behind. Anax let her run. One day, she wouldn't run from him and their connection.

One day, she'd run towards it.

FIVE

LEXI

"Welcome to Eritea, capital of Herkleios..." Lexi tuned out the overhead announcement as she shoved her belongings into a suitcase. Kynna had told her much about her new home planet over the last four days, but that hadn't stopped her anxiety from skyrocketing this morning. Prince Anax knocking on her door multiple times a day hadn't helped. Each time, Lexi had told Kynna to say she was ill. Once they arrived on the planet, would it be as easy to avoid him? She already dreamed about him nightly. Lexi couldn't become any more infatuated with the Crown Prince.

Lexi stacked the last of her bags on a droid-operated trolley before tapping the blue gem on her bracelet. The trolley beeped to life and floated off the ground. It buzzed from the room. Lexi once had her suitcase stolen off a luggage cart in Cabo, but Kynna assured her the trolley would safely take her stuff to her new apartments.

Kynna appeared in the doorway. "Are you ready, my lady?"

Lexi glanced around the room she had called home the last four days and nodded. "I am."

Kynna settled at her side. "Can you give me permission to transport you?"

Lexi pressed the green gem, switching it to red.

Kynna raised her wrist and said, "Two to transport to Lady Alexandra's apartments."

Lexi relaxed her shoulders as her skin tingled. In a blink, the transporters locked onto her location. She reappeared in a corridor with solid gold walls and blue marble floors lit by uncut crystal rock lamps. Large windows overlooked a bright, glowing garden. Herkleios. A freaking alien planet. Lexi walked automatically towards the windows, but a droid-trolley nearly ran her down. Lexi jumped out of the way. Palace staff bustled back and forth to prepare for the royal family's arrival. Some things were the same no matter the planet.

Kynna touched her arm. "I will give you a tour in an hour, my lady. Until then, perhaps it'd be best to get settled into your room."

Lexi reluctantly turned from the garden windows to the gold double doors. "If you—"

A figure transported into her path. A tall, horned figure with icy blue eyes, dark hair, and great abs. Kynna immediately dropped into a bow, as did every other attendant in the hall. The busy space had gone silent in under a second.

Anax nodded his head. "As you were."

The staff quickly jumped to their feet and returned to their tasks. Except for Kynna, who back away, her head bowed.

Lexi crossed her arms. "What do you want?"

Kynna flinched at Lexi's tone and backed further away, but Anax bared his fangs. "I've come to give you a tour."

"Why would I want to take a tour with you?" Lexi needed to spend less time with him.

"I also need to brief you on your assignment." Assignment? Lexi had an assignment? No one had told her that. Before she could ask, Anax continued, "As the heir, it's fundamental I learn all I can about our newest ally, Earth. You and I will spend quite a good deal of time together."

"I haven't even seen my room." Lexi tried to inch around him to the door, but his broad shoulders blocked the path. "I'm sure Kynna can give me a tour once I'm settled."

"Your attendant already has enough to do today. I can step in for this one task."

He gestured down the hall. Lexi glanced at Kynna, but her attendant hadn't raised her head. She sighed and walked in the direction Anax pointed. So pushy. But a small part of Lexi loved it. Not that she'd ever admit it.

Anax settled at her side, matching his long strides to hers. "Tell me more about yourself."

"Aren't we supposed to be focusing on Earth?"

"I'm taking a different approach," he said. "I think by learning how an Earthling spends their time, I can learn a great deal about their planet, Lady Lexi."

She twitched. "Don't call me that."

"You didn't like princess, either. What shall I call you?"

"By my name, obviously."

"Lexi," Anax said slowly, almost as if he were tasting her name against his tongue.

She shivered but focused on the corridor ahead. Attendants scurried from their path with furtive glances and light whispers. Lexi tried to put some space between herself and Anax, but her body gravitated towards his. She swallowed and tried to remember his question. "I'm a regular Earthling. My day-to-day isn't particularly interesting."

"I wholly disagree." His eyes stayed on her, an intense gaze. "Tell me everything."

Lexi flushed, heat traveling from her chest to her face. A tingling traced from her neck and down her arms. The words flowed to her lips, ready to share her entire life with this alien male. She dug her nails into her palms. She knew she shouldn't have come on this tour. Not that it was much of a tour. They had made it to the end of the long corridor, but Anax hadn't pointed at a single thing. She straightened. "You're an awful tour guide."

Anax threw back his head and howled. "Can't have that."

Before she could make some excuse to leave, Anax gently put one hand on her back and another on her wrist. With a smooth motion, he twirled her around the corner. Lexi let out a small yelp and almost lost her balance. Her hand landed on the bulge of his arm. The texture of his scales didn't bother her, nor did the heat radiating off him, but all of that became secondary to the feel of his muscles. She squeezed. Damn. Her mouth watered.

Anax cleared his throat, a growly sound.

Lexi pulled her hand away like he had burned her, but her skin tingled where it had touched his. She had groped him. Groped her hot brother-in-law. If her face could get any redder, it would.

Anax's lips split into a fanged smirk. But instead of making a comment, he gestured forward. "The corridor we exited houses guests of the Crown, but this one is for the royal family." They passed an ornate door made of gold and bright gems, blue and red in a rotating pattern. "The Chambers of the Sovereign. Usually a queen, but my father's mother, Queen Niobe, only had two sons. When my father's older brother passed, the throne went to him."

"Herkleios is a matriarchy?" Lexi looked at the palace with fresh eyes. Kynna had taught her much, but Lexi hadn't learned that fact. Maybe living on an alien planet wouldn't suck.

Anax nodded. "The dragon goddess Hyra declared it so. My father was the first king in nearly two hundred years."

"Then why are you the Crown Prince? You have sisters."

"I have eight marvelous sisters." Anax's smile changed, going soft. He truly loved his family. Lexi couldn't imagine having thirteen siblings. Kynna had drilled all their names into her head, but Lexi didn't remember half of them. "They would all make extraordinary queens, but Queen Niobe didn't want the throne to go to her brother's daughter. She had the laws changed, so the throne now goes to the sovereign's eldest child."

"Which is you."

Anax's smile disappeared. Why? Lexi wanted to know everything about him. She knew she shouldn't, but her heart controlled her actions, not her head.

He quickly gestured to another door, this one smaller but equally grand as King Xenobaccus's. "This is the door to my chambers. In case you ever need to know."

Lexi's heart near stopped. "And why would I need to know that?"

Anax approached, closing the small distance between them. Lexi backed up a step, but he continued to prowl forward. What was he doing? She scampered back, but that only increased the gleam in his eyes. Like a cat toying with a mouse. Like a dragon with its pile of gold. Like an alpha male with *his* female.

Her back hit something solid, blocking her retreat. Anax leaned forward, reaching—

For the handle of a door, which slid open and nearly deposited Lexi on the ground.

Strong arms wrapped around her waist.

Lexi tumbled into Anax's grasp. Her hands settled on the leather of his shoulder pauldrons. Anywhere but his scales. Not that she could avoid touching him. His bare chest pressed against her side. Her pulse kicked into double time.

She tried to summon some indignation, but her voice came out breathless. "You almost knocked me off my feet."

He bared his fangs in a slow, wicked grin. Her gaze drifted down the powerful angles of his nose and cheekbones to the curve of those temping lips. What would they feel like? Would they be smooth like a human man's? He only needed to lean down an inch for her to find out.

He closed the gap until his breath tickled her face. "I'd never let you fall, Lexi."

Lexi's mouth went dry. Heat flared within her chest, only to travel lower. It invaded her stomach, her core, and settled into an inferno between her legs. With a single sentence and the purr of her name, Anax had aroused her more thoroughly than any other man.

How could she survive him? She wanted him like no other. Needed him like no other.

But she couldn't have him. Lexi was an engaged woman.

She untangled herself from his grasp. Anax let her go easily, his cocky grin not fading in the slightest. Arrogant. He knew she desired him. Just like she knew he desired her. He wasn't hiding anything. Why would he? He was a prince—the Crown Prince. Lexi wanted to shout that she'd never fall for his tricks, but the words might be a lie.

She desperately wanted them to be a lie.

Lexi turned on her heels, putting her back to the Crown Prince. If she couldn't see him, maybe—

Her jaw dropped. Instead of more halls of gold and marble, Anax had led her outside to the courtyard garden. Leaves of purple, pink, and blue dangled from orange branched trees over grass the deepest magenta. A little path of gold stones cut between beds of unfamiliar, glowing flowers. Some were tiny like the buds of forget-me-nots, but others reached Lexi's height with petals the size of her hand. They swayed in the bright light from Herkleios's sun, the entire space alive and dancing.

A warm breath tickled her ear. "I saved the best for last."

Lexi spun, a giggle escaping her throat. A second ago she had tried to run from Anax, but that was all forgotten in the garden of her dreams. "This is the most beautiful place I've ever seen in my life."

"My mother planted this garden," Anax said, gently stroking a petal. "She loved flowers, too."

Lexi knelt at the edge of the path and reached out for a patch of sparkling pink flowers. "I wish I could grow these in my greenhouse. My customers would love them."

Anax frowned. "What is a greenhouse?"

The bulbs of the plant were smooth against her skin. "It's a place where humans grow plants inside if the weather outside isn't right. I'm a florist, so flowers and greenery are kind of my life."

"That was your occupation?"

When Lexi rose, Anax had stopped at her side and raised his

arm for her. She offered him her hand without hesitation. "I started an apprenticeship with a florist my mom knew after college. I worked at her shop for three years before opening my own store." Lexi sighed, thinking of her store. The tiny square of a room had been her heaven. It had hurt her to not re-sign the lease, but Uncle Grayson had offered her more money than she'd make in a lifetime. "To answer your earlier question, that's what I did all day. Created wonderful bouquets and arrangements of flowers for my clients in LA."

"I see." Anax led them under the shade of a blue willow-like tree, spotted with green-gold fruit. A carved wooden bench hid in the depths of the shade. It was the first seat Lexi had seen that wasn't levitating. "I will speak to our royal gardener if you wish. She hasn't had royal helpers since my sister, Elipida, got married."

Lexi pressed her hand against the tree's trunk. She had thought living in Herkleios might be miserable, but today she had hope. She might marry a male who didn't care for her while pining for his brother, but she had a beautiful garden to keep her company.

Anax gestured to the bench. "Would you like to sit?"

She settled into the seat. "It's so beautiful here. Thank you for showing me."

"It was my pleasure," he said, his voice a rumble.

She shuddered. Pleasure. The way he said the word rippled through her. She needed to ask something, anything, to break the tension building between them. "So... is this how you spend most of your time?"

Anax sat beside her. His arm brushed hers, hot scales against smooth skin. "It used to be. My duties have taken up most of my time in the last few years."

Lexi closed her eyes and breathed in the garden's scent. It filled her nose but couldn't entirely distract her from the feel of Anax at her side. "How many duties can a prince have?"

Lexi opened her eyes after a long moment of silence. Anax hadn't answered. He had turned his gaze from her, looking at his mother's gardens. From her research, she knew Queen Avra had passed away nearly two decades ago. Anax would have been a boy when she died.

"I'm actually my father's second son," he said after a long pause. "My father spent decades grooming my older brother, Eryx, to take the crown. Then, three years ago, my brother left in the middle of the night."

Anax had an older brother? Kynna had taught her nearly a dozen names, but she had said nothing about Eryx. Lexi reached for his hand. She didn't care if anyone saw. She didn't care if her heart stuttered at the feel of his scales. Pain etched Anax's voice, no matter how he tried to hide it. "He just left out of nowhere?"

Anax gripped her hand, his dark claws gentle across her skin. "Without saying goodbye to anyone. He left a letter abdicating the throne, no more. It was a shock to me. I always thought my brother and I were close." He focused his gaze on hers. The desire remained, but sadness overtook his expression. "Maybe I just didn't mean that much to him."

"You miss him?"

He paused. "Every day," he said, the words seemingly a surprise to him. "I wanted to look for him, but my father wouldn't allow it. He said I needed to focus on learning how to lead our planet."

"And what does a good leader need to know?"

"I have teachers for combat training, military strategies, history, the art and culture of our planet." He focused on their hands, still linked together. Lexi knew she should pull away, but she didn't want to. "Along with the basic understanding of the customs of our allies."

Which was why he needed to talk to her. Maybe his intentions were pure. Or half-pure. She hadn't imagined the heat in his gaze, the twist of his lips. "And that's where I come in?"

"Exactly."

"Is this how it's normally done? Learning about other cultures, that is."

"Not typically. But I don't want to be a typical king."

"You're anything but typical, Anax." Lexi looked up into his mesmerizing eyes. She never wanted to leave the garden. If she stayed here, in this moment, she'd never have to leave Anax's side. But she had to go before it became too late. She tugged her hand from Anax and stood. "Can you show me back to my room? I should unpack."

Anax straightened, the vulnerable side of him disappearing under a warrior prince's strength. His lips twitched back into that arrogant smile. With a flourish, he dipped into a light bow. "Of course, my lady."

SIX

LEXI

Lexi leaned over her balcony's balustrade and inhaled the thick scent of the garden. The morning breeze wafted the smells throughout her room. She closed her eyes. Sunlight flickered across her skin, a gentle warmth. Just like Anax's scales against hers yesterday during his tour.

Lexi immediately pushed him from her mind. After their walk in the garden, she had doubted her place here as Phintias's betrothed. How could she marry him when she was far more interested in his brother? But her mom had helped quash her doubts. She had used the palace's deep space relay station to talk to her mom for the first time since she left Earth. True to his word, Uncle Grayson had deposited the promised money in her mom's account. Lexi already heard the relief in her voice, the weight on all their shoulders finally lifted. While she still longed for home, Lexi needed to uphold her end of the bargain. Knowing her mom was well-taken care of spurred her into being a faithful bride.

Kynna cleared her throat behind her. Lexi jolted. Her attendant stood in the doorway to her suite, the rooms similarly sized to her home on the ship. A large bedroom overlooked the garden on the second floor, whereas the main floor held a sitting room and a few smaller rooms for her attendants. Not that she had multiple attendants.

"I'm sorry, Kynna." She pushed her elbows off the balustrade and stepped through the door into her apartments. "What's up?"

She glanced at the ceiling. "Up? The ceiling, my lady. Is there something wrong with it?"

"Oh, no." Not only were their facial expressions slightly different, but their verbal ones, as well. Lexi needed a guidebook to the Herkleian people as much as Anax needed one for Earth. "I don't mean literally up. It's an expression. What do you want to tell me?"

"There's a letter for you."

"A letter?" Even on Earth, letters were rare. She didn't expect to see one on Herkleios, where everyone had holo-screens worked into their bracelets. Lexi dug at the wax seal and pulled out a note written in gold, flowing calligraphy. Not in Herkleian, which her implant could easily translate, but in English. Someone in the palace knew English. Her eyes flicked across the beautiful words. Queen Chryseis had invited her to have lunch today.

Kynna folded her hands in front of her. "Do you have a response, my lady?"

"Please, Kynna, it's been five days. Call me Lexi."

"Lexi," she said cautiously. "But only when we are in private."

"Tell Queen Chryseis I'm accepting." Lexi placed the letter back into its envelope. She needed to make a good impression on her future mother-in-law. She hadn't seen Queen Chryseis since the engagement ball. The queen's glares still haunted Lexi's dreams. She glanced down at her sweatpants. "I need a dress that screams Herkleian bride-to-be."

Kynna tapped at her bracelet, sending Lexi's reply to the queen's attendants. "I have the perfect one, Lexi."

"WELCOME, LADY ALEXANDRA," a prim Herkleian declared before the doors to Queen Chryseis's rooms. Kynna didn't speak or step forward from where she stood behind Lexi, but she didn't need her attendant's help to know his gold epaulettes marked with stars meant he was the head of the queen's household. She had explained everything to Lexi before they left her rooms. Once she officially married into the royal family, Lexi would have a ranked staff, too. Until that day, all she had was Kynna. Not that she minded. A staff sounded terrifying.

She nodded a greeting. "Lord Steward."

His expression didn't change, but he gracefully slid out of the way, the doors to the queen's rooms sliding open with him. She placed her hands on her waist to smooth down her dress. Blue scales studded a mermaid cut dress, the exact azure color of a Herkleian's scales. Two decorative horns sprouted from the shoulders, a match to the clips holding her twisted hair in two nubs. Kynna had painted her nails black like Herkleian claws and dusted her cheeks with blue sparkles. Lexi didn't have fangs or slitted eyes, but in that moment, she became Herkleian.

She glided into the room with a glance at Kynna, who bared her fangs in an encouraging smile. Another attendant waited inside to lead her to the queen. Queen Chryseis's rooms mimicked the arched ceilings and ornate furniture of Lexi's own rooms, but everything was on a much grander scale. The sitting room she entered was twice the size of her bedroom, with four hallways leading to dozens of rooms. A large expanse of windows to her right showed the same gardens Lexi watched this morning, but the right side showed a modern city of sleek towers and twisting highrises miles past manicured purple lawns. Floating vehicles darted across the sky with glints of silver and gold, some little more than specks to her vision. They circled buildings, lowered to the ground, shot for the atmosphere, or even landed on a floating chunk of city over a spiraled structure.

Lexi stopped and stared.

The attendant gestured out towards a terrace. "Queen Chryseis, my lady."

Lexi snapped her jaw shut and emerged into the sunlight. She'd have years to watch and explore the non-palace parts of Eritea. Today, she had a mother-in-law to charm.

Queen Chryseis sat stiffly at a levitating table in the center of the balcony, her red hair wrapped in another elaborate updo around her spiked horns. The golden vines of her dress cinched her waist and wrapped around her wrists. Gemstones the size of a golf ball decorated her claws. Lexi dipped into a shallow bow. Kynna had taught her Herkleians didn't curtsey, but their bows required the tucking of the chin in order to bare their horns.

When the queen raised a hand, Lexi straightened. The tip of her heel sank into the groove of the stone tiles, nearly toppling her off her feet. Dammit. She had done a decent enough job when practicing in her room, but nerves had gotten the better of her. The attendant pulled out her chair and Lexi sat down, hoping the blue of her makeup hid her embarrassed blush.

Queen Chryseis bared her fangs into a forced smile, the look somehow menacing. Lexi's stomach twisted. The queen lifted a clawed hand from the table and pointed at the waiting attendant. "Would you like some zion?"

Lexi nodded. What was zion? Hopefully something like tea. The attendant disappeared into the suite for a moment before returning with two bowl-like cups. Lexi peered over the rim. Hot water steamed into her face, but otherwise, it looked exactly like tea. The attendant submerged a cloth bag filled with bits of colorful flowers into the water, dyeing it a light pink. Lexi sniffed. It had a vaguely floral scent but was also sweet and somewhat familiar. Lexi picked up the cup and took a sip. The heat of the liquid nearly singed her tongue, but a burst of sweetness exploded across her senses. Instead of Herkleian flowers, she imagined a county fair, with ferris wheels and carousels and... cotton candy? The zion tasted like cotton candy.

The zion's boiling temperature didn't bother the queen half as much as it did Lexi. Queen Chryseis took a long drawl of the drink before lowering the cup daintily back to the table. Lexi smiled, nervous. How did Herkleians make small talk? *Did* they make small talk?

Luckily, the queen filled the silence shortly after her first sip. "I see Anax has taken advantage of your time since your arrival."

Lexi stiffened. She had her answer. No need for small talk if the queen favored directness. "I don't mind too much. The gardens he showed me were quite beautiful."

The queen took another sip of her zion. "Not much happens here that I don't know about. Gossip runs rampant regarding Anax."

Lexi sipped at her tea. Dozens of attendants had wandered the hallways, witness to their conversation. But that was all it was—a conversation. Whatever the queen wanted to say, she needed to just come out and say it.

"He loves showing off his mother's gardens in his attempts to bed his latest conquest." Lexi's stomach dropped. "There's been music instructors, a translator tech, and countless ladies of the court."

Lexi kept her hand steady on the zion cup. Queen Chryseis was so casual in her cruelty. Lexi knew full well the queen had designed her words to hurt her. She refused to give her the satisfaction of getting a rise out of her. Lexi took a deep breath. It was no concern of hers how many females Anax showed the garden. There was no romantic future for them. His playboy status was irrelevant to her.

Entirely irrelevant.

If Lexi repeated it enough, perhaps it would become true.

Lexi put on her fakest smile. "I have no intention of forming any kind of romantic relationship with him."

Queen Chryseis growled, like the Herkleian version of a snort. "You wouldn't be the first female to say that, only to fall victim to his seduction later. A word of advice, my sweet child. He's all charm and smiles, but when it comes down to it, the females are replaceable and never last long."

"Thank you for letting me know," Lexi said with forced gratitude.

She needed to change this conversation. This was her future mother-in-law. If Queen Chryseis knew the depths of her attraction to Anax, it'd haunt Lexi to her grave. "I'm sure he was simply being polite. Your whole family has been so welcoming to me. I look forward to getting to know everyone better." Lexi paused, then added, "Especially Phintias."

At the mention of Phintias, the queen's entire demeanor seemed to change. She straightened in her chair and the suspicion left her slitted eyes. For all Queen Chryseis's faults, she truly loved her son. "He's such a good boy, but he's always off with his friends, racing gliders or at his father's other estates."

Lexi's smile twitched. Her father had always been there for her and her mother. She had dreamed of that for her own family. But Phintias hadn't put in the slightest effort to get to know her. Anax had shown up yesterday to give her a tour like she'd expect a fiancé to do. She hadn't seen Phintias since the engagement ball.

The queen saw her expression. "Don't worry too much about him, Alexandra. You won't be spending much time with Phintias, anyway. Once you become his wife, you'll spend your time amongst the court's ladies. I should start introducing you to some of them. Having no companionship must bore you."

"Oh, it hasn't been too bad. Kynna has been keeping me company."

"Who is Kynna?"

"Kynna." When the queen's face didn't change, Lexi elaborated, "My attendant."

"Oh." Chryseis snapped her fingers, her claws zinging together. "It's so hard to remember the help's names."

An attendant rushed in with a little golden plate. She fished the zion bag from the cup and dumped the herbs onto the plate. With a tiny spoon, the queen shoveled the herbs into her mouth. Lexi's eyes widened. They ate the tea leaves? Her stomach swirled. The attendant started to do the same with Lexi's cup, but she waved the female away.

The queen continued, oblivious to Lexi's shock. "I find it easier not to bother. Sweet child, there's no need to get friendly with your attendant."

If these females were anything like the queen, Lexi would much rather be in Kynna's company.

"The King is throwing a ball for my birthday two days from now," the queen said after a pause. "It will be the perfect opportunity for you to meet Herkleian ladies befitting a future princess."

She smiled politely and tried for a fake chuckle. Any human would have noticed the falseness of the sound, but it went over Queen Chryseis's head. "I look forward to it."

SEVEN

LEXI

A knock reverberated through Lexi's suite after lunch. Lexi was halfway down the stairs to her sitting rooms when Kynna opened the door. Anax strode in without even waiting for an invitation. "I'm ready for my next lesson."

After not hearing from Anax in the morning, Lexi had hoped he's given her the day off or became less interested in their so-called Earth lessons. Lexi's lunch with the queen had put her even more on edge. Lexi had always tried to stay out of drama in high school and college. She didn't feel at all equipped to deal with a court of gossip and infighting. She hoped it was only the queen who engaged in these behaviors but couldn't shake the feeling she was constantly being watched.

Lexi rushed down the stairs. "I really don't think we should be in my suite together."

Anax crossed his arms, his pecs flexing. "Why not? I'm the Crown Prince."

Heat spun in Lexi's stomach. She raised her attention to his eyes. A smirk had settled on his lips, flashing her half a fang. It spurred her forward. She pressed her hands onto his shoulder and tried to shove him from the room. "Get out, Anax."

He let her push him past the threshold. "If you insist. We'll have our lesson on Earth culture elsewhere."

Lexi glanced back at Kynna, who had ducked her head and settled against the wall. "Kynna can come with us."

"Why would we need a chaperon to watch us?"

"I don't want people getting the wrong idea."

His forehead creased. "And what kind of idea would that be?"

Lexi crossed her arms, mimicking his alpha male position. "That I'm just one of your flings."

The half-smile disappeared from his face. "You've spoken to my stepmother."

It wasn't a question, but Lexi answered it anyway. "I did. While you might not worry about your reputation, I do. I made a promise to your brother and I intend to keep it."

Something flickered in his slitted blue eyes at her words, but he put one hand over his heart, a warrior's salute. "Lexi, I assure you I would never do anything to hurt you or put you on edge. Nothing will happen."

"I still don't feel comfortable." Lexi glanced down the hall. None of the passing attendants glanced their way, but she couldn't relieve the feeling that someone's eyes were on her. "There are eyes everywhere."

"If it's the spies you're worried about, I have a solution. Do you trust me?"

Lexi paused. She knew she shouldn't. They hadn't known each other long, not enough for trust, but deep down, she knew she did. "Yes."

Anax reached out a hand. "I know a place where even Chryseis's spies won't reach us."

LEXI NEARLY TRIPPED over her skirt for the third time. "This was a terrible idea."

"We're outside the palace, are we not?" Anax asked with a boyish grin.

Anax's only solution to avoiding the queen's spies was to avoid the palace entirely—something strictly forbidden for Herkleios's heir. But escaping the palace had been easier than Lexi thought. Anax had removed his wristband and Lexi her bracelet, leaving behind the tech that tracked their every move. Kynna had loaned her a plain gray dress that all the palace attendants wore and a scarf to hide her horn-less head and scaleless skin. Anax had thrown on a guard's helmet, the vizier blocking half his face. They had exited through the staff door. In their new attire, no one so much as looked at them twice.

Once outside, the weight disappeared from Lexi's shoulders. She breathed deeper, enjoying the foreign smells of Eritea, the city. The palace was beautiful and pristine with a garden of her dreams, but it wasn't as real as the city, full of Herkleians living their day-to-day life. Buildings towered on either side of her, made of smooth metal straight from out of a sci-fi movie. Glowing plants and vines over-flowed in planters and wrapped around anything that didn't move. Everything was speckled with gold. Twenty feet above her head, vehicles zipped across the sky, submerging her in shadows for brief moments. Lexi didn't mind the shade. Herkleios had a variety of temperatures, but Eritea was near the equator, giving the sun an extra bite. As a Cali girl, Lexi was prepared for that. What she wasn't prepared for was the humidity, almost like a storm was forming.

Anax didn't tell her where he was taking her, the two of them falling into a comfortable silence on their walk. Not that she minded. She hadn't been alone with her thoughts since Uncle Grayson's staff shoved her into a dress for the ball. The last few days had changed her life a dozen times over. Anax let her be, drinking in the bright and colorful sights of Eritea.

A mouthwatering scent drifted past her nose on a warm breeze. Lexi inhaled deeply. She couldn't pick out any of the individual flavors, but they were all familiar. Like garlic, but not. Like sizzling meat, but not. Lexi turned to ask Anax when he held out a hand for her. "This way."

She gripped his palm, the warmth of his scales radiating through her. He led her down a narrow alleyway that opened to a little square lined with brightly colored stalls. Vendors shouted their offerings and promotions, their carts holding a range of products, from silky fabrics and fragrant spices to smoldering snacks and eight-armed monkey creatures.

"What are they?" she asked, pointing at the monkeys.

"Taferos. They excel at mathematics. Many business owners purchase one."

Her jaw had been open most of the walk, but it dropped further now. "You have monkey bookkeepers?"

"What is a monkey?" The crowds shoved Lexi tight against Anax's side. He wrapped his arm around her to keep them from being separated.

"It's an animal." Lexi gripped at his shoulder, not caring how close they were. "Looks like a tafero, but I don't know if they're good at math. Probably depends on the monkey."

He mirrored her smile, flashing her that intoxicating bit of fang. "Then, yes, we have monkey bookkeepers."

Anax walked with purpose to the far end of the market stalls before turning between two carts down a near invisible alley. Lexi bristled as they walked through the narrow space. She couldn't even stretch out both arms without hitting the wall.

"Where are we going?"

"Almost there." Anax made a sharp left off the alley into a quiet patio overgrown with purple ferns and glowing blue flora. The space had only a handful of tables and was entirely empty.

Lexi glanced around but didn't spot a sign. "Are you sure this isn't someone's backyard?"

Anax let out a howling chuckle. "Oh, I'm sure. As a matter of fact, this is the home of the best food on Herkleios."

He tapped at one table and the chairs floated back. Lexi settled into the seat before Anax did the same across from her. A narrow door slid open, revealing a Herkleian female, her purple hair streaked with aging gold. Anax rose at her approach, baring his fangs.

When the female got close, Anax lowered his head and tapped horns with the female. "Good day, Latona."

"It has been too long, little prince," Latona said, patting him on the shoulder. "Would you like your usual or do you want to show your friend the menu?"

Latona didn't blink at the sight of Lexi, even though her hood had fallen to reveal her human face. Lexi smiled and the female bared her fangs.

"We'll take a menu," Anax said.

Latona turned on her heels and back inside her restaurant.

Lexi leaned across the table. "How do you know her?"

"Latona worked in the palace kitchens when I was young. When my mother passed, I inherited part of her estate. I helped Latona buy this storefront. She wouldn't take much, but she's become one of Eritea's best in the last decade, despite the location."

Before Lexi could ask more, Latona returned with two pen-shaped objects. She placed them on the table in front of them. Anax tapped one. A menu projected into the air in front of him.

"Take your time to decide," Latona said before returning inside, leaving Lexi and Anax alone on the patio.

Lexi's eyes flashed across the menu. A bunch of unfamiliar words and pictures stared back at her. Her translator wasn't much help when there wasn't an Earth equivalent of the food.

"They have the best grilled simos," Anax said.

What was a simos? Lexi nodded vaguely before tapping her menu closed. "Why don't you decide? I trust you."

Anax's grin turned cocky. He tapped a few items on the screen and then closed his menu. The entire thing took under thirty seconds. Lexi had waitressed her way through college but getting orders instantly would have made her job a thousand times easier—and reduce the number of creeps who made gross comments.

She leaned an elbow on the table. "Do you come here a lot?"

"When I get the chance." He leaned back in his seat. Lexi fought to keep her gaze on his face and not his rippling abs. How dare Herkleian culture not include shirts? "We have chefs in the palace, but none are as good as Latona. Even if they were, it's nice to be somewhere where I'm not a prince. Only Anax."

"Latona doesn't care you're a prince?'

"Latona sees me as Anax. Nothing more. Her son, Dexus, and I played together as children. We later served side by side during my two years in the military. We were both stationed at Alphi Base on Kore."

"The moon?" Herkleios had three moons—the sisters, Kore and Ios, and a distance brother, Salane. All named for the children of dragon goddess Hyra. Lexi couldn't remember half of what she read on her holo-screen, but she remembered that. "Kore is like Earth's moon, right? Barren and gray?"

He nodded. "Herkleios hasn't been at war for decades. The military base is more for scientific discovery. Dexus served there for two years longer than me, but he wanted to be closer to his mother. He's a captain for the Royal Guard now."

A whooshing sound reached her ears, the patio door opening and closing gently. Lexi turned to watch Latona approach, two gold plates in her hands. Red-orange gravy covered hunks of blue meat, the plate spotted with green potato-like circles. Lexi inhaled a scent nearly like fried chicken. If whatever this was tasted like fried chicken, it'd probably become her favorite meal.

Lexi didn't hesitate this time to try the food. She grabbed her prong-fork and stabbed at one of the blue pieces of meat. Anax watched her as she brought the fork to her mouth. A spicy but buttery taste caressed against her tongue. Lexi nearly moaned. It tasted exactly like fried chicken, but a thousand times better.

Anax growled, a low chuckle. "You like?"

Lexi swiped her next piece through the red-orange gravy. "It's delicious. I see why this is your secret hideaway."

"The palace is my home, but it can be a lot. Everything gets back to my father and stepmother, eventually." He paused to take a bite. Lexi watched entranced as he licked his lips. "It's good to have a place to be myself."

"Chryseis really seems to have it out for you."

"She always has. She and my father started courting months after my mother's death. Eryx and I hated her." At the mention of the brother who abandoned him, Anax straightened. But the mask of the wicked prince didn't return to his face. He remained vulnerable with her. "My younger siblings seemed to have better luck. They're further down the line of succession, so perhaps she didn't see them as threats to her position."

"Your father didn't care that she was cruel to you?"

"Chryseis is a completely different person when he's around. I tried to tell him about her prior to their engagement, but he waved it away and said I was just upset because he was replacing my mother. It was one of the few times my father ever disappointed me."

"My dad was my role model, too." Lexi was almost shocked by the words. She never talked about her dad. It had been a decade since he died, but it hurt every day. "He always pushed me out of my comfort zone. I'm always a bit in my head. My dad wanted me to get out of my own way. He always wanted me to follow my passion and live in the moment. After he died, I burrowed deeper into my own shell."

Anax grazed his fingers against her hand. "I'm sorry about your father. I know how hard it is to lose someone."

Lexi didn't pull her hand from his as she finished her plate. If she hadn't been in public, she'd consider licking the dish clean. She leaned back in her seat, completely satisfied. Wetness pattered against her head. She glanced up. The blue sky had darkened to a rainy gray.

"We should get inside," Anax said.

Before Lexi could ask why, the few droplets turned into a heavy pouring. Lexi shrieked. Anax grabbed her hand with a growl. They ran for the sliding door and slammed into a bare hallway. Lexi couldn't stop giggling like a schoolgirl. But when she faced Anax, she choked. He shimmered in the light, the water gliding off his scales. The beauty of him warmed her chest. He looked down at her, equally entranced. Lexi almost laughed. She felt like a drowned rat, her hair soaking and a shiver setting in her bones. A shiver chased away by the heat of his body. She leaned forward—

Latona peeked out of a doorway down the hall, probably the kitchen. Lexi recoiled back from Anax, slamming into a wall.

The older female appeared at their side in an instant. "Go upstairs, dry yourself off. I'll be with you in a moment. I have some customers at the front."

Anax put a hand to his chest and bowed. "Thank you, Latona."

Lexi followed Anax up a flight of narrow stairs hidden behind delivery boxes. While the lower floor was half-kitchen and half-restaurant, the upper level was an open-concept apartment. A levitating bed hovered on the far side next to a small seating area. Lexi assumed she had entered a kitchen, but she wasn't sure. There was a bit of counter space, but a large rectangle occupied most of the room. Like a refrigerator without doors. The smooth surface was a screen. It lit up when Lexi approached, pictures of food flashing across the space.

Anax disappeared quickly into what was probably a bathroom and came back with two plush towels. He handed both to her. "I failed to plan to keep you warm and dry."

She tried to shove one towel back at him. "You need one, too."

"I'll be fine. Herkleians all burn with an inner fire, blessed by Hyra. We don't get cold the same way humans do. I will remember that and protect you next time."

Lexi snorted. "Protect me? I'm fine. A little hypothermia never killed anyone."

His forehead furrowed. "Hypothermia?"

Lexi waved her hand. "It's not a funny joke if I have to explain it. But fear not, I'm strong enough to handle both your rejection of my joke and a little water."

This time he did laugh, letting out that howl of his that made Lexi's knees go weak. Lexi tried to laugh with him, but it was forced. This close to him, his heat radiating out towards her, Lexi felt right, whole. As if her body belonged next to his.

But once they returned to the palace, she'd be his brother's fiancée again.

Nothing more.

ANAX

Anax didn't want to let Lexi go. Once the rain had subsided, they had walked through the city side-by-side, his arm over her shoulder, until they reached the palace. Even now, in the palace's dim, empty halls, their shoulders brushed. Each touch sent a spark through Anax's scales. His blood roared, demanding that he claim her. But he hadn't yet. She was his brother's betrothed, but that was simply an excuse. Every moment he spent talking with Lexi made him want another. He knew desire but had never wanted love—never expected love.

He wanted to scoff at the notion, but Lexi's hand brushed his and he had to resist the urge to capture it and place a kiss on her knuckles.

"Thank you," Lexi said as they turned the corner to her hallway. "It was nice to see the city."

"It was my pleasure."

A faint pink tinted Lexi's cheeks, like the color of trian flowers. He wanted to brush his claws against her face, but he clenched his fist instead. "Royal life can be a lot, but you'll get used to it in time."

She inhaled sharply—a snort, perhaps? "Will I?"

She would. Lexi was strong. He hadn't known her long, but their short time together had already shown him her spirit. She had moved across a galaxy for her people, her planet. She'd survive life at the palace. Better yet, she'd thrive. "You will—"

The door to her suite was jammed open. Anax stiffened and pulled his sabre in a smooth motion. With a click to the bottom of the pommel, the sword sparked with a flare of electricity. Someone had entered Lexi's suite. Still might be in her suite. His blood thundered through his veins, no longer lust but a protective urge.

Her eyes widened at his sword, but when she followed his gaze, her skin paled to a strange, white color. Fear. He didn't want her to be scared.

"Stay here," he whispered. "I'll be back in a moment."

"I'm not letting you go in alone."

"Lexi—"

She shook her head. "I'm not staying here."

As a male, as a prince, it was his duty to protect the females under his care. "You could get hurt."

She narrowed her eyes at him. "I'm coming, Anax."

He didn't have time to convince her otherwise. He pulled a knife from its holster at his leg and handed the blade to her. Even if she didn't come and let him protect her, it was better to be prepared. He couldn't leave her defenseless.

Anax kept close to the wall, his sabre raised and ready. He nudged the door. Voices sounded within Lexi's suite. One. Two. Three. He stopped and listened closer. Something was familiar about the third voice.

It clicked.

Anax lowered his sabre and strode inside. "Report, Captain."

Dexus straightened to attention at his arrival, as did the other two Royal Guards Anax had heard in the hall. Lexi's attendant, Kynna, sat on the closest couch, a shiver wracking her shoulders. Someone had wreaked the room, turning furniture upside down, breaking the wall's holo-mirrors, and scattering Lexi's few belongings across the floor. But worse still, whoever had done this spewed hanat flowers everywhere, the room poisoned by their putrid stench. The couches, the counters, the carpets, all lined with hanat. When the god Hadus had betrayed the goddess Hyra, she had banished him to the underworld. His castles and estates had rotted, all the gardens turning to hanat flowers.

The Herkleian flower of death.

A clear threat to Lexi's life.

Anax's vision went red, rage rushing through him. Someone had threatened his Lexi.

Lexi rushed past him and dropped at her attendant's side. "Are you okay, Kynna?"

Kynna jumped to her feet and dropped into a bow. "I am, my lady. I wasn't here during the attack."

"What happened?" Anax asked.

Kynna faced her prince, her head lowered. "I left to speak with the seamstress about having some dresses made for Lady Alexandra. When I returned, the room was like this."

The attendant had witnessed nothing of use, then. "Captain?"

Dexus touched a badge clipped to the straps of his pauldrons. A holo-screen flashed into the space between them, showing a choppy shot of the hall. It flickered, the time stamp changing by an hour. "Whoever did this tampered with the security monitors in the halls, Your Highness. We know little else. I have guards questioning the staff, but so far no one saw anything."

"Or they're simply not admitting it." The Royal Palace was impenetrable. Getting out had been easy, but when Lexi and Anax had re-entered the palace, they had to go through screening. Highly trained Herkleian soldiers paired with the best technology in the Intergalactic Alliance had verified their identities. To get to Lexi's suite, someone within the palace had to be involved.

"What do the flowers mean?" Lexi asked, picking up a stem. She brought the flower to her nose and dropped it with a gag. "What's that smell?"

"Hanat flowers. A symbol of death on Herkleios." Anax paused, but if he didn't tell her, someone else would. "This is a threat to your life, Lexi."

Her eyes widened. "On my life?"

"I agree, my lady," Dexus said. "Hanat flowers are often attached to death threats."

Lexi backed towards the door, like she might run from the room. "Who would want me dead? I don't even know anyone here."

"I don't know." When his siblings had gotten engaged, none of their spouses had received such threats. The Herkleian people were happy to strengthen the Intergalactic Alliance and gain access to new tech and resources. Earth wasn't as advanced as Herkleios, but they had many things to share.

It couldn't be because Lexi was an Earthling. Was it her engagement somehow? Phintias's maybe-former girlfriend wasn't capable of this. The time Anax had accidentally stumbled upon the two of them in the garden, the female had been shy and sweet. But what other reason was there? Anax didn't know. He hated not knowing. If he didn't know, he didn't have a target. Everyone became an enemy. Anax caressed the hilt of his blade.

"Is it safe to sleep here?" Lexi asked.

Dexus tapped his comms device. "I'll place two guards outside her door immediately."

"No." Anax settled his grip on his blade. There was only one path available to him. "Lady Alexandra is my family's guest. I will keep her safe myself."

"Yourself?" Lexi asked, her cheeks flushing that beautiful pink.

Anax turned to Kynna. "Notify my attendants."

Kynna tapped at her bracelet, but Lexi stormed into his path with her arms crossed. "Don't I get a say in this?"

Anax crossed his arms, too. Her eyes flickered down, drawn to the movement of his pecs. He couldn't stop his lip from twitching. "No."

She poked him in the chest. "No?"

"When it comes to your safety in this palace, no."

"I'm your brother's fiancée," she hissed.

Dexus cleared his throat. "The Royal Guard is capable of protecting Lady Alexandra, Your Highness. If she doesn't want to go—"

"She'll sleep in my rooms." He trusted Dexus with many things, but not with Lexi. The offenders might return and try to harm her again. "That's final."

Dexus didn't challenge him again. They had been friends during their youth and their time in the military, but here Anax was a prince, always obeyed. "Of course, Your Highness."

Anax refocused on Lexi. She remained rageful, her green eyes like the storms over the Azov Sea. He wanted her even more. She had a fire in her, one that called to the fire in him. "I'm not suggesting anything untoward, my lady. I will sleep on a sofa."

Lexi didn't budge. "I'm staying in my suite."

"It will take hours to clean, my lady," Kynna whispered, almost reluctantly.

Lexi sighed, long and hard. "Fine."

ANAX WATCHED Lexi survey his bedroom from the doorway. Luxurious soft fabrics covered his bed and dark curtains hung in his windows, blocking out all sources of light. The room was nearly twice the size of hers, as was the rest of his suite, with nearly a dozen rooms from multiple sitting areas to a training salon. Like everywhere else, the bedroom had few belongings. Any Herkleian could have lived in the room. Did she think it odd? She slowly approached the bed but said nothing. Other females had made comments before, but he had always told them some lie about his time in the military.

But if Lexi asked, he would tell her the truth. He'd tell her this was the heir's room—Eryx's room. Anax didn't feel right making it his.

She sat down on the levitating bed, testing the mattress. She hadn't spoken since they had left her suite. He would not force her.

The Anax of a few days ago would have used this opportunity to seduce her, claim her once and for all. Anax still wanted her. His cock twitched thinking about her, naked and exposed on the bed before him.

But things were different now. Anax couldn't have her once and forget her. She had wormed his way past his defenses. He wanted her now and forever. She had made her thoughts entirely clear on the matter. Lexi was to marry his brother. She had more honor than him. It only made him want her more.

Anax retreated into the hall before he punched a wall in rage. Phintias and Lexi, fucking. His vision went red. He couldn't surrender her. But he had no choice but to surrender her. Anax was the heir. He couldn't marry a human. Their union would ruin more than Herkleios's relationship with Earth, but Herkleios itself. As Crown Prince, as the future king, he needed to care about that.

He didn't.

He paced until his blood pressure lowered. He would find some way to make Lexi his. A hundred years ago, Herkleians had the right to challenge rivals for their spouses. Challenging Phintias would ruin his relationship with his father and all his siblings, but he'd do it for her. He'd do anything for her. All she had to do was ask.

Anax returned to his bedroom minutes later with a blanket in hand. His attendants had brought them extras, but Anax refused to let anyone else in the suite. He couldn't risk Lexi—both her life and reputation. His eyes immediately sought her out. She remained seated at the edge, staring blankly at her hands.

He approached and knelt at her feet. "How are you feeling?"

She tried for a smile, but the grin was small. In sadness, perhaps? She had lived a normal life before arriving here. She had probably never experienced a threat on her life. "I'm okay."

He placed the extra blanket beside her. He wanted to know what she was thinking, but he didn't push. He didn't want to do anything to hurt her. "If you need anything, I'll be in the sitting room across the hall."

She nodded. "Thank you, Anax."

He crossed the room, ignoring his body's urges to turn back, to answer the call of his blood. If they hadn't found those hanat flowers in her suite, this night might have ended very differently. But he couldn't seduce her now, not when she was vulnerable and scared. He cared about her feelings. When he claimed Lexi—and he would— she would be eager.

The door opened at his approach, but when he crossed the threshold, Lexi let out a long sigh. "You might as well sleep in the bed. It's big enough for two."

Anax's entire body stiffened, his heart kicking into a thunder. She had said sleep. She didn't intend anymore. Lying next to her and not being able to touch her supple skin would nearly kill him, but he'd do it if she wished. He'd do anything she wished. Anax turned to her, hoping the dimness of the room hid the lust in his eyes. Lexi had finally left the edge of the bed and crawled to one side. She grabbed at the spare pillows his attendants sprinkled artfully across the mattress, molding them into a little wall to divide the space in two.

Anax had to clear his throat to speak clearly. "I can sleep in the sitting room. Worry not, Lexi."

"I saw how long those sofas are," she said, still not meeting his eyes. "You'd barely fit." She glanced up briefly. "Besides, I'd feel safer having you close to me."

Anax nearly bared his fangs. He made her feel safe, the duty of every male. Herkleian females ruled their society, but the males were the protectors, the fighters. He might be a future king, but this was his duty. "Do not fear, Lexi. No one will harm you."

"Thank you, Anax." She tugged at the blankets and snuggled into the bed. Like the mattress in her suite, the cushion adjusted to her body, cuddling her close. "I'm exhausted, so if you don't mind, I'm going to turn in now." She paused, a bit of her fire returning to her gaze. "Don't cross my pillow line."

Anax dropped into a bow. "On my honor. I would never touch an unwilling female."

Lexi flushed at the mere mention of touching and quickly turned onto her side, giving her back to him. Anax gently climbed onto the bed. He felt her stiffen, but when he stayed on his side, she eventually relaxed.

Anax waited until her breath softened in sleep to close his eyes. He kept his hand on the hilt of his sabre at his bedside. If anyone at all entered the room, he'd awaken immediately. Anax wouldn't allow anyone to touch Lexi.

Not now, not ever.

Softs scales brushed across Lexi's skin, a touch of warmth that ignited the fire within her. She shuffled closer and inhaled, breathing in a deep, masculine scent. Anax. Even in her dreams, she couldn't escape him. The burning in her core turned into an inferno. She traced her fingers from his elbow to the crook of his shoulder, his muscles tensing beneath her touch. Like she'd never be able to touch him in reality.

But in her dreams, he was all hers.

Lexi traced her knuckles from his shoulder to the sharpness of his chin. She traced a thumb against his lower lip. Soft like a human man's yet somehow not. He opened his mouth, scratching the palm of her thumb with his fangs. Something fluttered in her stomach. She wanted him. More than she should. In a few years, he'd be her brother-in-law. He couldn't be anything more.

She needed to wake up.

Lexi pulled back her hand and pushed into unconsciousness.

Dream-Anax cupped her chin, his claws caressing her cheeks, and claimed her mouth in a kiss.

Everything stopped within her. Every thought. Every worry and concern. Only sensation remained. His rough tongue plunged into her mouth, taking and taking. She opened herself to him, letting him possess her. It was everything she had ever wanted.

Everything she ever wanted and would never get.

Except this once in her imagination.

Lexi thrust herself against his chest. Her shirt brushed against his scales, creating delicious friction for her nipples. A flood of warmth pulsed between her legs. She hooked one thigh over him. She needed him. Right now. A hardness pressed against her core. She whimpered. He groaned.

Lexi wrapped her fingers in the silky black of his hair, brushing against the base of his horns, and deepened the kiss. She wanted him. All of him. She ground her body against his. His cock twitched, growing harder.

With a growl, he rolled, pulling her on top of him—

The edge of his fang cut through her lip. A metallic taste exploded through her mouth.

Lexi sat up straight, propelled into awareness.

Anax's bedroom, the turquoise medallions carved into his ceiling bright in the morning light. Anax's bed, a levitating mass twice the size of an ordinary king, piled with soft blue pillows. Anax himself, underneath her, his slitted eyes tracing the lines of her face, his clawed finger clenching her hips where she straddled him.

Not a dream, but a reality.

Dammit.

Lexi pushed off him and nearly launched off the bed. Shit. It hadn't been a dream. She had kissed Anax. Threaded her hands through his hair. Ground against him. The warmth inside her turned sour, a twisting of her stomach. She put her hands on her thighs and tried not to vomit on his nice floors.

Anax was at her side in a moment, genuine concern in his eyes. "Did I hurt you?"

She shuffled away from his touch. "We shouldn't have done that."

"Lexi—"

"I need to go." She grabbed the outer skirts of her dress and rushed from the room. The path to the exit was a maze of sitting rooms, but Lexi tore through them all. The exit doors slid open. She tossed on her dress over her thin shift and glided through the door with speed. She nearly propelled herself into the wall on the other side of the hall. Lexi clutched at the nearest decorative table.

She had kissed Anax. Or accidentally kissed Anax. Who accidentally kissed someone?

Lexi needed air, needed to think. She was betrothed to his freaking brother. All the people of Earth and Herkleios expected their union. More importantly, her mother needed Uncle Grayson's support. He had paid off the worst of their debts, but billionaires were terrible enemies to make. What would he do to her family if Lexi broke off the engagement?

What would the continuation of that same engagement do to Lexi?

She shook her head. She had to go through with it. But her heart raced faster, the walls closing in. She needed to get out of this damned palace.

Lexi rushed down the hall before any attendant could approach —or worse, Anax. She focused on a single door, everyone in her periphery a blur. Nothing mattered but the beam of light.

"Lexi!"

Lexi all but ran into the garden, disappearing between tree-sized, pink-purple flowers shaped like pinecones. Anax was behind her, but she couldn't let him find her. She pushed off the path through a bush. Her skin brushed across fragile, soft petals. She closed her eyes and breathed, praying for the thick scent of nature to soothe her. But her heartbeat didn't calm, nor did her mind. Usually being in her element was enough to settle her, but it did nothing today.

Lexi had kissed Anax.

She opened her eyes and kicked at the underbrush as she walked. What had she done? She knew she had to stay away from him, but she had let him woo her. She had climbed into his freaking bed and invited him to lie beside her. What had she been thinking? Lexi pulled at loose twigs, but even in her distress, she couldn't find it in herself to destroy any of the beautiful flowers. This had been Queen Avra's garden, after all.

Lexi walked deeper and deeper into the maze that was the gardens. She didn't know where she was going at this point. As long as she kept moving, Anax wouldn't find her. She spun around a green-barked tree—

Only to slam into someone's back. She caught her balance, but nearly knocked the Herkleian from their feet. She grabbed their shoulder to steady them. "Oh, I'm so sorry—Phintias?"

Prince Phintias stumbled back from her, nearly yanking out of her grasp. Behind him, an orange-haired Herkleian female around his age howl-shrieked and tugged at her dress. Her hands crossed her bare chest protectively. Her bare chest. Lexi frowned, but focused on Phintias. When she had seen him at the ball, he'd worn a shirt. He didn't have one now.

Because his shirt was hanging from a purple bush.

Lexi had interrupted her teenage fiancé mid-foreplay.

"Uh." She backed away. "Sorry to interrupt."

The female's green slitted eyes widened on Lexi. She whirled on Phintias. "Is that... is that your fiancée?"

Phintias swallowed, looking between them. He grabbed his shirt. "Uh..."

The female sniffled and tried to hold in her emotions, but with one last glance at Lexi, she broke out in howling tears. Lexi flinched back.

"I'm sorry, Phintias," she sobbed. "I said I could do this, but I can't. I love you, but I can't."

Oh, God. Phintias had a girlfriend. Of course he had a girlfriend. He was eighteen and hadn't been engaged until a week ago. She wasn't even upset about it. Lexi wasn't marrying him out of love. She had thought herself the only one forced into the marriage, but she hadn't even considered the prince's situation. He had a freaking girlfriend and he had to marry Lexi. She pushed through orange-purple bushes in the exact opposite direction. "I'll go—"

Her heel caught on the edge of a glowing, crystalized rock and gravity dragged her down. Lexi slammed onto her tailbone. Her eyes watered.

Prince Phintias stared blankly.

His girlfriend gave a final sob, finished fastening her dress, and ran further into the bushes.

Lexi crawled to her feet, her back radiating pain. She was too old for this shit. "Aren't you going to run after her?"

"What?"

"Your girlfriend." Lexi pointed at the ruffling bushes. "She seems upset."

Prince Phintias gaped. "You're not angry?"

Lexi paused. She tried to summon anger, but she couldn't. She had just run from his brother's bed. Until they married, they owed each other nothing. "We're not married yet, Phintias, and won't be for years. As long as you're loyal then."

He straightened like a soldier to attention and nodded his head. "I would be. *Will* be."

Lexi twitched at the tense change but forced herself to smile. "Then run after your girl. Don't you dare break her heart."

"Yes, my lady." He backed away, dropping into a bow every other second. One benefit of raising males in a matriarchy. He paused suddenly. "You won't tell my mom about this, will you?"

Lexi almost laughed at the horror on his face. She couldn't see Phintias as a love match. He was a child. "I won't be telling anyone about this encounter."

His shoulders slackened. "Thank you, Alexandra."

"Go get her."

Phintias nodded enthusiastically and tore through the bushes. "Lexi!"

Lexi bristled. She had stood still for too long. Anax was closing in on her location. She didn't know what the hell she was going to do next, but she couldn't face the Crown Prince. Not yet. Lexi dashed in the opposite direction of his voice, back through the gardens until she found the path she had walked with him days ago. If she went left, she'd return to his rooms. Lexi took a harsh right.

Kynna had said it'd take a few hours to clean her room after the break-in. Lexi shivered suddenly. After what had happened this morning, she almost forgot someone had threatened her life yesterday. Who would want her dead? She didn't know. The royal family had been nothing but kind to her. Except for Queen Chryseis, but being rude and threatening death were miles apart from each other. The queen wouldn't want her dead, would she?

Lexi rushed back into the palace and went directly to the door of her suite. It was daylight, at least. The hallways bustled with activity, dozens of guards and attendants and droids going about their tasks. She didn't think she had anything to worry about immediately.

"Lady Alexandra?" A guard broke off from the nearby cluster of soldiers. Captain Dexus. He dropped into a small bow. "You shouldn't be out on your own. Let me accompany you."

She waved him off. "The door to my suite isn't far, Captain. I'm sure I'll be fine."

"I'd feel better if you were under my protection, my lady."

Lexi shrugged. It didn't hurt to have a bodyguard if her life was under threat.

Captain Dexus kept pace behind her as they walked the few feet to her room. When she approached the door, he gently touched her hand. "Allow me to go in first, my lady. In case someone is lying in wait. I'll check your suite, then call for more guards to stand outside your door."

Lexi peered behind her. Anax couldn't be far behind. "Thank you for escorting me, but I'll be fine from here."

Captain Dexus nodded. "I'll wait out here until your guards arrive. If you need anything, just ask."

"Can you find out where Kynna went?" Lexi would feel far more comfortable if she wasn't alone.

"Of course, my lady."

"And…" Lexi paused. "If Prince Anax comes by, tell him I'm not feeling well. I'm not to be disturbed."

Captain Dexus frowned slightly before washing the expression away. "Yes, my lady."

Lexi entered her suite, the doors sliding open with a quiet buzz. The uncut crystal rocks in the ceiling flickered to brightness. Someone had swept all the hanat flowers from the floor and righted all the furniture. Almost like yesterday had never happened at all. Lexi slumped onto the closest sofa. It didn't bob at the addition of her weight, despite its levitation. She slumped into the seat and dropped her head to her hands.

She had absolutely no connection with Phintias. Their conversation in the garden was the first time they had spoken outside a muttered hello at her uncle's headquarters. He might be young now, but she couldn't see herself growing to love him. At most, they'd be friendly for the sake of the alliance. She had always imagined a marriage full of love like her parents experienced. When her dad died, she thought her mom might never recover. She had loved him that much. Lexi wanted a heart-wrenching love with all her being.

When she closed her eyes, the ghostly touch of his hands traced her arms. It was Anax she wanted. Anax she craved.

But it was Phintias she had to marry.

Lexi jumped to her feet and kicked at the levitating coffee table. It glided across the air and bounced off a cabinet. Everything was unfair. She shouldn't be here, ashamed of her desire and confused about every single thing that had happened in the last hour. She glared at the coffee table. If she wrecked her room, it'd be Kynna's job to clean it up. No matter how much she wanted to turn her sorrow and hopelessness to rage, she couldn't give in.

Lexi lumbered to her feet and grabbed the edge of the coffee table—

The brightness of wrapping paper in the next room caught her eye.

Lexi straightened. The sparkly design was clearly Earth-based. One of Lexi's jobs during college had been at a department store in a mall. She could think of a hundred different wrapping paper designs off the top of her head, all thanks to hours wrapping gifts during the Christmas season.

The pang of the memory stopped her tears. Lexi approached the wrapping paper. Someone had stacked a dozen presents in a pile on the floor. Her engagement gifts. Kynna had mentioned them earlier, but Lexi had told her to put them to the side. She hadn't wanted to open them right away.

Now Lexi never did.

She picked up the top present. The tag said it was from an Italian ambassador. Lexi dropped the present to the floor and crumbled alongside it. She had to marry Prince Phintias. For her mom. For Earth. Both counted on her. If she left, what revenge would Uncle Grayson plot? What would happen to Earth's place in the Intergalactic Alliance? She couldn't risk it all for a silly kiss.

But Lexi's heart cracked at the thought, tears streaming down her face.

TEN

Lexi glanced at her reflection in the vanity's mirror while Kynna attempted to twist her hair into tight knots. Her attendant had easily adapted Herkleian make-up to fit a human face, dusting Lexi with blue, shimmering powder at her cheeks and eyes, but she still hadn't figured out the hair. The current fashion trend for Herkleian females was to wrap their hair around their horns in intricate patterns. Without horns to hold Lexi's hair in place, Kynna had to make do with an assortment of pins and hair gels.

Lexi ran her hands down the embroidered gold of her dress. The color was typically reserved for royalty, but King Xenobaccus had sent Lexi the gown for her to wear at the queen's birthday ball. The shape of the skirt was like a traditional Earth ballgown, but the gold embroidery changed to a wisp of soft feathers near the hemline. Lexi wanted to do little more than twirl around and watch the feathers dance. Queen Chryseis's staff had completed the look, loaning her a tiara that haloed out in beautiful sunbursts.

Lexi's gold bracelet buzzed. She tapped the jewel and the holo-screen flashed a message in front of her eyes. Two visitors were at her front door. She scanned the names and immediately jolted to her feet.

Kynna pulled back. "Lexi?"

"Anax and his father are at the door." Lexi had avoided Anax since waking up on top of him yesterday. Whatever Captain Dexus had said kept him from knocking. He had sent her a few messages, but she had left them all unread. She couldn't deny him now, not when he was with King Xenobaccus.

Kynna straightened. "I'll greet them right away."

Before Lexi could respond, her attendant rushed down the stairs to the main floor. Lexi took one last glance at herself in her vanity before following at a much slower pace. Herkleian heels were a thousand times more comfortable than any pair from Earth, but that didn't mean they were fast to walk in, especially not when wearing a ten-pound gold gown.

By the time Lexi made it down the stairs, Anax and King Xenobaccus had already entered her front foyer, Kynna dropping into dozens of bows. Anax had switched out his black casual pants for gold ones to match the swatch of fabric over his shoulder and his military medals. He paled compared to the king. His sunburst-shaped crown was twice the width of Lexi's and his sash embedded with red and blue gemstones. Instead of pants, he wore a toga-like skirt of shimmering gold fabric. He carried the same cane he had at her uncle's headquarters, his claws curled around the huge red jewel.

The king bared his fans when Lexi reached the bottom step. "You look beautiful, Lady Alexandra. Like a true Herkleian princess."

Lexi couldn't help her eyes from drifting to Anax at the words. His ice blue gazed burned as he traced her body. Almost more intimate than a physical touch. Lexi didn't know what to do about him. She had stuck to avoidance the last twenty-four hours like she should have at the beginning, but it was too late. Her heart fluttered in his presence.

The king continued, oblivious. "I heard you had a little scare and wanted to apologize. I'm sorry I could not find the time to do it sooner. The threat on your life is of utmost importance to me, Lady Alexandra. I have guards working around the clock to find the people responsible. We are fully committed to your safety and our alliance with your people."

Lexi dipped into a small bow. She hadn't trained in diplomacy, but years of customer service helped. "Thank you so much, Your Majesty. It was nothing. I'm feeling very welcomed here."

"I don't think what happened can be classified as nothing," Anax said, gaze intent on her.

Lexi flinched. Why did she have the feeling he meant more than the break-in?

King Xenobaccus tapped gently at Anax's shoulder. "Forgive my son. He's always had a flare of the dramatics." Turning his attention to Anax, he said, "I don't see any reason for you to scare the poor girl. I have alerted the guards. With no one hurt in the incident, I say it's best to let them handle the investigation."

"He's right, Anax. I'm completely fine." She paused. If Anax's words had had a double meaning, she might as well give hers one, as well. "Let's wipe it from our minds."

The heat dimmed in his eyes, but he recovered faster than Lexi, baring his fangs into that wicked half-smile. "I don't think I ever could."

Lexi's face heated. Hopefully nobody noticed through the blue of her make-up. She didn't reply. Anax didn't seem one to back down from a challenge. That was all she was to him. Another conquest, to claim and possess before moving on. Lexi wanted the time they spent together to be special, but it couldn't be. Not with him.

Maybe if she repeated it a dozen times, she'd believe it.

The king gestured toward the door. "We were planning to arrive at the ball together, Lady Alexandra. Would you like to join us?"

"Um..." How did one decline a king nicely? Lexi couldn't spend more time with Anax. She just couldn't. She didn't think she'd last thought another conversation without doing something she'd regret. She glanced at Kynna. "I still need to get ready."

Her attendant dropped her eyes but nodded gently. "I must add the finishing touches to her hair."

"It looks perfect to me," Anax said.

The fluttering in Lexi's chest moved downward. How the hell was she going to resist this male?

"Leave the lady to get ready at her own pace." King Xenobaccus tapped his cane and the door behind him slid open to reveal an entire retinue of staff. "Come along, Anax."

Anax propped himself against the door and crossed his arms, the flex rippling through his pecs. Lexi's mouth went dry. "With so many guests here tonight, the guards might be preoccupied, father. I'd rather monitor the Lady Alexandra myself."

"We can spare a guard to escort her." The king zinged his claws together, summoning an attendant to his side. "I'll assign someone right now."

Anax shook his head at the attendant, who paused awkwardly, stuck between the king and his heir. "I don't mind at all."

King Xenobaccus shrugged. "Suit yourself. I have guests to welcome. I'll see both of you in the ballroom shortly."

His attendants all shuffled around the king, getting into position. Before Lexi could ask what for, each member, including the king himself, tapped at their gold bracelet, turning their green gem red. Within a blink, the king and his retinue transported out of the room.

Without the king there to impress, Lexi frowned at Anax. "I don't need you to protect me."

Anax crossed the foyer in three long-legged steps. "Lexi, please—"

She backed away from his touch. She didn't have enough to resist him if he touched her. "I can't."

Anax lowered his hands reluctantly. "I know you want to remain true to your promise, but there's no reason we can't be friendly at a party."

A sharp cackle escaped Lexi's lips. "This isn't friendly, Anax. This is much more than friendly."

Anax pierced her with those slitted blue eyes. "Lexi—"

"The Lady Alexandra asked you to leave, Your Highness," Kynna whispered.

Anax whirled. In their emotion, both of them had entirely forgotten about the Herkleian female, standing invisibly in the corner. Lexi nearly pinched herself. She refused to become like the queen, indifferent to the surrounding attendants.

Anax folded his hand behind his back, becoming a serious prince once again. "You're right, Kynna. I've overstepped." Anax dropped to his knees before Lexi. The sharp tips of his horns nearly reached past her chin. "You told me no and I ignored your answer. Please, forgive me, Lady Alexandra."

The sight of Anax on his knees before her, the playboy prince and warrior begging forgiveness, melted Lexi's core into a hot wave of lust. How dare he be perfect and handsome and seductively masculine even when he was in the wrong? Lexi swallowed. At least the heavy embroidery of her gown hid the hard peaks of her nipples. "I forgive you, Anax."

He popped to his feet and bared his fangs. "I'll look for you in the ballroom."

"That's not—" Before Lexi could finish her sentence, he disappeared in the flash of a light. She sighed. What in the world was she going to do about him?

"My lady?" Kynna said hesitantly.

Lexi snapped out of it. She couldn't do anything about Anax now, but she could about Kynna. She reached for the attendant's clawed hands. At the touch, her slitted yellow eyes flashed to Lexi's face in surprise.

"I told you, call me Lexi." Lexi squeezed her hands. She wanted to give her attendant a hug, but Herkleians didn't do hugging. "Kynna, you've done a wonderful job with my hair and make-up. With everything, really. I don't know what I'd do without you."

Her cheeks glistened, the hint of a fang popping out at her lip.

"You're very welcome, Lexi. You're going to be the most beautiful female at the ball."

"I don't know about that, but it's kind of you to say." Lexi tapped on the gold wall, turning it into a mirror. She checked everything once and huffed out a sigh. Time for her first Herkleian ball. "Let's get this show on the road."

***

LEXI'S JAW dropped upon entry to the ballroom. The chamber was vast, wider than two football fields and higher than a six-story building. The first apartment building Lexi lived in could have fit comfortably inside. Glowing purple vines and spotted blue flowers wrapped around the gold metal of the domed glass ceiling. At the edges, where the ceiling met the wall, colorful titles created tiny, repeating mosaics that traced the entire room. Glowing, uncut crystals sprouted from embedded pillars and traced cracks through the mosaics. It was the most fantastic architecture Lexi had ever witnessed.

"Lady Alexandra?"

Lexi jolted. The crowds of Herkleians had mostly walked around her, but a male in his thirties approached. His hair was the darkest green, a perfect match to his eyes. His horns were tipped with gold and jewels, as were his claws. He wore a similar, toga-like skirt to the king, his chest only half-covered by the swoop of a sash. Unlike Anax, he didn't have any military medals. Something about this male was too delicate to be a warrior. "Yes?"

He dropped into a low bow. "I am Duke Iosif of Movro. Would you like to dance?"

"Um." Lexi heard the music, a soft rattling like rain against trees, but she had no idea how to dance to it. But the male waited expectantly and Lexi had never learned to say no. "Sure, I guess."

Iosif all but dragged her to the middle of the dancefloor, where Herkleians swayed gently to the melody. His hands dropped straight to her lower hips. Lexi nearly squealed. The male must have taken the noise for encouragement. He immediately began twirling Lexi in a circle, at much too fast a pace for the current beat. Other dancers dived out of the way. Lexi tried to smile at them, but it came out more like a grimace.

Someone cleared their throat at her side, a deep rumble.

Before Iosif could stop, Anax put a hand on the male's shoulder and gently shoved him out of the way. "I see you've met Lady Alexandra, Iosif. Unfortunately, she's already agreed to give me her first dance."

Iosif bristled, but Anax didn't give him a second glance. He whisked her away on a softer twirl, leaving the male standing in the middle of the dance floor alone. Lexi immediately forgot about him. Her world became Anax, his hands on hers, the heat of his chest reaching through her dress for her own heart. His ice-blue eyes ensnared her. A part of Lexi knew she should pull away, but she crushed that part of her.

She licked her lips, Anax's eyes tracing the movement. "Thanks for saving me from him."

"I did no such thing." He flashed her a smile full of fang. "I was serious about you owing me a dance and now I've come to collect."

"I never promised you a dance." Lexi glanced around, but no one seemed to care she was dancing with a male who wasn't her future husband. She didn't even spot Prince Phintias in attendance. King Xenobaccus circled the room, chatting with guest after guest. Some of Anax's siblings glanced their way, but they quickly lost interest. Even Queen Chryseis didn't care tonight, her attention held by the flock of courtiers who presented her with boxes upon boxes of gifts.

"Not in so many words."

Lexi pursed her lips. She could pull out of Anax's arms and cause a scene or continue to dance. Both her head and her heart were on the same page for once. She sighed. "You may come to regret the decision after I step on your feet a dozen times. I don't exactly know what I'm doing."

"Don't worry." Anax lowered one hand to the crook of her waist. The touch burned through her. "I'll lead."

Lexi's entire body tingled, the warmth in her growing and growing. She needed to keep her cool. She couldn't molest her future brother-in-law on the dance floor. That would be something to stare at. "Lead all you want. This is going to be a disaster."

He spun her around, leaned down to her ear, and whispered, "We'll go slowly."

A shiver racked her spine, followed by a rush of desire low in her belly. Lexi couldn't resist him. Not forever. She didn't even know if she was going to last the night.

Would it be so wrong to give into her passions?

Anax adjusted her hands, linking them around the back of his neck. He was nearly two feet taller than her, her feet nearly dangling off the ground. She held on as best she could and tried to focus on his eyes. If she didn't, she'd have front row tickets to his killer pecs, less than an inch from her face. Her mouth watered. Lexi turned her head abruptly. Maybe it was better to lean her head on his chest instead of ogling him. His heart pounded underneath his scales, in tune with her own. The warmth of him spread through her, down and down.

Anax was true to his word. He went slowly, guiding her through a simple one-two step. "You're getting the hang of this. Let's try a spin."

"I don't know."

"Try it." He spun her out and then back against his chest. For a second, Lexi felt like she was flying.

She couldn't help the smile that spread across her face. "Again."

"As you wish, my lady." Anax spun her again.

Lexi flew around in a gentle circle before landing back in his arms with a laugh. She couldn't believe she was actually having fun at what she thought would be a stuffy birthday ball.

Then Anax moved to dip her.

One of his hands slid up her back and the other lowered to her thigh. His claws traced tortuously against her. The rest of the ball disappeared, leaving only Anax, his slitted blue eyes, his long horns, the soft blackness of his hair. Her world narrowed to the strong lines of his face, so much like a man's but scaled and far more handsome. He inhaled deeply, like he was memorizing her scent. As intoxicated with her as she was with him. Lexi wanted to get even closer to him. The distance between their lips was nothing, a gap easily closed—

Some emotion flashed across Anax's face and he abruptly pulled her back to her feet.

The blood rushed straight to Lexi's head. The ballroom came back to her, the music, mutter of voices, and dim glow of crystallized rocks. She had almost kissed Anax in front of the whole ball.

Lexi no longer cared. Prince Phintias had no interest in her. Their relationship was political, nothing more. Why should pleasure come second to politics? She wanted Anax. *Needed* Anax. Had to have Anax, even if just for one night. It wasn't really cheating if she didn't love her fiancé. She didn't even know her fiancé. They hadn't married yet. Better she take her fill of Anax now than later down the road.

She took his hand and led him from the ballroom. Anax followed willingly, eagerly. The hunger in his gaze reflected her own. Her entire body ached with it. She had never felt this way with any Earthling man. She couldn't imagine feeling this way ever again. Whatever happened, Anax was special to her. Just like she was special to him. She wasn't a fling.

They slammed out of the ballroom and down a dark hallway. Lexi didn't care who saw them leave. She was almost running. Running after the moment.

Anax stopped. "Lexi, I—"

Lexi put a finger to his lips, halting his words. "Don't speak. I know I'm the one that said nothing could happen between us, but I lied, Anax. There's something between us. I know it. You know it. Why resist?"

His eyes devoured her. She loved the feral curve to his lips, like he was barely holding himself back. "You said so yourself, Lexi. You're to marry my brother—"

She gently lowered her hands to his chest. "Are you trying to talk me out of it?"

"No. Never." Something hard and long nudged her leg. The length of his cock. She needed him inside her. Just like he needed to be inside her. She knew it with every fiber of her being. "I want to fuck you, Lexi. I want you to break apart under my touch. I've wanted that since I first laid eyes on you. But you have to want it, Lexi. I won't force you."

Her mouth all but watered. "Anax..."

"Beg me to fuck you, Lexi."

ELEVEN

ANAX

"Fuck me, Anax." With the words, the entire planet shifted under Anax's feet. Yes. She had said yes. The urge to claim her spread like a fire through his body. His cock became an insistent rod. He needed her. Wanted her. Would have her.

Anax wrapped her in his arms and pressed her against the wall. He claimed her mouth in a kiss. Lexi moaned, a delicious sound. She wrapped her legs around his torso. His hardness pressed against the silk of her undergarments, her wet heat enveloping him. He groaned into her mouth as her breath hitched.

Anax needed her now.

He broke the kiss and tapped his wristband. "Two to transport. To my chambers."

Lexi's breath came out in gentle huffs, her cheeks a blue-powdered pink. She quickly tapped her own bracelet, the green gemstone turning red. He bared his fangs at her, a hungry look, but she swallowed his words, wrapping her hands around his horns and claiming his mouth as she had his.

His delightful, little mate.

Mate. The word echoed through him, but he knew it was true.

He'd thought about it before, but nothing else explained the desire burning in him, the rightness of her body pressed against his. Lexi was his mate.

His skin tingled as the transporters locked onto his signal. The air temperature dipped, going from the heat of the ball to the cold of his empty room. The music disappeared, his and Lexi's breathing a crescendo in the quiet space. Anax wrapped his hands tighter around her ass and stalked to his bed.

Lexi broke the kiss with a nibble to his bottom lip. "You're wearing too much clothing."

"As are you."

She grinned and tore at his sash, dumping it to the floor. His medals clattered against the marble. She trailed her hands down his chest, caressing at his scales. He shuddered at her touch.

"Put me down."

He did as commanded, lowering her to the edge of the mattress. Her hands didn't leave his chest. They lowered to his waistband, the gold fabric doing little to hide his erection. Her eyes widened at the width of him. She swallowed. Lexi was tiny, nearly a foot shorter than a Herkleian female. He didn't want to hurt her. He pulled back, but she dug her fingers into the fabric of his pants, holding him still.

He traced a claw along her chin. "Do you want to stop?"

She bit her lip and looked up at him with bright eyes. "No."

He wanted to howl with delight. Anax put his hands on hers and directed her to the button of his pants. She licked her lips. He grew even harder. He couldn't wait.

The moment she undid his fastening, he slid his trousers and boots off in a smooth movement, standing before her in nothing. Her jaw dropped at the sight of his massive, throbbing cock. After a pause, her hands reached out, tracing the scaled, ridged edges of his blue mass.

He groaned, almost coming apart with the single touched. He needed her. Needed to pound into her. Needed to listen to her scream and whimper. Needed her to come with his name on her lips. But he couldn't rush her, couldn't scare her—

Lexi stood and dropped her dress to the ground in a single motion.

Everything within him stopped at the sight of her body. The curve of her breasts and stomach, the intoxication of her hips. Her nipples peaked under his gaze, growing harder. He drew a knuckle gently against one of the buds. She inhaled sharply, leaning into his touch. He wanted to hear that sound, again and again.

He *would* hear that sound, again and again.

He stalked forward. Lexi tumbled to the bed, her eyes locked on his. Her legs parting, the thick scent of her arousal filling the air. He wanted to fuck her hard, but he pushed down his own desire. Her pleasure mattered more.

He planned to hear her scream.

He tapped his wristband, baring his fangs in a sly manner.

Lexi huffed in a bated breath. "What are you—?"

His bed beeped once before the levitation wrapped around Lexi. She gently floated into the air. She let out a slight squeak of alarm.

He put a hand on her hip, guiding her body to levitate before him. "Have you ever been fucked midair?"

She swallowed. "No?"

Anax parted her legs, her knees hovering at either side of his head. He retracted his claws and drifted a finger across her slit. She shuddered and jolted straight in the air. "Anax, I—"

He claimed her with his mouth. The taste of her wet desire flooded his senses. Delicious. She gripped his horns, her words turning into a loud moan. He wanted more of her. Anax grazed his fangs against the nub of her clit. Lexi gasped and arched her back. Perfect. With a growl, Anax took the nub into his mouth, licking and sucking. She squirmed at the sensation.

He inserted a single finger into the core of her heat, ripping another cry from her lips. Her hips bucked. She thrust against his fingers, eager and needy. He bared his fangs and scraped them across her sensitive folds. She almost came undone right then and there, her heat clenching against him.

Anax stopped, pulling back his head and glancing up the long line of her heaving body.

"What are you..." Lexi cleared her throat and tried again. "Why did you stop?"

Anax didn't reply. He raised his finger to his mouth. Without breaking eye contact, he sucked on the digit, swallowing her sweetness. Lexi shuddered. He bared his fangs at her, an arrogant grin.

He put one foot on the edge of the bed and propelled himself into the levitation field. As he floated upwards, he traced his fingers against the curve of her hip, the softness of her stomach, the hard buds of her breasts. When he arrived at her mouth, Lexi was shaking, her entire body in a desperate need. He traced the edge of his lips against the edge of hers, a slow, torturous move.

Lexi wrapped her leg around his torso and flipped him. They swirled in the air together over his bed. She gripped his horns and lowered down his body, until her wet opening nudged the edge of his throbbing cock. He wanted to thrust up and take her, claim her as his for all time. But Anax waited, the seconds painful as she lowered herself onto him. They groaned as one. Anax nearly spilled his seed.

Lexi shifted, taking his length in further. She was tight, his cock filling her to the brim. He had feared this. He didn't want to hurt her. Anax started to pull out.

She tightened her hold on his horn. "No."

"Lexi, I don't want to hurt you."

"You're not hurting me." She adjusted again, the ripple of sensation running through him. "I want you. All of you."

"Lexi—"

She leaned forward and stopped him with a kiss. "Shut up, Anax."

Lexi wrapped her legs around his back for leverage before pushing onto him in one quick movement.

Anax groaned. He rose to meet her next thrust, their bodies

merging into one. She clutched his horns as she rode him, coaxing them to a brilliant end. The force of their movements twisted them in the air, but Anax didn't care. Nothing mattered but Lexi.

She moaned and arched her back. Her core tightened around his cock, both of them seconds away from exploding.

Anax roared as his orgasm ripped through him. Lexi's entire body clenched, his name ripped from her lips in a scream. Her folds tightened around him, milking every drop of his seed. His body writhed in echo with hers. His mate. His Lexi. Now and for always.

Lexi slumped down into his arms, her body spent. He tucked the top of her head into the crook of his neck. He traced a hand through the silk of her hair. When a matebond solidified, a mark appeared on the back of the neck. She rubbed a thumb against the spot. He didn't notice a pattern of interlocking circles, but the spot near the base of her spine was red. Her mark hadn't formed yet.

A pang echoed through Anax's chest. One would appear. She was his as he was hers.

Lexi sighed happily and snuggled into his chest. Every beat of her heart vibrated through his scales.

"Are you alright, naika?"

"Naika?" she murmured, her voice thick with satisfaction. Before he could answer the word's meaning, she continued, "You're amazing. We were amazing. I never knew it could feel like that."

He pressed a kiss to the top of her head. "Neither did I."

She glanced up at him. "Really?"

He traced a clawed finger through her hair, pressing the damp strands from her face. "No one had ever made me feel as you do, Lexi."

She grinned, a bright smile. Anax traced his thumb against her bottom lip. He wanted her to smile like that every day. For as long as he lived, he made it his goal.

She tucked her head back against his chest. Anax wrapped her tighter in his arms, holding her close as they levitated over the bed.

TWELVE

LEXI

Golden-pink light trickled through the windows, urging Lexi into consciousness. Warm, powerful arms wrapped around her shoulders. Her entire body tingled, from her head to her toes, at every point her skin touched Anax's scales. Wrapped in his strong embrace, she had never slept better. Lexi burrowed into the blankets. She wished she might stay here forever, feeling the rise and fall of Anax's chest, his soft breath on her cheek.

He shuffled behind her, a hard weight pressing firmly against her thigh. Heat swelled in her belly, piercing through the quiet morning. Last night had been like nothing she'd experienced before. Like their bodies were meant to be intertwined. There was no way she could go back to Earth men now, not after the luxury that was Anax's skilled tongue and hands. She pressed herself back against him and his cock twitched. His breath hitched. She reached back, ready to wish him a good morning—

A knock sounded at the door.

Lexi sat straight, pulling the blanket to her shoulders. The heat within her died. She was in Anax's bed. If whoever was at the door came in—probably an attendant—rumors would spread through the palace before Lexi even decided what to do. She couldn't marry Prince Phintias anymore, no matter how much she didn't want to disappoint everyone.

Lexi nudged Anax's shoulder. His slitted blue eyes flashed open, alert instantly. She opened her mouth to whisper at him when the door slid open.

"Anax, you can't sleep all day..." A Herkleian female stopped dead in the doorway, her eyes locking with Lexi's. Turquoise hair wrapped around two black horns in an artful knot over a beautiful, sculpted face with deep purple slitted eyes and flush blue lips. Her six-feet of toned perfection wasn't dressed in a modern gown or the traditional toga-style garment, but in a green romper, the sides cut to reveal her fit, scaled stomach.

Anax sat up beside her, spine suddenly rigid.

"Hyra's Graces." The female shrunk back, her eyes flickering everywhere but the bed. "I'm... I'm just going to leave."

"Nicathra—" Anax started.

The female—Nicathra?—exited the suite at breakneck speed. Before Lexi could ask, Anax bolted out of bed and hastily threw on his clothes from last night. She'd never witnessed the calm prince so frazzled. Lexi's stomach swirled.

She climbed out of bed and grabbed her own dress. The warmth and elation she'd basked in five minutes ago disappeared, erased by the sight of a beautiful female who knew Anax well enough to charge into his bedchambers. "Who was that?"

Anax stiffened and didn't meet her eyes. "Nicathra."

"I gathered that." Her fingers trembled on the laces of her dress. The pit forming in her stomach grew heavier. He'd have an explanation. He would. She prayed for one. "Who is she? She just barged in like she owned the place."

He attached his sabre to his waistband. "She's a childhood friend."

He still wouldn't meet her eyes. Lexi charged around the bed and poked him in the chest. The same chest she had caressed not moments ago. This couldn't be happening. Not again. The last time she had felt like this, her ex, Josh, was a second away from telling her he'd gotten back with his ex-girlfriend, the real love of his life. "What are you not telling me?"

He gently grabbed her hand to stop her next poke and wrapped her small hands in his. His large, scaled, talented hands. "Promise me you'll give me the chance to explain."

She swallowed. "I can't promise that."

He met her eyes, clear and regretful. "Nicathra is my betrothed."

The words stabbed through her chest. Lexi stood there a moment, willing them to make sense. They didn't. And yet, they also did. All of Anax's siblings were engaged, Phintias the youngest and last of the brood. If Anax was the heir, the future king, of course he had a betrothed. Of course she was a beautiful Herkleian woman, probably from a noble family, ready to bear his children, the future heirs.

He had lied to her. He couldn't love a human. She wanted to mean more to him, but she was just another conquest.

Lexi pulled her hands from his and rushed out of the room. Her bare feet padded across the blue stone floors. She had left her shoes behind, but she didn't care.

Footsteps pounded behind her. "Lexi, please—"

She turned and slapped at his hands. "Leave me alone."

"Allow me to explain."

"I don't want to hear it, Anax." She stormed out of his suite and into the hallway. Three attendants cleaned and dusted, but Lexi didn't care if they heard. "Don't follow me!"

She wished she might slam the door in his face, but it was automatic. She turned on her heels and rushed across the hall to the garden. The quickest path to her rooms from his, through a beautiful collection of color and sound. The same gardens they had walked through days ago, Anax making her feel special. But she wasn't special. Queen Chryseis was right. Lexi wasn't anything but another fling for the Crown Prince. He had tricked her and ruined everything.

"Lexi!" Anax called from somewhere behind her. Lexi sped her pace. He hadn't caught her last time she had dashed from his chambers, the morning after the hanat flowers threat. This time, when he had actually committed a wrong, he stayed close behind. Lexi ignored him, her focus on moving her feet, one after another.

She pushed through the doorway to the hall outside her suite and sprinted across the small space. The door to her room didn't open fast enough. Lexi turned and slid through the crack of space. She waved her hand over the sensor, urging the doors closed. Anax appeared at the edge of the garden, the sunlight glittering across his scales—

The door to her room slammed shut in his face.

Lexi slumped to the floor, the energy that had propelled her through the garden dissipated.

Anax had a freaking fiancée.

Lexi was a fling.

She had slept with her betrothed's brother.

She had loved every second.

Lexi dropped her head to her hands and sobbed.

Anax knocked. "Please allow me to explain."

Lexi gave him no answer. She couldn't listen to another of his lies. She didn't have any willpower with him. How could she have been so stupid? The queen had warned her about Anax. That she was just his latest toy, his latest game. But Lexi had deeply wanted to believe there was something between them.

"You don't have to say anything," Anax continued. "Please listen. I never meant to lie to you about Nicathra. She *is* my betrothed, Lexi, but I feel no more drawn to her than you do Phintias."

Lexi had let her emotions get the better of her. Against her better judgement, he had drawn her to him like no male before. But she *should* have known better. Lexi couldn't face him again. How could she when the very thought of his face made her heart break all over again?

Lexi wouldn't put herself through that.

"I was wrong to keep it from you." His voice sounded desperate, not at all like the confident prince she knew. But he was lying. He had always lied. "Please open the door, Lexi. There's something else I have to tell you. Something important."

Lexi sat on the floor until the pounding on her door stopped. She almost waved her hand over the sensor to check the hall, but she resisted. Whatever Anax did now was his own business.

If only he had told her the truth. But the maybes and what-ifs didn't matter. He *had* lied. Lexi stood, dusted off her gown, and headed to her bathroom to clean herself up. She tip-toed past the door to Kynna's room. She didn't need to wake her attendant for this. Lexi had cleaned herself up after Josh broke her heart. This would be no different.

Crystalized rock threaded through the stone of the bathroom's surface, from the pink-purple of the sink to the deeper blue of the large, circular bathtub. Lexi tapped at her bracelet. The sink's faucet turned on, releasing a fresh stream of water. She adjusted the temperature with a flick of her fingers. Lexi scrubbed at the remnants of last night's makeup until her skin went red and raw. Kynna had used a miraculous cream last time to melt her makeup off her skin, but Lexi wouldn't ask.

Kynna wouldn't be her attendant for much longer.

Lexi combed through her hair, willing the repetitiveness of the action to calm her. She couldn't be the person Herkleios and Earth wanted her to be. Screw her uncle's money. Her mother would understand. There was no way she could marry a child, all the while watching the male who shattered her heart carry on as if nothing had happened between them. While their relationship meant little to Anax, Lexi knew it'd take an eternity for her own heart to heal.

She pulled her blond hair into a ponytail and unzipped her untouched suitcases. She threw on a pair of old jeans. Lexi would miss the beautiful dresses and dream gardens, but she couldn't stay for them. Working a second job to help her mom with the bills sounded better than spending one more day on this planet.

Dressed and cleaned, Lexi huffed out a long breath. Once she made this choice, there was no going back.

She tapped at her bracelet and sent a message to the king's steward.

A reply dinged back moments later.

King Xenobaccus was meeting with petitioners in his throne room. Lexi had never been to the room, but she pulled up the palace's map onto her holo-screen. There was no way to get there without passing Anax's room. She'd rather walk, but she couldn't run into Anax. With his persuasive tongue, he might convince her to stay. He could convince her of a thousand things with that tongue. Her body tingled, up and down where Anax had licked. She shuddered.

Lexi pinched at her own hand. Anax was the past. Nothing more than a one-night stand. She quickly sent her request to the nearest transporter station and tapped at the gemstone on her bracelet. It flickered to red. The transporters locked onto her signal.

Lexi took a deep, calming breath.

Time to break the news to the king.

Lexi tingled everywhere for an instant, the world going gray. In a blink, she appeared in a gilded antechamber, the walls to her left and right lined with petitioners sitting on floating chairs. Many of the Herkleians gaped at her. Most had probably never seen a human in a modern American outfit. She pulled at the hem of her long-sleeved, floral shirt and scanned for an empty seat.

Someone cleared their throat at her side. She turned to find the king's steward, the Herkleian female a mix between a librarian and Wonder Woman. She tapped at the holo-tablet in front of her, a stark contrast to her gilded pauldrons and sheathed sword. "Lady Alexandra?"

"Yes?"

"His Majesty, King Xenobaccus Yio'hyra, will speak with you now."

"Oh. Okay." Lexi cleared her throat. She could do this. "Let's go."

The steward ushered Lexi through two carved doors of solid gold. The throne room was a cavernous space, with a tiered, tiled ceiling over a wide expanse of floor. Everything was blue and gold—from embedded gemstones to paint to tiles. On the far side of the room, King Xenobaccus rested on a massive, gilded throne. Dragon-like spikes protruded from the edges of the throne, a harsh edge to the otherwise beautiful chair.

The king tapped at a holo-screen projected from his jeweled wristband. "Irys, I saw the Duchess of Agafyi's name on the list again. Tell her for the fourth time, I will not rescind her son's banishment—" King Xenobaccus halted, his grimace turning into a fanged grin. "Lady Alexandra, you're a sight for these sore eyes. I didn't expect to see you here today. How did you enjoy the queen's ball last night?"

Lexi dropped into a curtsy. "It was beautiful, Your Majesty. I'm sure Queen Chryseis loved it."

The king hmm-ed but didn't comment. "And how can I help you today?"

Lexi launched into her speech, afraid if she slowed down she'd chicken out. "I very much appreciate the kindness you've shown me, Your Majesty. But I don't think I can honor my engagement. I'm really not cut out for royal life. I'm just a regular girl. You could find someone else for Phintias, someone better suited to court. Your planet is so beautiful and your son so kind, but my place is on Earth."

King Xenobaccus raised a hand, his claws dotted with red-jeweled rings. "Slow down, my darling. You simply have to say you're not happy here. I'll organize a ship to return you home."

"Really?" She'd expected more resistance from the king. He was losing his son's fiancée and Earth expert, but he seemed very good-natured about it.

"Of course." The king stood from his throne and grabbed his

cane. He tottered to her side. "I can only imagine how homesick you must be. Phintias is still young with no rush to find a bride. And worry not about our alliance with Earth, it'll remain as strong as ever." He bared his fangs, a kindly smile. "It'll take a few hours to schedule the ship, but we *will* get you home as soon as we can, Lady Alexandra."

THIRTEEN

ANAX

Anax was a fucking idiot.

He slammed his fist through the trunk of a blue-barked pithi tree for the third time. When he removed his bleeding fist, the crackled bark smoothed and reformed, the nanites within the palace keeping everything clean and whole. The blue stain of his blood disappeared, like nothing had ever happened. He punched his other fist through the same spot.

If only he had told Lexi about Nicathra. Their relationship was no more real than hers with Phintias. He had known Nicathra since childhood, their betrothal announced when they were fifteen. Her father was Lord Solon, one of his father's closest advisors and an influential politician. Their marriage would unite the two houses, but he and Nicathra had never been more than friends. A younger Anax had tried kissing her when they were kids. He had thought himself irresistible. Everyone wanted to be with a prince, right? But she had kicked him in the shin in return and told him to never touch her again. He had respected that boundary ever since.

There was no romance between them, but he hadn't told Lexi. He had carried her back to his rooms last night and stripped her bare and fucked her out of her mind, all while hiding the truth from her.

Anax deserved this.

Deserved to be miserable, deserved to be alone. His own brother, his closest friend in the entire universe, had abandoned him without even a message. Lexi had every right to do the same, disappearing without a trace.

But he couldn't lose her.

She was his mate. He knew it. No female had ever made him feel this way, like his heart might fracture if he didn't get Lexi back. A mark hadn't appeared on the back of her neck, but he'd checked his own to find a faint outline of circles in shaped like a star. The beginning of a matebond mark. He needed to stop her. He couldn't lose her.

He tore out of the gardens, his pants and shoulder sash ruffled and speckled with shards of pithi bark. The staff might stare and snicker, but he didn't care. No one mattered but Lexi. He hadn't gone far from her suite after pounding on her door. He knew she needed space, but he needed to explain. It had been long enough. He marched in that direction. Nothing would get between a Herkleian male and his intended mate.

"She's not there," a familiar female voice said. "I knocked and spoke with her attendant. She's talking to your father."

Anax stiffened. Nicathra slithered out from the shadows of an archway, thumbing the heavy gold pendant of her necklace. Like Anax, both of them had lost their mother at a young age. While his father had ordered all portraits of Queen Avra removed upon his marriage to Queen Chryseis, Nicathra always had a reminder of her mother around her neck.

He wanted to be angry at her, but their years of friendship turned his anger into a slight bubble of annoyance. "Have you ever heard of knocking?"

"Well, hello to you, too," she muttered. "Yes, Anax, my trip was very enjoyable. Thank you for asking."

"Why are you even back?" Nicathra had spent the last few months at her family's home in the south. She was to return later this week, not today. If only she had stayed on schedule. He could have explained the situation to Lexi properly.

She shrugged. "Got bored."

He crossed his arms, but Nicathra only copied him with a baring of her own fangs. She had always loved to tease him. Nicathra might be his betrothed, but he had always treated her more like a sister. In a way, she was more his sister than any of his flesh-and-blood siblings, who had been raised by an army of attendants while Anax spent time with Eryx and their tutors. The heir and the spare.

"Want to tell me who was in your bed?"

"Her name is Lexi," he grumbled.

She frowned. "And by Lexi, do you mean Alexandra Seymour?"

"Lexi is a nickname." When Nicathra's face remained blank, he elaborated. "Earthlings sometimes call each other by shortened versions of their name."

"Intriguing," she said, though Anax knew she wasn't referring to the concept of nicknames. "When I was talking to Nefeli on my trip back, she told me you spent Chryseis's ball dancing with some Earthling. I almost didn't believe it." Nicathra let out a short howl. "She's your brother's betrothed, Anax."

Anax knew that. But being with Lexi had never filled him with guilt, for either Phintias or Nicathra. Lexi would be his. Fate had tied them together, a match ordained by the goddess Hyra. He had a growing matebond mark. She would have one, too, with time. If they had time.

But no matter what, Lexi didn't deserve the disrespect. His fist clenched. "Lexi isn't just some Earthling."

Nicathra propped her shoulder against the wall and smirked at his tone. "Could it possibly be that our playboy prince is finally in love?"

Anax released his fist. He wasn't angry at Nicathra. He was to blame for all of this. He wiped a hand across his face. "It doesn't matter anymore. I fucked it all up."

Her smirk grew. "Never told her you were engaged?"

"I kept waiting for the perfect time to tell her, but..." Lexi wasn't a fling. He had fallen for her, the matebond between them growing strong. He hadn't wanted to ruin their love story.

"Then what?"

Nicathra deserved to know. No Herkleian had reported a matebond in over a century. For him to receive one with a human was unprecedented. He didn't know what it meant for their society, their alliance with Earth, but for him, it meant he couldn't ever let her go. Not for Phintias or Nicathra. They had only ever been friends, but since Eryx left, Nicathra had trained to be the next Queen of Herkleios. She wouldn't mind losing the crown, but she would have been perfect in the role, a loving queen to her people.

He motioned her closer. When she approached, he turned and pulled the sash at his neck, exposing the matebond mark.

Her jaw dropped. "Is that..."

"A matebond mark, yes."

She reached out for the wall to steady herself. "No one has actually seen a matebond mark in a hundred years, Anax."

"I know."

"Do you know what this means?" she almost shouted it but quieted her voice when a passing guard glanced their way. "We thought Hyra abandoned the mark after Hadus betrayed her. But if you're receiving one, what the temple hypothesized isn't true."

Anax respected the goddess Hyra, but he wasn't as devout as Nicathra or her family. "I can't know the goddess's intentions. All I know is I have the mark."

"Does Lexi?" Nicathra asked.

He paused. She didn't. Her neck was slightly red, but that could be from anything. Were humans capable of receiving the mark? Or would he always have a half-formed matebond, never solidified? "Not yet."

"She is an Earthing. Maybe they can't get one." Nicathra stood straighter, something coming over her face. "I researched matebonds during one of my classes at Eritea University. There were a few recorded cases where only one partner had a visible mark immediately. However, if the second person's mark didn't form within the following week, the matebond would fade on the first. Hyra guides us to our soulmates, but it's our job to accept them."

His heart thudded. "Hers might still appear?"

"It might."

Anax wanted Lexi as a mate, but what would that mean for his family? He was the heir. His children would inherit his throne. Scandal had ensured when his father had married his mother to seal the Intergalactic Alliance. Herkleios had a century-long relationship with a neighboring planet, Eógan, and his mother had been born there, daughter to a half-Eógan noble and a Herkleian ambassador. Queen Avra had been three-quarters Herkleian, but some of the court hadn't thought it enough.

Nicathra touched his shoulder. "If Hyra wills it so, Anax, politics don't matter."

"It would be a disaster." And a miracle. A blessing. The answer to his prayers.

Nicathra shrugged. "It would annoy Chryseis that you stole her son's betrothed, but when is she not angry?"

He almost bared his fangs at the thought of his stepmother's anger. "Her face would be priceless."

"So what are you waiting for?"

"Lexi just wants nothing to do with me."

Nicathra linked her arm through his. Anax had a foot on her height, but he let the female steer him down the hall, towards Lexi's door. "Well, you did fuck her over."

Anax huffed out a grumbly sigh. "If I could redo everything I would."

"Then that's what you say to her," Nicathra said. "Tell her the whole uncomplicated truth, no excuses. She's probably back in her room by now. Your father wouldn't have wanted to talk to her for long."

Lexi's door came into view. Anax's heart fluttered like a virgin's. He straightened, puffing out his chest. He was a Herkleian male. He had served in the military and perfected the use of the sabre. He could face a tiny, enraged female, even if she was his mate. "You're a good friend, Nicathra."

"Oh, I know I am." She patted him on the shoulder, winked, and took off down the hall.

***

ANAX STOOD outside Lexi's door for ten minutes before she turned the corner into the guest suite hallway. She stiffened at the sight of him. His cock twitched. If he had had his way, he'd still be in his bed, worshipping her the way she deserved. Anax would give up the throne, give up everything for her to stay. For her to be his.

Lexi reached for her bracelet, probably to call for transport into her suite. Anax charged down the hall. She didn't flinch at the seven-foot-tall, horned Herkleian male running her way. A cluster of attendants dropped what they were doing and disappeared through whatever means necessary. Hyra's Graces. At least no one would overhear their conversation.

"Lexi—"

She crossed her arms, her green eyes hard. "I don't want to talk, Anax."

He dropped to one knee in front of her. Her entire body stiffened, something like panic entering her gaze, but she quickly hid it behind her anger. "Please, let me explain."

"There's nothing to explain. I'm leaving."

The word stabbed through his heart. Leaving. If Lexi left Herkleios, Anax might never see her again. He couldn't travel to Earth to find her. He was the heir to an entire planet. "Leaving?"

"I told your father I'm calling off the engagement." She poked at her bracelet and the time flashed across the holo-screen. "I'm getting on a ship in half an hour."

Then this was Anax's last chance to convince her. He would convince her. He had to. Lexi was his mate. He wouldn't live without her. "Lexi, Nicathra is a friend. Nothing more."

She snorted. "It doesn't matter, Anax. You lied to me. And at the end of the day, she's still your fiancée. You're going to marry her. You have to. You're the Crown Prince."

She tried to push past him, but he reached for her hands. Her soft hands, which had trailed his body and wrapped around his horns. His cock hardened, but he ignored it. All that mattered was her. "I won't. I don't care what my father or the people think, Lexi. I love you."

She pulled her hands out of his grasp. "You what?"

Anax pushed to his feet. He spread out his arms for the entire palace to hear. "I love you, Alexandra."

It was true. Anax hadn't known until he said the words. He loved her. He had never loved before. Females had come and gone. He had cared for a few of them, but not like this. If he couldn't be with Lexi, what was the point of living? He needed her like he needed air. She was his naika, the Herkleian term for a female mate. His naika. His female. His Lexi.

"It doesn't matter. It's too late." She swallowed, trying to regain her composure. "I won't home-wreck the freaking Herkleian royal family."

Anax wouldn't stop. "Lexi—"

"Please." She walked past him, avoiding his arms and his gaze. "Let me go, Anax. Please."

The despair and pain in her voice ripped through him. He had caused this. He had hurt her. He opened his mouth to plead, but she shook her head and ran for her room. The suite door closed firmly behind her. He could tear that door down. No one would stand in his way. But Lexi's words sparked something in him. She had said his love didn't matter. That didn't mean she didn't love him back.

She did. He knew. And if Lexi was no longer engaged to Phintias, that meant Anax could propose to her. If she were to be his wife, she wouldn't be home-wrecking the royal family, whatever that meant. If Anax made it official, Lexi would have to stay.

And if his father didn't agree, Anax would abdicate the throne just like Eryx had.

LEXI

Lexi sat fuming on the edge of her bed. How dare Anax try to change her mind? He had lied to her about Nicathra. She couldn't trust him. She wanted to trust him. He'd said he loved her. Lexi had heard the words before, said the words before, but she had never felt them in the core of her being. With Anax, with those three little words, the whole universe had righted for a second.

But Lexi couldn't stay. She couldn't marry Phintias. She couldn't watch Anax marry Nicathra. And a part of her remained distrustful of everything, including his proclamation. After Josh had left her for his ex, a part of her had wanted him back. She wanted Anax more than she had ever wanted Josh, but she couldn't have him. Lexi shouldn't have ignored the signs.

She itched at her neck. The sooner she got off the planet, the better.

Her bracelet buzzed. Lexi tapped the jewel on the surface. The holo-screen flashed, projecting a message from Commander Ezio Yio'aleta. The ship taking her back to Earth was ready for her. Lexi stood and pulled at the edge of her cardigan. She had no need for

Herkleian dresses anymore, leaving them all behind for the leggings and sweaters she had brought from Earth. The few other possessions she had brought all fit within a single suitcase.

Lexi pulled at the suitcase's handle and rolled it through the suite. Kynna waited by the outer door. Lexi took her attendant's clawed hands and gazed into her yellow slitted eyes. "Thank you, Kynna. For everything. I know Herkleians don't hug, but can I give you one to say goodbye?"

She opened her arms. Kynna's eyes widened, but she nodded. Lexi pulled the tall female into her grasp. Kynna stiffened, but after a moment, her clawed hands settled onto Lexi's back. Tear prickled at Lexi's eyes. Though they had only known each other for a week, losing Kynna was like losing a friend. If Lexi could stay, that's what they would've become.

Lexi gently pulled back from Kynna and unclipped her bracelet. "Goodbye, Kynna."

Kynna took the slim gold band and dropped into a final bow. "Good luck, Lexi. May Hyra bless your journey home."

Lexi shot her a small smile before pushing into the corridor. She locked her gaze on the ground but kept her pace quick. Around her, attendants and guards gossiped and whispered. Surely Kynna's reassignment and Anax's shouting at her door had already sparked rumors. Now she was back in her Earthling clothes, running down the hallway with a suitcase.

Running not only from their whispers and stares, but from Anax. If Anax came back once more, Lexi's resolve would crumble. She would stay, even if it was to be his mistress. She wanted him that much. That wouldn't go away for weeks. Maybe never.

But no one halted her path.

An attendant waited outside the transport room and led her inside. When she had arrived, the royal ship had landed in the gardens, but her departure ship was in the atmosphere and required special long-distance transportation. She stopped in a tiled circle in the center of the room. The attendant tapped his armband without looking or saying anything. There was no need to be polite anymore. She wasn't a future princess, but a simple traveler from the least-advanced planet in the Intergalactic Alliance. He hit a button on the wall, lowering the forcefield in the room and allowing the ship to lock on to her location. A tingle shivered up her spine.

The world flashed in an explosion of color.

When Lexi blinked, she wasn't in a bare room in the palace, but in the bustling bridge of a spaceship. Drones stationed at the various control panels around the circular room didn't react to her appearance, their focus on their duties. Her gaze drifted from them to the large windows on the curved ceiling. At her back, Herkleios glowed, a beauty of green and purple and blue. She ignored it for the darkness of space stretching across the front of the ship. She stepped forward, mesmerized.

"Alexandra Seymour?" A bald Herkleian male with yellow slitted eyes and three-inch horns rose from the captain's chair in the center of the bridge. "I am Commander Ezio Yio'aleta."

She tore her gaze from outer space. Once she returned to Earth, she might never see the stars up close again. It'd take years for the development of space travel infrastructure that a regular citizen could afford. Uncle Grayson certainly wouldn't pay for her, not after she ruined his agreement with King Xenobaccus. "Nice to meet you."

He snapped his claws and two males entered the bridge, wearing the same black pants all the military wore. Like the Herkleians on the surface, only the females wore shirts, the males' chests bare but for the crossing of straps holding their shoulder pauldrons. These males had an extra strap at their arm for a knife and one mid-thigh for a laser gun.

"The sergeants will direct you to your quarters."

Lexi nodded and followed the two males from the bridge. King Xenobaccus had said the *Acacia II* was a quarter of the size of *The Queen Niobe*, but that her chambers would be just as extravagant.

Lexi didn't care if they shoved her in a bedroom no larger than a closet. As long as the ship took her home.

The two males led her through the sleek, white halls until they arrived at a door flanked by two planters. The purple-pink flowers glowed dimly in the bright hall. Lexi ran her fingers along the petals. A little piece of Herkleios to accompany her on her journey home.

"Ma'am?" The red-haired sergeant asked, his horns short nubs. He gestured towards the door.

Lexi swallowed. Once she entered her room, her decision was made. Wasn't it already? But Lexi didn't take the last steps forward. Anax had said he loved her. They hadn't known each other longer than a week, but in Lexi's heart, she felt the same. She loved him. Could she leave him? If she had to. She could survive without him, but it'd be a half-life, devoid of color and pleasure. But with Anax, everything was right.

How could Lexi sacrifice that?

Lexi couldn't marry Phintias, but she couldn't leave Anax, either.

If she left now without at least saying goodbye, she'd regret it until she died.

"Um." Lexi cleared her throat. "Can I use one of your communication devices? I need to send a message to Prince Anax."

The guards glanced at each other, expressions unreadable. "You can do so in your room, ma'am. We'll be leaving the atmosphere shortly. Our comms are short range only."

Leaving the atmosphere? Lexi gripped the male's scaled arm. "I need to message Anax now."

"Enough of this," the green-haired guard muttered.

Before Lexi could ask, he grabbed her arm and dragged her through the door. It slid open. The space before her wasn't a suite. It wasn't even a bedroom. The bare walls and floor were utilitarian and white. A cot floated in the corner, nothing more than a slab of hard gold. A small screen on the opposite wall had two buttons: one for a toilet and another for a cleaning pod, the high-tech version of a shower.

This was a jail cell.

Lexi spun. An electric spark flared into the space between her and the guards. Her arm slammed against a forcefield. This wasn't right. Lexi was a guest of the Crown. The queen, the king—everyone had been kind. Why was this happening now? She pounded a fist against the field. "What are you doing? I demand to speak with Anax now!"

"Anax is unavailable," the red-haired male said.

Lexi gritted her teeth. "Then get me King Xenobaccus."

The green-haired guard howled and bared his fangs cruelly. "As you wish, Earthling."

He pulled something from his pocket and tossed it through the forcefield. Lexi ducked. A thin disk-like device clattered to the floor. Lexi reached down and poked its glowing button. She had seen nothing like it during her stay on Herkleios.

Light flared from the center of the disk. Lexi stumbled back. When her sight cleared, a holographic version of King Xenobaccus floated above the disk, projected into the air. The king tapped his claws against the red jewel of his cane. His friendly baring of fangs she had grown accustomed to had disappeared, replaced with a cold-eyed grimace.

"Alexandra." He shook his head and huffed out a growling sigh. "Look at the mess you've gotten yourself into."

Lexi's skin broke out in goosebumps. "What is happening?"

King Xenobaccus carried on as if he hadn't heard her. "This was never the plan. You have to understand, I wanted you to be happy. With Phintias. But I can't have you leading my heir astray. All you had to do was keep Anax at an arm's distance and enjoy the beautiful life we provided you."

King Xenobaccus knew. Of course he knew. Everyone in the palace must have known about her and Anax after their public conversations this morning. But that didn't explain why he had imprisoned her. "What are you talking about?"

"I warned you." The king shrugged, as if defeated. He dropped into a seat. Not the throne Lexi had seen earlier, but a simpler chair. Lexi couldn't see anything else of his room. "You ignored it. You continued to seduce my son."

He had warned her? Lexi's forehead creased. A warning... the hanat flowers? Anax had told her the Royal Guard was having the incident investigated. The king himself had told her finding those responsible was of the utmost importance. But if the king was responsible, then it was all a lie. "You sent the hanat flowers?"

The king slammed his cane into the floor, making Lexi flinch. "You don't deny seducing my son?"

There was no point denying it. She swallowed. Lexi wanted Anax with all her being, but she needed to say what the king wanted to hear. Maybe then he'd let her go. Then what? Would Anax believe her if she told him his father had sent the threat on her life? "Nothing will happen between Anax and I ever again. It's over."

"You say that, but my soldiers tell me you requested to speak with him. I can't allow that. Anax is the Crown Prince. After what happened with Eryx, I can't lose another heir. He needs a wife from a strong Herkleian upbringing and family that can enhance the Crown's treasury. He needs to marry Nicathra."

Lexi tried to repress her flinch, but the king saw it. The doddering old man was little more than a guise. His slitted purple eyes were sharp and devious. She crossed her arms to hold herself together. "Then send me back to Earth. You'll never hear from me again."

"I can't do that, I'm afraid." The king bared his fangs in mock sympathy. "Negotiating with Earth for a new bride for Phintias would take months. Months I don't have. I need an Earthling bride now."

Lexi shivered at the glint in his eyes. "Why?"

"You'll know when you're needed, my dear. Until then, I'll be keeping you tucked away on Gamta Base on Kore." He tapped at the gold of his wristband. A grumbling echoed through the ship, like the engines flaring to life. "My soldiers will teach you obedience. I can't have you messing this up again."

"Messing what up?" Lexi asked... no one. The light on the disk died, King Xenobaccus's image fading with it. Behind her, the sliding doors slammed shut. She stared around her cell—a freaking jail cell—as confused as before. What was King Xenobaccus planning? Whatever it was, it wouldn't be good. Not for Lexi. Not for Earth. Maybe not even for Anax.

FIFTEEN

Anax slammed into his father's study. "Father, we need to speak."

The high, vaulted ceiling echoed his words to a shout. His father glanced up from where he sat in the corner on a plush, levitating chair. Ancient tombs and bound books lined the wall opposite the door, centuries of Herkleian history and stories from before holo-books. King Xenobaccus placed a circular comms device on the table at his side, the light from the tall garden windows brightening the jewels on his claws to a shine. "Yes, Anax?"

He refused to shrink under her father's intense gaze. In his childhood, his father's tone alone would have had him running from the room. Anax stood taller, the pose of a king. "It's about Lexi—Alexandra Seymour."

His father picked up a red-covered book. "She's already left, Anax."

"You could summon her ship back."

With his father gazed at him again, the look was shrewd—something Anax had never witnessed directed at a family member. "And why would I summon the Earthling back?"

"She isn't a regular Earthling." Anax marched forward, ready to drop to his knees and show his father his neck. Ready to call off his engagement to Nicathra and demand Lexi's hand. The mark burned, fire flooding through his blood the further Lexi got. He was the first Herkleian to exhibit a matebond in a century. That had to mean something to his father. Hyra herself had blessed his relationship with Lexi. Maybe if Anax showed his father the mark, he'd listen to him.

His father slammed the book onto the table and stood. Anax towered over his father's shrinking frame. King Xenobaccus was still a warrior, the King of Herkleios and leader of the Intergalactic Alliance, but he wasn't young anymore. Anax's youth didn't intimidate him as he propped his cane in front of him. "You're right. She isn't some Earthling. She's your brother's betrothed. I know all about your dalliance, Anax."

Anax didn't flinch. The entire palace likely knew after this morning. "Father—"

"I've been patient, hoping you would lose interest. Earthlings are curious creatures, but enough is enough, Anax. You'll be the King of Herkleios when I return to Hyra's fields. To claim this kingdom, you'll need a Herkleian bride. You'll need Nicathra. That is the purpose of your marriage, just like your siblings' marriages uphold the Intergalactic Alliance."

If their people knew he and Lexi had bonded, they wouldn't care that she was human. She'd unite all of Herkleios. "Father—"

His father's gaze slid over his shoulder. Anax turned. A Herkleian with turquoise hair streaked gold with age, towering brownish horns, and red slitted eyes entered the room, his cape brushing the floor behind him. Nicathra's father, Lord Solon. Anax clenched his fists. He needed his father to listen, but Lord Solon wouldn't be happy when he learned Nicathra would no longer be queen.

King Xenobaccus tapped his cane against the floor. "We will continue this discussion later, son. I must speak with Lord Solon."

The burning at his neck intensified. The longer he waited, the longer it'd take for Lexi to return. But he couldn't bully his father into ordering Lexi's ship back to Herkleios. He needed to convince him with logic and words. Anax dropped into a shallow, stiff bow and retreated from the room.

Two of his father's attendants stood in the hall. Anax nodded to them as he passed—

A putrid stench filled his nose. He halted beside the attendant to his left. He didn't turn his head, but the scent was clear, if faint. His father's attendant had handled hanat flowers recently. The smell haunted a person for days, even if they wore protective equipment.

"Your Highness?" the attendant asked.

Anax didn't respond, but he walked towards the outer door like he hadn't noticed. Had his father ordered the vandalism of Lexi's suite? Because he knew how much time Anax was spending with Lexi? That seemed extreme, even for his father. But his attendants had direct access to the royal apartments and the guest suites. It would have been a simple task.

A stinging burned through the back of his neck, almost like Hyra herself had a message for him. He couldn't trust Lexi in the king's hands.

Anax took an abrupt left down a quiet hallway. When he and Eryx were young, they had explored every nook within the palace—including the secret passages in their father's quarters. Originally designed for attendants to move through the palace without being seen, kings and queens of the past had used them to listen in on their guests.

Anax twisted a tile halfway down the hall and slipped inside without anyone noticing. The passageways were pitch dark and made of plain stone, tall but narrow. His horns didn't scratch against the ceiling, but he had to tilt his shoulders to fit within the space. He shuffled quietly until he came to the right peephole.

"....Nicathra helped get rid of that Earthling as you expected, Your Majesty," Lord Solon said, standing in the same spot Anax had moments ago.

His father faced the window, his back to Anax and the rest of the room. His jeweled cane lay propped against his chair, out of reach. "It wouldn't have been possible without your help, Solon."

"No need to thank me, Your Majesty. As I've said from day one, it's my pleasure to help you expand Herkleian rule throughout the galaxy. With my family's financial backing, those primitive worlds won't know what hit them."

Rule? Anax stiffened. What was his father talking about? The Intergalactic Alliance's purpose was to share technology and resources, strengthening all the planets. It was the whole reason Anax stood here today. Without the alliance, his parents' marriage never would have happened.

His father approached a small table holding a decanter with sparkling bymo. He poured himself and Lord Solon a glass. "Exactly. And my newest acquisition, Earth, won't put up much of a struggle. They're savages in comparison."

"To our victory." Argyris raised his glass before taking a long swig of the bymo. "To your two decades of hard work. I wasn't sure initially if your long game would succeed, but you had the vision to bring it altogether, Your Majesty."

The king settled into his chair. "Since holding each of my children at their births, I knew I wanted to give them every advantage in the world. I was a second son. If I hadn't eliminated my brother, I'd be stuck as a prince with no country or purpose. My children will not suffer that fate."

"I simply would have divided our current territories amongst them, but your plan strengthens our planet."

"It wasn't easy to find twelve planets with suitable environments and peoples." His father tapped at his gold wristband, projecting a holographic map. Anax shuffled, but he couldn't get an unobstructed view. "Now that Phintias is tied to that Earthling, we're ready to move into the next phase of my plan."

"Your Majesty?" Nervousness crept into Lord Solon's voice. "Perhaps we should marry the Earthling to Prince Phintias now? To both strengthen our claim on Earth and remove all thoughts of the female from Anax's mind. Phintias is young, but the sooner he's bedded and impregnated the Earthling, the sooner Anax will get over her."

A heavy silence fell over the room. Anax couldn't see Lord Solon, but his father glared, his slitted purple eyes hard and cold.

"My apologies, Your Majesty, I didn't mean to offend—"

"The Earthling is no longer a problem," King Xenobaccus snapped. "Her ship is headed for Kore. She'll remain there until it's time for Phintias to marry her, perhaps after we conquer the last of our targets. A royal wedding will surely distract everyone."

Anax clenched his fists. He wanted to slam through the wall and impale his horns into his father's chest. How could the male who had been kind and generous to him his whole life be capable of such deception? And Lexi was caught in his father's plan. Neither of the three bases on Kore were fit for a gentle human. He ached at the thought of her in pain or fear.

"Of course, Your Majesty." Lord Solon was probably bobbing his head to appease his father. "We don't want another repeat of what happened with Eryx."

Anax stiffened. No. The rage in him spiked. What had they done with Eryx? His favorite brother, heir to the throne, had disappeared overnight. Anax had read the letter. He had believed his father's version of events. Was that a lie, too?

"I had such high hopes for Eryx. I thought he'd understand the merits of our military efforts." The king sighed. "Nonetheless, he knows if he reveals my plan, mercenaries would only be a few hours behind him."

Anax stumbled away. He needed to get off the planet. There wasn't anything he could do for Eryx. His brother was alive, at least. But who knew what terrors Lexi suffered? She might hate him for all of eternity, but he couldn't abandon her to Kore. Not his Lexi. He'd worry about his father's plans for universal domination later.

Anax had a mate to save.

SIXTEEN

The gentle rumble of the ship's engine died, ripping Lexi from her despair. She had spent the remaining hours of her short trip between Herkleios and Kore huddled in a corner with her knees pressed against her chest to stay warm. Anax hadn't been kidding when he said Herkleians didn't feel cold the way she did. Her breath literally frosted the air with every exhale.

The door clanked open and Commander Ezio strolled in, accompanied by the two sergeants. "Time to move."

Lexi pushed to her feet, but left her arms crossed. She didn't want them to think her afraid. "To where?"

Commander Ezio didn't answer. He marched forward into her space. Lexi couldn't hold back her flinch. He grabbed for her arms. She pulled from his grasp and tried to kick his shin.

The captain howled, a crude laugh. "Earthling females all have fire in their veins!"

"Fuck—"

He smacked her. The world went dark as pain radiated through her cheek. Lexi slumped to the floor, through the floor, melting into a puddle of fog. No one had ever hit her before.

Lexi pushed through the daze. Whatever the pain, she needed to know what was happening. She blinked, the ship coming back into focus. The sergeants had bound her hands and feet together with a glowing blue band that lifted her off the floor and levitated her behind Commander Ezio. Hogtied like a freaking pig. She tried to shout, but pain ripped through her jaw. Bastards.

Lexi slumped—as much as one could when held by levitating restraints. At the least, she could look, remember, learn. Anything might come in handy to help her escape. The glowing white corridors of the ship had disappeared, replaced by lifeless concrete slabs, painted with codes in Herkleian. The words didn't translate immediately. She squinted. The squiggles became coherent words. *Fleet hangar*.

Fleet hangar? Assuming their ship had landed in the main hangar, what was the fleet hangar? She got her answer a second later. Commander Ezio led them across a walkway with floor-to-ceiling windows. Tiny, circular ships filled the large room beneath her. Fighter jets. Herkleios had cut down on its military in recent years after signing a new treaty with the Intergalactic Alliance. She had known that from the reading she had done on her trip from Earth. Lexi couldn't imagine Kynna lying about that. Did no one know? Maybe King Xenobaccus had never reduced his fleet and simply stashed them elsewhere. Unlike the other moon, Selene, Kore was barren and uninhabitable. No one came here unless to visit one of the military bases.

She counted the rows of ships. Hundreds of them, on either side of her. King Xenobaccus had to have nearly a thousand ships in this single base. How many more did he have on the other bases nearby? Was he preparing for a war? He had to be. There was no other reason to have a shipyard this vast.

Lexi tried to get another peek, but they exited the walkway and turned down another boring corridor. Commander Ezio halted before a metal door. Her restraints jolted, digging into her wrist and ankles. Another two bruises, to match the mark on her face.

"Lower her," he snapped.

Her leg restraints buzzed and dropped her feet to the floor. The jolt ricocheted through her spine. Ezio waved his hand before a sensor by the door. Probably controlled through scanning his DNA like the doors in the palace. It slid open, revealing a small jail cell with a slab of a mattress tucked against one corner and an open toilet in the other. Ezio flicked his nails together, the sound a sharp zing instead of a snap.

Her restraints rocketed her forward and deposited her mid-room.

Commander Ezio bowed mockingly. "Enjoy your new home, my lady."

The restraints clicked and unattached themselves from her. They zipped across the room and into Commander Ezio's hand. She pushed forward, but her legs went weak. Lexi crumbled to the floor. Commander Ezio released that terrible howl-laugh again as the cell door slammed shut. His howling echoed down the hall as he stomped away, leaving Lexi with nothing but unending silence.

HOURS PASSED within the tiny cell. Lexi had examined every inch of the space, but she hadn't found a way out. Beside the toilet and a hard mattress, the only other thing of interest was an airplane-sized window. Not that it offered much of a view. Like Earth's moon, Kore was bland and gray, a cratered wasteland. From this angle, she didn't see any other bases or ships. If King Xenobaccus had an attack planned, there would surely be more shipyards nearby. But who did he plan to attack? All the planets with advanced lifeforms belonged to the Intergalactic Alliance.

Her stomach hollowed.

If the only planets to attack were Alliance members, then that was who the Herkleians planned to attack. Earth might be at risk. Her mom, her best friend, everyone she had ever known until a week ago lived on Earth. Even her bastard of an uncle. She didn't want to see any of them hurt.

Lexi had to get out. She might survive being trapped until the king decided it was time for her to marry Phintias. But she could never live with herself if she let King Xenobaccus destroy Earth.

But how was she supposed to escape? She was a human prisoner on a Herkleian moon base. She didn't know the first thing about their tech. She couldn't fight their soldiers. But she had witnessed no living beings beside the captain and the two sergeants. The only moving shapes in the ship and fleet hangar had been droids. Assuming she could get out, she'd only have Commander Ezio and his crew to avoid.

Three Herkleians too many.

Lexi's pulse kicked into overtime. She was doomed. Absolutely screwed. She'd never get out. Never see her mother. Never see Olivia. Never see the sun or a single flower ever again.

Never see Anax.

Lexi let out a sob. If only she had never left Anax. If she had listened to him, listened to her heart, she'd be warm on Herkleios, with strong, blue-scaled arms around her. Instead, she was here, freezing her ass off on a moon.

She took a deep breath. She couldn't change the past, only her future. Lexi was going to get out of here. She just had to clear her head. She didn't have any chance of overpowering the Herkleians, but maybe she could get around them somehow. If it was at all like a moon base in a sci-fi show, there'd be a command center with some way of contacting others. She might not get off this moon, but she only needed to send a message. While Uncle Grayson didn't care for her much as a person, if his satellites picked up her message, she knew his ego would never stand being tricked, used, and threatened.

Once the other Alliance planets knew, they'd stop King Xenobaccus. And once they stopped him, they would free Lexi.

The door buzzed open.

Lexi bounced to her feet. The green-haired sergeant stomped

into the cell holding a plate of purple goop. Lexi's stomach swirled at the sight and scent. She slapped a hand across her nose and mouth to stop herself from gagging.

Commander Ezio leaned in the doorway, on the other side of the forcefield. "Enjoy your meal, princess."

There was no way Commander Ezio was letting her out of this cell willingly. Lexi needed a reason for him to bring her into the hall. She didn't know what she'd do then, but even if she could outrun the Herkleians for a minute, it might be enough to plant the seeds of her escape.

She hadn't seen a fourth Herkleian, but they had to have a doctor, right? If Lexi pretended to need medical attention, they'd have to take her from the cell. This plan hinged on her captors caring about her condition. She wasn't sure they would, but Xenobaccus had said she had a role to play in his plans.

Lexi clutched her side and let out a tiny squeal of pain.

The Herkleian approaching with her tray jerked, nearly dropping all her food. He looked completely baffled. He must have never heard a human scream before. He backed away. "What is she doing?"

Commander Ezio had straightened, his bared fangs replaced by narrowed eyes. "What's wrong with you, human?"

"I think..." Lexi paused for dramatic effect. "I think I must have broken something when you dropped me on the floor."

Commander Ezio narrowed slitted yellow eyes. "Is that so?"

Lexi wasn't selling it. She dropped onto her levitating cot, like she could no longer stand. "Do you have a doctor?"

Commander Ezio didn't reply.

"You heard what King Xenobaccus said. He has plans for me. I don't think he'll like it if you let me die."

"Leave her plate, Paxos," Ezio snapped after a long-second. "We have many things to do today."

The soldier, Paxos, gave Lexi an uneasy stare, but lowered her tray to the ground. He backed out of the room.

Lexi jumped forward, barely remembering to clutch at her side. "I need a doctor. You can't just leave me in here to die."

"We don't have a doctor," Commander Ezio said. "They're untrustworthy, little bastards. Just like human females."

Commander Ezio lowered the forcefield to allow Paxos to exit. Lexi needed to stall. There had to be something she could say to get out of here. "What about a blanket? It's freezing in here."

Commander Ezio snarled in humor. "Maybe if you're a good, quiet human, we'll consider your request."

"Commander—"

"Until tomorrow, little human."

And with that, Commander Ezio waved a hand in front of the door. It slammed shut in her face. Lexi dropped to her cot. Tears pricked at her eyes. At this rate, it'd take years to get to the control room and send a message.

Lexi dropped her head to her hands and sobbed.

SEVENTEEN

ANAX

Anax approached the royal airstrip with a false ease to his step. It wasn't uncommon for him to take a glider out for a drive alone, leaving the guards who followed him whenever he left the palace on land to watch. He had learned all the tricks of spaceflight during his years with the military. None of the attendants or mechanics gave him so much as a second glance.

He opted for the favorite of his three gliders, a sleep arrow-shaped ship with two seats. It would get him to Kore the fastest and wouldn't be detected by their radars. He tapped the back of the ship and the mechanic trailing behind him rushed forward to re-fuel and complete a quick maintenance check.

"We'll monitor you from the ground, Your Highness," Dexus said from his left.

Anax nodded and crossed his arm to hide the clenching of his fists. His claws dug painfully into his palms. If his friend suspected what Anax had planned, he'd never get off the surface. Even once he was in his ship, he didn't have long to get to the base before someone reported him to his father. Anax's blood raced at the thought of the male. His father, planning to betray and dominate the Intergalactic Alliance. Anax wanted to deny it, but he had heard the truth with his own ears. And Lexi—*his* Lexi—paid the ultimate price for the king's deception.

"Ready for takeoff, Your Highness," the mechanic said, rubbing a towel against his greasy hands.

"Many thanks." Anax slapped Dexus on the back like he always did before a flight. "I'll be back shortly."

"Yes, Your Highness."

The glider lowered at his approach and the glass top slid open. Anax climbed in with a smooth step. He tapped a button on the screen, which lowered the top and sparked the engine in the same second. He placed his sabre in the space beside him but kept his laser at his waist. He didn't know how many guards he'd face on Kore. The moon had three bases, but his father had said Lexi was at the smallest and least-populated, Gamta Base. Since it was used mainly as a back-up and storage facility, Anax had only visited the base once during his years at Alphi Base.

No matter how many soldiers he faced, nothing would stand between him and his mate.

Anax grabbed hold of the steering wheel and shifted it upwards. The glider launched into the air without a sound. He didn't aim for the atmosphere immediately, but for the west side of the palace, over-looking the garden. He enjoyed seeing the bright bursts of color from up high. If he started there, Dexus might relax his guard.

He completed half of his regular route before cranking the steering wheel. The glider tilted, aiming for the sky. Anax's heart pounded out a quick beat. Lexi. Lexi. Lexi. If his father's soldiers had hurt her, he'd kill them without hesitation.

"Your Highness?" Dexus's voice sounded across the ship's comms.

He hovered a claw over the comms interface. One reply to throw his friend off, then he'd shut it down. Dexus wouldn't report him immediately, but there was no way to know who was in his father's pocket. "I'm fine, Dexus. Just testing her capabilities."

"But, Your Highness, as you well know, exiting the atmosphere requires a permit—"

Anax smashed the comms button, cutting off Dexus's voice. He flicked to another screen and activated stealth mode. He entered Gamta Base's coordinates before pushing his seat back. It was a simple journey that the glider's autopilot could fly on its own. Anax had nothing to do for the next hour except beat himself up for putting Lexi in this position. Never again would he let her come into harm's way. Once he found her, he'd guard her meticulously. From a close distance should Lexi decide to forgive him or from afar if she chose a life without him. The thought of never looking into her eyes or watching her fawn over every petal in a garden was a punch to the gut, but he'd let her go if it made her happy.

The blue of Herkleios dropped into his periphery, the darkness of space enveloping him in its embrace. The third moon, Ios, was on the other side of the planet and out of sight, but Kore and Salane hovered close together, named for the twin daughters of the goddess Hyra and her traitorous lover, Hadus. Salane was as bright as Herkleios, but Kore was inhospitable and gray. Once in the base, Anax's only escape would be through a ship, whether his glider or another in the hangar.

Anax aimed the tip of his glider at Gamta Base. Like all the military bases, the hangar bay remained visibly open, but a forcefield would stop any intruders. Anax would need to uncloak to enter and hope his military codes worked. As the Crown Prince, he theoretically had access to every military base, but if his father was keeping Lexi there, perhaps the base was being used for other secret reasons, as well.

He gripped the steering wheel tighter. Now or never. He tapped his screen, turning off his cloak and broadcasting his identification. The entrance to Gamta Base glowed before him. If his codes didn't work, he'd end up smashed against the forcefield. Anax braced for impact.

His glider slid gently into the hangar.

Praise Hyra. Anax set down his glider beside a larger Class-B vehicle, one designed for long-distance travel and observation. The ship meant to take Lexi back to Earth. He wanted to grab his sabre and leap from his ship, slicing limbs and decapitating heads. But if Anax tried, Crown Prince or not, he'd be shot on sight. The base surely had medical equipment aboard, but he'd be knocked unconscious, unable to save Lexi.

The second his glider touched the surface, alarms blared through the hangar, red lights flashing. Anax opened the glass top and climbed out, crossing his arms like a commander ready to inspect their base. He didn't know what lie he'd use yet, but hopefully the soldiers he encountered would listen before immediately contacting his father.

Three large Herkleians raced out from the main hangar door. His father chose well, taking no chance in securing Lexi. But while they might have had brute strength, Anax matched them in that.

One male stepped a foot in front of the others, his slitted, yellow eyes narrowing. His head was bald, a sign of shame to a Herkleian male. Was serving Anax's father penance for some unknown actions? It didn't matter. No Herkleian should imprison an innocent female, no matter who gave the orders.

"I am Prince Anax, heir to the throne of Herkleios," he announced, his voice booming throughout the hangar.

The yellow-eyed male placed his hand over his heart in salute, but the movement was mocking. "I'm aware, Your Highness. I am Ezio Yio'aleta, Commander of the *Acacia II*."

"Why are you at Gamta Base, Commander?"

"On orders from your father. Why are you here, Your Highness?"

Anax went with his first idea. "To inspect your work, of course."

The two other soldiers—sergeants given the marks on their sashes —glanced at their captain. Ezio narrowed his eyes. "We heard of no such inspection."

"As you know, Commander, the best inspectors don't give

notice." Anax had experienced that enough during his two years in service. Even as a prince, the military hadn't informed him of scheduled checks. He started marching forward. "Lead the way."

Commander Ezio pulled at something hanging from his waistband. A circular comms device used to project images. Like the one his father had in his study. If Commander Ezio reached out to his father, his hopes of breaking Lexi out went to Hadus.

Anax grabbed his laser with one hand and the hilt of his sabre with the other. The sergeants reacted—not nearly fast enough. He flicked his claw against the top of his gun, setting it to stun. The red-haired soldier dropped instantly. The green-haired one pulled his own weapon, but Anax kicked out. The laser skid across the hangar floor. With his sabre, he sliced at the commander's hand. The male pulled back, dropping the comms to the ground.

The light in the center of the device flared.

Anax flinched back. That was all the time the green-haired soldier needed. He rushed forward, slamming into Anax with his body. If he had lowered his head, his horns would have rammed through Anax's heart. The two males tumbled to the floor.

Instead of helping, Commander Ezio tapped at his gold wristband.

The comms light dimmed, replaced by an image of his father, face stern and annoyed. "I told you not to contact me, Ezio Yio—"

Commander Ezio spun the comms, facing it towards Anax. He had rolled atop the other male, pinning him to the ground with his forearms. His scales raked blood against the softer flesh of the sergeant's neck.

King Xenobaccus let out a long, tired sigh. "Anax."

He climbed to his feet but kept a boot on the soldier. "Father."

"When a mechanic reported that you'd left the atmosphere, I wanted to believe you didn't know." His father tapped his bejeweled claws against the top of his cane. "You overheard me speaking with Lord Solon?"

"After an attendant smelling strongly of hanat flowers passed, yes." He clenched his fists. He couldn't believe he had thought his father a decent male. "You threatened, Lexi."

His father sighed dramatically, a growly sound. "And neither of you heeded the warning."

Anax had lost his laser, but he still had his sabre. He twisted at the blade's hilt and electricity sparked across the weapon. The green-haired soldier flinched when Anax pressed the sharp tip to his neck. "Release her, father."

"There's no need for bloodshed, *son.*"

"I think I'll go with bloodshed," Anax growled.

"If you insist. I care not." His father tapped at his wristband. "But you should know, I control Alexandra's cell from the planet. It'd be quite easy to remove the life support from her room."

Anax nearly snarled. "You wouldn't. You need Lexi for your plans. Earth will fight with everything they have if you don't have a hostage."

His father stared up at him, purple-eyes clear and determined. "Are you willing to take that risk?"

Every muscle in Anax's body clenched, debating his next move. He couldn't hurt Lexi. He was here to save her. He reluctantly lowered his glowing sabre. When the blade touched the ground, the electricity flowing through it stopped. His father flickered his fingers. The green-haired sergeant jumped to his feet and grabbed Anax's arms. He didn't know what hurt worse. His father threatening his mate or his father imprisoning him. King Xenobaccus was not the male he proclaimed himself to be, not at all.

His father turned his glare on Commander Ezio. "Bring my son to one of the guest suites. You aren't to harm him. I want him afforded every comfort."

Commander Ezio gritted his teeth but bowed his head. "Yes, Your Majesty."

"And Ezio?"

The male stiffened.

"Fuck this up and you'll lose more than your hair next time. I'll have your horns."

The male swallowed, true terror in his eyes. Not a reaction Anax had ever witnessed to his father. "Yes, Your Majesty."

Anax nearly gaped. Taking a Herkleian's horns was a barbaric punishment, long discontinued. His father wanted to drag their people a century back in time to when war and strife ruled.

The light from the comms device disappeared in a blink, his father ending the call. Anax glanced at his sabre, but he didn't leap for it. If his father could control Lexi's room, he was probably watching the base through its security cameras. He clenched his fists, but marched forward when the sergeant pushed. The three of them exited the hangar, leaving the last soldier unconscious on the floor. Anax could fight two males. He could fight more. But would he be able to get to Lexi in time if he did? He had never been to Gamta Base. He didn't know where the cells or guest quarters were.

Commander Ezio led them down similar-looking halls, twisting and doubling back to confuse Anax's memory. By the time they reached a pair of gold-carved doors, Anax was entirely lost. He remembered half their path, but the second half... To escape, Anax would need to access the base's internal maps.

Ezio slid his hands in front of the door. With a few taps of his wristband, entering or exiting would require the male's DNA. Anax bared his fangs in a grimace as he passed, hesitantly entering a small suite with a floating bed and plush amenities. His father had ordered the best treatment for his heir, and Commander Ezio had delivered.

"Enjoy your stay, Prince Anax."

Anax spun with a snarl. The sergeant's knuckles paled on his laser, but the commander didn't flinch. He would once Anax made his request. "I demand to see her."

"You're not in the position to be making demands."

Anax bared his fangs, not in anger but in the cocky grin of a prince. "My father wanted me to have every comfort. I'd be comforted to see Alexandra Seymour. Without interruptions."

Commander Ezio started for the longest moment. He glanced back at the nearest security camera. The king was watching, then. The male clenched his fists, his claws digging into his palms. "As you wish, Your Highness."

EIGHTEEN

LEXI

The door to Lexi's cell clanked open. "Time to wake up, princess!"

Lexi jolted on the mattress and wiped at her blurry eyes. She automatically glanced out the window, but the blackness of space didn't give away the time. After failing to convince Commander Ezio to release her from the cell, she had paced back and forth for hours until the exhaustion forced her to sit. She had fallen asleep. Stupid. In that time, perhaps she could have escaped. Lexi scoffed at herself. She was a human, a florist. What chance did she stand against three Herkleian males? She pulled on her cardigan as the green-haired Paxos stomped into the room. He tugged her to her feet and from the cell.

She whacked his shoulder under his leather pauldron, but her fist touched pure muscle. "Where are you taking me?"

"Silence."

She bit her lip. It was better for her to conserve her energy for an escape rather than waste it on yelling. Lexi glanced around, but she didn't see anything useful to fight the Herkleian. But he hadn't restrained her like the last time they had moved her. Where were they taking her? King Xenobaccus had implied she'd spend at least a few weeks in her cell.

Before she could ask, Paxos dragged her into another hall and waved his hand in front of a gilded door. It slid open to reveal a luxurious suite with a levitating king-sized bed, plush couches near a floating fire, glowing rock ceilings, and holo-mirrors displaying the idyllic Herkleian countryside. Commander Ezio leaned on the wall by the door. Lexi's stomach tightened, but her gaze drifted across the room—

Anax stood from the couch.

Anax. Unharmed. Dressed in soft, black pants, sturdy boots, and leathered shoulder pauldrons. Not a prisoner.

Her heart cracked. Had he known about his father? That he stood before her in a suite instead of chains was answer enough. Not only did he have a fiancée, but he was part of King Xenobaccus's plan. Lexi's tight stomach turned into a swirling pit. She had slept with him. Let him touch her, caress her, give her pleasure no human man ever had. A silly part of her had even loved him. She had planned to go back for him. Lexi thought being imprisoned was the worst thing to happen to her this week, but nothing compared to the tear in her heart.

Lexi opened her mouth to call him something crude, but her jaw twinged, an echo of the pain from Ezio's smack. She clutched at her face with a mew.

Anax rushed forward. "Did they injure you?"

"Go away," she muttered.

He turned on Commander Ezio. "What did you do?"

The commander didn't answer. He gestured at his guard before exiting the room on the other male's heels. "Don't get any ideas, Your Highness. I'm placing my sergeants just outside this door."

And with that, the doors slid shut, leaving Lexi and Anax alone. Anax, who wasn't in on his father's plans. They wouldn't leave a guard at the door otherwise. She almost dropped in relief.

He reached for her elbow. "Are you going to pass out?"

Her anger flared through her, holding her on her feet. Even if he wasn't planning on attacking Earth and the rest of the Intergalactic Alliance, he still had a fiancée. A beautiful, toned-midriff-baring fiancée. She loved him, but he had lied. She whacked his chest. "What are you doing here?!"

He gently grabbed her wrist. "I'm here to rescue you."

"Rescue?" She cackled. Literally cackled, like a freaking witch. She pulled her wrist from his and stomped to the other side of the room. Away from the heat of his body. "How's that going for you?"

He bowed his head. "I know I failed you, Lexi, but no matter what it takes, I'll get you out of here."

"Why do you even care? Shouldn't you be back at the palace with your Nicathra? Or maybe there's some other advisor you can take advantage of?" Before he could answer, she raced back to him and whacked him again. "I don't need you to save me, Anax. I'd have escaped and gotten a message to Earth, but now you've put them on high alert. So outstanding job rescuing me, Romeo."

His brow raised, but he didn't ask who Romeo was. If he had, she'd have slapped him. Instead, he dropped to his knees. She jolted back, but a fluttering spread through her stomach. "I know you're angry, Lexi. You have every right to be. If you choose to never speak to me again after this, I'll respect that, but you have to know I love you, Lexi. You're the only one I've ever loved."

Her knees turned to jelly at the words, but she couldn't let him in again. Couldn't trust. "I want to believe you, but how can I after what happened?"

"Because I am yours." He dropped his head, the black of his hair spilling down either side of his neck. "Do you see the mark?"

"What—?" Lexi squinted. On the back of his neck was a swirling of lines a shade darker than his scales. It almost looked like a star. Her own neck tingled at the sight of the mark. "It's beautiful."

He raised his head and reached for her hands. She didn't pull away this time. "Many centuries ago, the goddess Hyra blessed my people with matebonds. Like your Earth concept of soulmates. Two halves of a whole, united through the matching marks on their necks."

The remains of her heart turned to dust. "Nicathra is your soulmate?"

"No, not at all. Our people haven't witnessed a matebond in nearly a century. I've known Nicathra for years, but my mark appeared this week, Lexi. It appeared because of you."

Her? The heat from his hand radiated through her, shooting straight for her core. She wanted him, loved him even, but soulmates? "Oh, how convenient for you. I'm supposed to believe your goddess wants us together?"

Anax's face fell. Lexi twinged. After her ex, she had lost the ability to trust. Anax had damaged that, but if Lexi wanted happiness, wanted a full life with him by her side, she needed to let him in. She exhaled, trying again. "If I'm your mate, where's my mark?"

Anax rose and raised his hand, like he meant to thread it through her blond hair. He paused. He had already touched in her places no man had gone before, but he still asked her permission. She took his hand and threaded it through her hair. His breath jolted at the touch of her silky strands on his scales. She swallowed, her throat suddenly dry.

He pushed her hair out of the way, but his forehead creased. Disappointment flooded his ice-blue eyes for a quick moment. "You don't have one."

Lexi didn't want to flinch at the words, but she did. "So I'm not your mate?"

His hand grazed the edges of her throat. "Sometimes the mark doesn't appear until both people have sworn themselves to the other."

"Like a wedding?"

"It's the swearing of vows, but without the ceremony and expense. The only people required are the mates themselves."

Lexi's heart stuttered. "And then the mark would appear? What if it doesn't?"

Anax grazed a thumb across her chin. The heat within her pooled low in her stomach. "The words themselves don't tie the couple together, Lexi. They must express what is truly in their hearts."

"Okay." Lexi stared into his blue slitted eyes. Eyes that had haunted her dreams since she first met him in her uncle's headquarters. She couldn't believe that had only been a week ago. She felt like she had known Anax for a lifetime. The cocky, arrogant prince was just a facade he put on for others. Underneath, he was loyal and kind. Committed to his people and family and determined to protect them at all costs. A warrior prince, who came all the way to Kore to rescue her. She had wanted to go back to him to see if he truly loved her. He had done more than tell her. He had shown her. "Then let's get on with it."

Anax stiffened. "What?"

She grinned, a bright look she only ever experienced with him. "We have nothing to lose either way."

"If the matebond forms, our souls will be tied together and won't survive without the other."

She put a hand on his chest. His heart pounded rapidly, but he leaned into her touch. Her presence was as magnetic to him as he was to her. "For the matebond to form, both parties have to love the other, right?"

"Yes."

"If you truly love me, I wouldn't be opposed to being with you." Lexi blushed. Until she had learned about Nicathra, she'd been happy with him. Why not let fate decide? King Xenobaccus could murder her tomorrow. All she had was this moment with Anax, their bodies pressed against each other.

He wrapped his arms around her and looked into her eyes. Her knees nearly melted, but together, they remained standing.

"What do I say?" she whispered.

"There are no set words from my understanding. We say how we feel about each other and we commit to spending our lives together."

She let out a nervous chuckle. "I have to come up with wedding vows on the spot? No pressure."

"Lexi." Her body tensed just at him saying her name. "I've never felt so strongly about someone as I have you. When I first saw you, my heart stopped. Though your beauty made me notice you, I have since fallen in love with your humor and willingness to try new things. The light and kindness in your soul draws me to you. And when I touch your skin, I want to bury myself inside you, to be one with you."

Lexi flushed, but the fluttering within her turned to itching heat. Her nipples hardened under her cardigan. She pressed herself harder against his chest. "I think you're getting a little off track."

He cupped her cheek. "Lexi, I love you and I swear to protect you until the end of time."

Lexi tilted her head, her mouth open and begging for a kiss. Anax leaned towards her. She wanted to grip his horns and climb his body, but if she didn't speak the vows now, maybe she never would. "Anax, to put it simply, I am yours and I always have been. I swear to spend the rest of my life with you, even if that means tomorrow when your father abandons us on a desolate moon."

His lips curved into a delicious baring of fangs. Lexi threaded her hands through the dark, silky strands of his hair. She grasped his horns as his lips met hers. He groaned into her mouth, but the roughness of his tongue didn't halt in its plunder. The inferno in Lexi's core threatened to burn through her body. She needed him inside her right now. His massive hardness pressed against her stomach. She wanted to impale herself on him.

His hands slid down to cup her butt. She hoisted herself into his hold, slamming her core back down onto his bulge. He growled as she moaned, the sounds a symphony of pleasure. She ground herself against him, a wonderful mix of heat and friction.

"Anax," she said as he broke the kiss, trailing his lips down her jawline, "I need you to fuck me."

He bared his fangs, a wicked grin. "As you command, mate."

He marched her across the room and swiped his hands across the surface of a narrow table. Something crashed to the floor, but Lexi didn't care. She wanted him, needed him—

Anax pressed one hand against the closest holo-mirror, changing the projection from Herkleian hills to a reflective surface. From all angles, she saw her body pressed against his massive form, her cheeks flushed and her hair wild. The heat within her spiked, becoming a burning need.

Lexi stared into his perfect blue eyes. His breath tickled her skin. "I'm going to watch your matebond mark form as I fuck you."

Lexi yipped as Anax spun her around. She met her own wild eyes in the mirror. Lexi had never liked her body. She wasn't overweight, but she wasn't fit, either. She hadn't wanted her ex-boyfriends to get a good look at her. But she hadn't cared that first time with Anax. And now, as his hands moved down her body, removing her cardigan, bra, and jeans, she wanted to watch every bit as much as he did.

She reached back to touch him, to feel him, but his hand caught hers and pinned it to the mirror. Hot scales pressed against her naked back. The sharpness of his fangs grazed her ears. He breathed into her for a second. The desire in Lexi built. It itched within her. She all but squirmed in his arms, begging to touch him.

Anax chuckled, a low growl. Everything within Lexi tightened at the sound. "I touch. You feel."

Lexi didn't have the chance to argue. With his other hand, he spread her legs. His knuckles grazed against her core. Something else followed them, a massive, burning length. Lexi might not have believed in Hyra a few days ago, but only a female goddess would create a cock ridged for her absolute pleasure. She shifted her hips, trying to impale herself on him.

Anax quickly clutched her side with a growl. "You're going to kill me."

Lexi's own face curved into a wicked smile, reflected to her in the mirror. She rubbed herself against him, tiny movements he couldn't stop. He groaned, his chin settling on her shoulder. The tips of his horns almost scratched against the mirror. "That's the intention."

She shuffled again, almost getting the right angle—

With a snarl, Anax lifted her hips. Lexi shot towards the mirror, close enough for her hitched breath to fog the mirror. He plunged into her, hitting her g-spot in a single, decisive stroke. Massive and ridged and all hers. She gasped out. Her vision nearly went white. In the mirrors, Lexi watched as Anax shuddered behind her, a look of pure bliss coming across his face. They were joined. They were one.

They were mates.

Lust roared within Lexi, an overpowering force. No longer sated but craving. She placed one hand on the table for leverage. When Anax pulled back, the movement in her body and the reflection, she launched. She met his thrust. Again. Again. Again. Every pound ripped a tiny, desperate sound from her lips. The noise became a symphony with Anax's groans, with the creak of the table.

Lexi's back arched, blond hair flying across her shoulders. Anax retracted his claws and trailed his fingers over her collarbone. Every touch burst into her senses. She could do nothing but watch as his scaled hands glided down her front, circling her pert nipples. They traveled over the valley of her stomach. When he reached the swell of her clit, his slitted eyes met hers in the mirror.

On his next thrust, he traced a thumb across the heat of her sex.

Lexi thrashed, nearly coming undone. He plunged inside her. His ridges stroked her. His scales rubbed against her back and his rough fingers down her front. Everything was Anax. The surrounding room disappeared, nothing but their flushed bodies and the mirrors. In the reflection, a thousand versions of Anax pounded into a thousand versions of Lexi. Each one of her cried out, voice pitching to a scream.

Her body clenched in a rush of warmth. Lexi arched her back. She grabbed hold of one of his horns. Her climax ripped through her like an earthquake. Without his cock inside her and his horn in her hand, the pleasure would have swept her into the storm. She thrashed and squirmed.

It was everything.

It was perfect.

He was perfect. Her mate, her freaking soulmate. He growled into her ear with another thrust, pushing Lexi higher again. Would she survive a second orgasm?

Anax shuddered with a roar. His fangs grazed across her neck. His thumb ground into her clit. His groan merged with her shriek. Anax spilled his seed all over her, within her, milked by her clenching warmth. Her mate. Her Anax.

Lexi went slack in his arms, utterly boneless. She stroked gently at his horn. He growled into her neck. "I love you, Lexi."

She smiled, a sloppy, exhausted grin reflected all around her. "I love you, too, Anax."

Anax traced the shape of their matebond mark on Lexi's neck, a light brush of his claws. She stirred, her back brushing against his chest—and other parts. His cock twitched. He had taken her three times before they tumbled to sleep on the bed. Each time she had shrieked with pleasure, a sound he wanted to hear every day for the rest of his life. A sound he *would* hear every day for the rest of his life. A sound he wanted to hear now.

He traced his claws down the length of her arm to the curve of her hip. She shuddered, her skin prickling, but her eyes remained closed. He pressed his lips to the pulse at her neck. She didn't wake. He grazed his knuckles along the roundness of her ass. She leaned into the touch, her legs parting ever so gently. Anax bared his fangs, a smile against the lobe of her ear.

He wanted his mate to wake screaming for him.

He retracted his claws before plunging a single finger into her depth, his teeth grazing the edges of her ear.

Lexi jolted, her eyes flashing open and spine stretching, flexing. A little gasp escaped from her lips. He gave her ear a final nibble before mumbling, "Good morning, naika."

"Naika?" she asked, breathless.

"It's what a Herkleian male calls his mate." He twisted his hand before plunging his finger into her wet core again, finding a steady rhythm guided by her panting. With the ball of his thumb, he found her clit and caressed the needy bead. His cock throbbed, aching, but he resisted the urge to pound into her, take her. This was about her pleasure.

"What do..." She bit off her word with a moan. Her back arched, her head pressing into his collarbone. The front of her body stretched before him, a feast for his eyes. Sweat ran in rivulets between the valley of her breasts, her nipples sharp peaks. "What do I call you?"

She had formed a full sentence. Anax couldn't allow that. He drew his finger up, brushing against the swell of her g-spot, before receding, circling her wetness around her clit. Lexi shuddered. He plunged in again, repeating the motion.

She clutched at his thigh with one hand and the bedsheets with the other. "Oh, God, Anax."

He chuckled into her ear. He loved watching her writhe. Loved to make her squirm. His mate. His for all eternity. He sped his motion, his fingers coming out wetter and wetter every time. Her climax built, a massive wave rising within her. His cock surged forward, settling into the heat between her cheeks. She jolted at his next touch, pulsing down onto him. He growled, the pleasure throbbing through him.

"Naikos," he groaned out.

Her fingers dug into his leg. "What?"

"Naikos..." She started thrashing, pulsing down to meet each caress of his fingers. The bouncing almost broke him. "You call me naikos."

Her entire body tensed, her mouth opening in a moan-turned-scream. The heat of her clenched on his fingers, holding him captive as she came in a roar of warmth. The shudder ripped through her body. Lexi's scream turned into a single word. "Naikos!"

Anax tensed at the word. His naika. His beautiful mate. All his, for evermore. He couldn't help himself. She thrust back onto his cock once more, tipping him into an explosion. Anax came, spilling blue seed on her, into her. Her warmth with his, like it was meant to be. Like *they* were meant to be.

His mate.

Lexi sunk into his arms, her breath coming out in little pants. She twisted and kissed the edge of his mouth. "My naikos."

Anax pushed onto his elbow and claimed her mouth in a deep kiss. Their tongue twisted together, making love like their bodies had. He traced his hand down her front, between that valley, before breaking the kiss. "My naika."

Lexi's circular pupils widened, her lips and cheeks flushed a bright pink. She pushed up to claim his mouth—

A knock sounded at the door.

Anax jolted. Gamta Base. His father's plan. He had let himself forget, but he couldn't anymore. He had ordered Commander Ezio not to interrupt, but it had been hours. They weren't safe. Lexi wasn't safe. This room had become their haven, but in truth, it was their prison.

He turned to Lexi, but she had already scrambled off the bed. She tossed him his pants. "We have to ambush them."

"Even if we do, we won't make it far."

"We don't have to make it far. There must be a way to get a message out? All we have to do is let the rest of the Intergalactic Alliance know your father's plans."

Anax jumped from the bed. "There should be a long-range comms device in the main control room."

"Then that's where we'll go." Lexi spun, but lost her balance on a pile of bedsheets on the floor. Anax reached out, catching her small frame in his arms. Her breath gasped out. She swallowed. "We have to do this, Anax. Not just for Earth but for everyone."

He pressed a kiss to her forehead. "You are a genius, naika."

She smiled, sweet and satisfied. "Why, thank you, naikos."

The guards knocked a second time. If he were any other prisoner, they wouldn't hesitate to barge in, but his father wanted him treated like the prince he was. "Your Highness?" one of them called. "Your father insists we return the human to her cell now."

Anax wanted to throw her over his shoulder. "Hide, my love. There are only three of them. I've faced worse odds."

"Nope." She pushed him towards the corner near the door. "I'll scream. They'll come in staring at me. You'll have a better chance."

"Naika—"

She nudged him again. "We're in this together, Anax. I am your naika and you my naikos. We do this together or not at all."

Anax wanted to throw her over his shoulder and hide her, but his Lexi would never forgive him for that. She was right. To escape, they needed to work together. Like the team they were. He rushed into the corner and put his back to the wall. Commander Ezio had taken his sabre and laser, but the greatest generals in the Herkleian military had trained Anax in hand-to-hand combat. He could take on his father's thugs.

He glanced at his mate, her short frame breakable but her eyes filled with fire. She nodded at him and he nodded back. Something filled his chest, part desire and part pride. His strong, beautiful mate.

Lexi let out a blood-curdling scream.

The guards didn't knock a third time. The two burly sergeants rammed into the room, their focus entirely on Lexi. Commander Ezio must be elsewhere on the ship, probably communicating with Anax's father. He couldn't waste this opportunity.

Anax came up behind them, his footsteps silent on the floor. The red-haired guard stomped towards his mate, but Lexi didn't flinch. Anax rushed forward and grabbed the green-haired guard around the neck. Lexi halted her scream and rushed around the couch, out of the Red Hair's reach. Anax grabbed Green Hair's laser, aimed, and fired in a single smooth motion. Red Hair dropped with a shudder, his face going slack into unconsciousness.

Lexi rushed to his side and grabbed his laser. Green Hair

thrashed, but Anax held on tight. When his arms went still, Anax dropped him.

Lexi kicked his side and stunned him for good measure.

His beautiful, vicious mate.

She grinned at him. "Let's get out of here."

He gestured to the door. "After you."

She stepped over Green Hair's fallen body. "Why, thank you, naikos."

Anax grabbed her hand and together they fled from the room. He didn't know the schematics of Gamta Base, but if it was at all like Alphi Base, the control room would be in the center of the complex. When they passed an interface, Anax stopped with a gentle tug on Lexi's wrist.

"What is it?"

He held the gold of his wristband to the little golden dot on the wall. Commander Ezio had taken the rest of his tech, but he'd left Anax his wristband and jammed it from outside communication. How short-sighted. "I can sync my holo-screen with the base. It will tell us where the control room is."

Lexi glanced nervously down the hall, her thumb stroking across her laser's trigger. "Is it far? I think the only Herkleians on this base are Ezio and his two sergeants, but I don't know."

He squeezed her hand. "Whatever obstacles we cross, we'll face them together, naika."

His wristband buzzed, finished its sync with the base. Anax brought up the screen with a swipe of his claws. Like he thought, the control room was in the center of the buildings two stories below them. He pointed. "We're here. We need to get here."

"That's not too far."

"It isn't." Anax scanned further down the hall. One doorway was marked with an upside-down triangle. "There are stairs ahead."

Lexi nodded. Together, they hurried down the rest of the hall. Anax kept his hand on the hilt of his laser. When the sergeants had heard Lexi's scream, it'd be protocol to call it in first. Commander

Ezio might be on his way to this floor right now. Anax wished for his sabre. With a blade in his hand, he was undefeated.

Anax pushed open the door—

Commander Ezio halted at the top of the flight of stairs. "And where do you think you're going, Your Highness?"

TWENTY

LEXI

Lexi raised her laser, ready to blast Commander Ezio's smug grin off his ugly face. He had threatened her. He had kidnapped her. He had hit her. But through it all, she had survived. She'd flourished. She'd found her mate, her Anax, and together, they would build a future together, for them and for their people. Lexi wasn't about to let anyone stand in her way.

She fired the weapon.

With a blur of his hands, Commander Ezio pulled something from his belt—a familiar gold hilt. Anax's sabre crackled in the bald alien's hand. With a swirl of the blade, he deflected the shot from Lexi's laser. Anax slammed into her side. The energy blast punched a hole through the wall above her head. Where her head once was.

She swallowed. That was too close.

Anax pulled her back to her feet. "Are you okay?"

"I wasn't hit." She trailed her hands across his scales, but he remained warm and whole. "Are you—Anax!"

Commander Ezio lunged behind them, the sabre raised and ready to take Anax's head off. Her mate grabbed her around the waist. He leapt back into the hallway. Not fast enough. The commander's sabre sliced down, grazing Anax's arm. Hot purply blue blood swelled to the surface and blanketed his scales. Her mate snarled in pain but swiped a hand across the door's sensor. It slammed shut on the commander.

"Anax!" Lexi ripped off her cardigan and pressed it against the wound. With her other hand, she raised her laser again. Commander Ezio pounded his fists into the door. It wouldn't stay closed long. Whatever command Anax had used, Ezio could override. "That bastard!"

"No, Lexi." Anax gritted his fangs together but he straightened, the strong, warrior prince. "You need to go."

"Go?" Lexi wasn't leaving him, not like this.

He slipped off his wristband with a hiss. The pain in his voice ripped through her heart. They had just found each other. She wouldn't lose him. She couldn't.

Anax tapped the band of gold a few times before handing it over. "Take this to the control room. It should auto-connect to the comms device. Record a message, not only for Earth but for all the Intergalactic Alliance. It will be played across the galaxy with my personal seal attached to it."

"Anax, no."

Commander Ezio slammed into the doors again. They started to slide open.

Anax put his hands on her arms, holding her in his warm embrace. "I'm not surrendering, Lexi. Not after we've just found each other. We will live a long and happy life together. You will be my wife. And if the Herkleians accept you, which I know they will when they see Hyra's mark, you will be my queen."

Lexi traced her palms across the scales of his face. "Oh, naikos."

He locked her mouth in a passionate kiss. His fangs trailed her lips and his rough tongue battled her own into submission. She melted into his arms. Lexi didn't want to leave him. After King Xenobaccus had kidnapped her, she swore she'd never leave again if she got back to him and he loved her. And loved her he did. Just like she loved him, like she had loved no other man. All of her ex-boyfriends paled in comparison to her prince, her soulmate, her naikos.

She didn't want to let him go, but she had to. If they didn't stop the king, millions would die across the galaxy. The rest of the Intergalactic Alliance wouldn't surrender without a fight. They would be no match for Herkleios's superior technology, but they would try to stand against them. King Xenobaccus threatened everyone Lexi had ever known. Her mom. Her best friend, Olivia. Kynna and Dexus. Literally everyone.

Lexi broke the kiss. She stared into those ice-blue eyes, trying to memorize his face. "Don't you dare die, Anax."

"I won't."

She squeezed his shoulder, wanting to hold him for as long as she could. "I love you, naikos."

"And I love you, naika."

Commander Ezio slammed through the door with a roar.

Lexi pulled out of Anax's arms and dashed down the hall. Tears flowed down her face, blurring her vision. The sound of flesh pounding into flesh ripped at her heart, but she kept moving. At her wrist, Anax's holo-screen flashed in front of her. He had charted her a path to the control room. All she had to do was run.

At the end of the hall, Lexi turned. Anax had rammed himself into the commander, pinning the other male to the wall. The top of his right horn pierced Ezio's shoulder. With a punch to the wrist, Anax made the other male drop his sabre. It skittered across the floor. They broke apart and both leapt for the blade.

Lexi forced herself through the door. If she didn't move now, she'd stay and watch, her heart not in her chest but in a battle for his life. Anax depended on her to get this message out. Everyone depended on her.

The little room she had entered must have been an elevator. It connected to Anax's wristband and buzzed, a quiet noise that shivered through her body. When the doors re-opened with a ding, she entered a quiet hallway. No Herkleian males battled for their lives. It was Lexi, alone on a freaking alien moon base.

The holo-screen projected the rest of her path to the control room. Lexi rushed down the paths, her focus on one thing. If she got the message out, she could return to Anax.

She rushed through an open door into the control room. Like the bridge of a spaceship, various screens and projections occupied the large space—

And a skinny Herkleian with blue-hair and short horns. He jumped from his seat. His black pants were military-esque, but he didn't have any weapons at his belt, only tools and gadgets. A technician, then. Lexi rushed forward and shoved her laser in his face. "Where's the comms station?"

The alien raised his hands, apparently the universal sign for surrender, and stuttered, "What?"

With her thumb, Lexi flicked the base of the laser, going from stun mode to kill. She quickly aimed at the chair beside him. The electricity rammed into the seat, which blasted halfway across the room and exploded. The technician squeaked. Lexi shoved her weapon back in his face. "I won't ask again."

The alien pointed, his clawed hands trembling. Lexi didn't let the technician out of her sight as she backed toward the screen. She tapped at it, but nothing happened. "Why isn't it working?"

"I can..." He swallowed when she glared at him. "I can make it work. Don't shoot me."

Lexi didn't know if she actually had it in her to shoot an unarmed person, but her hand didn't tremble as she motioned the technician over. He scrambled to her side. He didn't sweat, but his scales glowed with an odd sheen. Definitely nervous. He one hundred percent believed she'd shoot. Lexi smiled. She had never been one for poker, but apparently it was a game she'd excel at.

The technician quickly tapped a few buttons, his hands moving too fast for Lexi to follow. When the screen flickered to a blank-looking page, she nudged him. It looked almost how her bracelet holo-screen looked when she sent someone a message. "I can take it from here."

"What are you going to do with me?" the technician asked.

"Hmm." Lexi hadn't really thought about it. Guess she couldn't leave him to wander around. She flicked the laser back to stun. "Sorry about this."

"No, don't—gahh!" The stun wave hit him. He twitched and sunk to the floor. As his eyes closed, Lexi swore he muttered, "Fucking humans."

She snorted. Damn right.

Lexi pulled off Anax's wristband and lowered it to the screen. A symbol sparked to life in the corner, a twisting of lines within a triangle. His royal seal. His wristband had connected, then. All Lexi needed to do was record her message and hope the galaxy heard the sincerity in her words.

Lexi huffed in a big breath. She had never enjoyed public speaking. Now, everyone would hear her voice. She settled her mind, thinking of Anax and their future together. Her heart rate calmed. Lexi exhaled once and tapped the recording button.

"This is Lexi—uh, Alexandra Seymour of Earth, niece to Gravitas CEO Grayson Seymour and former fiancée to Prince Phintias Yio'hyra of Herkleios." She paused for a second, but no one interrupted her. Lexi sped on, emboldened by the silence, the waiting. The entire galaxy expected her next words. "A day ago, I tried to call off my engagement to Prince Phintias. His father, King Xenobaccus, was kind and generous, offering to take me home to Earth immediately. But he tricked me. His soldiers, led by a Commander Ezio, brought me to Gamta Base on Kore and imprisoned me. Why, you might ask? Because King Xenobaccus needs me, like he needs every one of his in-laws, to claim our planets when he tries to overthrow the Intergalactic Alliance. The base I'm on is filled with military gliders and ships. King Xenobaccus is not your ally. He means to be your overlord."

Lexi glanced over her shoulder. Anax hadn't returned to her yet.

Had Commander Ezio hurt him? Or worse, killed him? She turned back to the screen. A tear dripped down her chin and splattered onto the tech. "I only escaped my cell with the help of Crown Prince Anax. Right now... Last I saw him, he was battling Commander Ezio for control of this base. I don't know if he's alive. I don't know if we'll make it off this base. King Xenobaccus might blow us out of the sky when we try to return. All I can hope for is that you're hearing my message right now. Don't blame the Herkleians for this attack. Blame the king. He's your enemy."

A hollow thud rammed through the room. Lexi squeaked and jumped from her seat, laser rising. Anax stumbled into the room, dragging himself across the wall. Blood dripped down his chest, his shoulder, his cheek. Lexi lunged across the room. He all but fell into her arms. "Anax! Anax, my love."

He nuzzled her cheek. "Naika."

Her heart nearly cracked. She could barely hold his seven feet of pure muscle, but she held on long enough to drop him in her seat. The comms scream showed they were still broadcasting. She went to hit the off button, but Anax grazed her wrist. "I'll add the final touch. This is Prince Anax Yio'hyra of Herkleios. I attest that Alexandra Seymour of Earth has been truthful in her statement."

He tapped the screen, switching it to blank. Lexi didn't waste a second. She dropped to her knees in front of him and ripped at the frills of her floral shirt. If he bled out more, she didn't know if he'd make it back to the planet. "Hold this to your side, naikos. We have to stop the bleeding."

"Lexi—"

Her tears nearly blinded her. "I can't lose you. We only just found each other."

He let out a growly sigh. Or was it a groan of pain? Lexi couldn't tell. She pressed harder at the wound.

Anax pulled her into his lap with one smooth movement.

"Oh." Lexi looked into his blue slitted eyes. He bared his fangs at her, a tired but wicked grin. He wasn't seriously hurt. Lexi squirmed on his lap, trying to get a better view of his wounds—

Anax groaned, a firm hardness pressing into her leg. She stilled. An inferno sprung to life between her legs. Lexi had never gotten horny so quickly in all her life. Her eyebrows raised.

He chuckled. "Give me a moment to catch my breath, naika. Maybe then, I will satisfy you."

She whacked his shoulder. "You're hurt. I thought you were dying. You're obviously not."

"The blood on my face and arm is mine. But everywhere else belongs to Commander Ezio."

"Is he..." Dead? The thought almost relieved Lexi. Did that make her a terrible person?

Anax dropped his eyes. "He refused to surrender."

She traced his jaw, careful to avoid his injury. "You had no choice, Anax. If you didn't kill him, he'd have killed you. Then me. A whole intergalactic war would have taken out everyone else. You did what you had to do."

He flinched. "You don't hate me?"

"Why would I hate you?"

He met her gaze. "I killed someone, Lexi. I have been in battles before, but I have never taken someone's life. I am to be the King of Herkleios. I shouldn't be harming my own people."

"You did this for your people, Anax." She traced her thumb across his lips. "You're exactly the type of king they need. One that will fight for the people, not for your own gain."

He searched her face, but she had spoken the truth, echoed in her heart. He bared his fangs, a bit of the playboy prince returning to the tired warrior's smile. "I love you so much, Lexi."

She bopped her nose against his. "And I you, Anax."

TWENTY-ONE

LEXI

Lexi dozed in Anax's arms as his glider approached Eritea. The small space didn't allow them much room, but there was more than enough for their purposes. Lexi had been terrified when exiting the Herkleian atmosphere, but beyond thrilled at re-entrance. They had little to do but touch each other in the hour it took to return to the planet. Orgasms erased all her fears of turbulence.

"Lexi?" Anax brushed his hand across her arm to wake her.

She blinked open her eyes and traced the edge of his scaled jaw, the ice blue of his slitted eyes, the sharp tips of his horn. He was her Herkleian. Her naikos. Her alien prince.

"I've landed us outside the palace at an airstrip near the Queen Rhoxane Plaza." Lexi glanced through the windows and noticed the dozen other gliders and ships around her. "I must approach on foot."

Lexi straightened in his lap. "I?"

"I can't put you in any more danger." He brushed a strand of her hair from her face. They had used his glider's medical kit to clean off the blood from his scales, but the cut on his cheek couldn't be bandaged as easily as his arm. "If my father got his hands on you, I know he would hurt you to get to me."

She pushed off his lap onto the bench beside him. "You're going to leave me here?"

Anax tapped a button and the glider's lid slid off. "I'll arrange for safe passage to a nearby planet. If I don't reach out in three days, I'll have them take you back to Earth."

She grabbed his wrist. "No."

"Naika, please."

"Don't naika me." Lexi all but jumped out of the glider and started stomping towards the plaza. "Neither of us would've escaped Gamta Base without the other. We're a team now, Anax. We can get through anything, as long as we're together."

She didn't let him counter her. Lexi grabbed Anax's hand and dragged him forward. He came willingly. She continued, "What's your plan?"

He paused, but answered, "We need to find my father."

"That might be difficult." Lexi wouldn't even know where to look. She had barely explored half the palace in her week on Herkleios. Anax would have some ideas, but how long would it take to narrow down the list? King Xenobaccus could do ridiculous amounts of damage until they found him.

"We—" Anax paused and raised his head. Lexi frowned, but heard it a second later. A rumbling echoed through the plaza, a collective of chanting voices. The closer they got, the clearer the sounds became. Individual voices separated from the background, male and female voices, young and old.

"Allies don't fight allies!"

"No war! Only peace!"

"Say no to Xenobaccus's war!"

Lexi rushed around the corner into the opening of the plaza. In a little over an hour, hundreds of Herkleians had gathered, raising their clawed fists and shouting at the palace's outer wall. Guards lined the top, peaking between the stone crenulations, but none had exited the palace to face the protestors.

They had heard her message. Lexi had done this.

Anax pulled her back into the shadows. "No one can see us. We need the element of surprise."

"I know, but look at them, Anax." Lexi's heart swelled at the sight. "Your people oppose the war. There's no way your father can win."

Anax still didn't look happy. "He doesn't need to convince them. Only the senate."

Herkleios had a king, but much of the everyday governance was the job of the Herkleian Senate. Their chambers were attached to one of the palace's outer buildings, but Lexi hadn't ever been there. Kynna had pointed it out on a map, nothing more. "Is that where he'll be?"

"Probably." Anax took her hand and led her through the narrow alleyways. "Your message will have forced him to move up his time-line. He probably intended to woo the senators slowly, but he'll have no choice now."

"Okay." Lexi squeezed his hand. Together, they could accomplish anything. "We better get going if we want to reach the palace in time."

THEY APPROACHED the palace from the south side, sticking to the service roads. Lexi was glad Anax had been a rebel, sneaking out of the palace as a child. It had finally proven useful. He knew exactly how to evade the guards and what entrances were safest for them. She gripped his hand tightly the entire way. Once they arrived in the senate chambers, who knew what would happen to them? What if Xenobaccus had already convinced enough senators to his side?

"We'll try through here," Anax said, peeking through the doorway. They pushed into the gilded hall and crept towards another door—

It opened and someone pushed inside.

"Anax?"

"Shit." Lexi nearly dug her nails through Anax's scales. Queen Chryseis closed the small space between them. Like always, she looked absolutely fantastic. Opal claw rings matched the pearls dangling from the tips of her horns. Her red hair twisted around the base of her horns. The scarlet of her gown matched the dark orange of her slitted eyes. Lexi's shirt was ripped, her hair tangled, and her jeans stained with purple-blue blood. Not at all appropriate for a maybe-future queen addressing the senate.

Not that they'd get the chance. Once Chryseis sounded the alarm, the guards would throw Lexi in another jail cell. If she were lucky.

"Wait." The queen held out a clawed hand. "I can help you get to the senate floor. I assume that's where you are trying to go."

Anax narrowed his eyes. "And just why would you help us with that, stepmother? Have you set some trap for us?"

"I know you may not believe me, Anax, but I've always tried to help you."

"No, you haven't!" Lexi snapped. "You told me to stay away from Anax."

"Because that's what was best for you." Queen Chryseis nervously glanced behind her. Like maybe she was telling the truth. In all their encounters, the queen had always been arrogant and self-assured. "Better to keep a low profile so Xenobaccus didn't take too much notice of you. I knew he wasn't happy about how close you two were getting. I didn't want to see you hurt." Neither Lexi nor Anax lowered their guard. The queen nearly snarled with frustration. "I know what it's like to marry a stranger, Alexandra. I wish someone had warned me away from my husband's games. I never wanted you hurt. Either of you."

"Do you deny knowing about my father's plan?"

The queen flinched. "No. I've heard quiet whisperings for some months now. Some of your father's spies are actually my spies."

Anax clenched his fists. "You know and said nothing."

"What could I say? I know it was weak of me, but I wanted to keep my son safe. After what happened with Eryx—" The queen bit off her words.

Anax stomped forward. "What happened to my brother?"

"He's alive." The queen lowered her head. "He discovered your father's plan, much like you did. When he came to me, I told him not to challenge his father. But he did. Eryx is so headstrong. Just like you, Anax. Your father threw him off the planet when he refused to agree to his plan for galactic domination."

"Why would my brother go to you, Chryseis?"

"I know I was never there for you. I couldn't be. You father didn't like me spending time with either of you. You were his heirs. You didn't need coddling from a female, he said. Instead of fighting him, I abandoned you and focused on your siblings, but that doesn't mean I don't want to help you. Eryx knew that." The queen glanced up from her hands. "If you don't believe I'll do it for you, believe I'll do it for Phintias. He's happy as he is now. He doesn't want to be King of Earth. Nor do I want to see your sisters suffer. They have found love with their husbands. They would lose that in a war."

Anax looked to Lexi. She watched the queen's face, but she didn't see any signs of deception. Did it matter? They had little choice at this point. If they wanted to get to the senate floor, they'd need to trust Queen Chryseis. "Take us to your husband."

The queen nearly dropped with relief but bobbed her head and rushed back in the direction she had come from. She passed the first door and aimed for a gilded tapestry. She pulled it from the wall to reveal a hidden doorway. "Queens of the past used this passageway to spy on their senate's sessions in secret. Your cousin, Yna, showed it to me when she was last in Eritea, Anax."

Lexi peeked into the space. "This will get us close, but how will we get in?"

"There's an exit door into the senate chambers." The queen faced Anax. "Near your father's official seat."

Anax gave a quick nod. "Thank you, Chryseis."

"I'm sorry I didn't help sooner." With a quick yet sad baring of fangs, the queen strode down the hall. In a minute, she had disappeared. Anax kept his eyes on the place she had last stood.

Lexi reached for Anax's hand. "Are you okay?"

"I never even gave her a chance."

"There's no time like the present."

He bared his fangs at her. "You're right."

"Of course I am. I'm your naika."

Anax shook Queen Chryseis's revelations off and pushed into the narrow pathway. Lexi stayed at his back, a hand on his rippling muscles. Once the door closed behind her, they were submerged into blackness. Lexi nearly tripped over her own feet three times, but Anax didn't have any trouble. Could Herkleians see in the dark?

She didn't get the chance to ask. Nearby voices turned from murmurs to clear words. The speaker was male, but it wasn't the king. Lexi would remember his voice anywhere.

"This is our chance to rise to the greatest heights in our history. King Xenobaccus had done this for us. He's found us twelve planets to add to our empire."

Lexi's stomach sunk. "I had hoped there wouldn't be anyone on his side."

"That's Lord Solon," Anax whispered back. "Nicathra's father. I overheard him with my father earlier. They've always been allies."

Lexi nodded. Not exactly comforting, but not a blow to their chances, either.

"We shouldn't be considering the matter so lightly," a female senator said. "I move to adjourn until tomorrow after we've had time to go over the specifics of the matter."

"The news has leaked to the public, Senator Oriel," Lord Solon said. "It's only a matter of time before we have rebellion from the Alliance planets. We must strike now or completely lose our advantage!"

Anax reached back and grabbed Lexi's hand. "I've found the door, naika. Be ready."

She pressed her head to his back. "Ready, naikos."

"All in favor of conquering the primitive Alliance planets?" Lord Solon called over the murmuring senators.

Those were exactly the words Anax needed to hear. He pushed, ripping open a door with rusted, old-fashioned hinges. Lexi blinked, light streaming into her eyes. The senate chamber had a massive domed ceiling decorated with gold and sapphire-like jewels in a twisting, mesmerizing pattern. Three curved rows of seating hovered in the air across from a stage, where Lord Solon stood. Behind him, on a gilded throne, sat King Xenobaccus, tapping his fingers impatiently against his cane.

The king immediately jumped to his feet with a vigor that contradicted his cane and pointed to where she and Anax had appeared on the stage. "Guards!"

No one moved. Nearly a hundred Herkleian senators, staff, and guards stared open-mouthed at them. Lexi swallowed and touched at her tangled mess of hair. She wished she'd had time to change. But her self-consciousness disappeared when Anax glanced at her, love in his eyes. His wounds made him look like every bit the warrior prince, his dark hair wild but entrancing. If she looked to him the way he did to her, she was beautiful.

Lexi grabbed his hand and stood firmly at his side. Lord Solon's slitted gaze dropped to their hands. In the audience, a senator gasped at the scandal. Lexi didn't care.

"Before you vote," Anax said, projecting his voice throughout the room, "you should consider the voices of the people. Our people, who we serve as their leaders. I've come from the plaza. Protests have started already. The people are demanding we continue peacefully co-existing with our neighbors. We have new trading partners and new products boosting our economy." Anax pointed an accusatory claw. "My father wants you to conquer these people to obtain their goods and enslave them. Why is it necessary to take what they give willingly?"

"Because they are less than us," King Xenobaccus marched forward, utter hatred in his eyes. "They are not Hyra's blessed. We are the goddess's chosen people. She means us to rule. Not just the Alliance planets, but all the planets."

Some senators were nodding along with the king. Lexi stomped down her rage. Just because Earth wasn't as advanced didn't mean her people deserved enslavement. She took a step forward to punch Anax's slimy asshole of a father, but her mate wouldn't let go of her hand. Instead, he spun her until her back was facing the senators.

"If Hyra thinks the people of the Alliance planets unworthy, why would she bless a human with her mark?" His warm hands traced around her neck, making her shiver, and lifted her blond hair, barring her neck for all to see. "Why would she make Alexandra Seymour my mate, my naika, if she wanted us to conquer her planet?"

All at once, the senate chamber exploded into noise. Lexi couldn't see any of the senators, but their voices crashed into her. A few senators dropped into prayer, like Lexi having the matebond mark made her a messiah. Other simply shouted questions or disbelief. Lexi couldn't hear anything clearly, but Anax bared his fangs at her, a wicked, victorious grin. She couldn't help but smile back at him.

Out of the corner of her eye, King Xenobaccus pulled a knife from his robes and charged forward.

Lexi didn't have to scream. Her flinch was enough. Anax turned and struck, knocking his father off his feet with a single blow. The dagger slid across the stage to land near Lord Solon.

The king pressed onto his elbows. "Pick it up, you coward."

Lord Solon stared at Anax and Lexi in shock. "Is it true? Has Hyra blessed you with a matebond?"

Anax glared down at his father but took Lexi's hand and held it up proudly. "It's true, my lord. Hyra has blessed our union."

Something overtook Lord Solon's face, a wave of devotion. He must have been a religious male. He turned back to the senators and shouted, "Hyra has made her will clear, senators. King Xenobaccus had tried to kill his heir. All in favor of removing King Xenobaccus from the throne and crowning Prince Anax Yio'hyra in his place?"

The senators didn't shout assent but tapped at their wristbands and tablets. A holo-screen to the side of the stage flashed to life, quickly tallying the votes. 100-0 in favor of Anax.

"A completely unanimous vote," Lord Solon declared. He turned on the king, on his former ally, and gestured to the guards. "Remove this criminal from these holy chambers at once."

The king climbed to his feet and banged his cane into the floor. "I am your king! You can't do this to me."

"We can, father," Anax said.

Lexi couldn't help but grin. "The people have spoken."

"You're traitors, every last one of you." Guards approached King Xenobaccus, Captain Dexus at the front, but he whacked at them with his cane. "This is not over. It will not be over until every planet bows before Herkleios."

Anax wrapped his arms around Lexi. She snuggled into his side. No matter how much he hated his father, it must have been hard to watch the male he had admired fall so far. Lexi kissed his shoulder.

Anax glanced down at her. "This wouldn't have been possible without you, naika."

She grinned. "Or without you, naikos."

Anax leaned in to kiss her—

The king rammed the jewel of his cane into the floor. The red smashed, made of little more than decorative glass. Underneath, two gemstones glowed, one a strong blue and the other a dimmer green. The green gem switched to red. Exactly like Lexi's bracelet every time she lowered her personal shield for transportation.

She jolted forward. "No!"

King Xenobaccus disappeared in a flash of light.

EPILOGUE

LEXI

Lexi tucked her head against Anax's side and let out a long yawn.

"Did I tire you out, naika?"

"You did, naikos." Lexi kissed the scales at his shoulder. Anax threw a hand over his head and bared his fangs. Her heart stuttered at his proud grin. He had every reason to be arrogant. Pillows and blankets scattered the floor of their hotel suite, all torn from the bed during their lovemaking. Lexi didn't need fabric when she had a Herkleian male to keep her warm. If anyone got a glimpse through their window, their naked, entangled bodies might scandalize them, but that'd require scaling to the penthouse floor.

"Do you think we upset our guests by leaving early?" From her vantage point at Anax's side, she had a glimpse out paned windows, overlooking the Parisian nightscape. The Eiffel Tower glittered in the distance. When Anax had asked where Lexi wanted her engagement party, she had immediately known the answer. Every girl wanted to get engaged in Paris, right?

"I doubt they noticed we left, naika," Anax murmured, drawing his claws down the side of her face. "The music was blaring and they had just brought out a second course of that delicious meat. What was it called again? Loberster?"

Lexi snorted. Close enough. She had an entire section of the buffet set-up to serve lobster, from mashed potatoes to bisque to biscuits. It had been her favorite part of the ballroom until Anax arrived.

They had scheduled their engagement party to coincide with the re-signing of Earth's treaties. After King Xenobaccus fled Herkleios, the senate voted to install Anax in his place. They had crowned him within a day, but mending fences with the Intergalactic Alliance took far longer. Anax—now King Anax Yio'hyra—had traveled to each of the twelve Alliance planets to re-assure them their treaties were still in place. With Earth, they had even wanted them re-signed.

Lexi had spent the morning pacing the hotel while her mom and Olivia took turns assuring her that her fiancé wouldn't miss his own engagement party. She never doubted him. It was the Earth politicians she mistrusted. Not to mention her slimy uncle, who wanted his alliance even more now that Xenobaccus had fled.

But when Anax had walked through the ballroom's double doors, dressed all in gold, from his tight pants to jeweled pauldrons, Lexi's fears had immediately disappeared. Only to be replaced by the knowledge she wasn't going to make it through the night without jumping him.

She had lasted a little over two hours.

She drew circles across his pecs. The huge diamond-like stone of her engagement ring twinkling in the light. "Do you have any meetings tomorrow?"

"I'm all yours for the rest of the week, naika."

"The week? Don't we have to return to Herkleios?" Lexi had spent every moment she could savoring her home planet. Anax had even arranged for early flights for her mom and Olivia, giving Lexi every minute with her family. Both would attend her wedding, but the governments of Earth and Herkleios were still negotiating ordinary travel. Lexi couldn't beg for exceptions for her own family and friends.

He pushed up onto an elbow and claimed her lips in a single swoop. Lexi's tired body flared to life. She threaded her hands through his hair, aiming for the smooth base of his horns. Before she could grasp them, he pulled back. "You have spent the last two months by my side, travelling the galaxy to ensure the Intergalactic Alliance's future. I thought you deserved a rest. A treat. Earth is your home, Lexi. You need to spend time with your family and friends."

Her heart lifted. "I love you, Anax."

"And I love you, Lexi." His thumb came up to brush her lips. Electricity sparked between them.

Lexi couldn't wait any longer.

She threw one leg over him and climbed aboard with a smile on her face. His slitted pupils dilated. Lexi traced her fingers across his chest, his neck, his jawline. She gripped his horns. He growled. Beneath her, his cock hardened, the scaled ridges swelling for her.

She gave a gentle tug to his horns. "Here, boy."

Anax responded obediently, raising his lips to meet hers. She poised her wet core over his shaft, ready to impale herself—

A knock sounded at the door.

Lexi paused, the tip of him nudging at her entrance. She gazed into his slitted blue eyes. "I will kill whoever is at that door."

He managed a strained grin. "I'll happily assist you, naika."

"Your Majesty?" Captain Dexus called through the gilded wood. "I'm sorry to interrupt, but I have urgent news."

Lexi slid half an inch lower. She swallowed her moan, but Anax couldn't stop his growl. The tendons in his neck corded with the pressure.

After a few seconds, he managed, "Tell me through the door, Dexus."

"Are you sure, Your Majesty?"

"Yes," Anax and Lexi snapped together.

Captain Dexus paused. "It's about your brother, Your Majesty."

Anax looked a minute away from murder. "I have multiple brothers, Dexus."

"Eryx, Your Majesty. Prince Eryx has returned to Herkleios."

Anax froze beneath her as Lexi's jaw dropped. Eryx? The same Eryx who King Xenobaccus chased off Herkleios, breaking Anax's heart? Lexi started to climb off her fiancé, ready to let Dexus in—

Anax grabbed her thigh and flipped her onto the mattress. In a single motion, he thrust into her, his hard cock filling her to the brim. Lexi couldn't contain her moan this time. It escaped her lips, a high-pitched sound. Captain Dexus didn't reply, but he had certainly heard.

Lexi didn't even care.

"Tell me the rest later, Dexus," Anax said huskily. "I'm rather preoccupied at the moment."

"Are you sure?" Lexi burned with need, but this was Anax's brother. "You haven't heard from him in three years—"

Anax swallowed the rest of her question with a kiss. He hooked his thumbs beneath her knees and spread her legs wider. With his next thrust, he sank deeper. Lexi grabbed the headboard, her back arching. The rest of the room, the rest of the galaxy, disappeared from her mind. All that remained was Anax on top of her, his sharp horns, fanged smile, and azure scales. Like a god come to life, ready to fuck her brains out.

Almost like he sensed her thought, his smile turned wicked. "Beg me to fuck you, naika."

Lexi shivered. She'd never grow tired of that. Never grow tired of him. Her Anax. Her king. Her mate. "Fuck me, naikos. Fuck me hard."

Thank you for reading! Wondering what will happen

when Anax's brother, Prince Eryx, returns to Herkleios? He'll be right in time for an intergalactic royal wedding… and the return of Xenobaccus.

ANAX BONUS SCENE

LEXI

Chapter 4, where our star-crossed lovers meet in the ship's atrium, was originally from Lexi's perspective in our first draft. When we realized we needed to get into Anax's head more in the beginning chapters, we re-wrote it from his viewpoint.

Want to know what Lexi thought of our bad boy prince? Read on...

Lexi followed Kynna to a domed atrium in the center of the ship. While the hallways of *The Queen Niobe* were white and sleek, any space where the Herkleians spent time was colorful and cheery. Metal arches converged at the peak of the ceiling, twisted with glowing vines and flowers. Lexi ran her fingers across bright purple flowers near the entrance, the petals nearly the size of her hand. She knew the name of almost every flower on Earth. Now, she had an entire planet's ecology to discover. A warmth of excitement filled her chest.

"Thank you, Kynna."

"My lady." Kynna gestured into the center of the room, where various pitchers and kettles weighted down a levitating bar. Chatting

Herkleians in colorful garments and gowns occupied small oval tables scattered around the bar. A few of the aliens glanced in Lexi's direction, but they quickly turned their attention back to their own drinks. This must be the Herkleian version of a Starbucks.

Lexi approached the center bar alone. Kynna settled into a spot near the wall. Through the plants lining the room, Lexi noticed a dozen other attendants staying out of sight. Perhaps she would take her drink to go. She'd much rather stay with Kynna than nobility.

Lexi scanned the bartop, but nothing looked familiar. Bright, luminous liquid filled nearly a dozen glass pitchers. To their side, kettles steamed, boiling a brown liquid. Perhaps something like coffee. Unfortunately, there was no one to ask and nothing was labelled. Lexi grabbed a mug and filled herself a cup. She brought it to her lips, but someone cleared their throat behind her.

Lexi yelped and spun, but she knew who it was before she spotted him. Her heart fluttered at the sight of Anax. He had switched out of his tight gold pants, white sash, and military awards for the Herkleian version of casual. His pants were black and smooth over powerful legs, his boots reaching mid-calf. Her cheeks heated at the sight. The jeweled hilt of a sabre rested against his belt. His chest was bare like every other Herkleian male she had encountered, the rippling of his toned scales enchanting her eyes. He wore leather-like shoulder pauldrons, two straps across above his pecs. When she finally reached the ice blue of his slitted eyes, his gaze stabbed through her, reading every little hint of her desire. His lips twisted, flashing a bit of fang.

The fluttering in her heart spread to her stomach, but she straightened. This was her future brother-in-law. Nothing more. "Is there something I can help you with?"

He reached out. Lexi nearly fainted, but he traced his claws across the edge of her cup. "Krojs is extremely strong. You add a small amount to a glass of water to dilute the syrup. If you were to drink this whole cup, you'd be plagued by hallucinations for days."

Lexi nearly dropped the cup. "Hallucinations?"

Anax took the cup from her hand and placed it on the bar. "Probably. No human had ever tried it."

Lexi threw up her hands. "I just want something with caffeine."

"What is caffeine?"

Lexi pursed her lips. How did one describe caffeine? Spicy bean juice? "It's liquid energy. I need it to get through my day."

"The quinta fruit has properties that help people stay awake." He grabbed the red pitcher at the end of the bar and poured her a glass. Even though she hadn't asked for his help. Again.

She took the glass from him anyway. The quinta juice bubbled like an energy drink, but instead of tasting like a weird blend of chemicals and sugar, it reminded her of something floral with berry undertones. It was delicious. Hopefully the juice was as potent as her typical morning coffee. "You really have a thing for feeding people."

"It's custom for males to serve their female companions. I don't mind in the least." He turned his back to her to reach across the bartop. Her eyes went straight to his toned ass. She unconsciously licked her lips. Lexi jolted. She had to stop this. She chugged the juice to hide her feelings.

"I think I can take it from here."

His lips quirked, her heart twinging in response. "As you wish, princess."

She shuddered at the word. "Don't call me that."

"Then what should I call you?"

"You shouldn't call me anything." With the timber of his voice, he could call her anything he wanted. But he couldn't. She wouldn't ruin her betrothal, even if the alien she was meant to marry was eighteen and showed no interest in her. "Better yet, how about you stop speaking to me all together?"

Anax's lip quirked, flashing the sharpness of his fang into the light. How would it feel grazing against her skin? Lexi almost pinched herself. She needed to get away from him. She couldn't control her thoughts when he was near. "And I thought we were having such fun together," Anax teased.

"Look." Lexi crossed her arms and put on her most serious expression. She needed to end this, one and for all. "I'm not interested in this back-and-forth banter thing we seem to have going. As a matter of fact, I'm not interested in speaking to you at all. I am marrying your brother and I will join your family. There will be no funny business between us."

He flinched at the mention of his brother, but dropped into a smooth bow. "I will treat you as I would any female family member of mine, Alexandra."

"Lexi."

His forehead furrowed. "Pardon?"

"My name is Lexi." At his confusion, she continued, "Alexandra is my full name. I don't use it. People call me Lexi."

"Ah. I see." He clearly didn't. The cocky prince was gone, something more studious in his place. "Is this a common Earth custom?"

"I guess." She frowned. "You don't have nicknames on Herkleios?"

"What is a nickname?"

"I guess that answers my question," she muttered to herself. Lexi shuffled down to the end of the bar and stopped in front of a basket of pastries. The muffin-like objects were purple and dotted with pink berries. Lexi pursed her lips, considering, but she couldn't focus given the heat that was Anax's body at her side. He was like a radiator. Damn, Herkleians were hot—both physically and temperature-wise. She raised an eyebrow at him. "Can I help you with something?"

"I would do my family a disservice if I didn't ensure you had settled in well." He gestured at a muffin with blue specks. "Try one."

"What's in it?"

"Ganja berries. They're quite sweet." He paused, a playful look entering his eyes. "I love to suck on them."

Lexi's entire body jolted like she was hit with electricity. Her nipples hardened into nubs, eagerly volunteering to be sucked. She hoped they weren't poking through her dress. Lexi wanted to slap a hand across her chest, but instead she grabbed one of the muffins before turning on her heels and marching for the door. But in their conversation, they had circled the bar. Lexi was storming in the wrong direction. Crap. Anax settled at her side before she could turn around.

Lexi eyed him. "Can I explore the atrium on my own?"

He folded his hands gently behind his back, the pose of a gentleman—

gentlemale?—but his eyes hungry. "You could, but Herkleians are a social bunch and someone will surely approach you. You may think I'm bad, but you might feel differently if left alone to face the courtiers."

Lexi stiffened and eyed the aliens around her. She had noticed them peeking at her, but had ignored them. "Why? Are they not fond of humans?'

"They're used to all kinds of species at court, but there are a few who still believe Herkleians are superior." She paled. Lexi hadn't even considered that. What if everyone at her new home hated humans? When he saw her expression, he quickly added, "Fear not, my father has worked hard to make our planet a space where all our allies are welcome."

"Then how could they be any worse than you?"

"Because—" Anax leaned in close like he was going to tell her a secret "—

they're insufferable gossips."

A laugh slipped out of Lexi despite her best effort to hide it. Anax howled in response, a beastly sound that sent a shiver down her spine.

He noticed her tremor. "Forgive me, Lexi. That is simply how we show amusement, much like your laughter."

"No, that's alright. I liked it." She flushed. Liked it? She had, but she couldn't believe she had said it aloud.

"I like how yours sounds, too. Like the whistling bird in our gardens."

Lexi's cheeks went bright red. Shit. It was easier to resist him when he was being an asshole. If he started being nice and funny, Lexi was done for. Lexi forced her attention to the flower display around them, but she couldn't ignore his stare. It caressed across her skin, a warm prickle. A glance from a lover, not a brother-in-law.

Lexi needed to leave. Now. She couldn't let herself fall for the wrong alien prince. If that meant spending all her time in her room to avoid him, so be it. "If you'll excuse me, I must get back to my room."

She spun on her heel and ran from the room before Anax could even reply.

ERYX

BRIDE TO AN ALIEN PRINCE, BOOK 2

ONE

OLIVIA

"I hate space travel," Olivia muttered into the toilet, her knuckles white as she gripped the rim. The cabin rumbled, her stomach swirling again. She curled into a ball on the floor. Cars and planes made her queasy, but apparently spaceships were the real killer. The *USS Pegasus* had left Earth nearly two days ago. Olivia hadn't lasted longer than an hour before the motion sickness—space sickness?—hit her. The docking procedure didn't make it any better. The overhead speakers declared the *USS Pegasus* was docking with *The Queen Avra*. It'd been repeating the same message for ten minutes.

Ten minutes too long.

That was what Olivia got for trying to be supportive. When her best friend, Lexi, had told Olivia she was marrying alien royalty, Olivia did what any good friend would do—offer to help plan the wedding. But when Olivia imagined planning her friends' weddings, she always assumed they'd be looking at venues and stuffing themselves at cake tastings on Earth. Where else would they do it?

Everything had changed a year ago when the Herkleians made first contact with Lexi's asshole uncle, tech billionaire Grayson Seymour. The towering aliens with sharp horns and blue scales had offered Earth a position within the Intergalactic Alliance, a collection of twelve planets that shared technology and resources. But unlike the other Alliance planets, Earth didn't have a single royal family to seal the deal through marriage. The Herkleians had negotiated with Mr. Seymour instead—which was why Olivia's best friend was a day away from becoming a freaking alien queen.

When Olivia had first learned of the arrangement, she had tried to talk her friend out of it. Now, six months later, Lexi was happy and in love, her fiancé, Anax, not only an alien king but also her soulmate. Well, not exactly a soulmate. Lexi had said they were matebonded, but Olivia was sure the terms were close enough. Her friend really had hit the jackpot. How many others could claim a super-hot royal alien as a husband?

The rumbling stopped before a ding sounded throughout Olivia's cabin. "Docking successful. Welcome to *The Queen Avra*. An attendant will arrive shortly at your door to lead you to your new chambers."

Olivia peeled herself from the floor and crawled into the cabin. After pulling on her classiest pair of ripped jeans, she tied her black hair in a quick topknot. She didn't need a mirror to know it looked flawless. The benefits of being a trained hair stylist. She grabbed the handle of her suitcase, prepared to run from her tiny jail cell of a cabin. The sooner she left the *USS Pegasus*, the better. Everyone onboard was human, either friends of Lexi or delegates from various Earth countries. The medic had given Olivia some pills, but unfortunately her pain wouldn't go away until arrival on *The Queen Avra*, a Herkleian ship-turned-station. Her daydreams of its stabilizers and advanced medical equipment had kept her alive over the last forty-eight hours.

The door to her room swished as she approached. "Olivia!"

The ship rumbled out a final groan. Olivia slapped her hands across her mouth, her stomach rolling. Lexi stood in the doorway, eyes wide, her blond hair wrapped around a halo-spiked tiara and her gown decorated with sparkling burgundy scales. She was absolutely beautiful.

Olivia shoved past her and hurled into a potted plant.

"Oh, God, what's wrong with her?" A light hand touched her back.

"The doctor on board reported her space sick, my lady." From the corner of her eye, Olivia saw the outline of a second person, nearly a foot taller than Lexi's five-three frame. "Nothing too serious."

"Can you get some water, Kynna?"

Kynna. Lexi's Herkleian attendant. Olivia had heard about her during their video calls. What a great first impression for Lexi's new friend.

Olivia tried to push to her feet, but almost lost her balance. "You didn't tell me this would happen."

"It never happened to me," Lexi said.

Of course Olivia was cursed with space sickness and not Lexi. Her friend always had the best luck.

Hence the hot alien fiancé thing.

Kynna returned from the cabin. Olivia tried not to gape. She had seen pictures, but Kynna was her first in-the-flesh alien. Her blue dragon-like scales glimmered and radiated a gentle heat that Olivia felt across the hall. Herkleians had hair like humans—Kynna's the color of the midnight sky—but their bright-colored irises were slitted and black antler-like horns sprouted from their heads.

She offered Olivia a cup of water, her black-clawed fingers wrapped around the glass. "I added a refresher tablet to the water."

"A what?"

"The little square mounted to the wall beside your sink?" When Olivia stared blankly, Kynna continued, "We add refresher tablets to water for our breath. A little gift from the Herkleian engineers that helped build this ship."

So that wasn't a broken soap dispenser? Oops. Olivia took the glass cup and gulped the water down in a single second. When she huffed out her breath, she smelled something fruity. Nice.

Olivia tried on a tired smile and faced her friend. "Let's try this again."

"I'm so excited you're here!" Lexi opened her arms wide. "I haven't had a hug in months."

Without further explanation, Lexi crushed Olivia in a giant hug.

"In months?" Olivia choked out.

Lex squeezed tighter. "Herkleians don't hug."

Not the worst cultural practice. Olivia bit her lip to stop herself from saying so. Lexi was a hugger. Always had been. Once at a bar during college, Olivia had said she didn't like hugs. Lexi insisted on hugging her a thousand times that night. Like exposure therapy, a part of Olivia almost liked Lexi's hugs now. Almost. Maybe it was because she missed her. The friends hadn't gone over two months apart since Lexi's internship after sophomore year. Olivia didn't know what she was going to do without her bestie. It wasn't like the future Queen of Herkleios could visit Earth on the regular.

Lexi pulled away after a minute. "There's so much I have to tell you. But first, I want to show you something."

THE QUEEN AVRA was a marvel compared to Earth's first ship, the *USS Pegasus*. Instead of interiors that reminded Olivia of the military bases she'd grown up in, uncut glowing rocks threaded through the gold walls and ceilings. The floor wasn't boring black, but made of cobalt blue marble mixed with sparks of gold. Twisting staircases emerged from the stone and led to different floors. Strange, glowing plants swayed within the pot holders, bright pink and purple and blue petals near the size of Olivia's head.

Lexi hadn't stopped talking since they left the Earth ship, telling her about every little thing that had happened in the last six months. Olivia had heard most of it, but, damn, her friend had been busy. Olivia tried to take it all in, but she was still feeling shaky. When Kynna offered to take Olivia's bags to her new room, Olivia had almost begged the alien woman to bring her, too. She needed to crawl into bed ASAP to survive the wedding tomorrow.

"How much further to the venue?" Lexi had insisted on showing Olivia the options for their venue, whatever that meant. "Isn't it a little late to be making changes?"

Lexi waved away her concern. "It will make more sense if I just show you."

They continued down the hall. Olivia was glad to see Lexi so happy. While Olivia rarely supported marrying someone after only months of dating, she made an exception for Lexi. Though, Olivia wasn't *only* opposed to getting married quickly. More like marriage altogether. Olivia had watched her parents go through a bitter divorce when she was eleven and had decided then she'd never marry. Lexi's parents' love story had ended with the death of her father from cancer, making her as wary of relationships as Olivia... until her alien king had changed all that.

"Here." Lexi waved her hands in front of double doors, which slid open to reveal a bright white room. Olivia waited for her eyes to adjust, but they didn't. Everything from the floors to the walls was white with no end in sight.

She squinted. "What is this place?"

"It's super cool! When Anax told me about it, I knew it'd be the perfect place for our wedding."

Maybe six months on another planet had fried her friend's brain. "This white void of a room?"

"No, silly. Let me show you." Lexi grabbed her hand and dragged her forward. Once they stood in the center, Lexi tapped at a gemstone on her golden bracelet. A screen projected out of the gem, displaying block-shaped letters. After a second, Olivia's newly implanted translator switched the Herkleian words to English. "Scene 508."

The room plunged into darkness. Olivia shrieked. What the hell was going on? Before she asked, a light burst through the room. It didn't come alone this time. Sound and scent followed. Olivia now stood in a lush alien jungle. Green-blue moss climbed the base of towering trees, their purple-leaved branches creating a twisting canopy overhead. Birds and animals and insects chattered around her, but she didn't spot any on the twisting vines around her. Glowing flowers emitted thick but sweet smells, mixed with the familiar scent of dirt. No matter what planet Olivia was on, dirt smelled the same. But Olivia wasn't on another planet. *The Queen Avra* was a space station, parked halfway between Earth and Herkleios to allow people from both worlds to attend the royal wedding of the century.

Lexi twirled past her. "Isn't it amazing?"

Olivia could only gape. She accepted the room changing to *look* like a jungle, but not to *feel* like a jungle. Even the humidity seemed real. She drifted toward the nearest tree. Her hand didn't fall through the hologram but settled on its solid trunk. A real freaking alien tree. "What the hell is going on?"

"That's what I said my first time, too. Honestly, I have no clue how this works. All I know is the replication room can mimic the sights, smells, and sounds of any location."

"Any location?" Olivia tried to snap her jaw shut, but it was too much to take in. The Herkleians had amazing technology, but this was almost beyond her dreams. "So you can get married anywhere you want on Earth?"

"Not just Earth." Lexi threw her hands to the sky. "Anywhere in the galaxy. This scene is from a jungle on Yazd, one of the Alliance planets. Anax took me there once." She sighed, almost dreamily.

A brief pang of envy twinged through Olivia's heart. She'd dated, but no one had ever made her sigh like that. "I'll admit, this is probably the coolest thing I've ever seen, but you struggle to choose what takeout to order. How are you going to decide with literally endless options?"

"I know, right?" Lexi flicked at her bracelet again and two chairs appeared. She plopped into one. "Not really knowing what all the options are helps narrow it down a bit. But do I want a summer wedding? A fall wedding? A beach wedding? Maybe even a Guroverian desert wedding?"

Olivia dropped into the seat beside her. She tilted back her head and scanned the purple canopy. "Well, I have no idea what that last one was, but show me your favorites."

"Okay." Lexi sat straighter. "I have a top five. I know it's a royal wedding, so I'm not supposed to go minimal, but I think an outdoor wedding might mute the formality of it all."

"Outdoors it is. Like a beach wedding?"

"Maybe." She bit her lip and paused. "I'm not sure yet. Let me show you. Scene 245."

Olivia nearly tumbled off her chair as it sank into thick yellow sand. She jumped off it and spun. The jungle trees behind her had disappeared, replaced by an endless blue ocean, waves crashing against the nearby shore. Salty wind grazed across her face and tugged at the edges of her burgundy leather jacket. She raised her hand to block the bright sun from her eyes.

Lexi strolled past her, closer to the water. "Is it too hot? And what about the sand? It isn't real, but it feels real as long as you stay in the room."

Olivia shrugged. "At least your guests won't find any in the weirdest places days later?"

Lexi tapped at her bracelet again. This time, instead of a single chair, nearly a hundred popped onto the sand, separated into two sections. Tied to the back of each seat was an artful bow of pink peonies mixed with glowing Herkleian flowers. Exactly like the sketches Lexi had shared during their chats last month. In the aisle, larger flower displays exploded into life. Olivia hadn't thought to ask how her friend planned to get Earth flowers in outer space. Apparently, Olivia had her answer.

"It looks amazing, Lexi." Olivia walked down the aisle to stand next to her friend and the space for the altar. "Do you like it?"

She pursed her lips. "Hmm."

With another flick, the sky dimmed to night and torches flickered into place. "Herkleian wedding ceremonies are always at night."

"It's still beautiful."

Lexi settled into place at the end of the aisle. The air in front of her wobbled for a moment before a seven-foot-tall Herkleian with towering horns, silky black hair, and slitted blue eyes appeared. Unlike the chairs, flowers, and torches, he was definitely a hologram. Unless Lexi had somehow transported her husband-to-be into the room.

Olivia stumbled back. "Wow."

"Stand in the spot behind me." Lexi ran halfway down the aisle as a dozen other hologram-people appeared. Some had familiar faces —Lexi's mother, her friend from high school, and her two blond cousins. But the groom's party was entirely alien, starting with King Anax's best man. Under sharp, black horns and dark green hair, intense purple eyes pierced through Olivia's core. Her heart fluttered. The alien male had broad, muscular shoulders and azure scales marred by tiny scars, but she barely noticed at the sight of his ripped abs. Herkleian males didn't wear shirts, preferring shoulder sashes or leather-like pauldrons. Something she had thought would make a wedding uncomfortable until this exact moment. Olivia's eyes traced lower to powerful legs in tight, dark pants. Her mouth went dry.

"Olivia?"

Olivia ripped herself from her thoughts. Lexi had said something —possibly more than one something—but Olivia hadn't heard anything. She pointed at the alien. Looking into his intense purple eyes again made her flush, so she spun her gaze back to Lexi. "Who is that?"

Lexi's brow creased, but she answered, "Oh, him? Eryx. Anax's older brother."

His brother? Olivia internally smacked herself. She couldn't lust after Anax's brother. But she couldn't force her eyes away from the male, either. It was a cliché to hook up within a bridal party, but

Olivia had never wanted it more. Hot damn, he was handsome. And strong. And scarred. Warmth flooded her chest before sinking lower.

"Are you okay?" Lexi came forward and reached for Olivia's forehead. "You look flushed."

Of course she looked flushed. Olivia wanted to scale Lexi's future brother-in-law like a tree. "I'm fine. Perfectly fine. What were you saying?"

"I have no idea how we're going to get good pictures. My half of the bridal party is at least a foot shorter than Anax's."

"Oh." Olivia's eyes trailed back to Eryx. Olivia had a few inches on Lexi, but even she was short next to the seven-foot muscled alien. "I don't think anyone will notice. Not when we'll be standing next to half-a-dozen shirtless men."

Lexi snorted. "I will warn you, Liv. The males come off a little... strong."

"A little strong?" Olivia's inner feminist went on high alert. "Are you telling me any minute a man is going to come in here and tell me how to live my life? You know I hate it when they do that."

"Don't be so dramatic. I'm just telling you they come from a culture where females rule and males take on the role of protector."

Olivia crossed her arms. "Okay, so exactly like home?"

"It's all talk back home, but here actions speak louder than words," Lexi replied. "Just don't freak out, is all. I'll warn my mom, cousins, and Rachel, too, but I know it will bother you especially."

Lexi tapped at her bracelet, flickering to another scene, this one of a meadow filled with glowing flowers, but Olivia barely noticed. Her mind drifted back to Eryx. Too bad he'd be an overprotective alpha. Or maybe that was exactly what she needed him to be. Less chance Olivia would drunkenly flirt with him during the reception.

Less chance, but never zero.

TWO

ERYX

Eryx kicked back his seat, stretching his long legs out in the glider's cockpit. He sank into the soft fabric of the chairs, the fresh scent of Pithi wood wafting through the small space. He ran his claws against the elbow rests. In the marketplace on Hathor, he could fetch a hundred credits for the seat alone, much less the entire glider. Eryx gave a curt shake of his head. He wasn't on Hathor anymore.

"We'll reach *The Queen Avra* in the next ten minutes," his brother, Anax, said from beside him. "I'll message the rest of the fleet that we've almost arrived."

"No thanks to Senator Oriel." When the senate needed the king to cast his tie-breaking vote a few days before his wedding, no one had expected him to go back to Herkleios. Especially Senator Oriel.

Anax grunted in reply, a noncommittal answer.

"She tried to use your wedding to her advantage, Anax. Oriel thought you wouldn't return, thereby voting quickly and in her favor." Eryx had missed some things about his home, but the politics weren't one. But as Anax's best man, Eryx had offered to make the return trip with him. His brother wanted to fully understand the debate, something Eryx couldn't fault him for. It already made him a better king than their father.

"I'm dealing with Senator Oriel." He tapped at the holo-screen projecting from the glider's dashboard, keeping his eyes on the controls. "You don't need to worry, brother."

Eryx had returned to Herkleios four months ago, but Anax still rarely met his gaze. He couldn't blame his brother. Anax and Eryx had been close their entire childhood. The heir and the spare, a year apart in age but almost raised as twins. They had done everything together—the same tutors, the same military training, the same continental tours. But that had changed when Eryx was forced off their homeworld. When their father, King Xenobaccus, had shared his plans to conquer their allies, the king had expected loyalty from his son. Eryx couldn't give it.

What had happened next was a blur even three years later. All he remembered was going to sleep in his chambers with a plan to expose his father and then waking in the hold of a Sutekan pirate ship. If the pirates hadn't crash-landed in the Amun desert on Hathor, would Eryx have survived to see this day? Eryx didn't concern himself with hypotheticals, but what he did know was that Anax hadn't learned the truth until recently. For three years, their father let his siblings think he had abdicated and disappeared in the middle of the night.

His brother—now King of Herkleios after their father's removal from the throne—had welcomed him back into the family, but they still hadn't settled back into their old rhythm of casual banter. Eryx feared maybe they never would. He wasn't the same person he was three years ago. The easygoing, playful prince had died in the deserts of Hathor. Having to fend for himself on a war-torn planet controlled by armed militias had changed him. The hardships of those years weighted down his once thundering howl and crooked grin.

Despite it all, he was determined for Anax to enjoy his own wedding—which meant playing pretend for another day or two.

What would a normal brother say?

"Last chance for any second thoughts," Eryx said, breaking the silence as they approached *The Queen Avra*. Through the glider's front window, the ship-turned-station nearly glowed, the gold of its exterior reflecting all the light from the nearest system star. As beautiful as his mother, its namesake.

Anax let out a howl of a laugh in response. "I appreciate it, brother, but there's nowhere else I'd rather be than at my mate's side."

Mate. The concept still confounded Eryx. When news had reached Hathor that his father had been overthrown and his younger brother installed on the throne, Eryx had immediately started counting his credits. It had taken him two months until he had enough to board a ship to Herkleios—only to arrive and discover his brother wasn't only king, but also had a matebond with an Earthling female. It wasn't even the Earthling thing that had surprised him. The dragon goddess Hyra hadn't granted a matebond to one of their people in over a century.

Eryx tried on his old crooked grin. It stretched at his lips oddly. "You can't say I didn't ask."

His brother finally looked away from the screen. The two of them had similar facial structure, but Anax's eyes were a slitted blue to Eryx's slitted purple. Right now, they burned with emotion. Love. "One day you'll find someone who makes you feel the same way, Eryx."

"Perhaps." It wasn't the time to tell his brother he never planned on settling down. After the things Eryx had done, he wouldn't be a suitable partner. Hathor's civil war created the three main industries —fighting, healing, and scavenging. Eryx had trained in combat and quickly found himself in the warrior pits. Within a month, spectators were calling him the Butcher.

If it weren't for Doctor Sagara, he'd have become little more than an executioner and lost the last of his soul, drowned in blood. The Anpu militia had sat in the audience during his last fight, sizing him up. Instead, Doctor Sagara had offered him a small salary as a bodyguard and assistant. The Guroverian male had owned a practice on his homeworld, but had sold everything to fly across the galaxy and help Hathorian refugees. Travel between the camps was treacherous. But once the doctor realized who Eryx was—and the level of his education—he trained him as a pupil.

But two years of healing couldn't erase the stains on his hands. Nothing would.

A message flashed across the glider's holo-screen. Docking procedures were being initiated. The hangar bay doors slid open, revealing a massive, gilded space dotted with spaceships. Mostly Herkleian ships, but also from a dozen other planets. All of the Intergalactic Alliance members had sent at least one ambassador. Eryx taped his claws nervously against the elbow rest.

Anax noticed the movement and bared his fangs. "Last chance for any second thoughts."

"Not funny." Eryx no longer blanched at the sight of blood or pulled away from carnage, but diplomacy was a different issue altogether. This wedding wasn't a simple royal wedding—it was an intergalactic royal wedding. The uniting of Earth and Herkleios. Anax's bride, Lexi, thought her special day a dream, but Eryx imagined it a nightmare. Nothing could be worse than a station full of politicians and elite, all conniving and backstabbing. Eryx would rather be sentenced to an eternity in Hadus.

The glider landed in the hanger bay with a slight rattle. With a few quick taps, Anax shut the systems down. The glass canopy above their heads opened as a set of stairs expanded from the side. Three attendants immediately climbed the steps and grabbed for their bags in the back compartment.

"Take you time, Lord Steward." As Anax rose from his seat, he glanced at his gold wristband. "I won't be returning to my suite right away. Do you know where Lady Alexandra is?"

Areti, the Lord Steward of the royal household, dropped into a low bow, his horns almost touching the ground. "She went to the replication room with her Earthling friend, Your Majesty."

"Thank you." He re-attached the hilt of his sabre to his golden belt before nodding at Eryx. "Will you walk with me, brother?"

"Of course." Eryx would spend every opportunity he got with his brother. When he first returned to Herkleios, everyone had wondered if he'd challenge his brother for the throne. He was the eldest child of King Xenobaccus, after all. But Herkleios was no longer his home. He hadn't told Anax yet, but he planned on leaving after the wedding. Eryx wasn't sure where he'd go, but anywhere was better than the gilded cage that was the palace.

He reached for his travel bag, but Areti snatched it and placed it on a droid cart. The little robot hovered off the ground and flew away before he could say anything. Areti dipped into a small bow with a polite, "Your Highness."

Eryx tried not to frown. He couldn't even carry his own bag as a prince. "Thank you, Lord Steward."

As quickly as they had appeared, Areti and the attendants climbed back down the stairs. Eryx released his frown. Anax's half-smile turned into a full bearing of fangs. He smacked his brother on the shoulder. "Having a full staff isn't that terrible, Eryx."

"If you say."

Anax climbed from his seat to the stairs, Eryx following behind. When the two brothers stretched to full height on the platform, the hangar space around them fell silent. Dozens of technicians and engineers dropped into bows. Not at Eryx, but at his brother, Anax. King Anax. Eryx didn't want the title anymore, but he had grown up expecting it. Herkleians used to drop into bows at his father's presence.

"The same way they'll one day bow before you."

Eryx banished his father's voice from his memory.

"The replication room is on the other side of the station," Anax said. "We'll request transport."

The brothers both tapped at the green gemstones on their golden wristband, flicking them to red. With their personal shields lowered, the station's internal transporters locked in on their location. A tingling sensation slithered across Eryx's scales for an instant before the world around him changed. No longer was he standing in a busy hangar, but instead a gilded corridor with blue floors and glowing, crystalized ceilings. The hall wasn't busy, but it overlooked an open atrium, four floors of space over an idyllic seating area.

The fruity tang of tini-scented cleaning products wafted past Eryx's nose. His nostrils flared. He had once thought nothing of the scent, but after three years in the wild, he couldn't help but notice how fake it was. Like everything else here.

"Anax," a high-pitched, female voice shrieked.

Eryx turned from the atrium to watch his brother's mate, Lexi, leap at her fiancé. The human's yellow-haired head barely reached Anax's shoulders, but his brother helped, swinging her into his arms. In their spin, Eryx caught sight of their faint matebond marks—a unique pattern of swirling stars at the nape. His own mother, Queen Avra, had tattooed a mark on her neck in dedication to his father after their marriage. It had flaked off in a bout of the scale rot that killed her.

Eryx tried not to shudder.

Lexi placed her pink-skinned hands on Anax's face, caressing from his cheekbones to the base of his dark horns. Eryx glanced away. It wasn't taboo to display affections in public on Herkleios, but the Hathorians didn't even dare touch hands in public.

"You remember Olivia, don't you, naikos?"

"I do, naika," his brother replied, rubbing his nose against his mate's.

When his brother shuffled to the side, a second human came into sight. Eryx stiffened. Bright blue eyes looked directly into his. Hair the deepest of black curled into a neat ball on the top of her head, but a few loose strands tickled the pale-pink color of her cheeks. Her skin. Eryx hadn't ever wanted to touch human skin before, but he had to quench the urge to trail his fingers across her cheeks. His eyes traced down her slender body, almost like he was in a trance. She was taller than Lexi, but still a foot shorter than any Herkleian female. Her soft curves were clothed in a leather jacket and a ripped blue fabric. The pink skin of her knees peeked through the blue.

If only *all* her clothes were like that.

"... and this is Eryx, Olivia. You saw his image earlier," his brother's mate finished.

Eryx jolted at the sound of his own name. "She saw my image earlier?"

A brighter pinkness had crept up the second human's face as Eryx stared, but at his voice, her skin flared to red. A beautiful color. What did it mean? She said nothing in reply but continued to stare at him.

"In the replication room," Lexi said, unaware of the tension. "We were planning out the wedding ceremony. You have to come see, Anax."

His brother bared his fangs. "I will be happy with whatever you decide, naika."

Lexi dropped from her mate's arms and grabbed for his hand. "You should come, too, Eryx. With my maid of honor and best man, we can do a test run."

"Test run?" At this point, Eryx was simply repeating everything Lexi said. What was wrong with him? He had seen beautiful females before, from dozens of species. None had him reacting like a youngling. He scratched absentmindedly at his neck.

"Yeah." Lexi wrapped an arm around Olivia's shoulder. The female stiffened. "You'll walk down the aisle together, then we'll follow—"

"No." The answer came not only from Eryx's lips, but from Olivia's as well. Their gazes clashed again. He didn't know why she said no, but Eryx knew he couldn't touch her. If he touched her once, he'd want to touch her again. And this human female—no matter how delectable—would only be a distraction, a reason for him to stay.

Lexi's forehead creased, perhaps in confusion. "Why not?"

"Sorry, Lex." Olivia put a hand to her forehead. "I just wanted to lie down. I didn't sleep well and was sick the entire trip. But it's important to you and I want you to have the wedding of your dreams. We can do a test run."

"It's okay. It's not that big a deal." Lexi reached out to put her hand on Olivia's shoulder. "Does your head still hurt? Eryx can show you to the infirmary—"

"I can't." Three pairs of eyes—two human and one Herkleian—swiveled toward him. Lexi and Anax's in curiosity, but Olivia's in what almost seemed like anger. Like she knew he was rejecting her. He couldn't care. Eryx didn't belong in gentle civilization anymore. "I have to... I have to go."

Eryx couldn't stand there a minute longer. He turned in his boots and marched in the other direction. Anywhere but here. An intense gaze trailed down his bare back, lingering on each pale scar. Not his brother's. Not Lexi's.

Olivia's.

Even once he slammed into his own quarters, halfway across the ship, the tingles of her gaze still tickled at his spine.

THREE

OLIVIA

"How does my hair look?" Rachel shoved Olivia ever so slightly to get a better view in the mirror. Olivia stiffened, focusing on the mascara wand in her hand. If she didn't have such steady hands—a necessity for a hair stylist—she'd have a streak of black dissecting her eyebrow.

"I love it," Lexi's cousin, Brittany, said.

"Yeah. It's nice." Brittany's sister, Lynn, wasn't nearly as convincing.

Olivia peeked over and barely concealed her laugh. Human stylists had accompanied them from Earth on the USS *Pegasus*, but as soon as Rachel had seen Herkleian hairstyles, she demanded one. Two of Anax's sisters, Elipida and Hatria, sat in levitating chairs in the suite's corner, their dark strands wrapped artfully around their bejeweled horns. Rachel's didn't look nearly as good. The stylist had tried her best, but Rachel's red curls looked like two pointy nubs.

Rachel grabbed a glowing Herkleian flower from a nearby vase. "How about this, too? With a clip?"

Olivia sprayed setting mist over her makeup and crossed the room without meeting the other bridesmaid's eyes. Hair stylist though she may be, Olivia had never liked Rachel. She was a vain gossip, but when Lexi's dad had died, Rachel had provided support long after the typical condolence period. She recognized that even though Lexi put on a brave face, she still needed extra kindness. For that, Olivia let what the woman said slide.

Olivia raised her wrist and tapped at her new, golden bracelet. The Herkleians provided each guest with a similar device, which worked like a smartwatch. When her finger touched the blue gem, a holo-screen flickered into life. Her translator implant quickly switched the words from Herkleian to English. Ten minutes until showtime.

Olivia clapped her hands, drawing everyone's attention. The bridal party had set up in a suite close to the replication room, but it'd still take time to walk there. Hundreds of diplomats from across the Intergalactic Alliance were in attendance. Olivia might not have as many responsibilities as a normal maid of honor, but it wasn't like any of Lexi's staff were going to tell them they were running late. "Ten minutes, guys. Time to get this show on the road."

"Guys?" Hatria whispered to Elipida. "There are no males in this room."

"Earthlings are odd," Elipida replied.

Olivia didn't bother shooting the princesses a glare. They were princesses, after all. Or perhaps one was a queen. Out of the thirteen royal Herkleian siblings, all but two were married—Eryx and the youngest brother, Phintias. Their spouses were all royals from other Intergalactic Alliance families. Lexi was the first non-royal to marry into the line. During all their chats over the past six months, Lexi had never said her fiancé's family made her feel unwelcome, but Olivia noticed and she only boarded *The Queen Avra* twenty-four hours ago.

"Let's see if Lexi's ready." Rachel ran across the room as fast as her dress allowed. The four human bridesmaids wore blush-pink sweetheart gowns with off-the-shoulder sleeves, whereas Elipida and Hatria dressed in Herkleian-style, white robes. Ornate embroidery and jewels weighed down their gold bodices to the point of them nearly toppling over. It was customary for Herkleian royalty to wear only white and gold to formal functions, but Olivia would be so pissed if someone else wore white to her wedding. Lexi had assured her she didn't mind.

Rachel threw open the door to the master suite. "Lexi!"

"I'm ready." Lexi was practically glowing as she emerged from the master, her mother on her one side and Kynna on the other. She had opted for an Earth-style wedding dress, but was switching to a Herkleian gown at the reception. Her flowing skirt led up to a tight bodice with sheer sleeves, crystals and floral lace appliques scattered across the pale fabric. Her train trailed behind her, her flower girls grabbing the edges to help her walk.

Olivia's eyes watered. Her best friend was getting married. To an alien king. She was literally living out every little girl's princess dream. "You're gorgeous, Lexi."

Her bright smile spread across her face. "Let's get married."

Lexi led the way to the replication room, attendants scurrying across the corridors around her. After hosting an intergalactic wedding, all the Herkleian staff would need a week off. Olivia had done more than her share of weddings, both with friends and as a hair stylist. She muttered a plea under her breath to not look like a complete fool with the tears of happiness she was sure to cry. Olivia always cried at weddings, especially if the bride and groom wrote their own vows. Lexi had dubbed her a 'marshmallow' between their third and fourth college friend's wedding—dry on the outside, but gooey within.

The guests had already been led from the reception atrium to the replication room, but a party of towering Herkleians stood outside the double doors. They had switched their warrior pauldrons for flowing shoulder sashes, the groomsmen somehow making the fabric look badass instead of girly. Probably something to do with their scaled, muscular torsos and sharp horns.

Anax stood at the front of the crowd, his tight pants gold, his sashes decorated with medals, and his crown a jeweled sunburst.

When his slitted eyes met Lexi, they filled with a quiet wonder. The bridal party stopped as Lexi threw herself at her mate, a gentle 'aww' escaping from more than Olivia's lips. Olivia didn't believe in true love, but Lexi and Anax had to be fated. What other male would look at her friend that way?

A shiver drifted up Olivia's spine and stopped at her neck.

She stiffened. Olivia didn't need to look to confirm who stared at her. Eryx stood to the right of his brother, clawed hands crossed gently behind his back. His gold pants were as tight as Anax's, but whereas the Herkleian king was toned and in decent shape, Eryx was absolutely ripped. His back muscles had muscles. Olivia didn't want to admit it, but they had featured in her dreams last night. Along with the rest of the male. Dream-Olivia had trailed her fingers across the scars of his scaled chest, the edges of his cheekbones, through his dark emerald hair to the base of his horns. She had almost shouted his name as she woke. Thank God she had her own private suite, otherwise she'd never hear the end of it from Rachel.

After a minute, Lexi finally detangled herself from Anax's arms. "Okay, I'm ready. Rachel, you're walking down with Orrin. Elipida and Hatria, Vasilax will escort you both—"

"Both?" Hatria asked.

"Argrix has not yet arrived, sister," Vasilax said, speaking of another royal brother. Olivia didn't remember all of Anax's siblings' names, but Lexi had grumbled about Prince Argrix this morning. How rude was it to RSVP and then not show? "It would be my honor to escort two beauties such as yourselves."

His sisters all but preened under the compliment, crisis averted. Lexi almost dropped in relief. "Brittany, Lynn, you two can take Gavrill and Mius. And the maid of honor with the best man, of course."

The best man. Eryx. Olivia would need to touch him. Her heart kicked into double time. He hadn't been the politest when he ran off yesterday, but that didn't bother Olivia. It made it easier for her infatuation. If he wasn't interested, then he couldn't one day break her heart. She'd dream about the strong, handsome alien, but their relationship wouldn't ever be real.

Eryx stepped into place at her side. His body radiated heat. Literally radiated. Olivia's hands and feet were always freezing. Having someone like him at her side would be a blessing for her circulation. Not that he was at her side permanently. Only for a few minutes. At most. "Get it together, Olivia," she muttered to herself.

Eryx held out his arm. "Get what together?"

Heat flared through her face. "Nothing. Nothing at all."

His forehead furrowed, but before he asked, Olivia forced her hand to his thick, scaled forearm. Electricity sparked down her arm. He stiffened at the touch.

The sooner they got down the aisle, the better.

The doors slid open, revealing a midnight forest with glowing flowers of pink, purple, and red. Lexi had selected her favorite scene with Olivia yesterday, but the beauty of it all still stole her breath away. Over a hundred guests—humans, Herkleians, and other aliens Olivia didn't recognize—sat in gilded chairs. A band of Herkleians lifted gilded instruments and strummed out a sweet melody, almost like the threading of violins.

The paired-off bridal party entered the room two at a time. Olivia shuffled forward, Eryx at her side. From the corner of her eyes, she noticed him staring. She kept her gaze straight on the beauty of the replication room. *Not* because she was avoiding him.

Kynna gestured Lynn and Mius into the room, leaving Olivia and Eryx the last couple before the bride and groom. A camera droid whizzed overhead. The entire Intergalactic Alliance watched this moment from across thirteen different planets. Olivia straightened and clenched her hands. Olivia had worked among celebrities for years in LA, but the enormity of this event wasn't comparable.

"You're very tense," Eryx murmured, his claws brushing gently across her skin.

Olivia tightened her hand on his arm, but she couldn't repress her shudder. Goosebumps broke across her arm and spread through her chest, over her sensitive nipples. God, she couldn't get aroused at a time like this. "Sorry."

The word came out sarcastic and defensive. Eryx's slitted purple eyes narrowed. Lexi had told her Herkleians didn't always get human jokes, but he had understood her tone well enough.

"You—"

Kynna snapped her claws, a light clicking sound. "It's your turn, Your Highness, Miss Olivia."

Eryx stopped whatever he was about to say and started forward, his long-legged strides nearly three of her steps. Whatever Olivia had imagined for her friend's wedding, it didn't involve being dragged down the aisle. "You think you could slow down, buddy?" she whisper-hissed, her smile still in place. "We don't all have giant legs. Besides, we're trying to move gracefully and you knocking me onto my face isn't exactly graceful."

"I just want this over with," he muttered.

"Same here." Olivia loved that her friend had found happiness, but the spotlight of a wedding made her nervous. She increased her smile, hoping the aliens and humans on either side of her didn't notice the strain. "I'm not exactly a fan of weddings, either, but this is my best friend's day. I will do everything in my power to making it fucking magical!"

Eryx snorted, a light, growly sound. Heat sparked in Olivia's core. But he slowed his pace, just enough that Olivia didn't have to run up the platform positioned before a huge waterfall.

When they reached the altar, Olivia pulled her hand from his deliciously muscled forearm. Before she slipped into her spot, Eryx dropped into a bow, his sharp horns stopping an inch from her face. "Thank you for allowing me to escort you, Olivia."

Everything within Olivia clenched. She wanted to reach out and stroke the bases of his black horns, but she held her hands still. This prince was as abrasive and hard as the scars lining his muscular chest, but then he had to do this. Something almost gentlemanly. Gentle-male-ly? Lexi had said 'man' was a human word.

"Um." Her throat went dry. "Thank you, Prince Eryx."

"Call me Eryx."

And with that, he stepped into place with all the other groomsmen. Olivia shivered, suddenly cold without the alien prince at her arm.

The music changed, from some unknown Herkleian lullaby to an alien take on *Here Comes the Bride.* Shit. Olivia broke her gaze from Eryx's and scrambled into place. This was her best friend's moment. Olivia couldn't ruin it by overtly lusting after the best man. The guests rose as the doors slid open a final time.

Anax and Lexi walked into the room as one, her hand on the scales of his forearm. In their starburst crowns and wedding-day-best, they looked every bit like the King and Queen of Herkleios. Since Lexi's father was dead and Anax's a sociopath on the run for war crimes, neither had a male in the family to walk Lexi down the aisle. Not that Herkleians followed that custom. Herkleios was a matriarchy, and the females didn't need a male to walk them anywhere.

Tears prickled at Olivia's eyes, but she held them in until her friend arrived at the altar. Olivia stepped forward to take her friend's glowing bouquet. Lexi squeezed her hand and smiled. "Thanks for everything, Liv."

A tear streaked down her cheek. Olivia would not sob like a baby. She wouldn't. "I love you so much, Lex."

Lexi turned to Anax as the guests settled into their seats. A Herkleian female rose from the first row, the gold of her gown matching the pins holding her red hair in place around her horns. Anax's stepmother, Queen Mother Chryseis. Herkleian marriages were performed by the female head of the family. Once Lexi said 'I do', she'd become the queen and therefore the female lead, but until then, the role fell to Queen Chryseis.

"Today, we witness the merging of two worlds: Herkleios and Earth," the queen said, her voice projected. "As King Anax and Lady Alexandra become one, so do our customs and traditions. For those of you that don't know, it's an Earthling tradition to walk down an aisle surrounded by your family and friends. But it's a Herkleian tradition that we'll now follow. The right to challenge."

Olivia watched her friend's spine stiffen. The moment Lexi had been nervous about. Not all Herkleians accepted an Earthling as queen and this would be their opportunity to make that clear. Anax assured her no one had challenged a wedding in nearly fifty years. At the most, one of the nobility might snap their claws in offense.

What happened next was even worse.

Four aliens jumped to their feet at the back of the crowd. Olivia couldn't tell their gender—if the fishlike species even had the concept of gender. All had tall, spindly bodies under massive red cloaks, at odds to the aqua blue of their scales, fins, and gills. The fishman at the aisle edge pushed back his cloak dramatically and shouted, "King Xenobaccus objects."

Before anyone finished gasping, he pulled something out from under his arm, hidden in the folds of his cloak. *The Queen Avra* had technology that scanned for energy-based weapons used on twelve of the thirteen Alliance planets—but it didn't scan for a good, old-fashioned AK-47.

FOUR

ERYX

The Sutekans aimed the Earth weapons at the bridal party. The replication room exploded into sound, loud popping noises mixed with screams. Eryx leapt across the space, his focus on one thing. Not on Anax jumping to cover Lexi, knocking his bride to the ground. Not on the Herkleian guards swarming the platform. Not on his sisters ducking behind the altar's edge.

Only on the dark-haired human who had invaded his every thought since he met her.

Olivia.

She stared, jaw agape and skin pale. Eryx grabbed her arm and tore her to the ground. Olivia flinched. Not at his touch. A red stain spread across the front of her gown.

No.

He was too late.

Olivia collapsed into his arms. Exactly like Doctor Sagara. Eryx hadn't been able to save his mentor, but he could save her. Eryx tore off his sash and pressed it against her abdomen. He didn't know everything about human anatomy, but the pressure should help.

"What...? Eryx?" Her blue eyes clashed with his, shocked and confused. Before he responded, those beautiful eyes flickered shut, her head falling slack.

A fire within him roared, a spike of pain. No. Not Olivia. He raised a hand in front of her mouth. Faint breaths caressed his scales. Thank Hyra. She wasn't dead. Only unconscious. He needed to get her to the infirmary. Around the platform, Herkleian guards raised their wrists and activated the miniature shields in their gold armbands. They aimed their lasers at the attackers but couldn't get a clear shot. Outside their protective bubble, guests ran in all directions and ducked down underneath seats. Eryx's vision narrowed. The nighttime forest had turned into a war zone, exactly like the one he left on Hathor.

Someone touched his shoulder.

Eryx reacted with a growl. He grabbed his attacker's arm and twisted, ready to defend himself and the tiny female in his arms.

"It's me, Eryx." Anax pulled back his hand. "We must go."

Only his brother. Not a threat. Eryx suppressed that savage side of him, the Butcher born on the bloody sands of Hathor. That male wasn't needed now.

Eryx gathered Olivia into his arms, holding her while maintaining the pressure on her wound. He caressed a finger gently across the soft skin of her face. He had done his best to avoid her the last day. He didn't need another attachment to keep him in this life. But now, with her lifeblood dripping down his scales, the thought of not knowing her clawed at him.

Eryx would get her out of here. He wouldn't let her die.

Anax grabbed his bride's hand as the bridal party rushed off the platform. His sisters clung to Vasilax's arms, the same way Eryx's youngest brother, Phintias, clutched his mother. Chryseis's stern and determined gaze met his. She would throw herself in front of laser fire to protect her son.

Not all of their group was as lucky. Lexi's amber-haired bridesmaid lay stiff and unmoving on the platform, her chest pierced with the crude Earth projectiles. Like Olivia if Eryx hadn't dragged her down when he did. He forced his gaze forward. There was no point mourning in the middle of a battle.

"Look out!" A familiar voice called. The replication room had multiple emergency exits, the one the Herkleian party approached surrounded by Eógan soldiers. The green-scaled aliens were close cousins of the Herkleians, with shorter horns and poisonous ridges lining their spines. Eryx's mother had been a quarter Eógan and her half-brother had married the Empress of Eógan, Ailis. Eryx's cousin, Prax, popped out from behind his soldiers with a laser and nailed one of the Sutekans in the chest. Thank Hyra his cousin had trained at the same academy all Alliance nobility attended. Self-defense had been a core principle.

Prax ducked behind the Eógan shields to avoid a hail of projectiles, but his green-scaled face appeared a second later. He shouted again. "This way!"

The Eógan contingent split in two to allow the Herkleians behind their line. Through the emergency doors, a wall of soldiers surrounded Empress Ailis, her red eyes critically scanning every new arrival. Her forehead creased at the sight of the wounded female in Eryx's arms. "What is the meaning of all this, Anax?"

"I'm not sure yet." He angled his body, placing himself between his mate and the open doorway. He tapped at his gold wristband. "I'm calling in reinforcements, but would you care to assist, Aunt? If we split and combine our forces, we can leave behind soldiers to contain this situation."

Empress Ailis nodded and muttered something quickly to her lead guard. Half the Herkleian soldiers dropped into position behind the Eógans. The rest flanked the bridal party.

Anax gestured down the hall. "This way."

When his brother shuffled to the side, Lexi came clearly into Eryx's view—and so did Olivia in his arms. She tore out of her mate's grasp. "Olivia!"

Eryx's grip tightened. It took everything in him not to pull Olivia away when Lexi brushed at a strand of the female's dark hair. He swallowed, looking for the appropriate words. "I'm sorry. I failed her, Lexi."

She wiped at her eyes, filling with tears. "You saved her, Eryx. Now, we can fix her." Lexi spun on her mate. "We need to help her."

Anax took his mate's hand. "We have to get to safety first, naika. Once there, we can heal our wounded."

Lexi swallowed, but nodded. They started down *The Queen Avra's* bright halls. If it weren't for the contingent of guards at their front and back, or their blood-stained finery, Eryx would think the bridal party on a casual but brisk walk. He sped his steps to keep pace with his brother and Empress Ailis, careful not to jostle the delicate female in his arms. Eryx hadn't planned to stay, but if his family were in danger—from their *own* father of all people—he needed to be involved. "Any update on the situation?"

Anax flicked a claw against the holo-screen of his wristband. "Report, Captain Dexus."

The head of Herkleian security's voice projected across the comms. "We've apprehended two of the four shooters, Your Majesty, and are escorting them to the brig. The other two are dead."

"Good. The Intergalactic Alliance will prosecute them to the full extent of the law. Have they said anything? Do we know who is responsible?"

"They mentioned your father again, but we don't have time for the details now." The captain's voice flickered out. Some sort of interference? "Unfortunately, Your Majesty, I just received a report that a warship approaches at full speed. The invaders must have more people aboard *The Queen Avra*, too, since someone lowered the shielding on deck three."

Empress Ailis's green scales tinted red in anger. Eryx had been glad not to inherit the Eógans' color-shifting scales from his mother. He didn't need his emotions projected to everyone around him. "Your father has lost his mind, launching an attack like this."

Neither Anax nor Eryx disagreed. "How many more transported aboard?"

"Ten, perhaps?" The captain's voice cut out for a moment before returning in force. "We've locked down that area, but they're already on the ship. It will take time to flush them out. We must assume it's another attack on the Crown. I've advised your patrol to evacuate you immediately, Your Majesty."

His brother stiffened. It wasn't like a Herkleian to run from a fight. "I can't leave my people."

Eryx glanced at the female in his arms. Her pink skin had paled. Probably not a good sign. But he couldn't leave, either. Eryx hadn't had a choice three years ago. He had fallen asleep on one planet only to awaken on another. His family, his people, had thought he abandoned them. Eryx preferred the solitary life, but if Herkleios was in danger, he'd die to defend it. "Not to worry, brother. I will ensure your guests remain safe. I have experience in battles, and you're too important to risk."

"Eryx—"

"He's right." Chryseis slipped in behind them as they reached the stairs to the first deck. Their stepmother had never feared to announce her opinions. "A dead king is no good to his people."

Prax rushed to Empress Ailis's other side. "I'll stay, too, Mother."

Eryx had thought his aunt red before, but it was nothing compared to her rage now. "You'll do no such thing—"

Before Empress Ailis started yelling, Eryx said, "None of you will stay. You're your mother's heir, Prax. As important as my brother. You all need to get off this ship. Captain Dexus and I can handle this intrusion."

"At least I have one sensible nephew." Empress Ailis waved her hand over the green glasine gemstone in the center of her gown's chestplate and activated a small holo-screen. Eryx squinted, but the letters were too small for his translator to process. "Our ship is closer than *The Queen Niobe*. We would happily welcome you and your family aboard, Anax."

His brother clenched his fist and looked ready to ram something with his horns, but he bared his fangs in a polite but princely manner. "That's kind of you, Aunt."

"That's settled—" Olivia suddenly seized in Eryx's arms. His heart rammed into his throat. Lexi shrieked, the sound echoed by one of his sister's. Eryx rushed for a hovering bench and lowered her from his arms. He pulled at his now red sash and peeked at her injuries. Hadus. The damage was much worse than he initially thought. "Change of plans. I have to get Olivia to the infirmary now."

Lexi peeked over his shoulder, but nearly gagged at the sight. She inhaled deeply and faced her friend's wounds, anyway. "Can't we just grab the supplies and fix her on the Eógan ship?"

"She needs more than a few supplies." It didn't matter the species —if a creature lost all their blood, no matter the color, they lost their life. "Your friend needs a skilled hand and Herkleian nanotech. It's another few minutes to the trans-pod bay, then probably ten or twenty to my aunt's ship. She won't make it that long."

Lexi still didn't look convinced. "I can't just abandon her."

Anax wrapped strong arms around his mate's waist. "My brother knows his medicine, Lexi. I trust him with my life. He'll not only heal her, he'll protect her. I wouldn't leave Olivia with anyone else."

"Okay," Lexi said, biting her lip. "Promise me as soon as she's well enough, you'll get her out of here."

Eryx bowed his head. "You have my word."

Anax clapped a hand on his shoulder. "May Hyra protect you, brother."

"And you." Eryx nodded at his brother, at his aunt and cousin and siblings behind him. Even his stepmother regarded him gravely. His family. He hadn't interacted with any of them for three years, but the last few months had returned to normalcy. Those moments of reconnection and kinship suddenly cut to an end. Life on Hathor had been dangerous, but at least the war hadn't occurred on a ship where a stray explosion could breach the hull and kill everyone. This might be his last moment with them.

He drank them all in before plucking Olivia from the bench.

Directions to the infirmary flashed across his holo-screen. Eryx needed to run. With the enemy on board, they couldn't allow transportation requests within the ship. He walked down the hall until the bridal party moved out of sight. He didn't want to panic them. They would be off the ship and into safety in minutes.

The same couldn't be said for Olivia. She was losing blood fast. The tide trickled down his scales, but it slowed with every passing minute. Eryx ran. Even if he did, he didn't know if she'd make it. His vision tunneled.

Eryx shook his head. He couldn't let the dread pull him down. The first time he felt this, he and Doctor Sagara had arrived at a school collapsed by a bomb. The bodies of Hathorian children, scattered like dolls. He needed to stay focused now like he did then. He had saved those wounded children. He could save Olivia. Eryx couldn't lose her. He didn't know why, but she was important. As she bled out in his arms, it was as if a part of him was dying alongside her.

Olivia spasmed in his arms again. Pain stabbed through his neck, like in response to the agony she no doubt experienced.

Pain. In his neck. Eryx stopped outside the infirmary doors. Screams and shouting echoed from within the room, but it had faded when he glanced at the female in his arms. Impossible. But looking down at Olivia, his heart in tune with hers, it couldn't be denied. Eryx didn't need a mirror to see the back of his neck. He already knew what he'd find.

A faint swirling pattern, similar to the one on his brother's neck yet unique in its own way.

Olivia was Eryx's mate.

FIVE

OLIVIA

"Olivia!"

Rachel twirled in her gown in front of the mirror. "I love it, Lex."

Lexi's smile brightened the bridal shop's back room from halfway across the galaxy. The bride-to-be had returned to Earth for her engagement, but the rest of the preparation had to be completed distantly. Something that would be much more difficult without Herkleian holotech. If Lexi wasn't slightly translucent and hovering off the floor, Olivia would think she was actually in the room.

"I love the purple, but the blush pink works, too." Rachel spun again, this time stopping when she faced Olivia, Lynn, and Britney on the couches. Olivia jolted. A bright red blotch soaked through the bodice of Rachel's pink dress.

Olivia stood. "Are you—?"

Pain radiated through her middle. She glanced down. Blood. It stained her hands, her stomach, her ripped jeans. Why was she bleeding?

"Report, Captain Dexus."

"I love the blush pink." Lexi clapped her hands together and cheered. "We'll all look so great together. I can't wait, guys."

Olivia gently touched her injury. "Umm, Lex?"

Rachel squealed, a happy little noise, her joy at odds with the pallor of her skin and her stained gown. Lynn and Brittany didn't rise from the couch but smiled at their cousin. Scrapes and bruises marred their skin, blood splattering their blouses. Like they had recently escaped a war zone. The room around her crumbled and morphed, the couches tearing and the mirror shattering, but the bridal party continued to laugh.

Olivia's world spun. Why didn't anyone see what she saw? "Guys, what is happening? Why am I bleeding? Why is Rachel bleeding?"

"She won't make it that long."

Olivia jolted. That voice. Masculine and deep and rough. At complete odds with the bridal shop around her, yet oh-so-right. It echoed through her head, somehow both distant and close. What was happening? Whose voice was what?

Rachel hiked her skirts and skipped from the platform. She couldn't grab Lexi's hands, so she settled for nudging Olivia over with a quick elbow jab. The light tap turned to fire in her veins, ripping pain from her core. "Are we going to throw a Bachelorette party? I love planning parties."

"Oh, I don't know." Lexi glanced behind her, like someone on Herkleios had said her name. "It's not really a Herkleian custom. And I'm not sad to leave my single days behind. I found my prince."

"Aww," Lynn and Britney cooed.

"C'mon, Lex." Rachel's skin had paled to an off-white. The color of a corpse. Like Olivia's grandmother when she was eight. The open casket had haunted her for months. Olivia never wanted to see a dead body again, especially not one that walked and talked and acted like it lived. But no one noticed Rachel, just like no one noticed the blood on Olivia's hand. Olivia huffed in a quick breath. Was she hyperventilating? This wasn't real. None of this could be—

"Olivia?"

Light stabbed through Olivia's vision. She jolted awake. Awake. She sucked in a large breath and told her heart to calm down. It was a dream, nothing more. She and Lexi's bridesmaids had visited the bridal shops months ago to prepare for their friend's big day.

Lexi's big day.

The disaster of the wedding flooded back to her.

She sat straight. Or she tried to sit straight. Agony flared through her. She glanced down. On her stomach, a gauze-like cloth vibrated slightly, one end of it attached to a thin cord plugged into the side of the table. No, not a table. The gold metal surface floated off the floor and looked like a hard slab, but she sank into it like a cushion. She poked at the cloth and traced the cord to the slab. Where was she?

A warm, scaled hand gripped her shoulder. "Olivia?"

Her blurred vision focused on the face in front of her. Purple slitted eyes in a handsome, chiseled face under shoulder-length emerald hair. Eryx. He looked like he hadn't slept in days, but worry had replaced the exhaustion in his eyes. Behind him, an opaque barrier blocked the rest of the room, fluttering when someone passed. Like a curtained stall in an ER. Exactly like that. After those fishmen pulled their weapons, they had fired upon the crowd. Upon Lexi's wedding. She remembered nothing after they shot her, but someone had moved her here, to an alien ER in a floating bed aboard a freaking space station. Where was Lexi? Had anyone else been hurt?

She grabbed Eryx's hand. "What happened?"

He slumped back into his seat, dropping his head into his hands. If it weren't for the claws, horns, scales, and lack of shirt, he'd look like a hot Earthling man after a really long day. "A disaster, that's what."

"No 'do I want the good news or the bad news' speech?" Olivia bit her lip. She shouldn't have said that. Humor was often her way of coping with stress, but it didn't feel appropriate when her best friend's wedding had literally been shot up.

His brow creased in confusion, but he pressed on like she hadn't said anything. "It's been a day since the wedding. Seventeen of our guests died in the initial assault and eight were injured."

Olivia's heart skipped a beat. "What about Lexi and Anax?"

"The Royal Guard evacuated her and Anax. I received word from my brother that their ship is a day away from Herkleios. The rest of the bridal party accompanied them." He paused. "However, your friend, Rachel, did not survive."

"Oh." Olivia pulled her hand from Eryx's. Her skin chilled instantly when not pressed against his. Dead. Rachel had been yapping her ear off what felt like minutes ago. Now, dead. Olivia had never really liked the girl, but she hadn't wanted her dead. "My god, Rachel... But I'm glad Lexi's alive. She and Anax were the targets, weren't they?"

"Most likely." Eryx pushed from his chair and paced across the small space. Like a tiger in a cage. Something about this male was restless and wild, at odds to the prim and proper world of royals. "The Sutekans work for my father, Xenobaccus. I guess he thought by assassinating Anax and Lexi, he could restore himself to the throne."

Lexi had told Olivia all about her evil father-in-law. They had thwarted his plans for galactic domination, but his allies had transported him away before capture. No one had heard from him in six months. "But you stopped them?"

"Two of the assassins died during the initial assault. The third didn't survive transport to the infirmary. We imprisoned the last."

Olivia tried for a smile. Her entire body ached, but it sounded like Eryx hadn't talked to another person since the attack. She didn't know why, but she wanted to ease his pains. Not like she had anything else to do but listen. "That's good. Maybe things aren't as bad as they sound?"

Eryx's lips twitched, almost into a frown before returning to their brooding neutral. Olivia's heart sank. "I spoke too soon, didn't I?"

Those purple eyes scanned her, like a general surveying his troops. Like Olivia's father had looked at her compared to her brothers. His artsy, slightly goth daughter. Pale and willowy and frail. Olivia tried to sit taller in the bed, but she knew how pathetic she must appear.

But he didn't deem her incompetent. "After our guards contained the assassins, a Neithan warship approached and docked with us. *The Queen Avra* doesn't have the weapons to fight a warship. It wasn't deemed necessary this deep into Alliance space. Most of the guests were uninjured and took trans-pods to their ships, but we couldn't evacuate all the wounded."

Olivia shuddered. "So your father's men are on the ship? What do they want?"

"We have no idea, but they have control over the third deck, including the hangar bay. Nearly half the station." He raked a hand through his hair, his claws brushing against the edges of his horns with a zing. "We locked off the upper two decks, but without access to the hangar, we can't leave. There are more trans-pods, but they're on the rebels' side of the station."

When Olivia had left Earth for Lexi's wedding, she had always intended on returning. What harm was a wedding? But if there was no escape... Olivia swallowed. Her mom and brothers would be devastated, but she didn't leave behind children or anything. Just her cat, Gouda, who her neighbor would gladly adopt. "We're just waiting to die, then?"

"No one is going to lay a hand on you." The energy in Eryx coiled and changed, focusing on her. But not in a terrifying way. Her skin prickled at the possessive look in his eyes. "We have a good number of soldiers still aboard. We plan to launch a defense and take back *The Queen Avra*. Rest and all will be well."

Olivia tried for a calm smile, but her lip quivered. His eyes pierced through her. Her stomach fluttered again. Damn, how did anyone get anything done around Herkleians if they were this freaking hot? "You expect me to sleep at a time like this?"

"If you're unable to, I can have them give you something."

"No!" She didn't want that. So much had happened in the last day. The attack. Her wound. The alien at the end of her bed. She needed time to think, to process. "I'm sure I can fall asleep on my own."

The blue gem on his gold wristband flashed. Eryx tapped the gem with his claws and a message popped across his holo-screen. Olivia couldn't read it from her angle. "They need me in the control room. The surviving Sutekan assassin is awake."

Olivia shuddered again. She couldn't help it. She didn't know if this fishman had fired the gun that injured her, but it didn't really matter. He had aimed indiscriminately into the crowd. "Are you going to interrogate him?"

"I'll do what I must. As the last remaining royal on the station, the decisions fall to me." He puffed out his chest, his muscles rippling with the movement. Her mouth watered. Eryx must have confused her desire for concern, since his expression immediately shifted. "But I can order someone else to do it. Captain Dexus is quite capable—"

"No, you go. I'll be fine." Olivia waved her hand toward the door and relaxed onto her bed. She didn't want him to leave—why didn't she want him to leave?—

but Eryx wasn't her boyfriend or anything, sitting by her side while she healed. He was a freaking alien prince. Someone far more important than her needed his expertise and leadership.

He glanced toward the curtain, but hadn't yet budged. In his pacing, Eryx moved closer to her side. Olivia stared at the space between their hands. Screw it. She reached out and drifted her fingers against his knuckles. Friends touched each other's hands in comfort all the time, right? He flinched. She tried to pull back, but he relaxed and rubbed a thumb against her skin. The texture of his scales made her shudder. What would they feel like all over her? Olivia blushed. She was half-dead. Now wasn't the time to be lusting over a prince.

"I will return shortly." His voice came out gritty, dark. He cleared his throat. "I promise."

Olivia smiled. She didn't know what was happening. Not on the station and not with the alien at her side. Was it normal to feel like this after only a few conversations? She knew desire, but this was more than chemistry. She wanted to know this male, alpha tendencies and all. "Okay."

He rubbed his thumb against the skin of her hand once more before gently pulling away. "I'll tell Doctor Karvex you're awake. *The Queen Avra* has limited medical resources, but now that you're partially healed, he can transfer you to one of the more advanced medical beds."

"Thank you, Eryx."

Eryx nodded and dropped into a shallow bow, his scars at odds with the movement. A male of contradictions. Gentle and yet savage. Refined and yet rough. He backed toward the curtain and hesitated to leave, but eventually pulled himself away from her. The curtain swished behind him. Olivia slumped onto the table. Empty and cold.

Olivia couldn't wait for his return. Which was ridiculous. Olivia didn't need a man to make her happy... but that didn't mean she didn't *want* one. She hadn't thought she wanted one. Love only brought heartbreak. Her parents had gazed at each other lovingly once. They couldn't even stand in the same room now. Men only brought pain, but maybe Eryx would be different?

She pinched herself. Whatever drugs the Herkleians had pumped into her were making her crazy.

A Herkleian male pushed through the curtain, dragging her from her thoughts. Olivia almost yelped. He was a few inches shorter than Eryx and nowhere near as bulky, with long, narrow horns and burnt orange hair. His blue scales were lackluster. Maybe the Herkleian version of pale and tired? Like the rest of the males, he didn't wear a shirt, but the combination of an apron and scrubs covered his front.

He tapped at his wristband and a detailed holo-screen flashed into the air in front of him, displaying flickering vitals.

Olivia cleared her throat. "You must be Doctor Karvex?"

His yellow eyes skirted to her and then quickly back to his tablet. "I am, yes."

His bedside manner was terrible. "How am I doing, doc?"

His brow creased, like it annoyed him to answer her questions. Olivia didn't break eye contact. He let out a light growly nose, almost like a sigh. "The projectiles that punctured your abdomen went deep, but we got the bleeding under control. Luckily, no vital organs were damaged."

"Aren't all organs vital?" she asked, half-jokingly.

His eyes narrowed. "There is bad news, unfortunately. One of the projectiles nicked your uterus. Our nanotechnology repaired the lesion, but the scarring is permanent."

What? Every part of Olivia stiffened. "What does that mean?"

"You might not be able to carry a child..." He paused and tapped at his holo-screen "... Olivia."

"Oh." Olivia deflated into the bed like a balloon sucked of air. She always imagined children. Even if she never married, she didn't need a husband for kids. That dream faded and died. The option disappeared, taken from her by an alien king who wanted his throne back and didn't care about the damage he caused. Olivia stared blankly at her doctor, a scream and a sob lodged in her throat. Olivia needed her best friend. She needed a freaking hug.

Doctor Karvex tapped at his screen, not even bothering to meet her eyes. "I understand this news might devastate someone as young as you. We had a psychiatrist on board at one point. I can go see if she's still here and available to talk to you."

Olivia tried to slink further into the bed. Maybe the nanites would devour her whole. Dissolve her. She didn't want to talk to a stranger. Her conversation with Eryx had given her hope and energy, but without him, the terror of everything that happened—and everything that hadn't yet happened—weighted down her bones. "That's okay. I think I'll just sleep."

He grunted, a guttural sound, before slipping through the curtain.

Olivia dropped her head, letting it sink into the somehow-soft metal, and stared at the ceiling. She traced the rock's crystal veins with her eyes, a heaviness in her heart. She had been shot. She was trapped on a space station. She couldn't have children.

But Eryx would return shortly.

She grabbed onto the sliver of hope he represented and let it rock her into sleep.

SIX

ERYX

"Report, Captain." Eryx walked into the control room with his head held high, horns towering and strong. He couldn't let his soldiers know how it pained him to see his mate in such a state.

His mate. The concept amazed him, but he knew Olivia was his with certainty. Not that he knew what to do with her. The goddess Hyra joined mated pairs together, but it was their choice to seal their bond. Eryx wasn't worthy of her. But until she denied him, the swirl on the back of his neck solidified with every hour in her presence. Thankfully, Herkleian males wore their hair long, otherwise he'd have to explain himself to his soldiers.

Not that they were all technically his soldiers. Captain Dexus rose from his seat when Eryx entered and dropped into a shallow bow. The other Herkleian soldiers in the room mirrored the movement, but half of the room remained standing. Green-scaled Eógans left by his Aunt Ailis lowered their heads respectfully but did not bow. The three Guroverian soldiers, with their sand-colored skin and colorful feathers, barely acknowledged him and the seven ice-skinned Fens crossed muscled arms over their fur-edged breastplates.

He didn't worry about the Guroverian following his orders, but the Fens were an entirely different story. While their people were technologically advanced, they hadn't left behind some of their barbaric traditions like the Herkleians. His mother's youngest sister, his Aunt Rhiona, was Queen of Fenrik and her husband had promised his support, but if Eryx showed even a hint of weakness, he'd lose whatever little respect his soldiers had for an outsider.

Thirty-four soldiers. That was all that stood between the Sutekans and Olivia. The rest had all evacuated with the guests during the initial assault. The numbers made Eryx nervous, but Anax had called for reinforcements from Herkleios during the wedding and help should arrive within a day.

Captain Dexus cleared his throat. "Bad news, Your Highness."

"I've told you, Dexus. My title isn't needed." Eryx had told a younger Dexus the same thing years ago, before his father's betrayal and Hathor, but Anax's friend had never listened. "What is it?"

"My apologies, Your... er, Eryx. We received word from *The Queen Niobe*. The Neithans have formed a blockade around Herkleios. None of our warships can get through without attacking. Your brother doesn't wish to provoke them and risk our people, so *The Queen Niobe* has changed course to Eógan. But that unfortunately means reinforcements won't arrive for at least two days. Empress Ailis of Eógan has pledged her fleet to your brother, but it will take time for them to arrive."

"Hadus." Eryx settled at the head of the table and slammed his fist into the surface. His father had planned this well. Herkleios was the closest planet to *The Queen Avra*. If Anax couldn't send a Herkleios warship, they were adrift with no support for an extra twenty-four hours. With every minute, the Sutekans and Neithans gained more ground.

He surveyed his paltry troops. They had the upper hand. This was their station, under their control. They could survive two days. They *had* to survive two days. "We have two choices. Attack or wait to be attacked. The longer we wait, the longer our invaders have to get acquainted with the station."

The largest of the Fens, an eight-foot-tall beast named Helgi, pounded a fist into his chest. "I say we attack."

Eryx held the male's pale gaze. The Fen had height on him, but Eryx had bulk. Years on Hathor had strengthened him. He wasn't a prince trained in battle and combat through holo-simulations but through firsthand experience. "It would be reckless to rush into a situation we know nothing about."

"Then what do you suggest?" The Eógan captain, Berach, asked.

"They've cut the cameras in the hangar bay, so we don't know their numbers or what weapons they possess. I suggest we try to get eyes on the enemy while I interrogate the Sutekan we have in custody." Eryx faced Dexus, his ally in the room. "Dexus, you spoke with one of the station's engineers, correct?"

The male nodded and tapped at his gold wristband. His holo-screen synced with the table's holo, projecting a map of the station over the table. "We've sealed the entrances to the third deck, but there are air shafts connecting the entire ship. We have limited resources, but our engineer retrofitted a cleaning droid with a camera. With the data it provides us, we'll get a better understanding of our enemy."

"Any objections?"

The Fenrish warriors stayed silent, but the Eógans nodded and the Guroverians chirped in agreement. With no challenges, Eryx stood from his seat. "Good. We'll reconvene in two hours to examine the video and then make our plans. In the meantime, continue manning the control room and patrolling the halls."

Eryx twisted on his boot's heels, ending the meeting by walking in the other direction. Helgi glared a hole into his back, but he ignored the male. Their kind were violent fighters, but they didn't have horns. If it came to it, Eryx was sure he could impale the male before he moved in challenge. He had done so before. Hathor had demanded it of the Butcher.

Eryx tried not to shudder. He hated killing, hated causing pain.

But he needed to do this to survive—for himself, for the people on *The Queen Avra*, and for his sleeping mate.

The thought of Olivia calmed him, but he banished her from his mind. He couldn't think of her now. Not with what he was about to do.

A security droid parked itself in front of a door leading to the station master's office. *The Queen Avra* had a few holding cells in case visitors got rowdy or intoxicated, but unfortunately they were on the third deck. Eryx needed to make do with an office. The droid rolled out of the way when he approached, the door sliding open. Captain Dexus had pushed the hovering desk to the side, the space cleared to allow for two levitating chairs.

The Sutekan's gills flared when Eryx stepped inside, his beady black eyes following the prince's every movement. Their kind had evolved from the sea on Sutek, growing legs and arms while retaining their ability to swim and breathe underwater. The pirate's hands were bound before him, his webbed fingers tapping against the leg of his pants.

The Sutekans had always unnerved him, both physically and culturally. They had no interest in joining the Intergalactic Alliance or finding harmony—only in profit. But this time, his only response was the boiling of his blood. This male had killed his brother's wedding guests. He might have fired the projectile that wounded Olivia. Eryx would make the pirate feel the same pain he had inflicted on his mate, but for now he needed the male.

"Soon, little prince, our fates will be reversed and I will hold you prisoner," he said with a thick, nasally accent. Eryx was surprised his father had found a pirate who cared enough to learn Herkleian. His kidnappers from three years ago hadn't responded to his shouts as they crash-landed.

"Your partner has already started talking." His partner had died, but Eryx didn't need to tell the male yet. "If you want a deal, tell me what you know about my father's plan."

The pirate cackled, a high-pitched, whiney sound. "You've

entered a fight you have no way of winning. Surrender now and your father might grant you a peaceful death."

Eryx settled in the opposite chair. "Because of the weapons the Neithans have in the hangar bay?"

The Sutekan barred jagged teeth.

Eryx tapped his claws calmy against his knee. With every polite question the male denied, the closer Eryx got to the violence the Butcher within him craved. The violence he had never quite escaped outside of the fighting pits. "How much were you paid? I'm sure we can double it."

"Your father bought my loyalty, little prince."

"What a pity." Eryx pulled a single blade from a holster strapped to his thigh. It didn't spark with electricity or any other enhancement. It was a simple curved dagger, made of Hathorian metal. The Butcher could work wonders with a blade. "Whatever my father promised, he won't deliver. He only cares about himself. You'll come to see you are easily replaceable to him. If he could replace me, his heir, you are more than dispensable."

The Sutekan spat at his feet. "Do your worst, little prince. Herkleian torture doesn't scare me."

"Herkleian torture might not." Eryx slowly stood, letting the Butcher rise within him. Keeping the monster on a leash, but releasing him from his cage. For the civilians on this ship, for Olivia, he needed answers. "But Hathorian methods might."

The pirate's scaly blue flesh blotched in fear. Eryx bared his fangs and approached with the blade.

***

BY THE TIME Eryx returned to check on Olivia, hours had passed. *The Queen Avra* synced timewise with Eritea, the Herkleian capital. Back home, families and loved ones snuggled deep into their beds, unaware of the war taking place above their heads. Eryx wiped at his face as he entered the infirmary. The

Sutekan pirate was dead, but Eryx had learned nothing of use. The male had taken his secrets to the grave. Even worse, Captain Dexus's droid had recorded a dozen Sutekans and a hundred Neithans. Even without special weaponry, they were vastly outnumbered.

Eryx pushed those worries away. Rescue would arrive in two days. They needed to last that long. Not only physically, but morally. Eryx had sworn to never again be the male he became on Hathor. A healer, yes, but also a warrior. The Butcher. And who better to torture than someone who understood exactly how pain worked?

Doctor Karvex slumped on a chair in the corner, but pushed to his feet at Eryx's arrival. *The Queen Avra* only had a single doctor and three nurses. The Herkleians hadn't thought to staff it further, not when every attending dignitary had brought their own ship and medical supplies. Something Eryx regretted. The male looked ragged. His scales didn't sparkle in full health, his hair mussed and unkempt. The once-tidy infirmary matched its doctor, crammed with curtained stalls and sleeping patients. Blood stained the floors, from deep purple to orange to red.

Red like a human's.

He clenched his fists. Olivia was fine. He told the doctor to report to him immediately if anything happened to her. Eryx wished he could have stayed behind to watch her himself. He hadn't trained with all the latest Herkleian technology like Doctor Karvex, but if the doctor was busy with another patient, Eryx's war zone medical skills were better than nothing.

Doctor Karvex stopped before Olivia's stall and tapped at his wristband, calling up a holo-screen. "The human's recovering well, Your Highness. She's very receptive to our nano-bandages. I had my doubt as they've never been tested on a human before." The doctor scrolled quickly through her vitals, too quickly for Eryx to read. "I might write a paper on it."

"And the rest of your patients?" Eryx wanted nothing more than to enter Olivia's stall, but he had to appear objective.

"All survived. I discharged three, but the remaining five will be here another couple of days."

Days they might not have. If the Alliance didn't arrive in time, everyone aboard *The Queen Avra* would be at the mercy of his father and whatever else they had on the Neithan warship. "What about Olivia? When will it be safe to move her?"

The doctor's forehead furrowed. "Move?"

Eryx glanced around, but all the patients he spotted were sleeping. "There's one remaining trans-pod. We can fit all of your patients as soon as we can move them. Especially Olivia. Lady Alexandra herself tasked me with protecting her friend."

At the mention of the future Herkleian queen, Doctor Karvex wouldn't ask questions. Eryx pretended to be neutral, but he wasn't. He couldn't let his mate die on this ship with the rest of them. He would stay. If she never knew about their bond, she could live the rest of her life in happiness. Eryx wasn't deserving of a mate, wasn't deserving of happiness, but goddess Hyra had blessed him with one, so the least he could do was protect her while he breathed.

The doctor's eyes narrowed, but he held any comments to himself. "If her healing continues at this rate, she should be able to travel in a day or so."

Not as soon as Eryx liked but that only meant more motivation to keep the pirates away. "She's doing well otherwise?"

"Apart from her uneasy sleep." The doctor swiped away his holo-screen. "She tosses and turns quite a bit, mumbling indiscernible things."

Nightmares. Another thing Eryx had in common with his mate. "Thank you, Doctor."

Doctor Karvex bowed his head, barring his horns before nobility, before turning on his booted heels and returning to his chair. The male would sleep in the room until the nurses returned for their next shifts.

Eryx pushed through the curtain hiding Olivia from the rest of the room. She had kicked off half her blankets, her dark hair a halo against the gold metal of the med-bed. His heart stuttered. Beautiful. Absolutely enchanting. Her lips parted in sleep, muttering small sounds. His cock hardened. If only she weren't injured. If only pirates hadn't attacked the station. He'd never get the chance to know her. Never get the change to pound into her sweet warmth and hear those little mutters turn to moans.

Eryx shook her head. He was here to protect her, nothing more. He settled into the hovering chair. His knees bumped against the edge of her bed in the small space. Not that he'd be able to sleep, anyway. Neither in the space nor the situation. He might as well watch over her.

Olivia twisted, making a strange little noise. Like a strangled cry. It wasn't a sound Herkleians made, but he thought it distress. Perhaps she was having another nightmare? He wished he could reassure her and caressed his hand down her arm. Her skin was fragile and soft and warm, though nowhere near as warm as his. He nearly retracted his claws to keep her safe, but he had witnessed his brother touch his mate dozens of times without harm.

Olivia flinched. He recoiled, fearing he woke her, but she grabbed his hand. Eryx looked towards her face, her eyes still firmly shut. She squeezed his hand, her cries subsiding like the warmth of his scales chased away her nightmares. He might go numb in her grip, but he didn't care. As long as she was happy, nothing else mattered.

Eryx leaned his head back, intending to close his eyes for a single moment.

Someone cleared their throat.

Eryx jolted. His gaze went straight to his hand, joined with Olivia's. Then traveled up her arm and across her neck to meet blue eyes, open and aware. He had fallen asleep, holding her hand throughout the night. For once, the memories that haunted him since Hathor hadn't turned to nightmares.

He was very much pleased, but his mate not so much.

SEVEN

OLIVIA

"So you just sat there staring at me all night?" Olivia crossed her arms and tried her best to sound fierce, but a part of her was secretly pleased. No man—male had ever sat at her bedside while she was injured. Olivia had once broken her leg at school and her own father hadn't shown up. He was always too busy for Olivia.

Eryx remained seated, watching her with those intense eyes. "I wanted to make sure you were safe."

Aww. Part of Olivia melted, but another part stiffened. Romance only brought pain and disappointment. Olivia had already experienced enough disappointment for a lifetime. She warred with herself, but the fear won out, turning her response into a snarky, "And did holding my hand ensure my safety somehow?"

Eryx paused at that. Some emotion swirled in his gaze, but she didn't know him well enough to understand his thoughts. She didn't know him at all. There was no reason to be so attached. Olivia pinched herself under the blanket.

His lips parted, but he stopped again before answering. She caught a flash of fang and shivered. But not in desire. Definitely not.

Her eyes trailed across his jaw and down his throat to the corded muscles of his scaled shoulders.

Quiet and brooding, exactly her type.

Olivia pinched herself again. She needed to get a grip. And some answers. Why Eryx held her hand didn't matter, not when the station was under attack. "Are the fishmen still stuck in the hangar bay? What about the two we captured?"

His forehead creased. "Fishmen?"

"Yeah, fishmen." She puckered her lips like a fish and flapped her hands near her head like a fin. Eryx's eyes widened. She continued the flapping. Maybe if she acted like her true, weird self, he'd figure out he wasn't interested.

"You mean the Sutekans?"

She snapped her fingers. She knew he'd said the word before. "Yes, exactly. The Sutekans."

His lip twitched upward, the closest to a smile he'd ever managed. He leaned back in his hovering gold chair, relaxing into the seat. Not at all like a male weirded out by Olivia's strange sense of humor.

Maybe he actually appreciated it. She crossed her arms in mock-fierceness. "What's so funny? They look exactly like fish."

"If so, you have odd looking fish on Earth."

She gaped. "Did you just make a joke?"

His lips twitched again. "I'm quite capable of jokes."

"Sounds like something a robot would say."

"I assure you, Liv, I'm not a robot."

Liv. Her heart stuttered. Only her parents and closest friends called her that. He couldn't just use her nickname like that. They had only spoken twice. Maybe three times. The last time, she had been mid-death. It didn't matter if he was the hottest guy—well, not really a guy—hottest male she'd ever seen. He couldn't *pretend* to know her.

He noticed her discomfort, immediately leaning forward in the chair. He bowed his head. "You didn't like that. I apologize, Olivia. I am unsure how these... what do you call them? Nickernames?"

Damn, why did he have to be courteous, too? "Nicknames."

"Yes." He brushed a clawed hand through his green hair, the strands brushing against the base of his horns. Like he was abashed. Him, a seven-foot-tall Adonis. "I'm unsure how these nicknames work. We don't have them on Herkleios. Hathor didn't have the custom, either."

"Hathor?" She didn't recognize the planet's name. It wasn't part of the Intergalactic Alliance, but there were hundreds of planets out there that didn't belong. Not everyone in the galaxy wanted peace— as proved by Lexi's wedding.

"A war-torn planet. I... spent some time there."

Olivia shuddered. A hint of pain flared through her wound, a reminder of the bullets. When her parents had been married and her father overseas, her mother had watched the news every day, plas- tered with images of bomb-ruined buildings and starving citizens. Olivia screamed at her to turn it off more than once. She hated conflict. "Why would you want to do that?"

"It wasn't my choice." He propped his elbows on his knees, his chest muscles flexing. This whole no-shirt policy wasn't the worst. "My father revealed his plans for galactic domination to me years before he actually attempted them six months ago. When I refused to help, he disowned me and sent me to Hathor against my will."

And Olivia thought she had daddy issues. "Oh, my God, that's terrible."

"Hathor was a dark time in my past, but I learned much there. Before, I loved the spotlight. Loved the adoration of the people. I was young and vain and Hathor helped me grow."

Olivia couldn't imagine a playboy Eryx. Surely, he'd been born brooding. "Just because it was important doesn't mean it wasn't terrible."

Those slitted purple eyes flickered to her. "No, I suppose not."

She flushed at the mere look. Olivia waved her hands and glanced away. "Gah, I'm sorry I brought it up."

"I've never talked about it with another."

Then he definitely shouldn't talk about it with her. They were nothing to each other. Absolutely, positively nothing. "And now you're stuck in another war zone."

"I've been in worse places."

Olivia surveyed the infirmary. As little as she could see from her bed, that was. The blue floors and rock-threaded gold ceilings were nice, but it had the worried vibes of any medical facility. "This little square doesn't rate very high."

"We can change that." He tapped at the blue gem on his gold wristband and made a quick selection on his holo-screen. The curtains around her flickered. Flickered. She blinked. Within the space of a second, the dull little square she had called home over the last day turned into a bright garden of orange and yellow flowers under red-leaved trees. The high-pitched chirping of birds reached her ears. While she couldn't smell the garden, she imagined the scent.

"Wow," Olivia gasped out. If it weren't for the fluttering of the curtains, she would actually think she was looking out at a crimson meadow. Olivia wished she could pitch a tent right in the middle of the field. "It's so beautiful."

"The Mehet Fields in Hathor. Not all the planet was terrible."

She smiled. No matter what her head said, her heart wanted to melt every time he shared a piece of himself. "Well, aren't you an optimist?"

His lips pursed, like he had never considered the idea before. "I guess I am."

She dropped her head back onto her pillow. His eyes flickered down the length of her neck to her collarbones. Her skin prickled, her chest heating. If only she weren't wearing a thin hospital gown. She was entirely exposed to him. Olivia pulled her blanket to her chin. "Then optimize our situation, Mr. Optimist."

"I don't need to." His lip twitched, sharing that irresistible fang. "Sitting here by your side is already perfect."

Oh, God. The heat in her chest melted her heart and traveled down to her stomach, to her core. If she weren't wounded and trapped in a levitating, alien hospital bed, she'd probably jump him right there. Why couldn't he just be a pretty face? Why did he have to be sweet, too? If he were the asshole she initially thought he was, she'd have no problem jumping into his bed one night and out of it the next. Olivia couldn't put her heart on line. She *couldn't*.

She tried to push the smile from her face and smother her desire. "Do you have a plan yet? To get us off this ship alive?"

He let her change the subject, but that almost-smile remained on his lips. "We're in the midst of gathering reconnaissance."

Sounded like a non-answer. Her father gave those a lot. Comparing Eryx to her dad helped her quash the thrill rushing through her veins. "Meaning you have nothing."

"Not nothing. We've mapped out the ventilation system leading to the hangar bay and sent a droid to report on the enemy's movements."

"And if it finds too many people or weapons you can't handle?"

The smile slipped from his face. Eryx straightened, the warrior part of him shining determinedly through his eyes. "Then we will die trying."

"Like hell you will." Olivia couldn't stop the reply. Eryx couldn't die. He wasn't allowed. "Have you tried asking for help?"

He glanced behind him before leaning forward. His deep voice became a seductive whisper, but his words washed away her heat. "The Neithans have formed a blockade around Herkleios. They're the nearest Alliance planet to us."

"Damn."

"All isn't lost. We have access to one remaining trans-pod. Not everyone would fit, but we could send most of the wounded. Possibly one of the nurses. You wouldn't have to die here with us."

"Isn't everyone else in the infirmary a dignitary or some sort?" Eryx might choose her, but Olivia would *not* have her last act cause an intergalactic incident. Which meant she was going to die on a freaking space station. She'd never see her mom or her cat or her salon again. Or any of Earth.

Earth. The rest of the Intergalactic Alliance planets were on the far side of Herkleios, but *The Queen Avra* station was halfway between Eryx's homeworld and hers. "If Herkleios can't help us, then why not ask Earth?"

"The Neithan warship is much more advanced than any of Earth's ships."

Earth's *one* ship. The *USS Pegasus* had probably already arrived back at Earth, but could it return in time? "Never underestimate your enemies or your allies, as my father used to say."

"Your father?"

"I was a military brat." His brow creased in confusion. Guess 'military brat' wasn't an intergalactic term. "That means my dad was in the military and we moved around from base to base. He wasn't around a lot, but when he was, he drilled military tactics into me and my brothers on the off-chance any of us wanted to follow in his foot-steps. Both my brothers did."

"But not you?"

"Nah. I was always more into art and fashion, so I became a hair stylist." She gestured at her hair, which had looked great at the wedding. Two days ago. Probably a good thing she didn't have a mirror. "To his great disappointment."

"You'll never be a disappointment." He touched her hand on the edge of the bed. A spark of electricity shot through her. "Hair is sacred among my people. The goddess Hyra shaved off the god Hadus's hair when he betrayed her, a sign of shame to all that saw him. Your ability to style hair would bring you great honor on Herkleios."

"Too bad my dad's not from Herkleios."

"We won't listen to him."

She snorted. If only it were that easy. Olivia hadn't talked to her dad in a year, but his voice still haunted her. She couldn't *not* listen to him. "Except for when it comes to military advice."

That fanged almost-smile returned. "Perhaps."

EIGHT

When Eryx left, the temperature in Olivia's square in the infirmary dropped to freezing. She shivered. She tapped at her own bracelet, a second away from messaging him to return. But she couldn't. His soldiers needed him. She didn't. She *wanted* him. It was different.

Different and stupid and only going to result in heartbreak.

Olivia needed to get her mind off the hot Herkleian prince with solemn purple eyes. She pushed down her blankets. The nano-bandage plugged into her bed still pulsed warmth into her skin. She gently nudged a finger around its edge. When no alarm went off—both around her or under her skin—she peeled the bandage and peeked underneath.

"Wow," she breathed out. Instead of a gaping wound, a red scar marred her skin. A small patch near the line of her pants glistened, raw and unhealed, but when she straightened in the bed, pain didn't stab through her. Her abs didn't flare like they were on fire. Thank God for alien technology.

She blinked away sudden tears. Herkleian technology could only fix so much. She had tried not to think about the terrible news Doctor Karvex had given her. She'd never have children. Olivia slapped the bandage back in place and shook her head. If she didn't survive this station, her infertility wouldn't be a problem.

Nurse Eula poked her head around the curtain. "Are you ready for breakfast, Olivia?"

"Sure." Olivia tried for a smile. She took advantage of her almost-healed wound and propped herself higher on some pillows. She hadn't eaten anything solid since the wedding. "I'd love food."

Nurse Eula disappeared for a second, something rattling like metal on metal, before she popped back through the curtain with a golden tray. The Herkleian quickly tapped her bracelet, activating the tray's levitation. She lowered it in front of Olivia, where it dropped slightly before hovering over her lap. Juicy blue meat covered in orange-red gravy sat atop a pile of purple-green vegetables. Olivia inhaled the scent of fried chicken. Simos. Lexi had told her all about her favorite Herkleian meat. Her face fell.

"I can bring you something else if you prefer," Nurse Eula said. "Lady Alexandra wanted options for her guests and we have access to the wedding catering."

"Oh, no, I'm sure this is fine." Olivia plucked the two-pronged fork and stabbed it into the dish. Hospital food on Earth sucked. She couldn't let this royal-grade catering go to waste. She swiped the meat through gravy and shoved it into her mouth, prepared to moan in deliciousness no matter the taste. A flavor almost like fried chicken exploded on her tongue. "Oh, my God, this is amazing."

"It pairs well with the ovtro juice, I think."

Olivia plucked the cup and took a sip. Besides being the freshest-tasting juice she'd ever had, the sweetness contrasted nicely with the saltiness of the simos. "You're right."

A low growl emitted from Nurse Eula, the Herkleian version of a soft laugh. "It's my favorite dish from back home. My wife and I eat it yearly for our anniversary."

"You have a wife?"

"I do." Nurse Eula tapped at her bracelet again, calling forth an image of her and another Herkleian with long orange hair wrapped around her horns and blue eyes. "My wife, Pelaia."

"That's lovely. You both look so happy."

"I should let you get back to rest." Nurse Eula quickly checked Olivia's vitals before walking towards the exit. "Let me know if you need anything."

"I will."

Nurse Eula pushed through the curtain, but jumped back when Doctor Karvex nearly plowed through her. "Doctor, would you like to—"

"Not now, Eula," he snapped.

Olivia leaned out of her bed. "What's wrong?"

"Nothing, dear. I just wanted the doctor to look at your vitals." When Olivia narrowed her eyes, Nurse Eula kindly bared her fangs. "I'm sure he'll have time later."

Nurse Eula pushed her cart in the opposite direction of the doctor, dropping the curtain behind her. Her stall returned to the tranquil beauty of the Mehet Fields. Olivia tried to relax into her bed. She took another bite of her meal, but something itched at her. Doctor Karvex didn't have the best bedside manner, but she never witnessed him being rude to the staff. He was the station's doctor. If Nurse Eula or Olivia had a request, he should answer it. How much longer was she going to be bed-bound? When could she go to the bathroom without a hover-chair? When could the tingling nanite Band-Aid strapped to her stomach be removed?

If he wouldn't come to her, Olivia had no choice but to go to him. She nudged the tray, which shot into the sky above her head, and threw off her blankets with a dramatic flair. Olivia pushed her legs over the bed's edge. The medical room was set to Herkleian standard and her feet dangled off the floor. It wasn't a problem. With a tap to the side of the bed, a hover-chair slid out and snapped up to form a seat around her butt. She unhooked her nano-bandage. It wasn't more than regular gauze when not plugged in, but Nurse Eula had said yesterday she could remove it for a few minutes to float on over to the bathroom.

Not that Olivia was going to the bathroom, but the trip to Doctor Karvex's office took the same amount of time.

Her bracelet gently buzzed, a nudge from the hover-chair. Waiting for instructions. She glided her thumb across the holo-screen. When Nurse Eula first showed her the tech yesterday, she had expected Olivia to be a slow learner. And while Earth didn't yet have holo-screens and floating chairs, directing her seat around the infirmary was much like playing a video game on her phone.

Olivia's chair whirled out of her stall and into the main room. The doctor had discharged two more patients, but three stalls remained erected in the gleaming space. Neither Nurse Eula nor any of the other nurses were in sight. Olivia directed her chair towards the back of the room. Two doors led to the bathroom, but another two doors were tucked into the corner. Olivia directed her chair close to one. She waved her hand in front of the door's sensor. It slid open to reveal a supply closet, three hovering shelves stuffed to the brim with supplies. A few of the boxes were overturned, gauze, bottles, and other unknown medical thingamabobs scattered on the ground. A little droid zipped around the space, trying to clean the mess. Poor guy.

She motioned her chair out of the closet. Unlike the first door, the second door opened into a small space with a levitating cot and a side table topped with a glowing rock. Olivia halted. The nurses had had quarters down the hall, but she never asked about Doctor Karvex. She couldn't see him, but his horned shadow flickered across the wall. Paper and fabric ruffled, like they were being shoved into bags. She had known something was wrong, but what the hell was the doctor doing?

Olivia inched closer. Doctor Karvex came into view. The shower-esque cleaning unit all Herkleians had in their rooms was filled with clothes, like the doctor had materialized a week's supplies. He grabbed the heaps and tossed them into a black duffel bag, alongside papers and a book.

Why was Doctor Karvex packing?

There was nowhere to go. Eryx would have told her if their rescue had arrived. The doctor whirled around again. Olivia directed her chair backward, out of sight. She wasn't supposed to see this. The doctor's worried movement, his harsh tone. Wherever he was going, she suspected the Herkleians hadn't sanctioned it. *Eryx* hadn't sanctioned it.

When his footsteps pounded for the hall, Olivia quickly tapped at her holo-screen, directing her back into the supply closet. The door closed on her just as Doctor Karvex snuck past, his bag thrown over one shoulder. When the hallway went silent, Olivia floated out of the supply room. Instead of heading for the front door, he walked over to the elevator-like transporter near the bathroom doors. The transporters were offline at first, but the Herkleian technicians had locked the invaders out of their systems. But to be safe, no one could transfer into the infirmary. Only out.

Wherever he was going, the doctor didn't want anyone else to know.

When the transporter doors closed behind him, Olivia zipped over into the space. What should she do? If Doctor Karvex was up to something, she needed to report him to Eryx. But was one doctor really Eryx's biggest concern when half their station was under control of Sutekan pirates and Neithan soldiers?

Olivia waved her hand in front of the transporter, the door sliding open. Someone had to follow him. Since there was no one else that left her. The duty her father had drilled into her flared up within her. She owed it to everyone on this ship to ensure the doctor wasn't up to anything nefarious.

Besides, doctors weren't allowed to harm their patients, right?

Olivia stamped down on her nerves. He wouldn't hurt her. She directed her hover-chair into the elevator.

Her bracelet beeped, the hover-chair stopping at the elevator's rim. She tried again. Her bracelet beeped a second time, louder. Olivia glanced over her shoulder. The nurses hadn't noticed her or the doctor's disappearance. If her hover-chair started blaring an alarm, they definitely would. By the time they got her back to her bed, Doctor Karvex would have done whatever he planned with no witnesses.

Olivia wiggled her toes. If she wanted to get in the elevator, she needed to walk.

Olivia put both feet firmly on the floor. She paused there for a moment, perched on the edge of her seat. Her wound didn't flare. It twinged in discomfort, but discomfort wasn't pain. Yet. Olivia grabbed the transporter door's frame and pulled herself to her feet. A slight twinge pulsed through her stomach, from the lowest and most severe of her wounds, but her wound didn't burst with a wave of blood.

Olivia took two steps into the transporter and waved her bracelet against the panel. Three dots flared to life on the screen. All corresponded to another transporter on the ship, all on the first deck. Doctor Karvex hadn't betrayed them to their enemies then. But which location had he transported to? The first was a transporter near the control center, the second near the kitchens, and the third...

Oh, no. The third was the trans-pod bay.

Olivia tapped the third dot. The doors slid shut. Eryx had said one trans-pod remained, big enough to carry all the injured patients but not large enough for the soldiers, doctors, or staff. Like Doctor Karvex. Had he heard their conversation? Olivia didn't know if she'd get a space on the trans-pod, but whatever her feelings, it wasn't right to steal the only chance people on the station had.

The elevator buzzed with a slight rumble before the doors slid open into a cavernous room, golden walls and glowing rock ceilings like every other room on the station. A dozen doors lined the far wall, all closed except one. The last remaining trans-pod.

Which Doctor Karvex stood in front of, keying something into his holo-screen.

Olivia stumbled into the hall. "Doctor?"

Doctor Karvex nearly jumped out of his skin. "Hyra's Graces, where did you come from?"

Olivia put one hand against the wall for support and shuffled closer. She couldn't fight a seven-foot Herkleian even in the peak of her health, but perhaps she could talk him out of this? "You're betraying your planet if you do this, doctor."

He snarled, like the alien version of a cackle. "My planet has left me here to die. Eryx told me about this trans-pod last night. Even if I hadn't overheard your conversation, I knew it wasn't big enough for all of us. I thought at least I would travel alongside my patients. But no, I'm to stay and die with the rest of them, killed by Sutekans. Do you know what Sutekans do to their victims? What they did during the wedding was tame in comparison."

His voice ended in a shrill pitch, but Olivia didn't stop her approach. "You won't be left here to die, doctor. I'll talk to Eryx. You can come with us."

The doctor snarl-laughed again. "He doesn't have a space for me if he wants a space for you. And there's no way he'll let you stay behind. I ran a full diagnostic scan last night. I saw the mark on your neck."

Olivia touched her neck. "The what?"

Doctor Karvex was done talking. He tossed his duffle bag inside, tapped at his holo-screen, and then launched himself inside.

"No!" Olivia pushed off the wall. She didn't have a plan, but she couldn't stand by and watch the doctor doom everyone on the station. She slammed into the closed door. Through the window, Doctor Karvex lowered his eyes in shame. She banged on the window.

He pressed a button on his holo-screen, locking eyes with her once more as the trans-pod launched into space.

Olivia hit the window once more. "No! You bastard!"

Olivia pushed off the door—

Blood stained the front of her pale gown.

Pain flared through her gut, pain she had ignored during her adrenaline rush. Her knees turned to jelly. Olivia dropped to the floor. Blood dripped down her side. She was going to bleed out alone. Until the nurses pushed back her stall's curtain and noticed her gone.

They wouldn't notice in time.

As Olivia's vision greyed and fuzzed, she opened her holo-screen, her focus on one finding one name. She tapped out three words as the fog dragged her under.

Help. Trans-pod.

Eryx.

NINE

ERYX

Eryx slammed into the infirmary with Olivia in his arms. "Doctor!"

"The doctor's not here, Your Highness—" Nurse Eula trailed off when she noticed the dark-haired beauty in his arms. Bleeding in his arms. Dying in his arms. His one hand on her wrist, he felt the weakening of her pulse.

Before he could shout, Nurse Eula tapped at her bracelet, summoning the main surgery table in the center of the room. The gold detached from the floor and floated to waist-height. Eryx rushed toward it. Where in Hadus was the doctor? Eryx only had field medical training. The refugee camps in Hathor didn't have half the technology on *The Queen Avra*. Eryx didn't even know where to start.

When he lowered Olivia onto the table, a holo-screen flashed into life over her head, displaying her vitals. Her heart rate pulsed erratically. He ignored the rest of the data. "Nurse—"

"I messaged Nurse Tryph to check the mess hall for Doctor Karvex. He'll reply once he finds him. Until then, we need to keep her alive, Your Highness."

"Eryx. Call me Eryx." If they were going to serve side-by-side in a battle as treacherous as the one they all faced with the Neithans, Nurse Eula deserved to call him by his name. "We need to stop the bleeding."

Nurse Eula summoned the medical droid, pushing a floating basket filled with supplies. Eryx immediately grabbed for the gauze. First aid was the same no matter the planet. While Nurse Eula cut a slit in Olivia's red-soaked hospital gown, he pressed the gauze down on her wound. How did such a tiny body have so much blood? When Eryx had found her unconscious in the trans-pod bay, he thought her dead. He still didn't know what had happened to her. Perhaps the Neithans had found their way onto the first deck, to Eryx's mate.

Eryx's beautiful, courageous mate, who hadn't seen the mark forming on her neck and didn't know what she was to him. He hadn't planned to tell her, hoping to get her off the ship. But he had thought he'd die, severing their connection.

Not *her*.

He grabbed for more gauze, his hands drenched red. There was too much blood. At this rate, Olivia would bleed out before Doctor Karvex arrived. "I need a needle, a string, and a shot of nanites."

Nurse Eula finished hooking a plasma regenerator to her arm. "Eryx?"

He pointed at the golden cylindrical device. "Unless Herkleian science has upgraded their regenerators significantly in the past year, that won't be able to replace all the blood in her body. We need to stop the bleeding and we need to stop it now."

"I don't have the credentials to give her anesthesia," Nurse Eula said. "Only Doctor Karvex can operate—"

The doors to the infirmary slid open, Dexus rushing in. "What's happening? When you ran off, I had the computer send me your location. Why is the trans-pod bay covered in human blood—?"

"Not now," Eryx snapped.

Dexus's slitted eyes focused on Olivia. "Oh."

"Yes." Eryx packed Olivia's wound, his focus not on Nurse Eula or his captain. Everything was on Olivia.

Dexus backed out the door. "I'll wait outside."

Where he'd hover, stealing Eryx's concentration. He needed to put his soldier to use. "I want a report, Dexus. Who did this to Olivia and where in Hadus are they?"

"Of course, Your Highness. Sir. Eryx." The captain bobbled into a bow before rushing from the room.

"Eryx—" Nurse Eula started.

"If you can't administer anesthesia, then she won't get any." On Hathor, anesthesia had been rare if not unheard of in the camps. Anesthesia was a luxury he and his patients had never known. He brushed a hand across Olivia's arm. Her skin was cold to the touch. Too cold for a human? He wasn't sure. He hoped not.

Eryx couldn't lose her.

Eryx couldn't watch another person he loved die in his arms.

Like Doctor Sagara had.

"Live. Save the lives I won't be able to save."

Eryx pushed Sagara's last words from his mind. Now was not the time to relive old wounds. Doctor Sagara was dead, but his mate was not. He couldn't lose her.

Eryx held out a hand. "Nanites."

Nurse Eula didn't contradict him this time. She handed over an injector as the medical droid hovered at his side, a thread and needle arranged on a golden tray. Eryx laid a hand above her wound. If he inserted the nanites too close, they'd bleed out of her. He aimed under her ribcage. Her body twitched, but she didn't awaken. Thank Hyra.

This was going to hurt.

Eryx threaded the needle through his mate's delicate skin. It was like stabbing into himself. He grit his fangs. "Report?"

Nurse Eula tapped at the holo-screen. "The nanites are repairing the internal damage. There's permanent scarring along her uterus, but if we can keep her stable, she'll live."

"See if we have any human blood in the hold."

Nurse Eula nodded and sped-walk to check. The droid at his

side, the other slumbering patients in the infirmary, the invaders on the station—everything faded except for the needle in his hand and Olivia's skin. Eryx didn't let his hands shake as he stitched closed her wound. She'd live. She needed to live. Scarred like him, both internally and externally, but alive.

Eryx closed the wound and her vitals stabilized.

He almost dropped with relief, but kept himself standing. She wasn't safe yet. Nurse Eula returned with a single red bag. Combined with the regenerator, Olivia would have just enough blood to recuperate. She couldn't lose anymore. With a cloth, he wiped at her stomach, ever so gently. With her skin clean, he grabbed a nano-bandage from the droid's basket.

Now to watch and wait.

Without a word, Nurse Eula summoned him a chair. It floated over from the side of the room. He dropped into the seat, his gaze flickering between his mate and the holo-screen above her, pulsing with each beat of her heart. In the corner of the screen, the nanites reported their progress.

She'd live. His mate would live.

"Eryx?" Dexus's voice sounded at the comms in his ear.

Eryx straightened. His worry and fear had suppressed his rage, but now that his mate was stable, it flared up in a wave of fire. Someone had done this to his Olivia. Someone he planned to kill slowly. "Yes?"

"We reviewed the trans-pod bay's security feed. It was Doctor Karvex. He stole the last trans-pod."

The bastard. Eryx clenched his fists, his claws nearly piercing the scales of his palm. "Is it close enough for us to recall? If not, inform my brother. If that male lands on any Alliance planet, I want him arrested—"

"No need," Dexus cut him off apologetically. "The Neithans noticed the trans-pod's departure. They used their tractor beam to grab the pod and pull it in. We can't be sure, but we think they spaced Karvex."

Eryx shuddered. The Butcher had revived within him, the blood-thirsty monster imagining a painful death for the doctor, but nothing compared to the coldness of space. Eryx shook himself. Doctor Karvex was dead. He suppressed the warrior and summoned the prince. "What's our spy droid reporting?"

"Movement all over the third deck. I think they're preparing an attack—"

Hadus. Eryx had dreaded those words since the Sutekans attacked the wedding. The Eógan fleet wouldn't arrive for another day and a half. He had arranged a contingency, but they still needed time. "Clear the second deck and vent the atmosphere."

Dexus paused. "S-sir?"

"Backup is on the way, Dexus. We need to be alive to greet them. If we vent the second deck, they wouldn't be able to walk here. They'll have to hack into the transporters or get life support back online. That will take time. Time we need." When Dexus didn't reply, Eryx gritted his teeth, his fangs piercing his bottom lip. "Do it, Dexus."

"Yes, Eryx."

Eryx tapped at his comms, severing the connection. He dropped his head into his hands. For a moment, Eryx breathed. Exhaling Olivia's near-death, the darkness within him, the memories of Sagara's death, all in exchange for inhales of calm and peace. Eryx was a healer, not a killer. A leader, not a brute.

He raised his head, horns long and proud. "Eula?"

The nurse had hovered nearby, checking on their remaining patients and communicating with the rest of her team. At his words, she glanced his way. "Yes?"

"Do we have a transportable med-bed kit?" At her nod, Eryx continued, "Can you get it for me? Olivia will sleep in my quarters tonight. One less patient for you to manage."

Nurse Eula nodded. "Of course, Eryx."

Eryx took his sleeping mate's hands. He rubbed warmth into her skin. He couldn't leave her here alone, not when the infirmary no longer had a doctor. Not with an attack from the Neithans and Sutekans imminent. When Olivia woke to find him at her bedside, her annoyance would be a thing to behold, but he'd rather have her angry than injured or dead.

For as long as he lived, Eryx never planned to leave her unprotected again.

TEN

OLIVIA

Olivia drifted slowly into consciousness, cocooned in soft warmth. Not her hospital bed. The levitating metal was strangely comfortable, but it had nothing on this mattress. She turned her head into the pillow and inhaled. The thick scent of male reached her nose—primal and seductive.

Eryx's scent.

Why did her bed smell like Eryx?

Why did she have a bed at all?

Olivia rocketed into wakefulness. She sat straight—

Fire tore through her belly like a hot poker to the gut. A gasp escaped her lips as she deflated back to the mattress. Her wound had reopened. She had tried to talk Doctor Karvex out of stealing the last trans-pod, the last hope for the other civilians on *The Queen Avra*, but he hadn't listened. He had launched himself into the blackness of space as her bullet wound tore open, gushing blood through her hospital gown.

If she hadn't messaged Eryx, she'd be dead.

"Olivia?"

She tore her eyes from the purple crystals of the ceiling to slitted eyes a similar color. Like the last time she had woken, Eryx sat at her bedside. But this time they weren't in the infirmary. This looked like the suite the Herkleians had assigned her, her suitcase probably still spewed open on the bed. Golden metal posters twisted above a levitating king-sized bed across from a floating fireplace. Mirrors flanked either side of a little sitting area, the sofa's cushions a shade darker than the rock ceilings. A single pane of blackish metal served as the kitchenette, able to materialize any meal in a matter of moments. Olivia had wanted to try hers before the wedding but had never gotten the chance.

"Olivia?" Worry filled Eryx's deep voice as he leaned closer, reaching for her. She leaned into the touch, but instead of the heat of his fingers, he stopped an inch before her face. The blue gem on his wristband sparked. A holo-screen flared to life, projecting gibberish above her head. Her vitals.

Olivia buried down her disappointment. Checking her vitals wasn't a bad thing. It was exactly what doctors were supposed to do, right?

She tried for a carefree smile, but it didn't fit her lips. She had almost died. Her last thought was of the alien in front of her, a crease to his forehead as he flicked a clawed finger across the holo-screen. Olivia didn't know him. They had only spent two days together, but somehow, she found herself falling. It'd be easy to love him, easy to trust him.

Damn. This wasn't supposed to happen. *He* wasn't supposed to happen.

"Let me guess," she said, her voice a hoarse croak. "You single-handedly saved my life? Again?"

His lips curved, flashing a hint of fang. "Not entirely by myself, but something like that."

"Aren't you modest?"

He lowered his wrist, the holo-screen fading. "Princes are always taking all the credit, but we rarely do things alone. Nurse Eula helped me. You helped me."

She snorted. "By ripping my wound open?"

"By summoning me." This time, when he reached out, his scaled fingers grazed her chin. "If you hadn't, I don't know what I would have done."

"You'd have survived." Olivia barely managed the words. Her skin tingled where he touched, spreading down her chest to her stomach to her burning core. "You're a survivor, Eryx."

"I don't think I want to survive in a world without you."

Her breath hitched. "You don't mean that. We just met."

His purple eyes remained entranced by her. "I do. Olivia, I—"

She reached forward, placing a finger against his lips. Before she tore her wound, Doctor Karvex had said something about a mark on the back of her neck. Like the mark Lexi had, a swirling of stars the perfect match to Anax's. The matebond mark, she had called it. Was that what he had meant? Was Eryx her mate? Olivia never imagined such a concept, but it felt right. Like it was meant to be.

But what if it wasn't? She had thought her parents meant to be— until suddenly they weren't.

She didn't want him to say it, whatever it was. Either a break to her dreams or a confirmation. She didn't know which was worse. If Eryx wasn't her mate, her heart would break. But if he was and he died here, killed by his father's soldiers in an attempt to save her and the other civilians... That might kill Olivia like a slow-festering wound.

But they had this moment together.

Olivia would make the most of it.

"I surrender."

His forehead creased, so much like a human frown, but yet different. His blue scales puckered and his slitted eyes narrowed. But she didn't mind their differences.

"Surrender to what?" he asked, his voice a low rasp. He knew what she was saying. Knew and yet wasn't sure. Wasn't confident.

How could he not be confident? He was seven feet of pure, scarred muscle. She wanted to thread her hands through his silky green hair and grip the dark bases of his horn. She wanted to cut her thighs on his cheekbones.

She wanted him.

"The universe seems intent on making you my savior." She lowered her hand from his chin to the tops of his pecs. He wasn't close enough for her to truly touch, but he shivered at the kiss of her fingers. "I've almost died twice. We might die soon. Maybe one of us. Probably both of us. So I give up. I give in."

His tongue flickered out, like his lips had dried out at the words. It only sparked the fire deeper within her. Her eyes flickered down the length of his muscled chest to the dark belt of his pants. His straining pants. Dear God. Lexi had told her of Anax's, um, endowment, but she hadn't ever expected to see a Herkleian male in all his naked glory herself.

He pulled away suddenly. "You shouldn't."

The lack of him chilled her. Had she done something wrong? "Shouldn't what?"

"I'm not a good person, Olivia. I did terrible things on Hathor—"

"You father dumped you there. You did what you had to."

"I killed people. They weren't threatening me. I fought in the fighting pits in the Hathorian capital. Sometimes I went against other fighters, but other times they had me fighting animals, innocents." He dropped back into his seat, his head in his hands. Like the admission ruined him. "I could have killed them quickly, but I got paid more if I made it... entertaining. I needed the credits. I was filled with so much rage. I thought if I could afford a shuttle off Hathor, I could go return home and get revenge."

"That makes sense."

"No, Olivia." He nearly growled her name. "There's no excuse for cruelty."

Olivia wanted to grab him by the shoulder and shake him. His father had dropped him on a strange war-torn world. Survival didn't come for free. "But you became a medic, didn't you? You saved people. You saved me."

"In penance. My mentor, Doctor Sagara, rescued me from the fighting pits. He hired me to be his bodyguard, but within a month, I was assisting him with surgeries. I didn't choose to be a good person. It was forced upon me."

Olivia almost laughed, but she clamped down on the sound. She reached for him again. "You can't be forced to be a good person, Eryx."

He leaned away. "Olivia, please. I'd protect you with my life, but I'm not worthy of you."

Worthy of her? From what she knew of him, Eryx was worthy of her, of happiness. But Olivia wasn't asking for that. They might not live to see tomorrow. She didn't know if they could make each other happy in the long term. She hoped, but all either of them had was now. "Who said anything about that?"

Eryx stiffened, his entire body stiff and hard.

She shuddered at the ripple of his muscles, but continued, "We don't even know if we'll survive the week. It doesn't matter if you're worthy forever. You're worthy now. I want you now." When she reached for him this time, she touched, the heat of him sparking through her. She trailed her fingers down his abs. "We might only have this one night. I don't want to be alone. I don't want to be in pain."

He groaned when her fingers settled above the bulge of his cock. "Speak plainly, Olivia."

"You know exactly what I'm saying, Eryx."

"Say it anyway. I'm only a prince. I'm not very smart."

"If you're not very smart, I guess I'll have to give you instructions."

An almost-smile, playful and bold, emerged from his darkness. "Instructions?"

Olivia propped herself on an elbow. Any further and her wound flared painfully, but it gave her the perfect view of him. Did he not like her game? Some human men hated taking orders in the bedroom, but nothing turned her on more than an alpha on his knees. She'd even reciprocate.

At a later date, when she wasn't wounded.

"I'm badly injured," she nearly cooed. "You're my doctor, aren't you? If I'm the patient, you have to help me."

He could barely choke out the next sentence. "And what do you need help with?"

"Your pants, for starters."

He rose to his feet, his muscles uncurling slowly. She shuddered. He hesitated a moment. For a second, she thought his fear would win. But then he flicked a thumb under the edge of his pants and traced to where his cock strained against the fabric. "These pants?"

Olivia had to force her hands still at her side. Her body warred with her. Pull him to her? Touch herself? Both?

When she didn't answer, his lips blossomed into a full, fanged grin. It nearly broke her. "As you command, my lady."

A snap cracked the quiet air, his clawed thumb clicking against the fastening. With a single hand, he slid his pants down and off, tossing them in the corner to land on his boots.

When he rose to full height, Olivia's jaw dropped.

Scars marred the otherwise perfect azure scales of his powerful thighs, but her focus went entirely to his cock. Massive, blue, and ridged like her favorite vibrator. Damn. Her throat dried again, all the moisture in her body fleeing south. At this rate, the inferno between her legs would leak through his bed. Olivia tremored. She couldn't help it. She had an itch she needed scratched.

An itch only *he* could scratch.

"Is this what you wanted?" He wrapped one hand around his cock, stroking himself gently. She had never been jealous of another person's hand before. A deep groan escaped his lips. "What are your commands?"

Olivia wished she could leap off the bed and drop to her knees and take his marvelous length into her mouth. But she couldn't. She couldn't even stand. "I want to touch you."

He quickly closed the distance between him and her bed. Olivia drifted her fingers from his knee up the length of his hard muscle. He grew harder at the touch. Harder and longer. How would he even fit? She didn't know, but she wanted to find out. Olivia drifted her fingers across his cock until she came to his tip. Eryx flinched in her hand, his face pained.

"I wish I could take you into my mouth." She wrapped her tiny hand around the width of him and squeezed. "I wish I could suck you dry."

He nearly thrust into her hand. "I wish I could fuck you until you screamed."

She licked her lips. "But you can't."

"No, I can't. You're too injured for that." He pursed his lips, eyes trailing her body. "As your doctor, I must examine you."

She raised a brow. Olivia never had a doctor fantasy before, but she also never imagined banging an alien. "What exactly do you have to examine, doctor?"

He reached down for the sheets covering her body and flipped them off with a single movement. Cold air prickled up her bare legs. She was in another hospital gown, the fabric thin over her skin. Her dark nipples nearly cut right through.

He put a knuckle to the exposed flesh of her collarbone. "Where does it hurt? Here?"

She liked this game. "Lower."

He thumbed at the peak of her breasts through the fabric. "Here?"

She gasped and nearly buckled. He wasn't even touching her skin yet. "Lower."

He traced across the valley of her stomach, skirting around her wound. Everything tingled under his touch. "Here?"

"Dear God, Eryx." She gripped at the top of her hospital gown and teared at the string holding the fabric together. Warm air caressed her naked skin as she flipped the fabric off, barring herself to the world. To him. She grabbed his wrist and pushed him until his knuckles brushed the dark curls over her core. "Here. Right here."

His lips twitched. "Are you sure?"

"Yes, I'm—" Her sentence turned into a low whimper as he retracted those dark claws and slid a finger through her wet slit. He teased around her opening, but didn't plunge in. His eyes on her, he brought his finger to his mouth and slowly sucked on the digit.

Olivia almost came at the sight. "Yes, I'm sure. Right there. Right fucking there."

"I'll have to get a closer look."

Eryx nudged her legs apart, kneeling into the space between her thighs. Olivia dropped her head. Dear God. How in the world was she going to survive—

Eryx's hot, rough tongue licked her, following the path his finger had taken.

Olivia gripped a pillow. "Oh, God."

"You taste like Ganja berries," he growled into her, the puffs of his breaths on her sensitive flesh.

Hopefully that was a good thing. Before she said it, his head lowered again. He explored her with his tongue, from her depths to the bead of her clit. She almost pounced off the bed when he swirled his tongue around her most sensitive spot. "Eryx, please..."

"Please, what?" he murmured.

A thousand commands swirled through her head. She settled on one. "Your fangs."

He grinned up at her, a devilish look. Olivia almost came on the spot.

Eryx caressed his fangs against the edge of her clit. Olivia nearly saw sparks. Her back arched. He found a rhythm of sucking and nipping, a torturous pattern. She threaded her hands through his emerald hair. He growled into her when she tugged too hard, but she didn't care. The fire in her burned, trying to consume her.

He plunged a finger into her depths.

Olivia moaned, a reckless sound. Her hands clenched on the base of his horns. His entire body tensed, his finger twitching inside her. Rubbing up against her inner walls. Like his cock would, if he thrust it within her, those perfect ridges finding the spot that made her scream.

Which his finger found a second later.

His scaled finger rubbed against her, once, twice. Olivia writhed in abandon. Nothing mattered but his fingers. His tongue. Eryx, between her knees, worshipping her. She stroked his horns, holding on as she crested, rising like she never had.

Olivia surrendered entirely.

Her body exploded in a wave of warmth. She shouted his name as he drank her in, consuming her. Like no man had ever done. Olivia collapsed onto the bed, her breath rushing out of her. Dear God. If that was Herkleian oral, how the heck would she survive the full thing?

Eryx moved between her legs and kissed her thigh, a glazed, sated look in his eyes. "You're amazing."

Olivia flushed. She wanted to grab him by the horn, leading that wicked mouth to hers. She tugged gently. "Come here."

Eryx crawled up her front, careful to hover his weight off her. His muscles tensed with the effort. If only she could lick every straining bulge. She trailed her fingers across the lines of his cheekbones. He had plunged his rough tongue inside her, but she had never kissed him on the lips.

She lured his mouth to hers.

His tongue clashed with her, her taste on his lips. She swallowed him whole. Needed more. Wanted more. Olivia threaded her hands through his hair—

Eryx pulled away. "You'll hurt yourself."

"Not touching you hurts more."

Eryx rolled gently onto the space beside her. His purple-slitted eyes faced her. "Olivia, I—"

She silenced him with another kiss. She didn't want to hear about their future. Didn't want to hear if they were mates or not. If they would survive or not. They had no guarantee of tomorrow. Only now.

Olivia snuggled into his side. "Hold me?"

He gathered her into his muscled arms. "As you command."

ELEVEN

Eryx traced his claws gently across Olivia's sleeping face. Her pink lips parted, releasing little sighs. His cock hardened at the sounds. What did he do to deserve such a perfect mate? What did he do to deserve a mate at all? Before his brother, the goddess Hyra hadn't blessed a couple with a matebond in nearly a century. Yet here he was, tucked into bed on a hostile space station, the twisting of a star-shaped pattern growing on his neck, the same as hers.

Olivia twisted in her sleep, turning her head away from him, barring her neck and her mark. It had solidified since he last checked it. As they had grown to know each other. A satisfied warmth filled his chest at the sight, but also a fear. She deserved someone better than him. More than that, she deserved to live. The Eógan and Herkleian ships were still a day away. If Olivia discovered their bond, would she be able to leave him? Even if she never learned of their connection and they parted, would she succumb like mates some-times did in stories from his great-grandmother's time?

Eryx didn't want to worry. He wanted to live in the moment, enjoying the softness of the bed and the warmth of his mate. But life on Hathor always had him looking to the future. When would their next shipment of supplies arrive? Would it get to the camp before the most critical of their patients died? Worse, would the militia attack, forcing him and Doctor Sagara to abandon those who couldn't flee? Medics caught in the field received no mercy at the militia's hands. Eryx had known that long before meeting his mentor.

When he was more Butcher than healer.

A sharp alarm pierced the quiet air.

Olivia jolted awake with a little shriek as Eryx sat straight, his hand automatically tapping his gold wristband. He had disconnected his external comms last night, wanting no interruptions with Olivia. He should have turned them back on. The station was a war zone and Eryx a commander.

"What's happening?" Olivia rubbed at her eyes.

Eryx scanned her with a critical eye. He had attached a portable nano-bandage to her wound hours ago. Hopefully, it had healed enough if they needed to flee. "Let me find out."

She nodded as his comms connected to *The Queen Avra*'s systems, a faint crackle in his ear. He immediately tapped Dexus's name. "Report."

"Our scanners detected another ship," the captain promptly replied, a huff to his breath. Like he was running. "I'm headed to the control room now."

Eryx pushed off the blanket and rose from the bed. Olivia made a funny noise behind him. When he twisted, her eyes were glued to his bare ass. If only he could climb back into bed with her. Fuck her like she deserved. He flashed her a grin as he bent to grab his pants. She licked her lips.

Eryx had to stop himself from groaning across the comms. "Do we know if it's Neithan?"

"It's a Class-A warship in stealth mode, which is why we didn't detect it until now. We'll know what side they're on when they come into sight. I'll report to you immediately."

"No need. I'll meet you in the control room, Dexus." Eryx strapped a laser to his thigh holster. He hoped the ship was an ally but feared another enemy. Eryx wouldn't be so lucky, not again. He used all his graces with the goddess to get Olivia. "Until then, stream all data through an encrypted message to my brother. If we're attacked, we might not have a chance to update them."

When Eryx turned, Olivia had climbed from the bed, the blanket wrapped around her body. "Eryx?"

He rushed to her side. "Sit. I don't want your wound to re-open."

"It feels fine." She waved her pale hand, brushing away his concern. "What's going on?"

"A ship approaches. We don't know who." He tried to lead her back to bed. "I must go to the control room, but I'll be back."

"I'll come with you."

"Olivia—"

"Eryx." She held out a hand, the blanket sliding down her side. His cock twitched at the sight of her skin. "Just because you gave me the most amazing orgasm of my life does not mean you get to tell me what to do, Mr. Alpha."

Who was Mr. Alpha? His confusion washed away under a wave of pride. The most amazing orgasm of her life. He couldn't stop his lips from twitching. Eryx hadn't smiled this frequently in three years.

She gently whacked his shoulder. "Don't smile at me like that. I'm serious."

He clasped her small hand. Her skin was soft, breakable, like her tiny frame and fragile bones. Eryx would never forgive himself if something happened to this female. But if he left her here and they were attacked, would he have the chance to return? "I'll carry you to the control room."

"Don't be—"

"It's my one condition."

She let out a huff of air. "Fine. Carry me, Mr. Alpha."

After materializing Olivia an outfit, Eryx plucked her into his arms. She crossed her arms the entire way there, perhaps in annoyance, but she leaned into his side. Her one hand drifted across his pecs, sliding between the groves of a scar. Eryx never wanted to put her down, but his quarters were only two hallways from the control room.

Within minutes, he lowered her back to her feet before the double doors.

He waved a hand before the door's sensor. "After you."

Olivia walked into the control room before him. Through the flashes of her dark hair, their matebond mark wasn't visible. His was hidden, too, barely covered by the strands of his green hair. Thank Hyra. Eryx was torn between telling Olivia and keeping her in the dark, but the information should come from him. Not one of his soldiers.

The Herkleians, Eógans, Guroverians, and Fens all circled the main command table, a blank projection flickering above the space. At their entry, Captain Dexus emerged from the crowd. "The ship will be in view within a minute, Eryx."

"Do we have shields?"

"They're still down from the Sutekan sabotage."

Hadus. "And our unwelcome guests?"

"The Neithans can't raise their shields while docked." Dexus flicked to a different screen, relaying the cleaning droid's feed. A group of furred Neithans and gilled Sutekans played Cubes, their dice clattering across a table outside the hangar bay. "We think they're aware of the ship, but they don't care about its approach. Their focus remains on hacking our systems and trying to restore the atmosphere to the second deck."

Not a good sign. If the ship was an ally, the Neithans had good reason not to worry.

Eryx took Olivia's hand and approached the table. Some of the soldiers stared at where they touched, but none said a word. He pulled the head chair from the table. Olivia settled into it.

Eryx faced the soldiers around him. "We won't go down without a fight. We may be outnumbered, but I stand among the greatest fighters from across the Intergalactic Alliance. We will make these invaders regret every laying eyes on this station."

The Fens burst into a war chant, echoed by Guroverian chirping and Herkleian growling. Eryx joined in. He wasn't half as confident as he sounded, but there was no point putting extra stress on his soldiers. Mindset was half the battle.

Olivia reached out for his hand. "Men," she muttered, light enough that only he could hear.

Eryx raised her hand and lowered his lips to her knuckles—

Something flashed across the screen.

"Incoming transmission from the new vessel," Dexus said.

Eryx straightened. "Do we have a visual yet?"

"Not yet. They're still cloaked."

"Accept the call." Eryx prayed to Hyra that it wasn't another enemy. They could barely hold off the current intruders.

Static crackles against the line for a minute, the control room dropping into silence. Olivia clenched his hand. He rubbed his thumb against her skin. No matter the threat, he'd keep her safe.

"*The Queen Avra*, this is General MacKenzie of the *USS Pegasus*."

Olivia jumped from her seat. "Yes!"

The control room burst into relieved cheers. Eryx bared his fangs at his mate, but his smile slipped when she slumped back into the chair. Eryx's heart nearly stopped. If her wound reopened...

She saw his expression. "It's okay. I just stood too fast. I'll be fine."

"Are you sure?"

"Of course." She smiled gently at him. Almost hesitantly. Like she was as scared of this thing blossoming between them as he was. "Thank you for calling Earth."

"You were right, Olivia. It doesn't hurt to ask for help."

The connection to the *USS Pegasus* crackled again. "When we received your hail, Prince Eryx, we turned our ship right around. We're here to offer our allies assistance and protect all civilians on board, human or not."

"We very much appreciate the help, General," Eryx said. "My brother will be grateful for your actions."

"While we struck our alliance with Xenobaccus, we want what's best for all our planets. Earth is ready to fight to keep King Anax on the throne."

Eryx glanced down at his mate. He had called Earth for Olivia, not only because he trusted her, but because he needed her and the other civilians off the ship. Without them to worry about, Eryx could focus on holding the first deck until the Eógan fleet arrived. Whatever his father wanted, he couldn't let him get it.

But Eryx wished he'd told Olivia that before entering the control room. His fiery mate would be pissed.

"We need to get the civilians off this ship, General. Once we accomplish that, we can talk about transporting some of your soldiers over."

"Wait." Olivia turned on him. "What?"

Dexus cleared his throat with a growl. "We're still shielding from all inter- and intra-ship transportation, Eryx."

Eryx ignored his captain to focus on his mate. She had climbed to her feet and poked him in the chest. "You can't just kick me off the station."

"You are so brave, Olivia." Eryx cupped her face in his hands. Dexus quickly averted his eyes, as did the other Herkleians, Eógans and Guroverians. Helgi and his Fens outwardly leered. "I admire your spirit, but I gave my word to Anax and Lexi to keep you safe. I always keep my word. You must get off this station before it becomes too dangerous."

She tried to glare, but his hands on her cheeks caressed away the worst of her anger. "And how do you plan to do that? Throw me out with the garbage?"

Eryx pursed his lips, almost in consideration. Olivia swatted him on the shoulder. He captured her flailing hands and pressed a kiss to her soft skin. He never wanted to stop kissing her. But he had to let her go. Had to get her out. Once she was on the *USS Pegasus*, he'd concern himself with the other civilians. Olivia was the last remaining Earthling. She belonged with her people.

And there was only one way to get her there.

Eryx glanced over her head at Dexus. "If the civilians were to go outside the ship, the *USS Pegasus* could lock onto their location and transport them aboard?"

Dexus's eyes widened. He tapped quickly at his holo-screen, scanning the station's schematics. "Yes. The shields only operate within the ship."

"I'll bring the *USS Pegasus* into range," General MacKenzie said.

Olivia's jaw dropped. "Putting aside the fact that I'm not leaving, you think it's a good idea to just throw me into deep space until I *suffocate?*"

He rubbed his thumb across her palm, soothing her. "You won't suffocate. We'll get you a suit and tether you to the ship. If the USS *Pegasus* can't get a lock on you, then we can easily accept your return."

"My return." She pulled her hands from his and even stomped her foot a bit. Like a galaf bear challenging another female, staking a claim on its territory. Eryx didn't think she was doing that exactly, but the anger was implied. "I'm not some ill-fitting shirt. I'm a person!"

What did shirts have to do with anything? Eryx repressed a shudder. Unnatural things. Herkleian males saw no reason to hide their muscles, Eryx no exception. He flexed unconsciously, Olivia's eyes enraptured by the movement. She shook her head, snapping out of the trance. "I'm not going."

But she had to go. Eryx couldn't lose her. He stepped back from the table, pulling her away from his soldiers. She came reluctantly. Eryx stroked his hands down her arms and ducked his head until his eyes were near level with her shorter frame. "It kills me to know I can't ensure your safety if you stay with me. I don't want you to leave, either, but if you're still here when the invaders break into our deck— which they will, eventually—I know I'll be distracted thinking about if you've fallen into their hands. And that isn't fair to my soldiers.

They need me fully present." He lowered his forehead to hers. "I know it goes against your nature to walk from a fight, but right now leaving is the best thing you can do for everyone."

Tears pricked at her eyes. "Eryx..."

"Please, Olivia. For me. Leave for me. Live for me. For what we could've been."

She sniffled, her arms still crossed. No longer a shield but a brace, holding her together. She closed her eyes, a battle across her expression. When she opened those blue eyes, the tears streamed down her cheeks, but hard determination replaced the sadness and rage. "You better not die."

He squeezed her arms. "I don't plan to."

Olivia traced a knuckle against his jaw before thinking better of it. She wrapped an arm around his head, luring his mouth to hers. Eryx gave in, surrendering. Her mouth clashed against his. He wrapped her in his embrace as she curled her hands through his hair, nudging at the base of his horns. He nearly groaned into her mouth, but instead plundered her with his tongue, claiming her. If he didn't survive this, she'd never know she was his mate, but if he did, he didn't plan to leave her. He'd done nothing to deserve her, but Eryx couldn't resist her anymore. The Herkleian palace and life of a prince was no longer his—but Olivia could be his home, his life.

He would protect his mate with his last breath.

TWELVE

OLIVIA

Olivia gawked at outer space. Actual outer space. Seeing it through the windows of her cabin didn't at all compare to standing in it, the magnets in her boots and the cord at her back the only things keeping her from floating away. Never in a million years had she dreamed this possible. Millions of stars flickered all around her in a silent darkness. Everywhere she turned lay a desolate beauty of blackness and bright.

"Olivia?" Eryx's deep voice crackled in her ear.

"Oops." Olivia wasn't here to stare at her surroundings. She had to get far enough from the doors for the *USS Pegasus* to get a lock on her location. "Got distracted."

"You have to go another five feet."

Olivia nodded. Not that Eryx was within her line of sight, but he said he'd watch her through the external cams. She didn't know where they were, but hopefully he saw the nod. Olivia raised a boot. She pulled to get the magnet off and then pushed to her next step. Like walking through water, but worse. Like walking through molasses? Olivia had never tried that.

"God, this is a lot of work."

"Is your wound hurting you?"

Her hand went down to her stomach, her gloves hitting the suit. She didn't think so? Eryx had stitched her wound by hand and applied a nano-bandage. Together, they could hold long enough for her to get off *The Queen Avra*.

"Am I far enough yet?"

"A few more steps."

Olivia wanted him to keep talking. She didn't know if she'd hear his voice again. If she'd ever see him again. The male who had stolen her guarded heart in a matter of days. "Eryx?"

"Yes?"

"Just say something. Anything."

"I surrender."

Olivia halted. "What?"

"I surrender to you. What I feel for you. I feared this thing between us but not anymore. You're right. We might die at any second—"

Olivia glanced at the open, deadly space around her. "Maybe not a great time to bring that up."

He chuckled. "I'm sorry." Eryx paused, almost like he was nervous. He, a seven-foot-tall, muscled alien warrior prince. "This could be the end. I couldn't have you leave without knowing. I never imagined a life with someone before, but I can imagine one with you."

Olivia's tears started again. Instead of dripping down her cheeks, the little droplets floated through her helmet and splattered against the glass like rain against a windshield. "You're making me cry."

"I don't want you to cry."

She snorted. "Well, I am. Eryx, how can I leave you now?"

"One more step, Olivia."

Olivia inhaled, forcing her tears to a trickle. One more step. For her. For Eryx. She twisted back to the ship, wishing she could see him on the other side of the gilded door. "Goodbye, Eryx."

Olivia took the last step—

A white light flashed across her vision.

Olivia raised her head. Her jaw dropped. A ship floated above *The Queen Avra*. Empty space turned to metal, twisting words painted on the side. Not Earth words. And not an Earth ship. Olivia had watched *USS Pegasus*'s first launch from her apartment in LA. The sleek, car-like ship didn't look at all like the donut-shaped dome spinning above her.

Damn.

"Olivia!"

"Eryx..." Olivia licked her lips, suddenly nervous. "Who is that?"

"More Neithans."

Olivia nodded to herself, a cloying thickness spreading through her chest. If she weren't in space, adrenaline pumping through her veins, she'd break into hysterical laughter. "Wonderful."

"Hold on." Eryx's comms distorted. The flash of voices pulsed in and out in her ear. "...lower...now...Olivia...dead!"

"Well, that doesn't bode well," she muttered, staring up at the Neithan ship.

As the Neithans stared down at her.

Something mechanical twisted on the bottom of the donut-ship. Something far more threatening than a donut. It extended toward her like a mechanical arm with a bright, swirly bit on the end. As it reached out, the bit got brighter and brighter.

Was that a fucking space laser?

Olivia shrieked as the laser's glow harshened, weapons powering—

The world went dark as tingles crawled her spine.

Olivia hit the floor.

She patted at her shoulders, her torso. Everything accounted for, the suit and all. Through her helmet, she spotted crystal rock ceilings. Familiar ceiling. Eryx appeared over her a second later, his mouth moving. She didn't hear any words. Her eardrums had popped like a bomb had gone off.

Or like Eryx had beamed her inside right as the Neithans shot at her.

Her hearing returned. She flinched. An alarm blared, twice as loud as the one that had summoned her from Eryx's bed. Voices shouted around her as something crackled and flared. A feathered, sand-skinned alien ran past, holding the intergalactic version of a fire extinguisher. The Neithans had freaking shot at her—and through her, the hallway. She glanced at the wall nearest to where she'd stood. A fried, black splotch marred the once-gold surface, but thankfully the hull wasn't breached. The deck below was probably a mess. Olivia stared dully.

She had nearly been shot by a freaking space laser.

Eryx grabbed her hand and pulled her to her feet. Thankfully, Herkleian spacesuits weren't as bulky as Earth ones, but the movement was still awkward. Pain flared through her gut.

She bent over. "Oh, God."

Eryx dropped to his knees, tearing at the clasps of her suit. "Are you hurt?"

"I think..." She swallowed. "I need to sit."

He leaned closer, but the helmet obscured her words. He unclipped it and ripped it from her shoulders. "What?"

Olivia slumped into his arms, the only answer Eryx needed. He caught her in his firm grasp. All the strength fled her body. Her stupid, weak body. If Eryx was the one with the life-threatening stomach injury, it wouldn't slow him down for an instant. Olivia tried to push off him, but her legs were noodles.

Eryx nestled her within his arms and rose.

Olivia curled into his warmth. "You really have a thing for carrying me."

"Always, Olivia."

The heat from his arms spread to her chest. Eryx was too good to be true. Too good to be hers. He had to have a flaw. Olivia squinted at him, but he simply pressed a quick kiss to her nose.

He turned to a nearby Herkleian technician. "Status report?"

The female tapped at her holo-screen. "Minimal damage to the first deck, sir. The second looks worse, but I don't think it was breached."

He nodded before tapping his ear. "Dexus?"

Olivia didn't hear the captain's reply, but Eryx's face sagged in relief. She tugged at his arm. Olivia might fulfil every part of the damsel-in-distress role, but she wasn't about to let a bunch of alpha aliens keep her in the dark.

"The second Neithan ship has powered down their weapons," he said. "They were trying to stop you, nothing more. If they had wanted to do more, they'd have fired at full strength."

"And the *USS Pegasus*?" If Olivia had just destroyed Earth's only spaceship, she'd never forgive herself. If she hadn't suggested it to Eryx, General MacKenzie and every Earthling on board would be home right now.

"Retreated. They don't have the firepower to fight two Neithan ships."

"Do we?"

He swallowed. "No."

Damn. Olivia tightened her hold on Eryx's shoulders. "What are we going to do?"

"*We* aren't going to do anything." When she frowned, he tapped a finger against her lips. "You're returning to my room. You need to rest."

She snorted. "Like I could relax at a time like this."

"You need to heal."

"We need a plan to get off this station. My healing doesn't matter if we don't."

He frowned. This time, she tapped his lips. His rough tongue flicked out a quick kiss. "While you rest, I'll return to the control room. We have other options."

She hooked a thumb over her shoulder at the airlock she had walked through minutes earlier. "Wasn't that your last option?"

Eryx clutched her tighter to his chest. "Wars are constantly changing, Olivia. We'll adapt to this setback like we do all others."

She snorted. "That sounds like a bullshit answer to me."

His lip twitched. "It is."

Olivia didn't know how he retained his sense of humor at a time like this, but it was oddly reassuring. She should be panicking, but in Eryx's arms, everything was right. She could no longer hide her feelings for him. That realization was like a weight being lifted off her shoulders. She lowered her head onto his shoulder. "Fine. I'll rest. But the moment you guys have a plan, you message me."

"You'll be the first to know."

They arrived quickly at Eryx's room, his long strides covering twice the distance than her shorter legs. Not that she had ever walked into Eryx's quarters herself. He carried her over the threshold and into the bedroom. The bedsheets had righted themselves, a pile of golden pillows fluffed and artfully arranged near the twisting gold headboard. Certainly not the way either of them had left it, not after the thrashing Olivia did.

Her face flushed, desire welling in her core.

Eryx growled. "You need rest."

As he lowered her to the bed, she tugged him down. "So do you."

He smiled against her lips. "What you have planned isn't rest."

Eryx pulled back, drenching her in cold. But he didn't leave entirely, instead sitting at her side. Olivia tried to pull him closer, but she melted into the mattress. Exhaustion slammed into her. The pillows and bedding were smooth. Had the bed been this comfortable last night?

He stroked her forehead, lulling her into sleep. "I'll return shortly."

She yawned. "You better."

"Olivia, I—"

The overhead speakers dinged. Eryx straightened, a frown creasing his face.

"Are you expecting an announcement?"

Eryx tapped at his wristband. "Dexus didn't say—"

"You've made quite a mess of things, my dear son," a growly voice echoed through the room. Eryx's scales dimmed, his version of pale. Olivia gripped his forearm as the message continued. "Come to Father and maybe I can salvage the situation. My soldiers have restarted the life support on the second deck. Meet me in the replication room in thirty minutes. I'll come alone and unarmed. I expect you'll do the same."

The overhead speakers dinged again, marking the end of the message. Olivia was too terrified to ask. Eryx never showed fear—until now. Like a ghost from his past, returned to haunt him.

Or worse, his murderous bastard of a father, Xenobaccus.

"And so my firstborn son returns."

Eryx stiffened as the replication room's door slid shut behind him. Since no one had turned off the wedding scene, his surroundings remained a Herkleian forest glittering in the night. Overturned chairs scattered across the once-clear aisle, the flower bouquets torn and stomped upon. Hints of dried gunk smeared the scene—blue on the ground, green on the banners, red on the platform where his father sat. Dried blood. His father tapped his booted foot in the exact spot Olivia had fallen.

Her dried blood marred his shoe.

Eryx pushed down a storm of rage. He'd sworn to his mate he'd return. Eryx didn't trust his father, not entirely. Olivia and Dexus had thought this a trap and tried to convince him to stay, but Eryx knew his father. Xenobaccus had a plan, one Eryx wouldn't like, but it wouldn't be to kill him. His father wanted something and thought Eryx could give whatever it was to him. He had nothing to lose by listening. If anything, it bought his soldiers time to prepare.

Not that Eryx was entirely safe. In his father's presence, he once again became that naive prince, betrayed and banished. Eryx clenched his fists, his claws digging into his scales. He had buried that boy in the sands of Hathor. That was where Prince Eryx of Herkleios had to stay. He wouldn't let his father get under his scales.

Eryx strolled across the aisle, pretending he was indifferent to seeing his father after all this time. The closer he got, the smaller the male became. Aging gold streaked his father's black hair, his shoulders slumped and his hand gripping the hilt of his cane. In Eryx's youth, his father had been a warrior, towering and muscled. The last three years stole much of that strong king, but Eryx knew it was partially another trick. When his father confronted Anax and Lexi six months ago, he had forgotten his cane in his anger.

His father's vanity hadn't changed, though. Jewels threaded through the white of his robes, his shoulder sash weighted down with real gold. His horns and claws were further adorned with blue zafers and bits of gold, the colors of the Herkleian flag.

"These past years have treated you well, my boy." He looked Eryx over, already accessing him for weaknesses. "Look at the muscles you've formed. I can tell you've matured greatly."

Eryx crossed his arms over his chest. "If you call having to look death in the eyes every day for three years maturing."

Xenobaccus snorted, a growly sound. "Don't be so dramatic, my son. You were never in any real danger."

Eryx stiffened.

"You really think you could hide from me?"

Impossible. He had escaped his father on Hathor. The last three years of torture and blood couldn't be his doing. "The Sutekans you hired to kidnap me died in the crash."

"A crash I arranged." His father plucked his cane from his side and used it to tap the seat across from him. Eryx ignored it. He wouldn't sit with his father like they were friends. "Who do you think gave those dirty pirates such a nice ship?"

No. Eryx stayed stoic on the outside, but on the inside, the carefree prince revived and screamed. Not only had his father banished him and lied to his family, but also sentenced him to the cruelty of Hathor's wars. "Why?"

"Hathor isn't part of the Intergalactic Alliance. Its leadership had the chance to join twenty years ago when I wedded your *beloved* mother, sealing the agreement."

His mother. Eryx tensed. His father had mourned her, but Eryx was the one who had sat by Queen Avra's bed as the scale rot claimed her. It wasn't something any child should witness. But before he even managed a growl, Xenobaccus snapped his claws. The replication room exploded into color, the forest replaced by a stretch of desert, a loud crashing in the distance. Eryx twisted. In the distance, a militia ship dropped bombs on the remains of Inaros.

"This is what happens when you let savages rule themselves." Eryx had to strain to hear his father's voice over the distant scream. "Therefore, we Herkleians should rule all planets."

The Anpu militia had bombed Inaros a week before Eryx heard the news about his brother's ascension. A week after Doctor Sagara's death. This scene couldn't be a coincidence. His father had truly been watching him. And for what? "You want me to see your side? To agree with you?"

"I could have sent you to a dozen other planets if that were my only aim," Xenobaccus said. "When you learned the plans I had for you and your siblings, to make each of you a king or queen of an Alliance world, you turned your back on me. And not even out of morality issues like Anax. You and I know it was because it'd require action, but you preferred partying with your friends." His father climbed to his feet, his cane forgotten. Eryx started to back away before halting his feet. "I had failed you, my son. Sending you to Hathor was my way to fix you. Make you a male worthy of Hyra's might."

Eryx imagined pulling his blade and piercing it through his father's eye. "So you're claiming my years spent in a war zone were for character development?"

"It worked, didn't it?" Xenobaccus slapped him on the shoulder.

Eryx clenched the hilt of his blade. "Yes, it was a risk. You could have died or learned nothing, but that was the gamble. And look at how well it turned out. You're a better male for it. You've witnessed the destruction of a civilization and became a warrior."

A warrior? Eryx had become the Butcher in the fighting pits, less male and more monster. If it weren't for Doctor Sagara, he'd be a beast. His father didn't deserve credit for his dead mentor's work. "I became a healer."

"Eventually." His father circled him like the predator he was. "I was disappointed by the path you took at first. I paid the Anpu militia handsomely to attend your fighting pit performances. But in that, I was wrong. You witnessed suffering firsthand in trying to save lives. Perhaps more than if you were the one causing the pain."

Eryx's focus narrowed to a single sentence. Everything around him disappeared, from the beaming Hathorian sun to the screams of the dying. "You *paid* the Anpu militia?"

"I paid them to do a lot of things." His father bared his fangs, an unpleasant look. "Do you want to know Doctor Sagara's last words?"

"Go, Eryx." The memory of Sagara overwhelmed him. The male had shoved him, but Eryx barely stumbled at the push. His mentor's once-strong body weakened to malnourishment and injury, but his eyes remained clear and determined. When he dropped his hand, it was stained orange with blood. *"If you stay here a moment longer, boy, the Anpu will kill you, too. Live. Save the lives I won't be able to save."*

Eryx grabbed his father's sash with a snarl. He left Doctor Sagara to succumb to his wounds, the Anpu militia closing on their location. Eryx tried not to imagine his mentor's death. When it snuck into his nightmare, the Anpu found him still alive, shoved their claws into his wounds, and laughed as he squirmed.

Eryx's nightmares had been right.

His vision flashed red, all ration fleeing in the beast's path. Eryx pulled his knife, ready to plunge it through his father's throat. Whatever his father had ordered, Doctor Sagara didn't deserve. His aim focused on his father's pulse—

The buzzing tip of a laser tapped the back of his head.

Eryx stiffened. His father's grin widened, even as a drop of purple-blue blood trailed his throat. If the two Sutekan pirates at his back had been a second slower, he'd have killed his father, severing the major artery in his neck. Eryx nearly laughed. Did he thank the pirates or curse at them?

What kind of male killed his own father? What kind of monster?

The pirates nudged their weapons into Eryx's head. He growled out a sigh and lowered his blade. Of course his father hadn't come alone as promised.

Xenobaccus gestured to where Eryx's claws stabbed through his sash. "Release me."

Eryx glared but dropped his bastard of a father. "You broke your word."

The male rearranged his sash. "I'm old now, Eryx. My soldiers would have remained cloaked had you not threatened me."

Invisibility cloaking was still being tested by the military on Herkleios. What other assets had his father stolen when he fled? Eryx shook away the thought. His father liked to drop hints, little threads that he tugged on. Luring him with a complex web like the Therios spiders did their prey. Eryx couldn't play his games anymore. His father would twist him into the monster he left behind on Hathor— not a male worthy of Olivia. "What do you want?"

His father settled back into his chair. When he touched the armrest, the wedding chair became a gilded throne. "What I've always wanted, my son. To carve out an empire that will stand the test of time for my descendants."

Eryx rolled his shoulders, the Sutekans retracting a step. "And to remove Anax from the crown?"

"I am the rightful king by the divine will of Hyra, just as you are my rightful heir. I know you care for your brother, Eryx. I promise you when I take back the throne, I'll spare Anax. He'll spend the rest of his life under house arrest, but he can keep that little mate of his. She's sure to provide me a grandchild eventually."

Eryx gritted his fangs. "How do you intend to defeat him? You know these mercenaries will be no match for Herkleian warriors."

"Which is why I've allied with the Neithans," his father said. "King Akhen has always been my puppet and his dearest daughter is your brother Argrix's wife. The king does what I want and Neithan technology is comparable to our own."

Olivia and Dexus were right. If Eryx hadn't come, he wouldn't have to experience the dread pooling in his gut. "Then why are we having this discussion?"

"There is another piece to the puzzle." Xenobaccus lazily picked at his claws. "When I attacked this station, I wanted your brother dead. But since he escaped, I will have to settle for you."

The dread coiled into a spark of fear, but Eryx refused to show it. He stayed silent, waiting. His father wanted an audience for his mastermind. He had a captive one.

"I'm sure you've heard a Neithan fleet surrounds Herkleios. With a single command, I could have them attack, but the battle between the Neithan and Herkleian militaries would destroy our dear planet. I won't commit such a blasphemous act." He glanced from his claws, a maniacal look in his purple slitted eyes. "But when your brother arrives with the Eógan military, he'll allow you to transport on board."

No doubt with an army of Neithans at his back. Eryx wouldn't betray his brother, not for anything. "Why would I help you?"

"Well, if you don't, I'll kill everyone on this station."

"So you're threatening my life again if I don't align with you?"

"Oh, no, Eryx." Xenobaccus howled, a slightly insane laugh. "I would never kill you. If you die, the death of your beautiful mate can't claw at your conscience."

His beautiful mate. In three words, Eryx's world exploded. His father knew about Olivia.

His father *threatened* Olivia.

He launched forward with a growl, but the Sutekans grabbed at his arms. He tossed them off with a quick movement. Fuck maintaining the peace. No one threatened his mate. He pressed his blade to his father's throat again. This time, he wouldn't hesitate. "How?"

His father didn't need elaboration. "I have spies everywhere. When I heard about your tryst with the human, I knew she must be your mate. Your brother abandoned all sense when he met Alexandra. Will you sacrifice it all for a human, too?"

It'd be so easy to slit his father's neck. Watch the purple-blue blood stain his father's sash, his jewels, his fake throne. Eryx could revel in it. Smear it across his face like war paint as he did in the fighting pits. The death would stain him forever, but he'd do it for Olivia. To protect his mate, who didn't even know the threat she faced.

Didn't even know she was his mate.

But if he did this, he didn't deserve her. Worse, it almost guaranteed her death. Without his father holding back his army, Eryx's soldiers stood no chance. The Butcher slithered under his surface, craving blood. He needed to reign it back like he had for two years.

Eryx pushed away from his father's throne. "We're done here."

"I'll give you until tomorrow morning to reconsider." His father flicked his claws, banishing Eryx from the room like a king to a peasant. "If I don't hear from you, Olivia Harper will not live to see another day."

FOURTEEN

OLIVIA

Olivia paced the short distance between the bed and the couch for the thousandth time.

She hadn't wanted Eryx to speak to his father. The ex-king had nearly killed her best friend, not to mention desired to enslave Earth and every other 'savage' planet. He didn't deserve anyone's time, especially not from a son he'd banished. But a part of her knew it was the right decision. If the enemy wanted to talk and the chance of ambush was unlikely, opening a channel of dialogue could only bring more information.

"Egh, I sound like my dad." Olivia slumped down onto the couch and dropped her head in her hands. It didn't matter what she thought about Xenobaccus. Eryx had left to speak with him. Whatever happened, happened.

Which was another thing her dad said.

Olivia needed a distraction. She followed the swirling lines of glowing purple crystal in the ceiling. Lexi had told her the crystal rocks came from the caves where ancient Herkleians lived—a connection to a distant past. Her hand rested on her chest above her wound. The nano-bandage buzzed with a soft heat, busy at work healing her torn skin. Eryx said she'd need to wear it for another day or two.

Hopefully she had another day or two.

Olivia straightened. God, she needed a drink. Herkleians couldn't get drunk, but surely Lexi had ordered some for the reception.

The door behind her dinged and opened. Olivia jumped from the couch—

Strong, scaled arms wrapped around her shoulders, followed by Eryx's intoxicating scent. His chin rested on her head as Olivia glanced up. He clung to her like she might disappear at any moment. He inhaled, breathing her in like she did him.

"I'm guessing it didn't go well with your father?"

Eryx squeezed her tighter at the mention of Xenobaccus. What the hell had the bastard said to him? "He wants me to help him get onboard the Eógan ship with Anax when it arrives."

"That's crazy." Olivia turned in his arms. "Even if you did, how would that help him? I thought Anax held the support of the military. How does he plan to overthrow a warship, much less an entire planet?"

"The Neithans are a match for us technologically. We've been sharing inventions with them for decades. They owe a lot to my father."

Olivia's heart dropped. "And if he can get one planet from the Intergalactic Alliance, he can turn others."

Eryx nodded, the pain in his eyes reflected in hers. How had they only known each other a few days? Looking into his face, it was like Olivia had known him a lifetime. She wanted that lifetime. A part of Olivia warned her, screaming to pull away. She ignored her, instead leaning closer to rub a hand down his back. "None of that matters, Eryx. You have no reason to do what he wants."

Eryx ducked his chin.

Oh, no. "What does he have?"

Those beautiful purple eyes met hers. "He knows about you."

"What about me?"

"He's threatened to kill you if I don't comply." He paused. "And everyone else on the station, but especially you."

"I'm nothing special, but thanks, I guess."

He caressed her cheek. "You are special, Olivia."

Emotions swelled within her, a mess she couldn't decipher. "I think you're pretty special, too."

Something warred across his face, a brief flicker, before determination entered his eyes. "I don't know how much Lexi told you about the matebonds, but in Herkleian culture, the goddess Hyra grants the mark to two people whose souls are the same, showing to all that they belong together."

Olivia's throat went dry. She knew Eryx was special the moment she first saw him. But soulmates didn't exist. If they did, they were meant for people like Lexi—women who married princes and became queens. Not Olivia, with her ripped jeans and weird sense of humor.

Her neck tingled, but Olivia ignored it. There couldn't be a mark there. "Eryx, I—"

He dropped to his knees, his head bowed low. His emerald waves of hair slid to either side of his neck, barring his scales—and the star-shape twist upon his nape. Olivia's stomach fluttered. It couldn't be true, but she had never wanted anything so badly. Olivia traced the sapphire-colored mark. The shape's outline was a circle, but within thousands of tiny lines formed their own unique star. She had never witnessed anything like it. She shivered, a full body shudder trailing her neck.

"And I suppose you think I have the matching mark on my neck?" She tried to sound nonchalant, but she knew if she didn't, her heart would break into a million pieces.

"How could you doubt that?" Eryx raised his head and took her hands. "I've never experienced this before. I loved my mother. Anax and my siblings. My father, once. But none of that compares to what I feel for you, Olivia. My heart bursts when you're nearby. I feel complete, whole. You are the naika to my naikos. You're my heart and will always be everything to me."

Olivia had never heard such a declaration. He didn't even need to look. He knew. He trusted. A rush of warmth spread through her body. She grabbed his chin and lowered her lips to his. Even though he knelt, she didn't have to bend far. Olivia captured his mouth. Eryx surrendered to her completely.

His arms wrapped around her as he stood, cradling her gently. He didn't break their kiss. He deepened it. His rough tongue battled with hers. Olivia couldn't help a moan.

He pulled back. "Am I hurting you?"

"Never." She couldn't keep her lips from him. She trailed kisses up to his temple.

"Olivia, I—"

She gripped his black horns and gave them a gentle jerk. He stiffened and growled. She grinned down at him. "Less talking. More fucking."

Eryx's slitted eyes narrowed like a cat with his mouse. A Herkleian prince with his mate. She clenched her legs around his torso, directing him to the bed like a cowboy did a horse.

Instead of following her commands, Eryx dropped onto the plush couch.

Before she argued, the movement jolted her, plopping her down onto his lap. Onto a huge, hard bulge. They groaned as one. She shifted on him, rubbing her thin pants against his clothed warmth. His muscles corded, strained. "You're going to kill me, naika."

When the heat of her settled properly over him, she stilled. "That's the plan."

With a growl, he bit at her lips. Her heart stuttered, fanning the flames within her. Oliva couldn't wait. She had dreamed about him since the night they met. Since he went down on her, the dreams had invaded her waking hours.

She bent her legs, pushing off Eryx onto her knees. He tried to pull her back down until she snapped at the clasp of her pants. His hands stilled. Olivia shuffled them down, but the fabric was too tight.

"I think I'm going to have to stand..."

Eryx raked his claws against her tights, shredding her pants in a smooth motion. Olivia cackled. With a quick tug, he tore at the material until she was bared to the world.

Bared to him.

Bared and dripping wet.

Olivia grabbed for the buckle of his pants, ready to free him—

Eryx retracted his claws before sliding a gentle finger through her dark curls.

She gripped at his horns, needing something to hold her down. If she didn't, she'd float away on the sensation. "Eryx."

"Olivia."

His fingers teased her entrance as his thumb rubbed at her clit. Olivia clenched her eyes shut. She had planned to ride *him* like a horse, not his hand. But she couldn't stop from grinding into his movements any more than she could stop her whimpers. Her nipples pierced her dark shirt. Olivia wanted all of him. She pulled at the edges of the fabric.

Eryx's hand caught hers. "Leave that on."

"Why?"

"I'm your mate, Olivia, but also your doctor." He bared his fangs into that rare, full smile she loved. "I plan to fuck you hard. That shirt might be the only thing to save your nano-bandage."

Olivia pursed her lips, but Eryx kissed the annoyance from her face.

"Fine, Doctor."

His hand gripped her face. "Naikos. It's what a Herkleian female calls her mate."

A thrill tingled through her. There was Mr. Alpha. "Yes, naikos."

With a hand still on her face, he grumbled, "Unclasp my pants."

Olivia licked her lips. She loved taking charge, but receiving orders worked just as well.

She trailed her hand down his chest, over his scarred pecs and abs to where his cock strained to be free. Licking her lips, she pulled at the clasp. It didn't need much motivation. With a single click, his massive, ridged length sprung free.

Olivia tried wiggling over him, ready to impale herself.

Eryx grabbed her waist, rubbing his thumbs against the grooves of her hips. This time, Olivia was ready to complain. But before she opened her mouth, Eryx picked her straight off his lap and twisted her around.

Her breath gasped out at the change in direction—and the change in potential pleasure. A tsunami of heat burst through her. Eryx's hand trailed up her thighs, over her ass. Every touch was a surprise, a gift. She dropped her head back onto his shoulders.

His fingers found her clit.

She arched her back, crying out. Olivia needed him. She couldn't wait anymore. She slid her knees back until the tip of him brushed her entry. Eryx kissed down her shoulder, nipping and pulling on her skin.

Olivia plunged down onto him.

She gasped, his length stretching her to the brink. His ridges rubbed perfectly against her inner wall. She almost came instantly. He was perfect. Her male. Her mate. She didn't know if they'd survive the day, but none of that mattered with him here, inside her. Completing her.

Eryx bit down gently with a groan, his hand stilling on her clit. "You *are* trying to kill me."

"Most definitely," she said, her voice already reduced to pants.

Eryx growled against her neck. Her neck. Which he could clearly see, including her matebond mark. Olivia hadn't seen it, but she believed it was there. Believed it with her whole body.

She pulled off him before thrusting down again. Joining with him, again and again. With each landing, he rubbed against her g-spot. Olivia writhed. Only his hands on her kept her from falling. With one hand, he rubbed against her clit, but his other snaked up her side. He threaded his hand through the fabric of her shirt and flicked against her nipples.

Her rhythm stuttered. The fire within her built. No, not a fire, an inferno. Olivia twisting, wanting him with every touch. His mouth caught her. She arched. Connected, like they were meant to be. She reached up and wrapped one hand around a horn, pulsing onto him once more.

Her climax hit her like a wave, ripping her under. She screamed his name into his mouth. Her entire body shuddered as her core clutched at his cock, his big, delicious warmth. Behind her, his own body shook and trembled. His hands gripped her hips. She anchored him as much as he anchored her. Hot seed splattered into her, filling her.

Her mate. Her naikos. Together at last.

FIFTEEN

Eryx traced his fingers down his mate's face as she lounged across his chest. His mate. He couldn't believe it. He knew for days what she was, but seeing the mark of stars on her neck, a match no doubt to the one on his, made him want to roar his claim to the world. Eryx had done terrible things. Killed people. Abandoned people. But he had also saved people, using the skills Doctor Sagara taught him for good.

In Hyra's eyes, it made him worthy of a mate.

Worthy of Olivia, the perfect match to his soul.

"I want to lie like this forever." Oliva twisted in his arms until her chin pressed against his pecs. "Forever and ever."

He traced her lips. "Did I wake you, naika?"

"Not at all," she murmured. "It's almost sunrise."

Eryx had tried not to think of his father's deadline with wrapped in Olivia's arms, but the thought had crept further into his awareness with every minute. "It is. I can't let you die, mate."

"There's more at stake than you and me." Olivia brushed her fingers through the grove of a scar. "My best friend and your brother, along with everyone who stands with them. And do you think your father will be satisfied with Herkleios? How long before he's at Earth's doorstep? How long before he conquers planets not from the Intergalactic Alliance?"

Eryx frowned. His mate was right, but he didn't want her to be. He'd committed his life to saving others for two years. For once, he wanted to be selfish.

Olivia tilted his chin, meeting her eyes. "Why are you looking at me like that?"

He sighed out a growl. "I don't know if I should be proud or heartbroken. You're right, naika. I just don't know how to let you go when we've only just found each other."

"I wish we had more time together, but I wouldn't be able to live with myself if we didn't at least resist your father." She pushed onto her elbows. "There must be a way to stop him."

"My soldiers will fight until their last breath. All we have to do is last until Anax and the Eógan fleet arrive." But that wouldn't happen for hours. His father's deadline was in minutes. Xenobaccus would win. Again. He had claimed Eryx's happiness for years and would finally claim it for eternity.

Olivia grasped his hand, pulling him from his dread. "But what if he tricks Anax somehow? He must have a contingency. We need a plan besides hope and courage."

The answer came to Eryx instantly, but he bit it down. It was too final. Too harsh.

Olivia noticed and tugged on a strand of his hair. "What?"

He swallowed. She deserved to hear it, no matter how harsh. She wasn't a fragile female, but a warrior like him. Her father was wrong in that regard. Eryx would only be so lucky to meet Olivia's family one day, but he'd have to temper down the urge to hit her sire. "The station's self-destruct."

"Oh." She bit her lip. She opened her mouth multiple times, picking and discarding thoughts. "No one would survive that, would they?"

"Both Neithan ships would also be destroyed if they maintained their current distance."

Olivia closed her eyes, but opened them resolved. "Let's hope it doesn't come to that, but if it does, it's what we have to do. Your father won't be able to take Anax hostage if he's dead. If he can't do that, he can't take Herkleios back."

"No." Eryx traced the lines of his mate's fate, memorizing them for whatever time he had left. "It would stop him rather permanently."

Olivia wiped at her eyes. With a sniff, she pushed off him. Eryx wanted to pull her back down to bed, but they didn't have that luxury. He pushed onto an elbow and tapped at the holo-screen of his wristband. A second later, the blue gem on Olivia's bracelet blinked.

She stared down at it. "What did you do?"

"Shared my access codes. If something happens to me, you'll need to set the self-destruct."

Her skin paled to a waxy white, but she swallowed and nodded.

Eryx climbed out of bed behind her and pulled her gently into his arms. "It's a backup, nothing more. Believe all will be fine. Hyra wouldn't help us find each other only to tear us apart."

Olivia leaned into his grasp. "What do we do until then? I'm going to go mad with worry."

He kissed the top of her head. "It's time to tell my father our decision."

Olivia nodded and stepped from his arms. They dressed in silence, gentle and welcome. Neither of them felt the need to fill the space with sound. They existed, the two of them together in peace. If they survived the day, was this what their life would be like? Eryx dreamed of finding somewhere quiet to settle, but he never imagined sharing the space with another.

Now it was all he wanted.

Eryx strapped his laser and his knife to his leg by the door as Olivia pulled on her boots. They settled at each other's side. Eryx held out a hand. If she grasped it, they moved forward with their plan. If she didn't want to move forward, he'd do anything to make her happy, anything to save her.

Olivia took his hand.

He brought it to his lips and kissed her knuckles. "I'm not worthy of you, naika."

"I feel the same, naikos. Which is maybe why your goddess led us to each other."

Eryx bared his fangs. Hand in hand, they approached the door—

A low buzz emanated from the other side. A familiar sound. That of energy lasers, powered-up and aimed.

Eryx pulled his mate behind him, shielding her body with his own.

A soft gasp escaped Olivia's mouth. "What's happening?"

The door slid open before he answered. Eryx's slitted eyes met pale blue irises in a face carved from ice. Fenrish features weren't always harsh. His half-Herkleian cousins took after their father more than his aunt, but Eryx never felt cold stab into his heart just by looking at them.

The same couldn't be said for Helgi.

The Fenrish captain stood in front of three of his soldiers, their laser raised and aimed at Eryx's gut. He clenched his fist. He had known Helgi didn't like him, but to betray him—and through Eryx, his king—was another thing altogether. "Step aside."

"No can do, Your Highness," Helgi nearly hissed the word. "You weren't the only one to receive an offer from your father."

Hyra's Graces. Of course his father had a contingency. Olivia even said it, but Eryx expected to have until the deadline. How stupid of him. Xenobaccus was as traitorous as Hadus. Always had been. Always would be.

Helgi grinned. While the Fens didn't have fangs, the look was menacing. "What do you say to your father's offer, princeling?"

Olivia shoved to Eryx's side and grabbed his hand. "What do you think, asshole?"

One of the Fens turned their weapon on her. Eryx growled, but his bold mate wouldn't cower beside him in fear. Her hand squeezed his. She'd stand beside him. His heart lifted at the thought.

And gave him the courage to declare, "We say no."

A dramatic sigh floated down the hall, followed by the tapping of a cane. Eryx's grip tightened on Olivia. Her blue eyes widened, but she'd never met his father. She didn't know what approached. Eryx twisted, blocking her from the direction of the sounds.

Xenobaccus strolled around the corner and down the hall, followed by a miniature army of red-furred Neithans and gilled Sutekans. Hadus. Eryx hoped maybe only Helgi and his soldiers had rebelled. But if the enemy breached the first deck, all Eryx's soldiers were incapacitated.

Only he and Olivia remained.

His father snapped his claws in disappointment. "You disappoint me yet again, son."

Eryx rammed forward, but Helgi shoved his laser to his chest. "Where are my people?"

"Detained. These fine Fenrish soldiers lowered the transportation shields around the first deck. It was all too easy to overwhelm your pathetic crew."

Helgi frowned. He helped Xenobaccus, but he didn't like the male any more than he did Eryx. "Our reward? We want passage off this station now."

"Not yet, Helgi." His father stopped a few feet away, surveying Eryx and the female beside him. His lip curled in disgust. "The terms were, if I remember correctly, a reward in exchange for my son."

Hadus. Eryx dropped Olivia's hand and moved, reaching for his laser. But Helgi grabbed his left arm, another two Fenrish going for his right. He tried to shake them off, but there were too many. Eryx growled.

"Eryx!" Olivia shrieked, but the fourth soldier plucked her off her feet. His mate hollered, kicking out. The Fen tightened his hold, constricting her waist. Constricting her wound.

No. If she bled out again, Eryx didn't know if he could fix her. He fought harder, but the Fenrish had him in a tight hold. Eryx was trapped.

Olivia went slack.

His heart nearly stopped. If they killed her, his naika, nothing mattered. He stilled. "Don't hurt her. Please. I surrender."

"Eryx, no," she gasped out.

Helgi slammed the hilt of his laser into his shin, knocking Eryx to his knees. Xenobaccus towered over him. He handed his cane to the Sutekan at his right as the Neithan to his left passed him a case. When his father tapped a button on the side, the gold box's levitation activated. Xenobaccus used both hands to pry the lid open.

He wrapped his claws around a gilded injector, filled with some strange liquid. "I had the scientists on Kore's base working on this for months in secret. It combines our standard memory serum with another dozen chemicals and a boost of nanites. Do you want to know what it does?"

Eryx glared. He wouldn't give his father the satisfaction of seeing him beg.

"Eryx, please!" He couldn't see his mate, but he heard the tears in her voice. Wished he could wipe them from her face and whisper that everything would be okay. But it wouldn't be. If Eryx fought, they killed Olivia. If Eryx surrendered, they still might harm her, but she had a chance. He clung to that chance.

His hope died with his father's next words.

"With it, I can temporarily control your mind. I wanted you to be willing, son, but his method works well for me, too. When you next open your eyes, your dear brother will be my hostage and the Eógan fleet in ruins. And your beloved mate will be dead at your own hands."

Eryx snarled, a battle cry. His vision pulsed red. He should have killed his father when he had the chance.

If Eryx killed his mate, he could never live with himself.

Helgi and a soldier pressed down on his shoulders, holding him still as his father lowered the injector. The tip pressed down into his scales. The world around him twisted and blurred. Eryx's muscles went slack. As he drifted, his mate wailed behind him, a battle cry of her own.

His last thought as he faded was a prayer to Hyra.

Please let Olivia get out of this alive.

OLIVIA

"Let go of me." Olivia kicked out as a Fenrish brute carried her into the control room like a sack of potatoes.

She didn't expect him to listen, but suddenly gravity wrapped around her limbs. She dropped to the floor, pain flaring through her side. Bastards. She ignored it to scramble to her knees. Eryx was somewhere behind her, unconscious and unguarded. She crawled in that direction.

A laser pointed at her face. "With the others," a Neithan soldier barked.

Others? Olivia glanced around. A miniature battle had occurred in the room since her last visit, laser blasts scarring the walls around once-levitating chairs and tables, their exposed wiring sparking and crackling. She ignored multi-hued blood puddles and examined the people. Xenobaccus had corralled the civilians on one side, the remaining soldiers on the other. How many had died in the invasion? She couldn't tell, but their forces looked smaller.

The Neithan nudged her with the laser again. Olivia scrambled backward until she crouched with the other civilians. They didn't bother wasting restraints on her, the nurses, technicians, and few remaining wedding guests. Olivia met Captain Dexus's eyes across the space. He scanned her quickly for injury, but his attention was stolen away by who entered the room last.

Two Sutekans pushed a floating stretcher into the room, Eryx sprawled across the space. One booted leg flopped over the side. He twitched in his sleep, his eyelids flickering with movement. Olivia's heart hurt. Watching the Fens knock her mate to his knees before his father had nearly destroyed her. But seeing Xenobaccus inject him as he struggled had truly done her in. She sniffled, but her tears had long since dried.

Nothing else in her remained.

Xenobaccus would have Eryx kill her. She wouldn't blame him. Her last words would be to relieve his guilt, however little impact it might have. But until that moment came, Olivia would remain brave. She stiffened her spine, turning it to steel. She would not cower. She would not beg.

She would do what needed to be done.

Olivia shuffled further back among the civilians. Only three Neithans watched them. If she could just get her wrist out of their sightline—

Nurse Eula shuffled in front of her, blocking her from sight.

Olivia met the Herkleian female's steely gaze. She nodded, warrior to warrior. Not everyone on the ship was aware of her relationship with Eryx, but Eula had watched them interact in the infirmary. She trusted her prince and through him, his mate. Olivia had never been so grateful for the nurse's support.

She tapped the blue gem on her bracelet and activated the self-destruct.

All the holo-screens in the control room flashed. 00:05:00.

A Neithan technician scrambled across the controls. "Uh, Your Majesty?"

Xenobaccus surveyed his new station, the people around him

dolls in his game. At the technician's voice, he snapped from his delusion. Slitted purple eyes narrowed at the holo-screens. "What's happening?"

"Someone activated the ship's self-destruct, Your Majesty."

The ex-king grabbed the technician by his furry auburn scruff. "Who?"

"Uh..." More furious tapping. "Your son, Your Highness."

Xenobaccus pointed his bejeweled claws at Eryx's body. "My son is unconscious."

No sooner had he said it did he realize the truth. Xenobaccus twirled with a snarl and stormed toward Olivia.

She pushed to the front of the civilians. Xenobaccus would cut his way through innocents to reach her. Her pulse stuttered as the seven-foot, horned ex-king stomped at her like a monster from her nightmares. She dug her fingers into her palms to hold herself still.

"You!" Xenobaccus held up his cane like a sword. His thumb pressed a button hidden among the hilt's jewels, sharpening the end to a dagger's point. It crackled with blue electricity. The tip pricked Olivia's neck. "You filthy humans are such a nuisance. Deactivate it or die, Miss Harper."

Olivia swallowed, but she had expected this. Xenobaccus wouldn't let the station go without a fight. "No."

The ex-king's slitted eyes narrowed. His gaze swiveled to the alien next to her, a green-scaled Eógan in the uniform of a technician. "Bring her."

One of the Neithans grabbed the Eógan female and dragged her forward. She shrieked, but a swift smack to the side of her head quieted her.

Olivia tried to climb to her feet, but the Neithan behind her held her down. "Stop that! It's me you want, Xenobaccus."

"If you're anything like my son, threatening another's life will be far more effective." He pressed his cane-sword to the female's neck. She closed her deep red eyes and whimpered. "Deactivate it or I kill her."

Olivia dug her nails so hard into her skin, warm blood flooded to the surface. If the self-destruct launched, the female would die alongside everyone else on the station. But watching the Eógan die before her wasn't the same. Somehow, it felt more personal. Like Olivia sliced the blade across her throat herself.

Olivia imagined Lexi, Anax, her mother, and her brothers dying at Xenobaccus's hand. Even her father. All because of the king's war and need for domination. She imagined an entire galaxy bleeding at his jeweled feet.

Olivia didn't want to watch someone die, but she couldn't sentence thousands to death, either.

The Eógan female opened her eyes, meeting Olivia's gaze with resignation. With acceptance. With strength.

Olivia swallowed, swelling with pride. Everyone aboard this ship would die to protect their homeworlds. Especially if there was no alternative but death. Better to die saving their homes than die for Xenobaccus's pleasure.

Though they didn't speak, though Olivia would never know the Eógan's name, they both understood that.

Xenobaccus snarled, reading Olivia's decision on her face. He struck out, slicing the technician's head from her shoulder with a sizzling zap. Olivia's stomach swirled, but she didn't puke. She faced Xenobaccus, ready to die. If he got angry and killed her, at least it'd spare Eryx the terror.

Olivia switched her focus to her mate. His peaceful, handsome face. Lexi had told her matebonded pairs sometimes died together, but she hoped Eryx would live. Someone had to stand up to his bastard of a father. Someone had to fight for those that couldn't.

But Xenobaccus didn't strike her down next. His cane switched back into regular gold and clonked onto the floor. "We'll wait for my son to awaken. I want you to see how little he cares for you now. I want you to suffer as your mate kills you."

Before Olivia responded, Xenobaccus swirled and stomped back to the technician. "How long until the self-destruct launches?"

"It was five minutes, Your Majesty, but I've managed to change it to fifty."

"Can you override it?"

"Your son gave her the kill code," the technician said. "Even Prince Eryx will not be able to disable it when he awakens."

"Disable what?" a familiar voice asked.

Olivia stiffened. Her hope shriveled. Xenobaccus bared his fangs, a cruel and terrible grin. Together, they twisted toward the levitating stretcher.

Towards her mate.

Eryx propped up on one elbow, rubbing at his forehead. He blinked around the room, frowning. His purple-eyed gaze slid over Olivia, cold and detached, before settling on his father.

Olivia wanted to cry out for him to recognize her, to remember, but she wouldn't give Xenobaccus the pleasure.

"You were knocked unconscious during the attack, my son." Xenobaccus clapped his son on the shoulder. "These dirty rebels tried to kill us and overthrow Divine Hyra's will."

Eryx still must have been out of it because he nodded, accepting that as truth without question. If Xenobaccus erased his betrayal from his son's life, that younger Eryx wouldn't think to question his father.

Olivia was doomed. She hoped he'd awaken and remember her. That the bond between them would spark, reminding him who he was. But even Hyra's power didn't have anything on pure Herkleian science.

"For their crimes, these rebels will be sentenced to death, but we must do it quickly, son. I fear they triggered the auto-destruct and we can't turn it off."

"We should leave them on here to go down with the station." His tone was harsh, dark. Not at all like the Eryx she knew and loved. "If they want it to blow so badly."

"I thought that, too, my son, but I have a better idea." Xenobaccus turned his grin on her. With a chuckle-like howl, he sentenced her to die. "For their disloyalty, these traitors will be executed via airlock. As my heir, you must oversee every death."

Eryx nodded. "Yes, Father."

SEVENTEEN

ERYX

Eryx rubbed a hand across his temples as his father's soldiers dragged the traitors towards the airlock. His head had pounded since he woke. If it weren't for his location—*The Queen Avra*, a space station he didn't remember being commissioned—he'd think he spent last night partying in the seedy alleyways of Eritea, smoking synfo flower until the sun turned the sky golden.

One of the traitors cried out, drawing Eryx from his thoughts. The pain in his head crawled down his neck in a wave of tingles. A Sutekan mercenary wrapped slimy, scaled fingers around the pale arm of a female. He wasn't familiar with her race—short and slender with pink skin instead of scales, her head covered in dark hair without horns. His cock twitched. Eryx frowned. Her species might be compatible with his, but she was guilty of high crimes, a danger to his people.

What was wrong with him? Every step toward the airlock was a drag to his feet. Now he desired a traitor? This was not like him. He straightened, rising to his full seven-foot-five stature, his muscles rippling with the movement. He lowered a clawed hand to the laser at his belt. He erased the pain and attraction in his eyes, replacing it with cold intent.

He was Eryx, Crown Prince of Herkleios. His father's son. The heir to a dynasty.

Eryx turned the corner, the hallway to the airlock stretching before them.

The male at the front of the line—a Guroverian soldier—flailed at the sight. His elbow slammed into his guard's middle. The Neithan bowed over in pain. Before anyone could stop him, Eryx raised his laser, flicked the switch to kill, and fired. The electricity slammed into the male. With a high-pitched shriek, the Guroverian dropped to the ground. Dead. A mercy given the alternative.

Eryx couldn't stop his eyes from flicking back to the dark-haired female. Her mouth gaped open—shock and horror in her blue-eyed gaze. Something flickered within him. Shame? No. It couldn't be.

It didn't matter. In a few minutes, she'd be dead. All the traitors would be dead.

"Open the airlock door," Eryx ordered, his voice deep and emotionless.

The Sutekan at the front of the line glanced past him, only a flicker of his murky black eyes. To his father, strolling behind him. Eryx didn't have to look to know his sire followed. King Xenobaccus trained Eryx alongside his younger brother, Anax, but never trusted either to get a task right.

Eryx would prove him wrong.

Eryx marched forward, past his soldiers, past the prisoners, tapping at his wristband's holo-screen as he approached the airlock. The first door slid open. Eryx grabbed the arm of a Herkleian techni-cian and tossed him into the small square of a space. He dropped to her knees, barring his head and his horns. "Please, sir, please don't—"

Eryx closed the door on his pleas.

"There is no mercy for traitors," he announced, making sure his voice carried. To the end of the line, where the dark-haired female stood. To his father, a fanged-grin splitting his face.

And with that, Eryx tapped his holo-screen again.

The second airlock door slid open. The uncaring hands of space wrapped around the Herkleian male. In a blink, he disappeared with one final, silent scream.

Sucked into the vortex.

An image flashed across his eyes. The dark-haired female, clawing at the airlock door as he sentenced her to death. It stabbed through him, almost a physical pain. The back of his neck flared. Eryx scratched at the scales, keeping his expression stern. She was a traitor. Traitors deserved to die.

He repeated it, over and over.

"Next."

Two Sutekans pushed forward a Fenrish soldier. His own comrades had turned him in, saving Eryx and his father from the worst of the traitors' plans—

"Stop this, Eryx!"

He stiffened.

The dark-haired female tried to shake her guard's hold, but the male didn't let her go. Not that she cared. Her glare flickered to him momentarily before returning to Eryx. "You're better than this, Eryx."

Why did she speak to him like she knew him? "There is no greater honor than executing traitors."

She searched his gaze, like she was looking for something. "Don't let him win."

Him? Who was she walking about?

"Ignore her, son." His father's cane tapped the azure-stoned floors as he approached the female's side. He snapped his claws, an order to her guard. The soldier pulled his laser. "Stun her. She's caused enough trouble."

"Yes, Your High—"

Eryx nearly launched himself down the hall. His vision reddened, flickering in tune with the blood in his veins. No one could hurt the female. He didn't understand the impulse. He didn't know her.

But if anyone hurt her, Eryx knew a part of him would die, too.

He slammed the Neithan soldier against the wall. Something snapped like the crackling of bones. The male slumped to the floor, but Eryx ignored him. Every soldier in the hall had raised their laser and pointed it directly at him.

Eryx dropped the Neithan. What had come over him? Was he mad? Scale rot had made his mother do incomprehensible things in the months before she died, but Eryx hadn't noticed any discolored scales. He'd need to see a healer when they returned to Herkleios.

Whatever the reason, Eryx failed his father. As he always did. He faced the shorter male, his head bowed. "I'm sorry, Your Majesty. I don't know what came over me."

His father's face flickered into a frown before he smoothed it over under a sunny baring of teeth. "She may look innocent, son, but she is not. This female leads the rebels. She is behind the plot to see us murdered. Not only you and I. We would gladly die for our planet. But your stepmother, Chryseis. Your young brother, Phintias. Hadus, they even wanted your cousins dead. I couldn't save your mother, but by Hyra's might, I won't let these scum hurt her nieces and nephews."

Eryx couldn't help his gaze from trailing to the female. Whatever this strange emotion within him was, he needed to ignore it. She was a traitor. She needed to die.

The sooner, the better.

Eryx couldn't suffer any distractions.

He grabbed her arm. "Let's go, traitor."

A spark zapped through contact with her supple skin. It trailed through his body—wrapped around his heart, teased his cock, and tingled along his spine. Eryx almost pulled away, but he forced his hands to stay on her. He lightened his grip. When he first touched her, she'd flinched. Eryx would end her life, but he saw no reason to cause anyone unnecessary pain.

He tugged her toward the airlock.

The confusion and heat in her eyes faded, a wild panic taking root. She ground her heels into the floor. It didn't even trip up Eryx's step. If only it weren't so easy. Everything within him yelled he was making a terrible mistake.

Eryx passed the front of the line—

A Herkleian soldier launched from the crowd, slamming into Eryx's side. Eryx dropped the female's arm and grabbed for his curved blade. Someone else wanted to die prematurely? Eryx would gladly acquiesce. He aimed his blade for the gut.

Right toward Dexus.

Eryx stopped. Dexus. Son of his favorite palace chef and pseudo-sibling to both Eryx and Anax. Eryx lost touch after his time at The Royal Academy in his late teens, but Dexus and Anax had rekindled their friendship during a military placement on Kore's moon base. Last he remembered, his old friend joined the Royal Guard, quickly rising in the ranks.

What was Dexus doing among the rebels?

The male clasped his shoulder. "Don't do this, Eryx."

A Neithan and Sutekan guard tugged him back into the prisoner line. "Silence, prisoner!"

Eryx's frown deepened. Now that he thought about it, why were their guards all Neithan and Sutekan? Beside Eryx and his father, the only Herkleians in the room were with the rebels. Where were his people? If this station followed the design of others, it carried over a thousand people.

He stumbled back. Something was terribly wrong. This wasn't right. The pain in his head spiked, echoed by that strange tingle in his neck. Eryx rubbed at his forehead. He spun away—

To find the dark-haired female at his feet.

She must have fallen when Dexus charged from the line. She lay on her side, adjusting a nano-bandage under her shirt. Was she injured? Eryx's pulse jumped.

He knelt down beside her. "Let me help."

She jolted. "What?"

Eryx reached out. He had received basic medical training during his studies, enough to know how to apply a nano-bandage. Before he touched her, he stopped, hovering off her skin. Her heat reached for him. The fire all Herkleians carried within sparked in return.

He swallowed. "May I?"

She lowered her hand from the bandage. "Sure."

Careful not to rake through her skin with his claws, he gently re-adjusted the bandage—

The cold end of a laser pressed against his head. "You're a disappointment after all, son."

Eryx stiffened at the voice. "Father?"

"Stand."

Eryx did as ordered, twisting slowly. A deep and bitter rage clouded his father's expression, his slitted purple eyes narrowed.

He didn't lower his gaze, baring his horns to his father. Over the male's shoulder, he met Dexus's gaze. His old friend begged him with his eyes. To do what, Eryx didn't know, but it had something to do with the female.

Maybe the same something that had his father ready to kill him?

"I thought we could finally be a family, Eryx." King Xenobaccus flicked his finger against the edge of the laser, switching from stun to kill mode. "I guess I was wrong after all."

"What are you doing, Father?" With one question out, the rest poured. "Where are all our soldiers? Our citizens? Why is Dexus one of the rebels? Why has my neck itched and my head pounded since I awoke?"

"Walk toward the airlock, son."

Eryx didn't move. "Answer the questions. Something isn't right here."

"You're what's not right." His father lowered the weapon and leaned forward, crowding Eryx's space. "What kind of son betrays his father?"

"What kind of father betrays his son?" The question escaped

Eryx's mouth before he even understood the thought. Betray? When had his father ever betrayed him?

When he'd sent Eryx to Hathor.

Eryx frowned, the thought unbidden. Hathor? He'd never been to Hathor.

Yet he had. Two years he had toiled through fields of broken bodies, saving all that he could in penance for the terrors he committed during his year in the fight pits. The Butcher deserved no rest. The Butcher deserved no peace.

But the Butcher had found peace.

He'd found a mate.

Olivia.

With her name, everything came back to him. Every smile. Every touch. Every comment, snide humor or not.

His mate. His naika. His Olivia.

Who his father had tried to make him kill.

The pieces reformed in Eryx's mind, forming a complete picture. His whole memory. Eryx remembered crouching at his father's feet, struggling against the injector.

Eryx remembered the concoction dragging him under.

But he surfaced, three years of rage and anger clinging to his scales. His father had abandoned him. His father had tried to overthrow the Intergalactic Alliance. His father had tried to kill his mate.

Eryx pulled the simple curved dagger at his waist.

Xenobaccus saw the change in him, his hands raising slowly. "Now, son—"

Eryx knocked the laser from his father's hand while twisting him around with the other. By the time the Neithans and Sutekans had their weapons trained on him, he held the blade to his father's throat, the male a shield to their weapons' fire.

EIGHTEEN

Olivia had never been so relieved to see someone held at knifepoint.

She scrambled from the floor, her heart in her throat. So close. Too close. If Eryx hadn't snapped out of his father's control when he did, he would have ejected her into the cold of space. The beauty she witnessed during her spacewalk would have been her last sight. That and Eryx's distant face, the strong jawline and eyes she loved twisted into hatred. Her body broke out in shivers, but she forced herself to her feet. She wasn't dead.

Not yet, at least.

Every Sutekan and Neithan soldier in the hall had raised their lasers, converging on Eryx, the curved edge of a blade held to his father's throat.

"Don't shoot," Xenobaccus half-shrieked.

"Tell them to lower their weapons."

A low growl emitted from Xenobaccus's throat. The rage in it made Olivia shudder, but Eryx only tightened his grip on his blade's hilt. "Tell them!"

"Lower your weapons," Xenobaccus said, grinding his fangs.

Slowly, all the Sutekans and Neithans placed their lasers on the ground before standing with their hands raised, a universal sign for surrender. Before Eryx even barked out another order, the remaining prisoners moved, uncuffing the Alliance soldiers and grabbing for weapons. Olivia scrambled forward, too. The Sutekan laser dwarfed her palm, but she held it steady in her hands. Her father's fingertips ghosted across her shoulder, correcting her posture like he always had in the firing range.

Eryx grabbed the long black strands of his father's hair. "I should launch you out the airlock for your crimes. For what you planned to do to my mate."

"Eryx—" Olivia started.

Xenobaccus interjected. "You wouldn't dare. I raised you, boy."

"Raised me and then betrayed me." A line of purple-blue blood streaked the ex-king's neck. "You know what I endured on Hathor."

"You were soft," Xenobaccus snarled. "Trained in combat like so many lordlings but blind to the terrors of battle. I made you the male you are today. I might be responsible for your scars, but also your achievements. You are nothing without me!"

"I earned these scars."

"In the end, my efforts didn't matter." Xenobaccus continued, not even listening to Eryx anymore. His eyes took on a fevered, almost fanatic-like glaze. "Your mother's blood won out. Her compassion. You left the Butcher behind to become a healer. Nurturing the wounded like she did her gardens."

"Don't speak of my mother."

"You're weak—"

Olivia flicked her thumb across the base of the gun like she had watched Eryx do. With the settings changed from stun to kill, she pressed the barrel up against Xenobaccus's face. "Stop talking. Eryx isn't weak. His kindness, loyalty, and honesty make him stronger than you'll ever be. He survived Hathor, not only physically but mentally. I doubt you'd last a day in actual warfare."

"You bitch—"

"Don't speak to my mate that way." Eryx turned his hard eyes on her. The purple softened, filling with a light. Love. He loved her. Her naikos. She wanted to melt under that gaze. "You don't deserve to look at her."

Xenobaccus growled again, but couldn't speak. Not with a blade to his throat and a laser to his face.

Eryx nudged his father forward. "Move!"

"Where are we going?" Captain Dexus held two Neithans at bay, a laser in both hands. His soldiers had quickly followed suit, but all of them looked rather disheveled. What had they endured at Xenobaccus's hands?

"To the hangar bay. Take the rear, Dexus. I'll lead the way." To the whole hall Eryx said, "Cooperate and Xenobaccus will live. Fight and you'll all die, starting with your precious leader."

Eryx pushed his father forward, heading back towards the control room. Olivia didn't lower her weapon as she fell into step beside him. "We don't have much time. The self-destruct will go off in under ten minutes."

"I know." Eryx peeked at her from the corner of his eyes, almost shyly. "Olivia, I'm so sorry."

She grabbed his hand, the one not holding a massive blade, and kissed his knuckles. "It wasn't you, Eryx. Your father injected you with one of his freaking science experiments. You weren't in control."

"But I remember every second of it. I killed people for him. I almost killed *you*, Olivia."

"You saved me. If you hadn't remembered—"

"I could never forget you, naika. Even if my mind does, my heart never will."

Her eyes nearly watered. "That's the sweetest thing anyone's ever said to me."

Xenobaccus scoffed in front of them. "You're both pathetic."

Olivia glared. "Can I shoot him?"

"We need him to get off this ship."

"And after?"

Eryx frowned. Was it bad Olivia wanted him dead? She had

never wanted another person dead before. "His crimes are against all the Intergalactic Alliance. Surely the people should decide his fate."

Olivia lowered her laser an inch. Her mate thought himself a bad person, but he was better than her. She glared at Xenobaccus's bejeweled horns. "Fair enough, I guess."

Instead of heading for the control room or stairs, Eryx led them to a room with a giant gilded platform like the elevator-like transporter in the infirmary. He pulled his father and Olivia off to the side as the rest of their former captors and colleagues entered.

Dexus nudged the two Neithans in front of him onto the platform.

"Where are you sending us?" one of the Neithans asked, his voice low and somehow hollow-sounding.

Dexus glanced at Eryx. He pushed his father forward and placed the knife at his throat. "Back to your ship. We're not monsters like you. If you try to attack us, either on this ship or when we flee, I won't hesitate to kill your leader."

"Tell King Akhen—" Xenobaccus choked when Eryx increased pressure on his blade.

"No talking." Eryx flicked his claws to the others. "Get them on."

The Alliance soldiers pushed all the Neithans and Sutekans onto the platform. Olivia tensed, waiting for them to attack. *The Queen Avra*'s crew outnumbered the invaders, but not by much. It'd be too easy for the tides to turn.

Dexus raised his wristband and tapped at his holo-screen. "Transporting in five... four... three..."

One of the Sutekans launched forward with a hiss. Eryx spun his father out of the way, the older Herkleian falling into the grasps of a burly Eógan. With a single slice of his blade, he severed the male's throat, puncturing through his scaly gills. Silvery blood exploded from his neck. The attacker fell to the floor with a twitch.

"One," Dexus finished, not even halting his countdown. In a bright flash of light, the rest of the Sutekans and Neithans disappeared, frozen in awe at the sight of their dead comrade.

Or not their comrade, but Eryx. The fishman hadn't stood a chance against her mate.

Once they escaped this ship, Olivia couldn't wait to have all that strength under her fingertips.

Eryx hiked a thumb at the platform. "Now the rest of us."

"King Akhen won't let you get away with this." Xenobaccus tried to push from the Eógan's grasp, but the male refused to release him. He huffed indignantly. "I have allies, son. If you bring me before the Intergalactic Alliance, they will find me innocent and release me."

"Are you arguing for your own death?" Olivia asked.

"Of course not," he sneered at her. It made Olivia want to shoot him even more. "Release me now and we can part ways as... *friends*."

Eryx didn't even bother to reply, but Olivia couldn't stop her laugh. "Yeah, right. Get on the platform, buddy."

The Eógan shoved Xenobaccus back into Eryx's arm. With his spare hand, Eryx reached for his mate. Olivia grasped him tight as she settled at his side. The last time she'd been transported, she almost died minutes later.

Dexus settled at the front of the group and raised his wristband. "I'm transporting us to the hangar bay. Be on your guard. The droid reported most of Xenobaccus's pirates back on their ship, but we don't know their full numbers."

Xenobaccus bared his fangs. "You won't get off this station alive."

Eryx raised his knife, ready to threaten should they meet resistance. "On your count, Dexus."

"Three... two... one."

A tingle crawled Olivia's spine before the world flashed white. She clenched her fist on her laser. Until they got on a ship and off this station, they weren't safe. It still crawled with unknown enemies—not to mention the self-destruct. She didn't need to check her own holo-screen to know they had little time remaining.

In a blink, the brightness of the hangar bay stabbed into Olivia. She flinched, but didn't drop her weapon. The bay stretched across all three decks, though the only doorways existed onto the third deck.

Dozens of medium-sized ships and car-sized gliders from across the Alliance parked in the open space. Not all were in one piece. The invaders had begun to strip some ships for parts. Through the window in a set of closed double doors, a group of Sutekans quickly grabbed a crate and ran off. The Neithan warship was cutting it rather close.

As were they all.

Eryx dragged his father backward, towards a gilded bus-sized ship. Hopefully the Sutekans hadn't gotten to it yet. "Get everyone on board, Dexus."

Dexus tapped at his wristband as the group ran. The ship's back entrance lowered to the floor. The survivors scrambled up the ramp and settled into the rows of seats lining each side of the interior. Two of the soldiers rushed to the cockpit and started prepping the engine. Olivia found three seats near the back beside Nurse Eula. She smiled at the Herkleian female as she lowered into the chair. Freedom. Only days ago, she arrived on *The Queen Avra*, excited for her friend's wedding. Now she couldn't wait to leave the station and never set eyes on it again. She turned to grab Eryx's hand—

Eryx hadn't moved from his spot at the base of the ramp, his gasping father still in his grasp. She followed the line of his sight.

Olivia jumped with a gasp. "No."

The Fenrish brute from earlier had appeared from around another ship, his laser aimed and pointed at her mate.

The soldiers nearest her rose with her weapons, but Eryx waved them down. He faced the Fenrish male. "Let us go, Helgi. My father gave you a ship. We can all get out of here in time."

Helgi grinned, his smile like shards of glass. "Surrender the king first."

Eryx didn't loosen his grip. "What for?"

"He'll fetch enough credits to last a lifetime. Either from King Anax or King Akhen."

"Credits you won't get if you die on this station," Eryx said.

Helgi didn't lower his laser. "Now, Your Highness."

"You can't shoot us all."

"No." Helgi's grin didn't fade. "But I can shoot your ship's thrusters to your right. Good luck accelerating out of here without them."

"Dexus?" The captain perked at the sound of his name. "Raise the ramp and get out of here."

Olivia's heart stuttered. No. "Eryx?"

"Go, Olivia."

Olivia shook her head. "I'm not leaving you."

"Naika, please." Eryx couldn't twist around to look at her, but she knew his face well enough to imagine the expression. "You must leave. You must live. For me."

Olivia stomped down the ramp and grabbed his hand. "We do this together, Eryx. I don't want a life without you in it. I refuse to live in a universe without you."

Eryx peeked at her, still keeping Helgi in his line of sight. "If we stay, we might die."

Olivia didn't flinch from his gaze or his words. Her father didn't think her soldier-material, but she now knew he was wrong. For love, she'd stare down the end of a laser. "I know."

Eryx didn't doubt her choice. "Dexus."

The captain hesitated, but hit the button at the end of the ship. The ramp raised. With a click, it shut. Eryx pushed his father forward and Olivia followed behind. The ship's engine started with a rumble. Wind ruffled Olivia's hair. Helgi's gaze lifted, but Olivia didn't glance behind her to see her last chance off *The Queen Avra* rise into the air and zip through the forcefield holding space at bay.

"Now what, Helgi?" Eryx asked.

Xenobaccus squirmed. "Let me go, you fool. I'll go with the Fen and we can all get off this wretched station. Preferably before it explodes."

"I don't think so, Father."

"You'd doom your mate to death for this?"

"To save others from your cruelty?" Olivia crossed her arms. She didn't want to die. She had so many things to live for, staring with the male beside her. But some things were bigger than them. "Yes."

Xenobaccus snarled.

Helgi echoed the sentiment. "That's it. Hand over Xenobaccus Yio'hyra or..."

The laser in his grasp drifted, aiming for Olivia. A clear threat. Olivia raised her own laser—

Eryx pulled back his hand and threw his knife.

Helgi stiffened as the blade embedded in his neck. The male choked out something before dropping. He twitched as his body bled pale blue blood onto the azure stone floors.

Olivia almost slumped. Her heart pounded in her ears and ripped through her chest. That was too close.

"Don't just stand there, you idiots." Xenobaccus tried to grab for her, but Eryx grabbed him. The ex-king raised his own wristband, his holo-screen displaying the countdown. 0:00:59. "We need to go now."

Olivia pushed away one near-death experience for another. "Will we be able to clear the explosion in time?"

"We can try." Eryx scanned the ship until he settled on a sleek glider. When he tapped the gem at his wrist, the roof of it raised like an expensive sports car. "Let's go."

They ran for the ship. Eryx shoved his father over the edge and into the backseat. The male squawked before disappearing with a thunk. Olivia climbed into the passenger side with a boost from her mate. While Eryx jumped in behind her, she twisted back, keeping her weapon trained on Xenobaccus. "Don't try anything funny."

"Funny? We're about to explode, girl. Now isn't the time for funny."

Eryx settled into the driver's seat and tapped at the holo-screen that appeared. "This might hurt."

What might hurt? Olivia didn't have the chance to ask before the ship started rumbled. With a thrust, Eryx launched the ship into the air and aimed for the forcefield exit. He tilted a nob into the red zone.

A warning flashed across the screen, but he ignored it. Olivia clutched at the edge of her seat. Why weren't there seatbelts?

Before Eryx hit it, he glanced over at her. "I love you, Olivia."

Her heart shuttered, this time in happiness instead of fear. "I love you, too, Eryx."

He grinned at her, a beautiful, final sight.

Then he slammed onto the controls.

The glider launched through the forcefield, from zero to hundred in a second flat. They launched into darkness. The timer hit zero. She tried to scream, but the pressure nearly flattened her into the seat. In the corner of her vision, something exploded like fireworks. *Approaching* fireworks. The metal of her elbow rest grew hot. They wouldn't make it. The glider would be consumed by flames—

A tickling zipped up her spine as the world went white.

NINETEEN

ERYX

Eryx blinked away blindness, the flashing red lights of the glider's control panel and the fire at their rear replaced by bright white. He blinked. In a second, the whiteness passed. He dropped back to reality. The pressure holding him to his seat disappeared. Eryx's body started to slacken into his seat, but he quickly pushed up and grabbed for Olivia. Someone had locked onto the glider and transported it. Was it the Neithans? He wouldn't let anyone hurt his mate.

Xenobaccus cackled in the backseat. "You've lost, my—"

"Eryx?" Anax's voice sounded through the glider's speakers.

Thank Hyra. Not Neithans. His father slumped in the backseat, pursing his lips, but Eryx focused on the view outside the glider. He found Olivia's hand as he looked into a silver hangar bay, similar to *The Queen Avra*'s yet different. Eógan technicians rushed through the space, but his sight settled on two males below them—Anax in dark pants and black pauldrons, their cousin Prax at his side.

Olivia jumped from her seat. "Woo! Take that, Xenobaccus."

For once, his father remained silent.

Eryx lowered the glider to the ground, settling into the spot nearest to where his brother and cousin stood. The roof of the glider raised. Anax gestured with a single-clawed finger and soldiers stormed forward, weapons raised over the edge and aimed at the ex-king.

Xenobaccus scrambled to his feet, his slitted eyes calculated. "Anax, my son. I've missed you—"

"Take him to the brig," Anax snapped. "For crimes against the Intergalactic Alliance and the attempted murder of Queen Alexandra Kor'hyra, I place you under arrest, Xenobaccus Yio'hyra."

A flying droid dropped out of the sky and tried to place cuffs on the ex-king. Xenobaccus slapped at them. "Get your hands off me. I am royalty, descendant of the Goddess Hyra herself. How dare you touch divinity!"

"Oh, hush, you," Olivia said, quieting the ex-king with a single vicious look. No one spoke to divinity like that, either—with the exception of his mate. When she turned on Anax, a glowing smile replaced the hatred. "My best friend is a queen?"

"Lexi insisted my father not ruin our wedding day. We married on our trip to Eógan."

"Aww," Olivia cooed.

Two more droids dropped into the ship. Together, they tackled Xenobaccus to the glider's floor. When they floated away, he floated with them, dragged by the cuffs on his wrists. He dropped beside the guards. "What disappointments my sons are, mated to uncivilized Earthlings of all creatures."

Anax rounded on his father. "Say that again and I will not hesitate to kill you, father."

Eryx rose from his seat and climbed from the glider. Another droid pushed a ladder to the edge, which he settled on before reaching for his mate. "Nor will I. You'll have to rot in jail knowing all your children have disappointed you."

Xenobaccus' grin turned sinister. "Not all."

Eryx stiffened.

"Your brother, Argrix? Wed to Princess Kashta of Neith? He does as I command unlike the two of you." Xenobaccus cackled, a sharp howl. "You're a failure, Anax. In less than six months, you've destroyed the alliance I spent thirty years maintaining."

Anax clenched his fists and stalked forward, but Eryx slid into his brother's path. "He's not worth it."

For a second, Eryx thought his brother might not heed his words. He prepared for the king to shove him out of the way as his gaze flickered quickly to Prax. His cousin crossed his muscled arms, but the curve of his lip told Eryx everything he needed to know. Prax would take bets on the sideline of their fight before lending a hand.

Not that Eryx could blame him. This business was between brothers.

But Anax's shoulders slackened. "Take him to our coldest cell."

The head guard nodded. "With pleasure, Your Majesty."

Xenobaccus was nudged toward the exit. His father jumped from their hold, pulling at his sashes and jewels. "I am a king, fools. I can walk myself."

And with that, Xenobaccus strut from the room with dignity, the doddering, cane-using guise completely forgotten.

Anax, Eryx, and Prax stared after him long after the doors slid closed.

"So that's why Argrix wasn't at your wedding," Prax mused.

"I need to speak with the Empress," Anax said. "I doubt Argrix will try to contact home, but he might try her or Aunt Rhiona."

"Probably my mother." Prax ran a hand through his burnished hair. "Aunt Rhiona scares me."

Eryx grinned. "Doesn't she everyone?"

Prax frowned at him. "Did you make a joke? And smile?"

Olivia settled at his side. His hand reached for hers automatically. Both his cousin and his brother stared, their gapes traveling from his expression to the touch of his mate's hand. It wasn't like they hadn't ever witnessed him smile. Anax's new responsibilities weighed him down, but the three of them had once done little more than party. They had watched him smile and joke before.

But not since he returned from Hathor.

Not since Olivia.

Eryx raised to full height. When he glanced at his mate, it was like she read his mind. She stepped closer to his side, closer to his family, and smiled at them. "Your Majesty, may I present to you my mate, Olivia. We've been blessed by the Goddess Hyra, but as you're the head male of the royal family, I ask for your approval."

Anax tried to stay stern, but a wide grin split his face. "Of course, brother. You have my every blessing." His brother faced Olivia. "Lexi would be jumping up and down if she were here right now."

"She'd be hugging everyone on the ship." Olivia leaned into Eryx's chest. Exactly where she belonged. "Is she well? Did everyone make it to safety?"

"With the exception of the bridesmaid, Rachel." His brother's smile faded as quickly as it came. "When we joined with the Eógan fleet, she and all our civilians continued on in *The Queen Niobe.* They arrived safely on Eógan."

"That's good."

Eryx squeezed his mate's hand. "You will be reunited with your friend soon enough, naika."

She gazed into his eyes. "As long as we're together, Eryx, that's all that matters."

"Given that..." Prax started, his cousin's expression slipping into a crooked smile. "I had planned to offer you a room near the other survivors of *The Queen Avra.* They escaped the blast range and will land any minute, but I assume you'll want to stay with my cousin."

Olivia smiled at Eryx. "Yes. Forever."

Prax tapped at his silver wristband. "Then I'll give you the suite next to Anax's quarters. I've sent you the location, Eryx."

The blue gem on Eryx's own wristband flashed. "Thank you, cousin."

Eryx took his mate's hand and started for the doors. He matched his long steps to his mate's. His mate. When he met Olivia, accepted Olivia, he never thought he'd survive *The Queen Avra.* But now, the entire future stretched out before them.

A seed of doubt crept in. What if she didn't want him anymore? His own father had rejected him. Eryx became a new male on Hathor, but the pain of that rejection stung. It always would. When Olivia first called him naikos, she thought she'd die in a day. They both had.

But Eryx wanted her. His imagined future didn't involve him on his own, but with Olivia, making her happy.

When they exited the hangar bay, Olivia turned on him. "What's wrong?"

He wouldn't hide his thoughts or pains from her. "You said not to think about the future and to focus on the present. But we survived the station. We're together. What now?"

Her forehead creased, a little mark between her brows he wanted to kiss away. "What do you mean, what now?"

He stopped and took her other hand. "Do you still want me?"

"Are you serious?" Olivia's eyes widened, but after examining his face, her jaw dropped, as well. "You are, aren't you? We've been over this, Eryx. You're smart and loyal and brave. You're everything I could want. I should be asking you this question."

His brow furrowed. "You? You're perfect."

"I wasn't good enough for my father, either." She wrapped her hands around his waist—half his waist. Her arms couldn't reach all the way around. "I'm not a warrior like him and my brothers. Or at least I wasn't until today. I'm a hair stylist. I live on my own with a cat and wear too much leather. What would a super-hot Herkleian prince want with that?"

Eryx stared. He didn't know what a cat was, but it didn't matter who she lived with or what she did. She didn't see it, did she?

He'd show her.

Eryx swept his mate off her feet. An Eógan technician grumbled as he passed and another outright stared, but Eryx ignored them all.

She squealed. "What are you doing? There's people around."

"Our Eógan cousins are quite amorous. They won't mind."

"But I can walk on my own."

"I enjoy carrying you." Eryx started down the hall towards their new quarters. "You are a warrior, Olivia. You always were. You left your planet in order to attend a wedding. You've faced down Sutekan pirates and Neithan soldiers. You yelled at my father. You think I'm smart and loyal and brave, but that's what I think of you. It doesn't matter that you're a hair stylist and I'm a prince. Those things don't make us who we are." He tapped her chest. "But what's in here always will."

Olivia stared. Had he shocked her into silence?

"Put me down." Her voice deepened, almost like the Earth version of a growl. But not in laughter or rage...

In desire.

Eryx's cock twitched. "What did you have in mind, naika?"

He turned a corner. She looked around the silver hallway lined with doors. "Are any of these storage closets?"

He frowned. "Perhaps?"

She grinned at him deviously. "Let's find out."

A hungry fire spread through Eryx's chest, a combination of joy and love and desire. Eryx dropped her to her feet. She ran forward and opened a door, peeking inside. Eryx did the same with the other side. The Eógan soldiers inside the room looked up curiously, but Eryx didn't even care.

His mate raced down the hall to the next door and he scrambled to follow. The Butcher didn't deserve a mate, but the Butcher was dead. Eryx wasn't that male anymore. He never would be again.

He had his mate forevermore.

EPILOGUE

OLIVIA

Olivia wrung her hands as she stared at the silver-latticed door. "What if she doesn't like me?"

"How could she not?" Her husband and mate struck an imposing figure in the empty waiting room, his heat filling the cool, green space. Eógans were close cousins to the Herkleians, but they didn't run nearly as hot—or have the same obsession with gold patterns. Eryx stroked a hand across her shoulder. Olivia leaned into the touch. "You're perfect."

She grinned at him. "You only think that because you're my mate."

"I think that because I love you."

The warmth from his hands spread through her belly to her core. Five months they had been together, but Olivia didn't think she'd ever grow tired of her mate. If only they weren't in public. She wanted to peel off his tight black pants, climb onto his lap, and ride him where he sat.

Eryx's slitted pupils dilated. Attuned to her desire like he always was. He leaned closer until his breath tickled her ear. "What would you do to me if you could, naika?"

Olivia licked her lips, her throat suddenly parched. She glanced around. The head matron of Saint Ailbhe House had left them here almost twenty minutes ago. What were the chances she'd return now? Olivia angled her body, putting her back to the door and in front of Eryx, and trailed her fingers down the scales of his chest. Her simple gold wedding band traced across every scar. When she met the edge of his pants, she slipped a hand under the tight fabric and grasped his hard cock—

The door opened behind her. "Meri is ready for you now, Your Highnesses."

Olivia nearly jumped a foot in the air. She pulled her hand back from Eryx quickly, almost as if his scales had burned her. He was hotter than a human, but not that hot. Her face flushed red.

Eryx smiled over her shoulder. "One minute, please, Matron Fiadh."

Matron Fiadh must have nodded, since the door clicked closed behind her a second later.

Olivia dropped her head to his chest. "She's never going to approve our application now."

Eryx kissed the top of her brow. "Fear not, naika. I doubt she serves many chaste applicants."

"I doubt any of them are mid-hand job when she walks into her waiting room."

Eryx tilted her chin until her eyes met his. A swoop of emerald hair brushed his scaled forehead. She pushed it back behind his ear as he rubbed his nose against hers. "We won't be denied, Olivia."

The thought brought tears to her eyes. They couldn't be denied. Olivia placed a hand over her stomach, her skin sensing the faint line of her scars even through the fabric of her shirt. She didn't regret attending Lexi's wedding. If not for her time on *The Queen Avra*, she wouldn't have Eryx. But while Herkleian technology could remove the exterior scars, it couldn't fix her fertility. "Eryx—"

He took her hand and walked towards the door. "Come, naika. Let's meet our daughter."

Olivia's heart swelled at the word. Daughter. Her daughter. *Their* daughter. Her tears ran freely down her cheeks. She sniffled them back. Bawling her eyes out wouldn't be the greatest first impression.

Matron Fiadh led them through a twisting maze of corridors, the green of the walls not paint or metal but vines and plants. The Eógans loved nature even more than the Herkleians. Olivia had first visited the planet two months ago after Eryx planned a surprise camping trip. Eryx's cousin, Prax, had loaned them his family's hunting lodge. They might even settle here once things on Herkleios calmed, but with Xenobaccus's trial looming, Eryx didn't want to be far from home. Both of them couldn't wait to start a life away from the politics and games of the nobility.

The green corridors widened into a room filled with toys from across the galaxy. Floating Herkleian toy ships mixed with clay-made dolls from Eógan and Hathorian dice games. Olivia imagined the room echoing with laughter, but only a single voice let out a small hum. The girl was no older than seven, with the striped, sand-colored skin and vibrant red hair of a Hathorian. Matron Fiadh had met Eryx during his time in the Hathorian refugee camps, offering shelter to as many orphans as she could fit in her glider.

Meri was the oldest Hathorian left.

Olivia's heart broke for the little girl, but she wiped away another round of tears. God, becoming a mom had turned Olivia into a crier. *Almost* becoming a mom. Meri had a home today only if she wanted it.

Eryx stayed back as Olivia approached. She dropped to her knees beside the girl. "Hi, Meri. I'm Olivia."

The girl stayed silent at first. All of Matron Fiadh's orphans had implanted translators, so it wasn't a language barrier. But if Olivia had witnessed the horrors this girl had by the age of seven, she'd fear talking, as well.

She focused on the girl's doll. "What's her name?"

The girl peeked at her, her eyes a kaleidoscope of turquoise and orange. "Renpa."

"That's a lovely name." Olivia plucked another doll from the floor. "And this one?"

"That's her sister, Aua."

"Does Renpa want to play with her sister?"

The girl giggled like Olivia had asked a silly question, but before she answered, her gaze shifted over Olivia's shoulder. Her jaw dropped. "*Shedi?*"

Shedi? Before Olivia asked, Meri launched off the floor and ran straight into Eryx's side. She wrapped her scrawny arms around the towering male's leg. Eryx blinked down at the girl, the emotion in his slitted eyes part confusion and part heart-wrenching joy.

"*Shedi* is a Hathorian god that saves people from danger," Matron Fiadh said. "Meri is from one of the camps you assisted, Your Highness. I didn't think she'd remember you."

"Meri?" Eryx bared his fangs in a small smile. The girl didn't shy away, but instead revealed an entire mouth of pointed teeth. He plucked her from the floor and into her arms. "I remember you. How could I not?"

Olivia's heart almost melted at the sight of the tiny child in her mate's arms. She crept to Eryx's side. He immediately clasped her hand in his, joining the three of them together. Like a family.

"Would you like to come with us, Meri?" Olivia leaned into Eryx's side, seeking his strength and his warmth. "Would you like to be a family with us?"

She pointed her taloned finger at Eryx. "Father?"

Eryx grinned, a bright look. The Olivia of five months ago, grasping his arm as he all but dragged her down the aisle, wouldn't believe the joy on the stoic warrior's face. "Yes."

Meri twisted her hand, pointing her talon at Olivia. "Mother?"

Olivia melted. Absolutely melted. She had never wanted love. Never wanted a family. But how could love hurt her if it felt like this? It was worth every moment.

Eryx and Meri were worth every moment.

"Yes, Meri, I'll be your mother."

Meri pursed her lips for a second before the grin returned to her face. "Okay, but Renpa and Aua have to come, too."

Olivia laughed, tears leaking from her eyes. "Of course they can come."

Eryx wrapped them all in his arms. "We'll all be your family, Meri."

And with one sentence, the world became right.

Thank you for reading! Our next alien prince is Prax, Eryx's roguish cousin! After he "accidentally" kidnaps a feisty Earthling named Scarlett, they'll be forced to fake-date in order to stop dangerous blackmailers.

ERYX BONUS SCENE

OLIVIA

"Can I open my eyes yet?"

Eryx rubbed a thumb across Olivia's shoulder, the heat of his body radiating at her back. "Not yet, naika."

Grass tickled across her heels as he directed her up what felt like a small hill. They hadn't left the forest then. While neither Olivia nor Eryx wanted to settle in Eritea, the Herkleian capital, they couldn't just abandon their responsibilities after what happened on *The Queen Avra*. One month had become three in a blink. Olivia had nearly abandoned her hope of ever getting out. Until two mornings ago, when she'd awoken to find Eryx packing an overnight bag for a camping trip on Eógan. "Are we almost there?"

"Close."

She smiled at the grin she heard in his voice. After two days of the blackness of space, Olivia had gaped out the glider's window at Eógan's deep emerald fields. When they had landed in a meadow near a small town, Eryx had handed her a blindfold. Olivia had nearly refused to put it on. She didn't want to miss a second of the countryside.

His warm hands settled at the back of her head. "Ready?"

"Always."

Eryx cut through the blindfold with his claws. Bright light stabbed through Olivia. She blinked, rubbing at her eyes.

And opened them to paradise.

Emerald vines and foliage twisted up the side of a hunting lodge made of a deep black wood. The little building nestled in the middle of a clearing of bright flowers, pink and orange and red. Animals and birds trilled in the treetop canopy, strange but familiar noises. Olivia's heart warmed. She had always loved the wild. Despite being a city girl, the country held her heart in its grasps.

"It's wonderful."

Her mate settled at her side. "It belongs to my uncle, Daniil. He inherited it from his father, who used to take all his children here, including my mother. Prax let us borrow it for the week."

"Only the week?"

Eryx had promised her quiet, just the two of them together. Now seeing the lodge, Olivia was worried she'd never want to leave. Did she really have to? Lexi had just learned she was pregnant and Olivia had promised to throw a baby shower. They'd have to return for that.

But that was months away.

"I love it." Olivia rushed forward, ready to explore every nook and cranny. "What—?"

Eryx wasn't following her. Olivia turned, frowning—

Her jaw dropped.

Eryx crouched on one knee, sinking slowly into the long green strands. His hair matched perfectly with the forest around him, like he belonged here. A toned and scarred god of the woods.

"My brother told me about this custom." Eryx pulled a small box from his pocket. A little box Olivia had dreamed about but never expected. "Olivia Grace Harper, I should have asked you this months ago. The moment we escaped *The Queen Avra*. Will you—?"

Olivia squealed and jumped at Eryx, unable to contain her shouted, "Yes!"

Eryx landed on the grass with a soft *ooph*, Olivia splayed across his chest. She traced her hands across the scales of his pecs to his neck to the angles of his chin. "Yes, a thousand times, yes. I'll marry you."

His lips twitched, flashing fang. "I hadn't even finished the question."

She slapped at his chest playfully. "Was that not the question?"

He chuckled, a deep growl that sparked heat in her core. "You know it was, naika."

God. At the word, that spark of heat turned into a burning flame. Olivia threaded her fingers through his hair and gripped his horns as she lowered her lips to his. She claimed his mouth, swallowing the ends of his chuckle. Her Eryx. Her mate. Her naikos. He opened his mouth to her, his tongue battling with her. Both trying to plunder the other. Olivia's legs slipped to the grass until she straddled him. His thick erection pulsed against the thin layer of her underwear.

Olivia groaned into his mouth. "I need you."

Eryx nipped at her chin. "Where all the neighbors can see?"

She tugged at her dress, slipping it down her body until her breasts rubbed against his scales. The friction turned her nipples to peaks. "We're in the middle of a forest. We don't have neighbors."

Eryx's grin turned hungry. "Right again, naika."

Olivia pushed onto her knees and grabbed at the buckle of his pants. His hands trailed up her legs until he thumbed the edge of her underwear. In the same movement, she unsnapped his buckle, his beautiful cock bursting free, as his claws shredded through her underwear. Spring air caressed her bare warmth.

She didn't look at their lodge, at the forest, at anything around her. Only Eryx, his purple eyes alluring as she met his upward thrust. He slammed into her. Her back arched. Perfect. All hers.

Her mate.

Eryx rose to meet her lips as she plunged down on him. All but bouncing on his cock. Her eyes nearly rolled back into her head. Eryx nipped at her lips. She surrendered her mouth to him and he took it. They groaned as one, swallowed the sound as one. Olivia gripped his horns, palming at the base. Eryx shuddered, a growl rising in his chest—

He flipped them, the beautiful forest around them a swirl. The brightness haloed his head, bringing out the emerald of his hair. She nearly gasped at the sight—and did when he hooked one of her legs over his shoulder and thrust into her. His ridges slammed against her g-spot, perfectly caressing her inner folds. Olivia shuddered. She needed him more. Needed him deeper.

Needed to be one with him.

Her orgasm nearly ripped out of her at the thought. Her entire body clenched around him as she whimpered and cried and groaned. Claiming him. Her naikos.

Eryx shuddered with a roar, exploding in harmony with her. His warm seed flushed through her. She tightened her legs around his torso. Holding them together, the way they were meant to be.

Eryx slumped onto her chest, his head nestled between her breasts. She brushed her cheek against the tip of his horns. "Let's get married now."

He smiled lazily at her. "Now?"

"I can't wait to be one with you, Eryx. I can't wait to be your wife. Your naika. I don't need the fancy wedding or the pretty dress." She titled his chin, his slitted eyes fastened to her. "I just need you and this lodge."

"Me, this lodge, and the female head of my family."

Olivia snorted. "Lexi won't mind if we find a stand-in."

He kissed her nose. "For you, naika, anything."

Olivia almost burst with joy. "And then we can return to this cottage..."

"Mhmm." He slowly crawled down her body.

Her core heated immediately. She'd never tire of this male. "And fuck on every surface we can find."

"That might take a few days. There are so many surfaces."

"We have time. The entire week, if we must."

He parted her thighs and breathed in her thick scent. "Just a week?"

"A month. No one back in Eritea will miss us," Olivia said, but her focus fixed to his mouth. His tongue flickered out—

She fisted her hands in the grass as he licked up her slit. His rough tongue circled her slit twice before grazing the little bead with his fang.

Olivia almost jumped off the grass. "Yes, let's stay here. Forever."

"Forever?"

"Don't talk with your mouth full."

"As you command, naika."

PRAX

BRIDE TO AN ALIEN PRINCE, BOOK 3

"For the love of Christmas," Scarlett shouted, nearly falling out of her seat as a loud drilling sound reverberated through her makeshift office. She glared at the ceiling. The PR firm above Davies & Brown started renovations two weeks ago. Scarlett had vibrated in her chair in her actual office down the hall, forcing her to a spare room filled with boxes. Of course they'd move the construction over her head the moment she settled.

She turned her glare back to her papers. Craig Newcastle's rather smug-looking mug shot stared back at her. She flipped him off. Thankfully, the human trafficker and all-around scumbag wouldn't be present at her court case tomorrow. But if not for him, her client, Saima, wouldn't be in the UK. If not for him, the horrible things done to her, transcribed on the papers before Scarlett, wouldn't have happened. If not for him, Saima wouldn't have been caught using false documentation to flee the country and sentenced to a year in prison.

Gah, just the thought threw Scarlett into a rage. She rose from her chair to pace the spare office, weaving in and out of the stacks. In court, she always kept her cool, but in private, she wanted to scream at the world. She paced to the windows and back. Of course her poor client was in more trouble than her abuser. All Saima wanted was to return home—

Scarlett stopped halfway across the room. What in the heck was outside her window?

She pulled at the blinds, revealing the bricks of the building next to her... and on the streets, a crowd of journalists and paparazzi. Scarlett was used to cameras at her high-profile cases. She hated all the extra eyes watching her, but it came with the job. But why were they flocking outside her building?

"Did you see?" Her co-worker, Zack, poked his head into her office. She didn't work with him on many cases, but everyone knew the blonde was a major gossip.

Scarlett pressed her face against the glass. "Does it have anything to do with the people outside?"

"It's the aliens."

That had Scarlett pulling back. "The what?"

Scarlett knew about aliens, of course. She didn't live under a rock. A year and a half ago, some American tech billionaire—Seymour something?—received a message from deep space. A race of advanced blue aliens called the Herkleians had reached out on behalf of the Intergalactic Alliance and offered Earth membership in their little club. After much bickering among politicians, Earth became the alliance's thirteenth member. But it wasn't until recently that aliens started appearing on Earth.

Not that they usually strolled down the street.

"It's some prince," Zack said before rushing from her closet-office. Probably to get a better view.

Scarlett glanced back at her desk. Her files called to her, but she needed to leave soon to pick up her daughter from school, anyway. Might as well take a peek.

After slipping on her red blazer and grabbing her purse, she followed Zack to the lobby. Large windows overlooked the street from a pristine but muted lobby. Most of the photographers stood on the nearby sidewalk, but the major commotion was across the street in the gardens of a massive, white-stoned cathedral.

"He doesn't look blue," Marcie said, the short receptionist squinting through the glass.

Zack shook his head. "I don't think he's a Herkleian prince."

"Thank God," Robert muttered, sipping on his seventh tea of the day. "None of them should be allowed on the planet after the old Herkleian king tried to enslave us."

"That American girl married the new king, right? So of course they're going to allow them to visit." When Scarlett stopped at Marcie's side, the receptionist perked up. "You're American, Scarlett. What do you think?"

Scarlett resisted a frown. Marcie always asked about things back home, even though Scarlett moved to the UK a decade ago. She was an expert on immigration law, not American politics. "About Queen Alexandra or policy on letting aliens visit?"

Marcie blinked at her slowly.

Robert launched forward, touching the glass. "There."

The four of them huddled closer. Even Scarlett couldn't resist. Though she'd never admit it, she had watched Queen Alexandra's televised engagement parties with a wine glass in one hand and a charcuterie board in the other. Seeing the five-foot Earthling side-by-side with her seven-foot Herkleian man was always fun. He was almost twice her size—length-wise and width-wise. How they were now expecting twins was a mystery. Wouldn't he crush her?

Scarlett squinted across the street, looking for a big, blue alien—and instead found a green one. Her heart stuttered. Scarlett didn't have a clear view, but the male was nearly two-feet taller than every human around him. His chiseled face wasn't any less handsome given his emerald-colored scales and burnished bronze hair. Unlike the Herkleians, he had short horns and sharp ridges along his spine that poked through his shirt.

She nudged Marcie out of the way. "Who is that?"

Zack pulled out his phone. "Prince Prax M'Etein. A cousin to

King Anax and the son of Empress Ailis of Eógan. He's here on a PR tour according to his Wikipedia page."

Scarlett resisted pressing her face against the glass. She couldn't tear her eyes away from the prince. What was wrong with her? What was wrong with *him*? Aliens had no right to be that attractive.

Marcie echoed her thoughts. "He's hot!"

Zack snickered. "You said that about King Anax, too."

"And his brother? The scarred one who leapt across the platform when terrorists shot up the king's wedding?"

"Oh, yeah." Zack waved his hand casually, like he was the resident alien expert. "Prince Eryx."

"Yeah." Marcie almost purred. "Who wouldn't want a scarred prince willing to take a bullet for you?"

Scarlett snorted. Violet had recitals the night of the wedding, so Scarlett hadn't watched it live. Thankfully, since she hated gore. But the news had splattered pictures of the wedding-turned-battlefield across every screen the next day. "Isn't he married now, too?"

Marcie pouted.

Her watch buzzed. Scarlett glanced down. If she left now, she'd arrive outside Violet's school just in time for the bell. With reluctance, Scarlett stepped away from the window and the prince outside. "Well, this was fun, guys. I have to pick up my kid."

Zack snorted. "Best of luck with *that* traffic."

Scarlett squinted back through the window. The alien prince stole all of her attention, but she wasn't special in that regard. Everyone on the street stared, too. Cars clogged the road both ways as drivers slowed down to get a peek at Earth's newest visitor. "Crap."

Without another word, Scarlett spun on her heels and marched for the door. By the time she reached the first-floor lobby, her arches were screaming at her. On a normal day, she changed out of the four-inch death traps strapped to her feet before leaving. Her runners weren't the best match to her pantsuits, but as a thirty-four-year-old working mother, Scarlett no longer gave a shit.

"Crap not shit," she muttered to herself. Scarlett loved to swear, but she had tried to curb the habit given how Violet repeated every-thing she said. It was adorable in her little British accent, but the other mothers at her daughter's school wouldn't appreciate their kids dropping casual f-bombs.

She pushed outside onto a crowded sidewalk. For whatever reason, the alien prince and press had left the garden of the cathedral and approached the street—exactly near where Scarlett had parked her car. Assuming it was still there. She couldn't see her little buggy through the throngs of people.

Why the heck was her boring corner of London part of this press tour? To show aliens walking among Earthlings like regular Joes? Didn't sound like too bad of a PR idea, but why outside her office? And out of all the days they picked today. Her ex-boyfriend had Violet for the weekend and planned to pick her up tomorrow after school. He wouldn't be late... but at this rate, Scarlett would be.

"It's not a competition," she muttered to herself. Except that it was. Scarlett had once loved Andrew, but when he learned she was pregnant, he up and disappeared. Violet didn't know that, though. On the rare weekends he spent with her, he spoiled her rotten. From her daughter's perspective, she had a cool dad and a busy mom.

Scarlett clenched her fists. God, she hated that man.

The only benefit of aliens outside her office was that she didn't need to hightail it to a crosswalk. Scarlett weaved between the grid-locked cars, her eyes on the drivers. No one was paying attention. It would be just her luck for a car to hit her in front of an alien prince.

When she finally reached the other side, the crowd had shuffled closer to her. Scarlett couldn't stop her eyes from focusing on the prince. She never thought she'd see an alien in the flesh. The prince's emerald scales glistened in the dim sunlight, the strong lines of his face sharper in profile. Damn, he was handsome. A little tingle spread across Scarlett's skin, starting in her arms and working its way up to her neck. She shuddered.

The black paint of her car came into view. Almost there—

A tabloid reporter with a camera backed into her path.

Scarlett slammed right into his side with an *oomph*. The air knocked from her lungs. Her complaining feet abandoned her to gravity's cruel hold. Her hand released her purse and flailed for something to grab, but there was nothing nearby.

She dropped ass-first onto the pavement.

"Fuck!" Scarlett couldn't stop the swear from escaping her lips. Pain radiated through her hipbone. What was the point of the extra ten—fine, twenty—pounds on her ass if not to protect her from falling?

The tabloid reporter glared down at her. "Get out of the way."

Her pain disappeared under a wave of rage. "Excuse me? You bumped into me, asshole."

He pointed toward the crowd and the alien. "We're in the middle of—"

"Are you well, my lady?" a deep voice crooned as a shadow fell over Scarlett.

She stiffened. Under her blouse, her nipples peaked just at the sound of that voice. Without looking, Scarlett knew exactly who settled at her side. The entire street dropped into silence and focused on her.

And on the alien prince crouched beside her, offering her a hand.

It almost looked human—if human hands were large, scaled, and clawed. Scarlett followed the lines of his corded forearms to muscled shoulders. While Herkleian males didn't wear shirts, the Eógans were obviously different. The prince wore a tight-fitting, brown leather ensemble, almost like something out of a superhero flick. The straps across his chest strained against his pecs and looped around the sharp ridges protruding from his spine. Scarlett licked her lips, a fire bursting into life in her core. Those spikes made the perfect handholds for riding him...

Scarlett straightened. Riding him? Scarlett didn't even know the man. When was the last time she had sex? A year ago? Two?

The thought disappeared from her head entirely when her gaze clashed with his, the sight a shock through her system. His irises were a dark red around slitted pupils. So foreign, yet the expression in them was one of familiar concern... and desire? No. That couldn't be. Not that Scarlett wasn't attractive. Sure, she wasn't bad. But why would a hot alien prince be interested in a curvy, single mother?

When she didn't take his hand, a frown creased his brow, but he kept a wide, inviting smile on his lips. "Do you need medical attention?"

Goosebumps ran up Scarlett's arms. Damn, having a voice like that needed to be illegal. "No, I'm fine, thank you."

Before he said more, Scarlett's smartwatch beeped again. The twenty-minute mark to Violet's school bell. It splashed a bucket of ice water on the desire curling in the pit of her stomach.

"Fuck." Scarlett grabbed the alien's hand without a second thought. A jolt of electricity spread through her arm at the touch. A gasp escaped her lips. If she affected the alien prince, he didn't show it. He gently pulled her to her feet. "I'm going to be late."

"For what?"

"For Violet's school." Why Scarlett answered him, she wasn't sure. It wasn't like he actually cared. But he sounded like he cared. He focused entirely on her, almost enraptured. "I'm going to miss the final bell."

"And that is... bad?"

She faced him again. And behind him, the gaggle of reporters, their microphones aimed to absorb every word. A blush crawled up Scarlett's face. What was she doing? Flirting with an alien prince outside her office? She had to go.

"Uh." She patted him awkwardly on the shoulder. "Thanks for the help, um, Your..."

"Prax M'Etein," he supplied, completely forgoing titles. "But you can call me Prax."

"Um, yeah, that." What was wrong with her? Scarlett never got tongue-tied. She couldn't when so much of her job relied on convincing judges at a moment's notice. "I have to go."

Scarlett caught sight of her car through the throng around her.

Her vision narrowed. Without so much as a goodbye, she bulldozed her way through the reporters. She needed to pick up her daughter. *Not* an alien prince. Camera lights flashed and reporters threw questions her way, but she ignored it all. Her focus narrowed to her escape.

But not entirely. Tickles shivered down her spine as Prax's eyes remained intent on her back. When she closed her car door, she caught his gaze again.

His cocky smile had only widened.

TWO

PRAX

"At noon, we have your first talk show appearance scheduled, Your Highness..."

Kasey prattled on, the human publicist waving her hand with excitement rather than nerves. Nothing seemed to phase her. Not even having an alien as a client. Prax shifted on the odd sofa in his suite's sitting area. It thankfully didn't levitate like everything Herkleian—the close cousins of his people were always trying to relive the glory days when their kind flew around breathing fire and ruining things. But the stiff backing made sitting with his ridges impossible.

Prax propped an elbow on the plush edge and tried to appear attentive. He was heir to a throne, for the Empire's sake. He could sit through a briefing.

His clawed fingers drifted toward his silver wristband. With a single tap, he could project his holo-screen—

No, Prax had to focus.

But he didn't want to focus. Couldn't focus. All since yesterday, when that delectable human female fell into his path. His cock hardened just at the thought of her. He couldn't help it. Her soft curves and delicate features haunted him. No female had ever enraptured Prax before. He had dined with great beauties from across the stars, but none had him resisting his primal urge to hunt them down. No other female had piqued his interest the way she had.

When he inhaled, the ghost of her scent teased his nostrils. Even in this busy metropolis of a city, he could trace her from the spot they first met. Eógans excelled at hunting. It'd be too easy to find her and drop to his knees and take her sweet warmth into his mouth... Prax grew harder, his desire a dent in his pants.

Which wasn't appropriate, not on Earth. His cousins' human brides had sent him an entire manual—of which he'd only read half, but he vaguely remembered something about taboos.

He stood and dropped into a deep bow. "Excuse me."

"Oh, um..." Kasey sputtered, her skin flushing an odd red color. His scales only shifted to that tone when he was in great anger, but on a human it meant embarrassment. Why she was embarrassed, he wasn't sure.

Without rising, Prax backed out of the sitting area and into his rooms. Like the rest of the suite, everything was gilded from the chairs to the carpets. Something a Herkleian might like, but Eógans preferred to decorate with nature itself. He pushed open the window, letting a cool breeze waft across his scales.

He needed to find her. Prax wouldn't be able to focus if he couldn't, and the last time he couldn't focus... He shuddered, his ridges bristling. He couldn't repeat what happened on Yazd.

Unfortunately, the terrible memories didn't lessen his erection.

He growled down at his cock. What terrible timing it always had.

Kasey knocked on the door. "Your Highness?"

"I'm feeling unwell," he nearly snapped. "Come back in an hour."

"But the brunch—"

"An hour." When the publicist didn't leave, he added, "Please."

Kasey didn't respond, but her footsteps padded away. He'd have to beg for her forgiveness later. It wasn't polite to talk to a female that way. If she took him to court before his mother, Empress Ailis would declare her well within her rights to have him whipped.

But thankfully neither his mother nor her three consorts were here. Prax was the highest ranking Eógan on Earth. And as the highest ranking Eógan, there was no one to stop him from climbing from his window and scaling the red-bricked building to the ground floor.

When Prax hit the dirt, he dropped into a crouch and placed his hands on the grass. He closed his eyes and inhaled deeply. Every scent on Earth bordered on familiar, but nothing entirely matched the smells of his homeworld. Prax filtered through the exhaust and smoke for the scents of living creatures, then dug deeper for a *particular* living creature—

"What are you doing?"

Prax opened his eyes. His first sight was dull yellow-green grass, half an inch from his face. He twisted and glanced up to spot a tiny Earthling holding an even tinier stick with a bright red circular top. His nostril flared at its nauseating sweetness.

His cousins' brides hadn't forbidden him from speaking to children, had they? "I'm hunting."

She plopped the red circle in her mouth. Without removing it, she murmured, "For what?"

"A female."

"Are you going to eat her?"

Prax didn't sit up, but his ridges quivered in confusion. The tiny Earthling nearly dropped her treat. "Why would I do such a thing?"

"Because you're a monster?"

"I'm not a monster. I'm from a planet called Eógan."

"You're an alien?"

"To you."

She paused. "Which *is* a monster, so..."

"I assure you, I'm not a monster." He'd normally rise and bow, but he didn't want to scare her. At seven-feet tall, he'd tower over her. "I'm a prince."

Her fear disappeared under a bright grin, one of her front teeth reduced to a dark void. Did tiny Earthlings do battle? If not, where had her tooth gone? "Do you live in a castle?"

"I do."

"What's that on your neck?"

His forehead furrowed. Prax hadn't talked much with humans, but he didn't think they all bounced from topic to topic like wild mhonilts between treetops. "Scales?"

"Not the scales, silly. The pattern."

A mark. On his neck. Impossible. "What does it look like?"

He knew her answer before she said it. "Like stars. A bunch of stars in a circle. It's pretty."

The Herkleian matebond mark. Through his father, he was half-Herkleian and nephew to the ever-missed Queen Avra, mother to his royal cousins. His father had told him stories in his youth, but no Herkleian had experienced a matebond in nearly a century. When his mother had caught them one night, she had forbidden his father from ever speaking of it again. The matebond was a blessing from the Herkleian dragon goddess Hyra. Eógans worshipped no gods but their ancestors.

He had witnessed the mark bloom between his cousins and their brides, but Prax had never imagined a mate for himself. Not when he didn't believe.

Not after what he'd done.

"Charlotte!" an older female shouted, wrenching Prax from his thoughts. The tiny Earthling remained at his side but twisted at the voice. "Who are you talking to?"

Charlotte pointed with her red treat, but a trimmed hedge hid Prax from view. "An alien."

A long sigh. "I don't have time for this, sweety. We have to go."

The tiny Earthling nodded at her mother before waving to Prax. "Goodbye, alien prince."

Prax couldn't help a smile. "Goodbye, tiny Earthling."

She giggled as she ran off. Prax stayed low to the ground. If the tiny Earthling thought him monstrous, how would he venture into the city to find his female? His mate? He hadn't noticed the mark on his neck last night, but if it was there, forming for all to see, it had to be because of the female.

The soft skin of her hand caressed ever so gently across his scales when he helped her stand. What would she feel like all over him? Trailing his abs, gripping his ridges, lowering to his cock...

Prax jerked to his feet. Fuck what the humans thought. People had flocked to stare at him his entire time on Earth, but nothing would stand between an Eógan hunter and his prey. He stalked forward onto the street, his nose primed... There. A sweet musk, diluted in the breeze. A shiver crawled Prax's spine to his neck.

He'd find the female. And if she was his mate, he'd do everything in his power to claim her.

THREE

SCARLETT

Scarlett pulled into the school parking lot and snagged one of the last spots.

Violet bounced forward in the backseat. "Mummy, can we get frozen yogurt after school with Daddy?"

Scarlett hated spending time with Andrew, but she was putty in her daughter's hand and rarely said no. Not that she had to say no often. Her kid had great ideas, like skipping school to visit the zoo or that Friday nights were always pasta night. "If I can get out of court on time. But if I can't, you and Daddy can go together."

"Brilliant!" Violet's British slang, along with an accent that made her sound like a miniature butler, still took Scarlett aback from time to time. She couldn't replicate her daughter's prim and proper tone even if she tried.

They climbed out of the car, Violet with her backpack and Scarlett with her daughter's overnight bag. She ruffled Violet's blond curls. Andrew didn't deserve her. Heck, even Scarlett didn't deserve her.

Hand in hand, they strolled to the school's front steps. Scarlett's stomach dropped. The PTA Pack—as she had so kindly dubbed them

—had grown in numbers since the school year started. The yoga-pant-wearing mommies congregated at their daily meeting spot right by the main door. Scarlett sighed. She had no choice but to join them. What kind of working mom guilt would they throw at her this time? Scarlett braced as if heading into battle. She only had to survive a few stupid niceties until the school bell rang.

"Scarlett, how nice to see you," Vivien, the head mommy, greeted her in a fake posh accent. She didn't know why Vivien even bothered. It wasn't like people couldn't use Google to see she wasn't always so affluent. Scarlett didn't care about social class, but lying had always rubbed her the wrong way. "It's been so long."

"Hello, Vivien. I saw you just two weeks ago."

Vivien gave a fake but polite chuckle, as if Scarlett had made a joke. She hadn't. "I know, it just feels like such a long time for those of us who make drop-off and pick-up a priority every day."

Scarlett gritted her teeth but forced a grin. Had Vivien noticed Scarlett picking her daughter up late yesterday? All thanks to that hot, dreamy alien, but Vivien wouldn't take any excuse, not even extraterrestrial intervention. Scarlett's skin prickled just at the thought of Prax, but it washed away under annoyance. She couldn't put words to how much Vivien grated on her nerves.

Handing Violet her overnight bag, she gestured her daughter forward. Once she entered the building, Scarlett could flee. "Have a good day at school and behave for your dad this weekend, okay? Text me if you need anything. Anything at all."

"I'm not a child, Mummy."

"Of course not."

Scarlett watched her daughter climb the school steps, a pang in her heart. How had her baby grown up so fast?

"This is Bethany." Vivien tore Scarlett from her thoughts. She turned with a frown to find Vivien gesturing at another mother. Maybe a new face to the PTA Pack, but Scarlett couldn't tell. "Her son, Charlie, just started in our girls' class last week." Turning back to Bethany, she added, "Scarlett is Violet's mom."

"How enchanting," Bethany said. "You both have color names. I considered giving my children B-names like myself, but then thought it might rob them of their autonomy."

God, she was going to despise this woman, too. "Yes, it's so funny we're both named after colors."

Scarlett hadn't even made the connection when she first chose her daughter's name. That was the problem with completing a birth certificate while still loopy on sedatives. There was no one else for the nurse to hand the papers to since Andrew hadn't shown up.

The last school bell rang as the doors crashed open. Violet disappeared inside with a wave and an enormous smile. And good timing, too, since Scarlett wasn't sure how long she could stand small talk with these mothers. Scarlett didn't have any patience for women that tore down other women. Nor any time, not with Saima's trial today.

"Have a nice life, Vivien." With that, Scarlett turned on her sneakers and legged it to her car.

SCARLETT CIRCLED the block twice before finding a parking spot close to her office building. She slid a hand down the ruffles of her pantsuit before grabbing her purse and heels. It was still an hour before most people started their workday, but Scarlett needed to pick up her files before her case. She couldn't lose. A woman's entire life was at stake. She hit the lock on her car and recited her list of files she needed as she crossed the street.

Her gaze drifted to the sidewalks near the cathedral gardens. The light touch of scales shivered across her hands. There was no universe where the alien prince found her remotely attractive, but that wouldn't stop her imagination. He'd haunt her until the end of her days. Every time she looked out the window of her office, she'd remember.

Scarlett unintentionally released a dreamy sigh. Maybe she'd get a green vibrator and name it after him—

A man in a nondescript trench coat stepped into her path.

Scarlett frowned. "Excuse me."

"Scarlett Moore?"

She normally wouldn't have answered, but it was well within reason for someone to be looking for her outside her office. "Yes?"

"Don't scream."

"What?" Everything within Scarlett stilled as the man pulled something small and black from within his coat. A gun. Her skin prickled. Guns were for police officers, movies, and cases—not her real life. What would Violet do without her? Oh God, Andrew couldn't raise her. He was barely interested enough to see his own daughter for a weekend. A cold sweat broke across her palms, making her purse's handle sticky in her grip.

But on the outside, she remained calm. Cool and collected, a trained lawyer. "How can I help you?"

"Drop Saima's case."

She narrowed her eyes. "You're one of Craig Newcastle's goons, aren't you?"

"That bitch has ruined all of our lives. Drop her case. You're doing it for free, right? She won't be able to afford rep without you and then she'll rot in jail like she deserves."

Scarlett swallowed, her eyes following the sway of the gun. How much would it hurt to get shot? Scarlett hated pain. When she had arrived at the hospital during Violet's labor, the first thing she had asked for was all the meds the doctors could legally give her. *All* of them.

But no matter the pain, she couldn't agree to this man's terms. She went to law school to help people. To protect those who couldn't protect themselves. Like Saima.

"I can't do that," she said, everything within her focused on keeping her voice steady and her gaze ice cold.

The butt of the gun pressed into her stomach. "I will shoot you in broad daylight. I have nothing left to lose."

She stared into his dark eyes, searching for a bit of humanity to appeal to, but all she spotted was desperation. Saima's testimony had led to Craig Newcastle's arrest. The trafficking ring crumbled around her, and the police caught more of the dirtbags involved every day.

Like this man would be. Killing Scarlett wouldn't stop that.

The ridiculous things people did for revenge.

"My answer hasn't changed."

"You bitch." The man pulled back, and Scarlett's heart nearly burst in relief, but the click of the safety sounded in her ear. Rung like a church's bell, a deadly omen. Scarlett hadn't prayed in years, but she slipped into the habit easily. *Please, God, protect my daughter. Give her a good and happy life...*

The man's beady gaze flickered over her shoulder. His skin paled to an unhealthy off-white. The gun lowered again, but this time as his arm slackened, muscles releasing in fear.

Before Scarlett could turn, a hauntingly familiar voice said, "Are you well, my lady?"

FOUR

PRAX

The last time Prax had seen a human gun, he'd been at his cousin's disaster of a wedding.

This one was tinier, more like a knife than the sabres he'd trained with at the Royal Academy, but that wouldn't stop the pellets from tearing through flesh. Three of his mother's honor guard had succumbed to the weapons at the wedding. Soldiers Prax had known for years and even trained beside.

And now some human pointed the weapon at *his* female.

Her scent had lured him halfway across London, growing stronger with each step towards where he met her yesterday. She must have worked nearby. When he first spotted her, his heart had nearly stopped. She had wrapped her pale-yellow hair pristinely at the back of her head, leaving her slender neck on full display. The fabric of her strange outfit clung to her perfectly, molded to her skin. Part of it frilled out at her waist, accentuating her delicious curves.

Prax's cock jumped at the sight, his desire surging through his body.

And at the back of his neck, above his top spike, his scales tingled.

His mate.

His.

The fire of desire turned into a burning rage. How dare this human male threaten his mate?

Prax had asked his female if she were well, but neither her nor her captor had answered, too busy gawking at him. He used the shock to his advantage. Prax rammed forward, pushing all his strength into his legs. Before the human male reacted, Prax ripped the weapon from his hands and tossed it down to the end of a narrow alley between the red-bricked buildings.

The male raised his hands. "I don't want any trouble."

"Then don't threaten innocent females." Prax lashed out, his fist slamming into the human's nose. He pulled back at the last second. With his strength, he might smash the male's skull.

The male ricocheted back and slumped into a puddle on the sidewalk.

"Holy shit."

Everything within Prax tightened at the voice. He turned slowly. The female wasn't staring at him in fear, but her brown eyes couldn't stop flickering between him and the human male's slumped body. Impressed at his strength, perhaps? Prax couldn't help but flex, the exposed muscles of his arms rippling. Maybe that was why his Herkleian cousins didn't wear shirts.

His movement grabbed his female's attention. Her tongue flickered out across her red lips. Prax's cock became an irresistible throb. What would her mouth be like on his scales?

Suddenly, she straightened and smoothed a hand down her front, almost as if realizing his thoughts. "Um, thank you for the rescue, Prince..."

"Prax," he said. "I told you to call me Prax."

Red flared across her cheeks. "You remember that?"

"I'll never forget."

"Oh. Well. Um." She waved her hand expressively in front of her, from the unconscious male to him to the buildings at their side. "I have to call the police."

He stepped in front of her path. Another offense worthy of the whip but he'd happily surrender to her any day. "Why did this male attack you?"

"This male?" Her forehead creased, the hair above her eyes—eyebrows?—fluttering. "Oh, him. He works for a terrible man who wants my client to suffer."

Her client? He didn't yet know his mate's career, but he understood one thing. "Then you're not out of danger?"

"Probably not, but that won't stop me from—Get your hands off me!"

Prax's instincts reacted before his brain did. He clamped a gentle hand on her arm. His fingers wrapped entirely around her bicep. Too tiny. Too fragile. If this bad 'man' she spoke of tried to hurt her again, how could she possibly defend herself?

The human male behind him twitched and groaned, spurring Prax's emotions to a fever. No one would hurt his female. No one.

Prax couldn't let any harm come to his mate.

Because she was his mate. He was certain. When Prax looked into her eyes, he knew in his heart she was his. But how could he convey that to someone who'd never heard of the concept?

Before he could stop himself, the words, "You're mine," tumbled out of his mouth.

Her eyes narrowed. "Excuse me?"

Prax tapped at the silver band on his wrist, connecting the comms to his ship in orbit. He couldn't take her back to his hotel. His ship was the only option. *Etein's Might*, a Class-A Eógan warship, carried dozens of smaller ships within its hangar bay. If he got her on board one of those, got her away from Earth and its weapons, she'd be safe. He'd have the chance to get to know her. To protect her.

"Two to transport," he said.

The female jolted in his grasp. "Two to transport where?"

"To my ship. I'll keep you safe."

"You can't just kidnap me." The female tugged, but Prax didn't let go. "Let me go, asshole!"

Asshole. Prax would pay for this for a thousand years, but it was a price he'd gladly accept to keep his mate safe. She whacked at his broad chest, but he barely felt the thuds. Around them, more humans flocked to the streets. He needed to get his female off this planet now. He didn't know Earth. He didn't know her enemies.

His mate pulled something from her bag, jagged-edged pieces of metal jingling on a circle. She tried to jam him with one. It rebounded off his scales. Prax didn't have time for this. When his mate was safe, he'd explain. He twisted a silver ring on his finger and pressed it against her flesh. The sedative flashed through her veins. Before she grabbed another weapon to use against him, she slumped into his grasp.

Prax pulled her into his arms, cradling her delicately. His heart pattered as he looked into her sleeping face, a hint of anger still on her lips. She was a rageful, little thing.

But because of him, she'd live to be angry another day.

"Your Highness?" a voice crackled through his internal comms. All the crew on *Etein's Might* knew he planned to spend another few days on Earth.

"Two to transport to the imperial hangar bay." He didn't leave any room in his voice for questions. Once he got her onto the *Might*, he'd take her aboard his vessel, *The Carthak*. His people wouldn't approve of his choices, even if there was no other way to save his mate's life. He couldn't give them a chance to message the Empress.

A tingle tickled its way across his scales. Within a blink, the transporter locked onto his signature and that of the female in his arms. The streets of London disappeared in a flash of rainbow light. When he blinked, Prax stood within a silver hangar bay, vines twisting across the walls. Whoever had fulfilled his transport request had set him right next to *The Carthak*, the silver and green cruiser spotless and polished. He requested it be refueled before leaving for his tour and thankfully, the hangar technicians had finished the task right away.

He tapped at his wristband again, careful to keep his mate's weight balanced in his arms. A door slid open on his ship. He quickly slipped inside. The size of a small home, the Class-B vessel had four bedrooms arranged around a mess hall and central control room. It wasn't nearly as fast as *Etein's Might*, but it'd get Prax and his mate where they needed to go.

Not that he knew where, but he'd figure it out. Prax was always one to act first and figure out the plan later.

The door to the control room slid open as he approached. He nudged a box of homemade arrows from a soft bench before gently lowering his mate to the surface. She remained asleep. Prax approached the main control panel. Three droids flew between the various sections of the ship's navigation, but Prax enjoyed taking the steering wheel for himself.

He tapped at his comms again. "Clear for take-off."

A long pause, before another confused voice said, "Your Highness?"

"I'll return shortly." Prax didn't know if that was true, but he didn't want to explain. Not that anyone on the *Etein's Might* had the authority to stop him.

The hangar bay doors lumbered opened, the forcefield flicking as it held back the cold of space. With a rumble, *The Carthak*'s engines flared to life. Prax glanced at his unconscious mate. When Prax had imagined speaking to her, she had gladly accepted his offer to court her. He'd have flown her off to some romantic date.

Instead, he had abducted her from her planet without even asking her name.

"I'm sorry, naika," he whispered to her, the Herkleian word for a mate slipping unconsciously from his lips. "I can't let another female die on my watch."

FIVE

The strange beeping initially tipped Scarlett off that she wasn't where she belonged.

She crawled into consciousness, a fog over her mind. She blinked at a silver ceiling of narrow pipes and dim lights, almost industrial but still somehow pleasing. But the ceiling was far less confusing than the row of crossbows bolted to the wall, some glimmering, high-tech marvels and others carved from wood. Scarlett groggily shifted. The surface beneath her was soft yet covered in a foreign fabric almost like leather. What had happened to her?

She rubbed her temple. She had dropped Violet off at school before heading to work to retrieve her files... The gun. Craig Newcastle's associate.

The alien prince.

Fuck. At this rate, Scarlett would need to dump her entire week's earnings in the swear jar when she returned home, but that didn't matter now. Had Prax kidnapped her? Had the apparently kind and definitely hot alien prince fucking *kidnapped* her?

Her gaze flickered to her left. Little robots buzzed between control panels in what had to be the control room of a literal spaceship. Her kidnapper sat at one panel, his ridged spine to her. She closed her eyes and hoped he didn't notice her awakening. Scarlett literally defended human trafficking victims—now she felt like one.

She almost huffed out a frustrated breath, but instead held herself steady. It was probably best to appear asleep while figuring out a plan. She needed to clear her head. *Fuck.* She had zero experience with this. What kind of plan could she come up with? Through the large windows on the other side of the control room, the blackness of space stared back at her. She couldn't get away from him. At best, she could lock herself in a storage closet and hope he'd leave her alone. But what good would that do? She was at his mercy.

Her skin tingled. *His* mercy. Scarlett nearly blew her cover by smacking herself in the forehead. How dare she have the hots for her kidnapper? Damn Stockholm Syndrome. She hadn't even been conscious in his presence for more than an hour.

But despite everything, she was still attracted to Prax. She wasn't about to seduce him to get out of here. Could she try to overpower him? His bare shoulders rippled with scaled muscle, so probably not. The self-defense classes she took at the YMCA wouldn't be a match for this alien. And even if she overpowered him, it wasn't like she knew how to fly a spaceship.

Rage bloomed in her stomach. Scarlett always had a bit of an anger issue. She had thought herself grown out of it, but it returned with a vengeance. How dare he kidnap her, even if he had the physique of a literal god. Screw it all. She might as well just bite the bullet and attack the guy. He deserved it.

Scarlett peeked open one eye. The alien prince still hadn't turned in her direction. There were no weapons nearby, but her purse lay on the floor at her side. She slipped her hand inside. If only she carried around a Swiss army knife. She had dropped her keys earlier, and the only other potential weapon she carried was a bottle of perfume.

Scarlett hefted the bottle in her hand. Maybe if she threw it at him...

Scarlett launched into action. She bolted out of her seat, tossed the bottle at his head, and made a break for the door.

Which slammed shut in front of her.

She banged her fists against it. "Fuck!"

"Let's not throw things at each other, female," he drawled, his deep voice slithering over her.

Scarlett's nipples hardened. Damn traitors. She spun, putting her back to the wall. Prax rose from his chair yet didn't approach. His massive frame engulfed the room, the tight fabric of his shirt straining against his muscles. His scales had shone like emeralds in the sunlight, but the sheen didn't diminish in the harsh artificial lighting. He reached up and rubbed a hand around his horns and through his bronze hair, a nearly boyish action. Her eyes traced his arm as it flexed in the movement.

Oh, wait, she had thrown something at him. That was why he touched his head. Because he was a creepy, gross kidnapper.

She crossed her arms and sent him her best glare. Known criminals had withered under her gaze. "You try to stop me. And my name is Scarlett, you jerk. Not female. What year do you think it is?"

"Scarlett," he repeated, almost as if testing how it sounded against his lips.

Her traitorous nipples got harder.

Without another word, he sat, his legs stretched out before him. Not that his ease put her at ease. "There's no need to try that again, Scarlett. This is just a minor disagreement—"

"A minor disagreement, my ass! You literally kidnapped me. What's your plan? Am I to serve or to sell?" She nearly vomited at the words but if Scarlett were to survive this, she needed to know. She *would* survive this and return home. Andrew couldn't raise Violet under any circumstance.

For some reason, her kidnapper looked offended. "I would never do such a thing to a lady. They're to be honored and protected."

"Then explain why you kidnapped me."

He rubbed a hand down his forehead in another too-human

action. "We really need to start over."

She just glared at him.

"I'll start, then. When we met yesterday, I felt an immediate pull to you. I couldn't get you out of my head all night. Based on the mark on my neck, we're mates."

Scarlett held up a perfectly manicured hand. "And it just keeps getting worse. Now you want to mate with me?"

"Not *with* you. You *are* my mate."

"I don't really see how grammar changes the situation."

"Matebonds are supposedly a blessing from the Herkleian goddess Hyra—"

Nope. Scarlett didn't really believe in any human gods, much less alien gods. Certainly not enough to go along with this delusion. "Let me stop you right there. You think a non-existent alien goddess wants me to mate with you?"

He didn't look annoyed at her interruptions. Good. Damn kidnapper. "I don't really know. My cousins would know more. Two of them have mated with human females recently."

When Scarlett had watched the engagement party videos, she imagined the alien princes as dreamy and sweet. But if King Anax and Prince Eryx were anything like their cousin, maybe they were assholes, too. Scarlett glared. "Gee, I hadn't heard."

"You have every reason to be angry—"

"That wasn't anger. That was sarcasm."

"Which is almost anger."

"Don't talk over me, Prince Mansplainer." Scarlett strut forward, her fear forgotten. She crossed the room like she crossed the court-room in front of a judge. "I know all about Herkleian matebonds. Thanks to Queen Alexandra, there's a dozen articles on the subject. Cosmo even did an interview with her on it."

"Then you know how powerful emotions are within a matebond."

"So you kidnapped me because emotions overcame you?" She jabbed a finger into his chest and nearly bounced off his muscles.

Damn. The heat in her chest lowered to her core. Scarlett straightened and put a step between them. *Not in a thousand years, matebond.*

"I... overreacted."

"You think?"

"When I saw the male with the gun... when you said they'd try to hurt you again..." His red eyes filtered to her, piercing her to the spot. "I overreacted. I wanted to get you to safety. I wasn't thinking. This isn't how I wanted our first meeting to go."

Scarlett's heart tugged. Lord, at this rate, her entire body had turned traitor against her. He had acted with good intentions, but the result was less than stellar. Those crimson eyes continued to search hers, pleading, and she almost softened to him. *Almost.*

She crossed her arms against her chest. "Take me back to Earth."

She couldn't help but notice the flicker of pain across his face. The male was an open book. Powerful and commanding, yet open and vulnerable. If he hadn't fucking kidnapped her, he'd be the perfect guy. How rare was it to find a guy in touch with his feelings and as buff as Captain America?

The ship rumbled, a harsh jolt. Scarlett flew off her feet—and landed straight in the alien's lap.

Heat sparked between his scales and her skin. Scarlett's breath knocked from her chest at his touch. She tried to pull out of his embrace, but her hand trailed across his shoulder and down his chest.

The ship rumbled again.

Prax's arms tightened around her, holding her steady.

She looked into his eyes, too close. Like his lips. Like his whole damn self. Scarlett pushed from his lap. "What's going on?"

Prax cleared his throat with a deep grunt before spinning his chair around. He tapped at the control panel in front of him. His forehead furrowed as his entire body tensed. "A larger ship has trapped us in a tractor beam."

None of those words were English. "So get us out of it?"

"This ship doesn't have any weapons."

Scarlett's stomach dropped to her feet. "What do you mean, you don't have any weapons? The kind of aliens who steal women from their workplaces don't have weapons on their own ships to defend themselves?!"

"This is a luxury spacecraft meant for brief trips between planets within the Intergalactic Alliance. There's no need for weapons in friendly territory."

Scarlett pointed at the window—not that she could see any ship from this angle. "That's obviously not true. Hasn't your evil king of an uncle declared war on everyone?"

"My uncle is in jail. And we're less than an hour from Earth. No one would attack this close to your protected space."

She gestured wildly at the shaking ship around them. "Wrong again."

"Whoever's doing this will pay."

"Are you going to punish yourself for kidnapping me, too?"

Prax didn't have the chance to answer. With a final rumble, their ship slipped through the gigantic doors of another ship and lowered to the ground. Scarlett pressed herself to the glass, but she couldn't see anything beside a basic silver-grey hangar, like straight out of *Star Wars*. Not that she'd be able to identify another alien race if she saw them. Until yesterday, she'd only seen the Herkleians and Eógans in photographs.

Something thunked behind her. Scarlett spun. Prax had pulled a panel off on the wall, filled to the brim with gun-like weapons. Guess the crossbows were ornamental, then. He strapped a dozen sharp knives to various parts of his body before grabbing a sword that crackled with electricity. After a moment, he sheathed it at a hostler across his back and settled for a flickering laser gun.

A second clang echoed somewhere else on the ship. Prax aimed his laser at the door. As furred hands pried it open, he shifted into stance in front of her. "Just stay behind me, Scarlett."

Scarlett rushed to the hidden armory and grabbed a laser. "Like hell I will."

SIX

PRAX

Prax's fiery mate settled at his side right as a dozen auburn-furred Neithans rushed into the rooms, lasers raised and aimed. Fuck. Prax held his weapon steady, but Scarlett's grip faltered for a second. There was no way they were shooting their way out of this one. Even his mate, with her limited battle experience, could see that.

"Hello, cousin."

Prax had started to lower his weapon when the sharp voice echoed down the hall. In a smooth move, he stepped forward, putting Scarlett behind him.

She nudged him with the tip of her laser. "Excuse me?"

Prax didn't have the chance to answer her. Prince Argrix, third son to Xenobaccus Yio'hyra and his aunt Avra, strolled into the room. His dark-purple hair brushed down his back and his slitted eyes remained permanently narrowed. Despite living on Neith since his marriage to Princess Kashta years ago, his cousin remained in Herkleian formal dress, golden pants and a sash of white over his blue-scaled chest.

Prax reluctantly holstered his laser. Last he'd heard, Argrix had sided with his father and the Neithans against the Intergalactic

Alliance. Which meant they wanted Prax alive. What for, he didn't know. But whatever it was, it was Prax's only way to get Scarlett out. He had trained in combat with the rest of the alliance royals, but he couldn't take on a dozen soldiers single-handedly.

"What are you doing?" Scarlett hissed at his back.

He twisted toward her, keeping his cousin and the Neithan soldiers in view, and spoke softly, "Follow my lead and I promise to get you out of this alive."

"I wouldn't be here if not for you."

The words ripped through his heart. She was right. If he had remained on Earth and courted her there, he'd never have left the Eógan fleet—and therefore his protection—behind.

Damned matebonds.

Not that Prax could blame it entirely on that.

"What do you want, Argrix?"

"Always the smooth negotiator," Argrix said mockingly. "Where have your manners gone? You haven't even introduced me to your companion."

Prax held back a snarl. In his mind, he lunged across the room and knocked his cousin off his feet. But this time, it wasn't only his life on the line. This time, he'd think before acting. He didn't want Argrix getting anywhere near Scarlett. He was her last line of defense.

"Come now, Prax, you must be tired from your..." His purple slitted eyes flickered between Prax and Scarlett "... journey. Let's talk aboard my ship."

Argrix said it as if it were a kind invitation, but Prax knew from the soldiers surrounding him he couldn't refuse. He inclined his head anyway. Better to let Argrix think Prax believed himself still in charge, like the cocky male his cousin remembered from years ago.

With that, Argrix strolled from the control room, half of the Neithan guard flocking behind him. The remaining six stayed behind, dark eyes on Prax and his mate. He started forward, but made sure to pull at the collar of his shirt. Herkleians wore their hair long, making matebond marks easy to hide, but Prax's bronze hair barely brushed his neck. If Argrix saw his mark, what would he do to Scarlett?

His mate nudged an elbow into his arm and whisper-hissed, "Where are they taking us?"

Etein's mercies. Prax, Argrix, and all their soldiers had implanted translators, but Scarlett didn't. They'd understand everything she said, but she'd only understand if they spoke English. And it wasn't like Prax could convince his cousin to have a conversation in a foreign alien language. If things went to shit, she'd have no advanced warning.

"To their ship," he answered, his attention remaining on the guards beside and behind him. "My cousin, Argrix, wants to talk."

"The Herkleian is your cousin? Which makes him King Anax's brother?"

"His younger brother, but don't mistake family ties for alliances. Argrix has sided with Xenobaccus in the war."

The flush drained from his mate's cheeks. "What news-report-level shit did you get me involved in? King Xenobaccus? Seriously?"

"Unfortunately."

"I need to get home." A frantic look entered her eyes. "I need to get back to Violet."

He frowned. Return to violet? His cousins' brides' handbook had included some common human phrases, but not that one. How did one return to a color? Was it a flower?

Prax reached down and gently took her hand. She didn't push him away. If anything, she clung to his side. Just moments ago, she had been anything but cordial. At least she trusted him to keep her safe when it came down to it. That was a good sign. Perhaps, with time, she might come to feel the bond between them.

They exited *The Carthak*'s ramp into a silver-grey hangar bay. Neithan ships were massive, circular rings with domed ceilings and little decor. Practical and cold like its people, despite living on an achingly hot planet. Prax had traveled to Neith once for his cousin's wedding. He remembered little of it besides drinking sweet khamra. Thank the Empire alcohol worked on him despite his Herkleian genes. Prax rarely got wasted at official functions, but it had been the universe's most boring party—if you could even call it that.

A few feet from the end of the ramp, the Neithans had placed three sturdy chairs carved from dark ptah wood. Argrix settled into the grandest seat like it was a throne. His wife, Princess Kashta, occupied the other seat, her auburn fur gleaming in the light and threaded with hundreds of glittering beads. She picked at her sharp nails, looking like she'd rather be anywhere else.

Prax settled beside the remaining chair. He wouldn't sit if his mate couldn't, but he also didn't feel confident offering her the seat. If any sort of fight erupted, he wanted Scarlett beside him.

Without speaking, Scarlett arrived at the same conclusion. She stopped next to him and crossed her arms, her face settling into a blank glare.

"Please sit, cousin. I feel like an ungracious host."

"You *are* an ungracious host." Prax kept his tone polite, but he saw no reason to play games with his cousin.

"You are an ungracious guest," Princess Kashta said acerbically, her voice an accented Herkleian. "As always, Prax M'Etein."

"I see you still haven't forgiven me for your wedding, Your Highness. I was simply trying to liven things up."

"By swimming naked in the palace's fountain and flirting with all my sisters?"

"You have lovely sisters." Prax's gaze flickered to Scarlett, but her face remained blank. Perhaps it was good she didn't understand the conversation. "But we're not here to talk about them."

Argrix leaned forward in his seat, his black claws tapping against his chin. "I will get to the point, then. I need a simple favor from you and then we're free to part on amicable terms."

Prax's spine ridges bristled. "And why would I do you a favor?"

Argrix bared his fangs. "Because I know what happened on Yazd six months ago."

Prax stiffened, the venom glands within his ridges activating. He tried to keep his face blank. Argrix couldn't know. His friend, Prince Keveh of Yazd, had promised to have the evidence erased. "I don't know what you're talking about."

Argrix's smile turned cruel. "Then you won't mind if I play the footage from *Zaghan's Rage* to jog your memory."

Without waiting, he quickly tapped at his gold wristband. A holo-screen projected into the air, an image frozen on the screen. An image of Prax patting Prince Keveh on the shoulder before his friend left him alone at the *Rage*'s tables.

Before Prax committed murder.

"That's not necessary."

Scarlett discretely poked him. "What's happening?"

He didn't answer, but he couldn't stop his gaze from falling on her. She remained bravely at his side, but she frowned at the image of Prax. Even if she didn't understand what they said, she'd never look at him the same way if she knew his crimes.

Prax desperately wanted to win her over. He couldn't lose her now.

"What do you want, Argrix?"

"I want you to break my father out of prison."

Prax paused before bursting into laughter. When his mate stiffened at his side, he stopped and cleared his throat. "You're insane. How am I supposed to do that? Anax choose Herkleios to be his prison for a reason."

"I'm aware. No one can get onto Herkleios that isn't welcome. My grandmother—Hyra bless Queen Niobe's soul—was many things, but she wasn't stupid. No other planet's shielding compares." Argrix slumped back into the seat like the lazy, arrogant bastard he was. "While I'm no longer welcome, there's no reason you can't enter. Especially since I understand you have an invitation."

Prax clenched his jaw.

"You were invited to Queen Alexandra's party for her newborns, correct?"

"A ridiculous concept," Princess Kashta said. "She hasn't even birthed her spawn yet, and she's already throwing them a party."

"I agree." Argrix tried to place his hand on his wife's, but she tugged away with a glare. "Nevertheless, you *have* an invitation, Prax."

"I turned it down. I'm supposed to be on Earth."

"Make up an excuse. I don't care."

Prax crossed his arms, his position a mirror to Scarlett's. "And how do you suppose I'll break your father out? I might have access to the palace grounds but not the prisons."

"If you don't want to bring shame to your family with your past behavior, you'll find a way."

Prax ground his teeth. Etein's mercies. He wanted to spear Argrix with his ridges and watch him choke on poison, but the guards would tackle him to the ground before he even reached his cousin. Prax's hold on his emotions slipped. The green of his scales tinted red with deep rage. "The Empress will be... displeased to learn of my actions on Yazd, but she'd kill me herself if she learned I released Xenobaccus on the galaxy. I have to decline."

Argrix glared, fury in his gaze. After a long moment, his slitted eyes flickered to Scarlett. "Kill the human."

The Neithan guards raised their lasers, the energy a murderous buzz within. Scarlett gasped, but Prax quickly moved in front of her. "Don't you dare."

"What did you say to them?" Scarlett asked at his back. "Why do they want me dead?"

He ignored her. It took everything within him, but he forced his gaze forward. Prax narrowed his eyes at his cousin. If he agreed to help, would Argrix let Scarlett go? He couldn't leave her here with the Neithans.

He'd say anything to get her off this ship.

"Fine. I'll free your father. If we leave now, we'll arrive at Herkleios in time for the party."

"The human stays with us."

"The human *goes* with me."

"You think you're in a position to negotiate?"

"She's a necessary part of the plan," Prax said, scrambling for a reason. He reached down and took Scarlett's hand. She tensed, but didn't push him away, not in front of the Neithans. "She's my beloved."

Argrix released a disbelieving growl. "Not you, too, cousin. Humans are disgusting—"

Prax didn't let Argrix finish his sentence. If he doubted his relationship at all, what would happen to his mate? Nothing good. Prax spun toward her and murmured, "Don't hit me."

She frowned. "Don't what?"

Without another word, Prax swept Scarlett off her feet and claimed her mouth in a kiss.

SEVEN

Scarlett stiffened, her entire body a live wire as Prax kissed her. His lips were soft, talented. Warmth flared to life in her core. A little sound escaped her, more a moan than a yelp. She wanted to lean into his touch. She wanted to push him away and sock him in the jaw. She wanted and wanted, warring with herself.

Before either side of her won the battle, he broke the kiss. She reached out and fisted a hand in the dark leather of his shirt. Whether to pull him closer or stop herself from falling, she didn't know. A grin settled onto his lips, the look a secret just for her. If he were any other man—or a man at all—she wouldn't resist him for a minute.

But Scarlett wouldn't be falling for her royal kidnapper. Not today.

She stepped out of his arm and fidgeted with the buttons of her blazer. Anything but focus on the heat in her cheeks and the prince at her side.

Prax's cousin, Argrix, made an unpleasant growl before snapping something at Prax in whatever alien language they spoke. The stiffness in Prax's shoulders slackened. For a second before the kiss, Scarlett was sure she was going to die. But Prax's response—had the kiss been part of the response?—saved her.

She hardened her heart to him. She wouldn't need saving if it wasn't for him in the first place.

Prax and his cousin exchanged a few more clipped words before coming to some sort of understanding. Her questions for her kidnapper grew by the minute. What did Argrix want? Why did they keep mentioning the former king turned tyrant, Xenobaccus?

And why did Prax freak out when Argrix showed him that security footage?

The guards around the blue Herkleian and the Neithan princess stepped back, allowing space for others to pass. Prax reached for her hand. "We're to go with them."

Scarlett remained blank-faced. "I assume that's not up for debate."

"Unfortunately not."

Scarlett sighed inwardly and took the prince's hand. Together, they marched forward. Most of the soldiers flocked to them, but three Neithans split off from the group and entered Prax's ship.

"What's happening?" Scarlett asked, voice low.

"I'll tell you everything, but for now, we're being escorted to a room while my cousin makes... adjustments to my ship."

"Bad adjustments?"

"Bad adjustments," he agreed.

"Fuck." Screw the swear jar. It wasn't like Violet was around to hear her swear again. At this rate, would Scarlett ever see her daughter again? "Double fuck."

She shook away the thought. Not going there. Scarlett *would* see Violet again.

The Neithan guards led them from the hangar to a room off the main hallway. When the door slid open, Prax's ridges bristled. He was almost cat-like in a way, the movement of his spikes as telling as the red flush that crept his scales during the peak of his anger. Scarlett glanced into the room and her own spine tensed. The tiny square had a single mattress tucked into the corner on the floor and a cracked sink.

The Neithan guard grunted something, his beady eyes flickering to Scarlett.

"Absolutely not," Prax replied in crisp English. "My beloved stays with me."

Beloved? Scarlett immediately skipped over *that* terror to the more important part of the sentence. "Hell, no. I'm staying with him."

Despite her not understanding them, the Neithan guards seemed to have no issue with the reverse. He grumbled something else. Probably insulting. Scarlett was a second away from planting her foot in knockoff-Chewbacca's ass when Prax squeezed her hand. "Scarlett will stay with me, unless you'd like to tell my cousin that our deal has ended because of you."

The head guard growled a bit, a high-pitched wheezing sound, before turning on his boots and starting down the silver-gray hallway. The soldiers at their back nudged them forward. Scarlett and Prax followed silently, hands still clasp together. For a moment, she was grateful for the prince. If anyone else stood at her side, they'd have abandoned her the moment Prince Argrix made his threats.

The second room the guards led them to was a significant upgrade from the first. A low divan-style bed with bright red blankets occupied most of the floor space opposite something like a kitchenette. A door in the corner probably opened into a small bathroom— or whatever the alien equivalent was. Scarlett swore to never spend another night in a cheap hotel room once she finished law school, but better this than a cell.

The guards lined the hallway outside before slamming the door shut behind them. Something whirled like the mechanics of a lock. Apparently, the Neithans didn't want them walking freely around their ship.

Scarlett paced to the far wall. "This is definitely an upgrade over the last room."

Prax snorted. "Anything is an upgrade over that mess."

From the corner of her eye, she watched the alien prince settle into a chair. Scarlett wished she had the patience for that. She faked it in court, but this was not her comfort zone. This was a freaking alien ship and nothing good would come of it. She crossed her arms, but continued her pacing, the energy inside her an itch. "What's going on?"

"My cousin is blackmailing me."

"And?" That didn't explain why Prax had called her his beloved before sweeping her off her feet or why they were currently locked in here.

"If I don't break my uncle out of jail, Argrix will release something... incriminating against me and my family."

"Like?"

He clenched his jaw.

"Fine, don't tell me. I don't care. I still don't get how this concerns me."

"They were going to kill you," he said, grinding out the words. "I told them you're my beloved and that my cousins would expect you when we arrive on Herkleios."

Scarlett tried not to gape. "I'm not going to Herkleios."

"We have no choice, but once I'm there, I don't intend to break my uncle out of prison. He threatens the entire galaxy with his insane plans."

"At least we're the same page with that, then."

His brow crinkled. "What page?"

"The same..." Lord, she was explaining metaphors to an alien. "Never mind."

"I'll find us a way out of this, Scarlett. Trust me."

If only she could. She reached the end of the kitchenette and twirled, heading back the way she'd come. Her sneakers squeaked on the floors. Scarlett glared down at them. "Well, whatever we're doing next, I need a change of clothes. I'm sure I look amazing, but a pantsuit is not the best attire to outthink intergalactic blackmailers."

Prax pushed from the seat and stalked across the room toward her. Her throat dried. The male knew how to walk. His seven-feet of muscle radiated out toward her, a warmth she wanted to curl into. The ghost of his lips tickled against her skin. God, she hoped he kissed her again.

Hoped and yet didn't.

Scarlett stayed rooted to the spot until he stood less than a foot from her, staring down at her with a light quirk to his lips. The tingles in her lips trailed down her chest, tightening her nipples and whispering over her core—

Prax cleared his throat. "I'm trying to access the door behind you."

"Oh, shit." Scarlett immediately skirted out of the way. She had forgotten the bathroom door behind her. It wasn't entirely out of character for him to just approach her all sexy and menacing for fun.

Prax tapped on the edge of the door, sliding it open. The rectangular space was no larger than her closet back home and almost entirely empty. A shower-like pod with odd, glowing buttons occupied half of the space.

Prax pointed to two indents in the wall. "Tap that for the toilet and the other to clean your hands."

"Uh, thanks." Scarlett peered around him. "And the change of clothes?"

He gestured at a button with a squiggly triangle-esque shape carved into it.

Scarlett arched a brow at him. "I press the button for clothes?"

"It won't have many options."

What did that mean? Scarlett shrugged and walked into the bathroom. She had figured out how to care for a baby by herself in a foreign country. How difficult could it be to work an alien shower?

Scarlett waited for the door to close firmly behind her before kicking off her sneakers. She dropped her blazer next and her blouse, but kept on her bra. She'd paid far too much money to leave it behind. Most stores didn't sell size DDD, unfortunately. She wiggled out of her pants before shuffling into the shower space. There wasn't any nozzle for water. Scarlett squinted at the buttons and then shrugged.

She hit the first one Prax had pointed at, vaguely clover-like. With a flash of light, Scarlett erupted in tingles. "Bloody hell!"

Scarlett shrieked and jumped, but the light faded almost instantly. She slapped down at her skin. All the day's sweat had disappeared in an instant. How in the world? The Intergalactic Alliance had started sharing technology with Earth months ago and they needed to put this pod on the list ASAP.

The door slammed open. "Scarlett—"

Scarlett shrieked again and raised her hands, but she didn't have a towel. Thank God she'd only taken off half her clothes. Prax's jaw dropped. His eyes dropped, trailing over her breasts to the curves of her hips. Her skin puckered where his gaze landed.

"What are you wearing?"

"Nothing?"

"No, I mean." He gestured at her bra and matching panties. "What are those?"

Scarlett raised an eyebrow. Did aliens not wear underwear? Heat raced to her cheeks, but not in embarrassment. Her younger, bolder self flamed within her, awakened after a decade of sleep. "Like what you see?"

His scales darkened to a deeper emerald. "Very much."

Scarlett kept the eyebrow raised, trying for unimpressed. "Good. Now get out."

Prax swallowed, but did as she said. As he backed out of the room and slid the door closed, his gaze remained latched to her. She didn't move a muscle, not even on her face, but within she burned. No man had ever started at her like that, like she was the most beautiful thing in the galaxy.

When the door clicked shut, a small grin tugged at her lips.

She almost smacked herself. No matter how smoldering hot he was, Scarlett would *not* fall for her kidnapper. She glared at her reflection in the silver of the shower pod and raised a scolding finger. Bad.

Properly chastised, she hit at the last remaining button on the shower pod. In a blink, a form-fitting black one-piece covered her lacy underwear. Scarlett whistled. Damn. Her friend, Denise, always tried to get her to wear rompers, but Scarlett had never found the style flattering on anyone above a size 6. Yet here she was in what was basically a catsuit and her ass looked fantastic.

Scarlett's gaze flickered toward the door. Would Prax even survive this?

No time like the present to find out.

Scarlett pushed out of the pod and into the main room of their suite-cell, her blond hair tickling her shoulders. Prax had settled back into the seat by the small table, a steaming platter of food in front of him. His narrowed gaze fixed on the front door, almost daring someone to come open it, but he gravitated toward her when she entered. Though his jaw didn't drop, his eyes widened, the darkening of his scales returning in full force. Scarlett didn't let it trip her up. She settled into the seat across from him.

He cleared his throat and tried on a wide, cocky grin. "I thought you might be hungry, so I had the materializer create osha, a common Neithan dish. They had no better options."

"Osha is fine with me." Scarlett plucked a spoon from the table and pushed at the mound of orange-red beads. Maybe the Neithan version of rice? She scooped some into her mouth and nearly choked on the spice. "Wow, that's really..."

"Flavorful," Prax finished for her. "But tasty?"

Scarlett chewed. "It's not bad. The taste reminds me of Indian food, but the texture is a bit... chewy."

"And Indian is good?"

"Indian is delicious."

"I hope to try it one day."

One day? Wasn't he forward? "Assuming we get off this ship."

"I doubt we'll be here that much longer."

"If that's the case, I should know what blackmail is being held over your head."

In a second, his entire demeanor changed. He sat back in his seat as far as his ridges allowed, the flirty grin slipping into a frown. "It doesn't matter."

"It obviously does."

"I made a mistake."

Shit. Scarlett had heard this before. Not only from Prax, but from dozens of clients. He had easily confessed to kidnapping, so what could be worse? "Prax, whatever it was, I need to know. If we're going to do this, I can't be in the dark."

Prax opened his mouth, but no words came out. For a male who had joked with a laser pointed in his face, that spoke volumes. Scarlett pushed from the table.

He reached for her. "I'll tell you, Scarlett. Please, just hear me out—"

The door clicked open behind her. "The mistake he made was taking another's life."

Scarlett stiffened. She backed away from the table and the door, putting both Prax and his cousin, Argrix, out of reach. "Prax?"

He stood to face Argrix. "You were listening in."

Argrix leaned against the doorframe. "I never promised privacy."

"I don't care about him," Scarlett snapped. "Is what he said true, Prax?"

He lowered his head. "Yes."

No. She didn't know when it had happened, but despite the kidnapping, she had started to trust Prax. Started to let her desire flower without shame. Prax didn't seem like a person capable of killing. "Was it out of self-defense?"

Argrix did his eerie, growly laugh. "Go on, Prax! Tell her the truth. Was it out of self-defense?"

His head remained lowered, but those red eyes flicked to her. "No."

Scarlett lowered to the edge of the divan, her legs shaking. Argrix seemed to take pleasure in suffering, but she had no doubt he was indeed telling the truth about Prax. The emerald-scaled prince hadn't even denied it. Scarlett had been kidnapped by a freaking murderer. And now they were now off to free an ex-king who thought her planet the perfect addition to his empire.

Argrix bared his fangs cruelly. "No time to let you two sort this out. Your ship's ready, cousin."

EIGHT

Scarlett hadn't met Prax's gaze since Argrix informed her he was a murderer.

He'd wanted to deny it, to say it was in self-defense, but that would be a lie. Prax had already fucked up things with his mate to a state nearly beyond repair. He couldn't lie. Not to her. But she deserved the full truth instead of his cousin's warped summary.

Once they were alone on his ship, he'd tell her everything.

Argrix bared his fangs and said in perfect English, "Still want to take the human with you, cousin?"

Scarlett stiffened, but didn't slow her pace. If she did, his cousin's guards would happily drag her back to the hangar bay.

Prax's scales reddened. "Shut up, Argrix."

The male threw back his head and howled. If Prax had been on any alliance spacecraft, he'd have knocked the teeth out of his cousin's stupid face. "As you wish. But if she ruins your chances to break my father out of prison, the consequences for you will be the same."

"I understand."

Scarlett shot Argrix the darkest glare imaginable. "So do I."

It only made Argrix smile wider. "She *does* speak."

Never mind. Her glare somehow got darker. "Of course I speak, you moron."

"Scarlett…" Prax angled himself between his cousin and his mate. He'd die to defend her, but he'd rather live to see her out of this mess.

"Don't 'Scarlett' me," she said, mocking his tone. "I'll say what I want and deal with the consequences. I'm a big girl, Prax."

The doors to the hangar bay slid open before them. Neithan technicians surrounded Prax's ship, tapping at holo-screens and whispering between themselves. What had they done to his ship? Installed spyware of some sort? That would make getting Scarlett out of this mess more difficult, but nothing would stand in Prax's way. He'd return his mate to Earth. He wouldn't release his uncle from prison. And if Argrix released his blackmail video to the whole of the Intergalactic Alliance, he'd deal with the consequences of that, too.

A Neithan with the orange band of a medic around his arm approached when Prax, Scarlett, and Argrix entered.

Argrix paused, his slitted gaze flickering between Prax and his mate. This time, he spoke in Herkleian. "I assumed your… beloved didn't have an implanted translator. If she's going to be of any use on Herkleios, she'll need one."

Prax's ridges bristled. "You won't be injecting anything into her."

Scarlett elbowed him in the side. "What's he saying?"

Argrix answered before him, "You'll need a translator if you're to go to Herkleios."

A crinkle formed between her brow for a moment before she smoothed it away. "And you're opposed to this, Prax?"

"I am."

"You think it's a trick?"

Whatever anger his mate had toward him, she still trusted him. *Had* to trust him. "It could be."

"It's not a trick," Argrix said. "If I wanted you dead, you'd be dead."

"How blunt." Scarlett crossed her arms and examined his cousin for a minute before giving a curt nod. "Fine. Give me the translator."

Prax opened his mouth to reply, but bit down on an answer. Given the narrowing of his mate's eyes, it was the correct answer. He didn't get a say on what she did. Not now. Maybe not ever.

The medic approached with a flat, silver circle in his palm. Without care for her personal space, he pinched the device to her forehead. Scarlett stiffened and flinched, but otherwise remained silent. With a few taps to his holo-screen, the medic deployed the translator nanotech. Prax kept his eye on the medic's movements. He didn't have medical training, but he'd watched enough translator implantations to know if something was off.

"Done," the medic said gruffly, plucking the circle from Scarlett's temple.

Scarlett rubbed at her forehead. "Was that it?"

Prax nodded.

"I've had more painful sneezes."

"Our technology is far more advanced than yours." Argrix didn't sneer the words, but the implication was clear. He dismissed Scarlett with barely a glance, his attention locked on Prax. "We have a deal, cousin. You release my father, and I'll keep your murderous little secret from your poor mother and the rest of the galaxy."

Prax gave a clip nod. Without another word to Argrix, he motioned Scarlett toward his ship. She hooked her fingers in the pockets of her tight, military-issue pants and strolled forward. Prax did everything in his power not to stare at her ass. When she had come out of the bathroom in her new uniform, he had nearly died. The odd human suit she'd worn had hidden the true depths and valleys of her curves. He wanted to take her supple cheeks into his hands and squeeze.

"And, Prax?" His cousin's voice cut through his desire like a knife. "Don't think of betraying me. I had our technicians install cameras and a little... surprise if you decide not to complete your mission."

"Surprise?"

"Take a peek in the engine room," Argrix said. "Under the main turbine."

Scarlett stopped halfway through the door. "What's he talking about?"

Prax glared across the hangar at his smug bastard of a cousin. "Nothing we can change, unfortunately."

Once they entered *The Carthak*, the doors slid closed behind them and the engines flared. Prax turned left and started straight for the engine rooms.

Scarlett followed behind him, keeping distance between them. Now that they were out of Argrix's grasp, they returned to untrusting allies. "Who's flying this thing?"

"The auto-pilot," he said. "I'm sure the Neithans already programmed our destination."

"Great."

Prax shoved through the engine room doors. The slight buzz across the ship became a crashing rumble within the heart of his ship. The main core spun and twisted, crackling with blue electricity. He paced around it to where three turbines spun at an even pace. With the ship running, he couldn't put his hand inside to feel around, but Prax dropped into a squat and glanced under the largest turbine. A circular black device the size of his palm blinked a soft yellow light.

"Fuck."

"What is it?" Scarlett yelled from the door.

What to tell his mate? Scarlett backed to the other side of the hall as he rushed out of the engine room. When the doors closed firmly behind him, he rubbed at his forehead. In the silence, the only answer that came to him was the truth.

"An explosive device. And given its position, it'd magnify the energy of the core."

Her skin paled to a sickly off-white. "Which means?"

"If we don't do what Argrix wants, we'll explode." He met her eyes. "Worse, once we arrive, everything nearby will be at risk."

She nodded slowly, but her pallor didn't improve. "What's the plan, then?"

"Getting you home is my first priority."

"And how will you do that if this ship is rigged to explode?"

Prax wanted to say something brave and intelligent, but he couldn't give her false hope. His cousin had trapped them at every turn. It wasn't only Prax's reputation on the line, but their lives and, once they landed on Herkleios, the lives of others. "I don't know."

Scarlett pushed off the wall. "I'm going to die in space."

He rushed to her side. "You aren't going to die in space."

"Says Mr. No-Plan."

With his height advantage, he easily pushed in front of her. She stopped and glared up. "I don't know what we'll do once we get to Herkleios, but I won't be responsible for my uncle's escape. He's hurt too many people."

"So have you according to your cousin."

"There really is more to the story."

"I don't particularly want to hear it." Her stomach rumbled, the osha from Argrix's ship left mostly untouched. "I want something to eat. I want to take a nap. I want to go home."

Prax repressed a flinch, but she had every right to her feelings. He clenched his hands behind his back. "I'll show you to the mess hall."

Scarlett crossed her arms, but followed Prax down the hall. The chill of the space between their bodies ached in his chest. He wanted her. She was beautiful and brave and funny. His mate. But when she stared at him, it was clear she wasn't interested in him. Only angry. Prax wouldn't force her into a connection, but maybe she might grow to feel something for him, too. They had two days until they arrived on Herkleios.

Prax pushed into the mess hall, the small room dwarfed by a large rock table, taken from the base of Etein's sacred mountain in Drest. Streaks of silver and gold threaded the dark stone's jagged edges.

"Oh, wow." His mate drifted a hand across the stone. "That's beautiful."

Prax tapped at his wristband, ordering two chairs on opposite sides of the table to push back. Scarlett didn't yelp at the movement, but her brown eyes widened. She sunk into the seat while he approached the black paneling on the far wall. "It's a reminder of home. My people see no reason to alter nature, so much of our furniture keeps its original shape."

"I guess you weren't a fan of what you saw on Earth, then?"

Out of the corner of his eyes, his mate leaned back in her chair, her lips twisting into half a grin. He didn't turn. Once he faced her again, that tantalizing expression would leave her face. "Earthlings like to think of themselves as separate from nature rather than a part of it."

"True, I guess."

Prax pressed his clawed finger to the materializer's screen and scrolled through the options. "Before arriving on Earth, I wished to try some of its cuisine, so we have a few options. Is there anything in particular you'd like?"

"A burger?"

"A bur-grr?" Prax scanned through the option until he came to the unfamiliar word. He hadn't tried this on his trip to Earth. It didn't look natural, but for Scarlett, he'd do anything. He selected the option. A slot opened within the materializer and pushed out two plates, strange pale sticks surrounding a piece of unfamiliar meat in a bun. At least it smelled better than it looked.

He placed Scarlett's plate in front of her before settling down across from her.

The smile had left her face, but she hadn't returned to glaring. "It smells like a normal burger."

"Our materialization technology is quite accurate."

Scarlett plucked the bun and meat combo with her hands right as Prax stabbed into it with a two-pronged fork. He paused and watched as she bit into it, grease and sauce oozing from the sides. His stomach rolled. Disgusting. But something euphoric rose across his mate's face like the two suns of Yazd, bright and hypnotizing. "This is the best burger I've ever had."

Prax couldn't help a smile. "I'd love to take credit for it, but I did little to prepare it."

She laughed, all the tension between them forgotten. "I could certainly use a materializer at home."

Home. No matter what happened next, Prax had to get his mate back to where she belonged. Which, unfortunately, wasn't with him. He tapped at his wristband, pulling up a quick diagnostic. Argrix had said the Neithans had planted devices all over the ship, but would they have added one in the mess hall? In the little time they had, it made sense for them to only install in the control room and around the engine. His holo-screen flashed into the air above his hand. Clear of listening devices. "Speaking of your home, once we reach Herkleios, I'll have King Anax secure safe passage for you back to Earth."

The joy slipped from her face as Scarlett straightened, returning to business mode. "And won't it be suspicious if I have to leave right after arriving for a visit?"

"We'll have to stay for a day or so, but then we can create some reason why you're needed back on Earth."

An odd expression settled over her. "Like... because I need to go back for my hypothetical daughter?"

"Yes, exactly like that." Prax hesitantly picked up the bur-grr, dwarfed in his large hands. "Anax's human wife, Lexi, would surely sympathize with that excuse."

She narrowed her eyes at him, but he couldn't figure out why. "And then what?"

"Once you're safely on your way home, I'll launch my plan."

"Which is?"

Prax had no idea. He bit into the bur-grr, savory flavor exploding into his mouth. The meat melted against his tongue. "This *is* rather exceptional."

"No distractions."

He licked at the grease on his lips. "Distractions?"

Scarlett's eyes followed the movement of his tongue. Ah. Distractions. Prax hadn't even done that intentionally. Maybe there was hope for him and his mate. He grinned. "I didn't say that to distract you."

She picked at the pale sticks. "Your plan?"

Prax's grin widened. She was adorable when angry. "I can't give you an answer before I've done any reconnaissance, but it doesn't matter for you. By the time I've made my decision, you'll be happily back at home."

"Won't Argrix get impatient waiting that long?"

"He will, but he'll have to trust me for a few days at least."

"You seem very assured of yourself."

"Confidence is half the battle."

She grimaced at that, but swallowed the last of her bur-grr. She lowered her hands awkwardly to the table, trying not to touch anything with the grease. Why did humans eat such messy food with their hands? He whistled, summoning a service droid, which detached from the wall. It floated down in front of her and pointed one arm at her.

"For your hands," he explained at her blank look.

Scarlett raised her hands for the droid, which lasered away the dirt and grease. Her eyes widened again. So many things about his daily life were magical to her. He wanted to watch her experience every moment.

But he wouldn't get that chance.

Prax lowered his gaze to his food. "The way I see it, if I'm successful, Xenobaccus stays in jail and that security footage is never released. At worst, Argrix ruins my life but peace continues for the Intergalactic Alliance."

When Scarlett didn't answer right away, Prax glanced up. She chewed on her bottom lip, that odd look in her eyes again. She wiped it away when his eyes met hers. "I guess it's good you don't know. I don't want to be an accessory to the plan, anyway." Scarlett pushed back her chair. "You said we have two days until we arrive. Is there anything else to do other than staring into oblivion?"

Prax offered his hands to the droid. "You're not impressed with the stars?"

"I've gotten used to them by now."

Prax stood, too, towering over his small mate. Did her eyes follow the rippling of his muscle or was that his imagination? Prax had never been so unsure with a female. Whatever her thoughts about him, he knew a challenge when he heard one. "So you're telling me I need to find something more impressive?"

"Like you could."

Definitely a challenge. "I can."

Scarlett raised an eyebrow. "You're rather confident."

Prax started for the door and gestured her into the hallway. "After you, my lady. I aim to please... and I always succeed."

As Prax marched toward the door at the hall's end, a grin spread across his face. When he waved a hand in front of the sensors, the door opened with a small whoosh of air. He motioned Scarlett inside. She raised a brow and kept her arms crossed. What could he have on this ship to beat the literal stars?

"Trust me," Prax said. "When my father first showed me this as a child, I stared at it for an entire day."

With a sigh, she started forward. And stopped dead in the center of a pure white room, the walls and floors softly glowing.

"Um, what?" Scarlett looked back at Prax. Weird, yes. Super impressive, no.

The door slid shut behind him, but Scarlett didn't tense at being alone with the prince. After a day together, she knew he wouldn't hurt her. Especially with the smile on his face. How dare such an imposing male have such a wide, goofy grin.

"If you could be anywhere in the galaxy right now, where would you be?"

Her brows stayed arched. "Honestly?"

"Yes, honestly."

Scarlett chewed on her lips. With her daughter, but she couldn't say that. Prax couldn't know about Violet. He hadn't reacted negatively to the idea of her having a child, but he hadn't known she was serious. She couldn't risk it. "I'd be back in my flat in my living room."

His grin wavered. "Flat?"

"My house."

"Ahh, I see." He tapped a panel on the wall, which slid open to reveal circular devices the size of a coin, almost identical to the device the Neithan doctor had used. Prax handed her one and pointed at her temple. "Put this on."

Scarlett pressed the silver circle to her forehead. It pinched slightly before warming to her skin temperature. "What is it?"

"You're a bit too specific for the tech," he said, clarifying absolutely nothing. "Imagine your living room now."

"I..." The room flickered from all-white to color in the blink of an eye. Scarlett gaped. She rubbed at her vision. Had she had a stroke? Her feet no longer rested on white tile but dark hardwood, the same shade as her living room. Prax now stood next to her pink velvet couch in the entryway to her kitchen, her TV and balcony at her back. Scarlett spun and pressed herself to the glass. Outside, cars zoomed down the streets and people walked, engines and voices melded together into a familiar symphony. When she gasped and inhaled, the sweet scent of sourdough bread from the bakery down the street filled her nose.

"You have a teleporter on your ship?" If Prax had a freaking teleporter, Scarlett would claw his pretty eyes out of his head. He could've returned her to Earth immediately, not got her wrapped up in an intergalactic incident.

"Oh, no, it's all virtual reality." He snapped his claws together, returning the room to the eerie white box. "There's no such thing as long-distance teleporters."

"It didn't feel virtual."

He tapped at his own forehead, and Scarlett pulled the little device from her skin. "The replication room builds realities from people's memories. All the scents and smells are things you remember."

She handed him back the device. "Okay, I'll admit, that is super cool."

"Where else do you want to go?"

"What do you mean?"

"Thousands of people across the galaxy have added locations to the database. Anywhere you want to go, we can go."

The whole world—the whole *galaxy* spread before Scarlett like a buffet. Where should she even start? Hawaii? Tahiti? With a young child and a demanding job, she had rarely travelled over the last decade.

But where her heart yearned to go wasn't a tropical location. "My grandma's farm outside Cleveland."

As Scarlett finished the words, the room around her flickered. Soft grass tickled at her ankles under a watercolor sky, the sun setting over the horizon. Three white silos and a burnt red barn spotted the fields, the only buildings blocking her view for a near mile. She twisted to find Prax behind her, her grandmother's old white house sitting near the road. Tears prickled at her eyes.

The ground crunched as Prax settled at her side. "You love it here."

"I haven't been here since I was a teenager." Scarlett yearned to walk forward, climb the steps to her grandmother's porch, and push through the creaking door into the old wallpapered kitchen, but seeing it empty might destroy her. "After my grandmother passed away, my parents had to sell the farm."

He hesitantly reached for her shoulder. When his scales touched her, her skin tingled. "I'm sorry."

She wiped away tears. "It was a long time ago."

"We can change the setting if it hurts too much."

She faced him. On another day, she might bask in the dying light until the sun set, but she couldn't be vulnerable with Prax. At any minute, he could turn on her. "What's your favorite place?"

"My father's hunting lodge." Within a blink, the room changed to an emerald forest. A tiny cottage crawling with vines nestled within the trees. Something about it was almost Earth-like, but the leaves were cylindrical shapes and the brown of the bark rippled with an odd texture. In the canopy above, animals made strange, pitched squawks. "I spent much of my childhood here."

"Not in a palace?"

"Not right away."

Scarlett scanned his face, but he didn't seem bothered by it. "Can I ask why?"

"My mother, Empress Ailis, lived in the palace, but my siblings and I were raised by our fathers until we were teenagers."

Scarlett's jaw dropped. "Fathers?"

"My mother has three consorts."

"Is that... common?" Scarlett hadn't been able to wrangle one boyfriend, let alone three husbands. She shivered. Not that she was entirely opposed.

"Not anymore." Prax kicked through the foliage. "My mother did it to arrange multiple alliances, but most Eógans only have a single partner."

He glanced at her while he said that last bit, but Scarlett didn't turn from his gaze. Not going there. "And do Eógan fathers normally raise their children alone?"

"Not usually, but there were too many assassination attempts by rival families at the palace. My mother wanted us to have a normal life. For as many years as possible, at least."

Scarlett smiled and nodded, but the world around her kept grabbing at her attention. She started along the path and drifted her hands through the nearest shrubbery. The tangle of branches brushed against her skin. How could this *not* be real? "You were right."

"About?"

"This is impressive."

Prax laughed at her side, a deep thunder that spurred the heat in her core. Scarlett didn't turn to him. She couldn't. In a few days, she'd go home, leaving him to his fate. There was no reason to get attached to her kidnapper. Even if he did claim to be her soulmate.

When they rounded the next bit of greenery, a little alcove opened within the bush. Branches curled into a twisting bench, set back in the shade from the bright alien sun. Scarlett halted, but Prax settled into the space like it was his home. Because it *was* his home. Like her grandmother's farm held her heart, this cottage held his.

Scarlett closed the space between them and sat at his side. For a long moment, they basked in the silence.

Scarlett exhaled. She might leave him soon, but she still wanted to know. This male couldn't be a cold-blooded murderer. "I wasn't going to ask, because why receive more scary news about the guy you're stuck with, but you don't seem like the type. What happened in that security footage Argrix is holding over your head?"

Prax paused, almost as if he wouldn't answer. "It's a night I try not to think about, but even months later, it haunts my dreams. I never wanted it to happen, but I take full responsibility for my actions."

"That's not an explanation."

He sighed. "A few months ago, I visited a friend on Yazd, one of the alliance planets. We've always been rather wild when we come together. My mother hates when I visit Prince Keveh."

Scarlett nodded, willing him to continue. Whatever it was he'd done, his guilt was real. It etched the plains of his scaled face.

"We went to *Zaghan's Rage*, a not-so-respectable gambling den. We'd visited dozens of times before over the years." Prax sucked in a deep breath. "The one male, Eztl, wasn't doing well and had lost most of his credits. The more he lost, the angrier he got. This beautiful female hung off his arm, and I watched his grip get tighter and tighter on her all night. I should have said something then, but I didn't."

Scarlett's stomach sunk. She'd heard this story before or, at least, some version of it. "And then?"

"When it was clear there'd be no way he could win, he insisted we take a break and commanded the female to dance. She initially refused, which angered him even further." Prax turned, meeting her gaze. "He hit her. Over and over. No one so much as raised a finger to help her. Keveh went to find his guards to help, but I couldn't wait any longer. When I got in his way, Eztl tried to fight me. I didn't mean to kill him, but I was drunk and..."

Scarlett put a hand on his arm, her palms tingling at the contact. "When Argrix asked you if it was self-defense, you had to say no because you were defending someone else."

Prax nodded. "When Keveh returned with his guards, they removed the body and paid off the staff of the *Rage*. I thought they wiped the security footage, so I'm not sure how Argrix got a hold of it."

Nothing technological was ever truly erased, something Scarlett had been grateful for many times. Electronic trails had helped her build cases. But in this one instance, she wished it had failed. "But won't the tape show you defending the female?"

"It will, but Eztl was a well-respected shipping mogul."

Scarlett flinched. Damn. She didn't even have to ask. "Powerful men get away with everything on my planet, too." She tilted back her head, letting the sunshine caress her face. Prax hadn't meant to kill someone. He wasn't a cold-blooded murderer like Argrix made him out to be. Thankfully. "Do you regret it?"

"Saving that girl? No, but I wished I hadn't taken Eztl's life. He should have paid for his crimes in court. With my testimony, he would have."

The answer warmed her heart. "Will your mother *really* be that mad if this gets out?"

"It doesn't reflect well on Eógan." Prax climbed to his feet like he was unable to sit still any longer. His height blocked the light, but she didn't mind. "Worse, Eztl is Zocastan, part of the Intergalactic Alliance. They could consider my actions an act of war. Eztl had many powerful friends." He rubbed a hand down his face. "I named my ship after an Eógan warrior. Carthak sacrificed his life rather than betray the matriarch of my family line, Empress Etein. If it comes down to it, I'd sooner make that choice than cost so many people their peace."

"It won't come to that." Scarlett wasn't sure how, but there was no way in hell she'd let Prax lose his life to this. Without thinking, she took his hand and squeezed. He flinched at the touch, looking at where her skin met his scales with wonder and confusion. Scarlett didn't let him go. It didn't matter if she never spoke to him again after this week. He needed her. "You'll get out of this, Prax. You have to."

TEN

Scarlett paced between the door and the bed. Prax had offered her his room, the largest of the four bedrooms on *The Carthak*, but she had turned it down and claimed the one furthest from his door. Her feet sunk into plush rugs decorated with Eógan forests as a little fountain in the corner emitted a soft, almost floral scent. If she didn't know she was on an alien spaceship, she'd think this was a Scandinavian spa.

But it wasn't the luxe amenities or the spaceship part that bothered her. It was Prax. She shouldn't be sympathizing with a murderer, but his intentions felt so pure. He had killed to defend someone else, someone like Scarlett's clients. How many women were beaten and killed because there wasn't anyone to protect them? She couldn't fault him for that.

Despite the accidental kidnapping, he'd been nothing but kind. He hadn't tried to take advantage of her or sell her off like a piece of meat. He had protected her from his cousin and the Neithans. If she were giving him a grade—which she was—he'd score around a perfect gentleman. Which was more than she could say for her ex or any other assholes she'd dated.

More than that, his stupid smile made her chest ache. When he was near, her heart raced and her neck tingled. She hadn't yet checked for a matebond mark and Prax hadn't pushed it. A part of her didn't want to know. Scarlett hated being told what to do. If the fates—or a Herkleian goddess—said she was meant to be with Prax, she'd do everything to fight it.

Scarlett stopped by the door. If he were a regular man and they weren't on a spaceship, what would she do?

The answer was simple. Scarlett fought for what she wanted. And what she wanted was an alien prince.

She smoothed a hand down the tight black material of her outfit and strutted into the hall.

After Prax had bid her goodnight, he had headed to the control room to muck with Argrix's 'upgrades'. Scarlett quickly retraced her steps to find the door to the control room open, faint music spilling into the hall. She noticed his shirt first, hanging off the edge of a chair. Her pulse thundered, but she took the final few steps into the doorway.

Prax leaned back onto one muscled forearm, his bare torso twisted as he poked around under one of the three control panels. The scales of his chest glinted a beautiful emerald. He tore out a bit of wire and tossed it to the floor, where a little droid collected the scrap, and bit a wrench-like tool between his teeth to free his second hand. His abs flexed at the movement. Scarlett's mouth watered.

She licked her lips. "I want to help you."

Prax stiffened before peeking out, his red eyes piercing through her. He slid from under the control panel and stood in one smooth motion. It took everything within Scarlett to keep her jaw clamped shut. "Why put yourself in danger?"

"This is bigger than you or me." She inched forward, keeping her gaze focused on his. Her words were the truth, but she left half of it unsaid. There was something about Prax that made her want to abandon all logic. "You can't do this alone. If you try to get me out, you risk the Neithans blowing up this ship and everything nearby. With my help, maybe we can find another way."

"It's dangerous, Scarlett."

She stopped less than a foot from him. "So is life, but that doesn't mean we shouldn't live it."

The intensity of his stare pierced hers. Waves of heat radiated off his body across the tiny space between them. Scarlett couldn't help herself. She reached out to stroke his scales, warm and supple and soft. Prax stiffened, but didn't push her away.

She lazily drifted her fingertips across his chest, along the grooves and ridges of his scales. At her touch, the emerald darkened to a green nearly black. She pulled back. His scales had shifted to red before, but she hadn't asked given all the chaos around them. "Is it supposed to do that?"

"It is." His voice grated against her insides, fueling the fire. "My people's scales change color during strong emotions. Red for anger. Yellow for sadness."

"And what does this color mean?"

"Happiness." He placed one of his hands on top of hers. "It means I very much enjoy your presence... and your touch."

"Good." She glanced into his red eyes, nearly burning with desire —the same look reflected in her own. Her fears of the future faded away. "Because I plan to touch you."

The smile that spread across Prax's face tugged hard at Scarlett's heart. She wrapped her hands around his shoulders and lured his lips down to hers. He came willingly. Eagerly. When he captured her mouth with his, they groaned as one. Despite the scales, his lips were soft and delightful. She nipped against his lower lip, summoning a deep, primal growl from within him. The sound vibrated up her spine, leaving behind a path of tingles.

But Prax wasn't one for teasing. Like Scarlett, he took what he wanted. His rough tongue invaded her mouth, a welcome force. Scarlett's nipples hardened into tiny beads. When she walked in here, she had only imagined kissing him. Now she wanted more.

Needed more.

Scarlett threaded her hands through his burnished hair and wrapped a fist around one of his small horns. Prax shuddered at the touch. She smiled against his mouth. With him in hand, she had perfect control. She broke the kiss with a last nip and said, "This changes nothing between us. I'll help you on Herkleios. When this is over, you'll return me home. Understand?"

For a moment, she thought he might object, but he nodded. "Whatever you want, Scarlett. Always."

"What I want..." Scarlett slipped her thumbs under the waistband of her pants "... is for us to be wearing less clothing."

Without another word, she slid the fabric over her hips. The ship's cold air caressed across her bare skin, drawing goosebumps to the surface. She didn't feel it, not with Prax staring at her in utter rapture. The look spurred her on. She pulled off her top and reached for her bra—

Prax gripped her elbow. "No."

"No?" Scarlett glanced down—at herself, but also the tent in Prax's pants. Her eyes widened. At seven-feet-tall, with hands those large, she hadn't considered what other parts of him might be supersized. Her mouth dried. "So, you don't want me to be naked?"

"Of course I want you to be naked. This is the best day of my life." Those large hands wrapped around her back. "I simply want to do the honors."

Scarlett flushed from her head to her toes. No man had ever considered seeing her naked as an honor. She put her hands on his chest, his heart pounding beneath his scales. With gentle fingers, he slid the clasp of her bra and lured the lace from her skin. Her breath escaped her in pants.

Her bra dropped to the floor.

Prax didn't speak. He didn't need to. His eyes roamed across her skin, more intimate than any touch. Scarlett's entire body tensed from her nipples to the wet heat of her core. She ached, the distance between them nearly physical pain.

"Prax—"

In her voice, he heard her question. He closed the space between them, his hands trailing down her body and cupping her ass. Scarlett twisted her hands through his hair as he lifted her into his arms. No human man had ever lifted her before—few human men *could* lift her. But to Prax, she was practically petite. Scarlett wrapped her legs around his torso. When she rubbed against the leather of his pants and the hard length encased within, she moaned.

Scarlett bit at his lips. "Take your pants off."

"Make me."

Scarlett grinned. Legs still around his hips, she threaded her hands under that soft fabric. Prax's breath hitched against her face as she stroked a hand across the base of his shaft. His warm, massive shaft. Her hand barely fit around it. Her own heart jumped. Fucking Prax might literally kill her.

If only she didn't kill him first.

She squeezed, Prax's entire body tensing under her touch. "Take. Off. Your. Pants."

He obeyed instantly, lowering Scarlett to the control panel and sliding free of clothes in two quick moves. Scarlett leaned back on her elbows, giving him a magnificent view while enjoying her own. The muscles of his thighs darken to the most perfect emerald before becoming nearly black at his cock. Scales lined his length, creating glistening ridges. The heat of her tensed, quivering in anticipation at the sight. He was perfect. He was beautiful. He was hers.

For today, at least.

Scarlett pushed down all her worries, all her concerns and trust issues. They didn't matter now. Nothing mattered now but Prax.

Who hadn't moved forward to fuck her brains out, but instead stood frozen, his eyes rapturously devouring her.

Waiting for permission.

Scarlett spread her legs in the most blatant invitation. Elbows on the upper edge of the control panel, she twisted her fingers down her stomach and through the dark curls over her core.

Prax pounced forward, a hunter with his prey.

He gripped her wrist, stopping her an inch from touching herself. "You're mine."

She wrapped one leg around his thighs, pulling him closer. "Am I? Because I don't feel—"

Prax retracted his claws and rubbed a knuckle through her wet heat. Scarlett yelped, nearly coming off the control panel. With his other hand, Prax clenched a hand on her shoulder and held her in place.

"You're mine."

Scarlett didn't object this time. His finger plunged into her warmth, stealing all her thoughts. Her back arched, head falling back to the chilling metal. His hand followed and drifted down her front. The trace of his fingertips burned brands across her skin.

"Say it." With one hand, he circled a thumb around her nipple while his other mirrored the movement around her clit. "Say you're mine."

"I'm..." Scarlett lost the words on the edge of a moan. "I'm..."

Prax's hands got harsher, faster. He twisted at her nipple and her clit while plunging into her heat. "You're...?"

Scarlett twisted a hand around the control panel's edge, but it didn't ground her. Her body cried and ached, Prax stroking her into a firestorm. God, she needed him now. Wanted that thick, ridged warmth to ram into her. Wanted tears to water at her eyes, the pain and pleasure so good. Wanted him, all of him.

"I'm yours." She wrapped her other leg around him and pulsed him forward. "Oh, God, I'm yours. Now, fuck me."

Prax grinned in triumph. "As you wish."

Prax plunged into her depths, filling her to the brink. His ridges pulsed against her walls. Scarlett moaned and buckled, undone. With a single stroke, he claimed her, ruined her. How could she push him away when he made her feel whole? She couldn't. Not now. Scarlett pushed up on one elbow, wanting—no, needing to touch him. To make him hers as thoroughly as she was his.

"No." Prax wrapped a hand around her collarbone and pressed her to the display. Electricity danced up Scarlett's spine. "You're mine."

She gripped his hand and led it upward until it wrapped around her neck. "I'm yours."

Prax's eyes widened for a moment before lust flooded through his gaze. She raised her hips, meeting his next thrust. His hand around her throat tensed with each meeting of their body.

It was perfect. He was perfect. Scarlett gripped at his wrist, holding her to him as he stoked the flames. As he pushed her to the edge. As he fucked his claim into her.

And with his next thrust, she went over.

Scarlett tensed, her entire body clenching around him. She thrashed, his name ripped from her lips in a rush of heat. It burst behind her eyelids like literal fireworks. No man had ever made her explode like this. No one had ever come close. But with Prax, she came easy as her body submitted to his will.

With a roar, he came, too, his body shuddering above her. He pulled his hand from her neck and slammed it into the control panel. The barely-contained strength made her nipples tightened. Scarlett's breath hitched. He hadn't even pulled out of her, yet she wanted him again.

And again and again. As many times as she could have him until they reached Herkleios.

The planet's name drenched at her desire. She had a home and a career and a daughter, all things to return for. No matter how much a part of her wanted to, she couldn't stay in space for her alien prince.

Scarlett pushed those worries away and pressed onto an elbow. She trailed her fingers between the rivulets of his chest, across the glimmering scales until they curved at the length of his neck.

Prax pressed a kiss to her forehead. "You're incredible."

"So are you." She nipped at his chin and he groaned, his cock twitching back to life inside her. "On the plus side, I've discovered what I'm going to do for the next two days."

He lowered his mouth until his lips brushed hers. "And what is that?"

"You."

Prax grinned wickedly.

ELEVEN

SCARLETT

Scarlett stiffened as a loud ding echoed through her quarters on *The Carthak*. Her skin prickled, the sound far too similar to when the Neithans boarded. But at least the sound didn't catch Scarlett off guard this time. Prax had told her planet security would send them a hail when they arrived outside Herkleios's orbit.

Scarlett tapped at her new wristband's holo-screen, closing the romance novel she had spent the last few hours devouring. Not that she could entirely focus on the plot. Why fantasize about a regency-era duke when she had her very own prince? When Scarlett wasn't in her quarters—her self-declared sanctuary—she and Prax were fucking on every surface they could find. The last two days had passed in a blur of sweat and orgasms.

And now that they had arrived at Herkleios, that had come to an end.

Prax knocked on the door. "Scarlett? We're here."

She slipped on her blazer and slid a hand across her blouse. In between their sex-scapades, Prax had connected to some intergalactic wi-fi network and downloaded half a dozen human outfits to the ship's materializer. Most weren't in Scarlett's style, but one had included a pleated, floral skirt, sling-back heels, and a simple blouse. Classic and professional, just how Scarlett liked it.

She glanced quickly at herself in the mirror, fixing a stray piece of hair into her top knot bun, before waving a hand in front of the door's sensor.

Her heart jumped at the sight of Prax leaning in her door frame. He hadn't worn clothes most of the last two days, but the sight of his muscles concealed in a tight black fabric twisted in her core. Did all Eógans dress like a cross between a hunter and a superhero or was it just him?

But despite the urge to touch him, Scarlett crossed her arms, locking her hands in place. She had set a boundary, and Prax had promised to respect it. Once they arrived at Herkleios, they were partners in crime—not in any other way. It'd hopefully make their inevitable parting less painful.

Prax's lips quirked. "We haven't arrived on Herkleios yet."

"Prax—"

"I'm sorry." He straightened and backed out of her way, allowing her access to the hall. "I couldn't help myself. We'll find a way out of this mess and then I'll take you back to Earth. On Etein's honor."

Scarlett knew little about Eógan's founder and Prax's ancestor, but from him, it seemed a sincere promise. "How exactly do Eógan couples behave? We need to make a good impression on your cousin and his wife."

"We can behave however we want. Herkleians are formal, but my people are known to be more... wild."

"Well, I've spent the last decade in London, so you're not getting wild from me." When Prax frowned, Scarlett flushed. "The English aren't big on PDA."

"PDA?"

"Public displays of affection."

"Ah, I see." He clearly didn't. "Worry not, Scarlett. My cousin will surely greet us in person, but he and Alexandra will have hundreds of guests to manage. I doubt they'll analyze our relationship in depth."

When they entered *The Carthak*'s control room, the main control panel—the one Scarlett couldn't look at without blushing—flashed with a red light. Prax settled before it and reached out. "Are you ready?"

She reluctantly took his hand, his large palm swallowing hers. "Let's do this."

Prax tapped at his wristband, and the control panel flickered. A projection shot in the space between them. Scarlett flinched at the sight of the big Herkleian strapped with weapons and wearing a gladiator-esque helmet. When his expression didn't slip into Argrix's greasy smile, she relaxed at Prax's side.

"Please state your business," the soldier said briskly.

"I'm Prince Prax M'Etein, heir to the Imperial Throne of Eógan. I'm here to visit my cousin, King Anax Yio'hyra, alongside my Earthling guest, Scarlett Moore."

"For the baby shower," Scarlett added.

"Yes, for the showering of babies."

Scarlett repressed a snort. She had never understood the fuss over baby showers. When she was pregnant with Violet, she was so tired she just wanted her guests to finish their pretty tea sandwiches and get out of her flat. Queen Alexandra probably didn't have that problem.

The soldier typed something into his own gold wristband's holo-screen. "Our records say you declined your invitation, Your Highness."

Scarlett's hand tensed in his, but Prax remained loose. "I changed my mind. As a Prince of Eógan, I should have general approval to visit Eritea and the palace."

The soldier flicked through his holo-screen for another long minute. Even in outer space, guards at security screenings liked to take their grand ol' time. If Prax wasn't a prince, would they throw them in the alien version of an airport prison cell? Given her fake boyfriend's arrogance, probably.

"Approved." As soon as the soldier said the word, *The Carthak*'s engine revved, and the ship started forward. "You have permission to land at the Royal Palace's airstrip under the grace of His Majesty, Anax Yio'hyra."

Without another word, the soldier's hologram disappeared. Scarlett almost fell onto the bench in relief. "Step one, check."

"That was never going to be the hard part."

"I'm all about celebrating the small victories."

A range of emotions crossed Prax's face: curiosity followed disappointment and resignation. That Scarlett could read him so clearly terrified her. They hadn't even known each other for a week. He couldn't be more than a one-night—or two-day—stand she had to play nice with until she returned to her life. To her daughter, her job, her home.

The thought of Violet panged through her chest. Prax had mentioned his ship had long-range communicators, but Argrix had bugged them. Scarlett couldn't risk their blackmailers holding something over her, too. When she missed her court date, had someone reported her missing? Hopefully. Her daughter had always planned to spend the weekend with her father and wouldn't mind an extra few days with Andrew.

And if that son of a bitch didn't take their child until Scarlett returned, she planned to skewer him with some finely placed words.

"Are you well, Scarlett?" Prax settled into the seat next to the main control panel, his intense gaze on her. Was it worse that he could read her the same way she read him?

She opened her mouth, the truth about Violet almost slipping free. But if she opened to him, shared herself, he became more than a hookup. She forced a smile. "I'm fine."

Prax furrowed his forehead, but didn't question her.

She slid her gaze from him to the view outside the control room's floor-to-ceiling window. Anything but those probing eyes. Her jaw dropped. "Wow."

As Prax twirled around, Scarlett climbed from her chair and approached Eritea. The capital of Herkleios was a jumbled skyline of sharp gold towers wrapped with purple-blue vines and traversed by flying spaceships of all sizes. A small section of the city floated over the rest, but Scarlett didn't have a chance to absorb that marvel when the palace came into view. A wide expanse of manicured purple lawns made way for a palace of white columns and golden walls.

Prax's warmth settled at her side. "Welcome to Eritea, gem of the Herkleian monarchy. My people's ancestral home."

"It's beautiful." Scarlett all but pressed her face to the window. "It's so..."

"Gold?"

"It's a lot, yeah."

"Our cousins have never been one for subtlety."

She nudged his shoulder. "So you're saying Eógan palaces are better?"

"Spectacularly. The Imperial Palace is carved out of the side of a mountain."

"That sounds amazing. Maybe..." Scarlett bit her lip. Maybe one day she'd visit? That was entirely against her plan. This alien prince had already involuntarily brought her to one new world. She wasn't seeing a second.

Thankfully, Prax didn't press her to finish her sentence.

Within minutes, *The Carthak* landed with a light thunk on the Herkleian version of an airstrip, the great views of the palace replaced by gilded hangars and over a hundred ships. Without speaking—what was there to say?—Scarlett followed Prax to the main doors. She took his hand as it slid open and tried on her best smile.

Three Herkleians, one shirtless male and two females in long, gray dresses, dropped into bows on the tarmac. The female in the middle stepped forward, her slitted eyes a dark orange under twisting horns and black hair. "Welcome to Herkleios, Your Highness. I'm

Zopha, your attendant during your stay at the palace. May we take your luggage?"

Shit. Luggage. Scarlett hadn't even considered they'd look out of place without at least a day bag.

"No need," Prax said. "We didn't bring anything. My beloved wished to get a good look at Herkleian fashion before committing to any dresses for the party."

The frivolity of it sounded exactly like something Prax would do. The attendants must have thought the same, since none appeared weirded out by their lack of bags. Not that their expressions flickered in the slightest. Zopha waved a blue-scaled hand. "In that case, allow us—"

"No need, Zopha," a deep voice said. "I can escort my cousin myself."

Scarlett didn't need to ask, not with Prax stiffening beside her and the attendants all dropping into deep bows. A huge, dark-haired Herkleian approached the ship, hand in hand with a petite blonde with a massive belly. King Anax and Queen Alexandra. Did Scarlett curtsey? Neither of the female attendants had. Dammit. Instead of spending two days naked with Prax, she should have asked questions.

Prax only bowed his head, so Scarlett did the same. "Your Majesties."

"Not necessary, Prax." As the two of them stepped off *The Carthak*, Anax moved forward and lowered his own head. He tapped his longer, black horns to Prax's shorter, brown ones. Some sort of alien greeting? "To me, we'll always be family first."

Queen Alexandra waddled forward, her green eyes fixed on Scarlett. Before Scarlett could even process what was happening, the tiny queen pulled her into an awkward hug.

"Um." Scarlett patted her on the back. "Nice to meet you, Queen Alexandra?"

"Call me Lexi," she said, giving Scarlett a squeeze. "I'm sorry. You're the first human I've seen in two months. Herkleians don't hug, did you know? I saw an opportunity and took it."

Anax frowned, a hint of fangs in the expression. Scarlett shuddered. Thank God Eógans didn't have fangs. "I hug you plenty."

Lexi nudged his shoulder. "Not in front of our guests, naikos."

Naikos, the Herkleian word for a male soulmate. Scarlett hadn't wanted to ask Prax about the matebond, but the wristband he gifted her had supplied the basics. She'd seen a flash of Prax's mark, which he now hid with his collar. Scarlett had finally bitten the bullet and checked her own skin. Her nape was red, but there was definitely no twisting of stars. A tangle of emotions had panged through her chest, ones she stuffed down and ignored.

When Anax and Lexi started walking in the palace's direction, Scarlett and Prax followed. The three attendants lagged behind them, giving their charges space.

"It's a pleasure to see you again, Lexi," Prax said politely.

Lexi smiled, but it wasn't as bright. "You, too, Prax. Hopefully under better circumstances this time."

"This time?" Scarlett asked.

"We met at my wedding."

Scarlett shuddered. The bloody photos stamped across *The Telegraph*'s front page would stick with her for years. "Ah."

"Exactly. Ah." When Scarlett stiffened, Lexi waved her hand. "Oh, no, don't mind me. It all worked out in the end, uh... Sorry, I didn't ask your name. How rude of me."

Scarlett held out a hand. "I'm Scarlett."

Lexi's grin widened, seemingly delighted at the idea of a handshake. "It's so nice to meet you. And you're Prax's...?"

Before Scarlett replied, Prax said, "Beloved."

The shiver that ran up her spine started in the heat of her core. How dare such an old-fashioned but intimate word have that effect on her? But she couldn't pull away from him. If they didn't want to attract attention, she needed to be convincing. Scarlett rested her hand on his forearm. "Girlfriend is the Earthling term, babe."

Prax leaned into her touch. Fire burned through her body, rendering her reasoning useless. Scarlett pressed the heat down.

Hopefully, Anax and Lexi couldn't see it on her face. Not that Scarlett needed to concern herself about that. The way she responded to Prax's touch probably helped sell their story. Anax and Lexi would think they were passionately in love, just one touch between them sending Scarlett over the edge.

But going over an edge wasn't what Scarlett needed right now. She needed to find a way out of this—without causing a war.

"It's a pleasure to meet you, Lady Scarlett," Anax said, his voice a deep rumble. "We're excited to have you both here for the baby ball tomorrow evening."

"It's a baby shower, naikos, not a baby ball." Lexi snorted and rolled her eyes, but she clutched at her husband's hand. With her enormous belly, the human queen set the pace to a quiet meander. "I'm happy you decided to come, too, Prax. And you, Scarlett. I didn't know other Earthlings were pursuing romances with aliens. Well, besides Olivia and Eryx, of course."

"It's still rather new," Prax said, gazing down at Scarlett, his red eyes glinting like flames in the light. "I just couldn't help but claim her."

Scarlett couldn't hold back a laugh. Finally, some truth to their story. He *had* kidnapped her after only laying eyes on her twice.

"Yes, I remember the immediate attraction." Anax wrapped a hand around his wife's waist, every ounce of his attention on her. Scarlett's heart twinged. No one had held her like that when she was pregnant. Anax probably massaged Lexi's sore feet and helped her pick things off the floor. The madness of their lives over the last year hadn't diminished their love.

Lexi didn't let her husband distract her. "We'll let you settle into your chambers, but I'd love it if you would join me for a walk in the gardens this afternoon, Scarlett."

"I'd love that." It wasn't like she could say no to a queen. But despite her title, Lexi appeared very kind, and Scarlett didn't even have to fake her enthusiasm. Speaking to another human woman was exactly what she needed.

They finally reached the edge of the tarmac, the vast lawns stretching between them and the gilded palace. At this pace, they'd arrive at their rooms in an hour.

Lexi must have had the same thought. "You two must be tired from your journey. Zopha can lead you the rest of the way." The queen plopped onto a levitating bench. "I need a break."

"Are you sure?"

"Just because I'm a lumbering sloth doesn't mean everyone should be subjected to my pace."

Zopha slipped around Prax to Lexi's side. "This way, Your Highness, Lady Scarlett."

Scarlett tried not to look too relieved. The sooner they got to their chambers, the sooner they could decide on a plan.

The sooner she could release Prax's arm and stop the tingles across her skin.

Prax bowed his head. "It was lovely to see you again, Lexi."

The queen smiled, but it was her husband who replied, "Perhaps we can go hunting later?"

"I would be honored."

Anax sat at Lexi's side as Zopha spun on her heels. As they followed, Prax reached for Scarlett's hand. He squeezed it tightly. Some of the tension left Scarlett's spine. Since their first meeting with the King and Queen of Herkleios had gone well, maybe they weren't royally fucked.

TWELVE

Scarlett was royally fucked.

When Lexi had said chambers, Scarlett had imagined a sprawling suite fit for a literal prince. But unfortunately, because Prax had RSVP'd no and hundreds of guests were staying at the palace, their options were limited. Zopha led them to a gilded chamber with high ceilings of glowing rock, a levitating bed, and stark azure stone floors. Scarlett peeked through a second door, but it only led to a bathroom with a deep tub. Scarlett glared at the pillows piled high on the mattress. Sharing a bed was going to make detoxing from Prax almost impossible.

Unless she didn't. His touch was almost like a drug to her now.

She banished that thought from her head, but their two days together on *The Carthak* refused to be forgotten. Prax's hand clenched on her. The glide of his scales against her skin. The talent of his fingers. The throbbing weight of his cock at her back. Scarlett tore her gaze away from the mattress and faced the window.

She had a job to do. The sooner Prax's situation was resolved, the sooner she could see her daughter again.

Not that she or Prax had a solution yet. He had disappeared into the bathroom, muttering something about water helping clear his head. Without him, Scarlett didn't have the first idea where to start.

They couldn't free Xenobaccus. Yet, if they didn't, Argrix would release the blackmail he had on Prax and blow up *The Carthak*. Either way, they were screwed.

Scarlett's heels were minutes away from tapping a hole into the floors when the door to the bathroom whooshed open, a cloud of steam escaping the smaller space. Of course her dramatic prince of a companion had taken a bath.

Scarlett jumped to her feet, ready to interrogate Prax into a plan, when the prince stepped into the main room—in nothing more than a towel. Her jaw dropped, the dewy mist glimmering on the surface of his scales. His ship had no real bathing facilities. A real shame. Imagine the things she could have done to him in a bathtub...

Scarlett twisted away. She couldn't even trust her own brain. "Do you mind?"

"I need the materializer." Prax pointed at the circular platform by the window, like something straight out of a bridal boutique. She had nudged it with her shoe earlier, but hadn't figured out its purpose. "If I'm to hunt with my cousin today, I need the proper attire."

"Couldn't you have chosen clothes before you entered the bathroom?"

He paused, one foot on the platform, and grinned. "And miss seeing your expression?"

Scarlett crossed her arms, but her resolve weakened every second they were together. "Prax..."

"Nudity means very little on my planet, Scarlett." He disappeared from her periphery, probably standing fully on the platform. A light swoosh reached her ears, like fabric hitting the floor. Her heart stuttered. "No Eógan would consider this a seductive act."

"I'm not Eógan."

"I know."

At the smile in his voice, she almost plucked a vase off the nearby table and chucked it at his head. Everything he said grated on her nerves... and sent a flash of heat through her stomach. How could she be so aroused and annoyed at the same time? "You're done with your bath, so what's the plan? How are we getting out of this, Your Highness?"

"Always so serious."

Scarlett's hands twitched. God, she wanted to strangle him. Screw it. She'd seen him naked before. Scarlett spun around. "I want to get—"

Prax stood before her like a Greek statue brought to life. He had twisted and stretched, running a hand through his burnished hair and around his horns. The ripples of his muscles and scales glinted in the Herkleian sun. Her gaze drifted from his strong abs to his massive cock to the powerful lines of his thighs. Her hands twitched again, this time urging to wrap around something other than his throat.

His lips twitched into that inviting smile. "Something wrong?"

In her distracted state, she had closed some of the distance between them. Scarlett clipped her heels together. "Can you please put on some pants? This is a serious discussion, Prax."

"As you wish, my lady." Prax's grin widened as he tapped an option on the materializer's holo-screen. His chest remained bare except for two bandoliers of knives straining across his pecs, but Scarlett couldn't focus on those when she saw the rest of his outfit. The bottoms were a mix between a kilt and a toga, the pale fabric ending mid-thigh. A thick, black sash crossed his midsection, part decorative and part functional thanks to the slung for a laser and a real-life sword.

Scarlett couldn't help but gape. "You're going to hunt in that?"

He straightened. If the bandoliers could scream at the tension, they would've. "As is Herkleian tradition."

Scarlett slumped back into the seat. It bobbed a bit at the addition of her weight, but leveled off after a second. This wasn't her world. *Wasn't* her life. If she didn't understand the rules and Prax didn't take anything seriously, how would they get out of this without starting an intergalactic war? "We're screwed."

"Screwed?"

"This is hopeless, I mean."

Prax's pride slipped away, replaced by concern. He stepped off the platform and crouched before her. "This isn't hopeless, Scarlett. Not for you, at least."

"Which means?"

He wouldn't meet her eyes. "We can't release my uncle. If I take my ship when I go hunting with Anax and fake some engine trouble, I can get *The Carthak* away from others."

"And the blackmail?"

"I killed a male." Those crimson eyes flickered to hers. "It's haunted me every day since and a part of me has always known I'd have to pay."

The energy flooding her body at his nearness turned into nerves. "But you said it could start a war."

"Not if I speak to my mother first. If we get ahead of it, we can salvage the Intergalactic Alliance."

Her heart skipped a beat at his tone. "At what cost?"

"My title as Crown Prince, at least." His hand clenched on the armrest of her chair. "At the most... perhaps my life?"

Scarlett launched up in her seat. No. Without thinking, she closed the space between them by grabbing his shoulder. "That's not an acceptable answer."

His eyes searched hers. This close, her world narrowed to his red irises, so alien and yet comforting. Prax couldn't die. He'd return her to Earth when this was all done, ending their adventure together, but she didn't want to imagine a universe without him in it. Knowing he was out there would bring her comfort.

Her gaze flickered to his lips. Her body begged for one last taste, but it wouldn't be the last if she closed the distance between them. Scarlett couldn't give her heart to this prince. They didn't exist in the same world.

Prax decided for her. In a smooth motion, he stood and receded to the edge of the bed. Respecting her space, like she had asked.

"Worry not. I'll speak with my mother when she arrives tomorrow and arrange your return to Earth. She'll honor my promise if I can't."

If he couldn't. She didn't want to focus on those words, on that possibility. "What are we supposed to do in the meantime? Play happy couple with your cousin and his wife?"

"Argrix can't know anything is amiss yet. He undoubtedly has spies in the palace or some way to watch our movements. Otherwise, how would he know when to detonate my ship?"

Scarlett shuddered. "I can't just make small talk with Lexi while you ruin your life."

"You're not ruining anything. I said what I said to Argrix to get us off his ship, but I always knew I wouldn't get away entirely." Prax's gaze pleaded with her. "Help me fool him. I have no right to ask, after what I did to you, but I'm asking anyway."

"God, you're insufferable."

"Is that a yes?"

"I'll help you." Scarlett bounced to her feet and crossed her arms. "But I'm not spending the afternoon with Lexi just for appearances. If I can find you a way out of this, I will."

"OH, WOW." Scarlett couldn't help but gape at the nature around her. Flowers in glowing orange and yellow and blue dotted a field of magenta grass within an enclosed courtyard. Some plants looked familiar, but others had petals the size of her head and swayed despite the lack of breeze. The flowers didn't even creep Scarlett out, not in this beautiful wonderland. The manicured pathways turned the entire space almost into a maze of towering trees and shapely shrubs.

At Scarlett's side, Lexi settled a hand on her belly. "That's what I said the first time, too."

"Everything is so bright."

"So bright and so alive." Lexi let out a little happy sigh. "I love it. I was a florist before I came here, so this is my happy place."

Scarlett pursed her lips. Every media outlet had splashed stories of Herkleios' queen when her engagement was first announced. But none of the articles she'd read had mentioned anything about her career, only that she was a billionaire's niece. "I didn't know that."

"Most of the news you saw was PR bullshit from my uncle." Lexi started forward down one path, her flip-flops clapping against the stone. Scarlett was glad she hadn't changed into any Herkleian dress. Lexi had replaced the gown she'd worn earlier with sweatpants and a floral top. "He wanted me to sound like his little heiress, not someone he barely knew or cared about."

"That sucks."

"It doesn't matter. I stopped talking to Uncle Grayson months ago. It's all in the past." Lexi jolted back into a smile. "How did you meet Prax?"

Scarlett almost had to shake her head to push off the conversation's whiplash. "Oh, wow, right into the details."

"I kinda just speak my mind. I think it's gotten worse now that I'm a freaking queen."

"No, totally fine." Scarlett couldn't imagine going from florist to alien queen in less than a year. How did one adapt to that? "We, uh... we bumped into each other at work."

"Aww, a workplace romance," Lexi all but cooed. "I love it. Where do you work?"

"In London. At a law firm." Scarlett wanted to make her life sound more exciting than that, but it really wasn't. She internally flinched. She wanted her daughter back, but could she return to Earth like nothing had happened? This wasn't her life, but the old Scarlett wasn't her anymore, either. "Immigration law."

"London? That's so cool. I always wanted to visit. Are you English? These translators can do funky things with accents."

"Huh." Now that she thought about it, every alien she encountered had sounded American. "I'm from Ohio. I moved to the UK after law school and never looked back."

"I wish I could've done that. But then I wouldn't have met Anax, so I guess it was for the best." Lexi stepped off the path next to a blue tree with dripping leaves, almost like a willow. "You could probably keep walking, but I'm about to fall over. Mind if we sit?"

"Of course not."

"This is actually where Anax took me on our first date." Lexi pushed through the leaves. At the base of the tree, moss crawled the legs of a little wooden bench. It was the lowest tech object Scarlett had witnessed in space. "Well, at the time, I didn't really consider it a date, but it's a great spot, anyway. You can see all the beautiful flowers."

Scarlett settled beside the queen and inhaled, breathing in the quiet nature. "It really is beautiful."

For a moment, both of them sat in silence, letting the swaying of plants and chittering of critters weave a symphony around them. Scarlett peeked at Lexi from the corner of her eye. She had told Prax she planned on collecting intel, but Scarlett's questions were best asked after hours of study. Not that this was a cross-examination. She tried to relax her shoulders. Something natural should do the trick. "When are you due?"

"The doctors aren't sure. If I were Herkleian, they'd say a month."

"Must be terrifying to not know."

"It is, but I'm just happy they're healthy." She rubbed at her belly. "My little prince and princess."

Just a single toddler was already hell on wheels. She couldn't imagine having two at the same time. "Any name ideas?"

"Yes, but we're keeping them a secret." Her green eyes went distant. "Also, there's tradition, you know. Not something us regular folk consider, but in the Herkleian monarchy, they usually name the heir after a grandparent."

"Ah."

Lexi tried to keep her smile, but it dimmed at just the thought of Xenobaccus. Scarlett hoped to never meet the former king if that was all it took to drag down the bubbly Lexi. "Anax is hoping the girl is born first. It would be good for the planet to be ruled by a queen again."

Scarlett frowned. "They let a queen rule alone?"

"Herkleios was a matriarchy. Now the firstborn inherits the throne, but yeah, they've had a bunch of queens. Makes sense given their supreme deity is the goddess Hyra."

A tingle crawled Scarlett's neck. She had avoided researching anything beyond the basics of the matebond, but Lexi was a real Earthling who had experienced the phenomenon, not a clinical database. She couldn't help but poke. "The same goddess who gave you your matebond mark?"

"According to Anax." Lexi shrugged. "Not sure if I believe in a giant dragon goddess guiding the love lives of mere mortals, but whoever or whatever did it was right. Anax is like the other half of my soul."

Scarlett repressed a twinge. Somehow, those words felt right. Prax was obstinate and impulsive, but who else would tolerate her Type A attitude and sharp tongue? If they were a puzzle, their jagged edges matched up perfectly. "That's sweet."

"I wish everyone agreed."

"Don't they?"

"Anax's father didn't."

There he was again, Xenobaccus lurking over the entire Herkleian royal family, cousins and all. "Isn't he imprisoned?"

Lexi nibbled at her lip and nodded. Not a lie, but not the whole truth, either. Maybe Scarlett could find out exactly where. Not that she wanted to need the information, but better to have it than to wish she had asked.

"Then you have nothing to worry about. Don't they have an alien supermax?"

"Herkleians are big on reform and giving back to the community.

There is one major prison, but Anax wanted his father close." Lexi shuddered. "That's why I don't walk the gardens alone anymore. Herkleians build their prisons underground and these gardens have emergency hatches into the subterranean level."

Scarlett almost bolted out of her seat. "Excuse me?"

"That's exactly what I said. But the sub-level isn't all prison, so I guess it makes sense to have backup exits."

"You don't sound convinced."

Lexi glanced over and tried to force that radiant smile again. "I trust Anax. If he says it's secure, it's secure."

Scarlett grinned back, but it stretched awkwardly at her face. If only that were true. But Prax and Scarlett had already invaded layer upon layer of security. If Argrix had any more aces up his sleeve, it would be far too easy to jailbreak an evil ex-king.

Prax stepped from *The Carthak*, his boots crunching in the forest's deep grass. He adjusted his crossbow in his arms. It had been too long since he relished in the thrill of a hunt. Earth had not been conducive to his people's ways—except for when he hunted down Scarlett. When Prax inhaled, the scents of the forest paled to the smell of his mate, clinging to him like a specter. If he closed his eyes and walked, his nose would lead him straight back to the palace's gardens where she walked with Lexi.

Though they had only been separated for minutes, he longed for her presence. Nothing could have prepared him for the intensity of feelings that came with the matebond. The stories his father had told him made it out to be an all-encompassing love, but that didn't even begin to put it into words. In less than a week, Scarlett had become his universe. Her quick wit charmed him. Her reluctant smile at his antics made him want to take her into his arms. Her bravery astonished him. When he returned her to Earth as promised, every day without her would be torturous.

But whatever she desired, he would go to the edge of the galaxy to satisfy.

A shadow flickered at his side, settling into the form of his cousin, his gold finery and crown replaced by his hunting garb, his sash a brilliant blue. "Captain Dexus reported the wild zevra pack in these woods."

Prax glanced back at his ship. Dexus, the captain of Anax's royal guard, had insisted on accompanying them to the Vasilos Forest, a wild space to south of the palace, but he didn't want to intrude on their hunt. It was tradition for a father to hunt before the birth of his child, a practice the Eógans and Herkleians still shared. Usually the father's own father and siblings accompanied him, but Xenobaccus had forfeited that right and all of Anax's brothers were off-planet. Prax's eldest cousin, Eryx, had planned to attend, but he and his human mate spent most of their spare time assisting war orphans. Having a dozen sick children on hand was a worthy excuse.

"To the river?" Prax asked.

Anax nodded. "A good starting place."

The two males started forward. Before leaving the clearing, Prax glanced back once more at his ship. He had snapped a wire in the engine room when collecting extra arrows. Dexus hopefully wouldn't notice the error until they returned with their hunt. If the guard went to fix it, he'd notice the clear sabotage. Prax hated lying to his cousin, but it was the only way to guarantee everyone's safety. Argrix wouldn't hesitate to harm innocents, including his Scarlett. Keeping her safe gave him the will to carry on with the deception.

After tomorrow, after he told his mother the truth and suffered the punishment for his crimes, Argrix wouldn't have a hold on him any longer.

Until then, Prax turned his focus to the hunt. There weren't any zevra on Eógan, but he had hunted the orange spotted beasts years ago during a prior visit to Herkleios. He flipped through his list of scents. With his next deep inhale, he caught the right trail. Heading towards the river was the right choice.

Prax and Anax kept their footfalls light as they approached. Pale blue water sparked in the sunlight and peaked between the red-vined trees. Prax held out a hand, ordering Anax to stop. His cousin obeyed his orders. With another hand gesture—the sign language the Royal Academy had taught all its members—the two males dropped behind the shrubbery.

Prax raised his crossbow. Four zevra grazed at the water's edge, the brightness of their fur stark against the purples and blues of the forest. The creatures had six thin legs and massive, meaty torsos. They reminded him of a creature he'd seen on Earth, a large but tame animal the human police rode around the city. Zevra were far less aggressive but twice as fast. Once they fired into the clearing, the rest of the herd would flee in the blink of an eye.

Remaining quiet, Prax lowered the tip of his crossbow and gestured to Anax. The new father should make the kill. Prax was the better hunter, but it was Anax's right. The king didn't need the meat to feed his young—not with his resources and the food materializers— but Hyra blessed the hunter who made the kill. A younger, more obnoxious Prax would have made the kill without a second thought. But not anymore, not after killing Eztl and meeting Scarlett. The matebond mark tingling at his nape under his collar, urging him to be better.

Anax raised his own crossbow, an ancient thing carved of wood and gilded with zafers jewels, and after quickly lining up the shot, fired.

His arrow hit his target before a spark of electricity charged through the animal, killing the beast instantly. By the time the two males returned to their feet, the remaining pack had bounded off into the surrounding trees, less than a flash of orange to Prax's vision.

Prax clapped his cousin on the shoulder. "Good shot."

Anax growled, a light laugh. "Coming from you, that's high praise. You were always top of your class in archery."

"So were you."

"Only because you're younger and weren't my competition."

"True." Prax pulled six cuffs from his belt and attached each to the zevra's hooves. Once all connected, the devices flashed with blue light and levitated the animal into the air. While Herkleians enjoyed taking part in their ancestor's hunts, they didn't replicate them entirely. Neither Prax nor Anax wanted to carry the carcass back to the palace by hand.

With the zevra floating behind them, the males headed back toward the ship. To the moment Prax had anticipated. Neither his cousin nor Dexus would object when he insisted on fixing his ship himself. Prax had always been particular about *The Carthak*. His father had purchased it to celebrate his fifteenth year.

Waiting for a Herkleian ship would add extra time to their journey, time away from Scarlett, but it was worth it to save lives from Argrix's threat.

From the corner of his vision, Anax bared his fangs. "You're looking well, cousin. Better than the last time we saw each other."

"The last time we saw each other was on a warship after your wedding."

"I meant you appear calmer. More at peace. Your female puts you at ease."

"Really?" Prax snorted. "I've never felt less at ease in my life. Most females are impressed that I'm a prince, but Scarlett doesn't care. She judges me for who I am."

"Earthlings are feisty like that, aren't they?" Anax slapped him on the back. "Don't worry, Prax. I can tell she cares for you."

"As Lexi clearly does for you. Are you excited to become a father?"

Anax puffed out his chest proudly. "I can't wait to hold my children in my arms."

"Hyra has blessed you greatly with twins."

Anax paused. "I thought you didn't believe in Hyra."

"I didn't." But then he met his mate, Scarlett—a fact Prax couldn't reveal, despite wanting to shout it to the world. Scarlett wanted to return to Earth, not be his mate. "After watching you and Eryx find love with your mates, I can't help but believe."

"I can't blame you." *The Carthak*'s silver and green edges came into view through the trees, but neither Anax nor Prax quickened their pace. "Even I was skeptical of Hyra until I met Lexi. But how else could I explain the events that brought us together?"

Prax smiled at his cousin, but his eyes had fixed on his ship, dread weighing down his stomach. He hated to betray his family, but he couldn't put any lives at risk. *The Carthak* couldn't return to the royal airstrip. Argrix wouldn't like it, but he wouldn't be able to do anything about it if he wanted Xenobaccus out of prison.

Captain Dexus appeared in the ship's doorway. "Good hunting, Your Majesty? Your Highness?"

"Very," Anax responded as Prax tapped at his wristband's holo, directing the zevra into the hold. "Start the engines, will you, Dexus?"

The captain bobbed his head before disappearing into the ship. Prax focused on not tensing his shoulders, remaining calm at Anax's side. He and Anax were halfway to the control room when the ship rumbled... but thankfully, didn't start. His cousin's brow furrowed.

"Etein's mercies," Prax mumbled. "Not again."

"Engine troubles?"

"Nothing I can't fix, but I need to get a new regulator. I hoped to at least make it home before having to make the fix, though."

Anax sent him a slightly disapproving look. "And if you broke down mid-flight?"

Prax grinned, slipping into cheer with ease. "Then I'd drink all the meod while waiting for rescue."

Anax let out a growly scoff, the way he had before at a dozen of Prax's antics. "You're going to get yourself killed one day, cousin."

"Hopefully not too soon." Had genuine fear leaked into his voice? Prax hoped not. He didn't think he'd lose his life to this, but Prax had never stood closer to death. Of course it happened when he finally had something to lose. He pulled up his holo-screen. "I'll have to order a new part. Until then, *The Carthak* is grounded."

"I should make you walk back to the palace."

It was no less than what Prax deserved, but he kept the smile on his face. "Don't be cruel, cousin. Who will regale Lexi and Scarlett with tales of your bravery?"

"When facing down a tranquil zevra?"

Prax laughed, a full and booming sound. Lying came easily to him. Too easily. If—no, when—he lost his title, maybe he'd try his hand at politics. "And *that's* why you need me there to tell the tale."

FOURTEEN

SCARLETT

"Are you sure you don't need any help, my lady?" Zopha asked, the Herkleian female's clawed hands crossed gently across her chest.

Scarlett flickered through her top options on the materializer's holo-screen for a third time. Lexi had sent over a hundred unique designs. Zopha had vetoed any of the too-gold designs—the color reserved for Herkleian royalty—but otherwise, Scarlett was determined to make her own decision. "You've been a help already, Zopha. Thank you."

The attendant dropped into a polite but shallow bow. "If you require any more assistance, I've shared my communication information with your wristband."

When the door clicked shut behind the female, Scarlett circled through the options again.

On the other side of the room, Prax propped one leg up onto a levitating ottoman-esque piece. "You'll look fantastic in whatever you choose."

"Easy for you to say," she muttered. Prax had ditched his superhero garb for dark pants and a twisting of green sashes, designed almost to look like vines. A silver coronet circled his forehead under his small horns. Like a shirtless god of the forest brought to life.

Scarlett wasn't insecure, not really, but she knew her body shape and dressed to accentuate it. Whoever had designed these dresses had Lexi in mind. Scarlett sighed and tapped the option with a cinched waist. She'd make it work.

In a flash of light, her Earth clothes were replaced by layer after layer of green tulle-like fabric, falling in a waterfall to her feet. Scarlett almost coughed on her next inhale. The dress was cinched, all right. Though there wasn't any corset, it almost felt like she wore one. Scarlett tried to tug at her stomach, but she didn't want to damage the silver embroidery and the expensive-looking green gems.

Scarlett glanced at herself in the mirrored wall by the window. Breathing issues aside, her boobs had never been perkier. "Does this look tight to you?"

Prax didn't respond.

"Prax—"

When she turned his way, she stiffened. Prax had climbed to his feet and crossed half the chamber, awe mixed with raw lust on his face. Another pang went through Scarlett's belly, this time not in pain. God, how she wanted him. Without thinking, she stepped off the edge of the platform.

Prax swallowed. "You're beautiful."

Scarlett flushed. In the last week, she had blushed more times than she had in the previous ten years. All thanks to her charming kidnapper.

She wanted the word to sting through her, remind her of the mess she was in because of him, but it didn't. Prax had taken her from her home against her will, but she didn't blame him anymore. He had done it to protect her, in a way that was completely Prax. Honorable but impulsive.

She wanted to throw herself into his arms. It would tear down the boundary between them but she didn't care.

And if her gown weren't strangling her, she probably would.

She returned to the platform, reluctantly. In this dress, she looked like she belonged next to Prax. Thankfully, Zopha had changed the color palette to match Eógan rather than Herkleios. Her second option should match, too.

Prax brushed a hand against her wrist, blocking her holo-screen. "What are you doing?"

"I can barely breathe in this."

"I can fix that." He moved behind her, his fingers brushing against the skin of her arm before settling at her back. Scarlett hadn't seen laces in the mirror, but he tugged on something and her midsection loosen. The burning fire in Scarlett's chest flared, enchanted by his touch. It took everything within her to not start panting.

As his hands moved down to rest upon her hips, Prax met her eyes in the mirror. "No female has ever looked more beautiful."

Screw it. Scarlett twirled in his hold and tilted her head until his lips brushed her. "When this is all over…"

Prax stiffened, the light in his eyes dulling. He pulled away from her.

This time, Scarlett put her hands on his wrists, holding him in place. "When this is all over, maybe we can go on a date. Assuming we survive, that is."

His scales flushed a deeper emerald. "I thought you wanted to return home and never see me again?"

"I did." She lured his mouth closer. "A girl can change her mind."

Prax's lips split into a fierce grin as he closed the small distance between them. At the touch of him, the burning within her turned to fireworks. Scarlett melted into his arms. Prax plundered her mouth, claiming her, possessing her. She threaded her hands through his hair and thumbed his horns. This was where she was meant to be. Being in his arms felt right. Though she had asked for a date, Scarlett knew what it would lead to. The tingles across her body crept across her neck.

Across the space that marked her as his.

Scarlett hadn't looked, but she didn't need to see to know the matebond mark was there.

Their wristbands buzzed.

Prax released her from the kiss and laid his forehead against hers. "While I'd love to stay here and ravish you, we have a baby shower to attend."

A splash of cold fear clawed at her heat. "You mean, you have a mother to confess your crimes to."

"I won't do it at the ball," Prax said. "But at the end, before she leaves."

"So we have to pretend for hours?"

"Her ship arrived an hour ago and hasn't even landed. She won't be saying long."

Scarlett didn't know if that was worse or better. She almost pulled from his arms and started to pace, but he didn't release her. If something happened to him, this might be her last time in his arms.

Prax pressed a kiss to her forehead. "Will you do me the honor of accompanying me to the ball, my lady?"

Scarlett couldn't help but smile. "The honor is mine, Your Highness."

WITHIN A BLINK, the gilded bedchamber around Scarlett turned into an open gazebo of twisted gold, strung with glowing rock crystals like twinkling stars. Her hand tensed in Prax's. When he said they were transporting to the baby shower, she had imagined opening her eyes within the palace. Not to a seaside cliff, the air salty and warm.

Her heels crunched through the purple grass until she neared the edge. Crystals studded the rock edge, thousands of times larger than the gazebo's decorative baubles. Below, a blue-green sea crashed against the shore.

"This reminds me of home," Prax said at her side.

"Lots of cliffs on Eógan?"

He nodded. "There are forest lowlands, but most of the planet is mountains."

Scarlett took his hand, but bit back her reply. She had started to imagine a life together, but if his conversation with his mother didn't go well—or worse, if Argrix interfered—her dream might die before it finished blooming. When she had discovered she was pregnant with Violet, Scarlett had pictured a life with Andrew by her side, surrounded by children. After he abandoned her, she had sworn to never daydream about men again.

Prax wouldn't abandon her but what if he didn't have a choice?

"Prax!"

Prax twisted as an unfamiliar alien male approached. Scarlett tried not to gape. His height and muscular build were similar to the Herkleians and Eógans, but in the place of scales, his skin glinted like ice. In the sunshine, he literally sparkled. But despite his skin, something about this male was warm and friendly, helped maybe by his dark beard and a dark blue flowing robe.

"Rivix?" Prax crushed the male into a giant hug. "I didn't expect to see you. Aren't you supposed to be training?"

"Sigrid needed a week off. Unfortunately, my parents heard and sent me here in their stead."

Prax tried to suppress a smile and failed. "So Aunt Rhiona isn't here?"

Rivix snorted, the sound a deep rumble in his chest. "My mother's not here, no. You're safe."

"Praise Etein."

Instead of being offended, Rivix laughed. His dark blue eyes—slitted like a Herkleian or Eógan, the only similarity—trailed to Scarlett. His smile crooked. "And you are?"

"Scarlett." She took Prax's hand. She hadn't yet broached the mate subject with her prince, so she added, "His girlfriend."

At Rivix's blank look, Prax said, "My beloved."

"Oh." Rivix's dark eyebrows raised. "*Oh.*"

Scarlett squinted at him. "Oh?"

"Forgive me, Lady Scarlett. I just never imagined meeting a female with the patience to handle Prax."

Prax punched him lightly on the shoulder. "Rude."

"It's true." Rivix turned his entire focus on her again and dropped into a bow. "Allow me to introduce myself formally, then. I am Rivix, son of King Skarde of Fenrik and Queen Rhiona Yio'elipida."

How did Scarlett respond to that? She raised her hand like a princess of olde, only for the ice prince to kiss it. His mouth lingered.

Prax growled. Literally growled. Scarlett had heard the sounds from Herkleians in joy and annoyance, but for Prax, a growl meant exactly what it did on Earth.

Rivix dropped his hand and dipped into another bow, but his lips remained twisted. "Forgive me, Lady Scarlett. You're such a beauty, I couldn't help myself."

Was every member of Prax's family such a tease? "It's fine, Your Highness."

"Just don't let it happen again," Prax said.

That only made Rivix's smile widen. "I'll keep that in mind, cousin." His blue eyes narrowed over their shoulders. "I know you think my mother's the scariest of our matriarchs, but she doesn't hold a flame to the Empress. I would rather fight a pack of wild ulves."

Scarlett stiffened. An Eógan woman in a gown of glittering green jewels approached, followed by a trio of guards. Her red eyes pierced the three of them—or two of them, since Rivix had all but disappeared. Empress Ailis. Not only the leader of an entire planet, but Prax's mother. Scarlett had met kings and queens this week, but nothing fazed her like the thought of a potential mother-in-law.

Prax didn't remove his hands from Scarlett. If anything, he moved closer. Did the Empress's red eyes narrow at that or was it just the brightness of the sun? Scarlett squeezed his hand back. From what he had told her, Prax really loved and respected his mother. It'd kill him to break her heart with the truth of Argrix's blackmail.

"I didn't expect to see you here," the Empress said, reaching for her son's empty arm. They clasped forearms, but Prax still didn't release Scarlett. His mother definitely noticed this time. "Especially after you abandoned your tour of Earth."

Prax winced. In between all the kidnapping and space drama, Scarlett had completely forgotten Prax had been touring Earth when they met. Her prince had, as well. "I'm sorry, Mother."

"Are you?" Despite the question, the Empress's tone remained light, almost like this was something she expected. "Who is your friend?"

"Scarlett Moore." Scarlett paused and then bowed her head. "Your Majesty."

"My beloved," Prax added.

Now *that* surprised the Empress. "Your beloved?"

Prax nodded. "I promised her a dance, Mother, but we can talk after."

A dance? Scarlett tried to hide her surprise, but the Empress didn't notice. The concept of Prax dating seemed to stun her. Scarlett sent a brief glare her prince's way. They hadn't talked much about previous relationships. Prax didn't even know she had a daughter.

But did that matter? Scarlett liked Prax for who he was today. His past didn't matter. Hers didn't, either.

Prax all but whisked her off her feet, leading her across the gazebo to an open space where aliens from half a dozen different races swirled beneath the twinkling gems. Within the crowd, Anax and Lexi slow-danced in the center, the large Herkleian cradling his petite wife.

Before Scarlett could wave, Prax twirled her. A buoyant laugh escaped her throat. "We're actually dancing?"

"Why not?" He twirled her back into his arms. "I'm a great dancer."

"I bet you are."

Though Scarlett didn't know the steps, the same wasn't true of Prax. He easily slid them into the space between two couples in tune with the twinkling music. "I'm sorry about my mother."

Scarlett clutched at his shoulders. "What about her?"

"She speaks her mind."

"So do I."

"You do, don't you?" His hands caressed up her side. Scarlett nearly choked as warmth whipped through her. How could the simplest touch from him stir such intense feelings? "And what's on your mind right now, beloved?"

Scarlett fell into the red depths of his eyes. Wrapping her arms around his broad shoulders, she pressed against his scaled chest until every part of them touched. The pulse of his heart reverberated against her skin. Prax brushed his lips against her forehead. The ghost of a kiss fanned Scarlett's flames into a wildfire. She had never wanted anyone like she wanted Prax. The thought only made her clutch him tighter.

His breath tickled her ear. "I wish I could take you back to our suite and fuck you like you deserve."

Scarlett's heart nearly stopped. She couldn't do this. She couldn't watch him destroy his life, his future. But what other option did they have? She grazed her knuckles against his chin. "I wish you could, too."

"Lady Scarlett?"

Scarlett jolted at the voice and pulled from Prax's arms. They had shuffled to the edge of the dance floor, where Zopha waited with her arms crossed gently in front of her. Scarlett forced a smile for the attendant. "Yes, Zopha?"

"May I speak to you?" Her slitted eyes flickered to Prax. "Alone?"

She frowned at her prince, but Prax shrugged. Scarlett patted him on the shoulder before turning toward the Herkleian. "Of course."

The attendant backed away from the celebrating crowd for a quiet corner of the gazebo, overlooking the violet fields. The gold towers of Eritea spired between the distant trees. Scarlett barely noticed them for Zopha's face, an almost pinched expression. Was she in trouble? Scarlett barely knew the female, but that didn't matter. No matter what world, Scarlett couldn't help but try to save people.

She settled a hand on the gilded banister. "What's wrong?"

Zopha dropped her gaze. "I'm sorry."

"What for?"

Zopha tapped at her golden wristband and held it in front of Scarlett. Together, their bodies blocked the sight of the holo-screen from the rest of the baby shower.

And more importantly, blocked the sight of a familiar face.

Argrix bared his fangs.

Scarlett's stomach hollowed. "What do you want?"

"My spies tell me you're making no progress on freeing my father." Argrix's face flickered, the distortion twisting his grin into something far more sinister. "Prax even tried to defy me by removing his ship from the palace grounds. Since he won't listen to reason, perhaps you will."

Argrix paused, waiting for her to respond, but Scarlett held steady. She wouldn't let him see her reaction.

He let out a little growl, but continued, "I just wanted you to keep in mind what *you* stand to lose if you don't do what I ask."

Argrix's image disappeared, blinking away to reveal a park of green grass, pathways surrounded by black wrought iron fences. But Scarlett barely noticed, not when the picture focused on two figures walking side-by-side. The dark-haired human man had one hand in the pocket of his canvas jacket while his other gripped the arm of the blond girl smiling up at him.

Andrew and Violet.

FIFTEEN

When Scarlett left his side, Prax couldn't prevent his gaze from drifting across the gazebo to his mother. The Empress chatted politely with a Fenrish ambassador, who nodded animatedly at the conversation. Once he told her what he'd done, who he'd killed, the polite smile would slip from her face into the mask of a warrior, Etein's own blood. If his grandmother were still Empress of Eógan, Prax would surely be walking to his death. His mother had her determination, but she loved her children. It wouldn't come to that.

It *shouldn't* come to that.

The baby shower had only started, but every moment Prax waited was another to build the tension. Dancing with Scarlett provided only a momentary reprieve. He never wanted to leave her side, but Prax had a responsibility to his mother, his people. He straightened his shoulders, the vine-like sashes across his chest ruffling with the movement, and took a step forward.

"Prax." Scarlett appeared at his side, a wild look in her eyes. Her small hands dug into his bicep, almost painfully.

His mother vanished from his mind. What had happened? Zopha had asked to talk to her in private, and Prax had thought nothing of the request. Lexi encouraged honesty among the palace's staff. He cupped his mate's chin, rubbing his thumbs along her cheeks. His fingers came away wet.

A rage boiled within him. Whoever had made his Scarlett cry would pay. "What happened?"

Scarlett opened her mouth for a second before snapping it shut. Her dark eyes skirted furtively over his shoulders. Glancing at the partygoers around them?

He lowered his hands and linked one of her arms with his. "Walk with me?"

She nodded, a moment of relief blossoming on her face. But it quickly disappeared, dragged down by the panic. A pit formed in Prax's stomach. His fierce yet level-headed mate never reacted this way. Even when Argrix's Neithans had boarded *The Carthak*, she had grabbed a weapon with murderous intent.

They strolled to the edge of the gazebo at a delicate pace before taking the stairs to the field. Around them, the music and laughing continued. Neither of his cousins nor his mother glanced their way. If they had, whatever upsetting news Scarlett had received would have become a public spectacle. Rivix, Anax, and the Empress were all far too smart to miss the way Scarlett brushed at her cheeks or the bristling of the ridges on Prax's back.

In the middle of the field, Prax pulled Scarlett into his arms. "Tell me."

She bit her lips, tears watering in her eyes.

"Don't cry, beloved." Prax kissed her forehead, then lowered his lips to each side of her cheeks. Salt stained his tongue. "Whatever it is, we can solve it together. There's no reason to be so hopeless."

"There is." She swallowed. "Argrix knows we're not upholding our end of the bargain."

His ridges flooded with poison as his scales flushed red. "The attendant. She passed you a message."

Scarlett nodded, still nibbling on her lip. When she glanced into his eyes, some new fear lingered there. "Argrix threatened my daughter."

My daughter. His heart stuttered with the words. "Your daughter? You have a child?"

"I do." She tried to pull from his arms, but he held her gently in place. "Her name is Violet."

"Violet." He sounded out the name, a wave of emotion crashing through him. Part joy, but also part terror. "And her father?"

"He left me before Violet was born."

Rage overwhelmed the relief. "I'll kill him."

Scarlett burst into a sharp, almost surprised laugh. "I want to say yes, but that would break Vi's heart."

Prax couldn't have that. He had always wanted to be a father, to spoil his younglings rotten. But if Argrix hurt his mate's child, he might never get the chance. "Why didn't you tell me?"

"I wanted to keep her out of all this, but I guess I failed. If Argrix hurts her—"

"He won't. He knows our bond. It's my responsibility to defend your offspring, and I will fight to the death to protect Violet."

Tears flooded her eyes again. "Most guys don't even want to go on a second date after hearing I have a child."

And after killing Argrix, Prax would decimate every human male who said this to his mate. "How dishonorable of them. I assure you, beloved, I'll protect Violet as if she were my own." He wanted to hold her, comfort her, but Argrix wouldn't have made this threat lightly. "I assume my cousin's threat has come with conditions."

"He wants us to release his father. Now."

Etein's mercies. Prax closed his eyes, but no obvious solution came to mind. Argrix's spies would see if he spoke to his cousins or mother. Prax hadn't cared when it was his sacrifice, but he wouldn't risk an innocent child. "Then that is what we must do to keep Violet safe."

"But Xenobaccus is a danger to the galaxy. The way you talk about him, the way Lexi talks about him—"

Prax squeezed her shoulders. "We'll worry about that when Violet is out of danger."

Scarlett gave a final sniffle before determination entered her eyes. "Are you sure?"

"I'm sure."

Scarlett searched his gaze for something, but whatever it was she looked for, she didn't find. She reached up and entangled her fingers through his hair, luring his mouth to hers. Prax couldn't resist. When her soft lips touched him, his control on his anger snapped. He plunged into her mouth, taking, claiming. She was his mate. His beloved. The naika to his naikos, though the Herkleian words meant little to him.

She was *his*.

She broke the kiss with a gasp. "I love you, Prax."

His heart nearly stopped. "You do?"

"Of course I do, silly."

Prax's scales darkened, his whole body light with elation. "I thought I was your evil kidnapper."

"You were but..." Scarlett lured him closer until his forehead dropped to hers. "I just couldn't resist you, Prax. I think you were right. I've never felt anything like this bond between us. It led you to me and me to you. And it was right. Somehow, it was right."

His own thoughts spoken from her lips made him want to roar with joy. If only Argrix weren't threatening their lives. He'd throw his mate over his shoulder and tear into the forest to sate his claim. His heart thundered, blood rushing to his cock. He wanted to hear her scream his name. "I love you, too, beloved."

"I can tell." She smirked up at him and wriggled closer, the jostling turning his rod to stone. But her smile was brief, a momentary flicker. "But we can't forget Argrix."

Prax groaned and pulled out of her arms. "We need to find Xenobaccus."

"Lexi said he's in the tunnels under the palace, but there are apparently dozens of entrances."

"If he's in the tunnels, I know where." Anax and Eryx had shown him and their other cousins the then-abandoned prison years ago. "But getting him out will be difficult."

"Argrix has a solution for that," Scarlett said, pulling something from her pocket.

He reached out a hand for the tiny golden ball. "What is this?"

"Argrix said it would allow Xenobaccus and anyone else touching it to transport to the beacon on your ship. Apparently, they put more than cameras and bombs in *The Carthak*."

"So that's how he planned to get his father out." Prax examined the ball's smooth surface once more before slipping it into his pocket. "My ship has clearance to bypass the planet's shields."

Scarlett shrugged. "All the sci-fi technical stuff is above me, but yeah, I guess."

"I'll bring this to Xenobaccus, then. You can wait—"

She gripped his arm. "Like hell."

"Scarlett—"

"I'm coming with you."

Prax clenched his jaw. "It will be dangerous."

"I know."

He pushed a strand of her blond hair from her face. "You're so brave, beloved."

She smiled. "I know that, too."

Prax couldn't keep himself from her. He pressed another kiss to her forehead. If he surrendered to the lure of her lips, he'd never let her go. "Then we do this together."

Scarlett nodded.

He tightened one arm around her waist and tapped at his wristband. "Two to transport to the Queen Avra Garden."

A tingle crawled across his scales as the transporters locked onto their location. When Prax opened his eyes, he and Scarlett stood on a stone pathway leading through blue trees with drooping branches. If he remembered correctly, the hatch his cousins had led him through was somewhere within the thicket.

Prax locked his hands with his mate's. "This way."

At a leisurely pace, they started through the bushes. Prax pushed at the branches, but some still snagged in Scarlett's gown. It didn't slow his mate down. No one would get between his Scarlett and her offspring.

If only Prax had brought a weapon. He didn't expect any resistance until they neared Xenobaccus's cell, but he could better defend Scarlett with one. Not that Prax wanted to injure any Herkleians, but there'd be no way out of this without conflict. He adjusted the silver ring on his finger. At least he had one way to neutralize any guards without permanent injury.

Scarlett squeezed at his hand. "What do we do when—?"

A twig cracked, weight snapping it in two. Prax pulled Scarlett down into a crouch. Through the trees, he spotted two Herkleian males, their faces obscured by helmets. Guards patrolling the garden. Would they attempt to stop Prax? He was a prince, but Anax might have given them orders to detain anyone who approached the hatches.

"What is it?" Scarlett whispered.

"Guards, I think. They might just be patrolling the area but..."

"Shit." Scarlett tried to shuffle forward, but a dull thunk echoed like her shoe hitting a root. She flailed her arms. Prax moved to catch her, but she fell through the hedge. Her leg kicked out, knocking him over. Together, they tumbled into the path, Prax landing on top of her.

Right in front of the guards.

The two males halted. One put a hand on the laser at his waist, but the other stopped him after noticing Prax's silver coronet. "I apologize, Your Highness, but this area is restricted until further notice."

Prax barely heard him, not with his mate's delicious body underneath him. She tried to straighten out her legs, resulting in him slipping between her thighs. His cock hardened at the movement. If he was going to be locked in a cell alongside Xenobaccus, he could at least have his mate once more.

He read the same thoughts in her dark eyes. Scarlett's breath hitched as her hands trailed his side, a gentle touch of fingers. She leaned toward him until her lips hovered over his scales.

And then she spoke, a light whisper, "Herkleians are prudish, right?"

Her implication settled in right as Scarlett brought her lips to his. Her hands threaded through his hair and grasped at his horns. The sensation jolted through him. Prax groaned into her mouth. The guards disappeared in his mind. Nothing remained but his mate, the touch of her skin to his horns and his scales, the softness of her mouth on his lips.

"Uh, Your Highness?" one guard said distantly.

Prax ignored them, focused entirely on his mate. Her legs parted beneath him, one foot hooking around his thigh. He nearly growled when his length settled over her heat. The rich, heady scent of her flared at his touch. The scent he had followed halfway across her human city, but so much stronger with her desire. Prax travelled his hands down her body until he reached her legs, her bare skin.

Scarlett moaned and nipped at his lips.

It was her moan that finally did it. The two guards stiffened, but one had backed away. All they needed was a push.

Prax reluctantly pulled from his mate, but Scarlett didn't stop, kissing a line down his jaw. He narrowed his eyes at the guards, the ridges of his spine bristling. "Go away."

"Your Highness—"

The one male didn't have the chance to finish, not with the other male pulling him away. "Do you know who that is? We can't…"

Prax tuned out their fading voices. Scarlett had worked her mouth down to his collarbone as her hands trailed to the edge of his pants.

When she slipped under the fabric, he couldn't help a growl.

His hands tensed in the thick soil beneath her head. "They're gone, love."

"So?" Her dark eyes glanced up, wild and dilated. She gripped his shaft with a harsh stroke. "I want you, Prax. I want you forever. But if I can't have you forever, at least I can have you now."

"Then you're wearing far too much clothes." Prax grabbed at her collar and tugged, shredding through the fabric of her gown with his claws. His eyes devoured the exposed, round globes of her breasts before he lowered his lips, devouring them with his mouth. He sucked on one pert nipple, lathering it with the bristles of his tongue. Scarlett's back arched. Such a responsive female. He raked his teeth against the sensitive flesh and chuckled against her skin when she nearly jumped.

"The other," she begged. "The other, now."

"So demanding." But Prax complied, kissing a path to her other breast, lonely and eager. He tugged and nipped and sucked until Scarlett writhed, gripping at his horns.

"You're going to kill me."

"That's the plan," he murmured against her skin.

She shuddered. "Prax, I..."

He kissed down her stomach. "Yes, love?"

"I..." She tugged at his jaw, directing his face towards her. "Prax, I need you to fuck me right now."

Fire spread through Prax at the words, a primal urge. With a growl, he picked her up and flipped her, his mate's knees digging into the edge of a flower bed. He hiked her skirts as she tugged at her underclothes. The need pulsed through him, a rush of desire equal to hers. When the curve of her ass came into view, he nearly came right there, spilling seed onto her pale skin.

But he wouldn't.

Not without making her scream first.

Prax circled one hand around her leg, his claws retracting. He rubbed a knuckle through her heat. Scarlett dropped her head to the dirt, her moan shuddering through her body. He pulled his fingers away wet with her sweet scent.

He chuckled, the sound pulling another shudder from her. "Are you ready for me already, love?"

Scarlett pushed onto an elbow. "Dammit, Prax, just fuck—"

Prax pulled her to him as he thrust forward, sliding into her heat with a single stroke. Etein's mercies, she was tight. Her soft walls encompassed his girth, the ridged edges of his cock, every part of him. Like their bodies were meant to be. Like they were meant to be.

Scarlett cried out in pleasure but also pain. Prax pulled back—

She reached around, grabbing his leg. "Don't you dare stop."

A wave of arousal and love flooded him. His Scarlett. His mate. He grabbed her thigh and pulsed forward, joining with her again. And again and again. She bounced against him, an intoxicating dance. Fuck, Prax wasn't going to survive this. His hands wrapped around her hips, both holding on and driving her into him.

Her fingers dug into the dirt, into his leg, tensing with every thrust. He wanted to hear her scream for him. Wanted her to clench around him, milking his seed. Then, and only then, would he release. His thrusts turned erratic, a losing battle, but Prax wouldn't come until his mate was undone before him.

"Prax, I... I..." Her sentence was lost on a crying moan.

Prax slipped a thumb across the bead of her clit. "Yes, mate, come for me."

Like on command, her body shuddered. With the final tease, she clenched around him, releasing her beautiful scent into the air. She cried his name into the grass. Her body arched. Intoxicating. *His.* Every part of her belonged to him, like every part of him belonged to her.

With a final thrust, Prax exploded with a roar.

SIXTEEN

PRAX

Prax pressed his shoulder to the jagged wall of rock and peered around the corner. The long, cavernous path ended in a solid metal door, two guards blocking the prison's entrance. Neither seemed on high alert. The soldiers they had encountered in the garden hadn't reported them, then.

He turned back to his mate, who brushed the dirt from her skirts. Prax couldn't resist a grin. In the light of day, the tears in her gown—both thanks to nature and Prax—were clearly visible, but her human eyes could barely see in the tunnel's dimness. "You look beautiful."

She snorted. "I look like I just rolled around a garden."

"We *did* just roll around a garden."

"True." His mate let out a light sigh. "What's the plan?"

"There are two guards," Prax said. "They'll let me approach and once I'm closer, I can attack."

"And if you lose? They have weapons."

He gripped her hand and squeezed. "I won't lose. Not with Violet at risk."

She tensed at her daughter's name, but remained cool-headed and serious. "What if we repeat our garden trick?"

Prax's cock twitched. "Our garden trick?"

"Not the sex," she said with a quiet whack to his shoulder. His scales heated where she touched. "But let's say I have a kink for prison cells. You said they haven't used this place in years. If you thought it was empty…"

"Hmm." If Prax approached alone, it put Scarlett out of harm's way. But his arriving with a beautiful human on his arm would certainly stun the guards. They wouldn't expect the Crown Prince of Eógan to be here for Xenobaccus, but they might wonder. Scarlett's presence would be a simple answer, silencing any lingering questions and doubts.

"Hmm?" Scarlett locked arms with him and tugged at her gown, exposing more of her enticing skin. "You know it'll work, so let's do it. We've already wasted enough time."

"Wasted?"

"You know what I mean."

Prax kissed her temple. "I do."

Her arm skirted around his side and caressed down the lines of his abs. "And once we get to the guards?"

"Just follow my lead, love." Prax mussed at his hair. Not that it needed much work after their garden tumble. The only thing he couldn't fake was the darker hue of his scales. Both Herkleians and Eógans had great night vision, but hopefully the guards wouldn't notice.

Prax wrapped a hand around Scarlett's waist and all but twirled her into the hall. Her surprised squeak quickly turned into a full laugh. If they were going to be intoxicated lovers with a jail kink, they might as well go all the way.

The guards raised their lasers. "Halt. This is a restricted area."

They nearly slammed into the opposite wall, but Prax stopped them right in time, his back to the soldiers. If they fired, they'd hit him and not his mate. Prax hated leaving his back open, his spine ridges flaring—

Scarlett wrapped a hand around his neck and lured his mouth to her. In her gentle embrace, he relaxed, falling into the role expected of him. Prince Prax, carefree and nearly careless.

Footsteps pounded behind them. "We said, this is a restricted area!"

Prax reluctantly pulled from his mate but before he answered, Scarlett peeked around her shoulder and let out a high-pitched laugh. "Look! They have guns. You didn't say there'd be guns, Praxxy?"

Praxxy? He didn't even need to fake his smile. "There weren't any last time, love."

"Sir, ma'am, please leave—"

The male's voice halted the exact moment he noticed Prax's coronet and put it together with Scarlett's slurred *Praxxy*. He threw an arm around Scarlett's shoulders before the two of them stumbled forward. "No reason to be so hostile, brothers. Can't a male show his lady our dungeons? Not like anyone's been in them for years."

"Your Highness," the second male started.

Prax let go of Scarlett and moved forward, nearly tipping into the first guard. He clapped a hand on the male's shoulder beside his pauldrons. With a slight twitch of Prax's finger, his ring would do the rest. "Between you and me," he whisper-yelled, "my lady has a thing for restraints. If you know what I mean."

The second guard closed his eyes, likely throwing up a prayer to Hyra, but it was the first Prax watched. Slowly, the male loosened and slipped his laser back into his holster. "Be that as it may, Your Highness—"

Prax struck, twisting his ring and jabbing the sharp edge between the male's scales. He stiffened, but it was too late. As he slumped to the ground, Prax twisted at the second guard, who reached for his laser. His boot connected with the weapon's edge, sending it spinning across the hall. Prax rammed into the other male and slammed his hand against his chest. The guard blinked, slightly stunned, before slumping into the wall.

A second later, he crumbled next to his partner, a soft snore echoing through the tunnel.

Scarlett stared, open-mouthed. "Holy shit. Where did you learn karate?"

Prax readjusted his ring, making it safe again to touch others. "What is kaa-ra-tee?"

"The, uh..." She mimicked a kick, but it wasn't very high in her skirts. "The boom-boom, punch-punch."

"All nobility are trained in martial arts." Prax grabbed the first guard by the wrist and pulled. At the question in his mate's eyes, he said, "I need to move him closer. These doors require the right DNA and the right wristband."

She followed slowly behind. "Are you going to drag him all the way to the cell?"

"I hope not, but there's no way to know until we reach Xenobaccus." The last time Prax had entered the prison, Eryx had led them through the first door and the cells inside had all stood open. He hadn't cared enough to ask any more questions than that.

Once he reached the door, Prax waved the male's wrist in front of the sensor. Gears turned and clicked within before it opened, revealing pale light and stale air. No one had visited Xenobaccus as of late. Not surprising. The ex-king had betrayed all his family and former allies. The only person to remain on his side was Argrix.

Prax pushed through the door, but paused at the threshold. He reached for Scarlett's hand at the exact moment she reached for his. "Xenobaccus despises humans. Whatever he says, ignore him."

"I can handle a grumpy, imprisoned king, Prax. Maybe it will remind me of home. Some of my clients' traffickers think they're kings, after all." Her eyes dimmed. "What if this doesn't work? What if Argrix hurts Violet anyway?"

"He won't."

"You don't know that."

Prax raised her hand and kissed her knuckles. "You're right. I don't. But until my cousin has his father, he won't harm her. He needs her."

Scarlett reached up and brushed a strand of burnished hair from his cheek. Prax had never imagined a true love, one who made his heart nearly hurt. Yet here she was, standing in front of him. If Hyra hadn't given him a mark, would he have found her? Without it, he might have continued on his PR tour. Safer surely, but a much lonelier future. In this one, he could have a real family instead of siblings he barely knew and a mother who had to care more about her empire.

"Don't lurk in the doorway," a deep but unpleasant voice called. "Come in and face me."

His ridges bristled. Prax let out a sigh and released his mate. "He's dramatic, too."

Scarlett nodded, suddenly pale. Prax pushed in front of her and into the prison. He wouldn't let Xenobaccus get close. All of the tunnels beneath the palace were carved from the rock, but the prison was once a natural cave. The ceiling glittered with jeweled stalactites like the starry night outside. It was a far more beautiful view than the sight from Eógan's sky cells, one wall open to the cliffside. Far more comfortable for its prisoners, too. Only one of the six cells was furnished, the remaining five full of little but dust. With a gush of air, the dirt swirled and zapped against the forcefield lining the outer edges, but air travelled freely between the holes in the rock between the cells.

Xenobaccus pushed up from a cushioned bench. The Herkleian king had aged since Prax last saw him, his long, dark hair yellowing and his horns shrinking. But his slitted purple eyes remained sharp and calculating.

"Uncle," Prax said simply.

Xenobaccus bared his fangs. "Prax, my boy! What a pleasant surprise."

Scarlett remained behind him out of sight, but she sniffled and coughed at the stagnant air. The ex-king peered around him, gaze narrowing. "Who else have you brought with you?"

His mate said nothing, but she shuffled to his side, head held high. Scarlett crossed her arms across her chest, fierce despite the tears in her gown.

Xenobaccus growled. "A human?"

Prax nearly charged at the forcefield. "She is none of your concern."

"Defensive." His uncle settled two feet on the ground, sitting on the bench like it was a throne. "Have you also fallen for the charms of a dirty human?"

"Do you want our help or not?" Scarlett snapped.

Xenobaccus glanced at her, his lips twitching. After a moment of contempt, he returned to Prax. "Have you come to your senses and realized I'm meant to sit on the throne?"

"No, but Argrix can be very convincing."

Xenobaccus threw back his head and let loose a roaring crackle. "Good to hear one of my sons still remembers his father." His hands curled into fists, sharp, black claws digging into his scales. "Did Eryx marry that human of his, too? Meddling bitch."

Scarlett stiffened at his side, but didn't reply. There was nothing to say. To save Violet, they had to release Xenobaccus. But he didn't want to move forward. Didn't want to release this scourge upon the galaxy. He had harmed and killed too many innocents already.

It was Scarlett who broke the silence. "How do we open your cell?"

"You can't. Only Anax can."

Etein's mercies. His mate's panicked eyes met his, but Prax shook his head. There was no way to override that feature. "Then we've come here for nothing."

"Not nothing." Xenobaccus pushed to his feet and approached, the fabric of his white robes trailing across the ground. Anax had stripped his father of his jewels and his crown, but the male still knew how to command a presence. "There hasn't been use for this prison since my grandmother's era, so they updated it quickly for my arrival. Anax controls the forcefield locking me in here, but there's only rock on this side. If you can get into that cell—"

"And cut through solid rock?"

The humor fled the king's face, leaving something chilling

behind. "If Argrix's escape plan requires me walking out of here, he's just as much of a disappointment as his brothers."

"Then how do we get into the other cell?" Scarlett asked.

"I don't know. I don't design prison cells, I lead armies."

His mate scoffed. "Not from in here, you don't."

Xenobaccus rammed forward, a breath from the forcefield. "How dare you continue to speak to me, human? It disgusts me that my sons have fallen for creatures like you. Once you've released me, I think I'll start with your planet first. Your people are simple and your defenses are weak."

Scarlett clenched her fist, looking near murderous. "You're a sick son of a bitch."

"And you're—"

Prax pounded a fist into the forcefield. While solid on his side, it sparked on Xenobaccus's, causing the ex-king to leap back with a yelp. "I see your imprisonment has taught you nothing, Uncle. You're somehow crueler."

He pointed at Scarlett. "You can't honestly think she is an equal to us."

"You're right. She isn't. She's so much more than us. She's kind, compassionate, and generous in ways we will never understand. Anax and Eryx are all the better for meeting their mates just as I am for meeting mine."

"Your mate?" Xenobaccus's face twisted like he tasted something rotten. "*Your* mate? You're only half-Herkleian, and Hyra gave you a human mate, too?!"

Both Prax and Scarlett shuffled away at the tone. It was worse than Prax feared. His uncle wasn't only filled with hate. He had lost his mind. The king twirled around and paced to the other side of his cell, murmuring to himself. Prax caught snippets of it, both pleas and curses to Hyra.

"We can't release him, Prax. He's mad."

"I know." Prax pulled his mate into his arms. When Scarlett had told him of Argrix's threat, he wanted to march in here and free the male. Anything to save her daughter, the child he desperately wanted to meet. But how could he live with himself if he released a murderous maniac on the galaxy? "I know we can't my love."

Scarlett sniffled. "What are we going to do?"

"Did Argrix have Violet?"

"I don't think so. It all happened so fast. He showed me an image of her with Andrew, her father."

Prax twitched at Andrew's name. For the sake of his mate and new daughter, he wouldn't eviscerate the male when they first met, but he'd make him uncomfortable for the rest of his life for leaving Scarlett at their daughter's birth. "If we leave now, it's four days to get to Earth. *Etein's Might* is likely still in the atmosphere. If we can get off the planet and away from Argrix's spies, I can have soldiers I trust sent down to protect Violet and Andrew."

"And if Argrix finds out before?"

Prax wished he could erase all her pain and fear, but even a prince didn't have that power. "There is no path where Violet isn't at risk, love, but we risk her more by releasing my uncle."

"And the security footage?"

"I'll embarrass my family, but they'll survive. Violet is more important."

Scarlett nudged her chin in Xenobaccus's directions. "Should we tell him?"

"I don't want to hear the shrieking."

"Good plan."

Xenobaccus tore at a shelf of books in the corner of his cell, still muttering to himself. With as little noise as possible, Scarlett backed toward the door, Prax following behind. He shot his uncle one last glare. Though Anax and Eryx had both desired to kill the male, they thought he deserved a fair trial. Prax hadn't agreed then and he still didn't now. By the time the Intergalactic Alliance got through their bureaucracy, it'd be too late.

Back in the tunnels, Scarlett glanced at the unconscious guards. "Will they be okay here?"

"Xenobaccus can't get out to hurt them. But we only have half-an-hour before they wake. That's the time we have to get off Herkleios."

"Then let's—"

At the exact same moment, Prax and Scarlett's wristband dinged, the emerald jewel on its face flashing. Down the tunnel, the guard's devices blinked, too.

Scarlett flicked at it, calling up the holo-screen. "What's this?"

"A public announcement," Prax said, opening the message. "I didn't know there was one scheduled—"

An image flashed across his holo-screen, the still of a video.

A grainy security footage video from the *Zaghan's Rage.*

SEVENTEEN

SCARLETT

"No, no, no. This can't be happening. This isn't real." Scarlett's heart nearly stopped at the sight of the video on her holo-screen. Almost as if it heard her, the video flickered to life. Prax, facing an alien male with leopard-patterned skin and a tail. The two males huffed, already halfway through their fight. Argrix didn't care to show the whole video, the whole truth. Only the part that mattered. Their muscled bodies clashed together before one dropped to the ground, a dagger dripping with orange blood sticking from the leopard man's chest.

The video cut out and started again, trapped in a terrible repeat.

When Scarlett tore her attention from the screen to her mate, Prax's scales had flushed a sickly yellow. His red eyes fixed on the scene, the moment the easygoing prince had taken a life and changed his fate. Projected across both their screens.

Projected across the entire planet?

"You said 'public' service announcement?"

Prax swallowed. "Argrix's Neithan ship has relay technology. If they aimed it at Herkleios and had help from within the broadcasters..."

She dropped her arms, refusing to look at the video looping another time. "So everyone can see this?"

"Probably."

Damn. Scarlett pushed away the sudden nausea in her stomach and wrapped her large prince into her arms. "I'm so sorry, Prax."

"I knew it was going to happen." He curled into her grasp, his chin brushing the top of her head. "I was expecting it, but not like this, not this soon."

Scarlett squeezed. If only she could erase all his pain. In the few days they had known each other, they had experienced disaster after disaster. Their entire life wouldn't be like this, would it? "Why would Argrix do this?"

Almost as if his name summoned him, Scarlett's wristband blinked again. Zopha's name flashed across the holo-screen. She wanted to smack the decline button, but her finger reluctantly accepted the call. Instead of the Herkleian attendant's face, Argrix's smug grin filled the screen. Her nausea turned into a bubbling pit of fire.

"Did you get my video?"

Before Prax snarled into the screen, Scarlett shouted, "Fuck you!"

Argrix let out an amused growl. "Do not cross me again, human. I have a listening device in the transporting sphere my spy gave you. Walk away from my father again, and I'll kill your spawn."

Scarlett only hated a few people in her life, but Argrix easily made the list. "You're a lying—"

"Mummy?" a soft, accented voice asked. "Mummy, is that you?"

Violet's voice punched into Scarlett's gut. A cold sweat broke out across her skin, tingling down her arms. No. Her knees went weak. If she weren't in Prax's arms, Scarlett would have crashed to the floor. Not her baby, not Violet. The heat from her mate's body pulsed into her, but it wasn't enough to halt the chilling panic.

"This is your final warning. Release my father or your daughter dies."

Her holo-screen went dark, flickering away. Scarlett dropped her arm. Her body shook with her inhale, somewhere between terror and rage.

Prax rubbed at her skin. "We'll get her back, love."

"How?"

Prax kissed her forehead and said softly, "The only way we can."

Scarlett glanced back at the door to the prison. Xenobaccus. To save her baby, she'd release a mad alien into the universe. Every person he hurt or killed after would be a stain on her conscience, but Scarlett would carry that burden if it meant Violet lived.

"Can you stand?"

Scarlett straightened in his grasp. "I can."

He said nothing more. Even her chatty prince had no comforting words. They were trapped. Argrix had Violet. Even if they thought to risk it and try rescuing her, Argrix had trapped Prax on Herkleios the moment he showed his face. The blackmail video ensured that.

Her mate gripped the wrists of the first guard by the prison door and started tugging. If they couldn't open the cell beside Xenobaccus, what would she do? Scarlett gave a harsh shake to her head. She wouldn't go there. Not if she didn't have to.

Scarlett drifted around her mate and aimlessly entered the prison. Her feet didn't stop once she got inside. She paced past Xenobaccus's cell before looping back. How long did they have before someone thought to check here for them?

"How dare you leave me?" Xenobaccus narrowed his purple eyes at Scarlett's pacing and Prax's dragging, but his curiosity didn't stop him from being a petulant brat. "I am a king. You're not dismissed until I say so."

Scarlett flipped him off as she passed. "Oh, fuck off."

Xenobaccus hissed. "You're as vile as the rest of them, human."

"Choke and die."

Stopping next to the neighboring cell, Prax dropped the first guard with a thud. He raised the unconscious male's wrist toward the forcefield, but nothing changed.

Scarlett's heart nearly stopped. "Does it not work?"

"We might need both guards. I'll get the second one."

As Prax exited the prison into the tunnels, he glared at the ex-king. Scarlett forced herself to stop beside the guard. She chewed at her lip. In a second, she'd be gnawing on her nails, a habit she hadn't fallen into since high school.

Xenobaccus's lips twitched, almost like he enjoyed her distress. What a creep. "Have you two deciphered my genius son's plan?"

"He gave us a device that will transport you to Prax's ship."

He bared his fangs, a full grin. "I'll be able to fly away easily, then."

"Not entirely." Scarlett jumped at Prax's grunted words as he dragged the second guard through the doorway. "I'm sure Anax ordered my arrest as soon as Argrix's blackmail went public. If you encounter resistance, blame your son."

"Blackmail?" Xenobaccus almost sounded excited. "What in Hyra's graces did you do?"

Prax dropped the guard next to his colleague. "It doesn't matter."

"You killed someone, didn't you?" Xenobaccus slapped his leg in laughter. "How wonderful. If my wife were alive, she'd be disappointed in you as her kin, Prax."

"Stop talking," Scarlett snapped.

"You don't give orders to me, human."

Scarlett approached the forcefield. "Until we get out of here, I do. Unless you'd like to rot."

Xenobaccus slithered as close as he could to the field. "No one gives me orders."

"Stop being an ass, Uncle." Prax lined the two guards beside each other. "Can you take the second guard's wrist, love?"

Scarlett reluctantly backed away from the forcefield. Settling next to the guard, she gripped his wrist. His blue scales were like pavement in the sun against her skin. She copied Prax's movement, bringing the male's wrist to the forcefield's edge. When a screen flickered across the film, Prax tapped an option. A quick buzz echoed through the air before the forcefield dropped.

Scarlett's shoulders slumped. "Thank God."

Together, she and Prax approached one of the small holes in the rock wall between the cells. Scarlett had to pop onto her toes to see through the space, but Xenobaccus was over six-feet tall. He glared through at them. "Hand me the device."

Prax pulled the golden sphere from his pocket, but didn't hand it over. "We're going with you."

"Hand it to me!"

Prax raised the sphere to Scarlett. She linked her hand over his, the little ball in between them. Whatever happened next, she had her mate. They'd get through this. "We're not letting you out of our sight until my daughter is returned."

Xenobaccus glared but didn't speak, which was as close to agreement as they were going to get. Prax offered his uncle a hand through the crevice. Scarlett shuddered as their scales met. Just the thought of touching him disturbed her.

"Hold on." In their joined hand, Prax squeezed, his palm pressing against the sphere's top. It clicked and beeped before a wave of tingling flooded Scarlett's body. The world went hazy and flickered out of existence, almost like she had stood too fast. Scarlett blinked and rubbed at her eyes.

And opened them to *The Carthak*'s control room.

A roar split the air, raising the hair on Scarlett's arms. Xenobaccus stood within arm's reach, his head thrown back in triumph. Scarlett nearly backed away, but Prax stood firm at her side. Her mate's muscular arms twitched, almost like he wanted to throttle the ex-king.

If he tried, Scarlett would sit back and cheer.

Without warning, *The Carthak*'s engine revved, the panels flashing with launch procedures. A little droid settled into place at the controls and tapped at a button. A holo-screen blipped into life in front of the front window, displaying a life-sized Argrix. The male lounged on his dark wood throne, tapping his dark claws against the armrest. His eyes quickly scanned the three of them before focusing on his father. "Your Majesty."

Xenobaccus settled into the chair at the main control panel and clapped his hands together. "I will reward you for this, my son."

"I want to be your sole heir, Father," Argrix said almost immediately. "No more plans of dividing the alliance planets among your children."

Xenobaccus's eyes narrowed slightly, but he quickly replaced it with a bared grin. "Your siblings are traitors. They'll live peaceful lives as our prisoners but will inherit nothing."

"Good." Argrix turned his gaze to Scarlett and Prax, his greedy grin twisting into a frown. "Why are you and your human still here?"

Scarlett raised her chin. "We're not leaving until you return Violet."

"Violet?"

"My daughter?"

"Ah." Argrix lazily waved his hands. "I don't have her."

Everything within Scarlett scratched to a halt. She stared blankly for a long second before screeching, "What?"

"Are you deaf, human? I don't have her."

Was this a trick? If only she could ask her mate, but both father and son kept their slitted eyes on them. Prax looked equally stunned, though. "We heard her voice, cousin."

"I had my spies take an audio recording in addition to photos. We used the sample to create what you heard."

Scarlett launched forward, hands fisted at her side. If only she could grab Argrix by the throat and squeeze. "I don't believe you."

"Why would I lie? I don't want your little spawn running around my ship." Argrix tapped at his golden wristband and expanded the hologram's view. He sat before a wide desk, schematics projected across the screens around him. Scarlett couldn't read the star charts, but Prax probably could. "We're a few hours from Herkleios, within the edges of Neithan space. Not only did I lack time to return to

Earth, but I couldn't risk getting blown out of the sky by *Etein's Might.*"

Scarlett glanced at her mate. She didn't think he was lying, but Prax knew his cousin and his ways far better than she did. "I can't take your word for it."

Xenobaccus threw up his hands. "I frankly don't care if you believe him. Get off my ship."

"It's not your ship, Uncle." Prax approached the left control panel and tapped the screen. "Violet's father has one of those human communication devices, yes?"

It took Scarlett a second to figure out what he meant. "A cellphone?"

Prax nodded as Scarlett approached his side. When she saw the numbers on the screen, the solution clicked in her brain. If Argrix didn't have Violet, then Andrew did. She dialed his number, thankful she had memorized it all those years ago. A ring echoed through the ship.

"Pick up, you bastard," Scarlett muttered at the screen.

The phone clicked and connected. "Hello?"

Scarlett had never been so happy to hear his craggy British voice. "Andrew, it's me. Do you have Violet?"

"Of course I have her." His tone changed instantly to barely contained contempt. "No thanks to you. You're not a very responsible parent, Scarlett."

"Excuse me?" Both Prax and Xenobaccus flinched at her pitch, but Scarlett ignored all the staring aliens to focus her ire on her ex. "I've been picking up the slack since Violet's birth. Don't you dare give me a lecture."

"Is that Mummy?" Violet asked in the background. Scarlett's knees weakened at the sound, dropping her into the panel's chair. Argrix hadn't lied. Her daughter was safe. "Can I talk to her?"

"See," Argrix said. "Your daughter—"

Scarlett ignored him. "Put her on the phone, Andrew."

"Just a minute, sweetheart," Andrew said, obviously not to Scarlett. Muffled sounds echoed through the line, like the creak of footsteps and a door clipping shut. "Look, Scar, there's a game tomorrow night. If you're not back by then, I'm dumping her at the police station."

God, how was her ex somehow worse than a murderous king and his evil son? "You will do no such thing! How much do you owe this time?"

"More than you can give me."

Andrew's gambling problem had been a point of contention during their relationship a decade ago and he had gotten deeper into debt with every year. "Just give me the number."

"Fifty-thousand pounds."

"Fifty-thousand?! Andrew!" That would more than drain her savings. But if she took out a second mortgage on her flat... Maybe. For Violet, she'd do anything.

Prax crouched at her side, not wanting to be overheard. "Tell that asshole I'll give him double what he's asking."

Scarlett's eyebrows raised. "Really? You have that much money?"

"My siblings and I have a trust. It will have to be converted, but what's mine is yours, love." He grasped her hand, filling her with ease. Scarlett had never been overly affectionate with her men, but touching Prax made everything better in the world. Heat threaded through her core. "But make sure he knows he'll only get it if he takes care of Violet until we return."

"God, I want to fuck you right now."

Xenobaccus nearly gagged and Argrix curled her lip, but it was Andrew's confused "Excuse me?" that dragged her back to reality.

Scarlett flipped off the panel's screen, wishing she might project it across space at Andrew. "If you heard that, you heard everything else. You'll get your money and then some. Between the two of you, I'd say Violet has more common sense, so just do everything she says. Now put her on the phone."

"Female," Argrix started.

Scarlett turned her middle finger on him, but her rage faded at the sweet sound of her daughter's voice.

"Hi Mummy! Daddy and I are having the best time. He lets me eat ice cream for breakfast."

Scarlett's eyes watered. "I'm glad to hear it! I'm sorry I can't be there with you right now, but I'm on my way back. I love you."

"Don't worry about me, Mummy. I'm making sure Daddy wakes up and gets me to school on time."

"Glad to hear it. Just remember you're the boss, okay?"

"I know, I know. Men need to be led."

Scarlett laughed. She had raised her daughter to be strong and confident, the two things she'd need to survive in this world. The two things Scarlett needed to be right now, despite the exhaustion weighing her down. "I'll see you soon, Vi!"

"Bye, Mummy."

When the line went dead, Scarlett clawed at the last of her energy and remained upright. Argrix didn't have her daughter. Violet might be safe now, but they had just released Xenobaccus on the galaxy.

She couldn't rest until they stopped him.

"As I said, your spawn is safe," Argrix nearly growled. "Now get off my *father's* ship."

Scarlett turned to him, hardened her eyes. Like hell she was letting the male who wanted to enslave humanity—

Prax popped to his feet, nearly dragging her with him. "We're leaving."

Scarlett frowned. "Prax?"

He pulled her into his arms, his lips to his ear. "Trust me."

Scarlett didn't even hesitate. "Okay, we're leaving now."

His mate started for the door, Prax backing along beside her. Argrix and Xenobaccus were letting them go, but that didn't mean he could trust them not to attack when they turned their backs. Though they had destroyed Prax's life with the security footage, he still had more to lose. His life. His mate. His new child.

Prax refused to sacrifice any of those things—and that meant stopping Xenobaccus.

His eyes scanned his three crossbows mounted on the wall. For this to work, he'd need a believable excuse. Prax settled on the one carved from an ancient tree on Etein's mountain.

Argrix let out an immediate growl. "What are you doing with that?"

"This is my great-grandfather's crossbow." He grabbed a quiver from under the bench, a dozen of his homemade arrows within. He'd only need one. "I'm taking it with me."

"You—"

"Shut up, Argrix," Xenobaccus snapped at him. "If it gets them off this ship, then so be it."

Argrix grumbled but obeyed his father. "You have one minute, Prax. If you're not off the ship by then, we're launching without you. And I won't be hospitable this time."

Prax glared at his cousin. If only the male were actually on the ship and not a hologram. "Understood."

He didn't turn until he reached the hall, the door to *The Carthak*'s control room sliding shut behind him. Pain panged through his heart, but he ignored it. His father had taught him to fly in this ship. But it was replaceable, unlike their lives.

Scarlett reached for his hand. "What's the plan?"

Prax didn't answer, not right away. Together, they rushed down the corridor for the outer doors. The minute counted down in his head.

"Prax?"

"Not here." Prax didn't know if the Neithans had installed any cameras in the hallway, but he couldn't risk revealing their only chance at stopping Xenobaccus.

Scarlett didn't question him again. When they turned the corner, the exit slid open to reveal Herkleian forest in the bright afternoon light. Under his feet, the engine rumbled harder. Prax wrapped one arm around Scarlett's waist and pushed into a run. His mate gripped at his sashes, but didn't even shout as they burst into the open air.

A second after touching down, the door slammed shut behind them.

Etein's mercies. They'd made it. Hot air shot out of *The Carthak*'s engines, pushing Prax and Scarlett away from the ship. They approached the treeline. Scarlett put a hand over her eyes to watch the ship rise, but Prax quickly lowered his crossbow to the ground. He pulled a small knife from his back pocket, the weapon standard issue for a Herkleian guard.

The glint of the blade caught Scarlett's eyes. "Where did you get that?"

"Off one guard in the tunnel." At his mate's questioning look, he tapped at it, causing the blade to pulse with electricity. "Each blade has a power core in the hilt to allow for the electricity."

"Which is helpful, how?"

Prax pried the hilt open and gently plucked the blue, glowing core between his nails. He pulled an arrow from his quiver. Anax hadn't left behind the electric arrows from their hunt, but this was the closest thing. "If I fire this into the thrusters, it will explode. Not enough to damage the ship, but Argrix put an explosive device near the engine."

Her jaw dropped. "You're going to blow up your own ship?"

"*The Carthak* will never be mine again." Prax wanted to take her hand and convince her, but he didn't have time. His ship rose slowly into the air. Soon, it'd be too high for him to hit, even with his skill. "We have to do this, Scarlett. I can't let that male loose on the galaxy."

She didn't need more convincing than that. "What can I do to help?"

"I need something to thread through it and..."

Scarlett tore at one of the vine sashes wrapping around his chest, snapping it from the rest of his ensemble.

"That will work."

He threaded the sash through the metallic loop at the power core's end as Scarlett took the arrow from him. She held it before him as he twisted the fabric around the arrowhead's base. With the right knot, it would stay in place long enough to get chewed up in the thrusters.

Prax plucked the carved crossbow from the ground and threaded the arrow into place. "You should go."

"I'm not leaving you, Prax."

"I'll be right under *The Carthak* when it explodes. It won't be safe." Prax caressed his knuckles down her cheek. He wanted to spend a hundred years with his mate, but no one would get the chance to live a happy life with Xenobaccus on the loose. Prax had let him go. It was his responsibility to stop him. "Please, love, go to the trees."

She put a hand on his shoulder. "We do this together."

"Scarlett—"

She put a finger across his lips. "You said we don't have a lot of time left."

He scanned her face, committing it to memory. "I love you."

"I love you, too, Prax."

Prax let out a final exhale before turning and raising his crossbow to the sky. *The Carthak* twisted, its thrusters almost in the right position—

He aimed and fired.

His arrow shot into the sky and slammed into the left thruster. For a second, nothing happened. By the Empire. If the power core didn't explode—

The only warning Prax had was the crunching sound, like metal grinding together. He dropped his crossbow and wrapped himself around Scarlett's body.

Overhead, the ship exploded. Flaming parts spewed to the ground, followed by a wave of burning energy. It ripped Prax from his feet and slammed him to the ground.

Everything went dark.

A LOW BEEPING pulled Prax from the darkness.

He jolted awake, the harshness of his breath like an alarm in the silence. The sterile golden room had the glowing rock ceilings of the palace, but otherwise it could be any Herkleian infirmary. He sunk into the levitating med-bed beneath him, the metallic surface molding to his form. Nano-bandages lined his chest where his pain stabbed the worst. Like he had lost scales, his flesh a sobbing ruin. Prax grit his teeth, but he couldn't drop his head and surrender to sleep.

Not until he found Scarlett.

"You're awake." A Herkleian doctor appeared at the end of his bed, the female's eyes flickering between him and the holo-screen above his head displaying his vitals.

"Where—" Prax choked on the words, his throat tasting of ash.

"Let me get you some water," the doctor said. "There's minor smoke damage to your lungs, but nothing our nanites can't fix."

"Scarlett," Prax tried again, ignoring the uncomfortable scratching.

"Ah, you want to know about your human companion? She's sleeping in another of our med-beds—"

"Prax?" a voice croaked.

Scarlett. Prax tried to throw himself to his feet, but it was like his entire body burst into flames. He crashed back to the med-bed with a growl as the doctor rushed to his side.

"Idiot," she muttered. "You're going to tear your wounds."

"Is he okay?" Scarlett shouted. He still couldn't see her, but her voice echoed nearby. Prax closed his eyes and inhaled, searching for her scent. The intoxicating smell reached his nostrils. Close. So close.

"He's fine." The doctor tapped at the holo-screen projecting from her wristband. "You can ask him yourself, as long as you insist he stay down."

The wavering screen at the edge of the infirmary cubicle faded from white to translucent. Prax's heart stuttered when he met dark brown eyes. His Scarlett. A nano-bandage wrapped around her head and clumps of her hair had singed away, but she otherwise looked whole. She sat up in her med-bed, leaning as far as she could towards him.

When the doctor spotted that, she narrowed her eyes. "Not you, too. Stay in your beds."

"Having trouble with our patients, Doctor Gala?"

Prax stiffened as the infirmary doors opened and Anax strolled into the room. Without his crown and jewels, the male's exhaustion was obvious, his blue scales lacking their luster. No guards followed him, but Prax got a glimpse of a contingent in the wall, helmets a gleaming gold. He doubted they were there to protect the king. How many crimes had Prax committed in the last day? He couldn't even guess.

Doctor Gala dropped into a bow. "Nothing I can't handle, Your Majesty."

Anax bared his fangs briefly, but when he turned to survey Scarlett and Prax, his face cleared of emotion. "Are they well enough to talk?"

"The lady is," Doctor Gala said. "I don't recommend His Highness speak much for a few more hours."

"That will have to do." Anax settled between their two cubicles, locking his hands behind his back. Like a commander about to discipline his soldiers. "Thank you, Gala. Can you wait outside?"

She bowed again. "Of course, Your Majesty."

The doctor's soft steps retreated away from the door, probably towards an office. Prax hadn't ever needed to enter the palace's infirmary. Despite many of his childhood visits ending with scrapes and bruises, Prax and his cousins had always refused medical help.

But the male standing before him wasn't his friend, his cousin. Anax was King of Herkleios now, and that was who said, "You two have a lot of explaining to do."

"Anax—" Prax coughed.

He held up a hand. "What I know so far is that you broke my father out of his prison cell only to blow him into pieces less than ten minutes later."

"It's my fault, Your Majesty," Scarlett said.

"Scarlett..."

She didn't give him a chance to argue, not that he could in his current state. "Argrix kidnapped my daughter. Or, at least, we thought he did."

Violet. Prax's pulse spiked. Would Argrix have tried to hurt her in revenge? Certainly. Though his throat scraped, he managed to say, "We need to send someone to check on her right away."

"We saw the prison's footage, cousin." Anax's face softened for an instant at their concern. "As soon as your mate mentioned her daughter, Empress Ailis ordered soldiers from *Etein's Might* to go down to Earth and find her. She's well."

Thank Etein. No matter how furious his mother probably was, she wouldn't want to see an innocent child harmed. "Thank you—" The rest of Anax's words settled in his mind. "My mate?"

"We saw your marks, too. Congratulations."

Prax lowered his head to the med-bed. Announcing his mate to his family should have been a joyous occasion, not the somber event that this was. Not one fraught with betrayal. Prax closed his eyes. He couldn't regret his choices. With Violet on the line, he made the best decision he could. "I'm sorry, cousin. We shouldn't have lied to you."

"I understand why you did it. My younglings have not yet been born, yet I know I'd betray Hyra herself to protect them." Anax paused, a heavy silence. "The problem isn't my father's death, Prax. We reported to the rest of the alliance that he died in a failed escape attempt."

Scarlett answered him, voice soft. "The problem is the footage."

He nodded. "The Zocastans are enraged. Your mother is meeting with their emissary right now."

"I see," Prax managed.

"You'll probably lose your throne."

Prax glanced at his mate. His beautiful, precious mate with her sharp tongue and sharper mind. If he could travel back in time, even knowing what the future would bring, he wouldn't change a thing for her. "Some things are worth more than a throne."

When she smiled, his heart nearly burst. "Oh, Prax."

Anax awkwardly cleared his throat. "The Zocastans want a public apology, but I'll tell both their emissary and your mother that you're not well enough yet."

Prax nodded at his cousin but didn't speak again. He couldn't take his eyes off his mate. Anax exited the infirmary, the door sliding closed behind him. Leaving them together in silence.

"Scarlett, I—"

"Don't talk." She pushed at the blanket covering her and climbed from her med-bed. No alarms went off to summon the doctor from her office. His mate's injuries weren't as severe as his. Thankfully. She pulled at the levitating stool at his bedside and settled into the seat. "Anax is right, you need to rest."

"So do you."

"I'll rest easier when I know you're okay."

Prax took her hand. "With you, I'll always be okay."

"Let me worry, Prax. I'm your mate after all."

If only Prax were healed and whole. He'd pull his love into his lap and kiss her senseless. "I think that might be the first time you've said it aloud."

"It might be the first, but it won't be the last." She stroked her palm gently across his forearm. "I want to spend the rest of my life with you, Prax M'Etein. You're reckless and impulsive, yet brave and kind. Both my perfect balance and my perfect match."

Like she was to him. The doctor's orders vanished from his mind. Prax stroked a hand to her jaw and lured his mate's mouth to him. She came willingly. Eagerly. Before their lips touched, he murmured, "Whatever you desire, Scarlett. Always."

"Are you ready, love?" Prax asked, taking Scarlett's hand on the sidewalk before the three-story brick house crawling with blooming vines.

Scarlett bumped her shoulder against his. "I am. I think."

"You and Violet will love it."

If any other man said that, Scarlett would be inclined not to believe them, but so far neither she nor Violet had disagreed with any of Prax's housing choices.

As Scarlett climbed the steps, a sense of disbelief swept over her. She never could have imagined this eight months ago. Like Anax had said, Prax couldn't get away completely unpunished. The true events surrounding Xenobaccus's death remained a secret only known to the Herkleian and Eógan royal families, but the scandal with the footage from *Zaghan's Rage* quickly reached every corner of the galaxy. To satisfy the Zocastans and the rest of the Intergalactic Alliance, Prax had abdicated his place in line for the Eógan throne.

Not that Prax seemed to miss his old title. When she had asked, he happily agreed to move to Earth. Scarlett had expected him to want a little cottage in the woods like the hunting lodge he left behind on Eógan, but they had settled on a house in London. Violet had cheered when learning she could stay at her school, earning Prax a dozen points in the dad department.

But her mate took it one step further. After listening to her critiques of the dozens of home renovation shows they watched late at night, he set out to design the house of her dreams. He had consulted Scarlett on a few decisions but was set on surprising her.

Scarlett planned to love it no matter what.

She cautiously walked through the threshold, bracing for the unsteady planks she remembered previously there. But instead she stepped into a beautiful foyer, the perfect blend of modern and warmth. The marble she had picked out looked even better in person, but her eyes drifted to the hardwood circular staircase's commanding presence. Dozens of plants dotted the side tables, both Earth-grown and transported from Eógan. A blending of two worlds like their life.

"Oh, wow." Tears wet Scarlett's eyes, the emotion threatening to overwhelm her. "It's perfect, Prax."

He chuckled. "You've only seen one room."

"It's enough."

"You can't live in the foyer, love."

"Watch me."

Prax laughed and propped himself against the wall, one finger hooking through the belt of his jeans. The first time he had worn human clothing, Scarlett had torn them right off him. Who knew aliens looked so great in jeans? Stretched jean, the fabric straining over his muscles.

Heat flushed through Scarlett, making a beeline for her core. Despite being together for eight months and married for six, Scarlett couldn't get enough of her mate. She'd never grow tired of him.

She propped a hip against a table. "Want to show me the bedroom next? Violet's at school for a few more hours."

Prax prowled forward, closing the space between them. "I have a better idea."

"Better than the bedroom?"

He winked before grabbing her hand and leading her through the living room. Plush couches surrounded an empty accent wall of dark wood. Small holo-screens became recently available on Earth, but Prax had ordered one from Eógan in the place of a TV. They'd be the envy of all their friends and neighbors. Scarlett had already planned a housewarming party to coincide with the opening ceremony of the Intergalactic Games. She wouldn't have nearly enough room to fit everyone who wanted to watch Earth's first space competition from a high-def, alien screen—nor enough room to fit all the rival factions. Scarlett couldn't decide between Team Earth and Team Eógan and Prax made it worse by informing her his cousin, Rivix, was part of Team Fenrik. Could she cheer on all three?

But thoughts of space sports and house parties all disappeared from her mind when Prax turned the corner, walking her into a kitchen. Blue cabinetry with silver decals contrasted perfectly with a massive marble-like stone island. Scarlett brushed her hands against the surface, threaded through with silver like the rock from Prax's ship. Exactly like the rock from Prax's ship.

"Is this from Eógan?"

"A wedding present from my mother," he said. "White stone from Etein's mountain is quite rare."

"I love it." Scarlett spread her arms wide, nearly hugging the countertop. The cold of the stone made the heat within her burn to a fever pitch. "Goddamn, this is a sexy kitchen."

Prax paused behind her. "I thought you might like it."

Scarlett turned and hopped onto the counter. Slowly, she crossed her legs, giving Prax a peek up her skirt. "I love it! Just look at this island."

But Prax didn't come forward. He circled around her like a barely restrained predator. "Do you need a moment alone with your kitchen or do you still want to see the bedroom?"

She batted her eyelashes at him. "The activity I have in mind doesn't require a bedroom."

His scales darkened to that forest green she knew led to endless pleasure. Prax stopped his pacing, settling before her. His cock strained at his pants, already fully erect and threatening to break free.

She unhooked her legs and pulled at the top button of her blouse. "I see kitchens seem to do it for you, too."

"Not exactly, my love." He reached forward and grabbed her knee. Scarlett gasped at the touch, a tsunami of wet heat flooding through her. "What turns me on is the thought of pounding you against the rock again and again."

Scarlett licked her lips. "That's one way to test out a counter."

Prax's hand trailed down her inner thigh. "Is that a yes?"

She grabbed the lapel of his shirt. "It's always a yes from me, Prax."

He settled between her legs, the scruff of his jeans pressing against the thin cotton of her underwear. Scarlett bit off a moan. His hands circled her hips and settled on the curve of her belly. In a few more weeks, Scarlett's pregnancy would show, but right now their little Eógan-Earthling prince or princess was a secret between them. Once they told Violet, it'd be impossible to keep the news quiet.

When she met his red-eyed gaze, Scarlett's heart nearly burst. She wrapped her legs around his waist and pulled him closer. Prax came willingly with a growl. She threaded her hands through his hair and gripped his horns. His mouth closed over hers. Absolute perfection. Scarlett moaned and wiggled, wanting him closer. Wanting him in her.

He bit at her lip. "Patience, mate."

Scarlett flicked at the button on his pants. "When have I ever been patient?"

Prax chuckled, a deep, resounding noise, but he choked off when Scarlett wrapped a hand around his thick length.

Before she could speak, the world twirled as Prax flipped her over and hiked her skirts. Her breasts pressed into the cold of the stone. She dropped her head as his fingers slid into her warm depths. Her mate. Her everything. Her world.

"I love you, Prax," she panted. "I love you so, so much."

"I love you, too, beloved."

***

Thank you for reading! Our next alien prince is Rivix, the ice-skinned flirt from Chapter 14! After terrorists attack the Intergalactic Games, the prince will have to work together with his rival, a bold Earthling named Ivy with a troubled past.

Scarlett paced the foyer of her flat for the hundredth time, almost stuck in a little loop between her umbrella rack and mirror. When she glanced down at her smartwatch, only three minutes had passed. She let out a frustrated sigh and plopped into the chair by the entry.

Violet settled next to her, the tulle of her skirt brushing Scarlett's knuckles. "It's okay, Mummy."

Scarlett smoothed her daughter's blond hair. Less than two weeks ago, she had thought her daughter kidnapped, alone and afraid on an alien ship. While that had been a ruse, the four days it took to travel from Herkleios to Earth weren't any less torturous. Her mate had done his best to distract her—a great talent of his—but nothing truly stopped her worry until she had Violet in her arms.

And today, her two worlds would collide. Both Scarlett and Prax agreed it was best for her to spend a few days alone with her daughter before making an introduction. Not only did it allow Scarlett to explain everything to Violet, but it also gave Prax time to attend to his princely duties. Namely, trying to avoid an intergalactic incident.

Scarlett pushed that from her mind. Alien politics weren't her concern today. Her daughter was. There was so much riding on this meeting. She loved Prax and wanted to be with him, but what if Violet hated him? For Violet's entire life, it had been just the two of them. Her father made the rare appearance, but mother and daughter were inseparable.

How would their dynamic change once Prax entered the picture?

When the knock echoed through the flat, Scarlett's heart jumped. Before she climbed from her chair, Violet ran to open it. Scarlett flushed like a girl on her prom night, ready for her parents to evaluate her date. But then the door opened and Prax was there, his large, emerald-scaled frame filling her doorway. He was just as gorgeous as she remembered. Maybe even more so given his dark-washed jeans and V-neck shirt. Scarlett wanted to throw herself into his arms, but she held back to let Violet receive him.

The ever polite and very British Violet stuck out her hand. "A pleasure to meet you."

Prax's lips twitched as he took her small hand in his. "I've heard so much about you."

"I know," Violet said in all seriousness. "Mummy loves to tell everyone how great I am."

Prax's red eyes flickered to her, his smile now barely contained. "She certainly does. I hear you're top of your class at your academy."

"It's called school, silly. I have a lot to teach you about Earth now that you're Mum's boyfriend."

"I'll take all the help I can get. Earth is still new to me." As Violet backed from the door, Prax followed her into their flat. Together, they settled onto separate sides of the couch. The sight of her small human daughter and a massive, horned alien on her pink velvet sofa nearly made her cackle.

Prax shuffled forward, the ridges of his spine stopping him from fully sinking into his seat. "It smells great in here."

"Thanks." Scarlett quickly popped into the kitchen to grab a tray. When she re-entered the living room, Prax's eyes lit with excitement. "What better way to welcome you to London than with tea and scones?"

"I helped with the scones," Violet chimed in.

"We're really more bakers than cooks."

"That's an understatement." The moment Scarlett lowered the tray to the (table), Violet grabbed for a blueberry scone. "We eat take-away multiple times a week."

Scarlett flinched as she lowered to the armchair. "We're trying to make a good impression, Vi."

"He's going to figure it out once he tastes your food."

"I'm really not that bad—"

Prax chuckled. "I'll order a materializer immediately."

Violet's brow furrowed. "What's a materializer?"

"It's a Herkleian invention that can create any food instantly."

Her mouth rounded into an O. "Any food I want at the touch of a button?"

He snapped his claws together. "In the blink of an eye."

Scarlett arranged the three tea cups and started pouring. "I hope it has a child lock or someone's going to have cavities."

Violet ignored that. Her daughter plucked her teacup from the tray and sipped delicately. Her brown eyes keenly examined Prax. After a moment of silence, she said, "Prax, what are your intentions with my mum?"

"Well, Violet, I'd like to spend the rest of my life with her."

"Would you marry her? Mummy's never been married before."

Scarlett blushed again, her face near burning red, but Prax only smiled and sipped at his tea, "Only with your blessing."

"Good answer." Violet sat back, like a principal about to make a judgement call. Her daughter would make an amazing CEO one day. "Mummy, do you love him?"

"I do."

Violet nodded, like that settled something. "Then I do, too."

Scarlett nearly slumped into her chair. What a relief. The two pieces of her life slotted together, fitting like pieces of a puzzle. Prax reached for her hand and squeezed. At the touch of him, she nearly jumped. God, how she had missed him. How had they only been parted for mere days?

"Are you going to have a baby?"

"What?" Scarlett almost choked on her scone. Sure, she was blunt, but Violet always gave her a run for her money.

Prax wasn't nearly as phased. "Would you like a sibling?"

"Yes! I want a brother and a sister, so you'll have to keep trying until you get one of each."

Prax winked at Scarlett. "I think we can arrange that."

Scarlett playfully slapped at his hand, but she couldn't help but laugh. She hadn't imagined a future with a husband or more kids. The Scarlett of a month ago would be aghast at all her life's changes—especially at how quickly they occurred. But with her mate at her side and her daughter smiling, everything felt right.

For once, everything *was* right.

RIVIX

BRIDE TO AN ALIEN PRINCE, BOOK 4

ONE

IVY

Ivy leisurely twirled her ankle, careful to hide her twitch of pain.

No one paid any attention to her, but she couldn't risk showing weakness. Her competitors—both alien and human—sat around tables in *The White Serpent*'s mess hall. A dozen skaters she knew from the contest circuit on Earth had invited some of the long-haired, ice-skinned Fenrish to join them, their conversation echoing through the room. Not that Ivy wanted to join them. She didn't mind being alone. A bit of an introvert, she was content doing her own thing. But that didn't mean she didn't envy them.

Ivy tried not to stare, instead focusing on the glinting silver walls interspersed with frosted white glass. The Fenrish commissioned the spaceship specifically for the Intergalactic Games and put in the design hours to match. Ivy commended their dedication to the planet's colors, but after a day onboard, she was sick of all the monochrome.

Still, it beat the planes and buses she normally took between events. In the last decade, Ivy had traveled to competitions in Helsinki, Gangneung, and Sochi. Never would she have imagined an actual flipping spaceship taking her to skate in another galaxy.

Well, she wasn't exactly skating, not with her ankle.

As if thinking about the body part summoned its wrath, shooting pain stabbed up her leg. Ivy flinched, but squeezed her hand, jabbing her nails into her palm. Few people knew the story behind her transition from skater to coach and she didn't feel like telling it to anyone. She had fractured her ankle landing a jump nearly two years ago. It was a fairly common injury for a skater, and at thirty, Ivy was already towards the end of her career. But early retirement was just a part of the deal, a consequence of throwing your body into the air and making gravity-defying spins.

So here she was, a washed-up skater on her way to an alien planet. At least she had never imagined competing in the Intergalactic Games. Ivy had suffered her injury weeks before first contact with the Intergalactic Alliance, a collection of twelve planets spread across the galaxy.

A towering alien female with vibrant feathers in the place of hair and sand-like skin passed her table, causing Ivy to nearly spit out her coffee. Transportation between Earth and the alliance planets had only opened to regular folks a few months ago, and Ivy hadn't spotted any aliens in Chicago. Her encounters before this week had been limited to the news on her TV. The leaders of the alliance, the Herkleians, had received the most coverage, so Ivy had prepared for seven-foot, blue-scaled aliens with towering horns.

What she hadn't prepared for was the dozen other species.

She tapped at the smartwatch-esque bracelet given to her on arrival and discretely scrolled through some pictures. A Guroverian, maybe? When the Games Committee had told her a Fenrish ship would provide her transportation to Herkleios for the opening ceremony, she had studied the Fens and figured she'd have time to review the others. But apparently the Fenrish ship had made some stops along the way to Earth.

"Can I go to a party with the other skaters when we land?" The voice shattered through Ivy's solitude as a blond teenager sat at the table and crossed her arms. Knowing Addison, pouting and eye-rolling were seconds away.

Ivy sipped her coffee. Yelling at eighteen-year-olds wasn't professional, was it? They'd already had this conversation. "You're too young."

"So? There's no legal drinking age on Herkleios."

"That's because they can't get drunk unlike you." New alien alcohols had appeared in supermarkets, but none from the Herkleians, who were literally incapable of drunkenness. "You'd either make a fool of yourself or be hungover the next day. We can't have either of those things."

Addison scoffed. "You sound like my mom. You know I've drunk before, Ivy? I'm not a child."

Ivy squared her shoulders, trying to put on her best stern face. She was new to all this, but she remembered the discipline her coaches drilled into her. Ivy had always rejected the wild ways of other contestants. "I'm not your mother, but I *am* your coach. You're an athlete, Addison. One of the first humans to compete in the Intergalactic Games. You aren't here to make friends and party, you're here to win."

Addison pursed her lips. "What about the opening ceremony after-parties? They're *almost* like official events."

Ivy sighed. Addison clearly wasn't getting the point. Ivy almost regretted taking this job, but she had been desperate for a student after her accident. Ivy had never placed higher than bronze during her fourteen-year career. "We'll discuss it after we land."

"Discuss it? What kind of deal is that?" Addison waved as one of her friends passed them. When she returned her attention to Ivy, it was like she'd forgotten the entire conversation. "Does the Intergalactic Games do medals? I don't want to miss out on my podium moment because these aliens don't know what's up."

Ivy resisted sighing a second time. "You didn't read the information package I gave you."

It was more a statement than a question, but Addison shrugged in response, anyway. "Nope, and I don't plan on it. I'm more of a hands-on learner."

Ivy tapped at her bracelet again, enlarging the holo-screen projection from a small square to the size of a tablet. Before the games, the Intergalactic Alliance had altered their tech to be compatible with cellphones, which allowed her to sync her files to this device. She pulled up her information package.

"Ivy—" Addison started.

"The Intergalactic Alliance began hosting games similar to our Olympics over thirty years ago when the first treaty was signed between Herkleios and Eógan." Addison's pout somehow grew larger, but Ivy ignored it. In their year together as coach and skater, Ivy had learned to disregard most of Addison's complaints. "The games combine the traditions of all twelve—now thirteen—alliance members. Some of their sports are unfamiliar to us, but there's also overlap, skating being one of them."

"None of that answers my medal question."

Ivy skipped forward a few pages until she came to a sketch of three stones. "There are medals, yes, but they're made of Herkleian rock. Rupini, topazi and zapher."

Addison leaned forward in her seat, eyes pinned on the blue rock hovering above the yellow and red ones. "So I'm aiming for the zapher?"

"Exactly."

"That's all I really need to know, then." Her student pushed to a stand—

Ivy snapped her fingers. "Sit down, Addison."

"Ugh, fine."

If Addison wasn't such a great skater, Ivy would've quit months ago. But she needed this girl. If she won, Ivy's reputation as a coach would be sealed. She'd have students lined up for the rest of her life. "We're headed to Herkleios for the opening ceremony. We should be there in two days and once we arrive, we'll only be there briefly before leaving for our competition planet. But not to worry, there's designated rink time for you to practice." Addison rolled her eyes. "All the skating competitions take place on Fenrik, which has a cold environment and a thousand or so frozen lakes."

"Ugh, I don't wanna go to a cold planet."

"We're skaters, Addison. We're used to the cold."

"Speak for yourself," she muttered.

Ivy opened her mouth to chide Addison when her breath caught in her throat. A Fenrish male stalked into the room, a towel thrown over his bare shoulder. Unlike the other Fens she had met, this one had dark hair and a sharp yet handsome face. Her eyes trailed the beard over his strong jaw before finding the muscled expanse of his shoulders. The skin over his rippled abs glinted like ice in the artificial light, but the odd color didn't stop Ivy's mouth from watering. Tall and menacing and self-assured, everything her terrible taste in men desired.

"Ivy?" Her student's voice ripped her from her stupor, but not fast enough. Addison had already twisted around. "Damn. I'd let him break me in half."

Ivy stiffened as Addison's voice echoed through the mess hall. Competitors a table over stifled their giggles. Ivy couldn't stop her face from flushing a red to clash with her hair. Sure, she'd been thinking the same thing, but Ivy never mixed business with pleasure. She looked but never touched. "Stop it."

But the alien had already noticed their stares—and instead of ignoring them, he aimed straight for their table.

TWO

Rivulets of frosting sweat dripped down Rivix's chest.

He grabbed his towel and wiped his face, letting the remaining drops trickle slowly to the gym's floor. Some stilled and froze, but his body heat combined with the ship's artificial gravity would take care of them. Thousands of years ago, his ancestors had power over ice. The ability still manifested, though it was rare and weak. Rivix couldn't freeze more than a tub of water even at the threat of a whipping.

And the monks had more than threatened him.

He twinged as his hand went to his back, the ghost of stinging pain flaring through him. His fingers met smooth skin. Brother Magnus had reluctantly dressed his wounds with nano-salve, the potent medicine leaving behind no trace of a scar. If Rivix was a regular boy, the abbot wouldn't have bothered. But when his mother visited, nothing had to seem amiss.

Rivix wiped down his equipment as his holo-screen downloaded his stats. Though he retired after winning zapher at the last Intergalactic Games and no longer had to keep up his vigorous workout regime, he enjoyed the activity. The females certainly didn't complain, either. More than that, Rivix enjoyed knowing he could fight should the occasion arrive. Not that he had to often. As the youngest of seven children, no one would challenge him for his father's throne.

He pushed into the hallway, towel thrown over his shoulders. The Fens around him gave him brief nods when he passed, but only a spotted Zocastan dropped into a dramatic bow. A decade ago, after returning from the monastery to civilization, Rivix had awkwardly paused at each bow, but now he all but ignored it. It helped his own people didn't care anymore. Rivix might have been a prince, but he didn't have any real power. Helga's skulls, his elder sister's six-month-old baby was ahead of him in the line of succession. But other members of the Intergalactic Alliance weren't as familiar with him and *The White Serpent's* hallways crawled with outsiders.

Rivix passed the door to the mess hall, but his stomach rumbled when a savory aroma drifted past his nose. Eating was another thing he forgot to do, even all these years later. The Osträsk monks ate one meal a day. His first week at the monastery had his stomach growling and twisting, but he had grown used to it by the time he left.

But he might as well eat now. He had little else to do until they arrived at Herkleios. Without a rink, he couldn't train Sigrid. She already had enough discipline in her life and didn't need his constant tutelage.

Rivix aimed for the wall of materializers, his eyes scanning the mess hall. Skaters from Team Fenrik had joined a group of Earthlings, but the room was quiet otherwise. There was an empty table in the back, past two Earthlings—

Everything within Rivix stilled. His gaze slid past the pale-haired, younger Earthling and settled on the other. Her bright red curls were a dramatic contrast to her cream-colored skin. Rivix had grown used to the color thanks to his cousins' human brides, but he had never found an Earthling appealing until now. His blood roared through his veins, practically singing. What was happening to him?

He tried to glance away, but his gaze refused the order. Their eyes clashed. She stared back at him, her skin taking on a pink tint.

He closed the distance between them, almost unconsciously. As he approached, the female's spine stiffened, but she couldn't look away, almost as enraptured as he was. Within arms' reach, her scent reached his nose. Gentle and floral like the blåis flower, the only plant to grow on the snowy mountains around the monastery. Rivix had collected them for All-Mother Gundhil's bedside when she visited the monastery.

"Um," the younger female said, interrupting his thoughts. She stood from her seat with a roll of her blue eyes. "This is weird, so I'm going to leave you two to continue staring at each other."

Rivix stiffened. The teenage human was right. He was just star-ing. *Wretched boy.* Brother Magnus's voice brought his practiced smile to his face like an ice-whip to the skin. Where were his manners? Where was his charm? He had spent years cultivating his persona after the monastery destroyed him. Rivix was better than this.

He grabbed the back of the chair, but kept his eyes on the female. Slowly, he raised a single eyebrow in question, the quirk of his lip following the upward movement. "May I sit?"

At the sound of his voice, the female jumped. "Oh. Um. I guess?"

Not the excited response he expected, but he'd take it. There was something about this female. Something that had his blood pumping, his fingers itching to touch.

With a single, graceful move, he swept into the chair and leaned back, exposing the muscled lines of his chest. The Earthling's eyes immediately dropped—not that her attention had stayed on his face for long. She had stared at his exposed body since he entered the mess hall.

"I'm Rivix." He raised his hand in what the Earthlings called a handshake. He had witnessed his cousin, King Anax of Herkleios, greet his mate's human family that way. The gesture was hopefully standard procedure.

"Ivy," she replied, her hands still flat on the table.

Ivy. He'd heard the word before from Queen Alexandra, referencing some type of Earth plant. Was it as prickly as this female? Something had entered her eyes, a stern shield over her earlier lust. But Rivix had seen it. He knew it was there. And he wasn't one to repress his feelings.

He propped his elbow on the table, watching as her eyes devoured the movement. It was all the confirmation he needed. "Do you want to fuck?"

Her mouth popped open to match the widening of her eyes. "Excuse me?"

He frowned. A Fenrish female would consider the request honestly, but Ivy seemed insulted. Why insulted? Wasn't it a compliment? The sight of her filled him with so much desire, he wanted her right here and now. If only his cousins were aboard. He had never asked about the culture of their human brides—an oversight he now regretted.

She pushed her chair away from the table, the pretty pink tint of her cheeks now a red to match her hair. "Who the hell do you think you are?"

Hadn't he introduced himself? Perhaps she hadn't listened, too concentrated on his body. "Rivix? Prince of Fenrik?"

A wave of emotions flashed across her face, the flush fading from her skin. "Prince?"

"Did I not say that?"

She swallowed and pointed upward at the ship around them. "So this is your ship?"

"It's my family's, yes."

Ivy stared at him for a moment before fixing him with a grin. If the expression could be called a grin. It was forced, jagged like icicles. "I apologize for my earlier tone, Your Highness, but no, I don't want to fuck."

He had said something wrong. But what? If only his cousin Prax were on this ship with him. From what Rivix gathered, Prax had insulted his human mate half a-dozen-times in their courtship. Now they were expecting their first child together.

Rivix stilled. Courtship? Children? What was wrong with him? He had sworn to never reproduce. If his children possessed his abilities, the Osträsk would come for them. The treaty between his father's citizens and the religious nomads demanded it. Rivix wouldn't subject another to his fate.

But that didn't mean he couldn't have some fun with the human. Fun and nothing else. "Perhaps another time?"

Ivy jumped to her feet, her tone rising. "Perhaps never!"

Her flush had returned, but her expression was different this time. Abashed, maybe? Certainly interested. "I doubt that."

"You know what—" She nearly shouted before wrangling her words under control. "It was... *nice* to meet you, Your Highness. Goodbye."

She turned on her boots and hightailed it to the door. Though she had the grace of a skater, she favored her right leg over her left. Brother Magnus had trained Rivix to recognize weakness at a moment's notice. Rivix smiled suddenly. This female wasn't weak. She'd deck him for the thought. The idea thrilled him, a shiver travelling down his spine.

If there was anything Rivix loved, it was a challenge.

"It was nice to meet you, too, Ivy," he called out.

She stiffened, the entire room quieting to glance between them. She twisted, just slightly, but it was enough for her to see him—shirtless, elbow on the table, chin in his hand, and lips twisted into a wide grin. Her eyes flashed at the dare in his voice. A feisty one, wasn't she?

Ivy stomped out of the room, but not out of Rivix's mind. He leaned back in the chair, propping a foot on the table.

The one thing Rivix loved more than a challenge was a win.

THREE

IVY

Ivy watched in awe as Herkleios grew larger and larger in the observation deck's window. Purple and blue and gold, the planet somehow looked like Earth and yet so foreign. She climbed from the bench and pressed her hands to the glass. Breathing in and out, she relished the sight and the silence. This early in the morning, all the competitors were in the gym or sleeping. Ivy couldn't do either. She avoided public gyms after her injury, but had spent most of her life hitting the ice at dawn. Ivy hadn't slept past 6 a.m. in decades. Now her mornings were her own, a time to enjoy the quiet and exist with no one's expectations.

As she scanned Herkleios, her stomach fluttered. Something important was about to happen. Something big. She had experienced a feeling like this before, the morning she won bronze at her last Olympics. It was like her body knew everything was about to change.

Addison would do well. Her student would make her career. But repeating that to herself didn't ease her nerves.

A ding echoed through the observation room. "Welcome to Herkleios. Please follow the directions on your holo-screen to disembark the ship."

Ivy let out one last breath and brushed off the feeling. With a quick detour to her room, she collected her already-packed bags and headed for the transport room. Only half-a-dozen other passengers were in line. Ivy checked her bracelet. Addison had messaged her an hour ago about heading to the gym. That gave Ivy another hour to get settled before Addison even left the ship.

"Next," the technician called. Ivy entered the room and stepped onto a circular platform next to two female Fens. They chatted lightly in their own language, but Ivy didn't eavesdrop. Just because she had a translator implant didn't mean she had any right to their conversation.

A tingle crept up her spine. Ivy stiffened. What was—?

The entire world disappeared in a rainbow of colors for a brief instant. Ivy nearly screamed, but before she formed the sound, the transporter deposited her in a gilded lobby. Bright sun beamed down on her skin through a glass ceiling and potted, glowing plants replaced the Fenrish ship's blandness. Ivy gaped. She didn't know what to expect on Herkleios, but the reality blew her wildest dreams out of the water. She unconsciously drifted toward the front door to peer at a modern city of sleek, gold towers and twisting highrises. High above, floating vehicles landed on a floating chunk of city over a spiraled structure. Ivy's breath caught. She couldn't help but stop and stare.

She was standing on an alien planet.

"Miss?" The voice pulled Ivy back into the present. She turned toward the sound to find a shirtless Herkleian male in pants embossed with the hotel's logo. Ivy blinked rapidly at his azure scales, tall stature, and sharp horns, but she quickly brought a smile to her face. The Herkleian barred fangs in return—his version of a smile. Finally, Ivy's studying had come in handy.

"Welcome to Eritea, capital of Herkleios. On behalf of the Intergalactic Alliance, we welcome you to the 33rd Intergalactic Games." The male gestured her toward the lobby desk, where the other guests congregated. "If you give me your name, I can direct you accordingly."

"Ivy Dawson."

The Herkleian waved a hand over his gold wristband and tapped at his holo-screen. "Ms. Dawson. Coach to skater Addison Everest. You'll be staying in room 378 in an adjoining suite with your student. May I share the details with your wristband and transport you to your room?"

Transport to her room? If only this tech existed on Earth. She'd never take the stairs again. "Yes, please."

Her bracelet buzzed slightly as the male tapped away. "Once you arrive in your room, we'll send you an information package with all the maps and schedules you'll need. If you require anything else, please send us a message through any of the holo-screens in the hotel."

"Thank you."

"Ready to transport?"

Ivy nodded. The sooner she settled into her room, the sooner she could examine Addison's schedule and make a training plan.

Strange tingles crawled her skin again. Within a blink, Ivy transported from the lobby to a gilded room with high ceilings. A levitating bed hovered in one corner opposite a window and blinking dais—a clothing materializer. Ivy immediately dropped her bag and rushed over. She had witnessed a demonstration of the materializer on a shopping channel back home, but a part of her still believed it was special effects.

As Ivy stepped onto the dais, her bracelet buzzed and her holo-screen flared to life, displaying a range of clothing options. Her mouth gaped at all the styles from across the galaxy. Bright and dark palettes clashed, adorned with feathers and leathers and furs. Ivy almost clicked on an option, but the little pricing symbol in the corner kept her finger hovering.

Ivy stepped off. One day, maybe, but not today. Not until Addison won gold. Zapher. Whatever.

IVY SMOOTHED down the collar of Addison's tracksuit, branded in the blue and green flag the Intergalactic Alliance created for Earth. Every time Ivy saw the colors, she flinched, so used to competing under the American flag. "Big smiles. You need to look friendly for the cameras, but not so much that the other competitors don't take you seriously."

"It's just the opening ceremony, Ivy." Addison pushed off her hands, eager to join Earth's athletes as they entered the stadium. As a coach, Ivy would have a front row view alongside the other coaches in her division. "Isn't this supposed to be fun?"

Ivy sighed. Addison worked hard, but if she wanted to be a winner, she couldn't take breaks. Her attitude was nowhere near to what Ivy deemed acceptable. If her jumps weren't the most graceful Ivy had ever seen, she would have dropped the girl after their first session together.

"Ooh, I see my friends. Bye, Ivy!" Addison ran off towards the gaggle of girls she knew from the skating circuit back home.

Ivy shook her head, but what could she do? She headed for the coach box. Three rows were closed off for the skating coaches, most of the seats empty. Ivy's bracelet dinged when she passed her aisle. She scanned the chairs until her name projected over one.

"Oh, Ivy!" A coach she recognized from the UK sat in the row behind hers. Vanessa something? Ivy was terrible with names. "How are you?"

Ivy forced a smile to her face. "I'm good, Vanessa. Are you here with Imogen?"

"Yes, isn't it exciting?" The woman threw up her hands. "Look at this! It's like Earth but filled with aliens."

"Something about it does all feel familiar." When would the ceremony start? Ivy despised small talk. More coaches found their seats in the rows around her. Hopefully soon. A shadow fell over her right as Vanessa's eyes focused on something at her side.

"So we meet again."

Ivy stiffened. She knew that voice. She had *dreamed* of that voice, though she'd never admit it. Ivy twisted around to see that cocky prick from the ship towering over her. At least this time he wore a shirt, a dark, form-fitting leather thing lined with white fur. Ivy's mouth watered. Maybe the clothes weren't an improvement? Ivy never had a thing for Vikings before, but looking at Rivix, it could be her kink.

She cleared her throat. Hot alien or not, she didn't have time for this. "This section is reserved for coaches, so if you would be so kind as to leave..."

"I *am* a coach," he said, pointing at the next chair. *Rivix Skardesen* flashed above it suddenly. "How lucky for me to be seated next to you."

Ivy ground her teeth. Crap. Of course he had to be a coach. Of course he had to be a *skating* coach. "Who do you coach?"

"You haven't heard of him?" Vanessa piped up from behind her. Rivix glanced her way, but quickly returned those intense, slitted blue eyes to Ivy.

Vanessa wasn't having that. She pushed herself closer to the royal, muscled god of an alien. "It's an honor to meet you, Prince Rivix." Turning back to Ivy, she continued, "Prince Rivix holds the most medals of any athlete from the Intergalactic Games. He's the one that advocated for Earth to join the skating competition despite Earth's different techniques."

"You give me too much credit," Rivix said with a smile, but it wasn't anywhere near as wide as his earlier one. When he really smiled, Ivy wanted to trail her fingers through his dark beard and swallow the grin—

Shit. No, she didn't. She didn't want to do anything of the sort. Competitors slept around during events on Earth, but she was a coach. She needed to remain professional, her focus on Addison.

If Rivix noticed her dilemma, he said nothing. He continued,

"The games were already open to Earth. All I did was point out your figure skating was on par with our skaters."

Shit, something about that rang a bell. "Who did you say you were coaching?"

"Sigrid Karlsdottir."

Double shit. Ivy had heard that name before. The Fenrish girl was Addison's major competition. From the intergalactic chat boards Ivy accessed, the bettors thought both girls would place in the top three. It was just a matter of who would be first.

Vanessa's bracelet buzzed. "If you'll excuse me. My girl is having some last-minute nerves I need to settle." She batted her eyes up at Rivix. "But I look forward to seeing you again, Your Highness."

A sudden rage took over Ivy. How dare Vanessa look at him like that? She tried to push the emotion down. There was no reason for her to feel this way.

Rivix took her hand and pressed a kiss to her knuckles. "It was an honor to meet you. And please, call me Rivix."

The flirt. Ivy dug her fingernails into her elbow rests. Vanessa stumbled away, almost awestruck, as Rivix settled beside her. He slumped into the seat, the move somehow lazily seductive. Those eyes scanned Ivy, taking in the tenseness of her body. "Jealous?"

"I'm not—"

The lights dimmed, a hush settling over the crowd. The last thing Ivy saw was Rivix's quirking lips.

The bastard.

A hologram of a familiar figure flashed to life in the center of the stadium. King Anax of Herkleios stood proudly in a gilded robe, his bare chest exposing azure scales over tight muscles. A blond human around Ivy's age stood at his side in an equally elaborate gown. Queen Alexandra had given birth to twins less than two weeks ago, but she insisted on attending the opening ceremony. Ivy had skimmed articles both for and against the Earthling queen's decision this afternoon. Personally, she found it inspiring.

"Welcome to the 33rd Intergalactic Games," King Anax said.

The crowd roared. Ivy clapped along, but the male at her side stole half her attention. Despite looking like an icicle, heat radiated off his body. Her arm twitched, itching to close the distance between them. His claws tapped against the armrest between them, a tempting melody. He was like a black hole, pulling her closer and closer to him against her better judgement.

"The last few years have been chaotic for all of us, my friends," King Anax continued. "But I won't let the harm my father caused to our alliance stop us from celebrating this momentous event. We have new allies on Earth, my beloved mate's home planet."

Queen Alexandra smiled and took her husband's hand. "Today, Earthlings will compete alongside Herkleians, Eógans, Fens, Guroverians, Yazadi, and Zocastans. Because no matter our origins, no matter our technology, we are all equals."

King Anax barred his fangs down at his mate, the love in his eyes visible for all to see. "Let the 33rd Intergalactic Games begin!"

The holograms disappeared as a hail of fireworks burst throughout the open-aired dome. Ivy leaned forward, joining in with the 'oohs' and 'aahs' from the crowd. Her arm brushed Rivix's. She tensed, the same movement flooding his body. How was she already attuned to him? Ivy twisted, colorful lights flashing across the lines of his face—

Suddenly Rivix stood, breaking her trance.

Ivy frowned and started to stand. Something wasn't right. She wasn't an expert on Fenrish body language, but anyone could see the tension in Rivix.

"What—?"

An explosion rippled through the stadium.

Something was wrong with the fireworks.

Rivix jumped to his feet, eyes fixed on the stadium's floor. Was there someone down there? He strained, but he wasn't close enough to distinguish between the shapes. As a prince and member of the Intergalactic Committee, he had access to the plans for the games. These fireworks weren't manual and security should've kept anyone from their base.

Someone moved at his side, and Rivix nearly grabbed for the dagger in his boot. But when Ivy's sweet scent reached his nose, he calmed. For a minute. Something was wrong, and Ivy was here beside him.

In danger.

"What—?" she started.

The stadium rumbled at his feet as an explosion ripped through the floor.

The screams of joy twisted, turning to cries of terror. Flames licked across the ground, spreading faster than wildfire. The remaining fireworks caught alight and whizzed into the air in all directions. Rivix grabbed Ivy and ducked. The female was like a block of ice in his arms, frozen in fear and stiff to the touch. He trailed his hands down her side, but she seemed unharmed under her thick sweater. Her amber eyes remained fixed and dilated. In shock, then. Rivix glanced around. All the athletes had waited in the tunnels opening to the floor, but coaches, media, and guests filled the stadium. They rushed to the exits in a panicked mass. Someone had turned off the high-pitched alarm, at least, but the repetitive "Please exit the Phaedra Stadium in an orderly fashion" wasn't helping much.

They needed to get out of here.

Rivix gave Ivy a gentle shake. "Ivy. We need to go."

Her lips moved, but the screams stole away her words. He leaned forward and down until his ear was near her lips.

Her breath tickled his skin. "I can't."

He almost missed it again, her voice barely audible. Did she fear fire? Whatever it was, it didn't change his objective. And if Ivy couldn't get herself out, he'd have to carry her.

"I'm going to pick you up," he said before scooping her into his arms. The fiery female he knew would've slapped him upside the head, but Ivy only curled into his chest, her eyes fixed on the flames.

He cradled her against his chest, relishing the feel of her in his arms, breathing in her scent. But Rivix couldn't focus on that. He had a responsibility to keep her safe. He quickly made his way down the steps to the crowded halls. He paused, looking behind him. He didn't want anyone getting hurt. Flying security droids had thankfully flooded the area to guide everyone out. Across the floor, a team of emergency droids battled the fire, allowing time to evacuate.

When they reached the exit, Rivix savored a breath of clean air. He pushed through the crowds, aiming to get far away from the building. His wristband buzzed. Perhaps a message from Sigrid? He needed to make sure his student was unhurt, but then he glanced down at his tiny human. She pressed firmly against his chest, eyes closed.

"Ivy, we're outside now," he murmured, not wanting to startle her.

She opened her eyes, blinking rapidly. In the bright Herkleian light, all sense returned to her. Ivy scrambled out of his arms. Rivix let her go, an ache in his chest.

"I'm fine," she said, more to herself than him. She rubbed shaking hands down her arms.

"Are you sure? You froze back there."

Ivy looked down at her feet and kicked at the violet grass. "I, uh, had an unpleasant experience with fire as a kid."

Saying the words worsened the flash of fear across her face, but then she met his eyes and embarrassment replaced the expression. Rivix's blood roared inside him. He wanted to wrap her in his arms and shield her from every bad thing that could happen. It tore at him to see her like this.

Rivix put his hand under her chin, lifting her eyes up to meet his. "You have nothing to be embarrassed about. We all have things in our past."

"Thanks." She nudged her chin, pulling from his touch. That was more like her. "I don't normally tell anyone about it."

Just like Rivix didn't tell anyone about his time with the Osträsk. Everyone in the palace knew, but it was treated like a secret to this day. "Let's get you back to the hotel. Unless you need to be checked by the medics."

She straightened. "No, I'm fine. I just want to put this behind me. But I need to find Addison, my skater."

Ah, yes. Rivix tapped at his wristband and glanced at Sigrid's message. "Addison is already on her way back to the hotel. Sigrid said they loaded all the competitors onto hoverbuses."

"Oh, thank God."

"I can take you back?" Ivy hadn't responded to him the first time. Still in shock, perhaps. Either way, Rivix wanted to have her full consent this time.

She glanced down again, but only momentarily. When she met his gaze, all traces of her nerves had disappeared. "Yes, please. Thank you, Rivix."

HOVERING above Eritea's golden towers, Rivix swiped across his holo-screen for the third time in a row. Vehicles flowing out of the stadium clogged the sky, but as a royal, Rivix had diplomatic status allowing him to drive in the priority lanes. But he never took advantage of the privilege and didn't want to start today.

Ivy sat in the seat across from him, glancing out the window. She had drifted into silence the further they got from the stadium. Perhaps she was another reason to slow their ride to the hotel? Every moment was an opportunity to learn more about her.

He opened his mouth, but quickly shut it. Why didn't he know what to say? Something about this female had all his thoughts spinning out of control. But whatever he asked, it had to be good. He'd face Brother Magnus again to get a single smile out of her.

An alert buzzed on both of their wristbands. It was a message from the Intergalactic Committee. Though Rivix was a member, he wasn't on the board and didn't receive updates. A little bit of PR, no doubt. Rivix didn't even open his. Whatever it said would be a lie and it could wait until later. He wanted to savor his time with Ivy.

Ivy didn't possess the same patience. She opened it, her eyes quickly flying through the message. "No one was seriously hurt. Some people are in the hospital for smoke inhalation, but everyone got out on time. They're looking into a backup location for the opening ceremony and the games set on Herkleios."

"And the fire?" Rivix asked.

"Apparently, it was a fluke accident. We have nothing to worry about."

"I doubt that." Though the general populace didn't know, there had been news circling amongst the royal families that Prince Argrix, brother to Anax, had threatened to stop the games by any means necessary. Argrix and his supporters still blamed humans for his father's deposal and later death. Rivix couldn't help but snort. He had been visiting Herkleios when King Xenobaccus died and his evil uncle had no one to blame but himself.

"What do you mean?"

Rivix considered his words. He had no proof. Most of the royals dismissed Argrix's threats, but Rivix knew his cousin. More than that, he knew Argrix's exact intent. His father, King Skarde, had received a communication indirectly from Argrix asking them for support. Fenrik had yet to associate with Earth and Argrix believed that meant they were hostile towards Earth, too. In reality, they simply had no time. Though Rivix had left the Osträsk over a decade ago, the peace between his kingdom and the nomad clan had yet to return.

"I don't think it was an accident," Rivix said. "I need to get you off this planet."

"Like hell you do." Ivy's spark was definitely back as she glared at him. "You think it was easy to get here? You think it's just a game? I've dedicated hours and hours to this. You have your reputation as a golden boy prince, but I need this if I want any credibility as a coach going forward."

Rivix loved the fire in her eyes. His cock twitched. One day, she would say his name with that passion.

But not if she got killed in the meantime.

"It's not safe here."

"Why not?"

"I can't tell you." His father had denied Argrix's advances and told King Anax. Rivix had sworn to both of them to keep quiet about what he knew. They couldn't give Argrix more power by fueling the fear.

"Well then, I'm staying. The Intergalactic Committee says it was nothing. If it's good enough for them, it's good enough for me."

Rivix shook his head. There would be no convincing her. But if she wasn't leaving, neither was he. At least the games would give him reason to stay close.

And if he was being truthful with himself, it wasn't just to protect her.

FIVE

IVY

Ivy rushed through the hotel's lobby doors with a quick wave back at Rivix. He started to follow, but thought better of it and paused by the doors. Ivy couldn't watch him watch her. He had witnessed her breakdown. How could she ever face him again? She sped-walked through the gilded space. When she reached the front desk, she immediately tapped at the large holo-screen and selected her suite number.

Tingles crawled her spine. Once Ivy solidified in her room, she sank to the floor. Alone, she could no longer hold back her tears. Her body shook with the force of her sobbing.

She hadn't thought about the fire in years. Ivy had tucked the memory away somewhere it couldn't hurt her anymore. But the stadium's explosion had brought the memories and years of anxiety back to the surface.

"Mama," Ivy yelled, trying to rush back into the burning house. Pain flared across her back from where she had neared too close to the open flames, but nothing hurt as badly as watching her home burn.

Her father's hand settled on her arm, a hard grip. She looked up and up and up at his face. As a child, she had thought him cold, but looking back, she recognized the terror. Her baby sister, Willow, cooed in his arms. He tightened his grip around her diapered bottom.

"She'll get out, Ives," Dad said. "It'll be okay. The firefighters are almost here."

And her father hadn't exactly lied. The firefighters had arrived minutes later and her mother had made it out—severely burned but alive.

But her life had never been okay again.

Ivy reached for her phone out of habit and set a timer for five minutes. Five minutes she would give herself to cry. When her mother had doubled her training hours, five minutes was all he had. Ivy breathed in and out, counting her breaths like her therapist had taught her. She was okay. Addison was okay. The explosion had injured no one and the Intergalactic Games would continue.

Ivy couldn't let fire deter her life again.

When the five minutes were up, she pulled to a stand and wiped away her tears. She threw water on her face to make herself look somewhat presentable. Ivy didn't have time to fall apart. Her entire future career hinged on Addison's success. That was something tangible she could focus on, keeping her fears at bay for a short time.

Someone knocked at the door. Ivy approached. Rivix maybe? She had run away from him, rather rudely given all he had done for her.

But the sound came from the adjoining door, not the hallway exit.

"Ivy?" Addison called. "Open up."

Ivy swiped at her holo-screen, unlocking the door.

The teenage girl barged in like she owned the place. Though Addison had arrived earlier than her, she had yet to change out of her Team Earth outfit. "The rinks are okay, thankfully, so we won't miss any practice time. Isn't that great?"

"That is, Addy," Ivy said, though her student's disregard for the explosion rankled her. Everyone was so quick to dismiss the fire as an accident, but Rivix's reaction made Ivy wonder if there was more to the story. But if everyone else was going to practice, her protégé would, too.

Addison popped onto her bed, giving it a quick bounce. "It's open skate now. Can we check out the rink?"

Ivy hadn't quite caught her breath yet, but she'd welcome this distraction. "Go get your skates, then."

"Yes!" Addison jumped to her feet. "I'm going to skate circles around these aliens."

Ivy sighed. "Not sure you're supposed to refer to them as aliens. This is *their* planet."

"Well, I can't keep track of where they're all from."

"They have their flag colors on their uniform."

Addison snorted. "You think I bothered remembering their flags?"

Ivy almost glanced upward to pray for patience. She imagined the gold-zapher—medal and the boost it'd give her career. That was all that mattered. "Addison, can you please try to take this seriously?"

"I am, okay?" She rolled her eyes. "I'll rephrase. My only competition is the girl in the super boring colors with the creepy mountain logo."

Meaning the black and white flag of Fenrik. "You mean Sigrid?"

"Yeah, her! We met her super sexy coach in the mess hall." Ivy's cheeks flushed at just the mention of Rivix, but Addison didn't notice, too busy pursing her lips and staring into space. "I guess that green girl is pretty good, too."

Ivy face-palmed. "Addison, you can't call someone by their skin color."

"You're no fun." Addison skipped for the door. "Meet you in the lobby in ten?"

Ivy shook her head and said nothing as her student left the room. Oh, to be that young and think you had everything figured out.

THE TENSION in Ivy eased as the rink's chilly breeze washed over her. This was where she excelled. This was where she belonged. As Addison rushed forward to throw on her skates, Ivy meandered behind, enjoying the serenity. This was her true home, cold and barren and perfect.

Ivy surveyed the rink. Though the shape was similar to rinks on Earth, only a forcefield buzzed around the edges, providing a perfect view of the skaters. Addison had picked the smaller of the rinks. Most of the other athletes probably wanted to practice on a rink more similar to the competition, but Ivy hadn't fought her on it. She couldn't handle spectators after what happened with her ankle.

Two skaters practiced on this rink, one a Fenrish girl with long white hair. Sigrid, perhaps? Ivy couldn't ask Addison, who had jumped onto the ice like an eager kid at a ball pit. Ivy scanned the stands for Rivix. He wasn't there. A pang echoed through her. Disappointment? Ivy shook it off. God, this was embarrassing. Was she developing a crush? During all of *this*?

But could she really blame herself? He was a perfect specimen, the kind of guy who belonged in magazines and movies—if movies starred ice-skinned aliens with slitted eyes, that was.

"Focus, Ivy," she chided herself as Addison looped around the ice toward her. Ivy wasn't here to make eyes at an ice-sculpted Viking of a male. She was here to train Addison. "Okay, let's start warm-up with a single axle."

Addison snorted. "That's so easy."

"Do it anyway."

"Fine."

Addison glided across the rink, picking up speed. When the time was right, she launched into the air in a flawless jump. The girl really could skate.

"Again!" Ivy called.

Addison did as she was told and Ivy yelled more instructions, the two of them settling into their regular pattern. A peace settled over

Ivy, the threat of the fire gone. Her ankle twinged when she stepped forward, but Ivy ignored it. Nothing could keep her from this.

Ivy barely registered the doors opening as a fourth skater entered the rink. When the girl passed, Ivy narrowed her eyes. Another Fenrish girl, this one with a short white hair cut at a sharp angle to match the lines of her icy face. Her eyes were cold and determined, but the expression only added to her hard beauty.

Without warning, the skater raced across the rink, moving seamlessly from a jump to a spin. Ivy gaped. What she lacked in Addison's grace, she made up for with her speed and power. It was like the beauty of the sport had been twisted into something fearsome and otherworldly. The Fenrish called it iskrigg, a form of ice combat. Ivy imagined this girl battling as the Fens had centuries prior. The concept had mesmerized her after she found a painting on the intergalactic chat boards.

Even Addison stopped to watch this girl, jealousy clear on her face.

Ivy snapped her fingers. "Addison, focus."

But Addison wasn't one to back away from a challenge. She skated faster than Ivy had ever witnessed and threw herself into a triple jump. When she hit the ice again, her legs tensed with the impact. Ivy's heart beat nearly out of her throat. If Addison didn't focus, she risked injury.

Ivy stormed forward. Thankfully, she had brought her own skates. She glided onto the ice to her student's side. "If you're going to show off, execute the move properly. Did you even try to extend your arms?"

"Like you could do better? How many Olympic medals do you have again? One?"

Ivy glared. "You don't have any yet. Why don't I demonstrate?"

Back home, Ivy skated in the early hours of the morning. Even after her injury, she couldn't stop her love for the sport. Ivy hadn't skated in front of others in months, but there was barely anyone here and Addison couldn't remain unchecked. She only hoped she could prove her point and land a clean jump.

She skated a few laps around the rink, buying time to psych herself up for the move. She picked up speed, bent her legs, and pushed into the perfect spin. When Ivy hit the ground, a wide smile split her face. She didn't need to watch a playback to know she had aced the move. Ivy's ankle burned as she skated toward her student, but her exhilaration numbed the pain.

Ivy crossed her arms when she reached Addison, but her student no longer had any gloat left in her. "Fine, Ivy. You win."

Applause echoed across the rink. Ivy stiffened. Before she even twisted toward the noise, she knew who she would find.

Rivix lounged in a seat three rows into the stands and continued with his drawn-out applause. When Ivy narrowed her eyes, he stopped and strolled forward. "Well, it seems you *might* have a reputation to rival my own one day."

Was he being genuine? Ivy couldn't tell. But if anyone asked, she blamed her flush on the skating. "That was just a warm-up, I haven't..."

"No, it was perfect. You couldn't have done a single thing better."

"Thanks." She'd always had more trouble accepting compliments than critiques. Compliments were useless, her mother had always said. Critiques gave her something to work on. What were you supposed to say to a perfect score?

"You should skate with me."

She stared at him for a minute. "What?"

Rivix stepped onto the rink. One moment his boots had flat soles and the next, blade protruded from their bottoms. Holy shit. Ivy needed skates like that. She was so busy staring, she almost missed his words. "It's customary for coaches to skate between the competition and medal ceremony. We could do a few tricks for the crowd."

Skate with Rivix? A multi-zapher winning Adonis made of ice? In front of thousands of people? Ivy almost laughed hysterically, but he was serious. "I'm not a pairs skater."

"With your talent, there isn't anything you can't handle."

"I'll pass."

"Suit yourself." Rivix skated a circle around her, the movement somehow both languished and predatory. "It would be fun to show off a little for the crowd. If you change your mind, let me know."

"I—you—" Ivy turned back to Addison, who suggestively quirked an eyebrow. Ivy glowered. "Do some laps, Addison."

"But Ivy—"

She skated as far as she could get from Rivix. He was a distraction, nothing more. "Now, Addison!"

But Ivy felt his eyes on her for the rest of the practice.

SIX

RIVIX

Rivix surveyed the Fenrish Embassy's foyer from the top landing of the stairs. The vaulted ceilings dripped with ice sculptures, frozen solid despite the warmth of the glittering lights, but his gaze travelled past the art to the guests mingling below. Fenrik hosted all the ice-related events and athletes from every planet in the Intergalactic Alliance had reason to attend their party after the opening ceremony.

After what happened in the stadium earlier today, Rivix should have ditched the party for a meeting with his father and King Anax, but ruling wasn't his responsibility. It never would be—exactly the way he liked it. What he did care about was Ivy. Surely she'd attend, even after their little encounter at the rink. He had saved her life this morning. More than that, they had a connection. She felt it, too. She had to. Just the thought of her sent shivers up Rivix's spine.

Once she arrived, they'd finally get the chance to talk.

He'd finally say the right thing to impress her.

But the minutes quickly turned into half an hour. Dozens of guests had approached him, but Rivix hadn't left his spot overlooking the door. Would Ivy not come? She wanted to make a career out of coaching. He had researched her after their first meeting and discovered she stopped skating abruptly three years ago. Perhaps for the same reason she now favored her left leg? Certainly she'd attend, if only to make connections in the community.

The doors opened, admitting a wave of people—including one with bright red hair.

Rivix's heart skipped a beat. Her pale blue gown clung perfectly to the curves of her breasts and hips. The shimmering train hovered off the floor, revealing odd, dagger-like shoes. How regular humans balanced on those was beyond him, but Ivy had been raised on the ice. Even off the ice, even with her injury, she had a grace others couldn't compete with. Her red hair tumbled loosely across the gown's high neckline, flickering like a flame. Rivix wanted to thread his fingers through the strands. He didn't care if he got burned.

"...your win four years ago," a skater from Gurov was saying. What was the male's name? Rivix couldn't remember.

He slapped the male on his feathered shoulder. "I'm sorry, my friend, we'll have to continue this conversation later."

Without another word, Rivix hiked for the stairs, his gaze on the bobbing redhead. With all the towering Fens, Herkleians, and Eógans around, Rivix could easily lose sight of her. He reached the main floor and swerved through the crowd with the skill of a Fenrish ice warrior. If Brother Magnus could see him, the cruel abbot might actually complement his moves for once.

Ivy paused before the beverage table, surveying the dozen options.

"Can I get you a drink, my lady?"

Ivy spun in confusion, but her expression turned into a formidable glare when she saw him. "There're hundreds of people here. How did you find me?"

"I looked."

Her frown deepened. "And why did you do that?"

"You're the only person here I want to see."

She snorted. "Isn't this the Fenrish Embassy? Should you be saying that out loud as a Prince of Fenrik and all?"

Rivix slithered closer. "My parents and siblings and cousins are the politicians, Ivy. I'm here for the sport... and for you."

Ivy's eyebrows shot up an inch. She didn't believe him? Fine. He'd prove himself to her. Rivix didn't close the space between them, but he lowered his voice, luring her in. "Maybe here, at the Fenrish Embassy, I might have a better chance of winning the back and forth we have going."

His trick worked. Ivy leaned in to listen, almost unconsciously, but seemed to notice. She crossed her arms, guarding her heart like a plate of armor. "Do you do this for every woman you want to fuck?"

Rivix repressed a flinch. He'd made a mistake being so forthcoming during their first encounter. Earthlings didn't like that, apparently. How could he fix this?

Honesty was the only answer.

"I'm not here for that, Ivy." His interest in her went beyond that. He wanted her forever, to cherish and hold. Even though the feeling was foreign, he didn't fight it. "I'm here because I enjoy your company. I thought you might feel the same."

"Vanessa is just across the room. I'm sure she'd welcome your advances."

Vanessa? Rivix followed her gaze to the human he'd met at the Opening Ceremony. Was Ivy jealous? "I don't want her. I want you."

Ivy's eyes widened at the intensity in his voice. Helga's skulls, even Rivix was shocked by it. He hadn't meant to be so forthcoming, but he couldn't hold back when he was with her.

Ivy pointed at herself. "*You* want *me*?"

"Why would that be surprising?"

"Well, I'm not the prettiest, friendliest, or even the nicest."

Rivix reached out, drawing a hand down her arm. She shivered at his touch, but leaned even closer. The rest of the party disappeared, a blur in the background. "That's only how you want to be seen. I want to go deeper and learn your every thought."

Ivy stared into his eyes, almost as enraptured as he was. This close, her breath dusted his face. What would she do if he leaned down and claimed those red lips?

But the better question was, would he care?

A guest gave a high-pitched barking laugh, startling Ivy. She blinked around like she had exited a fog and stepped back. Helga damn these partygoers for interrupting.

She cleared her throat and ducked her head. "Well, right now I'm thinking how annoying you are."

A lie, but Rivix wouldn't fight her on it. There was another path to her heart. "How about this? Let me make some introductions."

"I've already done extensive research on Addison's competition."

"I would expect no less, but influential figures of the skating world are here in person. Donors, winning athletes, journalists." Her eyes lit up, a spark he recognized. That feeling lived within him, too— the desire to win. "If one were trying to launch their coaching career, this would definitely be the place to do it."

When Ivy sighed, he knew he had her. She was too dedicated to refuse the opportunity. He slid his fingertips across her arm and gripped her hand. Before she could think twice, Rivix led her across the room.

"...AND when Rivix finished with that jump, I knew he'd win zapher," Atlacoya said, the Zocastan female barring dagger sharp teeth in a smile. "I always back winners."

"And that was his first time at the games?" Ivy asked, glancing wide-eyed between Rivix and the metal baron. Rivix had almost elbowed his way through the crowd when he spotted his first patron. She always told the best stories about him.

Atlacoya nodded, her spotted-fur covered with a jungle-green gown that imitated leaves. "Everyone thought King Skarde had encouraged his selection. And after that nasty business with the Osträsk, why wouldn't they?"

Frost flared across the edges of Rivix's glass. He exhaled out a long breath, begging it to stop. No one mentioned the Osträsk to him. But Atlacoya wasn't Fenrish. She either didn't know or didn't care.

Probably the latter.

"The Osträsk?" Ivy frowned at him.

"Well, that's the story, anyway." Atlacoya put a hand on his shoulder. The fur lining his collar protected his skin and stopped his flinch. The memory of whips flashed through his mind. He had begged to be trained at a younger age than the other boys and received it because he was a prince, but if Rivix had known what Brother Magnus would put him through, he never would have asked. "Rivix here has never confirmed or denied it, but where else would a Fen learn the art of iskrigg? The Osträsk monks won't share it with anyone but their chosen few—"

"Rivix!"

Rivix twisted around, grateful for the first time in years for the sound of his mother's voice. Queen Rhiona approached, her gown a dragon-like hide made of pure zapher. The shade perfectly matched her patches of azure scales while still complimenting those that were Eógan-green. But the nods to her homeworld of Eógan and Herkleios ended there, her long dark hair cascading down her back in a mix of knots and braids. Silver tipped the edge of her horns, the metal sharp and harsh like the Fenrish themselves.

"There's my youngest." Queen Rhiona beamed up at him before turning a more demure smile on Ivy and Atlacoya. "Lady Atlacoya, what a pleasure."

"The honor is mine, as always, Your Majesty." Atlacoya's deep orange eyes twinkled when she glanced between Rivix and her mother. Rivix's insides twisted. The baron knew. He had never thought her so manipulative. "We must talk later, Miss Dawson. I'd love to talk about Addison's future—and yours, as well."

Ivy flushed, this time in happiness.

Atlacoya leaned closer to him. "I'm staying at your hotel if you want to visit me. It can be like old times."

Though his mother didn't hear, Ivy flinched. Rivix forced a polite smile to his face. Atlacoya had invited him to her bed many times, and he always accepted. Not anymore. Though she told great stories, he could never forgive her for mentioning the Osträsk. He'd do everything in his power to keep the baron away from his female. If that was how she spoke to a prince, how would she speak to Ivy once the fanfare disappeared?

Wait. *His* female. Rivix had thought of Ivy as his. He blinked down at her in shock. When had that happened?

Queen Rhiona bared her fangs at Ivy, a charming Herkleian smile. "It's a pleasure to meet you..."

"Ivy Dawson." Ivy reached out her hand, but then doubted herself and dropped into a half bow. "Your Majesty."

When his mother's forehead quirked in question, he added, "She's a coach to one of Sigrid's adversaries."

"I see." Her eyes flickered between the two of them. Though she had been blind to the way the Osträsk treated him, she never missed a romance. "And how are you liking your first Intergalactic Games, Ivy?"

"I'm amazed to be here. Fires and all."

Queen Rhiona's eyes dimmed, but Rivix only noticed because he knew his mother. "That was such an unfortunate accident, but no one was harmed, thankfully. And how are you enjoying our party?"

"It's lovely, Your Majesty. Your embassy is beautiful."

"And my son?"

Ivy's cheeks flared a color to rival her hair. "Your son?"

Queen Rhiona nodded. "How are you enjoying him?"

Rivix winced. "Mother."

His mother didn't break eye contact with Ivy, who grasped for words and couldn't find them. "I... uh... what?"

For whatever reason, that response made his mother's grin widen. What did she have planned? She always meddled. The gossiping courts of Eógan had raised her well.

"Mother—"

"Well, it's a pleasure to meet you, Ivy. Do you mind if I steal my son for a moment?"

"Of course." Ivy nodded quickly, almost thankful for the conversation's end. That was something they had in common. "He's been glued to my side for some time now."

"Glued?" Rivix asked, but Ivy made a break for the refreshment table, an embarrassed hunch to her shoulders. Rivix couldn't help a grin. She felt something for him, then. There was no other reason for her reaction—

Queen Rhiona twisted him around and grabbed at his collar.

"Are you well, mother?"

"You've found your mate!"

Rivix blinked at her slowly. "I've what?"

"That human. She's your mate, gifted to you by Hyra."

"She's what?" His mother wasn't overly religious, but she told him the same stories of the Herkleian goddess her father told her as a child. No one had formed a matebond in a century until King Anax met Queen Alexandra. Since then, two of his other cousins and countless Herkleians across the stars had found their other half. But Ivy and Rivix? His attraction to her had been instantaneous, but surely not. The ancient gods of Fenrik had their claws in him already. There certainly wasn't space for a foreign dragon goddess.

"A mother knows these things. I could see it in your eyes as you looked at each other."

"And my neck?" Rivix asked skeptically. Those selected by Hyra had a str-shaped symbol appear on their nape, individual to each couple. It bound them together for all to see.

Queen Rhiona pulled at his collar once more and frowned. "There's no clear mark yet. But that doesn't mean one won't appear. Trust me, son, that female belongs to you as much as you belong to her."

Rivix glanced Ivy's way, their eyes immediately meeting across the crowd. And somehow, Rivix suddenly knew what his mother said was true.

SEVEN

IVY

Ivy took advantage of Rivix's distraction and wandered down an empty hallway. Though she had made great connections, the party's volume made her brain pound. Meeting all those people hadn't helped, either. Even though Ivy could make small talk for days, she remained an introvert at heart. People drained her. And that wasn't even considering the whole Rivix situation.

Her breath caught at just the thought of him. Why did she feel this way? She barely knew him, but each second they spent together, she fell further and further down the rabbit hole. No man ever made her so flustered and angry and happy at the same time.

When Ivy reached the end of the corridor, she spotted a wide-open door. Ivy ducked out of the party. In the silence—semi-silence, that was—she exhaled. In the quiet, she finally had a chance to think. About her career. About Rivix. About everything.

When she opened her eyes, her jaw dropped.

The office blended familiar elements like a desk and sofa, though everything appeared carved of ice. How did it not melt in this heat? But that wasn't even her biggest question, not when the far wall displayed dozens of zapher medals. A holo-screen in the center of the shelves displayed a life-size image of Rivix standing on a podium. Younger, but just as bright and bold. Ivy approached. The whole thing was almost shrine-like, but Ivy couldn't fault the Fens, not when he'd won so many times. They had a good reason for their pride.

But maybe seeing this was good for her. She needed to remind herself that he was nothing more than a cocky prick. One with a reputation, too. Atlacoya had propositioned him with absolute confidence in his acceptance. She traced the lines of his face. Damn that *hot*, cocky, playboy prick.

Was looking at it really the best use of Ivy's time? She shook her head and turned on her heels, but immediately bumped into something solid—and warm and in a warrior-esque leather ensemble lined with fur.

Ivy had walked straight into Rivix's muscled torso.

She bounced right off. "Oh shit, I'm sorry."

"You aren't, but perhaps you should be."

Ivy froze at his tone, her cheeks flushing. He grinned like a devil —if devils were made of ice instead of fire. Ivy was seriously in trouble. But she didn't move, letting his gaze trail down her body as if he were taking off her clothes one piece at a time.

For a moment, she hoped he would.

"Rivix, I—"

The stern-faced skater from the rink earlier stumbled into the room, her white hair braided elaborately. Sigrid. She grinned sloppily, a huge change from the earlier girl Ivy had witnessed skating. "I've been looking everywhere for you."

Sigrid stumbled forward and all but fell into Rivix.

He sighed. "Sig, I told you not to smoke."

"Relax." She smacked his shoulder, exactly where Ivy had touched moments ago. Did her hand linger too long? "I don't compete tomorrow and it'd be rude not to enjoy myself at my own party."

"The Fenrish Embassy threw this party for the community."

"Sure, but I benefit. I saw you making the rounds."

Ivy's stomach did a flip. He hadn't made the rounds for Sigrid, but for her. Rivix hadn't talked about his star pupil at all, instead redirecting all questions to Ivy. Maybe he wasn't a prick, then? Not really. Even Ivy didn't have it in her to help the competition.

Rivix gripped Sigrid's shoulders and spoke slowly, "Sigrid, I want you to go find Helve and have her assign you to one of the guest rooms."

"I'm fine. I want to stay here with you."

"You will do as I say."

The ice in his tone brought her to her senses. She stood straighter, student to coach. But even one as disciplined as Sigrid couldn't stop her pout. Teenagers were the same no matter the planet. "Okay, fine, I'll go."

"Don't forget to get some sleep."

Sigrid didn't even turn around to acknowledge she had heard him.

When Rivix twisted back to her, Ivy crossed her arms and held the space between them. A minute ago, she had imagined throwing her caution to the wind and seeing what Rivix really had to offer. But Rivix wasn't a regular man. Ivy had to be careful. "I see it's an hourly occurrence that women throw themselves at you."

"Sigrid?" Rivix appeared totally confused. "She's just a kid."

"Do a lot of your students get that way?"

The confusion wiped off his face in an instant, replaced by a light of realization. "Do teenage girls giggle among themselves when they see me at the rink? Yes, they do. But I've never so much as flirted with any of them. I'm upset you'd think that of me."

"That's not what I meant. I know you wouldn't." Shit, Ivy had let her own jealousy spur her on to attack his reputation. That was low, even for her. "I mean, you could have any girl. Why bother pursuing me when anyone with eyes would drool all over you?"

"I don't want anyone, I want you."

Rivix looked her straight in the eyes. Under his intense gaze, she couldn't help but tell the truth. Maybe it was the tequila talking, but in this moment she saw no reason she couldn't enjoy his company. What was the harm? When else would she have the chance at a hot alien lover for a night?

It didn't have to mean anything.

Ivy only wanted to feel good.

"I want you, too."

This time, when Rivix reached for her, Ivy let it happen. He trailed his knuckles across her arm. Trapped in his eyes, her body tensed, goosebumps breaking across her skin. Her breath came out in a heavy sigh. Rivix's gaze flicked to her mouth, lured by her panting. Ivy's mouth dried. She licked her lips. Slowly. Intently.

As Rivix leaned his head down to hers, she raised on her toes.

Their lips clashed like blades on ice. Sharp and instant—but unlike ice, hot. Heat sparked through Ivy, burning her. Rivix plundered her mouth, his tongue dancing with skill. Ivy matched each move. She trailed her arms down the stark lines of his bearded jaw and wrapped a hand in the fur of his collar. With a tug, she pulled him closer.

A growl rippled through Rivix, but Ivy didn't flinch in fear. The foreign, animalistic sound reverberated through her core. Ivy almost whimpered. She hooked her leg around his torso, wanting to be closer.

Wanting him inside her.

Damn, Ivy had never wanted someone like she wanted Rivix.

He gripped her thigh, dragging her to him. The thin layer of her underwear brushed against the hardness of his leather—and something under the leather, something long and thick and too fucking big.

Ivy broke the kiss, her face flushed. Rivix was nearly seven feet tall. Of course, his, um, member, would be massive.

"Rivix, I, uh..."

He tapped his forehead to hers. Those blue slitted eyes searched hers, the question echoed by the rumble of his voice. "Do you want to stop?"

Did she? No. Should she? Yes. But Ivy had done what she *should* for years. Skated day after day to make her mother proud. Provided for her family after they invested everything in her after the fire. Worked and sweated for approval that never came.

For once, Ivy wanted to do something for herself.

"I don't."

Rivix grinned, as bright and sharp as sunlight off icicles. With a single hand, he lifted her. Ivy squealed, but wrapped both legs around his waist. If he had any experience with pairs skating—which he obviously did—he'd easily be able to lift her.

Ivy traced her fingers through his dark strands of hair and mussed the trims of his beard. She had never fucked a guy with a beard. She liked the tingle across her skin as he kissed her. How would it feel against her chest? Against her thighs?

Against her core?

"What are you thinking?"

Ivy bit her lip. She had never been shy with her partners and her pleasure. Just because she connected with Rivix in a way she had with no other didn't mean she'd censor herself. "I'm thinking about the feel of your beard against... me."

"Me?"

"My thighs."

His lips quirked. "Anywhere else?"

If he wanted to be cheeky, two could play that game. "How about you search and find out?"

"Search?" Rivix lowered her to the desk, but once she hit the top, he didn't stop until he was on his knees. Something about having a big Fenrish warrior between her legs thrilled her. "I don't need to search, darling."

"Don't you—Oh, God!" Without warning, Rivix parted the skirts of her dress and ran a finger across her underwear, over the center of her pulsing, wet heat.

"Nope. Not at all."

Ivy glanced sky bound. "Good. You don't need instructions, then."

"Words of encouragement are always helpful." He traced against her again, featherlight. "Do you need these?"

"What?" She glanced down. Rivix wrapped a single finger around the edge of her panties. "You mean my underwear? I guess not?"

"Perfect."

With a swipe of his claws, Rivix shredded through the fabric.

Ivy gasped as the chill of the air brushed against her sensitive folds. Almost through instinct, she tried to close her legs—only to bump against Rivix. Those blue eyes met her, filled with a deep hunger. Ivy shivered, a tingle crawling up her spine. It was like Rivix sensed the tingle, his gaze trailing across the bodice of her gown, her straining breasts, her curved waist... and focused on her exposed flesh.

He licked his lips.

Ivy moaned at the look. *Just* the look. How would she survive more if Rivix nearly made her come with his eyes?

Suddenly, he wrapped a hand around her ass and jerked her forward, spreading her legs wide, like an eager man before a feast. Ivy swallowed. Her nipples ached. Her core burned, aching through her. God, he better not disappoint. None of her ex-partners had ever really learned how to eat out a girl properly—

Rivix huffed out a breath—of frost, the sudden chill on her core eliciting a scream from her throat. Part pain, part pleasure, but all around a good time.

"Oh my God, what was that?"

"Some Fens have an... ability. The nameless gods gifted our ancestors with the power to control entire ice fields, but the gene has wasted away to little more than a trick."

She swallowed. "And this is how you use your god-given power?"

"Did you not like it?"

Before Ivy could reply, he huffed out another breath. Ivy's back arched, a little yelp escaping her lips.

"I'll put you down for yes."

"Yes," Ivy said through the huffs. "Definitely yes."

Rivix didn't need any more encouragement. He huffed out another breath before following the movement with a swipe of his finger, heat to clash with the cold. Ivy thanked whatever alien gods had blessed him with the gift.

With each touch, each batch of hot and cold and hot and cold, the pressure built in Ivy. She squirmed as it climbed, barely able to think. Her hands trailed down her front. Her thumbs circled roughly over her own aching nipples. She wanted more. *Needed* more. Ivy was starved, desperate for one thing.

She grabbed Rivix by the hair, jerking his head up. He obeyed, that arrogant smile on his lips.

She tried to speak, but hadn't caught her breath.

Rivix only grinned wider.

"Stop... playing... around!"

He reached up, tracing his thumb against her lips. "I'm only getting started."

"You—" Ivy's sentence tumbled and died as Rivix ducked his head and *licked* her. His rough tongue swiped through her, too slow and yet too fast. Within a second, it was over.

Ivy whimpered, a clear plea.

In response, Rivix swirled a finger around her entrance.

"I thought you said you didn't need directions."

Rivix didn't stop his swirling. What a tease. He swirled and swiped through her folds, stopping short of her clit and never daring to enter her core. Ivy squirmed, but Rivix clenched her thighs. Holding her still. Holding her in place.

Holding her for him to torture.

He was trying to kill her. That was the plan. Tease her to death, then claim zapher with Sigrid. Ivy could almost hate him if it wasn't such a glorious way to die.

When his mouth found her clit, everything went black. Ivy threw her head back, clinging to him for dear life. His teeth grazed her flesh. She hooked a leg over his shoulder, holding herself to the ground. If she let go, she was sure she'd float away.

"Rivix, God, don't ever stop." Ivy didn't register saying the words, but it was her voice, begging for more.

Rivix growled in reply, a reverberation that echoed through her body.

Ivy clutched her hands in his hair, sending him even deeper. His tongue glided through her folds. The teasing rhythm grew to unbearable. She needed him in her. His thick pulsing warmth spearing through her, making her scream. Ivy shifted her foot to his shoulder, planning to push him away and mount him like a goddamn horse.

Rivix plunged a finger into her core.

Ivy writhed. Her legs betrayed her, wrapping around him and pulling him closer. His tongue sucked her clit. His finger rubbed against her inner walls, the rough texture of his skin near deadly. All Ivy could do was hold on as the pleasure battered her around. It pushed her higher and higher until moans ripped from her throat—

Rivix slid his finger against her g-spot. "Come for me, mate."

Ivy obeyed. With a scream, she exploded, the world turning into a blur of sound and color and pleasure. She shuddered, the orgasm milled mercilessly from her body. But Rivix didn't stop, licking and sucking and nipping and pulsing.

Ivy writhed, everything out of her control. Instead of fighting it, she embraced it, submitting—

He picked up his speed, pushing her over the cliff of another mind-blowing orgasm.

Ivy shrieked his name for all to hear.

EIGHT

RIVIX

Rivix counted Ivy's soft breaths, each huff as intoxicating as the last.

The noises of the party faded into the background, a low rumble easily ignored. All that existed was his mate. *His* mate. What a concept. Twisted together on the sofa, she shuffled lightly in his arms. Every part of him tingled and burned where she touched. If only he could lie here forever. Neither one of them had to say anything. They simply enjoyed the others' presence.

But something had to be said. Rivix had to tell Ivy the truth about their connection. Lies served no one.

He pushed onto his elbow—

Ivy jerked, startled by the movement.

She jumped to her feet and adjusted the rumpled fabric of her gown.

Helga's skulls. "Lie back down, Ivy. I'm going to get us something to drink."

"No, I'd better go," she said, not meeting his eyes.

What had happened? One moment he was giving her intense pleasure and the next she was here, dressing like she couldn't wait to get away from him. "Please stay. There's something I must share."

"It's okay, Rivix, really." Ivy buckled the straps of her shoes and made her way to the door, keeping a wide berth from him. "I know what this was."

"And what was this?" Because he certainly didn't know. He grabbed his trousers, ready to follow her to the ends of Herkleios.

She twisted around, half-facing him. "Please, just let me go."

Everything within him yearned to go after her, but he forced himself still. She wanted to leave. He *had* to let her go. It stabbed at him, a deep, primal pain. She was *his*. "As you wish."

Ivy nodded and rushed from the room. He dropped to the sofa, his fists clenched. If he held anything in his grasp, he'd smash it against the wall. He inhaled a deep scent. The Fenrish didn't have the nose the Eógans and Herkleians had, but Rivix could still track her down. Like the nectar on his tongue, her sweet aroma was one he'd never forget.

He leaned back into the cushions and closed his eyes. Everything smelled like her. Her scent was driving him insane. He wanted her. Needed to possess her. To feel her body against his once again. His cock strained against his trousers.

Fuck it.

Rivix freed himself and gripped his shaft. With a groan, he threw his head back. He'd never regret pleasuring Ivy as he had, but that didn't mean he didn't crave her. Her legs had tightened around his shoulders as he devoured her.

He imagined those same legs around his thighs, her tight walls clenching on his cock.

Rivix squeezed and stroked. Hyra must hate him to send him a mate so beautiful and brave, someone he couldn't resist. To give him such a strong desire while she felt nothing for him in return. Rivix's neck corded as the pressure in him built.

She was torture. She was ecstasy. A wicked pleasure, both perfect and painful.

But maybe Rivix deserved the pain. He wasn't a bad person, but he had certainly done bad things. Fought. Partied. Fucked. After leaving the monastery, covered in blood, he had locked away the pain of his childhood for years.

Did Rivix deserve Ivy? No. Did he want her?

Yes. A thousand times yes.

With one last stroke, Rivix exploded, growling her name as he came into his hand. He dropped onto the sofa, used, spent, and also determined. He wouldn't give up on Ivy.

He'd tell her the truth and prove they were meant to be.

He would sacrifice everything to see her smile at him.

Even if that meant losing the games.

THE NEXT MORNING, Rivix was out of bed early, fully packed and ready to go. It used to take five days to reach Fenrik from Herkleios, but in the last few years, scientists had tested new warp-speed technology. Originally studied by King Xenobaccus and intended to help with his goals of intergalactic domination, the tech had finally been repurposed for good. With the new ships, the trip would only take a day. But the new vessels were a tenth of the size of a Class-A ship like *The White Serpent*. The athletes would need to travel in batches.

Which meant Rivix needed to get to the manifest before Ivy.

When he entered the shipyard's main terminal, only a dozen athletes wandered around, waiting for their assignment. Rivix went straight for the check-in counter. A Fenrish female sat behind the desk, tapping away at a holo-screen.

He quickly scanned her name tag. "May I ask something of you, Maja?"

The female straightened with interest in her eyes. He propped an arm on the surface between them, letting his muscles flex and charm. "Of course, Your Highness."

"What flight is Addison Everest and her coach on?"

"Hmm." The female flickered between pages on her holo-screen. "On Flight 416, Your Highness."

"And myself and Sigrid?"

"The one before, Flight 415."

That wouldn't do. If Rivix didn't correct this now, he feared he never would. He couldn't let his mate escape his grasp. "Is there any way for us to be on the same flight? Addison is Sigrid's biggest adversary this year." He leaned closer, whispering conspiratorially. "We need to learn everything about her to gain an advantage."

There was nothing a Fen loved more than victory. "Of course, Your Highness. Let me see what I can do." The female went silent for a minute, tapping away. "I've moved you all onto Flight 416, Your Highness."

He gently touched her hand. Though his stomach swirled—revulsion?—he thought about the time he'd have with Ivy. "Please, call me Rivix."

She batted pale eyelashes and all but purred, "Rivix."

"Thank you, Maja. Know your actions today were vital to our success."

Maja leaned closer and Rivix forced himself not to move away. "You make sure Sigrid wins zapher, yes? We can't lose the medal to an Earthling."

Rivix only smiled, a grin that meant everything and nothing, before turning on his boots. Ivy would be none the wiser and, during their transport, he'd discover what had her spooked—

Rivix walked straight into her.

Ivy narrowed her eyes and shuffled to the left, but Rivix mirrored the movement. Just because he gave her mind-blowing pleasure didn't mean he would be less himself. "We have to stop meeting like this."

"Get out of the way, Rivix," she hissed.

Was it something he said? Something he *didn't* say? "Ivy—"

She marched past him to the check-in counter. "When's my flight?"

Maja's gaze flickered toward him briefly before she responded, "You're on Flight 416, Miss Dawson."

Ivy hooked a thumb in his direction. "And him?"

"The same."

Ivy twisted and glared. "What a coincidence."

"My thoughts exactly."

Ivy sighed and stomped across the terminal hall to where her student sat with odd, rectangular boxes on wheels. Rivix didn't follow. If he went after her now, she'd bite his head clean off like Brother Magnus's förg snake did to the kitchen's vermin. Rivix frowned. Ivy didn't deserve to be associated with anything the old abbot had done.

Sigrid settled at his side, yawning. In one hand, she tossed her transportable materializer, containing all her belongings and outfits. "What's wrong with her?"

"I wish I had the answer."

"Why don't you ask?"

If only Earthlings were as blunt. "Apparently humans don't do that."

"Huh." Sigrid's gaze flickered from Ivy to Addison.

Rivix sighed. He knew that look. "Don't you dare, Sig."

She blinked innocently at him. "Don't I dare what?"

"You looked that way at Larrs Kristianson."

"And? It didn't affect my concentration. I fucked him over twice —once in the bedroom and once on the ice." Sigrid shrugged a sharp shoulder. "Not like you can talk. You're a minute away from kidnapping Ivy Dawson Osträsk-style."

Rivix stiffened. Before Sigrid, Rivix had discarded student after student all over the same question—what happened with the Osträsk? But Sigrid had never asked. She never mentioned his time with the monastery or the ice ability all children selected by the clan possessed. Sigrid didn't care about his past or his titles. Sigrid only wanted to win. "I'm going to pretend you didn't say that."

She immediately bowed her head at his tone. "I'm sorry, Rivix."

"Review your routine, Sigrid."

"Yes, Your Highness."

NINE

IVY

When Rivix claimed the seat next to Ivy's, she didn't even need to turn to confirm it was him. Her entire body lit up like a Christmas tree. That, and Addison and Sigrid giggled in the seat in front of her. Goddamn teenagers playing matchmaker. Ivy imagined reaching out and lightly whacking her student, but that would mean brushing past Rivix. Her skin already tingled from the base of her spine to her nape. She didn't need to make it worse. Goosebumps prickled across her arm and her nipples perked to life. Traitors, all of them.

But on her next inhale, his sensual scent reached her nose. It took everything within Ivy to resist sighing. Yes, he had gifted her the most perfect orgasms. Yes, she wanted him to spend the rest of his natural life between her thighs. Yes, she wanted to strip him naked and lick him like he'd licked her.

But Rivix was a playboy. In the little time she had known him, he flirted with both Atlacoya and the flight attendant. Ivy knew athletes like him. Ivy had *dated* athletes like him. If you could call it 'dated.' More like *wham, bam, thank you, ma'am,* followed by never speaking again.

She liked him, but he'd never like her. Better to distance her heart now and let the memories of him keep her warm at night.

Without speaking, Rivix held out a thermos-like mug in her direction. She angled away, trying to put as much distance between them as she could—

The rich scent of coffee reached her nose.

Ivy almost grabbed it from his hand. She had brought a supply of her favorite ground bean, but had chugged it all down in the days since leaving Earth.

Rivix pulled it back, luring her closer.

Fine. She glared into his too-perfect face. "It's too early for this."

"Too early for what?" He crooked a smile at her. "We're just two people sitting next to each. And yes, I'm offering you this *kaw-fee*, but if you don't want it, I guess I could leave."

"You can leave and the coffee can stay."

Rivix didn't release the mug.

"Fine." And with that, Ivy easily plucked it from his hands. "How did you even find this? No one I asked at the hotel even knew what coffee was."

"I have my ways."

Ivy quirked her brow at him. "That's not an answer."

Rivix watched her take her next sip like the act was holy. "Someone *may* have told me about your love of caffeine."

Ivy shot another glare at Addison, who quickly twisted around. That explained where her student had disappeared to in the terminal. But she didn't have it in her to be truly mad at her student.

"What's Earth like?"

Ivy almost didn't answer. She didn't *want* to answer. But when Rivix looked at her with that full, genuine smile, her whole heart melted. It didn't matter that her brain shouted warnings.

For the first time in a long time, Ivy ignored her instincts.

It also helped that coffee consumption put her in a much better mood. "It depends where you are, really. There's so many different climates and people."

"You know what I mean. What's it like where you live?"

"Born and raised in Chicago," Ivy answered. "It's a big, bustling city full of life and great food, but I spent much of my childhood travelling from competition to competition. Sometimes it doesn't feel like home."

"I understand."

Did he? Ivy twisted his way, welcoming the edges of him into her line of sight. "I always wanted to live in a palace when I was younger, but I guess it's not as glamourous as it looks."

"It wasn't, no."

He paused like he wanted to say more, but Ivy didn't want to hear it. If he shared his childhood, she'd owe him hers. Was she ready for that? "What's Fenrik like?"

Rivix took the bait, a softness entering his hard face. "Frozen perfection."

The passion he said it with... Ivy repressed a shiver. "You're setting high expectations."

"Outside the city, there are beautiful fjords and frozen mountains and forests covers in icicles. I'll have to show it to you. There's one place in particular I think you'll like. It's my favorite place to skate."

"Are we having a field trip?" As one, Addison and Sigrid peaked over the seat.

Ivy mock-glared. It seemed the girls had become fast friends. "There's no field trip."

"Come on, it sounds pretty."

"Please," Sigrid added.

Ivy narrowed her eyes, but Addison put on her best pout. Ivy released a heavy sigh. "Maybe if we have time."

"Awesome," Addison said before the girls sunk back into their seats.

Rivix chuckled lightly at himself. "That's what I get for trying to impress you with a fancy trip."

"You were trying to impress me?" Ivy couldn't stop her gape. Sure, she was decently attractive, but Rivix was... well, Rivix.

Their first conversation included a proposition. He only wanted her for sex. That was how it went. After a life on the ice and nearly two decades in competitions, Ivy knew what men wanted from her.

But then he shocked her again. "Of course I'm trying to impress you, Ivy. You're my..." He found a word, but discarded it. Ivy was his what? She didn't have the chance to ask when he continued, "What is it that Earthlings say? I like you."

"You *what?*"

"I like you. Is that so hard to believe?"

Ivy stared at him—his seven-foot of muscled, pale blue greatness. Guys with Rivix's body and Rivix's face and Rivix's smile didn't confess feelings for women. They didn't have to. There was always another option. "Yes?"

"Well, it shouldn't be." Rivix leaned forward, skimming his hand against her leg. "I've said it before and I'll say it again. I'm not playing games with you, Ivy. I want to get to know you. I want to spend time with you. Not Ivy Dawson, the skater or Ivy Dawson, the coach. Ivy Dawson, the person."

A rush of emotions flooded through her, overwhelming and overpowering. Tears prickled at her eyes. Ivy forced them down. "You'd be the first."

"What does that mean?"

"I won a medal, Mom," Ivy yelled as she rushed through their tiny apartment's foyer.

Her mother lounged on the couch, the long sleeves of her shirt covering the burns. She frowned when she spotted the stains on Ivy's skirts from the treat Dad had purchased, but the expression twisted into an ugly glare at the sight of the silver medal. "Only second? Second isn't good enough."

Her dad rushed into the apartment behind her, pushing Willow's stroller. "Bunny, we—"

Her mother plucked a remote off the side table and chucked it at the door. "Why did you feed her, Peter? She didn't even place first.

Does second deserve a treat? No! Treats will only make Ivy a fat, little piggy. How will she skate then?"

Ivy pulled from the memory. A hundred others flashed through her brain, all the same. Her mother had been too angry and her father too subservient. Either way, neither of them knew the real Ivy Dawson. "My own parents didn't want to spend time with me."

"What happened?"

"My mother was in an accident when I was younger. A fire. That was why I was so spooked at the opening ceremony. I remember it all." Ivy glanced up, trying to stop the tears. She had never shared this with anyone. Only Willow knew, her sister there in the background of Ivy's entire life. But for some reason, she wanted to share it today. She glanced at Addison, but neither she nor Sigrid paid them any attention. "What I remember most was her never being the same. She was a skater and tried to continue her career after we were born, but the fire ended it. From that day forward, I was Ivy Dawson, future Olympic medalist. Ivy Dawson, daughter, was dead to her."

Rivix squeezed her hand. "I'm sorry, Ivy. That's a terrible thing to endure."

"It could've been worse." Ivy shrugged and tried to laugh, but it sounded hollow even to her ears. "My dad tried his best to make up for the love I lost from her, but he always followed her lead. Even now that she's gone, he says things with her in mind."

"It's difficult when your parent won't stand up for you."

Something in his voice had her focusing on his face, ignoring the tear in her chest. "Do you speak from experience?"

Rivix glanced down, the first time he didn't meet her eyes. "I was sent away as a child."

"To a boarding school?"

"No. And yes." He sighed, but then came to some conclusion. Perhaps the same that Ivy had? She wanted to share. She wanted him to know about her and her about him. "I went to a boarding school when I was eighteen, but between the ages of twelve and sixteen, I lived with the monks of Osträsk."

Atlacoya had mentioned them, but Ivy still didn't know who they were. "Uh, and that's bad?"

"It was. Because of my ice ability, my father had to send me to live with the Osträsk people. They're a nomadic sect that follows the old religious ways of our people. Most have abandoned their ways for the future and technology, but they still hold a lot of spiritual power." He shrugged. "What matters is my parents let me go. Rulers of the past protected their children from the treaty, but my parents didn't fight for me. I remember the day they took me away. I screamed and cried and begged for my mother to let me stay, but all she did was stare at me."

"Your mom? You seemed on good terms with her last night?"

"It's never been the same between us."

Ivy wanted to leap across the seat and hug him. How dare he look so sad? How dare someone make him that sad! Ivy was glad she hadn't known this last night. She never had the chance to stand up to her mom. Bunny Dawson passed away a few months before Ivy won her first Olympic medal. By then, Ivy had accepted she might never come in first, but being third best in the world was still a feat. In her dreams, she sometimes played out that missed confrontation in her head.

But Rivix's mom was alive. Ivy would have screamed without a care in the world for the alien's crown.

"Rivix," a familiar, sultry voice nearly purred from the aisle between seats.

Ivy spun around. "Go away, Vanessa."

The British coach flinched at Ivy's tone, but she didn't care about being rude. Now was not the time. Rivix had shared something with her, something she knew stabbed at him like her own secret. It deserved a response.

But Vanessa didn't take the hint. She glanced past Ivy. "Have you decided if you want to skate with me? Coaches have to register today."

Irritation had flooded Rivix's face, but he hid it much better. "Vanessa—"

Ivy grabbed his hand. "He skating with me."

"He is?" Vanessa asked.

"I am," Rivix said, a feral grin spreading across his lips.

It took everything in Ivy to turn away from that smile. She faced Vanessa and tried not to gloat. After all, this could go terribly. Ivy hadn't skated in front of an audience in years for a reason. Even sitting here, her ankle throbbed lowly in the background of her mind.

But there was no way she was leaving Rivix to Vanessa. "Yup. We're going to a private rink tomorrow on Fenrik to practice."

"That we are," Rivix agreed.

Vanessa's lip curled, but the coach knew when to accept defeat. As she slinked away, Rivix leaned closer and whispered over her shoulder. "Consider that binding, Ivy."

Ivy shuddered at the promise in his voice. What had she gotten herself into?

TEN

IVY

Ivy stared out the windows of Rivix's silver glider in awe. Fenrik was like being engulfed in a winter wonderland. The capital, Älvsholm, seemed like a giant ice sculptor built atop a crossing of rivers, but when they left the glinting buildings and crowded laneways of hover-cars, the countryside revealed a simple landscape of snow. White dusted the towering trees, ice-covered streams, and mountain peaks as far as Ivy could see. No wonder the committee chose Fenrik to host most of the winter sports.

A calm quiet filled Ivy, as if the snow blocked out the unwanted noise from her everyday life. Was it weird she could imagine living here? Few humans had left Earth for Intergalactic Alliance planets, but it was theoretically possible.

"Do you like it?" Rivix hadn't interrupted her thoughts, keeping his hands on the glider's control most of the ride. But now he pushed back in his seat, leaning on an elbow to examine her.

Ivy couldn't help her smile. "It's amazing."

"I'm glad you think so."

"So where exactly are we going?" They had left Älvsholm nearly an hour ago, and Rivix had yet to reveal their destination—only that it'd be the perfect place to skate.

"What a convenient time to ask." The glider slowed as if prompted by his words. In under a minute, it lowered to the ground and parked between two pale trees. "We've arrived."

Ivy twisted in her seat, but besides rolling hills of snow, she didn't see anything. "And here is...?"

The glider's roof raised, exposing them to Fenrik's cold air. Luckily, thanks to the design of her Team Earth gear and some fancy Fenrish nanite pill, Ivy barely felt the breeze. Rivix leapt from the vehicle into the snow. By the time Ivy unbuckled her seatbelt, the alien prince stood at her side, offering her a hand.

What a gentleman—if gentlemen were seductive scoundrels, that was. But Ivy gave him the benefit of the doubt. He said he liked her. She would believe him. For one day, at least.

Ivy landed on the snow beside him, her boots absorbing the impact. She gently untangled her hand from Rivix's and peered around, blocking the light. "I still don't see anything."

"We're not *entirely* there yet." Rivix pointed up a hill. "There's a perfect rink at the top of this hill. I found it after returning from boarding school."

Ivy eyed the steep path. "Sounds great, but I don't want to die hiking up this icy path."

Rivix offered her his hand again. "I'm used to this terrain. I'll keep you safe, Ivy."

Ivy rolled her eyes, but took his hand. Even though fabric covered his skin, the heat of him radiated through. Though she was loath to admit it, the fear and tension left her body at his touch. Somehow, she knew Rivix wouldn't let any harm come to her at his side.

One step at a time, they climbed the hill, Rivix taking the lead and Ivy following. Thank God she was a skater. Without years of balance training, she'd have ended up on her ass a dozen times. The thick snow turned to rocks near the top. Ivy kept her eyes on the ground, watching every move her feet made.

Suddenly, the landscape leveled out. Though the pale rocks remained, they separated to give way to an undisturbed frozen pond. It glinted in the sunlight, a beautiful expanse of natural blue. Though Ivy had spent most of her life on artificial ice, she loved the excitement of natural rink.

"This is absolutely breathtaking," Ivy said with a huff, her breath turning to fog before her.

"Though I first learned to skate at the monastery, I didn't fall in love with skating until I came here. The monks taught me battle theory, but my own practice taught me grace."

"That can't be true. I saw those clips in the embassy's study. You're a natural on the ice."

Rivix surveyed the pond with something like fondness in his eyes. "Thanks, but it took lots of practice. I wasn't born with grace and talent like you."

Ivy looked down. If only her mother had taught her to receive compliments. What did one say in response? Did they truly mean it? "Thank you."

"It's true. You're a star."

And Ivy believed it. Somehow. After everything her mother said and done, how could she trust again? But she knew in her heart that Rivix was being genuine.

"Shall we?" Rivix offered out his hand and stepped onto the rink. Blades materialized on his boot mid-step. The Earthlings had brought their own skates, but Rivix had lent her a pair of the high-tech alien ones. She followed behind him, hesitating for a second. Like he promised, the blades appeared right as she touched the ice, but she hadn't prepared for the vibration in her boots.

Ivy stumbled. She caught her balance at the same moment Rivix caught her. Her hand flashed out to rest against his chest, holding an inch of space between them. Her eyes met his, their breaths mingling. Through her palm, she felt his heart skip a beat. Ivy leaned closer, lured by his warmth and scent. How could he be warm when they were surrounded by nothing but ice?

"Are you ready?"

Ivy nodded, though every cell within her screamed. Partially out of fear—she hadn't pushed herself on the ice in so long—but also because of Rivix's presence. This close, his scent nearly entranced her brain.

Rivix lowered her hand to her back, positioning himself like a dancer. Ivy never skated with a partner, though she had witnessed pair skating many times and knew this was the typical posture.

"How... Earth-like?" Ivy said, though all her focus was on the feel of Rivix against her skin. Would his touch ever fail to send a spark of electricity down her spine?

"I studied your planet's skating when evaluating you for the Intergalactic Games. The Fenrish don't dance on the ice."

As he talked, Rivix slowly moved, shuffling back and around. Ivy matched his speed and pace. Skating in unison claimed half of her attention. How did pairs do it? "You're dancing well enough to me."

"As are you."

After two laps around the rink, Rivix halted and asked, "Do you trust me?"

Ivy was at a loss for words. Did she trust him? It wasn't a simple question to answer. She trusted him to keep her safe, but was also somehow certain he'd break her heart. He had saved her at the opening ceremony and pleasured her into another galaxy, but he was a playboy and an athlete. What future could they possibly have together?

But that wasn't what he asked. "I trust you not to drop me."

Rivix lowered her hands down her body. "I'll take what I can get. How about we start with a lift?"

"As long as I don't have to do any jumps." Ivy's ankle couldn't handle the pressure today. "So you hold me up and I lift my legs into a split?"

He nodded. "Seems a basic move your people try."

"Probably easier said than done."

"It will be if you trust me." Rivix skated backwards, gradually picking up speed. "I won't drop you."

"I know you won't, but I still have to get past the fear I'll fall and crack my skull open."

They twisted around the edge of the pond, racing across the ice. "Don't you take that same risk when you land jumps?"

"I guess." Ivy huffed with the exertion, taking a pause as they raced to the other edge. Her competitive nature pushed her forward. "I just know I won't fall."

"And you have to put that same faith into me." And with that, Rivix lowered his hands to the curve of her ass and lifted. Ivy nearly shrieked. She tried to split her legs, but her body jerked violently, rebelling against her. The last time she had flown this high, she crashed back to the ice and ruined her ankle.

But Rivix didn't let go. He slowed his pace and lowered her to the rink, his arms not even shaking. To him, she barely weighed a thing.

Ivy huffed in a breath when she touched solid ground, the breath nearly a sob.

Rivix cradled her into his arms, blocking the world around her. "Look at me, Ivy. I've got you."

Ivy gazed into his slitted blue eyes, letting herself fall into their depths. She had made jumps before. Only days ago, she had showed Addison a spin on the rink, one she had done a thousand times. She hadn't ever skated with a pair, but so what?

Rivix wouldn't drop her.

"Let's try it again."

Rivix brushed a hand across her cheek. "Are you sure?"

She mirrored the action, grazing her knuckles against his beard. "I am."

Rivix didn't question her. Together, they pushed off, picking up their pace. They did one lap. Then two. The anticipation blossomed in her chest. This time, when Rivix wrapped his hand around her waist, Ivy glided gracefully into his hold. He lifted her up and spun while Ivy raised her arms and legs.

Ivy laughed, ecstatic. Her own coach had told her skating in pairs required chemistry and trust. At the time, she couldn't imagine willingly giving that to someone else. Yet now, she had no doubt Rivix would catch her every single time. It wasn't that pair skating wasn't for her.

She just hadn't found her ideal match.

When Rivix lowered her back to the ice, Ivy threw herself into his arms, a joyful giggle escaping her throat. Rivix chuckled, too. The deep sound reverberated against her. She leaned closer to him. She couldn't deny their connection any longer. Ivy wanted him—no, *needed* him. So badly.

Rivix abruptly slowed and pulled his hands from hers.

"What's wrong? I thought you wanted this as much as me."

"Helga's skulls, Ivy, of course I want you. From the moment I saw you, I wanted to taste and explore every inch of you. How could I not? You're pure perfection. But you aren't sure of me. I want this to be real between us. I can't have a taste of you and then lose it."

"I might be looking for more than a one-night stand, too." He didn't so much as chuckle, his face completely serious. Ivy brought her hand to cup his cheek. "I can't deny there's something between us any longer. I want you. Not just for now, but after, when the games are over. I'm willing to give us a shot."

"I'd be honored to be in your life... and your bed."

The tingling in Ivy turned to a burning heat. "Stop talking about what you're going to do and just do it already."

He brought his lips to hers. "As you wish."

ELEVEN

RIVIX

Rivix claimed Ivy's mouth, desperate and passionate and all-consuming. He had touched her before, kissed her before, but he hadn't realized how he longed for her taste until now. Her lips parted, letting him inside. He took and devoured, wanting every bit of her.

Needing every bit of her.

She was his mate. The naika to his naikos, if he used the words of his mother's people. Being here with her, touching her, was the way things were meant to be.

Rivix trailed his hands through her hair and down the sides of her neck. He didn't check for a matebond mark. He didn't need to see to know. When he reached the furs of her coat, he trailed his fingers under the fabric, brushing gently across her collarbones.

Ivy shivered and broke the kiss.

Rivix barely repressed his ravenous growl. But while his body burned and his cock throbbed, he'd do whatever Ivy wanted—

She unbuttoned her coat and tossed it down to the ice.

Rivix raised a dark eyebrow and glanced around the ice rink. Humans weren't made to survive in this intense chill, even with the warming nanite pill. "We could go back to my glider?"

Her lip quirked, a mocking smile he wore often. "Live a little, Rivix."

Rivix wouldn't argue with that. As Ivy tugged at her shirt, Rivix tossed his own fur coat to the ice. His eyes stayed locked on her. They didn't touch, didn't speak. Rivix discarded one piece of clothing after another, but he imagined her hands trailing down his body. Imagined trailing his fingers down her.

The tension in Rivix built and climbed at each revealed inch of skin. She was so pink and smooth and supple. The curve of her breasts intoxicated him. The valley of her belly had him salivating. She slid off her pants and underwear last, exposing curved thighs, a perfect ass, and that patch of dark red hair. Rivix's cock grew harder, larger.

With one hand, he freed his last piece of furs, standing as naked as her.

"Oh, wow." Her eyes widened at his girth. "You're, uh... big."

Rivix stared down at his rod. Females had complimented his pale blue member and come screaming when his ridges rubbed against their inner walls, but he had thought himself only average. "Human males must have disappointing cocks."

"Uh, well, yeah, I guess." Though she said the words, her eyes remained transfixed.

Rivix skated closer, closing the distance between them. "We will fit together perfectly." He trailed his knuckles against her cheek before following the line with his mouth. "I'll lick every inch of you." He kissed a trail down her neck. "And when you're moaning and wet, I'll plunge into your depths." He brushed against her nipple, the hair of his beard teasing against the sensitive skin. "You'll come so hard and so loud that Fens living miles away will hear you scream my name."

She shuddered against him. Before he could take the lovely pink bead into his mouth, Ivy reached between them and wrapped her hand firmly around his cock. Her palm barely fit around the width. "No more playing around."

An animalistic hunger exploded through Rivix. He needed her. Desperately. He picked her off the ice and plunged her down onto his cock in one swift motion.

Ivy gasped as he invaded her wet heat, the sound part pleasure and part pain. "Skipping the foreplay, huh?"

It took all of Rivix's brain cells to form a response. He almost fell to his knees as she clenched around him, adapting and expanding to his length. Helga's skulls, she felt amazing.

But she had issued a challenge. It deserved a response.

Rivix wanted to thrust into her, pounding and pounding until she screamed. But he didn't. He skated forward, slowly heading for where his pile of furs lay scattered on the ice. As he moved, he turned his attention to her budding chest. He slid one hand languidly up her spine and around to her front. When he reached the weight of her breasts, he cupped one in his hand. He circled her skin with the brush of his fingers, the warm heat of him awakening her skin.

And suddenly, without warning, his hand went cold.

Ivy gasped at the quick change in temperature. Her body arched, giving him access. Giving him permission. He rubbed out another few circles of cold before switching back to hot.

Ivy shivered, throwing back her head. With each rotation, he approached her straining nipple. The deep red bud screamed for his touch.

Rivix got closer and closer... then stopped.

Ivy raised her head and opened her eyes. "What are you doing?"

"Waiting."

She shuffled in his arms, her heat shifting on his cock. His other hand clenched on her waist. She grinned knowingly. "Do you want me to beg?"

He did. He wanted to hear the words. Wanted to hear her admit defeat. "I do."

She shuffled again. Rivix couldn't help a groan. "You first."

"Ivy—"

Adjusting her leg at his waist, she pulled off him an inch and rammed herself back. Ivy moaned, her light sound overpowered by his growl.

Fine. If she wanted to be fucked, he would fuck her like she deserved.

Rivix dropped to his knees, landing in the furs. Ivy squealed at the freefall, but he wrapped a hand around her back. He lowered her slowly to the ground and pulled at her hips. Her legs locked around his midsection. She splayed before him, her red hair a dash of fire against his white furs. Gods, she was beautiful.

Beautiful and perfect and all *his*.

Ivy pushed onto an elbow. "Rivix—"

"Do you want me to stop?" he huffed.

"What? No, I—"

He didn't let her finish. Not now. Not when he had the perfect angle on her sweet, burning core. He thrust into her depths, sinking into her heat. Ivy gasped. Her hands clenched into the furs.

She'd need to hold on to survive this.

Rivix gripped her legs as he pulsed. Gods, she was his. His mate. His everything. He had never wanted a female to call his own. Never imagined one who didn't fear his ability and his past. But Ivy didn't. She didn't care. She was as damaged as him, as competitive and ambitious.

His perfect match.

She began mewing, faint cries ripped from her throat. Rivix wanted to hear those sounds until the day he died. This is what he would do. Screw coaching. Fucking Ivy deserved his full attention. The ridges of his cock swelled, grating on her walls as he pounded in and out.

"Rivix, I'm—Oh, God." Her hands grasped for solid ground. Her head thrashed. Her breasts bounced, jostled by his movement. Her moans increased, rising and rising. With a few more thrusts, she'd tumble over the edge and explode.

Because of him.

He wanted to hear her scream.

"God, deeper," she yelled hoarsely.

Rivix picked up his speed, plunging into her with primal strokes. She matched his movements. Their moans morphing into one continuous sound. They were made for each other. Entirely in sync, their pleasure cresting as one. After experiencing this, there was no way Rivix could ever go back to other females.

Ivy was his one and only.

With a scream, she cried out his name. Her core convulsed around him, gripping him tight.

Rivix buried himself in her and exploded in an endless rush. His hips thrust uncontrollably. Rivix collapsed, landing on his elbow as the orgasm infused his every cell.

The pleasure ended one day or month or year later. Rivix didn't know or care when. He rolled onto the furs at Ivy's side. He had never felt so satiated in his life. He reached for her, intent on memorizing every line, every inch of her body.

Ivy snuggled closer and lay her head against his chest. "That was amazing."

He traced a line up her back to the nape of her neck. It was time to tell her. Higher and higher, he reached where her matebond mark—

Rivix encountered rough skin. He stiffened, Ivy echoing the movement. She tried to pull away, but he sat and glimpsed her upper back. A deep red welt splotched against her skin.

Rivix's fist clenched. "Who did this to you?"

Whatever reaction she expected, this wasn't it. The worry left her face, replaced by a flushed happiness. "No one hurt me, Rivix. At least not on purpose, anyway."

Even if it happened accidentally, Rivix would still commit a murder. "Explain."

"Remember I said there was a fire when I was a kid?" When he nodded, she continued. "My house set on fire one night while my family and I were sleeping. We all got out, but my mother and I suffered burns. My mom's injuries were far worse, so I got lucky."

Any burn was too much of a burn. Rivix traced it lightly. "Does it hurt?"

"Not anymore." She curled back into his arms. "Most of the time I almost forget it's there. Even the nightmares have faded. Until the fire at the opening ceremony, I actually thought I was completely over it."

"Everyone heals at their own pace."

"That's true enough." She smiled up at him, the look partially sad. "I never thanked you for pulling me out of the fire."

"You don't have to, Ivy. It was my duty as an honorable male."

"Still." She rose onto an elbow and kissed him hard. "Thank you."

His body awakened at her kiss, his cock twitching back to life. How, he wasn't sure. He would never grow tired of his mate. Not in a thousand years. "I think this is my favorite way to be thanked from now on."

"Well, I have a lot of reasons to say thank you. It's not every day a girl orgasms that hard."

Rivix traced fingers down her back until he came to the curve of her ass. He circled between her legs. Automatically, Ivy spread them, granting him access. Her breath huffed harshly against him as he murmured, "I'll be accepting thanks through kissing only now."

Ivy moaned.

She didn't stop for hours.

TWELVE

IVY

Ivy strolled through the monochromatic lobby, hand in hand with Rivix. The athletes and coaches congregating in the seating areas twisted and stared. Ivy couldn't fault them. She couldn't stop staring at Rivix, either. The sharp angle of his bearded jaw. His swoop of dark hair over intense eyes and a wicked smile. And his ice-carved body... Ivy flushed, a heat flaring in her core. Sure, figure skaters were fit, but Rivix had muscle upon muscle, perfect and delicious.

When they passed the concierge, Ivy made brief eye contact with Vanessa, the UK coach sending her a sharp glare. Ivy didn't care. Nothing could bring her down now. Rivix was interested in *her*—flaws and all.

When they reached a holo-screen, Rivix paused and pulled her closer.

Ivy laughed. "What are you doing?"

He answered her with a breathtaking kiss, slow and intimate. She moaned. Who cared if the whole lobby heard? Ivy had never been one for PDA. How people could be so affectionate under the watch of others had been a mystery to her, but with Rivix, she finally understood it. It was painstakingly difficult not to touch him.

He eventually pulled away, leaving her breathless. "I just can't help myself."

Ivy wrapped her hands around his torso. "Neither can I."

Rivix reached for the holo-screen. "Your suite or mine?"

The fire in her burst into an inferno at just the words. After they made love on the ice and again in the glider, Ivy had thought herself out-sexed for the week. But her hunger for Rivix bounced back at a remarkable speed. If only the Intergalactic Games weren't running. Ivy didn't want to do anything but fuck Rivix.

If they made *that* an official sport, Ivy would easily win zapher.

Ivy pressed her head against his chest and sighed. "I really need to check on Addison."

"I know," he said, both resigned and accepting. "I should find Sigrid, too. Dinner tonight?"

"Where do you want to go?"

He gave her a devilish grin. "I was thinking more like room service."

God, how was she going to survive the day? "Works for me."

Rivix tapped the holo-screen, selecting a spot in the hallways between their two rooms. Tingles crept across Ivy's skin, but she barely noticed them in Rivix's arms. When they appeared in the hall, she traced her hands along his chest and took one last inhale of his scent—

And almost choked. Ivy slapped a hand over her mouth. "What is that awful smell?"

Rivix stiffened before her, once again a firm block of ice, cold and unyielding. She sometimes forgot skaters in Fenrik weren't all harmless dancers, but warriors skilled in the art of iskrigg and inheritors of an ancient lineage.

He suddenly gripped her wrist and tugged at her bracelet. "Go back to the lobby."

"Like hell." Ivy fully pulled from his arms. He wasn't always going to be this bossy, was he? If so, they were going to have a problem. "I need to know what's happening."

"Fine, but if I say go, you run."

Ivy gave him a noncommittal shrug. Just because she wasn't a hotshot Fenrish warrior didn't mean she'd run from a fight.

He sighed and shook his head at her, but Rivix crept down the hall, the two of them following their noses. When Ivy spotted the ajar door, her heart nearly burst. It was her and Addison's adjoined rooms.

Ivy tried to rush past Rivix, but he grabbed her arm. She didn't need to glare this time. He let her go and gestured. Somehow, she understood. Together, they pushed into the room. Nausea burst to life in Ivy's gut. The sofas and chairs were toppled, the mattress nearly torn off the bed, and the table near the kitchenette shattered into a thousand piece of now-melting ice. Foul-smelling flowers scattered the floor.

Ivy rushed forward to the adjoining door. "Addison?"

Rivix followed on her heels, a stern set to his jaw. "There's no one here. We need to go check on the rest of Team Earth. Do you know where they are?"

"The rest of the skaters are on this floor." Ivy all but ran into the hall. Her ankle flared in pain, but she ignored it. Something was terribly wrong. She didn't understand what the flowers meant, but the overturned furniture was a clear sign.

She pointed at two doors in the opposite direction. "Check those!"

Rivix nodded and started knocking on doors. Ivy did the same in the opposite direction. No answer. Maybe some of the skaters were out?

Yes. That had to be it.

Ivy turned a corner, ready to pound on the last door—

Vanessa stood before it, hand on the knob. She took one look at Ivy's tear-stained face and snorted. "What's wrong? Alien prince bored with you already?"

Vanessa really had the world's worst timing. Ivy clenched her fists and stormed forward—

Rivix appeared at her back, placing a comforting hand on her shoulder. "Vanessa, have you seen anyone from Team Earth?"

The coach's entire demeanor shifted. Even though Vanessa had watched Rivix and Ivy in the lobby, she still got dreamy-eyed at the sight of the prince. "They're all eating lunch together in Addison's room. At least they were last I checked."

"How long ago was that?"

"Maybe half an hour?"

Ivy twisted around to Rivix. "Then they can't have been taken far, right?"

"Taken?" Vanessa asked, but Ivy ignored her.

Rivix stroked a hand across her cheek before his gaze flicked over her head. "Vanessa, can you go find the hotel's security?"

Ivy couldn't see the coach, but she must have nodded before tapping at her own bracelet. When Ivy pulled from Rivix's arms to pace, the hallway was empty.

What was happening? Why would someone take the skaters from Team Earth?

Or worse, had the kidnappers grabbed the *entire* Team Earth?

"What's happening, Rivix?"

Rivix had his holo-screen expanded before him, probably messaging his father and anyone else who might help. He quickly minimized it. "I have an idea."

"And?" Why was he suddenly so secretive? Or had he always been this way? He had told her a few details about his childhood and his time with the Osträsk, but how much did Ivy really know about him? "What do the flowers mean?"

"They're from Herkleios," he said. "Called hanat flowers. Herkleian mythology says after the god Hadus betrayed the goddess Hyra, she banished him and all the flowers around his palace turned to rot. It's the Herkleian death flower."

The word stabbed through Ivy's gut. "A death flower?"

"This must be Argrix's doing. Hanat flowers were a favorite threat from his father, Xenobaccus."

Hearing Rivix say the name of the former Herkleian king was mind-warping. He was a figure she heard about on the news, hardly even real to her. But as Rivix's uncle, all the stuff she'd read about throne stealing, terrorist attacks, and breakout attempts became reality. "Why would Argrix do that? King Xenobaccus is dead and his brother Anax is securely on the throne."

"Revenge? Queen Alexandra helped oust Xenobaccus. When he tried to get his revenge and attacked *The Queen Avra* space station, another human named Olivia helped to thwart the attempt. My other cousin, Prax, was partially responsible for Xenobaccus's death, alongside his human mate. In Argrix's warped sense, Earth is responsible."

Ivy rubbed at her arms. This wasn't good at all. Rivix tried to comfort her, but she side-stepped him. "How do we know this isn't just a prank from another team and the skaters are off at the rink?"

"No one leaves hanat flowers as a joke." He paused, wringing his hands together. "There's something you don't know, Ivy. Argrix has threatened the Intergalactic Games. That's why I was suspicious about the explosions at the opening ceremony."

Ivy froze and stared. "Argrix threatened the games, and no one did anything to stop him?"

Rivix lowered his gaze, but only for a moment. "The alliance leaders didn't want to worry anyone. After Xenobaccus's death, Argrix lost support from his last ally, King Akhen of Neith. All of his siblings and cousins sided with Anax. With no resources, we thought he was bluffing."

"We?" Ivy rushed forward, sudden rage flaring through her lungs. "*You* were involved in the decision to *not* even warn my people about the threat?"

He met her eyes, but Ivy wished she could erase the expression from his face. How dare he look so pitiful and guilty when it was her student and team members kidnapped? "Ivy, I honestly thought nothing of his threat until the fire."

"Which was days ago! We were in danger the whole time and you pretended everything was fine." Ivy nearly paced halfway down the hall before turning back. Her anger burned away the flare of pain in her ankle. "Would acknowledging the threat throw a wrench in your seduction attempts?"

"Ivy, please. You know you mean more than that."

"Do I? Because it seems to *me* you've been lying this whole time. What's one more lie if it gets you laid, right?"

Rivix flinched like she hit him. "Ivy, I love you. You're my... you're my mate."

A near-hysterical laugh bubbled up her throat. "I'm going to ignore the fact that you chose now as the moment to declare your undying love for me." Ivy squared her shoulders. She couldn't leave Addison to whatever fate awaited her. Ivy had promised Mr. and Mrs. Everest that she'd care for their daughter. Her relationship drama wasn't important. "Right now all I want is to find the skaters."

"You're right. They should come first." Rivix recalled his holo-screen, the pain washed away under the serious expression of a prince with responsibilities to his citizens. "I'm getting a security detail for you and any other Earthling in the hotel. Herkleios sent some of their soldiers with us and my parents will loan the palace's personal guards."

"I don't want protection. I want answers."

"And I'm going to get them for you."

Ivy grabbed his wrist. Her skin burned where she touched, but she ignored it. Listening to her lust got her into trouble in the first place. "I'm coming with you."

Rivix gently removed her hand, regret in his eyes. "I'm going to use every connection and advantage my position provides, but there's no way you're going to be allowed in talks of this significance."

"Fine." Ivy crossed her arms like a shield around her. But if she was honest, she was holding herself together more than holding Rivix out. The heat of him pulsed through the hall, luring her. How she wished she could lean into him. But he had lied, and Addison paid the price for it. She needed time to think.

Still, a tiny part of her won out and whispered, "Promise me they'll be alright, Rivix."

"I'm going to bring them back. I swear."

THIRTEEN

RIVIX

The Royal Palace in Älvsholm speared from the ground, a harsh building of silver and ice. Its peaks and towers always reminded Rivix of icicles dangling from the mouth of a cave outside the monastery. Some of the other children had dared Rivix to go inside, but he had never made it past the mouth for fear of the ice daggers impaling him. At least he had made it to the entrance. Most of the others were spooked by the whistling wind.

Once inside, Rivix didn't have to guess where his parents would gather to discuss the kidnappings. In the time it took him to fly to the palace, they had called a meeting of the Intergalactic Alliance. Rivix checked his wristband for more updates as he walked. The guards had searched the hotel and surmised only fourteen human skaters were taken. The news wasn't a relief. A quarter of Team Earth missing was a quarter too many.

As he approached the royal family's private library, the security thickened. He reached the door, and the guards stepped aside without question. Though Rivix wasn't anywhere close to being the next king and never wanted that responsibility, King Skarde always wanted his youngest son's opinion when it came to the Intergalactic Games.

When he pushed opened the doors, his gaze immediately focused on his parents. King Skarde paced the room, the nearly eight-foot-tall king in a cloak of white fur to match the paleness of his hair. His mother sat behind him on a sofa, stirring at a cup of steaming zion. As a foreigner, his mother didn't officially have any power as consort, but his father had always ruled with her by his side.

Between his parents and the massive shelves of ancient books, thin circular comms devices projected holograms of representatives from across the Intergalactic Alliance. He recognized his aunt, Empress Ailis of Eógan, and his cousin, King Anax, but the other representatives were high-ranking dignitaries he barely knew.

King Skarde turned at his entrance. "Rivix, good to have you here." His father's voice boomed through the room, echoing off the walls. "We have my son to thank for securing the official games' hotel. No one is getting in or out for the time being."

"Have we received any ransom videos?"

His father's face darkened at that. "We have, son."

His mother touched his arm. "You aren't going to like it."

"Play it for him, Rhiona," Empress Ailis said. Rivix tried not to stiffen at his aunt's voice. Even as an adult, she terrified him. The Empress of Eógan had survived numerous assassination attempts from rival families simply by killing the assassins herself—or so the rumors went. Even her son, Prax, didn't know the full extent of the truth. The stories had grown out of control between all the royal cousins.

Turning back toward the alliance representatives, his father selected an option on his holo-screen. "Here's the message."

A projection of Sigrid popped into the center of the room. Rivix's heart wrenched. He hadn't even thought to message his student. Of course she had been with Addison. He examined her, taking in her ruffled clothes and an off-white bruise forming on her cheekbone. "Humans are a dirty, inferior species. You bring great shame to the

Intergalactic Games by allowing them to compete alongside us. We warned you at the opening ceremony and you proceeded anyway."

Sigrid paused, her eyes flickering as she read the next line off camera. She stifled a sob. With that, Rivix knew what his student would say next. Sigrid never cried. "The human athletes will be put to death. Their execution will be broadcast in place of the next set of games."

Sigrid covered her mouth, trying to hold back her tears.

"Continue," a voice shouted in growling Fenrish.

Everything within Rivix shriveled. He *knew* that accent.

"Please stop," Sigrid pleaded.

Her protest was met with a quick slap to the face. Rivix's blood boiled. How could anyone show such disrespect to a child?

When she recovered from the shock of being hit, she continued. "The lives of the humans are non-negotiable, but if you want the Fenrish champion back, you *will* meet King Argrix's demands. Cut all ties with the dirty Earthlings."

King Argrix? His cousin had lost his mind. Even if Anax died, the Herkleians would rather crown his newborn twins or any one of Anax's dozen siblings instead. Argrix would never see his father's crown. Not only because of inheritance laws, but also because Rivix was going to kill him.

"He's allied with the Osträsk, isn't he?"

His father didn't deny it. Instead, King Skarde said to the dignitaries, "We received the message from the Osträsk ambassador. As some of you may know, they're a nomadic group who follows the old ways and worships the old nameless gods. Though not officially part of my kingdom, they still hold religious power."

"I thought you were on good terms with them, Skarde," Aunt Ailis said, her red eyes flickering to Rivix.

"The last decade has been... tense." Though his father didn't say why, everyone in the room knew. If Rivix had stayed as the treaty insisted, there wouldn't be bad blood between the Fens and the nomads. "But we remained amicable until today."

"Their actions make little sense," Rivix said. "All-Mother Gundhil enjoyed her peace too much to admit outsiders. Argrix isn't even Fenrish. Why are they doing this?"

Though it was barely noticeable, King Skarde flinched. If Rivix didn't know, then who would? He had disappointed his father—again. "We don't know. We're trying to make further contact with them to negotiate Sigrid's release."

Just Sigrid? A chill crept Rivix's spine, cooling the air around him. "What about the others? The next broadcast is set for tomorrow night. We're running out of time to save them."

"I'm deploying reconnaissance teams to the Osträsk Mountain, but we won't engage until we have more information."

"I'd like to go with them."

"I don't think that's a good idea, Rivix."

It took everything in Rivix not to challenge his father, but that was not the way they did things on Fenrik. Rivix had to listen to his elders, especially when the male standing before him was more than his father right now.

"I'll head back to the hotel, then." He stormed out of the room before anyone else responded.

Rivix was halfway down the corridor when his mother called after him. He stopped and waited for her to reach him. When her warm presence settled at his side, he said, "Mother, I know what you're going to say. I can't just sit by and wait for them to be killed. I can try to stop it."

"You misunderstand." Her mother put a gentle hand on his arm. "I will not hinder your rescue attempt. I only mean to assist you. Your father is a good king, but he cares about politics too much. I want these athletes rescued, for both their sake and your own." His mother paused, glancing around. She said the next bit quietly, "And for your mate. She'll never accept you if you don't do everything you can to help her fellow Earthlings."

"She can't even look at me right now." And she had every right. Rivix had lied. His instincts had screamed something was wrong, but he ignored them, too enraptured with Ivy. *Everything* she said was true.

"She's probably angry, but I believe she cares for you. I don't want you to spend the rest of your life longing for her. You must do what needs to be done."

He needed to make it up to her—to show her he was worthy. "I'm going to ready my ship. Will you keep Father busy until I'm gone?"

"Certainly. I've had people tracking the movements of the Osträsk since you left them. In case they decided to retaliate. Based on my last report, they should be encamped in the Heila Caves."

Rivix stiffened. The Osträsk only entered the Heila Caves when the old leader died and a new one needed to be selected. Had All-Mother Gundhil finally passed? Regret swarmed through him. Without the All-Mother, he never would've survived. "Thank you."

"It's the most I can do, given what I put you through."

Rivix stiffened. For years, he and his family had ignored the traumas they caused each other. "You didn't know they were abusing me. Every time you visited, I told you how happy I was to be learning iskrigg."

"I shouldn't have let them take you in the first place, treaty be damned."

A strange tangle of emotions burst through Rivix's chest at the emotion in her voice. His mother had cared. *Still* cared. Though Rivix was a male grown, the wounds of his childhood had never fully healed.

Perhaps now they finally would. Maybe then he'd be worthy of Ivy's love.

His mother must have sensed the direction of his thoughts. "Go to her, son. You don't know what trouble the Osträsk will cause. Say what you need to say while you both still have a chance."

FOURTEEN

IVY

When the knock reverberated through the door, Ivy knew who was on the other side. She crept closer, her entire body tingling at Rivix's nearness. Her every cell was a traitor, yearning for him. How dare he not tell her about the threat? If she had known Addison was in danger, she wouldn't have stayed in the competition.

Ivy imagined her student's reaction. Addison wouldn't have surrendered anything for the chance at her first major win. Ivy was the same way. So maybe they wouldn't have left, but if they had known, Ivy would have been careful. She certainly wouldn't have left her student unattended to go skate and flirt with a handsome prince.

Ivy pulled open the door and glared at the guard between her and Rivix. In their hours apart, her rage had grown into a beast of its own. "What do you want?"

Rivix turned on the guard. "Could you give us a few minutes alone?"

The Fenrish male nodded and marched down the hallway without another word.

Rivix faced her. Ivy faced him. God, she wanted to smack him and kiss him at the same time. How dare the dirty liar be dreamy and sexy?

Ivy crossed her arms and didn't move from the doorway. If Rivix intended to make things right between them, he had to make the first move. She didn't want a partner who didn't know how to communicate.

Rivix's dark eyebrows arched lightly. "Can I come in?"

"Do you have any information about Addison?" She also didn't want a man—*male*—who didn't correct his mistakes.

"I do."

"Fine." Ivy shuffled out of the way. "Come in."

As Rivix approached, Ivy moved back, keeping a wide space between them. She couldn't let him seduce her into forgiveness. In her youth, after her mother flew into a rage, she showered Ivy and her father with gifts and kind words. It never solved the issues, only buried them until they festered. Ivy didn't want anything with Rivix to fester. He was different.

They were different.

Ivy plopped down onto a single chair in the corner, her back to a windowed wall. When Rivix stepped into the light, the pale blue of his skin sparked, reflecting the gleam. A sigh automatically huffed from her lips, but she twisted it into a cough. "So?"

Rivix crossed his hands behind his back like a good soldier. "They're being held by the Osträsk."

"The same people who took you? Why?"

"They're not known for opposing our government, but I suspect Argrix offered them something."

Ivy focused on breathing. How did they end up in the middle of this? Ivy and Addison weren't anyone important. Her student didn't deserve to be used by a megalomanic prince with a hatred for humans. "And why would Argrix do that? What does he want with them?"

Rivix paused. "He plans to execute them during the next scheduled broadcast."

This time Ivy couldn't hold in her sob. Rivix started forward, but Ivy held out a hand. She desperately wanted his comfort, but Ivy wasn't a child, the pain of the world hidden through a hug. A hug rarely solved anything. Ivy needed action. "Is there any way to stop them? Can't your army do something?"

Rivix kneeled, his presence close but out of reach. "My father ordered more recon before engaging the enemy."

"But Addison and Sigrid don't have that kind of time."

"I agree with you." Rivix shuffled closer until he hovered an inch away. "That's why I'm heading out myself."

"Alone?" Nausea flared to life in Ivy's belly. She wanted Addison and the other athletes back, but not at the cost of Rivix.

Fuck it. She took his hand.

Rivix stared down at where they touched, her thumb skirting out to rub at her palm. "I'll be fine. I know the Osträsk."

But that wasn't necessarily a good thing. Though Rivix hadn't told her the whole story, she assumed his time with the clan wasn't entirely positive. And if he returned to the palace at sixteen, did that mean the treaty with the Osträsk was broken? Ivy was missing a layer of information, but she didn't have time for a Fenrish history lesson. "I'm coming with you."

"Ivy—"

"Addison is my student. The athletes of Team Earth are my people. Let me come."

Rivix clenched his jaw, but Ivy held his gaze. Sure, she didn't know how to fight. She wasn't versed in politics or negotiation. But Rivix couldn't go in alone. They were a team.

Ivy didn't know when *that* had happened, but the words rang true. If Rivix wanted this to work between them, they needed to be equal partners.

"You'll stay on the ship," he finally said.

Good enough for her. "Let's go."

IVY SNUGGLED into the front seat of Rivix's glider.

The Osträsk currently inhabited a mountain range three hours outside the city. The farther they got from civilization, the rougher the terrain. The hills grew steep, the trees scarce, and the sharp crevices between the fields of ice treacherous. About an hour into the trip, Ivy glanced out the window and spotted a three-eyed, wolf-like creature the size of a horse. Rivix had called it an ulv, his hands tensing on the controls. The ulv watched them pass overhead, but Ivy couldn't shake the image of it lunging at the sky like something out of a horror movie.

When they approached the correct mountain range, Rivix pointed. "See that? There's an opening to the Heila Caves there. It's an ancient place, thousands of years old. The Osträsk use it to commune with the ancient gods and confirm a new leader."

Ivy repressed a shiver. "And for holding human prisoners?"

"They must have cells, but I've only been inside once, when I first arrived. The Osträsk confirmed my ice ability there."

"So you don't know the whole layout?"

"I can guess," Rivix said quietly. "I'll remember that day until I die."

The tone of his voice nearly destroyed her. Ivy had always wanted to face her mom, but the actual concept had been paralyzing. Was that what Rivix felt now? The tension hadn't left his body since he returned from the palace. Still, he flew forward, not turning back or cowering away. For Sigrid, for Addison, for Ivy, he'd face his past.

Ivy hit the button at the side of her seat, releasing her from the chair's forcefield. The loud click echoed through the quiet space.

Rivix twisted. "What—?"

Ivy slid across the seat and into his arms. He kept one hand on the steering panel, but shuffled automatically, allowing her closer to his heart. "I'm sorry, Rivix."

"I'm the one that should apologize." He leaned his chin on the top of her head. "You were right. I should have told you when I suspected the danger. You deserved to know."

Ivy loved a male who could admit his flaws. "Thank you for saying that. And I'm sorry, too. I got so angry at you. Too angry, I think. It's something I have to work on."

"Neither of us are perfect, Ivy. I promise to never keep anything from you again if you promise to give me another chance."

Ivy pulled back far enough to gaze into his eyes. "Of course I'll give you another chance."

Rivix grinned like sunshine splitting through clouds on a rainy day. Ivy could bask in his warmth forever. She lured his lips down to hers. The kiss was little more than a quick graze, but it reverberated through Ivy's core, spreading warmth from her fingers to her toes.

Rivix grunted with contentment when he pulled back, but on sight of the mountain, his frown returned. "Since we're about to confront my childhood, there's something you should know."

"What?" Whatever it was, Ivy wouldn't let it ruin her day.

Rivix paused as if collecting his words. He hadn't broached the topic before, then. "The Osträsk take Fens with an affinity for ice, but it isn't a luxurious life. We're trained to become warriors, and it's a harsh way to raise a child. I was whipped, beaten, and starved during my four years."

Ivy stiffened in his arms. "Excuse me?"

"When I turned sixteen, I finally had enough. The Osträsk are ruled by a council of elders, with All-Mother Gundhil acting as the leader. She was kind, but the monastery where children like me lived and trained wasn't. The abbot, Brother Magnus, was cruel... except for when All-Mother Gundhil visited." Rivix paused, but Ivy didn't interrupt. When he was ready, he would say it. "One day, I couldn't tell his lies anymore. I told her everything and when he denied it, I lashed out at him. It turned into a fight. I won, just barely, but All-Mother Gundhil wouldn't let me kill him."

"That's good, isn't it?"

"It didn't make sense. My people are harsh, but the Osträsk are even worse. If you start a fight, you must finish it. But All-Mother Gundhil stopped me and sent me home." Rivix paused and swallowed. "I never looked back, but now I wonder if she did it to save me."

"Oh, Rivix." Ivy caressed his cheek. She had imagined his childhood a life of luxury, but the cocky prince she first met was a mask to guard the truth of him. "I'm sorry. That's no way to treat a child."

"It's in the past, but..."

"Things like that leave scars." Even if they weren't visible, the scars were still there. The damage on their psyches would take a lifetime to heal.

Ivy curled into him, providing comfort in the silence. The mountains grew larger and larger on the horizon. As they got closer, Rivix became colder and stiffer. Ivy rubbed a hand up and down his back, massaging away the pain.

When they reached the correct distance—whatever that was—Rivix tapped at the glider's control panel and lowered the ship to the ground. Between two hills, the glider became near invisible in the snow.

"We can't get any closer. The Osträsk don't use modern technology, but they have scouts."

"Are you sure you should go alone?"

"You'll be safer here, Ivy." Rivix tapped half a dozen buttons on the control panel in quick succession. A button flashed into the air. "If I don't return in two hours, hit this button. I've programmed the glider to fly back to Älvsholm and alert the Royal Guard."

Like hell. "I'm not leaving you here, Rivix."

"You have to." He grasped her hand, somehow the touch more urgent. "You're more than my heart, Ivy, you're my—"

An arrow pulsed through the glider's hood. Though the end was feathered, a bit of metal circled the arrowhead. It sparked with a blast of electricity. The energy ripped through the ship. The holo-screen fritzed, sizzled, and died, the entire glider going dark.

In the silence, Ivy couldn't help but notice the harshness of her breathing.

"Please tell me that wasn't an Osträsk arrow."

When Rivix didn't reply, Ivy muttered, "Shit."

This wasn't good.

This wasn't good at all.

FIFTEEN

RIVIX

Rivix grabbed the knob on the bottom of his seat. It twisted with a loud snap, dividing the front bench into two separate chairs. Rivix swiveled his seat around, Ivy firmly in his lap. Damn the Osträsk. Damn his cousin. There was no way the clan would have sensed his ship without modern technology. The kingdom hadn't provided any —though they had offered—which meant it all came from Argrix.

His mate gripped the front of his furs. "What are we going to do?"

Reaching over her, he slammed his fist into a button in the back row. The seat raised, opening to a storage compartment large enough to fit a full-grown Fen.

"You're going to hide," he said, tracing the lines of her face. "I'll lead them away from here."

Her nails dug into his arm. "Are you insane?"

"This doesn't change our plan." Rivix pressed a quick kiss to her lips. "I'll find a way to get Sigrid, Addison, and the others out. I connected your bracelet to my glider, so once it reboots, it will return you to Älvsholm where you'll be safe."

"But Rivix—"

He claimed her lips in another kiss. Helga's skulls, he could kiss her forever. "You're not leaving me, Ivy. You're helping me. If I know you're safe, I can put everything into saving the athletes. Right now, this plan is their only hope."

Ivy bit her lip, but her tears stopped and she nodded. She scrambled from his lap and into the compartment.

Before he closed the lid, she grabbed his hand. "I love you."

Rivix had never known how much he wanted to hear those words. If only he could scoop her into his arms and hold her until the end of time. There was so much she didn't know—about him, about their connection. He tried to tell her they were mates before, but she hadn't grasped his meaning.

Next time they spoke, he would make her understand. There *would* be a next time.

"I love you, too, Ivy."

And with that, Rivix shut the compartment. He didn't bother grabbing any weapons. He hit the manual lever and pushed open the roof with his bare hands. Rivix surveyed the area around the glider. Though he couldn't spot the Osträsk, he knew they were out there. They didn't need tech to hide in the snow.

With a final huff, Rivix climbed out of the ship with his hands raised.

When Rivix's boots hit the snow, they emerged from the landscape. Cloaked head to toe in the white fur of an ulv, he wouldn't have noticed them if not for the glint of their weapons. At least the blades weren't modern and sparking with electricity. It took everything within Rivix to stay still as they surrounded him. His instincts urged him to fight, but he shoved them down. He needed to lead them away from the ship. His own safety came second to Ivy's.

The tallest male came forward and sneered, "What an unexpected surprise, Your Highness."

Though Rivix hadn't heard the voice in over a decade, he recognized Frode's nasally tone. The older boy had been a favorite of Brother Magnus and become his second in later years. If Rivix could see through the layers of fur, he would probably recognize all the warriors around him, once brothers and sisters in arms.

Rivix didn't let it show. "I didn't expect such a warm reception."

"Of course you didn't. You always thought we were nothing more than primitives, Rivix." Frode pulled the arrow from the side of Rivix's glider and slotted it back into its quiver. "Thankfully to King Argrix, we now have a radar system in place to engage with the enemy."

"All-Mother Gundhil is dead, then?" Rivix had suspected it, but the arrow and radar confirmed his theory. The old All-Mother had refused to accept any technological aid. More so, she never considered the city-bound Fens enemies.

Frode snorted. "Here to pay your respects?"

"I'm here for the humans you have hostage."

"An easy enough request." Frode gestured with his blade and the two Osträsk at his back rushed forward to restrain him. "Tie him up and search his ship."

Rivix's blood boiled. He couldn't let them find Ivy. "There's nothing of use on my ship."

"Forgive me if I won't take your word." Frode turned to his warriors and shouted, "Take it apart."

Helga's skulls. His attempt to spare Ivy possibly made things worse for her. But the Osträsk had probably never seen a glider. Perhaps they wouldn't know to check under the seat. Rivix kept his expression blank as fabric ripped and electronics crashed. Frode watched him with eager blue eyes, waiting for the moment he flinched.

Rivix wasn't that boy anymore. He would *not* flinch.

Then Ivy yelped, yelling, "Let go of me!" Rivix clenched his hands behind his back, but he didn't react. If Frode knew what Ivy meant to him, the male would tell Brother Magnus and the abbot wouldn't be kind.

They dragged Ivy out into the cold and threw her to the ground.

"Asshole," she muttered into the snow. Without translators, the Osträsk didn't understand the word. Thankfully.

Rivix stepped forward to help her stand, but one warrior pressed a sword to his throat. Rivix glared first at the warrior before turning the sour look to Frode. "She's not a part of this. Let her go."

Frode grabbed Ivy and dragged her to her feet. He tore off her bracelet and tossed it to the snow. "You brought her here, so she must be important. I'm sure *All-Father* Magnus will save you the best view for her execution."

THE HEILA CAVES were just as Rivix remembered, a cluster of dark tunnels and open caverns lit by crystalized rocks. They didn't pass many Osträsk as they made their way deeper and deeper into the planet. Most of the clan stayed in their homesteads in the dead of winter. Only the council of elders would have travelled here to select a new leader.

To select Brother Magnus. All-Father Magnus now. If only they had made any other choice.

When they reached a fork in the path, Frode stopped. He gestured down one path. "Throw the female with the other humans."

No. If they were separated, Rivix might never see her again. He tried to lunge for her. Screw the Osträsk knowing about their relationship. "Don't hurt her!"

They tugged her away, Ivy's thrashing barely noticed. "It's okay, Rivix," she shouted, though her voice betrayed her fear. "We'll be okay."

When she disappeared into the dark, Frode stared down the other pathway. Rivix glared into the tunnel Ivy had disappeared into, but when the nearest warrior nudged him, he followed. If they brought him before the elders, there was a way out of this. Rivix knew the Osträsk. He knew their ways.

And unlike a decade ago, he wasn't a young boy. Rivix was grown now. Magnus couldn't bully him any longer.

They turned another corner, dragging him toward a chamber awash with blue light. Rivix's insides froze, his ability flaring at just the sight. At the base of the Heila Caves, the Elders' Chamber was where young Fens were tested for their gods-blessed ability. Those who didn't possess a strong enough gift never returned. Rivix still remembered the ice crawling across his skin, sliding down his throat. If he hadn't stopped it, the Osträsk elders would have frozen him solid.

The warriors stopped at the edge of the chamber's entrance and pushed him inside.

The first thing Rivix noticed were the bodies. Within the holy ice walls, hundreds of Osträsk elders and thousands of unworthy children made the chamber their final resting place. Becoming one with the gods, as the clan like to say. Rivix searched the closest faces, looking for All-Mother Gundhil. As the most recent elder to die, her body would have been placed in the upper layers of ice. Over time, as more elders passed and more children failed, she would get pushed deeper and deeper into the abyss.

He tore his attention away from that. The dead weren't his concern today. Sitting on blocks of ice in a semi-circle, the Elders of the Osträsk observed Rivix. He knew half their names, but some elders were unfamiliar faces, their predecessors long in the ice. But Rivix couldn't focus on them, not when Magnus sat in the high seat.

The bulky male barred crooked teeth, a pale scar splitting his lip. "We sent word to the King and Queen of Fenrik of your capture. Thank you for giving us even more leverage over the situation, boy."

Wretched boy. Rivix hadn't missed that. Magnus's tone remained as venomous today as it was a decade ago. "I'm not a boy anymore, Magnus."

"So it seems. I hear you're a champion. Using our sacred art of iskrigg to win little trinkets." Magnus clapped his leg and bellowed. "How mature of you."

"He's not even that good."

Rivix spun at the familiar voice and glared as Argrix entered the chamber. His Herkleian cousin wore layers of fur, his long dark hair and blue scales clashing with the white, but all of Rivix's attention went to his head. A gilded crown wrapped around his horns. It wasn't anywhere near as ornate as the true Crown of Herkleios, but a decent attempt none the less.

If there was one thing his cousin hated, it was mockery. "What in the skulls are you wearing on your head? It might be the ugliest thing I've ever witnessed."

Argrix stormed forward—

Magnus raised his hand, and his cousin stopped in place. The floors of the cave froze up around his feet. "You are a guest here, Your Majesty. Do not forget it."

"What is he offering you?" Argrix wasn't the one with the power here. Rivix had to negotiate with Magnus. "I'm sure the Fenrish Crown could match the reward... All-Father."

"Such pretty words. You always were such a smooth talker, boy. If you weren't, I wouldn't have trained you before all the other children." Magnus pushed from his seat and lumbered over. Rivix remembered him as a giant, but they were the same height now. "I want nothing from your parents. I've read all about you, Rivix. All your successes. You're the planet's favorite prince. But I know the real you. The real you is a coward."

"Is this all about revenge?"

"You challenged me, boy." Magnus closed the space between them, hissing the words. Gundhil hadn't told the other elders of their fight, then. She spared Magnus's ego. "And you did not win. You didn't strike the killing blow. You *are* a coward."

"There's nothing cowardly about sparing a life."

Magnus growled, a low rumble. "You sound like her."

Her? "Mother Gundhil?"

"She was a warrior in her youth like Queen Helga herself." He raised his voice, once again speaking to the room. "But she grew old and weak. The gods begged me to return her to their embrace, so I did as they commanded."

"*You* killed the All-Mother?" Rivix couldn't imagine it. Even though the female was nearing a hundred last Rivix saw her, her command over the ice hadn't faded. No one could touch her in a fight, much less kill her. He had imagined her dying of natural causes like the All-Leader before her.

"I did." Magnus circled the fire and plopped into his high seat. "And now I am All-Father of the Osträsk."

Rivix had always thought the male insane. But in the monastery, Magnus's power had been limited. He faced the other elders. The Osträsk loved strength, but they loved their peace and isolation more. "You're allowing this? Magnus is using you for revenge."

"Magnus bested Gundhil," the most ancient of the elders said, a shriveled block of ice given life. Elder Agda, if he remembered correctly. "Therefore, the gods chose him. We follow their will."

Idiots. "If you kill the humans, you'll bring the full rage of the Intergalactic Alliance upon you."

"The gods will protect them," Argrix said mockingly behind them. Rivix glared at his cousin, leaning casually on the wall. What was his grand plan? To kill a dozen humans and bring about the downfall of the Osträsk? That wouldn't get him any closer to the throne.

He couldn't do anything about his cousin. If he tried to make a move, the elders would stop him. Their guests had rights to protection. There was only one move Rivix could make. All-Mother Gundhil never officially banished him, so he was still Osträsk.

And though Rivix thought the practice long abandoned, any Osträsk could challenge for leadership of the clan. Like Magnus had All-Mother Gundhil.

For Ivy, he would do anything—even *this*. "Then as is my right, I challenge you, Magnus."

Magnus's eyes narrowed. "You are not one of us."

"Aren't I?" He glanced at the other elders. None of them

disagreed. "Even if I wasn't, when Queen Helga made her challenge, it was accepted as she ruled her own people. I am a Prince of Fenrik, too."

"We will not become one with your kingdom again," Elder Agda said.

"I don't expect you, too." Rivix bowed his head respectfully to Elder Agda before turning on Magnus. To him, he showed no respect. "Would you really ignore a direct challenge, Magnus?"

Magnus glared. The male had aged since their last fight, but he wasn't frail. His control over ice was a concern, especially if he used it to overpower the All-Mother. But Rivix could win this. Rivix *would* win this. He had no other choice.

"We fight tomorrow at dawn," Magnus finally said. "To the death."

"That was not our deal." Argrix tried to storm forward, but an elder flicked their finger and the ice trapped his hands to the cave wall. "I promised you technology. You promised me a public execution."

"Take His Majesty back to his guest quarters." The warriors outside the cave snapped to attention at Magnus's command. "And take Rivix to a cell."

"Take your hands off me," Argrix yelled, slapping at them.

Rivix didn't bother resisting. But he had one more thing to say. If he might die tomorrow, he needed to tell Ivy everything. "As a challenger, do I not have the right to prepare for my possible death?"

Magnus paused. "You do."

"Then I demand companionship."

Magnus sneered. "We'll send you a female, then—"

"I don't want one of your females," Rivix interjected as the warriors circled him. "I want the human female I came here with."

Argrix quit his shrieking to curl his lip toward his cousin. "Egh, not you, too, Rivix."

Magnus stomped his foot, shaking the cave with the might of his ability. Everyone fell silent. The old abbot had been practicing. Rivix couldn't let it scare him. He could win this.

For Ivy.

"Bring him his female," Magnus said with a wave of his hand. "And don't leave his door over the night."

SIXTEEN

IVY

Ivy thrashed and kicked as they dragged her deeper and deeper into the Heila Caves.

"Where are you taking me?" she shouted, but the alien warriors didn't reply. Did they even understand her? Rivix said they didn't like technology, so perhaps they didn't have translators.

If only Ivy knew how to make hers reply in Fenrish.

Not that it would help. No matter what she said, the Osträsk were content to ignore her.

After a few long minutes, Ivy was dragged to an open doorway and shoved into an icy cavern. Niches were carved into the space, making it the perfect dungeon set-up. The Osträsk had weaved together wooden beams to act as bars, fortifying them with a layer of ice. Ivy pulled in the warrior's grip again, this time to peer into the huddle of humans in the corner cell.

Addison's blond head rose from the mass. "Ivy!"

"Addy!" The warrior at her side tightened his grip, but only lightly. "Are you okay?"

"I've been better."

An injured Sigrid snuggled against Addison's side. "Where's

Rivix?"

The dread in her belly washed through her at the question. She tried to push it down before it drowned her. Ivy needed to stay strong. Rivix would get her out of this—get *all* of them out of this. "They took him in another direction."

Sigrid turned to the warriors around Ivy. One broke away from the group and put a hand on the bar, closing her eyes in concentration. Slowly, the ice around the door faded.

"Hey!" Sigrid pushed to her feet and stomped over. "Where's Prince Rivix?"

Though the words sounded English to Ivy, Sigrid must have spoken Fenrish. The warrior opened her pale eyes and glared. "With the elders. Now shut up." She jerked a finger toward Ivy. "Unless you'd rather the human stay with us."

Every cell in Ivy tightened and shivered at the clear threat. Sigrid bit her lips, but remained quiet. Thankfully. The warrior went back to concentrating. After a minute, the ice cleared enough for the warrior to tug open the door.

Ivy was tossed unceremoniously inside.

Her ankle twisted as she fell, pain flaring up her left leg. A scream ripped from her throat. Sigrid jumped forward and caught her. Addison helped, too, but her grasp was weak. Had they been fed? Or did the Osträsk just leave them here in the cold to slowly die?

"Ivy." Addison grabbed her shoulder. "What's wrong?"

"My ankle," she gritted through the pain.

"Let's sit." Together, Sigrid and Addison maneuvered her through the crowd of athletes. Most remained quiet with only the barest nods to Ivy. Once the warriors moved away, with only two remaining near the entrance, light chatter started up among the Earthling. Ivy closed her eyes. If she ignored the pain and invading cold, she could pretend she was in a café back home.

Addison snuggled up against her one side, with Sigrid on the other.

"You and Rivix came to rescue us?" Addison asked.

"That was the plan."

Sigrid leaned closer. "Where's the backup?"

"There isn't any." Ivy flinched at the disappointment on Sigrid's face, but she couldn't lie. "King Skarde planned to negotiate for your release, Sigrid, but..."

"I know." Sigrid put her head on Addison's shoulder. "I read their demands. They want everyone else dead."

Addison clutched her hand. "I don't want to die, Ivy."

"I know, Addy." Ivy squeezed her hand back. If only she had that kind of power. "I know."

IVY HAD FINALLY GOTTEN comfortable when the warriors returned to the cell. The harsh-looking Osträsk male from Rivix's glider glared through the huddle to Ivy. "Her." He said with a cruel point of clawed fingers. "That's his companion."

"What's happening?"

They didn't respond. Ivy glanced at Sigrid, who repeated the question.

The warrior sneered, but responded, "His Royal Highness has issued a challenge and All-Father Magnus accepted. As is tradition, the challenger gets a companion for the night, in order to make peace with their life."

A companion for the night? Sigrid nodded like it was common custom, but Addison muttered, "Eww. That's super rape-y." The girl straightened, looking abashed. "Not that I think Rivix is like that."

"It's okay, Addy." She patted her student on the shoulder. Addison was right, but Ivy pushed aside the bullshit implications. If Rivix was going to fight for her, for Addison and the other athletes, she wanted to see him. "Will you be okay here alone?"

"I'm not alone. I have Sigrid." Addison glanced at the warriors, standing firm. "And I don't think you have a choice."

Ivy sighed. Right again. She tried to push to a stand, but her ankle flared. "Help me up."

Sigrid and Addison helped her to her feet. Ivy limped toward the cell door. She twisted once she reached it, glancing back at the Earth athletes. This wasn't goodbye. Rivix would win the challenge and free them. Ivy had to trust him. This wasn't her world. But she would support him however she could.

When the cell door snapped open, the warriors grabbed her harshly. Ivy hissed in a breath. The lead Osträsk gestured, a quick flickering of fingers. Without warning, one warrior picked her up straight off the floor.

"Excuse me?" Ivy tried to protest more, but her stomach slammed into the male's shoulder, knocking out her breath.

The warriors slid into formation and quickly marched from the room. Ivy caught one last glimpse of Addison and Sigrid huddled together with the other Earthlings. She tried for a smile.

Before either of the girls could see it, they were out of the prison.

The warriors took a twisting path through the Heila Caves. Ivy kept her eyes on her surroundings, but even if she found the chance to escape, she wouldn't be able to navigate this maze. Besides, she wasn't leaving here without Addison.

Something clunked and squeaked, like a door pulled open. Ivy twisted in her captor's hold—

The warrior threw her headfirst through a doorway. Her knees scraped as she met the hard rock floor.

Ivy landed in a puddle at Rivix's feet.

He immediately crouched down and reached for her. Ivy threw herself into his arms. They had been parted only a few hours, but she had never worried so much about another being. What was it about Rivix? She loved him. She had admitted that before the Osträsk dragged them apart. But how was it possible to love another like this? The intensity of it nearly pained her heart.

Rivix caressed a hand down her back and glared at the warriors. "Watch it, Frode."

The lead warrior, Frode, laughed and slammed the door.

"Are you hurt?"

Rivix traced hands down her body, but Ivy gently grabbed them. "I'm okay. They didn't hurt me. Not intentionally, at least."

Rivix's intense slitted gaze focused on her. "What does that mean?"

"My ankle... it, um, sprained, I think."

Rivix glared at the door, but there was nothing he could do from within here. He scooped her up into his arms. Ivy finally got the chance to look around his room. No, *room* was too generous. This was little more than a cell. Carved from pale stone and speckled with glowing crystals, the sole furnishing was a pile of furs for a bed.

Rivix lowered her down to the furs and settled at her side.

She curled into his arms. "Frode said you challenged them. What does that mean?"

"It's the only way to get you out, Ivy." Rivix stroked a hand through her hair. "Magnus wants to punish me for fighting him all those years ago. I advocated for humans at the Intergalactic Games. He knows I'd never get over my guilt if the athletes in this cave are harmed."

The same Magnus who had beaten him? She didn't have to ask, not at the tension in his jaw. "What about Argrix?"

"Argrix is a guest, but barely. They treat him more like a prisoner. His opinion doesn't matter here." Rivix huffed out a breath. "If I beat Magnus, I become the new clan leader."

Ivy grazed her fingers against his chin. "You'll beat him. You did before."

"I was an enraged child before, with All-Mother Gundhil's assistance."

This wasn't like Rivix. He had never showed fear to her before. Ivy wanted to whisk him away from here, from what he had to do. She couldn't imagine having to face her abuser.

She didn't want to put bad vibes into the universe, but she had to know. "What happens if you lose?"

Rivix paused and held her gaze. "If I lose, I die. It's a battle to the death."

A claw of emotion ripped through Ivy's chest. No. Not Rivix. She couldn't watch him die. She *wouldn't* watch him die. He would beat Magnus. Everyone would work out.

But when had it ever? Ivy's skating career hadn't gone as planned. Addison's first major games were a mess. At this rate, she'd never coach again.

But those things didn't matter as much as they once did. Her mother probably rolled in the grave at the thought, but Ivy no longer cared. Winning wasn't everything.

Ivy closed her eyes and burrowed into Rivix's chest. He wrapped his warm arms around her, squeezing her tightly. If only they could stay in the moment forever. Nothing bad would ever happen to him. A deep ache filled her heart, confirming what she already knew was true. She loved him so, so much.

Ivy tilted her head. "Kiss me, then."

He tucked a strand of hair behind her ear. "You don't have to do this, Ivy."

Do what? Fuck him? Wasn't like it was a hardship. "I want to do this."

"You don't even know what it means."

She snorted and tugged at his furs.

"Ivy, I—" Rivix grabbed her hand. "You're my mate."

Ivy paused. He had said that before, but now she focused on the word. What it meant to her and what it meant to aliens were two very different things. Queen Alexandra wasn't just married to King Anax, she was his mate. Ivy thought it was only a Herkleian thing, some blessing from a make-believe dragon goddess. Though Rivix had a Herkleian mother, he didn't look like the scaled aliens. "Uh, what?"

He sat up and pulled at his furs.

She licked her lips. Why talk when he could strip? But Rivix didn't tackle her to the ground, ready to ravish her. He twisted around and exposed his nape—and the little star-shaped pattern marked on his skin.

Ivy traced the shape. Every matebond mark was unique in shape, or so Queen Alexandra said in a *Good Morning America* interview alongside two other human mates. "Is that what I think it is?"

"It is, Ivy. And it's for you."

Ivy touched her own neck, feeling at the damaged skin. Would she even have one? Or was it somewhere there beneath the burn marks?

But even if she didn't, did it matter?

No. No, it didn't.

Ivy pulled from his arms and settled on her knees. "That doesn't change anything, Rivix. Mark or no mark, you're mine. And I plan on using every last second I get with you, you big idiot."

Rivix's eyes widened, his pupils dilating as she pulled at her jacket, stripping away the layers of fabric. The cold of the cave brushed against her skin, but Ivy didn't care.

Rivix wouldn't let her freeze.

"Take off your clothes."

Rivix followed her commands, pulling away his own furs. Within seconds, he was naked, crouched before her in full, muscled glory. God, she would never get used to his body. His strong arms, his toned pecs, the lines of his abs, the swell of his beautiful cock.

Ivy wanted to take it into her mouth.

"Lie down."

Rivix leaned back, his eyes never leaving her body. Ivy was just as enraptured. His muscles flexed perfectly as he leaned back on an elbow. Like an ancient Greek god, splayed before her.

Ivy crawled forward, careful not to put pressure on her ankle. She traced her hands up Rivix's muscled calves to the thick width of his thighs. His cock jerked at the touch, straining forward. Big and blue and all hers. When her knees knocked against his, she stopped, examining him.

Rivix clenched his fists at his side. "Do whatever you want to me."

Ivy couldn't help a grin. They were imprisoned in an icy cave, hours away from a challenge that could kill him. Rivix. Her mate. She hadn't really believed in the concept an hour ago, but she knew it was true. She didn't need a mark to know what was in her heart.

He was hers.

She would make him so.

Ivy leaned down and took the tip of him into her mouth.

His taste flooded her senses, salty and deep and perfect. She flicked her tongue against the end, savoring the taste. Rivix's head fell back, his entire body tensing. His cock grew larger, more insistent. Ivy wouldn't keep him waiting. She tasted and teased, figuring out what he liked. When she licked the underside of his length, he shuddered. She massaged fingers against his balls for a moan.

When she drew her teeth against him, he let out a primal groan.

The groan reverberated through Ivy. God, she needed him. Her body ached, her core slick and wet. But she wanted to suck him dry. Wanted to feel him come into her mouth.

Ivy kept one hand beneath her, but with her other, she skirted between her legs and touched her pulsing warmth. She almost moaned onto his dick. She was so wet.

Her own heat spurred her on. Ivy took in as much of him as she could. His hips shifted, but he didn't thrust. She wanted him to. She wanted him to fuck her mouth until he exploded.

Ivy wanted to drive him mad.

She grazed her teeth against him again, gripping his balls in the same move—

Rivix jerked. "I don't... I don't want to hurt you."

"You can't hurt me, Rivix. *Fuck* me."

She took his cock back into her mouth and sucked hard. Rivix buckled. Yes. Just like that. Ivy pushed a finger into her own heat as she took him deep into her throat. She wanted him everywhere. Claiming her. Marking her as his.

"Ivy, I'm—" Rivix groaned, his entire body shaking.

She grazed her teeth against the underside of his shaft.

Rivix came with a roar. A hot rush of seed exploded into her mouth. Ivy sucked it down, drinking the salty nectar. She loved the taste of him. His skin. His seed. Him. She made her fingers pulse faster within herself, coaxed on by his wave of pleasure.

She let him go, releasing his cock to let out a deep moan. Rivix lifted his head. His eyes trailed the length of her body—her hard nipples, the sweat on her skin, her hand between her legs...

He leaned back, throwing a hand behind his head.

Enjoying the show.

Ivy almost came at just the look. No man had ever watched her masturbate. The act was even more intimate than her having his cock inside her. She pulsed a second finger into her depths. Her gaze locked with his. With each pulse, she imagined his fingers. His thick shaft. His rough tongue.

When her pants turned to whimpers, Rivix prowled forward—

"Now," she gasped out.

And with the command, Rivix plucked her up by the waist and rammed her down onto his hardening cock.

He filled her to the brim, his large width nearly painful to take in. But it was exactly what she needed. *He* was exactly what she needed. Ivy arched her back as an orgasm ripped through her. Her head thrashed. Her moaned echoed back at her, amplified by the ice cave.

Rivix's groan joined the melody as her core clenched around his cock. He reached up, swallowing her cry with his lips. They came together in a shuddering display, like fire on ice.

Like two souls uniting.

Like two mates accepting their bond.

Rivix collapsed to the furs, Ivy slumping on top of him. She kissed at his pecs, a light trail around his nipple, and shuffled her hips.

Rivix threw a hand over his face. "Don't do that."

And just like that, the fire within her flared back to life. Ivy shuffled again until she could whisper in his ear, "I plan to fuck you all night long, mate."

Without warning, Rivix flipped her over, his elbow at her head. "Funny. That was my plan, too."

SEVENTEEN

RIVIX

Rivix held Ivy in his arms until the first rays of light pierced the Heila Caves. Though he couldn't see the sun from this deep underground, the rock crystals brightened to a pale blue during the day. The color change had been the first thing he noticed after emerging from his testing in the Elders' Chamber all those years ago.

And today, he'd return to that chamber again under the threat of death. For that reason, Rivix hadn't slept. He didn't want to, not when he had to savor every moment with Ivy. He was confident in his skills, but the Magnus he remembered wasn't the Magnus that existed today. The old abbot Rivix had known never had the nerve the challenge the All-Mother.

But if he was going to die, he couldn't think of a better final night.

He gently nudged Ivy. Rivix hated to wake her, especially since she only fell asleep a few hours ago. But he wouldn't let the clan warriors drag her off naked.

She groaned and stretched. "How is it already morning? I'm still exhausted."

"You *did* exert yourself last night," Rivix said, winking at her. "I'm sorry to wake you, naika, but the warriors will come for us soon."

"It's okay." She grinned as she pulled at her pile of clothes. "What does naika mean? My translator didn't catch that."

Rivix grabbed his own garments. "It's a Herkleian term for a female mate."

"You're not Herkleian." She glanced at his slitted eyes, the one feature from his mother. "Not entirely, at least."

Though his mother had taught him the language, he didn't speak it well without a translator. "It *does* seem foreign to me."

"Then don't call me that."

"What should I call you?"

"Mhm." Ivy climbed to her feet, balancing most of her weight on her uninjured leg. "What do you want to call me?"

Rivix stood, too, eager to have her back in his arms. What did he want to call her? He had never used pet names with former lovers. But Ivy wasn't a lover. She was his mate, the match to his soul.

There was only one option. "Käras?"

"*Sher-as?*"

"It's an old Fenrish term, roughly translating as 'dear one'."

"I like that," Ivy said, chin propped on his chest. "I'm not ready to let you go."

"Thousands of years wouldn't be enough time with you, käras. But should something happen—"

Her eyes watered. "Don't even say that."

"You're right. We'll survive this, Ivy." Rivix had to. Not for himself—he would gladly die for Ivy. But he needed to live to save her and Sigrid and Addison.

That was all the encouragement he needed.

The door jerked open suddenly, admitting five Osträsk warriors. Rivix pushed in front of his mate as Ivy pulled on her last layer of clothing. Did any of the males leer at the rumpled furs behind them? Like the Fens, the Osträsk had few rules regarding sex, but Ivy wasn't from this world and the Osträsk hated outsiders.

Frode split from the herd. "It's time to die, Rivix."

He glared at Frode. "And my mate?"

The warrior bared cracked teeth. "She can come. Magnus wants her to watch him beat the life out of her prince."

"ARE YOU READY TO DIE, RIVIX?" Magnus intoned as Rivix entered the Elders' Chamber.

Rivix only glared in reply. He wouldn't stoop to the old abbot's level. When Rivix first arrived at the monastery, he had screamed and cried and argued. That had all been beaten out of him, the crying boy replaced by a deep well of rage. He had locked that part of himself away when he left, but today, for Ivy, he'd face the tragedies of his past.

Argrix chuckled from where he leaned by the entrance. "Everyone dies miserably, All-Father. Even a prick like Rivix."

Rivix hiked a thumb back at his cousin. "Does he have to be here?"

"King Argrix is my honored guest," Magnus said. "He wants to watch you die, so that's what I'll give him."

"And after, I want the humans dead, too."

Rivix growled, but when he tried to stomp toward his cousin, the warriors blocked his path. Instead, he shuffled in front of Ivy. She glared at Argrix, eyes narrowed.

"I don't like him," she muttered.

"No one does."

"Enough," Elder Agda said, pounding their walking stick into the ground. They sat with the rest of the elders around the sides of the room, patiently waiting for the challenge to determine their fates. Their passivity made his anger spike. If he snapped and somehow murdered them all, they would die thinking it was the ancient ones' will. "Let the challenge begin so we can know our gods' plan."

Magnus tossed off his outer layer of furs, dropped his belt of weapons, and stomped into the center of the chamber. Thick scars lined the male's chest, some from a young Rivix's blade. He'd add more today if everything went his way—if Magnus didn't have any tricks. So far, he had behaved honorably. But Rivix didn't trust him.

He twisted to give Ivy's hand a final squeeze. She smiled at him, but the expression quivered. Rivix gazed into her eyes. He didn't need to say anything. She knew exactly what she meant to him. She knew he would fight with everything he had.

Rivix stripped his outer layer of furs and entered the fighting ring.

The elders bowed their heads and started chanting. Rivix closed his eyes. To survive this, he'd need to pull on the full extent of his abilities. As the ice crept down the wall and across the floor, Rivix inhaled and exhaled. Sucked in the cold, only to huff it back out. He let himself become one with the ice. Rivix sensed exactly when the ground beneath him turned. His boots buzzed, blades materializing between him and the cold.

Rivix opened his eyes.

Magnus stood unharmed, his own skates materialized at his feet. It was the one piece of technology the Osträsk requested from the Fens. His parents had gladly handed pairs over to get him the training he desired.

He glanced into the thickness of the ice walls. If only he could thank the All-Mother one last time. Without her influence, he'd never have learned and survived.

Magnus followed his gaze and grinned sharply. "For extra motivation..." The All-Father snapped his claws at Ivy. "Put her against the ice."

Argrix almost clapped.

Ivy jerked against Frode's hold. "What?"

Rivix rushed forward, but Elder Agda raised their hand. The challenge hadn't yet started. If he fought now, he forfeited. "You'll kill her."

"Rivix!"

Magnus only laughed at Ivy's panic. "If you beat me in time, maybe you'll be able to save your female from the ancient gods' chill."

"Ivy!" Rivix skated forward, but he couldn't leave the rink. This was Magnus's plan. If Rivix forfeited, Ivy and every human in the Heila Caves died.

He needed to fight.

Frode pressed Ivy back against the ice wall. She screamed when she touched it, a wild sound. Rivix growled. Not at Frode, but at Magnus. When he became clan leader, everyone in the room would listen to him. He'd save Ivy.

"You may begin," Elder Agda said calmly.

Rivix launched himself forward.

Magnus spun out of the way.

Rivix ducked. If he hadn't, the male's skate would've lodged in his back. He spun as he ducked, putting space between himself and the old abbot. Behind him, Ivy thrashed against the wall. The ice already crept over her hands. How long could a human survive the touch of the ancient ice? Some Fenrish children died within minutes.

Rivix needed to make this fast.

He charged again. This time, he wouldn't let Magnus escape. He clenched his fists, willing ice to form up around his opponent's skates. Magnus tried to move, but his skate caught—

Rivix rammed into his side.

They crashed down on the ice. Rivix raised his knee, landing on Magnus's stomach. The air huffed out of the old abbot. He clenched his fist and punched down, hoping to knock him out in a single hit.

Ice wrapped around his fist.

Fuck.

The added weight threw off his hit. Magnus punched up, hitting Rivix in the sternum. He fell off, choking. Somewhere else in the room, beyond the elders' chanting, Ivy coughed, too. She couldn't breathe. Rivix needed to—

A club of ice smashed into his face.

Rivix flew across the rink. The world spun. He shook his head and coughed out pale blue blood. It splatted across the rink.

Magnus slowly skated forward, reforming the end of his ice club.

That single hit could have killed Rivix, and a second one surely would.

"Goodbye, cousin," Argrix said with a wave.

Rivix refused to surrender. He grabbed at a chunk of ice and willed it into a dagger.

Nothing happened.

Helga's skulls. With the pounding in his brain, how could he concentrate? Rivix narrowed his eyes. He needed to focus. But not on the blade. Rivix kept the ice in his hand, but looked past Magnus, past the elders, past the warriors, to where Ivy stood. Ice crawled across her body, her skin nearly blue. Her eyes blinked closed, exhaustion taking hold. Once she was sucked into the ice, the only way to escape was through sheer will.

Rivix didn't have time.

Rivix would *not* let his mate die.

He clenched his hand on the chunk of ice. It cut into his skin, a blade formed from his rage. All the whippings Magnus had given him. Every time he pushed him down during training, claiming a beating was just the thing Rivix needed to learn discipline. All the rude names. All the pain. But Rivix wasn't Magnus's wretched boy. He was a prince. He was a champion. Iskrigg wasn't Magnus's life and purpose—it was Rivix's.

His dagger expanded, growing out into a spear.

As Magnus raised his club, Rivix slammed forward.

With a rip, his spear stabbed through Magnus's gut.

Rivix let out a laugh, but Magnus's club slammed into his arm. He screamed as the bones cracked. Rivix drove the spear deeper in. He ground his teeth through the pain, glaring at Magnus. The old abbot hacked out a spray of blood. It splatted against Rivix's face.

"Wretched boy," he grumbled.

"Fuck you."

Magnus hacked out one last breath before he went slack.

His club smashed to the rink, but his body tumbled onto Rivix. He tried to push the male off, but his arm screamed in agony. Definitely broken. The injury would be easily fixed back in Älvsholm, but Rivix needed to maintain control. If any of the warriors sensed his weakness, they would think him easy pickings.

Clenching through the pain, he pushed Magnus off him.

The chamber was eerily quiet for a moment before the warriors devolved into feral growls. The elders raised their hands, silencing the protest. Through their laws, Rivix was now All-Father of the Osträsk, a position he'd hold until death.

Elder Agda rose from their seat. "All-Father."

Rivix ignored the platitudes.

Argrix pushed forward. When his foot touched the slick ice, he nearly tumbled onto his face. "This is bullshit. We had an agreement—"

Rivix snapped a claw in his cousin's direction. "Lock him away. Now."

Frode and the other warriors hesitated a second before jumping forward and dragging Argrix away. Or, at least, Rivix assumed so. He had bigger things to deal with.

Rivix skated toward the wall.

A sheen of ice blanketed Ivy. Her eyes were closed and her skin so pale she nearly appeared as blue as him. Rivix pounded a fist into the ice. If he pulled her out, warmed her up, maybe she'd survive.

"All-Father," Elder Agda started.

"Shut up." He didn't want to hear what they had to say. Ivy *was* alive. He would know if she was dead. His mate was his other half, a part of his soul. Surely he would know.

He couldn't have been too slow.

Rivix punched and punched until she tumbled into his arms. He cocooned her, willing her to live.

"Please, Ivy. Please."

EIGHTEEN

IVY

Ivy gasped as the ice invaded her lungs.

When the warriors dragged her toward the cavern's walls, Ivy had done everything in her power to stop them. But it hadn't been enough. She wasn't a giant alien warrior. What could she do against their strength?

The last thing she remembered before touching solid, true cold was Rivix shouting her name.

The chill ripped and tore at that memory, but Ivy clung to it. All around her, the world was white like an ice storm. It battered her, whacking her back and forth. The cold ravaged her skin, the touch nearly a burn.

"Ivy," her father shouted from somewhere, the smoke too thick to see through. "Ivy, where are you?"

Ivy curled under her bed, a pillow pressed to her face. The fire consumed half of her room, but a path to the door remained. If she crawled forward, she could make it—

Ivy jerked out of the memory. It wasn't time for flashbacks. There was nothing in there to help her but pain. Her father had dragged her out of the house, her back a searing flare of agony. The firefighters had gone in for her mother.

But there was no one to help Ivy here.

She tried to scream, but the ice only claimed the opening, the sound caught in her throat. She choked on it, just as she had the smoke all those years ago.

Ivy loved the ice. She had never imagined it hurting as much as fire.

A flare of red pulsed through the winter landscape. Ivy squinted, but she couldn't make the image out through the snow. Automatically, her body moved forward. Drawn by the light like a moth to a flame. The ice gripped at her ankles, her arm, but she pushed through it. Nothing around her was real. She was in the Elders' Chamber, the ice of the walls devouring her. Rivix fought for his life—for her life.

But she had to fight, too.

So Ivy pushed through the pain. She had pushed through so much in her life. Her mother's demands. Her father's inaction. Her coaches' training. Her injured ankle. Ivy pushed and pushed and pushed.

And watched as the spark of flame flared up and out.

Ivy gaped. She was dying. She had to be. Her brain was oxygen-deprived and showing her weird, freaky images.

Like that of the giant, blue-scaled dragon burning before her.

Was that... Hyra? The Herkleian dragon goddess? No. Impossible. Gods weren't real. But whatever it was, Ivy ran forward. Ivy had feared fire for years, but she didn't now. Not anymore. Her entire body burned with cold. Too cold. Her fingers looked nearly blue. Ivy ran toward the dragon, ready to embrace its flames.

As she approached, the dragon opened slitted blue eyes and met her gaze. The weight of it slammed into her chest, warmth and light and love—

Ivy hacked out a gallon of ice onto Rivix.

She screamed, her voice hoarse. Her entire body ached and tingled. God, how did she even feel anything? After that long in the ice, Ivy should have been dead.

"Ivy?" Rivix ran his hands up and down her body. When he didn't find any injury, he pressed her head against his chest.

She snuggled up against his warmth. Nothing would ever feel cold again compared to that, but she still shivered. "I'm fine. It's just shock, I think."

Rivix kissed her on the forehead. "I can't believe you survived, Ivy. I thought you were dead. Only beings from Fenrik have survived the ancient gods' test."

Ivy raised her head at that, meeting those slitted eyes—so much like his goddess's. Was that what had saved her? Her matebond? "It wasn't me."

"What?"

"I know this is going to sound ridiculous, but I saw a freaking dragon."

Rivix stared. "You saw... a dragon?"

Yup. Totally a hallucination. Ivy waved it away, her hand fluttering weakly. "It doesn't matter. All that matters is that we're together."

Together... with a dozen other people. Her vision cleared, focusing on the rest of the cavern. Argrix no longer stood by the door, making smarmy comments. The warriors weren't trying to kill Rivix, and the elders appeared as stoic as the rocks they sat on. Behind them all...

Ivy gagged. Was that a dead body?

Rivix twisted at her expression, dispassionately studying his old teacher. "I killed Magnus."

Shit, she was going to puke. "I can see that. You won, then?"

"I did." Rivix turned his gaze on the Osträsk. *His* Osträsk. "And as All-Father, my first command is to free the humans."

IVY SHUFFLED IN HER SEAT, bumping Addison in the side accidentally. Rivix had used the Osträsk communication relay to message his father and request a transport ship. Unfortunately, they had severely underestimated the size of humans. The dozen athletes packed tightly together in the military ship's hold, almost elbow to elbow. It at least helped with warmth, as the ancient ice wall had decimated the effects of Ivy's nanite warming pill.

Addison and the rest of Team Earth weren't nearly as lucky. One skater in the middle of the huddle wasn't doing well. Ivy suspected she had hypothermia from the cold, but the doctor had examined her and said she'd make a full recovery. Ivy didn't see how, but the Fenrish had technology beyond Earth. The doctor had waved some device over Ivy's ankle and returned it to normal—her normal, that was. The scar tissue wasn't easily as healed.

"Did I ever say thanks for coming to save us?" Addison pressed firmly against her side. When asked about it later, she was sure her student would blame it on lack of space. "I know I can be a real pain in the ass."

"Apology not needed." Ivy wrapped a hand around her and rubbed at her arm. Over her head, she made eye contact with Rivix. The doctor held the glowing device over his broken arm. Despite the agonizing pain, Rivix had carried her the entire way to the ship. "You're eighteen, Addison. Every eighteen-year-old is a pain in the ass. What matters is you're one of the most amazing skaters I've ever seen. If anything, I should apologize to you. There's more to life than winning. Life on the competition circuit isn't easy, and I only made it worse for you."

"It *is* a lot of pressure, but that's not on you, Ivy. I wanted to win." Addison kept her eyes on the ground. "Sometimes I wish I was like other kids with just school to worry about. They have time to hang out with friends and live their life."

Sigrid bumped her shoulder from her other side. "That's the price you pay to be extraordinary."

Addison blushed and grinned, her attitude returning somewhat. With her resilience, this incident was only going to make her stronger. Ivy pulled her in for a hug before the moment passed. "I'm honored to be your coach, Addy."

"You're not so bad yourself. Your boyfriend's pretty killer, too."

Ivy snorted. "Thanks, but he's not my boyfriend."

"You aren't going to try to deny it, are you?"

"We've all seen the way he looks at you," Sigrid added.

"I'm not." Ivy focused on her mate again. *Her* mate. "Rivix is my mate."

Sigrid gasped. "I knew it."

"Really?" Addison tried to bounce out of her seat, but she nearly kicked another athlete in the head. She settled down with an apologetic grin, but her energy hadn't faded. "Like King Anax and Queen Alexandra? And his brother and the hairdresser? And that lawyer? Like *that* mate?"

Ivy nodded.

"You're like a real-life fairytale princess."

"Hardly."

"No, exactly." Addison grabbed the front of her coat and shook her. "You have a true love and everything. I'm jealous."

Ivy's gaze flickered to Sigrid. Since Addison faced Ivy, she couldn't see the skater's moonstruck expression. "You have nothing to be jealous about. Your true love might be closer than you think."

Addison immediately eyed Sigrid and blushed even harder. "Stop it, Ivy. You're embarrassing me. Go make out with your mate or something."

"What a great idea." Ivy patted Addison on the back, climbed to her feet, and maneuvered through the cram of bodies. Addison deserved some alone time with her beau, anyway.

Sensing her movement, Rivix dismissed the doctor with the haughty air of a prince and turned toward her with a wink. Ivy's stomach twisted inside out. Who taught him to wink like that? She owed whoever it was a debt because it drove her insane. Despite being in an overcrowded ship, she felt like the only person in the world when he looked at her.

When she reached him, he immediately opened his arms.

"You good?" she asked.

"Now that you're here."

She whacked him playfully on his uninjured shoulder. "That's so cheesy."

He frowned. "That made absolutely no sense to my translator."

"It doesn't matter."

The doctor returned, carrying a briefcase-like box. She snapped it open, revealing what looked like half a dozen white plastic armbands. "A nanite brace to ease your pain, Your Highness."

Rivix plucked one from the box and pulled it over his arm. Somehow, the piece molded and stretched until it settled over his bicep. He looked a little bit like Cyborg with it on. Ivy stifled a chuckle.

"Would you like one for your ankle, ma'am?" The doctor said, turning on Ivy.

Ivy frowned. "My ankle?"

"I saw the way you walked on it. If you still have residual pain—"

Ivy tried to laugh it off. "Oh, no, that's from an old injury."

The doctor's pale eyebrows furrowed. "And? With the nanite brace, all past injures can be managed."

Ivy stared at the cheap-looking piece of plastic. "Are you serious?"

Rivix answered for the doctor. "Do they not have nanite braces on Earth yet?"

Ivy grabbed one of the braces, light and frail in her hands. "Hell, no. You think I'd choose to walk around in pain?"

"If I had known, I would have found you one sooner, käras."

Ivy melted in his arms again. Whenever he used that pet name for her, she became putty. If only they weren't in a tiny cargo ship with a rotating crew of soldiers around.

As if summoned by her thoughts, one of the Fenrish soldiers approached, replacing the doctor. "Your Highness? His Majesty the King would like a word."

He gestured behind him to the small strip of space between the hold and the cockpit. Ivy had witnessed soldiers streaming in and out, a forcefield popping into existence to hide the contents of their calls. She shuffled from his grasp.

Rivix tightened his hold. "My mate comes with me."

"His Majesty specifically said—"

"I don't care." Rivix rose, and Ivy went with him. "I didn't listen to them earlier, so why start now?"

The soldier hesitated, but Rivix strutted past him. Ivy didn't even have the chance to de-tangle herself from his arms before they reached the box and the forcefield activated. He tapped a section of the wall, summoning a levitating seat for her to sit on, and expanded a holo-screen. Ivy fiddled with the nanite brace. Had she really found the solution to all her pain?

Rivix handed her a tiny circular device the size of a coin.

"What's this for?"

"Put it on your temple."

Ivy shrugged, but followed his lead. The soldiers had done the same thing—

As soon as the device touched her skin, the military ship disappeared, replaced by a grand library carved of ice. Ivy gaped at the high ceiling, the elaborately carved dome a match for the Florence Cathedral. In the mural, some ancient Fenrish queen battled hordes of ulves in a scene right out of a fantasy movie. Was this the palace? She had glimpsed it through her hotel window.

Someone moved, drawing her attention. Rivix's parents rose from a plush sofa. Queen Rhiona's emerald gown swished when she stood, highlighting the small patches of green scales inherited from the Eógan side of her family, while King Skarde crossed thick arms across his fur-lined breastplate. The eight-foot-tall Fen was a giant compared to his son.

"It's replication technology," Rivix said at her confused look. "It creates a virtual reality built from participants' memories. We're still on the ship, but it's easier to communicate this way."

"Are you alright, dear?" Rivix's mother said, approaching.

He reached out a hand, squeezing his mother's palm. "I am."

But his father was all business. "Was the mission a success?"

"The mission you didn't want me to undertake? Yes, it was."

Ivy and Queen Rhiona flinched at the tone, but King Skarde didn't mind. In fact, he smiled broadly. "I know we disagreed, son. I thought I was right, but you proved me wrong. I welcome your input going forward."

Rivix glanced back at Ivy. Something in his eyes had her shuffling forward on her levitating seat. Sadness, perhaps? Why sadness? They had survived and saved the athletes. They were together now.

Ivy couldn't accept any other future.

"That's not going to happen, Father."

"Rivix—"

"We didn't escape." Rivix stood taller, linking his hands behind his back. He looked almost regal like that. "I challenged the Osträsk leader, the All-Father."

King Skarde paled to an off-white shade and the queen's blue-green scales tinged yellow. Ivy didn't know the Fens, Eógans, or Herkleians well enough to know what that meant, but it probably wasn't good.

Ivy was missing something. "What's happening, Rivix?"

Her mate faced her and took her hand, rubbing a thumb against her palm. "The All-Father rules for life. The only way to choose a new one is through death."

Ivy's heart dropped to her toes. "What are you saying? That you have to die?"

"No, of course not." Rivix crouched down until his perfect face was level with hers. "Besides Magnus, the Osträsk haven't had a challenge for leadership in centuries. When the old All-Leader dies, the potentials fight until one remains standing."

"You can't abdicate?"

He shook his head.

Ivy clasped a hand over her mouth. She hadn't known. Rivix didn't want to be a leader. Like her, he wanted to skate.

He had given it all up for her and her people.

Her mate couldn't bear to see her upset. Rivix wrapped his arms around her waist. "Don't, käras. I'd make the same choice to keep you safe. Besides, while Magnus did terrible things to me, they weren't all bad people. I have a responsibility—"

Queen Rhiona interjected. "You have no such thing."

"It's okay, Mother." Though Rivix kept his hands on Ivy, he faced his parents. Queen Rhiona clenched her fists in rage—not at Rivix but at herself. "You had to hand me over when you discovered my ability. I don't blame you for that. But both of you instilled a sense of duty in me. I never wanted to be a ruler, but it was the price I had to pay."

For a moment, both of Rivix's parents stood in silence. Then the king asked, "And Argrix?"

"Skarde!"

But Rivix answered, matching his father's professionalism. Like a true leader. "Argrix is imprisoned. I wanted to get the humans home first, but once I return to the Osträsk after the Intergalactic Games, I'll transfer him to you."

King Skarde nodded. "Thank you, son."

And with that, the king disappeared, poofing out of existence. Had he removed the little device on his temple? Though Ivy couldn't see one on the others, she knew Rivix wore one and could feel her own.

"Don't mind your father, Rivix," Queen Rhiona said. "Are you sure you want to do this?"

Rivix reached out for his mother's hand. She clutched at him, her knuckles paling with the tension. "I am, Mother."

Queen Rhiona swallowed and nodded. "I'll leave you alone to talk with your mate, then."

She reached up to her forehead and disappeared a second later.

Ivy grabbed Rivix's arm and pulled herself to her feet. Pain twinged through her ankle. She hadn't yet had a chance to put on the nanite brace. That didn't matter, not when Rivix's whole life was in upheaval. "You have to live with the Osträsk?"

"I don't have to, but I can't ruin their way of life. Even though they live isolated from us, they're the spiritual leaders of our people—"

"You don't have to convince me, Rivix." Ivy raised one of his hands to her lips and kissed his knuckles. "Does this mean I have to live in a cave?"

Rivix blinked down at her. "What?"

"You think I'm not coming with you? Of course I am."

"But... we can bring some technology with us, but it won't be at all like it is in Älvsholm."

Ivy snorted. For such a smart male, he could be quite dumb. "So? We can visit, right?"

"But what about your career?"

"What about it?" What she had said to Addison was true. Winning wasn't everything. Ivy had been so focused on being the best, on being number one, that she never truly lived her life. She loved skating, but not because of the medals. That was her mother's goal, not hers. "This is an ice planet, Rivix. I can skate anywhere. Besides, the Osträsk children will need a new teacher, right?"

Rivix stared at her for a moment, shock and joy clashing across his face. "Ivy—"

She held a finger against his lips. "Wherever you go, I'll follow. You're my mate, Rivix. I don't want to be parted ever again."

EPILOGUE

RIVIX

"There's nothing to fear, Ivy." Rivix stood behind her, rubbing his hands down her shoulder. Ivy twisted toward him and huffed out a long breath. Her nerves had peaked when Addison took to the rink, but hadn't eased even watching her student's excellent performance. Though Rivix hadn't said it to her, he didn't know whether Sigrid or Addison would come out victorious. The judges kept their scores hidden until the last moment.

But Addison's score didn't seem to be the problem.

"I don't think I can do this." Ivy tried to make a run for it, but Rivix blocked her in. "I haven't performed in years, Rivix. With my ankle..."

"What about your ankle?" Below them, underneath Ivy's glittering tights, a thin nanite brace pulsed against Ivy's skin. In the week since returning from the Heila Caves, Ivy had marveled at every moment without pain. "It doesn't hurt, does it?"

"No, it doesn't, but that's not the point, Rivix." She dropped her head to his chest, seemingly deflating. "Why am I doing this? There's so many people watching."

He tilted her chin, luring her mouth upwards. He loved that

sweet mouth of hers. The things it could do... Rivix let his lust gleam through his eyes. "Because you love the sport, Ivy. We're not going out there to win. We're going to skate. For ourselves."

Ivy nodded and huffed out a nervous breath.

"Citizens of the Intergalactic Alliance," the announcer said, their voice echoing through the stadium's dome, "may we present Earth's Ivy Dawson and Fenrik's All-Father Rivix."

The blood rushed from her face at the words, but color pinched back into her cheeks at the wave of applause. Rivix cupped her face in his hand and claimed her lips. She moaned, opening to him. With one hand, Rivix lifted her, wanting her closer. Ivy wrapped her legs around his waist. Even through her costume, the heat at her teased his cock, tempting and luring.

Abruptly, Rivix dropped her to the floor.

Ivy huffed out a breath. "What was that?"

"Motivation. The sooner we get this over with, the sooner we can fuck."

Red flushed through her cheeks, a lovely contrast to her wild hair. It always made Rivix smile. She was so stupidly beautiful.

Rivix took her hand and lured her to the ice.

Once their skates touched the rink, the stadium went silent. Hand-in-hand, Rivix and Ivy skated to the center. The judges were gone from their seats, probably to deliberate and tally scores, but everyone else—athletes, dignitaries, ordinary citizens—watched with eager eyes.

Ivy faced him. He dropped his forehead down to hers.

"We can do this, käras."

Something had changed. Maybe it was the applause, maybe it was the rink itself. There was a flame in Ivy. *There* was the female he loved.

Rivix and Ivy danced.

Eyes on each other, the rest of the world disappeared. Rivix moved for her, chasing her across the ice, his hands always a brush away. Ivy ran and jumped and twisted. When he caught her, they twirled into one, like souls combining. And when the music dropped, they broke apart, only to start the chase again.

It was their story, distilled into minutes. Chasing, catching, fighting, loving. Every little bit, the good and the bad melded together.

When they clashed together for the final pose, Rivix huffed, his heart beating nearly out of his chest. Ivy sucked in her breaths, too, her little puffs against his face.

As the audience exploded into a roar of cheers and claps and screams, Ivy wrapped her fingers through his dark hair and kissed him senseless.

"Ivy Dawson and All-Father Rivix, everyone!" the announcer cried, bringing Rivix back to reality. However much he wanted to, he couldn't claim his mate here.

Maybe they'd come back tonight once the rink was closed.

With the adrenaline wearing off, Ivy nearly dropped to the ground. Rivix held her up and waved. He skated for the exit, easily carrying her.

She wrapped her arms around his neck, tracing at his matebond mark. Though Ivy's wasn't visible through the scarring, they both knew it was there. "That was wonderful."

"You were wonderful."

She nuzzled against his beard. "Why don't we skip the ceremony—"

Addison and Sigrid nearly crashed into their side. "That was amazing, guys."

"A remarkable performance." Sigrid winked. "For two retired coaches planning on moving in with the Osträsk."

Rivix placed Ivy on the ground. "And you think you could've done better, Sigrid?"

Sigrid mocked Ivy's cross-armed pose. "You couldn't beat me—"

The rink suddenly darkened and quieted as a hologram burst into life in the middle of the rink. The top judge, a Fenrish male who started skating long before Rivix was born, surveyed the crowd before him. His gaze somehow pierced into all the contestants, each nearly biting their nails with anticipation. "The results have been calculated."

Rivix, Ivy, Sigrid, and Addison leaned forward as one.

Within a blink, a holo-screen flicked into existence and displayed a chart of names. Before Rivix could even find Sigrid's name, the projection re-organized. Ivy, Addison, and Sigrid crowded at his side, each trying to see—

Sigrid and Addison disappeared in a flash of light.

Rivix spun around and grabbed Ivy with a cheer.

"Where did they go?" she yelled.

The judge and three skaters transported onto the ice.

Ivy nearly climbed his shoulder when she spotted her student. "They're on the ice!"

He dropped her back down. "I thought you educated yourself on the Intergalactic Games."

"I didn't realize they transported the winners mid-step."

"In third place, we have Diyya of Gurov." The judge handed a feathered female a red rupini medal. "But as you can tell from the scores, Addison Everest of Earth and Sigrid Karlsdottir of Fenrik have tied."

Neither Rivix nor Ivy had read the board, each of them exclaiming and glancing up at the numbers. 200 to 200.

Ivy grabbed his arm. "What does that mean?"

Rivix didn't have a chance to answer. The judge snapped his clawed fingers and the topazi medal in his hand switched colors—to blue zapher. "Congratulations to our two zapher-medalists!"

Addison started screaming and Sigrid threw her arms around her co-winner. Ivy almost climbed Rivix's side again, wild in her excitement. Winning wasn't everything, but it still felt damn good. Rivix pumped a hand in the air with a shout. He couldn't have imagined a better outcome.

Then, Addison turned on Sigrid, wrapped her hands through her pale hair, and kissed her.

Ivy's eyes went wide. "When did that happen?"

Rivix grinned. Never mind. *This* was the best outcome. "Probably in the ice cave. They're aphrodisiacs, I hear."

"Oh, shut up."

Rivix plucked her into his arms. This time, he wasn't letting her down until he could strip her naked. "I love you, käras."

"And I love you, Rivix. Let's go home to our cave."

Rivix spun for the exit. "Not all the Osträsk live in caves."

"Too bad. They're aphrodisiacs, I hear."

Thank you for reading! Want to read more stories set in the Intergalactic Alliance? Try Marked for an Alien Prince, a standalone novella set after the events of *Rivix*.

RIVIX BONUS SCENE

IVY

Ivy leisurely twirled her ankle, marveling at the lack of pain.

"I got them!" Ivy's younger sister, Willow, crashed into the resort suite, holding a pair of fur-lined skates. The pale color perfectly matched the fur edges of Ivy's wedding gown. "The attendants were sharpening them again. Did you use them last night?"

"You could say that." Ivy couldn't help her flush. The Svarjörn Resort sat at the border between Fenrish and Osträsk territory, with a large ice field in the place of a garden. Ivy imagined the rink normally packed with guests, but the royal wedding party had reserved the entire resort. Rivix had lured her to the ice last night for some well-spent quality time.

And well-spent it was.

Ivy sighed.

"Eww," Willow said. "I don't want to know."

Ivy winked at her sister. "You really don't."

Willow paused. "But like how? Ice is so... cold and slippery."

"The slipping is the best part."

Willow plugged her ears. "You're right. I don't want to know about my older sister's sex life."

Ivy snorted, but waved Willow forward. Her sister dropped to her knees and offered Ivy a skate. When they were kids, Ivy always helped Willow put on her skates. Today, the roles were reversed. Ivy gently tilted her ankle, careful not to jolt the nanite brace at her left ankle. Without it, agony shot up her leg whenever she walked. But in the months since meeting Rivix and getting the device, Ivy had been pain-free.

With both skates on her feet, Ivy glided into a standing position. With a quick tap of the boots, the blades disappeared. She wouldn't need them until they reached the dancefloor. Ivy twirled on her thick heels. Gossamer lace crawled her arms and decorated the bodice of her full skirt, but the tinkling, frozen teardrops of water were Ivy's favorite part of the gown. When they caught the sunlight, she sparkled in the light just like her husband-to-be. Icy raced across the room—thankfully the hemline of her dress didn't pass her ankles—and shuffled on a white fur shawl.

When she turned, Willow stood stuck in place, her eyes watering. "You're so beautiful, Ivy. I can't believe my older sister is getting married."

Ivy faced the mirror, her reflection belonging more to a redheaded winter princess than her. "Neither can I."

Willow clutched her hand, the fur-lined mittens she had just put on turning her fingers into one large puff. Though her sister didn't need to say it, Ivy knew they both thought of their mother. Bunny Dawson was long gone, but Ivy wished for the woman she remembered as a child—full of light and love and happiness. Before the fire and her bitterness washed that all away.

Willow nudged her shoulder. "Who needs 'em?"

Ivy clutched her sister's hand. Willow was right. Ivy had her mate, her alien prince. She didn't need anything else.

The door slid open behind them with a light ding. Both women twisted around to see Fenrish attendants, dressed in solid black. Since Ivy had spent the last few months moving between Osträsk settlements, she didn't know any names. Why did royals need full-time attendants?

But even though Rivix was a seventh son and no longer in the line of succession, today was an official royal event. Ivy straightened her shoulders and glided forward. Little did everyone know, Ivy and Rivix had already married a week ago in a little hamlet outside the Heila Caves. Not even her sister knew. Ivy planned on keeping that day a secret—a moment for just her, Rivix, and the startled priest to remember.

Today was little more than a show—but Ivy was used to performing.

"The guests are still being seated," said the pale-haired attendant as they strutted down the ice-carved hallways. "But you've had a request, Your Highness, one neither Kind Skarde nor the All-Father can deny."

Ivy's brow furrowed. "A request?"

The attendant didn't answer, instead pulling open a door to an antechamber off the wedding chapel. A table to the side held a variety of snacks, both familiar and foreign, but Ivy's gaze skipped over the food to the sitting area. Three Earthling women twisted in her direction. When they spotted her, all three jumped to their feet.

Ivy recognized all three, but had only met the first, a curvy blond with a bulging belly. Scarlett waddled forward. Rivix had introduced Ivy to his cousin, Prax, and his expecting wife during their first trip to Earth after their engagement.

"You look beautiful, Ivy," Scarlett said, reaching for Ivy's hand and luring her forward. "Like an ice princess come to life. Are those crystals in the dress or...?"

"It's ice, yes." Ivy wanted to focus more on Scarlett, but her gaze couldn't leave the other two women. The taller one with dark hair was Olivia, mate to another princely cousin, but the short blond with green eyes was none other than Queen Alexandra herself.

"I..." Did Ivy bow? She wasn't Herkleian, but King Anax was head of the Intergalactic Alliance and therefore almost a king among kings. "Wow. I knew who was on the guest list, but it's so weird to see you in person. You've been all over the news for years, Your Majesty."

Queen Alexandra snorted. "Call me Lexi. All the title crap gets annoying real fast. You'll see."

"And I'm Olivia, sister-in-law and best friend." The dark-haired woman wriggled her fingers in a wave. "I've only been on the news twice and I was half-dead that one time, so..."

"I know who you are." Ivy had studied all the humans mated to Rivix's cousins. Both Olivia and Lexi had sent her engagement presents, but none of them had the opportunity to meet until now. When she wasn't with her mate or the Osträsk, Ivy guided Addison through her win at the Intergalactic Games. People across the Intergalactic Alliance were obsessed with Addison and her girlfriend, Sigrid. Netflix was even talking about filming a documentary special on the teen medalists.

Olivia took the lead. "We just wanted to wish you good luck and..."

"Welcome to the sisterhood!" Lexi shouted.

Ivy blinked between the three women. "The sisterhood?"

"Humans married to aliens," Scarlett said.

"Alien princes," Olivia expanded.

Lexi tapped her shoulder, adding a correction of her own, "Alien princes who are all cousins."

"If you ever need anything, just reach out. We girls have got to stick together." Olivia linked arms with Lexi, the two women grinning widely at each other. Scarlett mock-rolled her eyes. "We'll see you out there, Ivy. And congratulations!"

Scarlett patted her on the shoulder. "Congrats, girl."

The two Fenrish attendants appeared at the door again, seemingly out of thin air. One led the three human mates into the chapel, while the second waited at Ivy's side. Ivy glanced at the male. What did she do next? It was weird to have a staff of hundreds dealing with all the moving parts of her wedding. Even Willow, as maid-of-honor, didn't know what was going on most of today.

Speaking of Willow... "Where's my sister?"

"One of our colleagues brought her to the rest of the bridal party, Lady Ivy. They'll all join you in a minute."

"And until then?"

The door clicked open, answering Ivy's question.

Ivy twisted—

And stopped dead, her heart trying to beat its way out of her chest.

Rivix leaned in the doorway, all seven-feet of his muscles decked out in Viking glory. His dark hair contrasted with the mass of white fur that haloed his shoulders before turning into a long cape. Under the delicate fur, he wore plates of dark armor molded perfectly to his body. He rested one hand on the hilt of a silver sword and carried a bouquet of pale blue flowers in the other.

When her eyes finally returned to his face, his own bounced back, too, the same ravenous energy within him. Would the wedding guests care if they canceled? Ivy wanted to take him back to their room and have her way with him.

Rivix's lips twitched into his full, beautiful grin. He held out the flowers. "Consolation prize?"

It was like he read her mind. Ivy snorted, but she grabbed the flowers, anyway. It wasn't as good as her naked husband.

For now, it would have to do.

Rivix swept her into his arms. "You look beautiful."

Even after all the time they had spent together, Ivy still blushed. "You're the one who's beautiful. You look like a Viking lord."

"I don't know what a Viking is." Rivix dropped his forehead to hers. "But whatever they are, nothing compares to you, my Fenrish princess."

Her face went even more red. How did he do that to her? They *had* to attend this wedding. It was theirs, after all. Ivy closed her eyes and breathed in his deep scent. She could happily live an entire life as long as she never had to be parted from him. Today, they committed to that dream in front of a galaxy of people.

"Are you ready?" he whispered.

Was she?

The answer was simple.

Ivy leaned forward to claim his perfect mouth in a kiss. It was the only response he needed. Rivix's hands lowered around her waist, squeezing her butt. He parted her lips, marking her with his tongue. Ivy melted into the touch. Heat flushed through her body from her head to her toes.

Screw it.

"Get rid of the attendant," she muttered against his lips.

Rivix pulled back. "What?"

She pointed down at his pants. "How easy can you undo those?"

"I—" Rivix paused, a light entering his eyes. Lower down, something stiffened against her stomach. A long, hard something.

Ivy licked her lips.

Rivix immediately pointed at the attendant. "Out."

"Your Highness, the wedding is about to—"

"They can wait. You can't start without the bride and groom." Rivix plucked Ivy off the floor. She wrapped her legs around his waist and kissed a line across his bearded jaw. "Now. Get. Out."

The attendant got.

"I love you so much, Rivix," Ivy said, trailing her lips down his neck.

"I love you, too, käras."

MARKED FOR THE ALIEN PRINCE

BRIDE TO AN ALIEN PRINCE, BOOK 4.5

ONE

IZZIE

The three suns of Yazd streaked golden light through my windows.

I woke at the same time every day to watch them rise, starting with the smallest of the suns, Rosha. It shifted the sky from darkness to a murky red like the splatter of blood, but when its brighter sisters followed, Peri and Soraya chased away the blotching scarlet. For the scant minutes of brightness, I closed my eyes and breathed. The world was silent in between those seconds, the day still full of endless possibilities.

But it never lasted.

When all the suns broke the horizon, the bracelet at my wrist buzzed, notification after notification popping across the holo-screen. I flicked it closed and sighed.

It was time to get to work.

I pushed from my bed and crossed to my dresser, the width of my room travelled in three brief steps. The drawers squeaked when I tugged at them, carved wood scraping across carved wood. The piece had to be an antique, but Yazdi technology had stripped its value to zero. With a few taps of a materializer, gowns popped in and out of existence.

After dressing, I crept through the grand house, avoiding all the creaky points on the three flights of stairs between my attic room and the main floor kitchen. Mehze forbid anyone else be ripped abruptly from their sleep at dawn. My mother and sisters required a gentle awakening accompanied by a steaming pot of zion and warm breakfast.

I snorted lightly as I filled the kettle. No one in this house was a relative of mine and referring to them as so always filled me with revulsion. I swallowed it down and plated the breakfast trays. There was no point in wasting energy on that. My 'sisters' were their bitchiest first thing in the morning. Better to brace myself for any slights they would throw my way than wallow over calling them family.

Assuming I survived Parvaneh's wrath first.

When my holo-screen flickered again with an alarm, I pushed the levitating cart from the kitchen and up the stairs to the second floor. The double doors to the master bedroom were ancient things more tree than door, painted the green and orange of the Yazdi flag. Unlike other modern doors, these didn't automatically open with the wave of a hand. I knocked gently on the wood before pushing inside with a cheery, "Good morning, Mother," on my lips.

She didn't even glance my way as I circled her massive bed of lush pillows and placed her breakfast on her nightstand. She plucked at the cup, her orange-bronze skin spotted with age. "My zion better be hot this time, Isabelle."

"It is." I knew because I'd burned my hand touching the cup. I didn't have the same affinity for heat as my Yazdi keepers. My mother and sisters all wanted their zion scorching hot, just the way the Herkleians made the tea-like delicacy on its origin planet.

Parvaneh continued going through her mail on her holo-tablet, flickering in the air before her. Unless she was issuing a command, she never had anything to say to me. I moved to open the thick curtains, revealing a stunning view of the garden, a nearly wild space of orange and red flowers. Thankfully, the Yazdi liked their nature untrimmed. Parvaneh let go of the gardener last month, and I barely had time to complete my chores as is.

In the distance, over the rooftop of other houses, towered the purple Farzin mountain, capped with white tips. So much of Yazd was foreign even after a decade on the planet, but the snowy mountains always reminded me of home. Skiing in Utah with my real parents, my little brother racing me to the bottom. I had nearly forgotten Jacob's wild laugh, but I always remembered at the sight of the mountains.

"Race you to the bottom, Izzie!"

Jacob disappeared in a wave of white powder, clumps flinging against my face. I wiped them away with my gloves. "No fair, you have a head start."

"Guess you better catch him, then," Dad said, adjusting his goggles.

Mom whacked him on the shoulder.

Parvaneh let out a gasp, ripping me from my memory. One of my few good memories. I had been abducted at twelve, but barely remembered anything of my childhood. The Yazdi doctors said whatever the slavers gave me messed with my memory. Thanks to them, I only had a few recollections of Earth and nothing of my kidnapping. The sole flashes of that were reduced to something about the birthmark on my neck and a twinge of pain when I got the scar on my palm.

But despite Parvaneh's interruption, as I spun around, I released my clenched fists. Mother had a mean backhand. Better to let her think the angry child she had locked in her attic for weeks at a time had faded. This new Isabelle's only concern was her mother's happiness.

Had the zion not been hot enough? Parvaneh didn't look pissed. She had all but jumped from her bed, her silky nightgown flowing willowy down her six-foot frame. "Isabelle, you're going to be very busy today."

"What—?" I started, but Parvaneh swept past me from the room.

Odd. She never left the bedroom with her plate untouched or her dark, curved horns unpolished.

I followed behind her, dreading the orders that would follow. She made her way down the hall toward her daughters' rooms. She pushed through Esfir's door first.

In the darkness, Esfir groaned. "How many times do I have to tell you I want my breakfast later?"

I stopped at the threshold as Parvaneh all but tugged her eldest from her bed. "Esfir, I have news that is worth ending your sleep."

At her mother's voice, Esfir bolted up, rubbing sleep from her red and green kaleidoscope eyes. "What is it, Mother?"

She opened her mouth, but then decided against it. "Go get Esta, Isabelle."

Lucky me. Dragging her teenage daughter out of bed would be no pleasant task. With a few steps, I crossed the hall from Esfir's door to Esta's. I knocked once, twice, but she continued to sleep on. "Esta?"

No response.

I pushed open the door and peeked my head inside. "Esta?"

Before I ventured further into the room, Parvaneh stormed through the door, nearly knocking me off my feet. "Can you do anything right?"

I all but slammed into the doorframe, but bit my lip to stop my cry. I wouldn't give Parvaneh the satisfaction.

She rushed around her daughter's grand bed and pulled the covers, startling Esta awake. "Esta, wake up!"

Esfir followed her in, pointedly ignoring me, and settled on a cushioned futon near Esta's Rygian harp. Neither sister had an ear for music, but proper society expected all Yazdi daughters to play at least one instrument. With the exception of me, of course.

"What is it, Mother?" Esta asked, trying to pull her blankets back on.

Parvaneh clapped her hands together. "His Royal Majesty is throwing a ball and we're all invited."

Esta's jaw dropped, exposing a mouthful of sharp teeth, and Esfir let out a high-pitched squeal. I fought the urge to cover my ears. It was nearly as terrible as her singing voice.

Esfir rushed from the futon to her sister's bedside. "There hasn't been a ball in the longest time!"

"That's not even the best part." Parvaneh latched hands with her daughters, a terrible look of glee flooding her orange and blue eyes. "As you know, Prince Keveh is the last of the King's single children. In order to change that, the King has ordered every unmarried female must attend the ball for Keveh to pick a wife."

"I could marry a prince?" Esta shriek-asked.

Her sister shoved her. "The prince won't choose you, Esta. I'm older and prettier."

I swallowed my snort. The Yazdi were humanoid enough, but their beauty standards were as alien as their planet. Their skin had to be more bronze than orange, their horns more black than brown, and their teeth more blunted than sharp. Esta had a mouth like a shark and Esfir was like a walking carrot. Not ugly, but not traditionally beautiful, either. Certainly not enough to catch the attention of a prince.

"Hush, girls." Parvaneh pulled her fighting daughters apart. "You'll both get your chance to impress the prince tomorrow."

"Tomorrow?" The word slipped from my mouth before I could reel it in. Three pairs of kaleidoscope eyes flickered in my direction, ranging from disgust to annoyance. I stiffened my spine and pasted on a neutral smile. If the ball was tomorrow, I had a lot of work to do. Parvaneh would take her true daughters to the designers, but I'd have to whip something together from scraps. Not that Parvaneh cared about that. "It will take days to order a custom gown design, ma'am."

"Which is why we'll be heading to the designers right away, stupid girl." Parvaneh climbed from Esta's bedside and rushed from the room almost as quickly as she had entered. She called back, "Get ready quickly, girls. We'll have to beat half the city there if we want a decent selection for our materializers."

I followed Parvaneh, head down. Esta and Esfir started yelling at each other behind me, but I ignored seventy percent of what they said on a regular day. If Parvaneh planned to buy three new dress designs and the fabric of their materializers, I'd need to go to the market.

Once in her room, Parvaneh entered her closet. A circular dais occupied most of the space, the latest materializer design, but the left-hand side of the room contained racks upon racks of jewelry. The last vestiges of the Xanthi family wealth, stored in a form easy to sell. After her husband died, Parvaneh had been left to manage the estate. Her poor investment choices and lavish taste quickly bankrupted them. On the outside, the manor was well-kept with a beautiful foyer and sitting area, but there were wings of the house no longer in use. If guests couldn't see it, she left the rooms to crumble.

Parvaneh started plucking at the boxes. "Be discreet as always, but do it quickly. We'll need the credits in our account when we leave the designers today."

Though I hated when the words left my mouth, I said them anyway. "Yes, Mother."

When I turned on my heels, it took everything in me to suppress my smile. Parvaneh started sending me to the market to sell her jewels years ago. If she hadn't, I never would've amassed the credits I had stored under my mattress. It was the only place on the planet where I had something like friends. The jeweler and I had an agreement: he transferred most of the money into the Xanthi family accounts and skimmed a small amount off the top for me in old-fashioned coin.

And one day, once I had saved enough, I planned to board the next ship for Earth.

TWO

KEVEH

Soraya's Hope glided through the sky, the city far below my feet. Gulbar was an oasis in the middle of a desert, but from this height, the hustle and bustle of the city faded, only a beautiful melody of life remaining. It paired well with the dusky sky, a mix of vibrant purple and orange.

I sighed, wishing I could stay up here forever. This was the perfect altitude. I could still see the city's twinkling lights and the whiff of clouds over my head. Picturesque and quiet, away from the formality and duty of my life. As the youngest son of the King of Yazd, I'd never have the same responsibilities as my older brother, but I still craved a simpler life.

I had found one, too, for a moment. While stationed on Hathor, a neighboring, war-torn planet, I was simply Kev. My platoon trusted me to keep them safe. The comradery we formed while fighting the armed militias that overthrew Hathor's government was a bond second only to my friendship with my elder sister. But all of them were gone now—my friends returned to their planets and my sister long in the ground.

My comms crackled as Command issued instructions. "*Unit 425, engage in defense formation Code Shirian.*"

Out of the corner of my eye, two gliders of similar size to mine descend into my blind spot. This was what I'd been waiting for. Adrenaline pumped through my veins. I pushed at the *Hope*'s controls, spinning her into a perfect downward spiral. Beneath my 'enemies', I had access to their vulnerable engines. I fixed my laser systems on them but held my fire.

"*Mehze,*" Farro cursed from his glider. "*How did you do that, Your Highness?*"

I couldn't stop smiling. While this wasn't Hathor, I still had a purpose here. Training the next generation of Yazdi pilots was honorable. "I'll show you—"

"*Pilots, return to Royal Airfield.*"

I frowned. Since Yazd wasn't engaged in any wars, the drills we engaged in were short, but never *that* short. I had planned to teach my two students the move I used on them today. Perhaps the parliament had slashed funding for elaborate training exercises again? I needed to speak to my father. He'd listen to me, but what would he ask me to sacrifice in return? My father was pushing for me to settle down and that meant leaving my post in favor of a life at court.

As I touched *Soraya's Hope* to the ground, I noticed my attendant, Mavend, waiting for me. That was never a good sign. Mavend had served me for years, but he rarely reached out during the day. If he was here, there was a change to my usual schedule. I straightened my shoulders and climbed from the glider's front seat, bracing for whatever order would come next.

Mavend wasted no time. "His Royal Majesty wishes to speak with you."

"What about?"

"He didn't share the details."

How encouraging. "Alright, let me get cleaned up first."

Mavend winced. "Your father requires your presence immediately, Your Highness."

Of course he did. Patience was not one of King Adashir's virtues.

I let out a frustrated groan, but what could I do? "Lead the way, then."

Mavend and I walked through the palace's many courtyards in silence. We didn't need to speak, not after years together. As one, we turned into a smaller courtyard used by my parents to entertain dignitaries. Orange azaar flowers specked the entire area, the plant a favorite of my mother's. Like most Yazdi, she liked her nature wild, her flowers creeping over the surfaces of anything they could reach.

Under a veranda, my parents sat at a table of ornate metals and jewels. I almost stumbled at the sight. After my sister's death, she rarely ventured from her private suite. This must be important.

My father fussed over my mother, gesturing at the plates piled with steaming food spread before her. "Eat, Myna, please."

"I'm not hungry," my mother said, pushing away a plate.

"Myna..."

My father let his sentence trail off when I came into view. "Ah, Keveh. Come, sit."

I stopped before the table and bowed my head. Whatever my father wanted to say to me, he could say it while I stood. "Father. Mother."

My father's kaleidoscope eyes, both green and blue like mine, hardened. He crossed his hands on his lap, going from loving father to king in a moment. "You've been back from your tour for six months?"

"That is correct." He knew it was, so the topic must have been sensitive, even for a king.

"And despite the many females put forth by our allies, you've yet to choose a wife. Were they not up to your standards?"

Mehze. Not this again. Since I arrived home from Hathor, ladies from Yazdi houses and princesses from across the galaxy had found the time to visit our palace. My sisters-in-law had officially entertained them, but I knew why they had come. "They were all beautiful and intelligent, Father, but I'm not ready to choose a wife yet."

He slammed his hand on the table, making my mother jump. I

almost rushed to her side, but she settled quickly. "And yet you must, Keveh. It's your duty."

But I didn't want to do this. Did my feelings not matter? I focused my attention on my father as my mother appeared lost in her thoughts, her gaze over my shoulder. Unlike most Yazdi, her eyes were silted and solid-colored, inherited from her Herkleian grandmother. "In time, Father—"

"No. As you're not making a selection on your own, you've forced my hand. I will hold a ball tomorrow for you to select a bride from the eligible females. Only Yazdi nobility received an invitation. With your brothers married to royals from other worlds, you must strengthen our bond with our own people."

I gritted my teeth. "Is that an order, Your Majesty?"

My mother cleared her throat, stopping my father from shouting. "Please, Kev. You must select a partner. Building a family with your father and seeing my children grow has been the greatest joy of my life. I want the same for you, my son."

Saying no to my father was one thing, but fighting with my mother was not something I was capable of—not after Zyra's death. She rarely spoke when my father talked about royal business. This must be important to her. My claws nearly pierced my skin, but I managed a nod. "I will try, Mother."

She beamed back at me with a mouth of sharp teeth. I hadn't witnessed her smile in years. Maybe the ball wouldn't be entirely unbearable. I tried to grin back, but I couldn't manage it entirely. Every female interested in me had always wanted my title, not me, not Keveh. And now my father had gone and thrown a ball, inviting all the hunters to see their prey—me.

"Is that all, Father?" I asked.

He nodded. "For now."

"Then I have much to prepare." I hadn't attended a ball since I left for Hathor. What did one even do at a fancy party? "Good day, Father. Mother."

I turned on my heels and exited the courtyard. Mavend reappeared from where he had faded into the shadows, loyal and at my side, as always. But even with him, I couldn't fully connect. Since Zyra's death, I had been a stranger in my own family, in my own home. We all tip-toed around each other, stuck in our separate grief.

Dozens of females would compete for me tomorrow, but none of them knew what they were getting into. How could I inflict this mess on someone else?

But it wasn't like I had a choice.

THREE

IZZIE

Stifling a yawn, I gently closed the supply closet and pressed my forehead against the cold surface. The scent of fake azaar petals tickled against my nose, the front foyer polished to within an inch of its life. Or, more accurately, within an inch of my life.

In the twenty-four hours since learning about the ball, my step-mother had assigned me nearly a hundred tasks. My fingers ached from tailoring adjustments to my sisters' gowns all day and my own all night. Pushing from the closet, I rubbed at my hands, thumb grazing the straight line of my scar. The cleaning products had stained my skin a faint blue, but it would wash out. If not, it matched the shade of my dress perfectly. Yazdi rarely wore the color, and the markets had piles of the shade for almost free.

It wasn't like I would catch the attention of a prince, anyway.

I climbed the stairs, passing my sisters' rooms on the second floor. All three of my 'family' members had been stomping across the manor for nearly an hour. Wrapping their hair in elaborate hairstyles or applying the latest rouge, no doubt. I'd barely have time to brush my hair, much less style it.

Grabbing the banister to the third floor's staircase, I put a foot on the step—

A loud squeak echoed through the hall.

"Isabelle!" Parvaneh shrieked from her room. "What took you so long?"

I frowned. If anything, I was ahead of schedule, but none of my family had worked a day in their lives and had nothing to compare against. "I was finishing my chores. I'm done earlier than usual."

"Really?" Parvaneh appeared in her doorway. Behind her, Esta attempted to tighten the laces of Esfir's dress. "Are you sisters ready for the ball? I think not."

I gritted my teeth. My gaze drifted up the stairs, towards my room and my gown. Once I helped Esta and Esfir, I'd have to throw my dress on if I wanted to travel with the family. The invitation had included transport codes into the palace itself.

But I forced my lips into a smile. "I'm sorry."

Parvaneh slid out of the way as I entered her room. Esta had somehow strapped her sister into her dress, the eldest Xanthi sister seated before a vanity. I approached. Esta rammed into my shoulder as she passed, nearly knocking the breath from me. I gasped, but held myself steady.

"If the prince doesn't notice me, it'll be your fault, Isabelle," Esta said.

Esfir snorted, but I kept my smile large. "We have plenty of time."

A lie, but Esta didn't need to know. My second sister had yet to put on her gown, but between the materializer and my needlework, it'd fit perfectly. Helping the two with their makeup would be far more work. "You'll both be the most beautiful at the ball. No one will compare, not even me."

The room dipped into silence as Esfir twisted around and Esta stopped before the materializer. But it was Parvaneh who broke the quiet. "You?"

A chilling dread climbed my throat. "Of course. Your invitation said every eligible female—"

Esfir and Esta broke out into giggles.

"Can you even imagine her at the ball?"

"As if the prince would have any interest in a human."

I stiffened, but not at my sister's words. I knew that. I wasn't going to lure a prince. This ball was the only escape from this life of endless chores. At the rate I was saving credits, it'd take another decade to have enough for a ticket home. Earth only joined the Intergalactic Alliance a few years ago and had a single ambassador on Herkleios. There was talk of them opening more embassies, but until they did, I'd have to pay my own way back.

Until then, this was all I had.

"Girls, enough," Parvaneh snapped. My sisters quieted, annoyed pouts on their faces. "Isabelle is correct that every eligible female citizen is to attend."

I nearly gaped. Out of every response imaginable, Parvaneh siding with me was the least likely. She only defended me to her friends because she could use it to mention how generous she was in adopting a poor, abandoned human. For whatever reason, either through accident or intention, the slavers who abducted me from Earth abandoned me in an escape pod. The Yazdi found me after the pod nearly crashed into the moon. The event had made every news channel, both because of me—a child from a planet unaware of aliens —and because of the still-unsolved mystery of my slavers. Their ship hadn't registered on any alliance scanner. But how did my attending the ball benefit her?

"But she'll only embarrass us, Mother," Esfir whined.

Parvaneh bared her sharp teeth. "That she would... if she were going."

I tried to stay neutral, but I couldn't help my flinch. What was I thinking? There was no way Parvaneh would ever defend me. "But you just said I could, Mother."

She crossed to my side and stroked a hand across my cheek. Like I was a pet instead of a daughter. "You're not eligible, Isabelle. You're human. The King doesn't want a human bride for his son. That was trendy when Earth first joined the alliance, but not anymore."

"Please." I hated begging her for anything, but I couldn't keep the plea from my voice. At age twelve, my world had quickly constricted from an entire life on Earth to a slave ship to the four walls of this house. All my heart desired was a night of dance and food. Without it, could I hold on until I saved enough credits? "I promise I won't so much as look in the prince's direction. I just want to go to the party."

"Wearing what?" Esta jutted her chin at my stained dress. "That dirty apron?"

"You will stay at home." With a final pat to my cheek, Parvaneh crossed to her daughters. Her *true* daughters. "You'd only bring dishonor to this family's name."

My fingernails stabbed into my palm, but I needed to keep calm. If I tried to fight Parvaneh on this, she'd lock me in my room. But if I copied the transport code and waited for them to leave...

I smiled demurely. "Of course, Mother. I'll stay here."

FOUR

IZZIE

I inhaled sharply, my fingers hovering over my holo-screen.

Parvaneh and my sisters had left for the ball nearly half an hour ago. I wouldn't run into them on the way there, but what about once I got inside? If they caught me, what would they do? This was silly. It put everything I had planned for years at risk. If they searched my room and found my credits, I'd never get off Yazd.

But I was tired of working. Tired of mopping and scrubbing and polishing until my body ached. For one night, I wanted to be the lady people outside this house thought I was.

And tonight, I looked the part.

I brushed a hand down the glittering blue bodice over a full skirt of flowing fabric. When I had spun around in front of the mirror, the color had rippled like water. Yazd was mostly desert, but I had spent hours swimming in lakes at home. My mother—my real mother—had called me her little water baby. This was my homage to her, though she'd never see it.

But wherever she was, she'd want me to live my life to its fullest.

I tapped the transport code into my holo-screen.

A faint buzz tickled up my spine before the world around me

changed in the literal blink of an eye. The fake elegance of the Xanthi manor became a high-ceiling room of carved sand-colored stone, painted arches in the shape of a horseshoe dividing the space into separate halls. I appeared in the middle of the third hall, far from the music and dancing guests. Guards circled the carpeted 'landing' area, their breastplates displaying a gryphon-like animal, the royal shirian.

I peeked around the guards at the guests in the second hall, but didn't spot any of my family. Thankfully. The monsters had left an hour ago. In a room this size, hopefully we'd never cross paths. I might be an outlier in a crowd of bronze-skinned, horned aliens, but at my height, it'd be easy to duck around them and hide if my sisters spotted me.

A soldier waved me forward before tapping at her wristband. My own pinged back a reply. I was legally a Xanthi and probably on the guest list, but with the Royal Family at stake, security couldn't be too careful. The guard tapped at her holo-screen for a moment. The strong urge to slip off my shoes overwhelmed me, like at an airport back in the US.

The guard stepped out of my way. "Welcome, Lady Xanthi."

I almost snorted. *Lady* Xanthi. I was barely Isabelle Xanthi, much less that.

Out from the landing circle, I quickly swept into the crowd. Kaleidoscope eyes flickered my way, some with curiosity and others with familiarity. When I was younger, Parvaneh loved bringing me to all the society events. I recognized some faces, but I had never been privy to any names. While my sisters had run off with their friends, I was expected to stay nice and quiet at Parvaneh's side, more accessory than child.

And now that I was alone, that didn't change. Ladies and lords quickly turned their attention back to their drink and gossip. Some probably talked about me and my obnoxiously blue dress, but most dismissed me quickly from their minds.

Exactly how I liked it.

Through the crowd, I spotted a fountain lined with cups. I made a beeline for the refreshments. A little liquid courage couldn't hurt. I quickly dipped my cup before taking a sip. A flavor almost like an orange exploded within my mouth. I chugged it down, uncaring about whatever unknown effects the Yazdi alcohol would have on a human.

I drifted from the drinks to a table lined with sweet nibbles dusted with pink and purple kadaa nuts. I loaded an entire plate. I hadn't eaten this well in years. Parvaneh kept me fed, of course, but she relegated me to her scraps most days. The last time I had tasted a treat was when Lord Xanthi lived. It had been his decision to adopt me, saving me from an uncaring foster system. I couldn't be returned to Earth, not with the knowledge I had of outer space. If he hadn't passed years ago, perhaps I'd have been raised a true Xanthi lady.

A female in a red hoop skirt bumped into me, nearly launching me into the dessert table.

"Excuse me," I said, dropping my head.

Her eyes widened at the sight of me. "What is an Earthling doing here?"

I faked a smile and quickly skirted around her. Whatever happened, I couldn't draw attention. That should be easy enough. Most of the partygoers congregated at the far end of the third hall, where a massive stone dais erupted from the floor. One by one, Yazdi approached the thrones, where King Adashir sat alone. His wife, Queen Myna, had gone into seclusion after the death of their daughter years ago. Two of his other sons sat on small chairs around the king's throne, accompanied by their spouses, but the seat of honor at the king's right was empty. Prince Keveh had yet to arrive.

I picked a spot in the corner by a curtained hallway and settled in to people-watch. A nervous energy had settled over the crowd, lords and ladies eagerly awaiting the arrival of the prince. What would he think of their daughters? His brothers had married a Princess of Herkleios and a Duchess of Gurov. In comparison, Prince Keveh's marriage to a mere lady of Yazd was almost boring.

My eyes scanned the crowd again—and clashed with a pair of familiar orange and blue eyes.

Shit. Esta.

Without thinking, I nearly flung myself behind the curtain.

My heart nearly ripped through my chest, but I had to check. If she had truly spotted me, I needed to get home before Parvaneh did. I pulled at the curtain and peeked through a slit of space. My youngest sister pulled on Esfir's sleeves, a frown creasing her forehead. Esfir whacked at her hand while laughing at something one of her friends said. Esta continued to glance around, but she seemed more confused than sure of herself. Luckily she had seen me and not Esfir. There was no tricking that one.

I popped back behind the curtain, and back to the wall, I sunk to the floor. Thank Mehze. The Yazdi supreme goddess had looked out for me, for once. I inhaled to steady myself, but a little giggle escaped my lips. Whether it was relief over not getting caught or the absurdity of me, plain ol' Izzie, being in the palace, I wasn't sure. Or maybe it was just the alcohol? Borderline hysterical, maybe, but I didn't care.

"Are you well?"

I nearly shrieked. The hallway appeared empty when I first entered, but a male stepped from the darkness at the far end. Stupid Yazdi and their amazing eyesight. The figure coalesced into a tall figure with curved black horns over dark hair and bright bronze skin. Sun-shaped military badges lined his shoulder, marking him as some sort of official. Unlike my sisters, I had never learned to read rank. But my focus quickly left his chest, tracing the sharp lines of his chiseled face to a pair of enticing blue and green kaleidoscope eyes.

I swallowed, my throat suddenly dry. "I'm fine, thank you. It was just a little overwhelming out there."

To my surprise, he sank down into the space across the hall from me and propped a muscled arm on his knee. "I feel the same way. Which is why I'm hiding out here."

The warmth in his voice conjured a blush to my face. Was he

flirting? I wouldn't know. I had never talked to a male around my age. "Sorry to invade your secret spot, then."

"No worries." He extended his hand. "I'm... Kev."

I stared at his outstretched palm. His nails were long and dark, more like claws, but it was the scars on his hand my eyes traced. Not like the clean line of a slaver's knife on mine, but small little marks in the bronze.

When I didn't respond, he frowned. "Is this not how people on your planet greet each other? You're an Earthling, are you not?"

I jolted. What was wrong with me? Who became enraptured by the very sight of a male's hands? I swung my hand up and towards him so fast I nearly slapped him. "It is, but it's just been so long since I shook anyone's hand."

His lips flickered, a slight quirk at the edge of his mouth. He put his other hand on top of mine, encompassing me within his warmth. At the slide of those rough, scarred hands against my skin, tingles crawled by arm and down my chest. I shuddered. Noticeably, since his half-smile grew. "It's a pleasure to meet you...?"

"Izzie."

"Izzie," he repeated, like he was tasting my name on his tongue and enjoyed the flavor. An odd warmth pooled in my stomach. "I know we just met, but you wouldn't want to get out of here, would you?"

My mouth popped open. He wanted to go somewhere with me? That was definitely flirty, wasn't it? But I was a human—too short, too pale. Not at all attractive by Yazdi standards.

But despite that, I wanted to go. I had come to the ball to be a different person for a night, something more than a slave. But out there, I was either Parvaneh's pathetic rescue or a stranger from another planet. I didn't belong anymore here than I did at home.

In Kev's eyes, I wasn't any of those things. He looked at me—the real me, nothing else.

He might be a complete stranger, but I didn't care. He had been kind to me... and, yeah, he was insanely hot. I was either going to have the best night of my life or get murdered.

"Where to?"

He gave my hand a light squeeze before pulling me to my feet. "Someplace special."

FIVE

KEVEH

"Right this way, my lady." I pushed the branch of a leleh tree from the path, allowing Izzie to pass by my side unharmed. The untamed wilderness of Yazdi gardens called to a primal instinct within me, but I saw why other cultures trimmed their gardens. In the few minutes we had walked outside, I already had to stop three times and help untangle my companion. Thankfully, her gown was Yazdi-made and meant to withstand our nature.

She smiled up at me. "What a gentleman."

"Hardly." With the worst of the laleh branches behind us, I offered her my arm. Her hand warmed through my sleeve. "It's nothing less than my duty."

"And what else is your..." She gestured to my shoulder, where my sun medallions rested. "...duty?"

She somehow made the awkward question adorable—and also triggered questions of my own. She wore a Yazdi-style dress and spoke the language without the help of a translator, yet couldn't read my medallions? "I'm a pilot and completed a tour of Hathor last year. We helped the resistance fighters reclaim the capital."

Her eyes widened. "I read about that on the news. Is that why you were at the ball? Are you a war hero of some kind?"

I quickly pushed away my shock. She didn't know who I was? Surely all eligible bachelorettes had studied my profile before attending my father's farce of a ball. I almost told her who I was, but Izzie was a mystery I wanted to solve. And if I told her I was a prince, why did I have the feeling she might run and not give me the chance? "You could say that."

"Have you travelled to many planets?"

There was something in her voice, something unasked. "I've had the honor of seeing most of the Intergalactic Alliance."

"Even..." She paused, like she needed to summon the courage to say the word. "Earth?"

Out of everything she could have said, I hadn't expected that. She was an Earthling. Why ask about her home like it was forbidden?

"Twice," I replied. "Once as a child and once more recently as a friend of mine lives there with his human wife."

Her eyes widened, her pupils near black in the night. "I have so many questions from that sentence alone."

"That's exactly how I feel about you, my lady."

Red crept across her cheeks. "Uh..."

It took everything within me to suppress my smile at her embarrassment. But luckily, we had reached the edges of the garden, where shrubbery turned to dark tarmac. I tapped at my wristband, awakening the Royal Airfield. Lights sparked, illuminating a hangar made of stone with dozens of wide doors. One door raised as *Soraya's Hope* floated into the open air.

Izzie let out a slight yelp at the sudden light, but at the sight of my glider, a jolt flashed through her. "We're going flying?"

"I did mention I was a pilot, didn't I?"

She playfully whacked my shoulder, her earlier nerves completely gone. "Are we even allowed to be out here?"

"Don't worry about it." Prince Keveh was certainly allowed out here, but no regular military officer could use a royal plane without permission, war hero or not. But she started forward, too enraptured by the idea of my ship to think about the holes in my story. If I told her who I was, everything between us would fall apart. For some reason, I didn't want it to. I dreaded forced polite conversation with strangers, but despite only meeting Izzie minutes ago, all my reservations were gone.

When she had flung herself past the curtain into the hall, I had nearly stayed in the shadows. But the same thing that had me stepping forward was the same thing that made me want to speak with her even more. My father was certainly cursing my name to Mehze right now, but I didn't care about politics or marriage. Right now, all I cared about was Izzie.

I reached for her hand before crossing the tarmac to *Soraya's Hope*. As we approached, the roof slid open to reveal two seats in the front and two in the back. When we reached *Soraya*, Izzie drifted her hand across its sleek edges like one greeted a prized animal. I copied the motion beside her. In a way, my glider was like a pet, something to distract my mind and keep me company. I had more connection with its metal and wire than I did with my own family.

"What's her name?"

"*Soraya's Hope*."

Izzie glanced at me, her dark eyes curious. "After one of the sun goddesses?"

"You know your Yazdi gods."

"I've lived here for years."

Curious. Capital cities like Gulbar attracted residents from all Intergalactic Alliance planets, but Earth had only joined recently. Had I read something about an Earthling child crashing here years ago? I reached for the memory, but couldn't grasp it.

"Why Soraya?" Izzie asked.

"My mother always told me stories about Soraya running from her sisters." At her frown, I continued, "You know the gods, but not the stories?"

"No one ever shared those parts."

"I'll have to tell it to you someday."

Someday. Like this wasn't a fleeting thing, over in an hour. A splash of pink colored Izzie's cheeks, a beautiful shade. "I'd like that."

I tapped at my holo-screen, ordering *Soraya's Hope* to hover closer to the ground. When it lowered, Izzie almost yelped. She stumbled back into me. I caught her in my arms, my hands sliding down her soft skin. A tingle crawled from my palms to my shoulders, shivering up my neck and tracing down my torso. It sparked a heat within me, a pounding urge to claim her.

My entire body tensed, but I kept a smile on my face. I had never reacted like this to any female. Desire, yes, but not this overwhelming urge to mark her, make her mine. The Yazdi didn't mate like that, but something within me roared, uncaring.

I shoved it down, pushing it deep within me. Whatever it was, I couldn't let it surface, not now. Izzie was far too gentle, far too frail for that.

Instead, I waved my arm at the ship and offered her a hand. "After you, my lady."

She accepted my offering. "Thank you, my lord."

"I'm no lord," I said almost automatically.

"And maybe I'm no lady."

She said it with a smile, almost flirtatiously. I couldn't help but return the look.

After Izzie settled into her seat, I swung into the one beside her and synced my wristband to the steering. Holographic controls popped into the air in front of me. Izzie watched, enraptured, but didn't speak. When was the last time she had travelled in a spacecraft? I wanted to know everything about her, but asking all the questions I had would require the entire night.

With a final tap to my holo-screen, the engine revved. "Hold on."

Izzie gripped the sides of her seat, fear and excitement warring on her face.

I pulled back the controls, launching us into the sky.

Izzie scream-laughed as we climbed high into the air above

Gulbar. I roared alongside her. Nothing compared to flying, nothing at all. My heart pounded with the thrill—and with Izzie's presence.

When we reached the right altitude, I leveled *Soraya's Hope* out. From this angle, the city was a splatter of twinkling lights and distant music, alive and near yet also so very far.

Izzie let out a breathy laugh. "That was awesome. Like a roller-coaster ride, almost."

It took a moment for the Earthling word to register. "Yes, like a rollercoaster! I've been on one of those before."

"You have?"

"Long before Earth joined the alliance, my family went on vaca-tion there." Few other Yazdi families could say the same, but there were some benefits to being royal. "We used cloaking devices to disguise our appearance and visited Adventure Land."

Her eyes widened. "Actually?"

I nodded. Though the trip had happened years ago, I remem-bered it like it was yesterday. My sister, Zyra, and I had raced each other to the start of the rollercoaster ride over and over again. If either of us had been making the decisions that day, we'd have never left.

If we hadn't, maybe Zyra would still be alive.

My smile slipped, but I forced the expression to stay on my face. For Izzie's sake. In her seat, she seemed caught up in her own memo-ries. Were they a combination of joy and sadness like my own?

"I loved Adventure Land as a child," she said quietly, talking to herself more than me.

That wouldn't do. Izzie deserved happiness. I wanted to hear that euphoric laugh from her again. I tapped at my holo-screen and the storage between our two seats slid back and out of the way. "While Adventure Land's rollercoasters are fun, they can't top my glider."

Izzie perked at the sound of my voice, dragging herself from her thoughts. When she spotted my glider morphing, she raised her eyebrows. "Can't they?"

"Nope." With the storage unit out of the way, I flipped a switch. The bottom of the glider flickered from solid black to transparent flooring. Gulbar wasn't only on the horizon now, but like a moving piece of artwork at our toes.

Izzie squealed and pulled her feet off the floors, but that didn't stop her from leaning forward to get the best view. "Oh my, that's incredible."

"I could sit here for hours." I dropped my hands from the controls as the glider switched to autopilot. This wasn't a war zone needing my constant attention. I was here for Izzie. "I do sometimes."

"That sounds lovely."

My throat suddenly went dry. Was I nervous? No. But when I asked my question, I nearly stuttered. "Do you want to just... sit?"

"I'd love that, Kev."

SIX

IZZIE

When my feet again touched the tarmac of the Royal Airfield, I nearly crumpled, the tingles of thrill travelling through me almost numbing. I had witnessed both Earth and Yazd from space, but I had never flown over Gulbar. The buildings and twinkling lights were beautiful up close, but nothing compared to the view from the sky. Gulbar stretched across the desert, far larger than I ever comprehended.

I spun toward Kev. "That was the best date I've been on in years—"

Shit, date? That wasn't a date. We had escaped the ballroom together, but that didn't mean anything. "Or, sorry, the best outing..."

Kev grinned, flashing an edge of his fangs. Something stirred within me at the sight. "Why couldn't it be a date?"

That something turned into a flush of heat, spreading from my core to my face. "Uh, you seem great and I had a lot of fun, but, uh..." His eyes remained intently on me. "Um, dating isn't something I see happening for myself any time soon."

His smile didn't lessen, but it changed, quirking at the edges. "I see. We only have this one night, then."

But did he see? I couldn't date, not if I didn't have any time to myself. Parvaneh expected me to be on call all day and night. If I risked that with a boyfriend—or any friend—I risked my one way off this planet. "Um, Kev..."

He closed the distance between us. A panic welled within me until his large hands settled gently on the side of my face. His thumbs rubbed against my cheeks, the roughness of his skin creating sparks against mine.

"May I kiss you, Izzie?"

Everything within me went silent at those words. The universe narrowed to Kev's swirling eyes and the warmth flooding through me, like the glow of a fireplace. I should say no. I should turn him away and leave this place before I did something stupid.

"Yes."

The quirk at his lips became a full-blow grin. Kev closed the remaining inch between us. The softness of his mouth grazed against mine. At his kiss, the peaceful fire within me turned into a burning inferno. I trailed my hands across his chest and tangled them in his lapels. A soft sound escaped me, nearly a desperate whimper. Kev wrapped his arms around me, deepening our kiss. I skimmed my hands up his neck until I touched the silky edges of his hair. I didn't know what I was doing, but I didn't care. The solid heat of his body pushed me into a frenzy.

I gripped a hand around his curved horns. He growled, a deep rumble. The heat within me dipped, awakening something in my core. An itch I wanted to scratch. I pressed against him—

He nipped at my ear. "Come home with me."

His words splashed chilling water on my desire. I pushed at his chest. "What?"

"We can continue this in my bedroom—"

A flushing heat spread across my face. Bedroom? Did he want to have sex? I couldn't do more than gape at him. I had learned the basics in elementary school, but I was a virgin. Trapped in the Xanthi household, romance had never been on the table, never mind sex.

But for some reason, I wanted to say yes to him.

I had stared too long, the space between Kev's brows creasing. "That is if you want to?"

The heat within me dropped lower, twisting into an almost throbbing sensation. Hell yes, I wanted to. But I couldn't. I couldn't go to his house and spend the night like a regular Yazdi.

I was anything but.

I pushed out of his arms. "I... I... No?"

Kev let me go, but disappointment and confusion washed across his handsome face. "No?"

"I'm not..." How did I explain this? I wanted him, but I couldn't. "I can't..."

He straightened, masking his emotions. "I apologize, Izzie. I've made you uncomfortable. Allow me to escort you back to the ball."

What a gentleman. The urge to close the distance between us spiked. How dare he be perfect and kind and drool-worthy? The exact male I'd want... if I weren't basically a slave. I backed away from him slowly, careful to not trip over the trim of my dress. "Oh, no, it's fine. It's not far, I'm sure I can find my own way back."

"It would be no trouble."

I waved away his words and nearly ran into the garden. If I didn't leave now, I never would. "It was nice to meet you."

"But what if I want to see you again?" Kev shouted.

I HUMMED as I polished the post of the foyer's grand staircase. My knees and elbows were sore, but I barely noticed. Not after the events of last night.

I had transported back to the house after leaving Kev in the garden, beating my family home by hours. When they had returned after midnight, intoxicated and loud, Parvaneh had summoned me to collect their dresses and jewels like nothing had happened. Even Esta had forgotten she saw me. But why would they suspect anything? I had been obedient for more than a decade. Why would I start rebelling now?

I'd succeeded at my first real adventure. I had left the palace and pretended to be more than a maid for a night. A handsome Yazdi male had escorted me through a garden and stolen my first kiss in the moonlight. I couldn't wipe the smile off my face just thinking about Kev. He was one of the few people who had bothered to look past my human appearance and get to know who I was. Our conversations came so easily and he made me laugh genuinely for the first time in so long.

He had been perfect—well, perfect until he invited me to his bed. My cheeks flushed at the memory. If only I weren't a maid. Sure, I was a virgin and afraid of embarrassing myself, but maybe Kev would be an excellent teacher. He'd know exactly how to please a female. His mouth would trail from my lips, down my neck to my body...

"What are you in such a mood about?" Parvaneh's voice crashed through my daydreams. Given her tone, she was in a worse mood than usual.

"Nothing."

"Then stop your strange noises," she snapped. "Esta and Esfir are sleeping in today. Last night was a terrible letdown."

I clamped down on my humming and continued my polishing, but I couldn't hold in my question. "Why?"

"Have you not read the news, girl?" She tapped at her bracelet and enlarged her holo-screen, projecting an article at me. "Because this idiot didn't even show up to his own party."

I froze, Kev's piercing green and blue eyes staring back at me. The picture wasn't from last night, his military uniform replaced by a traditional Yazdi beaded robe and coronet. *That's* the prince?"

"You're so stupid." Parvaneh stormed up the stairs, ruining half my work. "Who else would it be?"

Upstairs, she slammed the door to her room. Thankfully, since I still stood there frozen. Kev, my Kev, was a prince. I had kissed an actual prince. Me, a nobody maid stuck on a foreign planet.

He must have thought I was such an idiot not to know who he was. How did I not realize Kev was short for Keveh? *Prince* Keveh. I laughed. I was the only female at the ball not looking to become his wife, yet I had snagged his attention. If Esta and Esfir found out, they'd never end their shrieking.

That thought brought me back to my senses. No one could ever know what happened last night. My life was already hard. I didn't need more misery. A few years ago, when money got tight, Parvaneh had threatened to sell me to Sutekan slave traders. Slavery was illegal, but so was making your own adopted child a maid. No one would envy the life I currently lived, but I knew my conditions would be worse if the Xanthi family grew tired of me. I had to be good until I had the credits to return to Earth.

An electronic chime echoed through the house at the same instance my wristband buzzed. A delivery, probably. I approached the door and tapped at my holo-screen. The cameras captured the image of a Yazdi male with dark hair and blue-green eyes...

I halted, hand almost on the doorknob. Prince Keveh. Mehze help me. How did he figure out where I lived? I guess it wouldn't be too hard to find a human in Gulbar. Shit, what was I going to do? My everyday clothes resembled that of what a maid would wear. I didn't want him to see me like this. I scrambled to the closet and grabbed a cloak, despite the day's warm temperature.

I huffed out a breath and smoothed my hair down. If I told him I was busy, surely he'd leave? He had to. But did I really want him gone?

I twisted my lips into a pleasant smile and stepped out onto the porch.

SEVEN

When Izzie opened the door, the brightness of Yazd's suns highlighting the darkness of her hair, my heart nearly burst. After she ran from the garden last night, it took everything in my power to tamp down the urge to follow her. I tossed and turned all night, the ability to close my eyes and fall instantly to sleep destroyed by her mere introduction into my life. Immediately upon waking, I tasked Mavend with finding her. It hadn't taken him long.

My hands craved the touch of her skin like my lips craved her own, but I stayed put and dropped into a shallow bow. "Izzie—"

She quickly closed the door and whispered, "You can't be here, Your Highness."

I repressed a twinge. She had discovered who I was. I should have told her when I discovered she didn't know, but I hadn't wanted to ruin our moment. Had I destroyed everything between us, anyway? "Good morning to you, too."

"I'm serious." With a furtive glance back, she pulled me away from the door and to the side of the porch. "How did you even find me?"

"It was easy enough to find out where the only Earthling in the capital lived." I tried to keep a smile on my face, but at the sight of her distress, it slipped a little. "I thought you'd be happy to see me. If you want me to go..."

She gripped my forearm. The touch of her sent tingles across my spine and along my nape. "No, I am. I just can't let my family see you."

Ah. Most Yazdi were rather open with affection and love, but some of the noble families were more conservative. I knew little about the Xanthis beyond what Mavend told me this morning. "So you want to keep us a secret?" She flushed at my tone and grin. "I'll play your game."

"It's not a game," she said, still glancing back at the house like her mother might storm out at any moment. I wouldn't give Lady Xanthi the chance.

I took her hand. "Come with me."

"I can't..."

"Let me talk to your mother." I lured her toward the door like a shepherd to his herd of orda. "I can be very persuasive."

"No, no. Don't go in." She almost threw herself into the doorway to block my path. She truly didn't want her family to see me, then. Or was something else the matter? Mavend had mentioned the Xanthis had financial issues. Perhaps there was something wrong with her house, but it appeared like every other stone manor on the street, with curving arches and wild gardens.

She opened the door. "Wait here. I'll... ask. Give me a few minutes, okay?"

My heart nearly leapt with joy. "As you wish."

I crossed my hands behind my back as she disappeared inside. I hadn't imagined our connection. Thank Mehze. If she had asked me to leave, I wouldn't betray her wishes, but Izzie wanted me here. I could tell. Even though she now knew I was a prince. Most females would be more excited upon learning the news, but Izzie remained the same. Another good sign for our future.

Future? I stiffened at the thought. But when I searched within myself, I discovered it was true. I imagined a future with this female.

After no time at all, Izzie rushed back out. She had removed her cloak for a plain gown in the bright green of Yazd's flag, like what females wore to Mehze's temple. Perhaps her family *did* ascribe to the old ways?

But none of that mattered, not when she was here, taking my hand with a smile on her face.

I brought her hand to my mouth and kissed her knuckles. "You look lovely."

She blushed, the pink of her cheeks heightened by the red. "Where are we going?"

When I had rushed here after speaking with Mavend, I hadn't planned exactly where to take her. Izzie had frazzled me, ruining my usual smooth seduction. I considered my options. Somewhere private, definitely.

An idea sparked. "I know just the place."

WHILE THE TRANSPORT vehicle lowered in front of the Isahan's grand staircase, Izzie pressed her face to the window, her eyes wide. Built in the reign of the Karimi dynasty, the Isahan complex was hundreds of years old. Like the palace, it had towering sandstone walls and painted domed ceilings topped with spires. Its ornateness was a visible contrast to the more modern buildings surrounding it.

"Wow," she said. "What is this place?"

"You've never been to the Isahan Zoo?" It was a popular destination for families across Yazd. Because of construction, it was currently closed, making it the perfect place for a private outing. If we were to go anywhere in public and someone recognized me, Izzie's face would be splashed across the news, just like it was when she arrived on this planet in her childhood. I didn't want that for her. Today, we were simply Kev and Izzie, our families and responsibilities forgotten.

"I haven't, no."

"You'll love it."

After we exited the vehicle, I took her small hand in mine. We walked up the marble steps toward the building. The buzz of construction became apparent as we stepped between towering columns and into the shade of the arcaded walkway. Through large doors, workers laid new tile in the lobby. But Izzie gaped past them to the ceiling, a mosaic of color soaring high above our heads.

"This is so amazing." She spun under the peak of the dome, head thrown back. "I can't imagine how much time it took. It takes hours to do my embroidery, and that's on a flat surface."

I stopped beside her and peered up at the ceiling. I had never stopped to appreciate the artwork or beauty around me, but looking at it through her eyes gave me a whole new perspective.

Someone cleared their throat. Under the archway leading out of the lobby, a Yazdi female in the uniform of an administrator dropped into a bow.

I tugged Izzie from the lobby, whispering, "That's not even the best part."

"Your Highness," the administrator said. "I have passes for you and your companion."

I tapped at my wristband, accepting the passes. "Thank you."

"Please, enjoy your visit."

While the administrator went left, I led Izzie to the right, down a simple hallway decorated with paintings. Her eyes bounced from side to side, enraptured by everything we passed. I almost felt bad for rushing her past the numerous masterpieces.

But when we pushed through doors to an open-aired courtyard filled with a symphony of animal cries and squeals, the look on her face made everything worth it.

Her jaw nearly hit the floor. "Wow."

Between wild hedges and fields of flowers, gilded cages contained animals from all across Yazd. Purple winged shirian lounged on man-made cropping of rocks, surveying their kingdom in the blistering sun. The horn of a kargadan peeked out from a deep pond, spraying water in the air with a snort. A massive aviary in the center of the courtyard held a multitude of birds, their plumage all colors of the rainbow. Izzie drifted between the cages, such excitement on her face. If she had never left the city, all of these creatures would be new to her.

After making two circles through the zoo, we took a seat on a bench in front of the aviary, sitting close enough that our legs touched. Relief speared through me at her presence. It was almost as if not touching her caused me physical pain. She must have agreed as her hand grazed across mine.

"If you don't mind me asking, how did you come to this planet?" Mavend had told me a bit and a news article shared more details of the story, but Izzie's arrival on Yazd was a mystery to most.

"My parents were astronauts—that's the Earth word for someone who spends time in space." I nodded, encouraging her to continue. "When I was twelve, my parents volunteered the family to live on a space station. Scientists wanted to know how children would fare, I guess. At first it was scary to be away from home and all my friends, but looking back, that was probably the best time of my life. My whole family was together in one place with no one but each other to keep us company."

"You were close with your family?"

"Yes." Tears welled suddenly in her eyes. She glanced away and wiped at them. "I'm sorry, this is so embarrassing."

"Don't apologize." I opened my arms. Without prompting, she leaned into me. "If you don't want to tell me, you don't have to."

She relaxed into my touch. "I've never told anyone before, but I want to tell you."

I waited for her to be ready. I wanted to know everything about Izzie, even the tough parts. I had cared for previous lovers, but I hadn't ever craved to know and be known like I did with this female. I stroked her hair, her body relaxing against me.

"I don't know how it happened, really," she stared hesitantly, searching for the words. "I don't remember much. We had lived on the space station for a few months when suddenly, I woke up on an alien ship. They must have transported me somehow. Earth didn't know about aliens back then and we didn't have any shielding technology." She rubbed at her hand, where the faint line of a scar marred her pale skin. "There were a bunch of other kids on the ship."

"How did you get away?"

"I don't think I did." She pursed her lips, glancing off into the distance. Past the aviary and the other zoo animals to something only in her memory. "They checked us for marks on our neck. I have a birthmark there, but when they saw it, something wasn't right. They cut my hand, and that somehow confirmed it. I don't really know how."

"How odd." I had never heard of kidnappers like that. Before fighting in the war on Hathor, I had worked to stop trafficking across the Intergalactic Alliance, both on ally planets and those under our protection. Izzie's story was unique. "Did the investigators ever discover more?"

"Some officers had me look at a catalog of different alien species, but none of them fit what little I remember."

"I'm sorry."

"It's okay. It's all in the past." With a small shake to her head, she twisted toward me, her dark eyes searching mind. "How about you? Any painful childhood memories you want to dredge up?"

I reached for a lie, my gut instinct, but I didn't want to hide my true past from Izzie. Life as a prince had more benefits than most, but not everything had been simple. "I watched my sister die in front of me."

She flinched. "Oh, Mehze. I'm so sorry, Kev. I shouldn't have asked."

"Don't feel sorry. I started this."

Izzie interlocked her fingers through mine. "How did she die?"

"My sister and I were the best of friends," I said, the words flowing far easier than expected. "We did everything together, including training. My parents wanted us all to know how to pilot gliders. I challenged Zyra to a race, but her engine failed." I glanced at our interlocked hands. If my sister had lived, would she have liked Izzie? In another life, they might have been the best of friends. "There wasn't anything anyone could do to save her."

"And you still became a pilot?"

My mother had asked the same question. In one of the rare few times she had exited her chambers since Zyra's death, I had told her about my plans to enroll in our military academy and become a pilot. She had shouted at me, her fear almost palpable. "When I'm in the air, it's like she's there with me. Zyra loved to fly."

Izzie squeezed my hand in response. I focused on where we touched, the warmth of her skin pulsing through mine. Pale white on bronze, Earthling on Yazdi. So different in so many ways, yet also similar. Though my family lived, I wasn't close with my father or elder siblings. I had only had my sister and mother. They were both gone now, out of reach in the same way Izzie's birth family had been for the last decade. I wanted to know why she hadn't returned to them when Earth joined the Intergalactic Alliance, but the mood had already dropped far enough.

I rose from the bench and offered her a hand. "We never shared a dance last night."

"Probably for the better." A wild flush crept her cheeks. "I've never danced with anyone before."

"Really? A girl from your social class?"

"My family doesn't let me out much. They think I'll embarrass them."

"That's ridiculous. You're absolutely perfect." I dropped into a bow, my hand still reaching for hers. "Izzie, may I have this dance?"

She nervously tucked strands of dark hair behind her ear, but after a moment, grasped my hand. "You may."

I whirled her into my arms, summoning a laugh from deep within her. Our pasts may have been dark, but this happiness here was our future.

I had never been more sure of anything in my life.

Meet me at the edge of Ravar Park.

When Keveh's message flashed across my holo-screen, I almost dropped the dress I was tailoring. It had been two days since Keveh and I had visited the zoo and danced between the cages, laughing and talking. I had almost convinced myself the time we spent together was a dream. A prince couldn't be into me, could he? It didn't make sense. I was plain Izzie, little more than a servant.

But he didn't know that. To him, I was Lady Xanthi, born on Earth but raised on Yazd.

That should matter to me, but I found it didn't. I want to spend more time with Keveh. Wanted to kiss him and touch him and know him. A tingle crawled up my spine just at the thought. I rubbed at my neck. It was almost like the star-shaped birthmark on my nape twinged when I thought of him.

My wristband dinged again. *Izzie?*

I glanced around. Parvaneh and my sisters were out having tea with a neighbor. If I left a note that I was going to the market, they wouldn't think anything out of place—unless I returned empty-handed.

Luckily, I had spent years cultivating the right friendships.

I messaged Keveh that I'd see him in half-an-hour before compiling my grocery list for Omid, the grocer. I'd have to pay from my own credits for the delivery, but it was well worth it to see my alien prince. If only the Izzie of a week ago could see me now, sacrificing my hard-earned money for a boy.

But with my grocery list sent and my maid uniform switched for the only other nice dress I owned, I headed off into the city, a skip to my step.

When I entered Ravar Park, I easily navigated to the edge of Ravar Forest. As Gulbar was a desert city, all the greenery was artificial, but that didn't take away from the beauty of the twisting trees and orange-flowered bushes.

I forgot all that beauty in the presence of Keveh.

He rose from a bench, a fanged smile stretching across his bronze face. I waved, already blushing. He was handsome, yes, tall and strong, but my attraction to him seemed deeper than that. Something that rippled through my very soul. Was this what love felt like?

I shook away the thought. It had only been a few days. I couldn't love Keveh, could I?

Once I was close enough, he pulled me into a hug. "Good day, my lady."

I breathed in his scent as he held me. Thick and woodsy with a hint of spice, a smell I knew well after this week.

I pulled back in his arms but didn't break his touch. "Where are we headed?"

"It's a surprise."

I hit his chest playfully. "That's what you said last time."

"And did you not enjoy the surprise?"

I mock-grimaced. "I did."

"Well, then you will again."

I gave an exasperated sigh, but honestly, it didn't matter where we went. I just wanted to be with him. Despite my better judgment, I *was* falling for this unabashed prince.

Keveh took my hand and led me into the forest. Oh, Mehze, how I wished he wasn't a prince. Maybe then a human would be a suitable enough partner. Even then, I would be pushing my luck. I wasn't born on an advanced planet and though I carried the Xanthi name, I wasn't a true Yazdi lady. Parvaneh would never bless my union.

"What are you thinking about?" He squeezed my palm, summoning me from my thoughts. "You look so serious."

"Nothing important." I wouldn't let my doubts ruin this. What if this was the only chance we had? If Parvaneh found out, she'd get rid of me instantly. I wanted this to last forever, but what if it didn't?

My only guarantee was today.

We walked in silence through the unbridled Yazdi nature, simply enjoying each other's company. I subconsciously leaned closer and closer to his side, reveling in the warmth his body gave off. After a few minutes, he led us off the trodden-down path into what appeared like a bush. But I trusted him. Wherever Keveh led me, the result would be magical.

Keveh pushed through a cluster of branches. "We're here."

"And where is here?"

He swept his arm forward, clearing the last bit of brush, and revealed a spring of crystal clear water. My exhale came out in a soft gasp. The water was the brightest blue, like a beach in the Caribbean I had visited once with my family. I had always dreamed about going back. Maybe I never would, but this was just as perfect.

Keveh kicked off his shoes. "The water's quite refreshing this time of year."

I stiffened, the implications settling in. Warmth pulsed through my chest, rising in me like a fog. "I didn't bring a bathing suit."

"What is a bathing suit?" he asked, tugging at his shirt.

Mehze protect me. "It's something you wear in the water."

"Why would you wear clothes in the water? It's so constricting." And with that, his shirt hit the dirt, exposing his chiseled bronze abs to the glistening sunlight. His muscles flexed with every movement, power contained within the layers of cord and sinew.

I somehow managed to form a sentence. "Uh, for modesty? To cover, er, certain parts."

Keveh glanced over at me, thumb slipping under his waistband. The grin that spread across his face just about killed me. "That takes half the fun out of the date."

"Kev—"

He peeled off his pants in a smooth movement. His toned legs and the curve of his ass belonged in a museum, but it was the length of his near-gilded cock that snagged my attention. I had never seen a naked man before, but I should've realized a seven-foot-tall male would have an enormous, erm, appendage. The warmth within me flared into a burning inferno, a wet heat that pulsed with every rapid beat of my heart.

Keveh winked—winked!—before turning and slipping into the spring. "Join me, Izzie."

Join him. I knew Kev wouldn't do anything against my wishes, but why did it feel like if I took this step, the outcome was inevitable? I instantly knew the answer. Because I wanted this. After years of pushing down my desires, keeping my wits to survive each day, I wanted to do something reckless. I needed to touch him, to feel him inside of me.

If I couldn't have Keveh forever, at least I could have Keveh today.

With my gaze locked in his kaleidoscope eyes, I reached back and unclipped my dress. With a gentle shrug, it slid off my skin and pooled at my feet. The warmth of the sun beat against my skin, but nothing compared to how he looked at me. It almost burned, the same hunger I felt reflected in him.

Keveh reached up, his hand an offer and a seduction. I paused at the water's edge. Sensing my hesitation, he said, "We can stop at any point. You're in control, Izzie."

"No, I want to. I'm just not quite sure how. I'm, uh... I've never done this before."

"There's nothing to fear." His fingers traced against mine, the touch a shot of electricity through me. "I'll take care of you."

I stepped into the water, my foot settling onto a rock edge. The water lapped gently at my thighs. When Keveh swam closer, tiny splashes tickled higher, eliciting a gasp from my throat. My entire body was like a live wire, sensitive to the briefest touch.

Keveh trailed his hands up my thighs until he cupped my ass. "You're beautiful, Izzie."

I wanted to say something profound, but all I managed was, "You are, too."

His lips quirked. But his eyes didn't stay on mine, instead lowering down my belly to the patch of dark curls over my heat. With me on the step and him in the springs, he was eye level with my core. I squirmed, both at the itch under my skin and in embarrassment. Did Yazdi females have hair down there? What if he didn't—

Keveh leaned forward and inhaled, the echo of a growl in the sound.

I shivered as bumps trailed a path up my skin and my nipples hardened. Oh Mehze. I wouldn't survive this. How could I, when he wasn't even touching me yet?

Keveh patted the rocks behind me. "Sit."

The word was a command, and I obeyed, lowering until my bottom pressed against the sun-warmed rocks. The rough sensation against my hyper-active skin made the burning need within me so much worse.

"Spread your legs."

My nipples somehow got harder. I didn't think it was possible to feel this much arousal. How didn't people just combust during sex? My legs trembling in anticipation, I did as he said, exposing myself to him. I shivered at the breeze against my most sensitive flesh—and at the look on Keveh's face. Like a starved man before a buffet, he licked his lips. I nearly twitched, the tension too much to handle.

His hand settled on my knee, holding me in place. As he trailed his clawed fingers from my knee along the inside of my thigh, he murmured, "I'm going to fill your delightful heat with my cock, Izzie, but first, you'll receive my tongue. I'm going to devour you until you come." His next exhale tickled across my flesh. "Do you consent?"

"Mehze, yes, Kev—" My sentence erupted into a groan as Keveh pressed a kiss to my core.

His other hand settled on my other knee, trapping me. Holding me still to receive this pleasure. To burn within it, writhing and screaming. His tongue slid through my slit before he stopped at the top. His fang grazed against my clit. I nearly jumped, but there was nowhere to flee.

Not that I wanted to run.

The edge of teeth turning into the caress of a mouth, gentle and sucking. My back arched, head flying back. I moaned, not caring if anyone heard. "Oh, Keveh."

He settled into a rhythm of licking and sucking and tugging and biting. My eyes nearly rolled back into my head. I floated within my own body, almost wild with his touch. I gripped his horns, grounding me to reality.

Keveh let out a groan, the vibrations making me yelp. I stroked a hand around the curve of his horn, from base to tip. He gave me a warning nip.

I grinned. Was that how he wanted to play it?

With both hands, I rubbed around the base of his horns—

Keveh plunged a finger into my heat.

I cried out again, my rubbing of his horns forgotten. The calluses of his skin stroked against my inner walls. I clenched around him, holding him tight, but he didn't stop. Keveh was determined to torment me.

Instinctively, I rocked my hips in response to the thrusts of his fingers, almost as if my body knew exactly what to do. I needed this. Needed him, needed release. The heat wound in my body, a tense build-up of energy that clawed within me like a beast.

With one final flick of his fangs, I came undone. The world exploded around me, light and color swirling into one as I collapsed into a puddle. Mehze, that was wonderful—Keveh was wonderful. I slumped into the water, sinking into his strong arms. He nuzzled at my neck, kissing along my jaw.

My hand lazily gripped at his shoulder. "Is that what it's always like?"

"No, shireen. That was so much better."

Shireen. Old Yazdi for 'dear one', a term husbands used with their wives. I flushed, a buoyant feeling in my chest. I might only get Keveh today, but he'd hold my heart forever. I shuffled in his arms—

A thick hardness bulged against my thigh. Keveh groaned. He had pleasured me, but what about him? I twisted in his arms until our lips grazed together.

He kissed my nose. "Don't worry about me. Rest, shireen."

"What if I don't want to rest?" I threaded by hand through his thick strands of dark hair. "What if I want to be bold?"

Keveh's mouth parted, but no sound escaped beyond a gasp. I grinned wickedly, a mimic of his own entrancing smile. I wanted this male. All of him. For as long as I could hold on to him. Wrapping my legs around his waist, I positioned the head of him at the entrance to my heat. When we brushed together, we both groaned.

"I want you, Kev. Right now and forever."

I impaled myself on him. His thick girth expanded me, stretching my body taunt. Tears wet my eyes, but I didn't care. Keveh stayed still, his muscles tensing with barely constrained strength. But he didn't thrust forward, didn't force himself on me. I took him, inch by painful inch. Slow and torturous, yet delicious and deadly.

My tight walls resisted him, but I used my leg around his waist to push him further in. My breathing became little more than pants.

Keveh gripped the rocks behind me, his claws digging in. "Izzie, I want to let you do this at your own pace, but you're killing me. Mehze, I might die."

"Same," I panted.

"Izzie—"

I trailed my hands through his hair and gripped his horns. I had surged forward as far as I could. My body hummed and hissed, an intoxicating mix of pleasure and pain. I glanced into his kaleidoscope eyes, wanting to stay within the twisting green and blue forever. "I'm ready, Keveh."

He snapped at the words. With a growl, he rammed into me, filling me entirely. My vision went white, a scream torn from my lips. My hold around his horns became a death grip. He was perfect. He was everything and too much.

He was mine.

Keveh's thrusts turned wild, each pound eliciting a scream from my lips. My body writhed and rattled. The water around us lapped at my skin, at my breasts. Every sensation was too much, too over-whelming. Keveh claimed me, *fucked* me. Branding me with every pound until my thoughts faded to a chant.

Yes, yes, yes, yesyesyes.

More, more, more, moremoremore.

I hadn't even caught my breath from the last orgasm, but my body surged again, pushed toward another. My back arched, head thrown back. A whimper escaped my lips, a desperate plea. There had to be a limit to have much pleasure the human body could handle. "I... can't... take.... anymore."

"You can and you will."

Keveh caught my lips with his own, swallowing my response. Swallowing my scream. I exploded into stars. My body shuddered as my hot core clenched around his length. His thrusts became uneven, short bursts before he shuddered, releasing a hot stream into me. Keveh broke the kiss to roar.

Together, we sank into the spring's water, merged as one.

NINE

When we finished, I carried Izzie out of the water, her body limp in my arms. I placed her down gently on a thick patch of grass and curled at her side. My arms wrapped around her. She let out a satisfied sigh.

For what felt like years, we lay in silence, complete and sated in each other's arms. Fate itself had brought her to me. I thanked Mehze that she had been in that hallway and found me when she did. I knew none of the other females I could have met that evening would bring me this happiness. No other female in the universe compared.

I rubbed my thumb along her chin. "Was it everything you expected?"

"That was..." She blinked slowly at me, almost blearily. "I just have no words. All I can say is I will never get enough of you."

I smiled and tugged her closer. She shuffled her thigh, grazing it against my cock. Blood immediately rushed from my head to the needy appendage. "And I will never tire of giving it to you, shireen."

She chuckled softly, but her eyes remained closed. The sunlight and our touching bodies kept us blissfully warm, a lulling temperature. I traced a finger along her jaw, across the cords of her neck—

I stiffened.

A twisting of stars marked Izzie's neck, the shapes tugging at something deep within me. Was this her birthmark? Impossible. I had witnessed something like it before, on a friend and his mate's nape. "Izzie, has your birthmark always looked like stars?"

"One star, yeah," she murmured.

One star. This wasn't one star. But she continued before I asked, "I think it's the reason the kidnappers chose me. All the other kids had star-shaped birthmarks, but none of the others had them on their neck." She shrugged, brushing her shoulder against the chest. "Maybe that was why they didn't want me."

"I don't think that was why." The insistent pull within me continued, urging me from my slumber. My heart stuttered out a rapid beat. It couldn't be, could it? "Can you look at my neck?"

Izzie finally opened her eyes, a frown spreading across her lips. I didn't give her the chance to counter me. I twisted and brushed my hair from my nape. Her gasp was the only answer I needed.

Her fingers grazed my neck. "Oh, that's so weird. You have one, too. But it's multiple stars in a circular pattern."

I twisted back to her, a sandstorm of emotions in my chest. I couldn't decipher them until one rose above the other, the warmth of pride. I caressed her cheek, exploring her face, her eyes with newfound wonder. "Impossible."

"What is?"

"My great-grandmother—my mother's grandmother—was a Herkleian noble."

The space between her eyebrows furrowed. "And?"

The stories my grandmother had told flooded back to me. "The Herkleian goddess Hyra supposedly blesses people with matebonds. The couple are the perfect match for each other, made for each other, almost. The bond only recently reappeared among the population, but in every case, the couple get star-shaped marks on their neck."

Izzie stiffened. "What are you saying?"

I took her hands within my own, so small and fragile on a female so strong. "Izzie, from the moment I first saw you, I knew you were special. And in this short time, I've come to love you. And now I know it's because we're meant to be."

She stuttered for a moment, eyes wide. "Don't be ridiculous, Kev. I've had this mark for years."

That was true. Hyra didn't always bless a couple right away with a mark, but it never occurred *before* the first meeting. But how else could I explain our matching marks? I certainly didn't have it during my last army physical. If only I could see the pattern and confirm it matched the twinkling of stars on her own.

But I didn't need to see the mark to know it matched. Izzie was my mate.

And suddenly, I realized the only possibility. "When did you go to Adventure Land?"

"What?"

"The theme park on your Earth?"

"What are you—oh." She covered her mouth with her hand. "You went there as a child."

I nodded, my head a quick bobble. It was the only possibility that made sense. "What if we met, even for just a moment? I didn't have a mark until recently, but if you had never gotten yours..."

She slumped back in the grass, bewildered. "Then I wouldn't be here today."

"Exactly." But was that a good thing? If it were true, the Herkleian goddess—or whatever biology caused matebonds—was responsible for all the pain Izzie had suffered. I wasn't worth that. In the few days we had known each other, I couldn't imagine her not being part of my life, but I would trade that for the childhood she deserved.

Izzie seemed to have the same thoughts. Her dark eyes stayed on the sky, a swirl of emotions within them. I reached for her hand—

A notification popped across my holo-screen, a message from Mavend. I swiped it away.

She grabbed my arms, holding me in place. When I glanced at her, her eyes were no longer on the sky, but fixed on my holo-screen.

More specifically, on the time.

"Damn it! How did it get so late? I've got to go."

I wiped away a frown before it even settled on my face. "I'll have my attendant send us a ride to the park entrance. We'll be home soon."

"Soon isn't good enough." She pushed from the ground and grabbed for her dress. A nervous energy rippled through her entire body.

Something wasn't right.

"What's wrong, shireen?"

She paused, almost as if to debate her answer. I didn't interrupt, letting her come to her own conclusion. Her shoulders suddenly slumped. "My family doesn't exactly treat me well."

My blood shot straight to boiling. "Tell me."

She nibbled at one of her pale nails before crouching before me. "I messaged them I was going to the market, but I've never taken this long before. They'll notice I'm gone."

I didn't understand. Didn't *want* to understand. "They'll be angry you were socializing outside of the house?"

"Yes." Her cheeks flushed, and she looked down, embarrassed. "They keep me busy with work inside the house."

"What are you keeping from me, Izzie? Whatever it is, you can trust me."

Izzie looked back up at me. "I'm not a Xanthi lady, Keveh. I'm their servant."

Rage rocketed within me, a blast of fury. I'd kill them. The Xanthis had adopted Izzie, paraded her around, only to treat her like a servant? Slavery was illegal on all the Intergalactic Alliance worlds, Yazd was no exception.

But the Xanthis had gotten away with it. Izzie was human, with no one to protect her.

I wanted to roar and run into the city, crashing down the ornate door to her fake family's manor, but instead I let the anger lurk, fester. Izzie needed me right now. I opened my arm for her, wrapping her in my heat. "I'm so sorry, Izzie. That's no way to be treated."

She shrugged listlessly. "It could have been worse. If I landed on another planet, I could have been sold into a sex trafficking ring. The Xanthis never forget to remind me of that."

I gently ran my knuckles across her jaw. "You deserve so much more."

How could I let her return home, knowing she'd be treated that way? The answer was I couldn't. Izzie couldn't return to the Xanthis. My hand traced down her jaw to her neck, where the matebond marked us as a perfect match. In all my life, there'd never be another like Izzie.

I swallowed, suddenly nervous. "You're aware I'm supposed to be looking for a wife…"

Izzie jumped from my arms like I'd set on fire. "Stop, Keveh. Please. I can't do this."

She paced to the forest's edge, but I followed her, a breeze against my bare skin. "Marry me, Izzie. Be my wife. My princess."

"I'm not the kind of girl you take home to your family, especially your royal family. I'm nothing. I'm a maid."

"I don't care about that. I want you. I want to spend every day with you, protect you from any harm." I reached for her, but this time she flinched. Had I rushed this delicate thing between us? "Don't worry about your family or mine. I can keep you safe from them."

She twisted toward me, eyes wet with tears. "Keveh…"

I pulled her back to me, her head barely reaching my shoulders. She remained tense for a moment, but with a soft caress, every bit of resistance melted away. "Yes, Keveh. I'll marry you."

I twirled her around and claimed her mouth with my own. My arms wrapped around her waist as I plundered her, a branding with my tongue. She moaned, sinking into my hold. Her hands trailed my chest, across my pecs to my abs. My cock twitched to life. Mehze, I'd never let this female go. "I love you, Izzie."

"And I love you." She brushed a strand of hair behind my ear. "But I still have to get home. You have to tell your parents and… I have to tell mine."

A part of me rebelled at the thought of being parted, of letting her return to that prison, but I'd do anything to make her happy. "One night. I'll tell my parents and send transport to you tomorrow. I won't let you be a servant anymore, Izzie. You're mine now, just as I am yours."

TEN

IZZIE

A smile stretched across my face as I mopped the kitchen floor. Yesterday with Keveh had been absolutely incredible. Muscles I didn't even know I had were sore, but I still craved more of him.

I couldn't believe that I had found love. Keveh filled my every waking thought. I'd think of something randomly and instantly want to share it with him. Despite my rather boring life—abduction aside— he was so interested in everything I said. In my ten years on Yazd, he was the first person who wanted to understand me. Just like I wanted to understand him.

I wanted to be with him forever. A single week wasn't enough. But I pushed that thought back. Keveh still hadn't contacted me yet. What if his parents said no? I didn't think that would stop him, but I couldn't be sure. The matebond mark on my neck flared at the thought. No, it was right, he wouldn't do that to me. But I couldn't be sure either of our families wouldn't get in the middle of us.

"What are you smiling at, Isabelle?" Parvaneh appeared in the kitchen doorway, a frown marring her bronze face. "You look deranged."

I immediately washed the grin away. "Nothing, Mother."

Her brow remained furrowed, but she pushed aside her suspicion —momentarily. At this rate, she'd find out about Keveh sooner rather than later. "I need you to show me Esta's dress for the party I mentioned this morning. The ribbons for her hair must match perfectly."

"Let me bring it down from my room." I leaned the mop against the wall and wiped my hands on my apron. "I'll meet you in the sitting room?"

"Does it look like I have all day?" Parvaneh snapped. "Take me to the dress, unless you have something to hide."

"Er, no." And while that wasn't the truth, Parvaneh would find no evidence of Keveh or my former escape plans in my bedroom. I hid everything dear to me, even though I couldn't remember the last time Parvaneh had set foot in the attic.

Nerves tingled through my arms, but I pushed the feeling away. She couldn't suspect anything, could she?

Either way, I had no choice but to lead her up the stairs.

When we entered the room, I went straight for the mannequin. Esta had picked the dress from a designer's widely available catalogue, but wanted adjustments to make it more unique. I'd shortened the train and added beading to the skirt. My fingers still ached from all the stitches. If only the Xanthis would buy a newer materializer, which allowed such tailoring without a scissor and needle.

Parvaneh observed from the threshold to my room. "That will do nicely, Isabelle."

"Thank you, Mother."

I expected her to leave, but she remained in the door. "Do you know what party we're attending tonight?"

"No?" Parvaneh and my sisters attended so many parties, I had lost track. When she had asked for a dress tailored at the last minute this morning, I thought nothing of it.

"The King invited us to the palace," she said, baring her sharp teeth.

A sinking feeling flooded my stomach. "He... did?"

"He did." Parvaneh pursed her lips in mock innocence. "Did you not get the message? Oh, wait, you wouldn't have, as I disconnected your holo-screen from our family plan."

I almost dropped to the floor. "You what?"

Parvaneh stormed into the room, invading my space. I had to crane my neck to see her face. "I know what you've been up to with the prince. Did you really think I didn't notice you sneaking around?"

"Mother—"

She slapped me. Pain exploded through my cheek, but I forced my tears to stay hidden. "Don't call me that. I'm not your mother." Parvaneh exhaled, a calming hiss. "Luckily for me, your tryst will benefit this family. Your prince didn't specify to his father *which* Xanthi girl he wished to marry."

"Keveh won't let you do this." Parvaneh was mad if she thought Keveh would go along with whatever sham she planned. We were mated, our fates aligned by a literal higher power. I clenched my fists and held her gaze for the first time in my life.

"If he wants you to live, he'll do so."

Fear invaded my anger as goosebumps crawled my skin. "You're going to sell me to slavers, then?"

"I wish, girl." Parvaneh rolled her eyes and tapped at her gilded bracelet, summoning her holo-screen to life. "But no, there was hardly time to arrange that. Your prince won't know it, but you're going back to Earth."

Out of every possibility, that answer surprised me the most. "What?"

"I've paid for your passage. The ship leaves in ten minutes." She flicked through her screen until she landed on a ticket with my name on it. "Isn't this grand news, Isabelle? You've wanted to return to Earth for years. Now that the planet is part of the Intergalactic Alliance, you can."

A week ago, I'd jump for joy at the idea of returning home. I still wanted to go one day. My parents and brother still lived there, Mehze willing. But if I returned to Earth, would I be able to come back? I had found Keveh, our paths entwined. "But—"

"No." Her claws dug into my arm, nearly drawing blood. "I have been gratuitous and kind to you for years, providing you a place to live and sleep. Dressing you. Feeding you. This is my last mercy. Pack a bag and return home, Isabelle. Yazd will never accept a human princess. My Esfir will make a perfect wife to Prince Keveh." Her grip tightened. "You're getting on that ship, no matter what. Even if I have to drug you."

No. If she drugged me, there was no chance of escape. But if I stayed quiet and obedient, surely I'd have an opportunity to run. Transport ships didn't make it a habit of imprisoning their clients. Once I was out of Parvaneh's grasp, I'd make my move.

I bowed my head, once again becoming the Isabelle Parvaneh expected. "May I get changed, ma'am?"

Her kaleidoscope eyes remained narrowed, but I could hardly travel in my maid uniform, stained with chemicals. "You have one minute."

Parvaneh left the room, but the stairs didn't squeak when the door closed behind her. She remained close. Too close. I rushed to my dresser and pulled out the first dress I laid my hands on. But if I wanted to guarantee my success, I'd need more than a nice dress. I ripped my uniform off and hurled the new gown on, already twisting toward my bed. I nearly tripped, but kept my footing. Dropping to my knees, I trailed my hands against the edge of the mattress.

When I touched the soft edge of my drawstring purse, I tugged.

The credits within the bag clattered lightly. Years of saving, only for Parvaneh to purchase my ticket. But if something went wrong, I'd need what little money I had. If I got trapped on the streets of Gulbar or even on another planet, I had another way to sustain myself for a day and hopefully contact Keveh.

Parvaneh barged in right as I shoved the purse into my bra.

I dusted a hand down my front, smoothing the ruffles in my gown. "I'm ready, ma'am."

She held out her hand. "Wristband. I can't have you contacting anyone."

Gritting my teeth, I handed it over.

"Good." She pulled a little circular device from her pocket. "Hold this."

"What is—" Parvaneh tapped at her holo-screen and a light blinked on the little device. A numbing tingle crawled my legs.

The world flashed white for a brief second before returning to color.

The tiny square of a room I'd known for years had disappeared, replaced by a ship's cabin of equal size. A bed pressed against the wall and an open sliding door led to a miniature washroom. The cheapest cabin, all Parvaneh needed for her human servant.

Former human servant.

For once, I was free.

But I couldn't revel in those feelings. I hiked my skirts and started for the exit—

Only to run into a muscled back.

With a gasp, I stumbled back. A huge Yazdi turned around and crossed thick arms across his robed chest.

"Uh, excuse me?"

He didn't move.

Parvaneh had hired security to keep me on the ship? What a bitch. I glared at the mountain of a male, but he didn't move.

Fine. If he didn't respond to that, I knew something he'd respond to. "How much did she offer you?"

He didn't move, but his kaleidoscope eyes remained on my face.

"Not much, I'm presuming. The Xanthis barely have any money." I pulled the drawstring bag from within my dress. "Here. Take this and let me go."

He weighed the bag in his hand. Did he not speak? Had Parvaneh hired a mute—

"Or I could take this and leave you locked in your room?" he grumbled.

I didn't let my shoulders droop under the despair. "This is a passenger ship. It has its own security. If I scream and tell them you're not here as my protection but as my jailer, whose side do you think they'll take? The fines for trafficking are ridiculously high. They won't risk it."

He glared, but shuffled out of the way.

I dashed from the cabin, not looking back. Few people wandered the hallways. This ship was probably minutes from take-off. I skirted down corridors like a rat in a maze, following the glow of exit signs.

The brightness of the Yazdi suns came into view, shining through a doorway. I tossed myself through it, disregarding the crew member who shouted we were nearing take-off. I didn't care. My feet on the ground, I ran from the ship.

Freedom. Finally.

I dropped to a bench, my adrenaline rush fading. My breath came out in quick pants. The crew member who had yelled at me shrugged and closed the door, locking it shut. The engines revved, blocking the sounds of the city around me. I watched the cruiser rise, heart in my throat.

I had evaded the first obstacle, but there was one more I had to conquer first.

I pushed to my feet, glad I hadn't changed out of my work shoes. The shipyard was on the far side of the city from the palace. Without any credits or holo-screen, I had a long walk ahead of me.

I straightened my shoulders and put one foot in front of the other.

For Keveh and my happy ending, I wouldn't stop.

ELEVEN

KEVEH

I brushed a hand across the medallions lining my shoulder for the third time in a row.

"You look splendid, Your Highness," Mavend said at my back.

Did I? I had never been self-conscious, but standing here, decked in the flowing robes of a prince, I had never felt more out of place. I had insisted on wearing the medallions, the glinting shirians I earned with blood and sweat and sacrifice. But would anyone even notice over the gilded coronet circling my head and my horns?

Izzie would.

I warmed at the thought of my mate.

My parents were overjoyed to learn I found someone, though my father didn't believe in Herkleian goddesses any more than he believed in Mehze. He had wanted to throw a grand ball to announce my engagement, but I insisted on a smaller event. Tonight would be family only—mine and Izzie's. Not that the Xanthis were her true family. As an engagement present to her, I planned on announcing their crimes and having them arrested. My father wouldn't abide having slavers at his dinner table, though he'd be enraged at me for not telling him of my plan.

I swiped at my holo-screen. No reply from Izzie. Her 'mother' had accepted my father's request hours ago. Had something gone wrong? There was never any reason to strike a female, but if Parvaneh Xanthi hurt my Izzie... My vision nearly went red, a growl climbing my throat.

"Your Highness?" Mavend asked, one dark eyebrow cocked.

I settled, forcing a smile to my face. "Thank you for your help, Mavend. You've always been the best attendant."

"Thank you, sir." Mavend's wristband must have buzzed, since he glanced down. His kaleidoscope eyes widened. "Her Royal Majesty is here."

Her Royal Majesty? I rushed to the door. My mother hadn't left her quarters and courtyards in years. My room wasn't far from my parents' suite, but everything outside her four walls was too far for my mother.

But when I pulled the door open, there she stood in her finest beaded gown, her horns twined with gilded wire.

Without warning, she tugged me into a hug. "My baby. My Keveh. You look like a male grown now."

Because I was, not that she would know. When Zyra died, she had all but abandoned me to be raised by staff. What fourteen-year-old didn't need his mother? But the thought didn't bother me as much as it had. I had never shared my strife, but now that I had Izzie, the burden I carried was lighter on my chest.

"Mother," I said gently.

She pulled back in my arms before I could continue. "I'm sorry, my son. I was a terrible mother. You deserved so much better than me."

I almost flinched. Out of loyalty and respect, I'd never say such a thing aloud. But I didn't have to. My mother had known all along. I searched within me for anger, but all I could find was sadness. "I understand."

"Zyra..." She swallowed and bowed her head. "Zyra's death does not excuse me for abandoning you. I should have been stronger." She gripped my shoulders, those slitted eyes on mine once more. "But here you are without me, chosen by Hyra herself. My grandmother told me many stories about matebonds. Her own parents had one. The goddess answered your prayers when I could not, providing you with the family we never gave you."

"You did your best, Mother." And she had. I couldn't imagine the pain of losing a child. Losing a sister had been terrible enough.

Mavend cleared his throat from farther into my quarters. "I'm sorry to intrude, Your Majesty, Your Highness, but the Xanthis have arrived at the dining hall."

"Thank you, Mavend." My mother smiled kindly at my attendant before offering me her arm. "Let me escort you, Keveh. After everything, it's the least I can do."

I tucked her small arm within mine. "I'd be honored, Mother."

We walked in peaceful silence down the long halls of the palace. When we entered the dining hall, the sandstone walls glistening with gold and gems, my gaze went straight to my father, kissing Parvaneh Xanthi's hand. In a lavish gown of feathers, the Matron Xanthi preened at all the royal attention. I resisted a scoff, an unpleasant taste in my mouth. How Izzie had become the female she was with Parvaneh as a role model astounded me.

But where was Izzie? Her sisters stood at Parvaneh's back, marveling at the grandness of our dining hall. If my brothers were here, they'd be making polite talk with my future sisters-in-law, but I had asked for only my parents to attend. There was no need to embarrass the Xanthis in front of my entire family. But none of that mattered, not if I couldn't find my Izzie.

I stopped in the shadows of the open doorway and gestured to a guard. He stood at attention. "Where is the third Xanthi daughter?"

The guard frowned. "There is no third, Your Highness."

Panic flared through me, but I kept it down. When enemies struck, a pilot had to keep their head if they wanted to survive. In a way, court politics were just as deadly.

But I refused to play games with my mate's life.

My mother immediately noticed the tension. "What's wrong, Keveh?"

Her voice echoed through the dining hall, silencing all conversation. My father and Parvaneh twisted toward me, as did the Xanthi daughters. A blotching of bright orange flared across the younger's cheeks, but the elder remained cold-eyed.

"Ah, Prince Keveh." Parvaneh crossed the dining hall to my side at a leisurely pace. Like she had already won. "I'm delighted to make your acquaintance. My daughter has told me so much about you."

I resisted the urge to sink my claws into her flesh. "Where is—?"

"May we speak in private?"

I glared, and Parvaneh flashed me an oily smile. My father's brows furrowed, but I pulled the Matron Xanthi aside. I didn't want him involved in this, not yet. King Adashir had a temper and might act first without thinking of the consequence—namely, Izzie's life.

When we were far enough away, I dug my fingers into her arm, careful not to break skin. "What have you done with Izzie?"

"What I should have done years ago."

Cold stabbed through my heart. "Sold her to slavers?"

"You'll never see her again." She pulled her arm from my grip. "But if you marry Esfir, I'll ensure Isabelle's safety."

"You're insane."

"No, Your Highness, I'm desperate," Parvaneh snarled. "You don't know what it's like to lose everything. You'll do anything to get it back. Marry Esfir and save Isabelle. That is my offer."

That was no offer. It was blackmail with my mate's life. I wouldn't stand for it. I searched Parvaneh's gaze. She was desperate, yes, but also over-confident. Another prince, once who didn't have experience with war and combat, might kowtow to her demands, but I didn't negotiate with criminals.

Especially when they were bluffing.

"Guards," I started.

Shouts echoed down the hallway and into the dining hall. One voice, pitched to a yell. A familiar voice, one I'd know anywhere.

Parvaneh grabbed at my sleeve, but I pulled from her grasp. Nothing would stop me, least of all her. Before I reached the door, the guard I spoke to earlier entered, his holo-screen displaying some message before him. "Your Highness, the gate guards apprehended an Earthling female claiming to be Isabelle Xanthi. We've brought her inside."

"Yes, yes, let her in," I shouted, barreling through the male.

Behind me, my father called, "What is the meaning of this?"

I ignored every question thrown my way as Izzie came into view. Two guards dragged her down the hall. She had twisted her dark hair in a bun, but strands escaped to form a fizzy halo around her head. The hem of her simple gown was ripped and stained with dirt. Where had Parvaneh sent her? Had she escaped and walked here on foot?

I rushed forward ready to wrap her in my arms.

"Keveh!" When the guards released her, she threw herself into my grasp. I pressed my face to her head and breathed in her sweet scent. We never should have parted ways. If I had brought her home with me and told my parents right away, none of this would have happened.

I patted my hands down her sides. "Are you injured?"

"I'm okay." She cupped my cheeks. "I'm fine, really."

"Keveh?"

I twisted, not releasing Izzie from my grasp. My father and mother stood in the hall behind me while the Xanthis crowded the doorway.

Gripping hands with my mate, I smiled down at her. "This is my mate, Father. Izzie, meet my father, King Adashir. Father, this is Isabelle Xanthi, Parvaneh's adopted human daughter—or should I say her live-in slave."

"Your Majesty." Parvaneh rushed forward.

My father held up a hand. "Silence."

But he didn't speak right away. He had wanted me to marry a Yazdi noble's child. While Izzie technically qualified, she was human. Not exactly what my father had imagined when I told him I mated with a Xanthi.

Whatever he said, nothing would change between me and my mate. Nothing could separate us.

My mother stepped forward first. "Welcome, Isabelle. I'm overjoyed to meet my new daughter."

Izzie flushed. "It's a pleasure, Your Majesty."

"Please, call me Myna."

My mother's acceptance was all my father needed to rip out of his thoughts. He twirled on Parvaneh and snapped his claws in her direction. My father wasn't the biggest fan of humans, but he hated slavers more. "Captain, arrest this female."

"Your Majesty, I—" Parvaneh cut off as guards surrounded her and grabbed her by the arms. She snarled, but couldn't break their grips. With one last roar, she turned on Izzie, "You little bitch, you always ruin everything."

Izzie watched her silently, dark eyes unfeeling.

"Are you well, shireen?" I asked.

She curled into my side. "I am now. She's just not worth my time. None of them are."

At that, Esfir and Esta flinched, drawing attention their way. My father frowned at them, but it was subdued. "Your mother's crimes are not yours. Leave my sight at once."

And with that, the two Xanthi sisters scurried from the hallway.

Mavend gestured after them. "I'll ensure they leave."

"Thank you." Nothing mattered besides comforting my mate. My mother tugged on my father's sleeve and gestured him into the dining hall. Within seconds, all the guards followed, leaving me alone with Izzie. I wrapped my hands around her and stroked her back.

"Really, I'm okay." She threaded her hands through my hair. "I'm finally free."

"And what will you do with your newfound freedom, shireen?"

Her lips twitched into a beautiful but mischievous grin. "I don't know, my prince. Did you have any plans?"

"I have one." With a quick call to my friend, Prax, I had consulted his human wife on what Earthlings expected from their future husbands. I reached into my pocket for the golden ring topped with a glowing orange jewel. Dropping to my knees, I held it before my mate, my shireen.

The only female for me in all the stars.

"Isabelle, will you marry me?"

She bent over and captured my lips in a quick kiss. I wrapped my hands around her and pulled her into my lap. Her moan spurred me deeper, claiming her with my touch. A heat filled me, racing to my cock. Would my parents be mad if I abandoned their dinner plans?

Yes, but I didn't care.

I picked Izzie up. With a quick yelp, she broke the kiss. "Where are we going?"

"I think I invited you there once," I said. "My bedroom."

Her cheeks flushed. "Oh."

I grinned, a wicked twist of lips. "You haven't answered my question."

"Haven't I?" Izzie kissed a path along my jaw until she reached my ear. After a tug to my earlobe, she said, "Yes, Keveh, I'll marry you. Of course I will."

It took everything within me not to sprint down the hall.

My mate. My shireen. My Izzie.

My foot tapped restlessly against the leg of the high-backed chair as I gripped the plush velvet elbow rests. The Eógan embassy in Houston had been a hotel in its former life and, while part of the building was under construction, the sitting room remained generically upper class. But the bland wallpaper, high ceilings with dripping chandeliers, and regal furnishings were the least of my concerns—all my focus remained on the clock.

Keveh reached across the little side table between our chairs and placed his hand on mine. "They'll come, Izzie."

I tore my attention from the clock to my mate's kaleidoscope eyes. "Are you sure? It's been ten years."

"You're their daughter."

Just the word almost triggered a panic attack. After a decade of dreaming, I had finally returned to Earth, to my home city. Everything was so familiar and yet so foreign. The cars, the technology, the clothes... nothing was like I remembered. Somehow, despite all the horrors the Xanthis put me through, Yazd had become my home.

All I needed was a family.

I placed my other hand on top of Keveh's, letting the warmth of him calm me. On the side table between us sat an ornate envelope, the reason we were here today. King Adashir had approved Keveh's proposal, but the wedding was still a month out. Between all the preparations, we had just enough time to fly to Earth and invite my family.

But we had to find them first. It hadn't been hard to do. As my parents were astronauts, there were dozens of articles about them. Keveh had requested access as soon as we boarded the ship. I had spent hours reading everything I could find. NASA had reported my disappearance as a death, probably at the insistence of the government. The whole world had mourned my loss, the first child to die in space. Unsurprisingly, my parents returned to Earth with my brother shortly after and continued their work from the ground. My father now had tenure at a university and my mother travelled the world as an author. If my brother's social media was any indication, he had recently started university and lived on campus with his girlfriend.

They had moved on, lived full lives without me. And here I was, trying to drag them back to the past.

I pushed from my seat. "They aren't coming, Keveh."

"Izzie—"

"I get it, I do," I said, holding back my tears. "They buried and forgot me long ago. They have lives here—"

Keveh gently tugged me to him, until my knees hit his. "They're just late, shireen."

"I don't need them." I tugged at my mate, trying to pull him to his feet, but he easily resisted. "You're my family. You're all I need at the wedding."

Keveh sat forward and wrapped his arms around my waist. He pressed his chin against my belly, looking up at me with those entrancing eyes. Warmth blossomed within me. I caressed a line down the sharp edges of his face. Mehze, my mate was perfect. Kind and handsome and somehow all mine.

The door clicked open behind us.

I pulled from Keveh's arms and spun as a green-scaled Eógan

attendant entered. Yazd didn't have its own embassy near my parents' house, but luckily Keveh's Eógan friend had put in a kind word for us. The attendant dropped into a shallow bow before saying, "Mr. and Mrs. Alwyn are here, Your Highnesses."

My heart nearly burst in my chest. They were here? The world started spinning, and I stumbled back. Keveh rose behind me and wrapped me in his arms. Holding me up and holding me together.

"Please show them in," my mate said.

The attendant disappeared out the door with a nod.

I twisted in Keveh's arms, my heart near racing and my breath escaping in fast pants. "Kev—"

"I'm sure they never stopped loving you, Izzie. Just like I'll never stop loving you."

"Oh, Kev…" I lured him toward me. He bent until my lips could touch his. A fire burned within me, a near constant since meeting Keveh, but I resisted the urge. I hadn't seen my parents in ten years. I didn't want our reunion marred by a heavy make-out session. I tapped my forehead to his, relishing his nearness.

"Izzie?"

"Is that you?"

Everything within me froze at the voices, ones I had imagined time and time again for years. An older human couple stood in the doorway, their dark hair streaked with grey and wrinkles lining their pale skin. My father had glasses now and my mother wore her hair short, but I'd recognize them anywhere despite the changes.

I licked at my lips, my throat suddenly dry. My father stayed in the doorway, but my mother drifted closer, their faces equally stunned. "Mom?"

"Oh, Izzie." She rushed forward with a cry and pulled me into her arms.

Tears rushed down my face. I sunk into her arms, once again a child. I had wanted this for so long. Dreamed of this moment from the second I woke on a slavers' ship. I wrapped my arms around my mother and inhaled, sucking in her scent. My exhale escaped in a sob.

I pulled from her grasp, but didn't go far. "Where's Jacob?"

"His flight will arrive in a few hours," my dad said. "He's attending Berkeley in California."

"I can't wait to see him." Though my parents didn't ask, their eyes drifting toward Keveh, looming over us. I gently separated from my mother and took my mate's hand. "Mom, Dad, this is Keveh, my... fiancé."

My mother's jaw dropped and my father's eyebrows hiked nearly to his hairline. I simply smiled and leaned into Keveh's side. I knew my return would be a shock, but I had never imagined it being quite *this* shocking.

Keveh dropped into a low bow. "It's a pleasure to meet you, Mr. and Mrs. Alwyn."

My parents still didn't speak, stunned into silence. Might as well drop the other bombshell. I plucked the envelope from the table. "We have so much to talk about, but first will you attend our wedding? We'll have to leave in a few days to reach Yazd in time."

"You're... getting married.... in space?" my dad whispered.

"Uh, yeah."

He tugged me and Keveh into a hug, his face streaked with tears. With another cry, my mother joined. "Of course, sweetie. We'd love to attend your wedding."

If my parents and mate weren't holding me up, I'd crash to the floor. Over my mother's shoulder, I meet Keveh's eyes. In them, I saw a universe of love and happiness.

This was my future. Not as a slave, but as a woman who loved an alien prince, surrounded by family on all sides.

I couldn't have wished for a better dream come true.

Curious about Izzie's mysterious alien kidnappers? Join Kate's newsletter to get updates on the upcoming series...

DID YOU KNOW?

Reviews are one of the most powerful ways you can support an author. If you enjoyed the *Bride to an Alien Prince: The Omnibus Edition*, would you consider leaving a review? It would make our day! You can find review pages on Amazon, BookBub, and Goodreads.

ABOUT THE AUTHOR

Kate Stevens is a writing pair who love sci-fi and fantasy romance with strong, quirky heroines and hot, alpha males. They've been devouring romance novels and soaking up every detail since they were far too young to be reading them. When not writing, you can find them comparing their favorite love interests, baking delicious treats, or cuddling with their cute-but-demanding cats. They both live in Toronto, Canada.

Find Kate Online

Facebook: @katestevensbooks
Twitter: @kstevensbooks
Instagram: @kstevensbooks
Pinterest: @kstevensbooks
BookBub: @kstevensbooks
Ko-fi: kstevensbooks
Amazon: author.to/katestevens
Website: kstevensbooks.com

9 781990 551086